Land's End

Land's End

KEVIN STARR

McGraw-Hill Book Company
New York · St. Louis · San Francisco
Mexico · Toronto · Düsseldorf

Book design by Anita Walker Scott

Library of Congress Cataloging in Publication Data

Starr, Kevin.
Land's end.
I.   Title
PZ4.S7972Lan   [PS3569.T33624]   813'.5'4   78–26795
ISBN 0–07–060880–6

123456789DODO7832109

Published in association with SAN FRANCISCO BOOK COMPANY.

For Ernest Scott

Know ye that on the right hand of the Indies there is an island called California, very near the Terrestrial Paradise and inhabited by black women without a single man among them and living in the manner of Amazons. They are robust of body, strong and passionate in heart, and of great valor. Their island is one of the most rugged in the world with bold rocks and crags. Their arms are all of gold, as is the harness of the wild beasts which, after taming, they ride. . . .

García Rodríquez Ordóñez de Montalvo
Las Sergas de Esplandián, ca. 1510

———◆———

*Though I am old with wandering
Through hollow lands and hilly lands,
I will find out where she has gone,
And kiss her lips and take her hands;
And walk among long dappled grass,
And pluck till time and times are done,
The silver apples of the moon,
The golden apples of the sun.*

William Butler Yeats
The Song of Wandering Aengus

Land's End

Chapter 1

DEBORAH TANNER wore a lavender summery dress to Mrs. Whiting's retirement party. It was just before the lunch hour. We all stood around the great round table in the Commission Room sipping Korbel champagne and wishing Mrs. Whiting *bon voyage*. Mrs. Whiting, a small, demure black woman, has worked in Technical Services as senior book repairer for some thirty years. She is enormously popular with the staff, and there was a big crowd at her retirement party. I gave a brief speech, which seemed to please Mrs. Whiting and also seemed to have some mollifying effect on Danny Parker, the Library's affirmative action officer, who had gotten the whole party together in the first place—partially, no doubt, as a show of black power in the Library, which is formidable, about a third of our staff being black. Deborah Tanner recently transferred to the main library from the Mission branch, where she'd been quite successful in establishing good relations with the Latino youth gangs. She insisted that she have fifteen hours of paid time per week to get out onto the streets and, as she put it, reach the people.

"You've got a literacy problem in this city," she told me over the telephone after Sarah Panel, the chief of branches, refused her request for a split schedule. "You've got kids who can't read either Spanish or English. They don't go to school. They just hang around. I want to get out there and reach them."

1

I overruled Mrs. Panel and gave Ms. Tanner permission to spend half her time on a literacy program aimed at Latino kids in the Mission district. Deborah had already worked out such a program with the reading specialists in the public school system. In civil service, it is dangerous to overrule permanent employees like Mrs. Panel, when you are an impermanent department head, the city librarian, appointed by the mayor over strong protest. In San Francisco municipal government, the tenured upper-middle civil service management holds the power, they and the unions. In any event, Deborah put together a fabulous program, revolving around a series of storefront literacy clinics. People were encouraged to drop in to have contracts or leases read, to be tutored in basic Spanish or English, and—the more literate of them—to be given simple books to introduce them to the joys of reading. Bea Potter did a profile of Deborah's program for the "Scene" section of the *Examiner*. This got the Library Commission all excited, especially Mrs. Mabel Storm; and so I had no trouble getting the commission to vote through a city-wide literacy campaign, sponsored by the Library in cooperation with the school district—with Deborah Tanner in charge, working out of the adult coordinator's office under the main rotunda. After she arrived, I managed to drop down every day to check her progress.

Deborah has a dynamite body—legs like an antelope's, a fabulous fanny that fills her Levis to capacity, and breasts that move languorously beneath her dress, with more than a faint suggestion of uncontained nipple. She rarely wears stockings, but tucks her bare feet into wooden Scandinavian clogs that make her even taller than her five feet, ten inches. The first time I saw her, at a branch librarians' meeting, I fantasized paying intimate attention to her, face to face in the standing position, which is hard to do unless a woman is as tall, or taller, than you are. Deborah wears her thick auburn hair in the Medusa style—a wild cascade of piled curls, jasmine scented as I found out on her first day in the main library when I bent over her at her desk to inspect a statistics sheet she was working on.

2

"Must you lean all over me, Dr. Norton?" Deborah asked.

"I find your statistics fascinating," I said.

"Who ever heard of statistics being kept in a brassiere?"

"You're not wearing a brassiere."

"That's what I mean. Must you lean all over me like this? Could you be one of the dirty old men who stalk the Library? Your specialty, I suppose, is foundation garments."

"How can I be a dirty old man? I'm only thirty-five."

"Then act your age. Stand up straight and quit leering."

Deborah Tanner has wit. You have to say that for her, despite her rad-lib style and her obsession with the streets. Most of the younger reform-the-world female librarians are too funky for my tastes, or lesbian, or worse, both funky and lesbian. But not Deborah Tanner. She's heterosexual: a Jane Fonda type with a touch of Nancy Sinatra, sort of half bad and incipiently juvy, like Nancy Sinatra in her boots, mini-skirt, and streaked hair singing "Jackson" in the mid-sixties: sassy, with a touch of country sexuality and Nashville glitter—like girls you sometimes see as sergeants' wives in the army or working as cocktail waitresses in airport bars—country girls, into the big city, getting laid since early high school, getting hard-faced by thirty or so, but now looking good in blond hair, glittery make-up, and pouty mouths that suggest they know how to blow real good; girls who like hamburgers, Coke, and Southern Comfort.

Deborah Tanner, however, is only partially this sort. She also has a streak of real refinement. She went to Mills College before getting her master's in librarianship at San Jose State. Something of the Mills College girl of my generation (I being thirty-five to Deborah's twenty-five) clings to her: a suggestion of the Seven Sisters that plays off marvelously against her Sunbelt sexuality. Deborah is originally from Phoenix.

Deborah Tanner received more than a partial education at Mills, having taken American literature from Franklin Walker and medieval history from Lynn White. She has a bookish side—rare, but welcomed, in a librarian, most of whom are into social work, not books, or the shadow boxing of symbolic revolution. The SLA could have easily picked up a few recruits

3

among the under-thirty female librarians on the staff of the San Francisco Public Library.

At the party, I sipped champagne and some Andre's Cold Duck, which black people seem to like, and tried to talk to as many of the staff as possible, while returning every so often for some badinage with Deborah. Through the great windows of the Commission Room I could glance out across the Civic Center to City Hall, which rises like St. Peter's Basilica across the western edge of the plaza, a grand Beaux Arts building, perhaps the finest neoclassic city hall in America. Right then in Room 200 on the second floor Mayor Claudio Carpino would be winding up the morning's affairs, prefatory to sweeping out to lunch with his entourage to this or that favorite place: perhaps to Señor Don's on Polk Street, owned by his brother-in-law, where you could get great Mexican food, or to the Villa Toscana on Hotaling Place, off the Trans-Pacific Pyramid. At this private club, plush-Tuscan in decor, using Pierro's kitchen, waiters in black tie serve marvelous slices of smoked salmon, which the Mayor enjoys with a Campari and soda as an aperitif before lunch. The gubernatorial primary campaign will soon be starting. Meanwhile, the Mayor is sticking close to home, attending to city business, his chief strategists having decided that performing as a busy mayor is the best way to play the first hand against State Senator Andy Soutane of Santa Barbara, whom everybody knows, whether they admit it or not, already has the edge.

"Who are you for in the primary next June?" I asked Deborah, knowing the answer already. She wasn't Mayor Carpino's type.

"Andy Soutane. It's my generation's turn to take charge."

"The generation of Aquarius?"

"The generation of raised consciousness and heightened responsibility."

I broke off. Political conversations are no way to get laid, and I desperately want to get laid with Deborah Tanner—not at the moment, but at some time down the road when the time is right. Politics, I find, suffocates eros. My temperamental conservatism angers most of the left-of-center women who are protagonists in the sexual revolution; who will, that is, get laid and demand that you talk about it all the time: how it was, where you were coming from, what you were into; the sort of Aquarian, Esalen, *est* bullshit that is the staple of contemporary San Francisco discourse. It drives me up the wall—getting laid, then having to rap about it *ad nauseam*. Too many female San Franciscans of the sexually available sort specialize in a certain attenuated connoisseurship of self-consciousness that I can't handle.

I don't think Ms. Deborah Tanner is that way—or not completely that way; for she has this Sunbelt side to her nature. Two types of expatriate women seem to come to San Francisco: East Coast drop-outs and girls from the Sunbelt. The East Coast types dress badly, are highly educated and ferociously women's libish. The Sunbelt sort are liberated, but also feminine in an old-fashioned way. Amidst San Francisco's decadence, they sustain a streak of old-style American orthodoxy. They wear Joseph Magnin's clothes and have their hair done. At the moment Deborah was wearing a JM dress and she was looking sexy Sunbelt, or at least Marin County tennis. Ms. Tanner's outrageous Medusa hairdo suggested one side of her nature, and her chic dress another. Somewhere in the intersection of chic and funk, Deborah Tanner has found her style.

"Do you like Art Nouveau?" I asked, returning from one round of diplomatic chatter, spent mainly on a vain effort to be charming to Miss Leah Mae Hyster, the Library's director of special programs, a black woman in whom racial militancy wars against an essentially bourgeois spirit.

"Yes, It reminds me of sex. Art Nouveau is all about sex."

"Are you?" I ventured.

"Am I what—Art Nouveau?"

"Yes, and all about sex also."

"Has anyone ever told you that you lack an element of wholesomeness in your character? I prefer clean, wholesome men."

I retreated to my duties, which consisted of making a farewell speech for Mrs. Whiting. I presented Mrs. Whiting

5

with a large photograph of the Main Library, matted and framed. Her son reached over to help her steady it since it was so heavy. He wore a light gray double-knit suit, with wide lapels, a blue shirt, a generous velvet maroon bow tie, and sharp shoes with moderate platform soles. He featured the usual Afro and Billy Eckstein moustache.

"Lest you forget the Library, Mrs. Whiting, I'd like to present you with this beautifully framed photograph of the Main Library, taken just after its doors opened in 1917."

The Library, a grand Italian Renaissance building, looked imposing and serene in the photograph, as it must have seemed on 15 February 1917, the day it was dedicated by Mayor James Rolph and the trustees, including Sebastian Collins (1848-1940), the well-known turn-of-the-century man of letters whose biography I hope one day to write. That first board of trustees—Sebastian Collins himself, his friend and former student James Duval Phelan, Horace Davis, the others—wanted the San Francisco Public Library to be a great institution serving a great city. They would not be pleased at what either the Library or San Francisco has become. The Italian Renaissance grandeur of the Library, like the Beaux Arts elegance of City Hall across the Civic Center, exudes an ambiance of overweening fantasy. Both the Library and the City Hall are the granite daydreams of San Francisco's betrayed *fin de siècle*.

Mrs. Whiting's son took the photograph from me. I had a momentary vision of it hanging in his home in the Ingleside, where Mrs. Whiting also lived.

"Did you mean what you said about her?" Deborah asked me.

"How can I tell?" I replied. "We all play our minor parts in San Francisco's provincial drama."

"Yours isn't so minor."

"It's way less than it looks. Have some more champagne."

She drank what I poured her, then herself refilled both our glasses. I was flattered by her attention. The reception was losing momentum, now that the lunch hour was approaching and people would be staying on their own time.

6

"I'll take a bottle back to the History Room. It's closed today. We can talk."

She looked amused but said nothing. My heart was pounding and my throat dry. Taking a last full bottle from the washtub of half-melted ice under the commission table, I left the room by the side entrance that led into the commission secretary's office. Marcia Pennyworth, head of the History Room, has decorated it magnificently in San Francisco Victoriana. I walked down the third-floor corridor, past my own office, and let myself into the locked History Room. It was cool and quiet and dim. Next to my office (which Mrs. Pennyworth has also decorated), the History Room is the most beautiful room in the beat-up, seedy Main Library. At one end is Special Collections, an open foyer lined with incunables and rare editions. The main research room also serves as a museum of San Francisco. A portrait of Mayor James Rolph, Sunny Jim of the Mission, dominates one wall. Mrs. Pennyworth has hung framed portions of pre-earthquake stained glass in front of the windows which open out to the empty Marshall Square, currently being fought over by the Library and the sponsors of the Performing Arts Center.

Penetrating the drawn blinds, the bright May sunlight passed through the stained glass, warming the room's oaken tables with the polychromatic radiance of lost San Francisco, vanished city of memory and desire. At the northern end of the room are the archives themselves. In its closed stacks are stored range upon range of books, records, manuscripts, prints, serial and newspaper runs—all containing the traces and leavings of the dusty, irrelevant, but to me at least, strangely iridescent past. It was because of the past, after all, that I had gone into history at Harvard and into librarianship.

I sat on the sofa in the Rare Book Room, sipping champagne from a plastic tumbler, studying the shelves of books. The glassed-in incunables, books published before 1500, ranged up before me in leathery splendor. The San Francisco Public Library, especially its main branch, may very well be a disaster, yet the Special Collections and History

Room passes distinction. I walked over to the incunable shelf and examined Francesco Colonna's *Hypneroctomachia*, printed by Aldus Manutius of Venice in 1499. It was a love story, superbly illustrated. Historians of printing generally agree that it is probably the most beautiful book ever produced. Special Collections owns a first edition, donated by Robert Grabhorn, and several later editions. All in all, the Library has more than a hundred incunables, donated over the years by local collectors. Had the earthquake and fire of 1906 not destroyed the nineteenth-century collection, the San Francisco Public Library—by 1906 already a good collection—might have achieved greatness. As it was, this room gestured, restrictedly but defiantly, against the mediocrity of the total institution. I was trying to improve it—to interest wealthy donors, to get a permanent curator with rare book experience appointed. The librarians' union had flown into a collective rage at my plans.

The buzzer rang. I opened the door leading out to the corridor. It was Deborah, holding a plastic tumbler of champagne in her hand. She entered and looked around.

"I've never been up here before."

"It's probably not your style."

"Don't play Harvard bibliophile to me."

"Sorry."

"I like books. It's just that we've got more pressing social problems to attend to."

She walked into the Rare Book Room.

"What's the use of all this when you've got people in this city who can't even read? Or a crappy branch system? Or a Main that's in shambles?"

"It's because of the larger disaster that we need this," I answered, pouring for us both the last of Mrs. Whiting's retirement champagne. "Let me show you the history section."

I turned the lights on in the research area and took her through the displays. Mrs. Pennyworth had just mounted an exhibit of glass-plate photographs of the 1906 earthquake and fire. The negatives were discovered by Sergeant Roncalli, the police department historian, in the Hall of Justice basement. Left there by a police photographer, they had sat in the old Hall of Justice on Kearny Street for more than sixty years, miraculously surviving the move of the Hall of Justice to new quarters on Bryant Street.

We bent over the display cases, our hips touching, and inspected the scenes of disaster: the smoke billowing up from a devastated Market Street, the crowds of refugees lining up for emergency rations, soldiers on patrol, a tent city in Alamo Square, a view from Twin Peaks of San Francisco in smoldering ruins.

"This is it," I said, "the primal trauma of San Francisco, the deepest, darkest self-image of the city—in ruins, punished by God and nature for its unrepented, unatoned-for sins." I was a little high. Champagne on an empty stomach always makes me even more voluble than usual.

"Pretty dramatic, aren't you?" she replied without looking at me. "But I get your point. The same thing could happen again, but this time for social sins, for crimes against people. San Francisco could once again go up in flames."

"Now who's being dramatic?" I asked. We walked over to a portrait of Mayor James Duval Phelan.

"Maybe I'm exaggerating, but I've been out there on the streets and I know how alienated people are. San Francisco has become a big-time corporate city, a Manhattan, and ordinary people are being pushed aside. They're angry, especially the minorities, and thinking of ways to fight back."

She faced me as she talked, as tall as I was, nearly six feet. Her abundant copper-colored hair radiated from her head like a sunburst, like the helmet of a Greek goddess painted by Arthur Mathews for a rotunda in one of the halls of the Panama-Pacific International Exposition of 1915; pastel, alive with Art Nouveau sexuality. Even Deborah's colors were *fin de siècle*: copper hair, green eyes, the suggestion of girlhood freckles on her face, her lavender dress of Grecian folds. The dress and, behind it, the ample athleticism of her body made me think, when I first walked into the Commission Room and

9

saw her, of Isadora Duncan, or a figure from the Mathews mural in the Oakland Museum of California girls in Greek robes dancing in a eucalyptus grove sometime around 1904, the one in the lead exposing a bare breast through an open yellow robe as she led the procession of dancers.

I leaned forward and kissed her. She kissed me back, closing her eyes for a flicker of a second, and returning the pressure of my lips, mildly, without opening her mouth but with a suggestion of interest.

"You're very beautiful," I said.

"I know. I've always been beautiful, even when I try not to be."

"Let's not talk about politics."

"What shall we talk about?"

"Us."

I said this, even though it sounded like dialogue from a thirties movie. I sometimes feel that my whole life is being played out according to some archetypal Hollywood script.

"What about 'us'?"

"We could be an 'us' if we wanted to."

"You talk a lot. You must be an intellectual."

We walked into the San Francisco archives, down through the dark stacks to an open area in the rear, where Louis Lurie's great rolltop desk was stored. We walked past files of *The Wasp, The Wave, The Argonaut, The Lark*; past the municipal records of 1849-1850 which has just turned up in the City Hall basement (like the glass-plate negatives of 1906, another great find, one that had gotten us a *Chronicle* story by Toby Wain). Deborah walked ahead of me. I noticed how broad her shoulders were, how her hair continued down beneath the nape of her neck in a slight auburn fuzz which disappeared beneath her dress. Reaching Lurie's rolltop desk, she turned, put her arms around me, and kissed me with an open mouth. I looked up over her hair and saw a large colored photograph of Louis Lurie and Maurice Chevalier, both in hamilton collars, tuxedos, and straw boater hats, celebrating Lurie's eighty-fifth birthday at Jack's. They each stood to one side of a huge birthday cake, which said HAPPY BIRTHDAY, LOU LURIE!

10

"You're probably asking yourself why I've brought you here," Deborah said.

"I thought that it was I who brought you here," I said.

"Then you don't understand women," Deborah said. "Which is not surprising. You're a thirty-five-year-old bachelor librarian who once studied for the priesthood."

"Why am I here?" I asked.

"You've been hanging around me like a priapic adolescent in the throes of puberty," she said. "I want you to grow up."

"I will!—if you'll help me."

"I'll try, but it won't be easy."

I kissed her again on the lips, then kissed her where the lavender of her dress swept across the swell of her breasts. Her skin was tan, then became white just as it disappeared beneath the cloth of her neckline. She smelled of sunshine and lemon soap. When I opened my eyes, I saw the beginnings of what at first seemed a rather large mole. In an unembarrassed gesture, Deborah pulled her neckline even further away. There it was, make no mistake about it: on the inside of her left breast was a tattoo about the size of a nickel—a delicately fashioned, subtly colored Art Nouveau rose.

"Where," I asked, "did you find a tattooist capable of Art Nouveau?"

"This is San Francisco. Good tattooists in the Bay Area are capable of anything: Art Nouveau, illuminated medieval, R. Crumb funk, or abstract Pollock."

I bent over and kissed the Art Nouveau tattoo on her left breast. I felt a thrill, incipiently fetishistic, as if I were doing something slightly forbidden and possibly a little wrong. She obviously felt something similar, for she shuddered slightly as I kissed her, as if enjoying a vaguely tabooed pleasure.

"I like your tattoo."

"My mother doesn't. Neither does my father."

"Why do you have it?"

"I love the Art Nouveau. My rose is modeled upon a floral design by Gustav Klimt."

"I could love you," I said.

"Perhaps. But don't feel obliged to. Just because you've

kissed me on a semi-intimate part and seen my tattoo doesn't necessarily mean we're engaged. After all, this is San Francisco 1975, and we're all liberated—even you."

"Make fun of me all you want," I said. "I think you're beautiful and I think I love you."

"Let's get out of here," she said. "Too much history gives me the creeps."

As we walked quietly down the outside corridor to my office, both a little subdued by what had taken place, I glanced over and we caught each other's eyes. We both seemed a little embarrassed.

Who is she, anyway? What was she like as a kid in the fourth grade? What does her father do for a living? The sexual revolution, in which I tried to be a willing and vigorous zouave (despite—or because of—my Catholic training), has no time for such questions. In San Francisco one frequently finds oneself in the throes of *soixante-neuf* with a young lady about whose last name one yet has doubts.

"I'd better get back to work," I said for want of anything better to say. I felt a little uneasy wondering what would be expected of me, what we would find to say to each other after such a precipitous rush into intimacy.

"Have you had lunch?" I asked, somewhat aimlessly.

"I'll eat a sandwich at my desk."

"I'll call you."

"That would be nice."

She continued down the corridor towards the elevator opposite the Commission Room: cool, unruffled, seemingly untouched by all that had happened: Isadora Duncan, Greek girl from a Mathews mural, whose mouth had clung to mine a few minutes ago, already becoming once again a stranger.

My telephone was ringing as I entered my office. It was Commissioner Mabel Storm.

"James, this is Mabel. Listen. This performing arts controversy is getting to be a disaster. They're moving to take Marshall Square away from us, and you know how all of us

12

have worked our fingers to the bone for the new Main Library on Marshall Square. We can't let it happen. Come to a strategy meeting with the Friends of the Library on the third at nine A.M. We'll plan our defense. Goodbye."

As usual, Mrs. Storm hadn't allowed me a word in edgewise.

I put the phone down and stepped over to the window overlooking Marshall Square—a full city block on the northern edge of the Civic Center, bounded by Grove, Larkin, Hyde and Fulton streets, named for the man who started the Gold Rush by discovering gold in the American River in 1848, the year Sebastian Collins was born. Marshall Square was presently being used as a parking lot and, on its Larkin Street side, as the site for the Planning Commission's headquarters. The Friends of the Performing Arts Center wanted Marshall Square for the city's new concert hall. The Library—in the form of Mrs. Storm—wanted it for a new central facility.

Seagulls lazed overhead in the clear blue June sky, groups of them settling occasionally on the Pioneer Monument at the southeast corner of the square, at Grove and Hyde near Market, opposite the BART station and the Orpheum Theatre. James Lick, an eccentric, self-made millionaire, left the money for the monument at his death in 1876. Marshall Square had been a cemetery until 1870. After that it functioned for a decade or so as San Francisco's Hyde Park, a place for soapbox orators, most noticeably Dennis Kearney, the fiery teamster who brought the city to near revolution in the late 1870s with his anti-Chinese campaign. Lick's monument hadn't been finished until the mid-1890s, by which time San Francisco's City Hall (containing also the Library) occupied the site. The Pioneer Monument is an allegory of California history from the arrival of Sir Francis Drake in 1579 through the mission era and the Gold Rush. There's a bear on the monument, and Indians, traders, miners, vaqueros, together with relief portraits of James Lick, John Charles Fremont, Francis Drake, Junipero Serra, and Augustus Sutter.

Naive city that allowed itself such monuments! That felt such a coherent sense of its own past! I sure as hell don't, although I am nearly obsessed with San Francisco's history—a proper passion in a librarian, but a rather useless obsession when it comes to running a battered and embattled city service such as the San Francisco Public Library.

What the hell is happening to both past and present? I ask myself this frequently. I tried to answer this question in a book, *San Francisco, Ordeal and Transformation;* yet it still baffles me, despite the elaborate argument I advanced in my book: namely, that in the decades since the Second World War, San Francisco developed, but did not destroy, the implications of its earlier provincial premises; that the old city is yet to be found beneath the manhattanized, polyglot surfaces of the new San Francisco.

Do I believe this? I vacillate in my certainty. Mayor Carpino, now running for governor of the great state of California, seems caught in the same vise of transition. Andy Soutane will beat him next year in the primary: I know this now, no matter what I want to believe as someone who has much to gain if Claudio Carpino becomes governor. Andy Soutane is the future, and the Mayor is the past, and I am probably the past also, although I am only in my mid-thirties, a few years younger than Andy Soutane.

I went over to my desk, sat down, and thought of Deborah. She seemed a luminous presence in my imagination. If she liked Mexican food, I'd take her for lunch to the Roosevelt Tamale Parlor out on Twenty-fourth and York in the Potrero. We'd go out together: have dinner at the St. Pierre on Pacific or the Washington Square Bar and Grill in North Beach, then a good movie, one that we could discuss together afterwards over Irish coffee at the Buena Vista or over a cappuccino at Tosca's. I could revitalize my Spanish and try to converse with her in it. Deborah speaks Spanish fluently. We could drive up to the Bohemian Grove on Sunday and picnic at my camp, or spend some time at John Howell Books on Post Street opposite the St. Francis Hotel, looking over rare books and maybe

14

buying something. I'd like to give a party at my place and have some friends over to meet her. We'd go to the opera on Tuesday night, I in black tie, Deborah in something long and clingy, Jean Harlow style.

Serena, my secretary, came in from lunch. Serena rarely eats at noon; she shops instead. Today she brought back a Joseph Magnin bag. Serena dresses beautifully and wears a lot of dramatic scarves.

"What's on the agenda for this afternoon?" I asked.

"Local Four Hundred's coming in for consultation," Serena replied, rolling her eyes, then laughing.

I like Serena. She lives in North Beach in a set of flats owned by herself and her three sisters, all of whom live there with their husbands. Serena has two grown sons, but she is still glamorous. She combines North Beach and chic: working-girl chic, as in the old days when women who worked in offices downtown dressed up to go to work. Serena is also peasant-smart, like her father, a bootblack who put enough aside to acquire considerable real estate in North Beach.

"What else is on?"

"You're due over at the Planning Commission at three to talk to Albert Esau about Marshall Square."

I leaned back in my chair (it once belonged to Lou Lurie) and composed myself for the meeting with Local 400. With Mrs. Pennyworth's help, I have made my office perhaps the most beautiful city office in San Francisco, next to the mayor's. The Lou Lurie estate donated the late, great Lurie's office furniture to the Library: a massive carved oak desk, a work table, a bar, a file cabinet, also of carved oak. I have decorated my office as a mini-museum of San Francisco. On one wall I've hung a photograph of Mayor James Duval Phelan in formal riding attire, putting his horse through dressage in Golden Gate Park sometime in 1901. On another wall I have a colored photogravure illustration of the Midwinter Fair of 1894, and opposite that, a rendering by Bernard Maybeck of an architectural fantasy he proposed during the Depression to be built with WPA funds atop Twin Peaks: a Grecian temple-like affair, from which water was to cascade downwards to various levels of reflecting pools. Behind my desk hangs a portrait of John McLaren, the creator of Golden Gate Park, a truly great civil servant, one of the finest this country has ever seen.

The shelves of my bookcase are adorned with artifacts dug up from the ruins of the city in 1906, my favorite being a stack of porcelain plates melted together by the heat of the fire that destroyed San Francisco. Directly behind me, I have a portrait of Sebastian Collins, taken in 1915, the year of the Panama-Pacific International Exposition. Bearded, portly, Collins is looking up from an open volume on his lap. Some people think he looks like the actor Monty Woolley or the actor Sebastian Cabot. Certainly he seems elegant and accomplished, at home with both himself and his city. The photograph is inscribed to Jack London and dated 20 February 1915.

Serena buzzed me on the intercom. "The Librarians' Guild people are here."

"Send them in."

Helen Huskett, a union activist who lives with a nurse on the staff of General Hospital, came in first. Helen wore no make-up and sported her usual thrift-shop look, a matter of Maoist affectation rather than income. As a Librarian Three, Helen could afford better clothes if she were at all interested. She threw herself on the couch opposite my desk and parted her legs so that my line of vision directly encountered her denim-covered crotch. Her vagina, I suspected for a moment, was probably protected by spiny growths, or perhaps a rudimentary set of teeth. Teddy Crato sat down next to her. Teddy is Bulgarian, and I suspect that he drinks a bit. He usually wears sunglasses. He was a teaching brother for a while. We at least had our time spent in religion in common. For two years I studied for the priesthood at St. Patrick's Seminary in Menlo Park. I like Teddy Crato, although he can be a total pain in the ass when it comes to union affairs, being Bulgarian and all.

The Librarians' Guild of the City Workers Union is among the best-organized union groups in city government. Many of

16

the librarians, especially the younger ones who formed hostile attitudes towards established institutions in the 1960s, throw themselves into guild affairs with ferocious passion. In a world of banished orthodoxies, they find in the union a common cause. The guild subsumes the leftish sentiment of their undergraduate days, bringing it to bear upon adult purposes. Held every other Thursday evening in the Commission Room, guild meetings, aside from assuaging loneliness, keep alive a sense of revolt in onetime anti-Vietnam demonstrators who had condemned themselves to the routines of civil service.

The guild meets and confers in groups of three, lest deals be made with management, so Ann Muse from Cataloging came along. A smallish, pert divorcee in her early thirties, Ann serves as shop steward to the guild, handling employees' complaints. A devout Episcopalian, she sends her ten-year-old daughter to the Canterbury School for Girls at St. Anselm's on Van Ness. Ann Muse, I suspect, likes me; or rather, being an educated woman of some imagination, she takes a certain amount of amusement in the drollery of my situation: a scholar trying to run (at Mayor Carpino's insistence) one of the most problem-ridden public library systems in America, a system grossly underfunded, overexpanded into twenty-eight branches, some barely blocks apart (one for every neighborhood in the city), a system having for its Main Library a hulking, inefficient building that over the years has become the refuge of bums, peeping Toms, the impoverished, the unsheltered. One particular old lady carries a portable television in a sling across her chest, which she constantly watches, listening to it through an ear plug as she sits in the Periodicals Room perusing *Playboy* and simultaneously watching daytime soap operas.

"What's this shit about Sunday hours?" Helen Huskett, president of the Librarians' Guild, never at a loss for words, opened the meeting.

"With the large numbers of federally funded employees coming here under the CETA program, more than a hundred I believe, the staff should seriously begin thinking about

17

opening the libraries on Sunday when ordinary working people can get to them. After all, that's why we're here: to help ordinary people."

"What a lot of crap, Norton." This, again, from Ms. Huskett (in case there is doubt). "What a lot of bullshit."

"Please explain your position," I said, trying, for Ann Muse's sake, to maintain some posture of drollery; although, in dealing with Ms. Huskett, to keep one's sense of humor is always difficult.

"We're already overcommitted here," Ms. Huskett shot back, her mannish physiognomy ruddy with anger. Freckle-faced, auburn-haired, Helen Huskett looks Irish, which she is: like myself, a fourth-generation Irish Catholic San Franciscan. Thirty years ago, with her tendencies, her will, her intelligence, Helen Huskett probably would have joined an order of nuns like the Good Shepherd sisters, who take care of delinquent girls. But with the collapse of Roman Catholicism as an American subculture, Helen is, I suspect, somewhat at loose ends. One gets the impression that being a radical activist librarian does not fully satisfy her. Maybe that's why she is so heavily into guild work. Helen is tough, treacherous, and a very competent negotiator. More than once, she's walked out of my office with more than I wanted to give away.

"You can't use low-paid federal employees to replace regular civil servants," Helen announced. "The CETA program is supposed to supplement regular librarians, not replace them. Besides, you've got a lot of other things to do around here before you open on Sundays—get rid of the backlog in cataloging, for instance, or get the shelves read. Half the books in the card catalog aren't on the shelves."

She was right. The place was a mess. The card catalog was a work of fiction, more fanciful than any missing novel not on the shelves. Intending to place me in a position of honor as city librarian of San Francisco, Mayor Carpino had made me, in effect, the captain of the *Titanic*—no, not the *Titanic*, for the *Titanic* at least possessed some elegance. You could enjoy a drink in the bar before it sank, and maybe talk to someone nice. The San Francisco Public Library was a garbage scow, or,

18

more charitably, a Liberian tanker breaking up on the rocks and spilling oil. My predecessor, William Holderson, came here as the hottest young library executive in America. Four years later, he barely left his office. He spent a lot of time there moping and staring at the ceiling. His predecessor, now at the Humanities Library of the University of Delaware, left after seven years at the SFPL with a bleeding ulcer, *tic douloureux*, and a string of unpaid psychiatrists' bills.

"The more service we give the public," I replied, "the more we'll have their backing come budget time."

"Bullshit." This from Teddy Crato. "The more we do, the more is expected from us—and the less we get to do it with."

To tell the truth, I agree with Teddy. Very few San Franciscans truly care about the Library. San Francisco just isn't a library town. It is an opera town, a symphony town, and, of late, a ballet town—but it is not a library town. I remember standing in the foyer of the New York Public Library on Forty-second Street and seeing the hundreds of names of donors carved into the marble walls—upstate Knickerbocker names, WASP names, Jewish names—all having given money to the New York Public Library to make it a great institution. James Duval Phelan and Sebastian Collins, founding trustees of our library, hoped that something similar would happen here in San Francisco, but it hasn't. Our endowment is nonexistent. What books we have are continually stolen. Drunken bums and Indians roam our corridors. Sex perverts haunt our restrooms or stalk the stack areas, looking above them into the skirts of women on the next highest level. Our patrons are the old, the sick, the tired, the shabby. On rainy days, when we are more crowded than usual, and when the steam heat, controlled elsewhere in the city, is turned up to the maximum, an unbearable smell fills the place: the smell of dirty wet socks and damp overcoats, of unwashed bodies, the human smell of bad breath and Lysoled hotel rooms in the Tenderloin, the smell of defeat. There are days when the library seems overwhelmed by indigents looking for a place to keep warm. Tattered clothes, rheumy eyes, the smell of alcohol: at best I can consider it Dickensian. At worst, it mocks the Italian Renaissance grandeur of the Library façade and the bold mottos carved upon the interior walls.

"Pioneers Leaving the East" is the title of the mural in the History and Social Science Department, while "Pioneers Arriving in the West" dominates an entire wall in Literature, Philosophy, and Religion. Frank Du Mond did these murals for one of the exhibit halls of the Panama-Pacific International Exposition of 1915. The arrival mural depicts sturdy pioneers, healthy and Anglo-Saxon of mien, striding joyfully into a golden land of milk and honey. One of our patrons, a fellow whom the staff calls Charlie Chaplin because he dresses in baggy pants, tattered cutaway coat, and a bowler hat (he also features a toothbrush mustache), often sits by the hour in Literature, holding an open, unread book, sometimes upside down, staring at Du Mond's mural. When the guards don't prevent it, he pushes along a Safeway shopping cart filled with old magazines and newspapers, which he sifts through and sorts endlessly when he isn't studying the arrival of the pioneers from the East.

"Here's what I propose," I said, wanting the interview over, for it was getting near to three and I was due over at City Planning to talk to Albert Esau. "The CETA people won't be here for two months or so. John Stickey will head a committee to arrange the staffing assignments of the CETA people. The three chiefs and the program coordinators will sit on it. You can select one union representative to sit on it also. That way, your input will be there from the start."

It was a generous, foolhardy move, but I was getting bored with the meeting and wanted it over with. Besides, if the union didn't like what I was doing with the CETA people, they'd complain to the commission directly, and the commission would come back to me, so I might as well have union input from the start. Stickey, the personnel officer, was tough and wouldn't give away any more than he had to.

Ms. Huskett, Mrs. Muse, and Teddy Crato filed out in silent satisfaction. They'd made it onto an administrative committee, a step forward for the soviet! Let them have it, I felt. I'm tired of pettiness and fighting over nothing.

20

I had a half hour before I was scheduled to see Esau at Planning. I reached into the lower left drawer of my desk and took out my Sebastian Collins folder. For the past few months I have been gathering material on the life of Sebastian Collins for a possible biography or Bohemian Grove play. Collins joined the Bohemian Club in 1894, the year of his return from Europe and belated marriage. James Duval Phelan sponsored him. I have in mind to do a Grove play evocative of old San Francisco, and Collins seems marvelously representative. He was born in San Francisco in 1848 and educated here through graduation from Boys' High School. He went east in 1867 to matriculate at Harvard, from which he graduated in 1873, having in the interim spent nearly three years as a soldier with the army of Pope Pius IX in the last years of the War of Italian Unification. The San Francisco financier William Chapman Ralston, then president of the Bank of California, paid for Collins's Harvard career and postgraduate education in Europe. Ralston envisioned establishing an art museum in San Francisco and wanted Collins to head it.

Collins took a doctorate at Heidelberg in 1876, writing his dissertation on the baroque sculptor and architect, Bernini. Under the sponsorship of Joseph Sadoc Alemany, the Dominican Archbishop of San Francisco, Collins obtained an appointment as *scriptor* in the Vatican Library, where he worked for some three or four years. Ralston died in 1875, a probable suicide after the failure of the Bank of California, and so Collins's future in San Francisco remained in doubt. He might have spent his life as a research scholar in the Vatican Library, had not Archbishop Alemany personally persuaded him to return to take an appointment as professor of art and philosophy at the Jesuit College of St. Ignatius, then at Van Ness and Hayes streets. Collins taught there from 1881 to 1888, the year he published his *Bernini, Eros, and the Transcendent,* by which he is yet remembered (if remembered at all!), a study, by the way, that won him the praise of Santayana in that savant's *Scepticism and Animal Faith.* From 1888 to 1894 Sebastian Collins lived again in Europe, having returned there in romantic pursuit of the San Francisco-born singer

Sybil Sanderson, later *diva* with the Paris Opera and mistress of Jules Massenet. Rejected by Sybil, Collins lived a rather vagabond life for a number of years (some might say debauched!) until experiencing a religious conversion in Paris. He spent a year at Grand Chartreuse in study, prayer, and meditation, then returned to San Francisco in 1894, the year he joined the Bohemian Club.

This is how I first encountered him in my Harvard researches: the beloved figure from *fin de siècle* San Francisco; friend of Mayor Phelan; adviser to Daniel Hudson Burnham in preparing a master plan for San Francisco; early champion of Frank Norris, Jack London, Willis Polk, and Bernard Maybeck; the charming essayist of the revived *Overland Monthly* and the *Argonaut*; the Bohemian extraordinary, a founding member in the Bohemian Grove of Esplandian Camp; the scholarly author. His many books include the masterful *Memoirs of a San Franciscan Bohemian*, published by Paul Elder in 1915, which I consider the single best account of early San Francisco—certainly better than Jerome Hart's *In Our Second Century*, which is better known. Fortunately for the San Francisco Public Library, Sebastian Collins was both a trustee and an inveterate collector. His collection of papers and *memorabilia* is now the glory of our History Room, along with the Eric Hoffer papers. I've been through the Collins papers for my research. I hope in the next few years to do a biography of Collins that will be a biography of San Francisco itself, for the late Sebastian Collins was truly what Ralph Waldo Emerson describes as a Representative Man. For me at least, he is San Francisco personified.

Aside from the material Collins collected, I've done my own searching at various libraries across the country. I have a rather complete file of his periodical essays and xeroxes of many of his letters, culled from various collections: letters to Josiah Royce from the Royce papers at Harvard; letters to James Duval Phelan, from the Bancroft Library in Berkeley; letters to Sybil Sanderson, now in the Sanderson Collection of the Library of Congress; letters to Archbishop Alemany from the archives of

22

the Archdiocese of San Francisco; letters to his boyhood friend Charles Warren Stoddard from the Stoddard papers at the Huntington Library in San Marino. Collins drafted, but suppressed from *Memoirs of a San Franciscan Bohemian,* a lengthy account of his years of *Sturm und Drang* on the continent after his rejection by Sybil Sanderson. It is now among his papers in the History Room. Also, there are cartons and cartons of sorted and chronologically-arranged *memorabilia*: his Harvard diploma, signed by President Charles Eliot (whom Collins detested); a diary he kept at Heidelberg and at the Vatican Library; a photograph of Collins in the robes of a lay oblate of Grand Chartreuse, taken in 1893; programs from performances by Sybil Sanderson, including the premiere of *Thaïs* at the Paris Opera on 16 March 1894, just days before Collins sailed for San Francisco; his commissioner's ribbon from the Exposition (he played a role in getting Maybeck the commission for the Palace of Fine Arts); a photograph of Collins and John McLaren standing in front of the just-completed De Young Museum; yellowed clippings of letters to the editor, defending the Library's right to the Larkin–McAllister site. There are autographed books from figures as diverse as Frank Norris—a copy of *McTeague,* inscribed: "For Sebastian Collins, protector of our City's scribbling tribe"—and Rafael Cardinal Merry del Val, the aristocratic papal secretary of state whom Sebastian had known as a young monsignor in the early nineties—a copy of *Sacred Strivings,* inscribed: "Sebastian, my friend, our debate on Bernini must one day be resolved."

Yes, I have the material, more than enough, in fact, for a Grove play. That is why I am thinking about doing a full-scale biography. When I really get busy on this project, I'll also do a series of tape-recorded interviews with Collins's daughter, Mrs. Marina Scannell, a very charming woman now in her early eighties who lives at St. Anne's Home on Lake Street. She comes in occasionally to go through her father's papers and seems to have more than all her marbles if one is to judge from the sprightly conversations she has with Marcia Pennyworth, the curator of the History Room. Her son, Collins's grandson, John Charles Scannell II, now in his fifties, heads up the Trans-Pacific Corporation. Aside from being a highly decorated war hero (Naval Air), Scannell is, I'd guess, one of the five or six most important men in San Francisco: an inhabitant of the almost exclusively private world of the upper business echelon—a suite in the Trans-Pacific Pyramid, the Pacific Union Club, an estate adjacent to Mickey Tobin's in Hillsborough, the presidency of the Society of California Pioneers—none of which constitutes a bad end for the great-grandson of an Irish-born army private (later sergeant) and his wife who came around the Horn to California in 1846 with the Stevenson Regiment. Yes, indeed, if I do Sebastian Collins, then I should do his parents also, and his daughter Marina, and her son John Charles Scannell II (if I could ever get his permission), for the Collins family story runs down from 1848 to the present and is in itself a capsule history of San Francisco.

The writing of *San Francisco, Ordeal and Transformation*, however, has left me temporarily worn out. I'm coasting now, hoping that administrative duties, my world of action, will refresh me, will reinvigorate my imagination with a wealth of new data and concerns. Experience heals, I once read in Rabelais, and I need healing, which is why, I tell myself, I took this job when the Mayor offered it: to restore myself through action for the public good.

"Bullshit," Helen Huskett would say. "You took the job because it pays $30,000 a year and you got tired of being Carpino's flunky." Helen would, as usual, be making some sense.

Serena came in. "You'd better get over to see Albert Esau. Also, Commissioner Storm called while you were with the union. She knows about the Esau meeting and she said that you are not authorized to give anything away or make any deals. That's the commission's exlusive prerogative."

I don't want to make any deals with anyone about anything. I only want to be part of San Francisco-in-the-making, part of

24

some great civic enterprise as envisioned, say, by Lewis Mumford, whom I knew when I was a tutor at Cabot House at Harvard. I have read and savored all of Mumford's books on urban culture, my favorites being *The Culture of Cities* (1938) and *The City in History* (1961). The grandeur and sweep of Mumford's vision linked up in my mind with what San Francisco should be, with what, in fact, people like James Duval Phelan and Sebastian Collins wanted it to be: a great city in the grand manner of Paris, Rome, Florence. Mayor Claudio Carpino is always talking this way, and I used to believe him—so much so that I resigned my appointment as a resident tutor in Cabot House (I had two years left on my contract) to come to San Francisco and work as executive aide to the Mayor. Claudio Carpino mesmerized me with his version of San Francisco's possibilities, and after eight years of Harvard study—M.A., Ph.D., and a library degree from Simmons College in Boston—I was ready, I thought, to play my part in some grand work of building the City Beautiful. I fantasized myself working as the Mayor's liaison with the park people, the museum directors, Kurt Adler over at the Opera House; putting the influence of the Mayor's office behind their projects; getting, for instance, a park promenade built along the bay from Fort Point beneath the Golden Gate to Fisherman's Wharf, shore land now in various stages of undevelopment, but consolidated in federal hands as part of the Department of Interior's newly created Golden Gate Recreational Area. This bayshore promenade could be landscaped. Viewing platforms could be built, benches set out, and some of Benny Bufano's animal sculptures (left by Benny to the city, now languishing in a warehouse) could be emplaced in a manner suggestive of Copenhagen.

Why not? I dreamed on, buoyed along by my own academic fantasies and by the Mayor's near-hypnotic powers of persuasion. Why not? The historical pattern was there, the precedent. San Franciscans accomplished something unique in the annals of city-building between 1906 and 1939: between, that is, the destruction of the city by earthquake and fire and

25

the opening of the Golden Gate International Exposition on Treasure Island. Out of their own vision, their strength of civic purpose, using local fiscal resources, San Franciscans rebuilt the city in little more than three years; opened a great world's fair, the Panama–Pacific International Exposition of 1915; built a Beaux Arts city hall and a civic center of magnificent proportions, which included one of the world's great opera houses; constructed a dam and aqueduct system carrying water from the Sierra to reservoirs in San Mateo County, which ranks among the engineering marvels of all times; spanned the bay with two bridges, one the Bay Bridge, and the other the Golden Gate Bridge, which is a work of high art as well as an act of bold engineering. They finished Golden Gate Park, built the De Young Museum, emplaced the Palace of the Legion of Honor on a cypressed promontory overlooking the Pacific. They established a zoo and studded local neighborhoods with playgrounds and swimming pools.

The end of politics—I ardently believed four years back when I drove myself and my books across country in a U-Haul truck—the end of municipal politics especially is to finish the work of the founders, to complete San Francisco, or at the least to take it forward to its next major stage of development.

As we had sat in the foyer of the Dana Palmer House, where Claudio Carpino stayed the night of his Harvard visit, the Mayor had outlined what was yet to be done. Did he know then that it was too late—for him, and, more tragically perhaps, for our conception of San Francisco? Did he know, as we sat amidst the late Federalist elegance of a long-gone American orthodoxy, did he know that he was finished, his world was finished, and maybe even I, age thirty-one at the time, was finished also? As he outlined what remained to be done, his Mediterranean mien, dark blue Brioni suit, and Gucci shoes made a striking contrast to the portrait of Richard Henry Dana, Senior, hanging about the Harvard chair in which the Mayor sat. Richard Henry Dana, Senior, as painted by Washington Allston, had a hawklike WASP Yankee face, hooknosed and ferret-eyed above a ruffled stock and backed by

26

a stiff, high Regency collar, a face characterized by both the bland serenity of the comfortably second-rate and the even calmer assurances of Cambridge caste in the early 1820s.

"We've got the Yerba Buena project to get moving," the mayor of San Francisco told me that iron-clad December night, just before we went down to Cabot House for a cocktail party and a dinner which the master, Matthew Hastings, Fisher Ames Professor of American Studies, had arranged in honor of all undergraduates from San Francisco. "The entire South of Market area is an empty lot, razed by Redevelopment. There are plans for a $550 million project. There's a new performing arts center to be built. I've gotten $5 million in revenue sharing funds set aside. A group headed by Harold Barrett of the Bank of Northern California is raising the rest. We should be sponsoring an annual conference on urban civilization in San Francisco, chaired by someone like Lewis Mumford. We could hold it at the old Flood Mansion on Broadway, now the Convent of the Sacred Heart. The madames would let us use the building in the summer. The film festival needs broadening. The museums should be expanded and an endowment program begun."

It began to snow outside. From where I sat I could look across Prescott Street to Harvard Yard and enjoy the sweep of Sever in its array of lighted windows. The Doric columns of Widener Library, lighted also, glowed in the snowy darkness. The Mayor and I walked past them on our way down to Cabot House.

"I want to drop by here tomorrow and see the Dante collection," he told me.

That was four years ago. Now I was in another library, the San Francisco Library (rather weak in books by or about Dante), riding down three floors in one of its antiquated elevators on my way to see Albert Esau of City Planning. Tina Mae Sperry was running the elevator. A black girl from the Bayview-Hunters' Point Area, large, essentially sweet in temperament, Tina Mae hates the monotony of her job. I

27

recently helped her get into a course offered by Civil Service for minorities desiring to improve their skills. Tina Mae is studying stenography, hoping to take the junior clerk-typist examination. She graduated from high school, but in San Francisco that means nothing. Half our high school graduates are semiliterate. I tutor Tina Mae in my office in basic grammar and writing skills. No one has ever really spent time on the basics with her. She learns quickly. She is about twenty-five, and I like being around her. I hope to hell she passes the steno exam, which is a tough one.

"Doctor Jim," Tina Mae said, "Doctor Jim." Tina Mae calls me "Doctor Jim" with a mixture of sly put-on and, I hope, with some affection. Like so many black people, Tina Mae hides her intelligence behind hip irony, but I know something of what is going on within her: she wants out, and she wants in; she wants something better than what she's got.

Tina Mae's steno books were piled on her chair, the top one open, as if she had been studying in the intervals between the incessant buzzes that summon her throughout the day from floor to floor, keeping her in a seven-by-ten box, filled, usually, with shabby, smelly people. Tina Mae keeps a lot of reading material near her, a fact which her immediate supervisor, Manny Vogel, secretary to the commission and head of support services for the Library, doesn't like. It keeps her from paying attention to her job, Manny claims. I have persuaded Vogel to let Tina Mae read when she isn't busy. Tina's love of reading, I told Manny, stands in such contrast to the nonbookish inclinations of so many librarians on the staff. Tina Mae likes glamour magazines—*Vogue, Mademoiselle, Harper's Bazaar*—diet books, and how-to manuals: how to cook, garden, improve your memory. After Christmas last year, she showed me a photograph of her sister and herself standing in front of a decorated Christmas tree in matching long red gowns, which Tina Mae had herself sewn, having taught herself from a how-to-sew manual.

About a third of the SFPL staff are black: all different, all individuals, and yet all unified by the destiny of color.

28

Black–white relationships are, of course, tragically flawed at their existential core. No one can atone to blacks for the ancient hurt offered them in slavery. Even the most humane and spiritually serene, like Mrs. Spellman, the head of the Religion and Philosophy Department in the Main Library, a woman of learning and compassion, must feel an edge of resentment in the face of the larger America, past and present. Blacks, it seems to me, are like Jews in that they bear the burden of a historical destiny which is both a blessing and a burden. Balance can never come easily. I've sat at fashionable dinner parties next to the most successful and accomplished blacks—a superior court judge; a bank vice-president who is San Francisco's first black socialite; a very lovely, very feminine, very dynamic television newscaster; a city supervisor. Despite it all, despite the home in the Marina, the appellation "Your Honor," the private wine cellar, the recognition by the maître d' at L'Orangerie (San Francisco's official social arbiter), the resentment, the tension, now and then shows itself: as if a serpent were suddenly to rear its head in a flower bank, hissing ominously.

I walked out onto Civic Center, passing, as I had a thousand times, the bust of Edward Robeson Taylor (1838-1923) that stands in the foyer. Taylor served as reform mayor of San Francisco from 1907 to 1910. A physician and an attorney as well as an accomplished literateur, Taylor was appointed mayor in June 1907 when Mayor Eugene Schmitz was convicted of extortion (a conviction later overturned), thereby losing his office under the city charter. Taylor served a total of 33 years as a trustee of the library, many of them alongside James Duval Phelan and Sebastian Collins. Taylor chose the inscription on the façade of the building, "May this Structure Throned on Imperishable Books Be Maintained and Cherished from Generation to Generation for the Improvement and Delight of Mankind": a sentiment that always makes me a little sad when I realize what these early hopes have come to some sixty or so years later.

Like James Duval Phelan and Sebastian Collins, Edward

29

Robeson Taylor brought nineteenth-century dreams into San Francisco's twentieth century. Taylor studied medicine on his own while clerking in a Sacramento store during the 1860s. He later received formal medical training at the Toland College of Medicine, since absorbed into the University of California Medical Center on Parnassus Heights. He studied law on his own while serving as private secretary to Governor Henry H. Haight and was admitted to the bar in 1871. Taylor wrote ornate, rhetorical poetry, filled with learning, moralism, and the sort of florid aestheticism favored by San Francisco's late Victorians, including Sebastian Collins.

As a library trustee, Taylor directed in 1917 that the names of the great writers of western civilization be inscribed on the new Library's outside walls. Sebastian Collins gave him some argument on this, feeling it a little too pretentious, hence provincial; but the majority of the Board of Trustees voted with Taylor. Sophocles, Aeschylus, Pindar, Virgil, Dante, Cervantes, Shakespeare, Goethe: these grand names are arranged around the San Francisco Public Library's granite walls like leather-bound tomes arranged on the shelves of a nineteenth-century gentleman's study; books read, remembered, cherished by frontier Californians who because of the remoteness of their circumstances sustained—as did Sebastian Collins—a special reverence for the high orthodoxies of European civilization. As young men, they read the classics in the Sierra by cabin firelight, or in Sacramento boarding houses after a day of selling beef and flour. A few years later, by the 1870s, when they had made some money and moved down to San Francisco, they read these books in overstuffed leather chairs by the glow of a gasjet. Had the fire of 1906 not destoyed the San Francisco Public Library's collection, many of these battered editions of the classics would still be on our shelves, annotated by this or that worthy of local obscurity or fame.

Old books offer a tangible suggestion of lives having been lived. For me at least, this is the palpable essence of history: a sense of the past perceived as cumulative lives, especially in personal moments surviving in physical fragments—a book, a letter, a miniature brought around the Horn in a sailor's breast pocket in 1846. That is why I became a librarian and a curator rather than an academic historian, why I got my library degee along with my Ph.D., and took an internship at the Boston Museum of Fine Arts: because I feel the past as an artifact and an ambiance as well as a sociological process or dialectic. For me history survives best in books and *objets d'art*, in manuscripts and curios. That is why I love museums and libraries. They preserve the physical feel of the past. That is why I once hoped to get something done for San Francisco.

Albert Esau, Director of Planning for the City and County of San Francisco, was brooding at his desk when I entered his office. Being an intellectual, Esau broods a lot. Being a left-liberal intellectual, he broods even more. Esau hates Mayor Claudio Carpino. This is fairly obvious to all of us. Whatever the personal aspects of the dislike, the ideological confrontation is clear-cut. Esau wants San Francisco kept on a smaller scale. He despises what he calls Carpino's "edifice complex." Carpino, on the other hand, has led the development of downtown San Francisco—manhattanization, it is called. The two, ever polite in each other's presence, carry on a nasty guerrilla warfare whenever they get the chance.

"Carpino," Esau says, "would like to turn this town into one goddamn skyscraper."

"Esau," Carpino says, "would like to turn this town into a Pacific Coast Williamsburg—a boutique city for limousine liberals, where they could promenade before an admiring peasantry."

As mayor of San Francisco, Claudio Carpino is Albert Esau's boss. As director of planning, Esau technically reports to the Planning Commission; but Carpino appoints the commissioners, most of whom are his personal friends. If Carpino were ever to push it, he could make it tough for Esau. But Carpino rarely pushes it—even when Esau nearly defeated John Charles Scannell II's Trans-Pacific Building, a pyramid-shaped skyscraper planned for the site of the old Sutro Block on Sansome Street, right in the heart of downtown San Francisco. Aggressively stylized, the Trans-Pacific Pyramid unambiguously celebrates the coming-of-age of San Francisco as an international corporate headquarters. It makes no apologies to anyone. It resembles, in fact, a neo-Babylonian temple to commercial enterprise.

"It's a phallic symbol, a goddamn phallic symbol," Esau says.

"Renaissance Sienna was full of phallic towers," Carpino answers. He wanted the building built—approved, that is—by the Planning Commission and by the Board of Supervisors, as required by the city charter. "Intellectuals, even Freudian intellectuals, shouldn't be allowed to arbitrate taste," the Mayor used to say—frequently, and loudly.

The Trans-Pacific Building was approved by the Board of Supervisors with only a one-vote margin. Esau agitated against it ceaselessly, and nearly won. The gleaming white pyramid now dominates the city's downtown skyline. It even appears in the logo of KLIB, the city's public television station, most of whose commentators opposed the building in the first place. The very sight of the Trans-Pacific Pyramid must drive Albert Esau crazy.

Esau helped defeat Carpino's bid to allow National Steel to build a skyscraper and ferry-port plaza on the Embarcadero near the Ferry Building. Esau also helped defeat Carpino's plan to develop a number of unused piers on the Embarcadero into an office, apartment, shopping, and boatel complex. Carpino wooed the Vatican Bank as a prime investor. Esau and the environmentalists were driven to a frenzy by the Vatican-backed plan. They fed data to the Bay Conservation Commission asserting that such a massive pier development would damage the ecology of the bay. The plan went down to defeat when the Bay Conservation Commission ruled against it.

For the past ten years, the Redevelopment Agency has been acquiring and clearing entire city blocks south of Market Street, an area that was once San Francisco's skid row. A $500 million complex is planned: a convention center, a sports auditorium, a furniture mart, a shopping mall, office buildings, residential apartments; the whole integrated through caseways and promenades into an urban beehive of commercial and residential life. The liberal intelligentsia are appalled by the vision behind this project: the vision of the future city, the future of San Francisco, as a mass-scale megalopolis. Three years ago Roger Kindus, a local radical activist, lodged a class-action suit against the project. It was never taken to the voters, he claimed. Inadequate provisions had been made to relocate displaced residents. No low- and middle-income housing was planned for the proposed apartment complex. For the past three years, the Yerba Buena project has languished in litigation. South of Market looks like a bombed-out city in the Second World War.

And yet, I thought, as I looked around Esau's office, with its view across the Civic Center to City Hall, has any American city been more redeveloped in the past twenty-five years than San Francisco? One wall of Esau's office is hung with photographs of projects now underway or already brought to completion. Between the work of the Redevelopment Agency and the manhattanization of the financial district, San Francisco has been totally transformed. No wonder the radicals are angry! They want the city kept scaled down. Redevelopment, in turn, has scaled it up—destroying the city's erstwhile Mediterranean skyline, thrusting San Francisco upwards to the sky, story by story. The new San Francisco emanates a mood of corporate power. The Levi Strauss Company, the Alcoa Corporation, Standard Oil, the Pacific Gas & Electric Company, the Bank of America, and assorted other companies have in the past five years all erected towering skyscrapers in downtown San Francisco.

As usual, Esau was in a grumpy mood. He shaves his head Telly Savalas style, and plays a Kojak role around City Hall: brusque manners, necktie pulled away from an open collar, glasses pushed up over his forehead. Esau's energetic East Coast Jewish temperament is continually running up against

33

San Francisco's more laid-back provincial pace. It's no secret that, fed up with his job, Esau has recently been negotiating for a professorship of city planning at Stanford.

Ignoring my entrance, Esau continued to write furiously away on a yellow legal tablet. Having nothing to do but wait, I studied examples of Esau's photography mounted on one wall. They were taken from a recent exhibition of Esau's work given at the Museum of Art. In the exhibit Esau celebrated what he likes about San Francisco: neighborhoods such as the Haight-Ashbury and Noe Valley where he lives along with many of the other intellectuals of the city; the Spanish districts of the Mission; picturesque North Beach with its Italian restaurants and second-hand bookstores; everything, in short, that counter-defines manhattanization. No wonder the man is frustrated! His rudeness has by now become a defiant pose against the forces that thwart his vision of what the city should be: Carpino, the Chamber of Commerce, big labor—the coalition, in short, that now holds power in City Hall: the sort of people whom Andy Soutane will be explicitly running against, "the Big Cigars," Toby Wain calls them. To Esau I am merely part of that coalition. I am just another flunky of Claudio Carpino's. I never expect, nor do I ever receive, much help from Albert Esau.

"How's the next mayor of San Francisco?" Esau asked sarcastically, throwing his flair-tip pen down on his desk with a sort of subdued violence, as if, symbolically, he were throwing me out of his office.

Two days ago *Examiner* columnist Walter Rosenfeld included me in a list of dark-horse candidates to enter the mayor's race this spring. Carpino's second term expires in January of next year. Rosenfeld also mentioned Johnboy Turfer, the brash self-made millionaire antitrust attorney who, ten years earlier, slept in his Edsel and dined on peanut butter sandwiches the first night he arrived here from Chicago. Turfer now rents an entire floor of the Hearst Building on Market Street and lives in a Spanish Revival mansion out in West Clay Park, overlooking the Golden Gate. I was there for New Year's Eve last year, and I must say that the Turfer home is spectacular: art, books, antique furniture, a slew of servants—everything to make a poor Appalachian boy from Chicago feel good about himself. Turfer features aggressively tailored pinstripe suits and smokes $1.50 Monte Cruz cigars. He's brash, arrogant, and colorful as hell. Come to think of it, either he or I would make a good mayor once Carpino steps down although neither of us has a chance of ever getting elected. Supervisor Sandra Van Dam, Judge Charles Fessio, Supervisor Al Tarsano, and the two state senators, Mortimer Engels and John Como, have already made moves to enter the race. One of them will be the next mayor.

"Don't believe everything you read in the papers," I replied. Esau's rudeness unnerves me. I always have trouble dealing with women and rude people. "Besides, like Oscar Wilde says: the next worse thing to being talked about is not being talked about." I hated myself for trying to please him. He stared blankly at me for a score of uneasy seconds, like I was some loathsome slug crawling across his garden lawn.

"What the hell is your commission trying to do?" he began *sans* preface. "They're never going to build on Marshall Square. This just isn't a library town. The performing arts people are ready to build. This square has been empty since the earthquake and fire. Let them have it."

Esau's shirtsleeves were rolled up and his tie yanked loose from his unbuttoned collar, Bobby Kennedy style. Outside, through the blue-tinted glass of the Planning Department (a temporary building in the modern style, thrown up just before the Second World War as a USO reception center), I could see the Beaux Arts grandeur of Arthur Brown's City Hall. Esau was right. The Civic Center should be completed. A performing arts center on Marshall Square would do the job nicely. There is no way in hell that a new Main Library will ever be built on Marshall Square, Commissioner Mabel Storm notwithstanding. Defending the Library's position, I am defending a lie—but it isn't the first time I've rushed to the defense of a dishonest orthodoxy.

"You know this, Albert, and I know it, but the commission is adamant. They'll fight any attempt to re-allocate Marshall Square."

"How can you go along with this bullshit? The Mayor wants the PAC people to have Marshall Square. He's allocated $5 million in federal revenue-sharing funds to get the center built. Harold Barrett and Harry Stern are raising the money. Plans are being drawn up. The Library could never get even halfway to this stage in a thousand years. You're the city librarian. You're protected by the Mayor. You can't lose your job, even if your commission gets angry. Tell the truth. What's the best thing, given public support, that could be done for the Library?"

I'd thought about this question on many previous occasions and had no trouble answering him, although I was a little surprised by my frankness. As I said: his brusqueness unnerves me.

"The best thing we could do right now is not to build a new main library, but renovate the old one. About a third of the space is unused anyway. The entire basement is unimproved."

"Exactly," Esau continued for me. He is smart, Albert Esau. He knows a lot about libraries, hospitals, parks, zoos, and the locating of police stations and firehouses. He knows a lot about cities—period, which is why even his enemy, Mayor Claudio Carpino, dare not can him. It would cause a scandal.

"Exactly. You get the new space-saving technology into the Library—microfilm and microfiche readers, things like that. You put your infrequently circulating materials into remote storage. You put your reference collection on a noncirculating basis. You automate the twenty percent of your collection that really circulates. There you have it—an automated, renovated library. No need to build a behemoth on Marshall Square at more than $90 a square foot, a useless, expensive book warehouse, another goddamn ego-edifice in San Francisco."

"What do you want me to do?" I asked.

"Tell the truth about what should be done when you go before the Planning Commission and Board of Supervisors.

36

The Performing Arts Center project is fragile. It can't stand a big public fight, especially against the Library."

"Why are you behind the PAC?" I asked. "I thought you disliked big buildings and big downtown projects."

I hadn't the nerve to suggest that two of the PAC sponsors were Stanford trustees and could be instrumental in getting Esau's professorship through or blocking it, depending upon how well he performed on his last big project as planning director: getting the PAC solidly underway, including nailing down the site. Esau was under a lot of pressure.

Esau was visibly annoyed by my question. Backing such a big Chamber of Commerce—Downtown project as the PAC is not exactly his style. Esau's crowd, the Noe Valley, upper Haight-Ashbury crowd, are all for the neighborhood arts— experimental theater; ethnic dancing; Black, Asian, and Chicano self-expression, that sort of thing. The PAC will be used to book concerts and performances originating in the East Coast or in Europe: nothing but big-name, big-time performers and performances, for whom San Francisco is just a road town. Already the neighborhood arts people are up in arms against the PAC. They've been around my office pledging support in the upcoming contest over Marshall Square: support I really don't want.

I left Esau's office and on impulse started to walk across the Civic Center to City Hall to see the Mayor. If you drop by at odd times, if nothing else is doing, and, most crucially, if Ursula Iraslav, the Mayor's irascible, loyal, sixtyish, appointments secretary is in a halfway decent mood (which isn't too often), then you might be able to get in. Actually, I like Ursula Iraslav, and I know that she is faintly amused by yours truly.

"Norton's a good librarian," she says, "even if he doesn't know where the books are."

She says this, and other things, in a rather loud voice. She is over six feet tall and has red hair. She pulls out a compact, 1940s style, three or four times a day and applies makeup, 1940s style, to her unambiguously Eastern European features. Ursula Iraslav is an old-fashioned executive secretary in an era

37

of women's lib, when secretaries think twice about getting their boss a cup of coffee.

"Jimmy, what's doin'? I was just on my way to the Library to see you. Got a minute?"

It was Tiny Roncola—*the* Tiny Roncola: failed seminarian (like myself, like Andy Soutane, our probable next governor), failed candidate for the governing board of the city college district, failed law student (evening division, the University of San Francisco), now getting by as a semisuccessful political handyman and behind-the-scenes City Hall kibitzer. Current employment: administrative assistant at Redevelopment. Being civil service exempt (the jobs there are handed out by the mayor), Redevelopment offers a safe haven for people like Tiny Roncola, political hacks who have done favors (Tiny worked on the Mayor's second campaign) and who now need to be tucked away until the next election time, when they can once again earn their keep.

As I said, Tiny and I were down at Saint Patrick's Seminary in Menlo Park together, trying on a cassock for size, around 1963. In both cases, the cassock didn't fit. We'd both graduated from the Jesuit-run University of San Francisco in 1962 and resumed our acquaintance, casually, when I returned from Harvard to San Francisco. Tiny likes to pull me aside and pump me for gossip from the Mayor's office, a tidbit or two which he can then pass on at strategic moments to the higher-ups at Redevelopment, thus preserving his reputation for being wired into City Hall.

Tiny Roncola pays me back once every six weeks or so in the form of Friday lunch, his treat, down at the Wharf—Sabella's, Castagnola's, the Franciscan—a two-martini, bottle-of-wine lunch, ending at two-thirty, which leaves very little remaining of the work day, which is usually OK by me because by Friday I've had it up to here with the goddamn San Francisco Public Library and the goofy people running around there, as in a squirrel cage, until their pensions come.

Tiny is a fringer, a parasite on real power (whatever the hell real power is!), but so am I, by the same token, a fringer and a parasite. What I care about most deeply in life (if I care about

38

anything!) doesn't in the long run count for much in San Francisco; but I can't play the martyr. Let's be honest. I like the money and the semi-status of being city librarian. I like the association with the Mayor. I like lunch around town in the big black Cadillac limousine. (A truck carrying the Red Garter band, playing downtown at noontime, once followed us, serenading the Mayor's limousine with "San Francisco.") I like sweeping into Trader Vic's after the opera in the Mayor's entourage, he with the evening's soprano on one arm, the restaurant breaking into applause. I like the throwing out of the first ball of the Giants' season at Candlestick Park. I like meeting visiting celebrities like Gina Lollobrigida, Pete Dawkins, Cyrus Vance, Tony Lukas (the Mayor took Tony to Tommy's Joynt for lunch and an interview). I like the Damon Runyon-like characters who cluster in the front office: Inspector Ted Potelli, the Mayor's chauffeur—bodyguard, who talks all day on the phone; Jimmy Driscoll, the Mayor's aide for neighborhood relations, who ran a bar out in the Mission for twenty-five years. I like, in short, the Last Hurrah quality of the Carpino administration, its lingering mood of the oldtime San Francisco when Sunny Jim Rolph was mayor and everyone in town seemed to be having fun.

"I was just going over to try to see the Mayor. No appointment, so no hurry."

We sat on the one bench free of derelicts. Civic Center hasn't been the same since they ripped out the park that used to be here to build an underground parking lot. Paved over in concrete, sparsely planted, relieved only by a nondescript reflecting pool, Civic Center now exists as a sort of no man's land facing City Hall, the State Building, where the Supreme Court sits, and the Library, against whose southern side a cluster of Indians, stumbling up from the Greyhound bus depot on Seventh, daily hold a drunken pow-wow.

"How's the primary campaign coming, Jimmy?"

Tiny, like everybody else, knew that the Carpino candidacy isn't going too well. The latest poll shows Andy Soutane ahead of Carpino two-to-one for the Democratic nomination for governor. Anyway, for the past half year my role in planning

39

for the campaign has been reduced to next to zero. A year or so ago, I belonged to a study group headed by Danny Pappas, the head of the mayor's Office of Economic and Community Development. Pappas supervises the enormous flow of federal funds coming into the city. We'd meet in Danny's office in the basement of City Hall an hour or so before work, drinking execrable coffee out of styrofoam cups, planning for the upcoming primary. There were Danny; myself; Nadia North, a UC–Santa Barbara graduate who'd married one of the Mayor's nephews and now worked with Pappas as a community planner; Hal Diamond, a Bank of America VP who took early retirement; and Terry Butterworth, a Planner Two, working for Esau, married, the father of two kids, who came out of the closet last fall at the opera when he showed up with a boyfriend, the two of them wearing matching bodyshirts and puka necklaces.

Danny Pappas would assign us topics—pollution, economic development, education, the aging—and we'd develop position papers for the Mayor to use in the primary. Of course, he never will use any of it. The inner circle of the campaign—dominated by Fred Carpino, the Mayor's cousin, a West Portal restaurateur, and Barry Scorse, head of civil service, the Mayor's most trusted aide—feel that the doubledomes should get the hell out of the campaign with their crazy doubledome ideas. The campaign, they say, should be run right and hard-line: by which they mean Labor, and Labor alone, should have the main say.

For the past four months Scorse has been shuttling the Mayor up and down the state on PSA commuter flights to meet with the leadership of nearly every union you can think of. Beefy guys in doubleknit suits move in and out of the Mayor's office like a longshoremen's convention—which is what they are: longshoremen, but also teamsters, plumbers, marine cooks and stewards, warehousemen, construction workers, the lot. These guys, Scorse tells the Mayor, ain't no doubledome fairies, but a bread-and-butter, meat-and-potatoes crowd. Come election day, these guys will deliver the vote—period. No issues, no highfalutin bullshit, just juice. That will be enough to get Claudio Carpino the nomination—juice.

Meanwhile, Andy Soutane, the other Democratic candidate, state senator from Santa Barbara County, age forty-two, a bachelor, and for some five years or so in his late teens and early twenties a student for the priesthood with the Franciscans at Mission Santa Barbara, is doing exactly the opposite. He's going up and down California telling people that California needs a New Spirit to fit the New Times. He's preaching austerity and a de-escalation of expectations. He's talking ecology and wildlife preservation. He quotes Buddha, St. Thomas Aquinas, Simone Weil, Ivan Illich, Herbert Marcuse, Bob Dylan. He walks the beach at Santa Barbara and warns of future oil spills. He wangles his way into the yard at San Quentin and talks prison reform. He throws open his home in a back canyon outside Carpenteria to reporters, and they in turn fill the newspapers and magazines with details of his austere lifestyle: the cot, the footlocker, the Quaker chair; the save-the-whale poster on the wall; the stir-fry he uses to whip up austere vegetable dinners; the books—Kierkegaard, Schumacher, *The Little Flowers* of St. Francis, Buckminster Fuller; the magazines—*Sierra Club Bulletin, Rolling Stone, New Republic*; the backpack and assorted camping gear tossed into a corner as if after recent use. Soutane dates a well-known movie star and an even better-known fashion model to establish his sexual identity. His advisers, I know, have warned him that his being single could develop into an issue. He gets his photograph with top-notch model Tara Malone in *Rolling Stone*, the two of them walking dreamily, hand in hand, along a deserted stretch of Malibu beach—she in jeans and a halter, Soutane in a three-piece Brooks Brothers suit with his tie loose, perfectly relaxed, as if he'd just dropped by from drafting a progressive piece of legislation.

"No," I said to Tiny Roncola, "the campaign's not going so good."

"You've got an image problem," Tiny continued, talking to

41

me as if I were in the thick of the Carpino campaign, which I am not. It's Tiny's way of flattering people (including himself). "Carpino has got a compromised image. Soutane is clean. He looks like Robert Redford. He's fresh—the future." So far, Tiny was belaboring the obvious.

"It's out of my hands, Tiny. I just want to survive, that's all."

"Yeah, you're right. The next mayor probably won't keep you, you being so close to Carpino and all. If Carpino doesn't go to Sacramento, you'll be on the streets."

Tiny was pushing it a little—but not very. It is a very probable scenario. Teaching jobs are next to impossible to find in the Bay Area. I live well—a flat on Telegraph Hill, a Porsche, a book collection, the Bohemian Club, an active social life. I need a minimum of $25,000 a year just to stay afloat at my present lifestyle. What would I do if I lost this job? I'm getting too old for *la vie bohème* in a Haight-Ashbury garret. Or worse, I might have to get a job in college teaching, spilling my guts out in the classroom about American culture for undergraduates who couldn't care less about any of it. I've tried so desperately hard to play some sort of role in what I consider the real world. How could I go back to being a thirty-five-year-old assistant professor, anxiety-ridden over tenure?

"There's got to be a breakthrough," Tiny continued, "some way of suggesting that Soutane's shit stinks like the rest of ours. We all know Carpino's shit stinks."

He laughed, then stared at me for a moment blankly, as if waiting for a reply. Knowing that Soutane's, Carpino's, and everybody's shit stinks, I could think of nothing else to say. I preferred our Wharf lunches. Tiny Roncola was amusing then. Now he seemed a little tedious. I made as if to get up.

"Now something like this might do the trick." He handed me an envelope. "Go ahead, look. Take a look."

There were photographs inside, in color, a series of them. They showed Andy Soutane in a series of interesting positions with another gentleman.

42

Chapter 2

M Y NAME IS SEBASTIAN COLLINS. I am sixty-seven years old. I was born in San Francisco in 1848, the year gold was discovered. Next year, in February of 1915, the Panama–Pacific International Exposition opens. My friend, the bookseller Paul Elder, has asked me to hurry along with my *Memoirs of a San Franciscan Bohemian*. He wants to publish it sometime during the Exposition. I have the manuscript just about ready, having been at work on it now for some two years.

Sixty-seven! Quite frankly, I never expected to live so long. When I was a young man, I broke off my studies at Harvard to fight in Italy with an Irish regiment of papal Zouaves. We were making a last-ditch effort to preserve the independence of the Papal States. In the course of my service I killed a man; and because of this I never thought that I would myself survive the war. In the horrible time after I realized that my love for Sybil Sanderson was hopeless, I thought I would drink myself to death, or worse, die of syphilis, or be stabbed one early morning outside a cabaret. When my wife Virginia died in childbirth, I was nearly fifty and I thought that the shock of her death would make me an old man and that I would just slip away.

But here I am: sixty-seven and in good health, the father of a nineteen-year-old daughter. For these past two years I have been reviewing my life and its tattered, surviving artifacts: artifacts, by the way, I am fortunate in yet possessing, for I had my books and papers removed to St. Helena in the Napa Valley just before that dark and terrible time some nine years ago when this city, this beloved San Francisco, was shaken to the ground by earthquake, then gutted by fire. I kept the house at Avila Vineyards which Virginia and I shared together for a year. I brought everything up there because I was spending more and more of my weekends in the country. Because of this I have not lost the tangible evidence of my past as have so many of my fellow San Franciscans, the accumulations of whose lifetimes went up in smoke.

From the vantage point of the study window in my flat atop Taylor Street, I have been watching the pastel fantasy city of the Exposition rise up on the once marshy acres called Harbor View. My study is crammed with the artifacts and remnants of my surprisingly long life. I have gone through them all, sorting and arranging them with the help of Marina, my daughter. Given her age and mine, Marina should be my granddaughter, but no mind: I am a Pacific Coast Prospero, shipwrecked in San Francisco with Marina, my sea-born daughter—only my Marina was born in St. Helena, amidst the vines. Marina seems to have a natural gift for imposing order on chaos, which probably arises out of her having kept house for a widowed father for most of her life—in between taking lessons at the Convent of the Sacred Heart and pursuing courses across the bay at Mills College.

"I insist, Father, that you organize your papers," Marina announced one Saturday morning *apropos* of nothing in particular.

"Do I look that feeble?" I asked. "Am I ready to slip off?"

"On the contrary, you look disgustingly healthy for someone of your advanced years. It's just that it's no good having everything lying about in disarray up in St. Helena. Let's bring it all back to San Francisco and organize it; and then you'll really have something."

"And what, pray tell, will that be?"

44

"Proof that you existed—or if not that, then at least some decoration for your study. This room is too bare for my tastes."

"Like a monk's cell?"

"You, dear Father, are no monk. I am living proof of that."

"Very well. I shall have it all brought down—but only on the condition that you help me organize it."

"I agree. It will give us something to talk about. Besides—I'm curious as to what you were up to in the half century of your life before I appeared on the scene to give some justification to your scattered, haphazard existence."

"You more than redeem me, my dear. Now be a good girl and fix lunch."

Marina and I have spent many happy hours together, sorting and arranging the scattered leaves of my sixty-seven years—although I will not let her read some of my letters. She can read them later, when she is older and I am dead, but not while I am yet around to be asked embarrassing questions by an impertinent Mills College girl. Now, some two years into the writing of *Memoirs of a San Franciscan Bohemian,* my study—as Jack London laughingly put it the other night when I had him over for a whiskey before dinner at the Bohemian Club—my study is like a Yukon cabin provisioned to the ceiling for a long winter: my winter obviously (although Jack did not say so) being whatever few years lie ahead.

There are my books, first of all: next to my daughter—and my memories!—the most significant items I've rescued from devouring time. My Heidelberg thesis, firstly, *Bernini, Eros, and the Transcendent* (1878), which I completed in the Vatican Library. Archbishop Alemany had secured me a position there when my patron William Chapman Ralston's plans for a San Francisco Atheneum (Sebastian Collins, Director) collapsed in 1875, along with everything else, with the failure of the Bank of California and Ralston's subsequent drowning off North Beach. Next to this on the shelf is my *Art of the Baroque* (1885), published—the very year I fell in love with Sybil Sanderson—by the Houghton Mifflin Company of Boston, which also published my friend Josiah Royce's *California*

(1884). Royce left San Francisco for Harvard in 1882, while I stayed on at my post at St. Ignatius College. Among my students there was James Duval Phelan, the former mayor of our city, the current United States senator from California, and my close friend.

"Here's Mother's book," Marina said to me reverently and a little sadly when we came upon the boxed manuscript of *Wine Prospects for California* (1895). Virginia and I jointly wrote this little monograph in the happy year of our St. Helena life together. I saw it through the press after her death. I saw Virginia's handwriting, so bold for a woman's. I took the ribbon-tied bundle from Marina and, holding the sheaf of papers to my face, I caught, or thought I caught, a trace of her scent. Virginia held Marina in her arms but once before the fever took her off. She looked at me with—what? Accusation? Fear? Resignation? I cannot decide even to this day.

My *A Call for California Literature* (1900) comes next on the shelves. Marina insists that we always order my few books chronologically. Some day this particular book will be a collector's item because of the wonderful inscriptions across the portraits of the writers I singled out for praise: Jack London, Frank Norris, Gertrude Atherton, John Muir, George Sterling, David Starr Jordan, Mary Austin, Ambrose Bierce, Charles Warren Stoddard, Agnes Tobin, Gelett Burgess, Porter Garnett, Nora May French and the others, so many of whom I knew—some too well!—from Coppan and Telegraph Hill circles, which I frequented some ten and more years ago despite my age and despite the fact that Charlie Stoddard and I should have known better. We verged upon making fools of ourselves, but we loved the gaiety and youth of bohemian San Francisco, not to mention its droll acceptance of Charlie and myself as survivors of an earlier era, the golden Literary Frontier of Bret Harte, Mark Twain, and Joaquin Miller. I feel a sense of some sadness when I pick up this book, written but fifteen years ago. So many of the people in it are dead—Charlie Stoddard, Ambrose Bierce, Frank Norris. Nora May French committed suicide on George Sterling's porch at

Carmel, and Jack London is not doing too well these days either. "To Sebastian Collins," Frank Norris wrote across the photograph of himself in *A Call for California Literature,* "Nestor of our scribbling bohemian tribe." Frank appears quite elegant in the photograph, sitting in a velvet smoking jacket by his books and silver samovar. He died the next year on the operating table.

How generous of George Santayana to review so favorably my *Theological and Literary Relationships* (1905), and for Rafael Cardinal Merry del Val, papal secretary of state, to write me so warmly upon its publication. His letter recalled our last meeting with the Tobin family in Burlingame upon the occasion of his visit to San Francisco in the autumn of 1899, when he was *en route* to Japan. Sitting on the veranda before a sweeping lawn, we ate cold salmon and sipped the very chablis Virginia and I had pressed from the good grapes of Avila Vineyards. Monsignor Merry del Val commented favorably on the wine.

Sybil Sanderson, A California Story (1910) is but half the book I might have written. The rest is written in my heart and in the few dozen or so rambling, tormented letters I wrote to Sybil from various cities of Europe in the years 1888–1892, as I wandered about in search of forgetfulness—a stupid, foolish forty-year-old dissipant, a comic lovesick *habitué* of brothels and stews, more wine-soaked than priapic, but copulating when and if I could, as if to regain time and stay the terror of my wasted life. None of this, for obvious reasons, finds its way into my biography of Paris's and San Francisco's great opera singer—although I do enter the narrative obliquely in my account of the opening night of *Thaïs* in Paris on 16 March 1894, the night before I left Europe to return to San Francisco, cured of my obsession.

My friend and confessor, Monsignor John Gleeson, rector of St. Mary's Cathedral, was immediately sensitive to the undercurrents and resonances of my account of Sybil's operatic career. He brought the matter up to me ever so subtly one night recently as we sat over cigars and claret, as is our wont

47

every fortnight or so. "I loved your evocation of *Thaïs*," he said between a sip of the claret and a puff on the fine Havana that Dunhill's on Post Street imports for us both. "You suggested in a most beautiful manner the opera *Thaïs's* intersection of sacred and profane love."

I fear that I might be too old to feel profane love. Yet I dearly love my daughter and will insist that she be cautious with her new young man, John Charles Scannell, although despite my prejudice against lawyers, I rather like him. Sacred love has either baffled or eluded me. I felt, however, the pointedness of Monsignor Gleeson's suggestion, for I once told him the whole story of my infatuation with Sybil. He kindly listened, repelled no doubt (although I tried to be delicate) by the rather blatant eroticism of my life after Sybil sent me away with gentle laughter—but also attracted to it. John Gleeson, despite his monsignor's robes and thirty years of celibacy, is also a man, possessed of a man's feeling, possessed also of great empathy for the life of art, which, after all, is not that different from the life of religion.

I will leave my books to Marina. Someday she can discuss them with her children or grandchildren: in some far-off year, 1940, say, when I will have long since been deposited in Holy Cross Cemetery, past memory or care. Will I be with Christ? What blinding vision, or what darkness, will greet me when I leave this life?

1940 has a nice resonance to it: a point of perspective for some chronicler upon the years 1848 to 19whatever that I have enjoyed. If I say so myself (and I do), I have not had a boring life. In my youth, fleeing from the ambiguity of what happened to me at Harvard, I wore on my breast the white cross of a papal Zouave. I was in the field against Garibaldi, assisting in 1867 in his arrest outside Rome. My *confrères* in the Zouaves found my enlistment humorous, America being a secular republic and all, but I convinced them that I was more Irish than Yankee, my parents both having been born in the old country and having come to California in 1846 as part of Colonel Stevenson's colonizing regiment of soldier—settlers.

48

Yes, I shall pass these books on (so few to show after a lifetime of reading and study), together with the boxes and cartons of letters and *memorabilia* Marina and I have sorted and arranged as if I were already dead, which I do not yet intend to be—dead. A marvelous determination has come over me of late, an appetite for life perhaps in bad taste for a portly gentleman of sixty-seven, a minor scholar and man of letters, recently retired from the James Duval Phelan Chair of Philosophy and Art History in the College of St. Ignatius. I have seen San Francisco grow up and be destroyed; and I want to see it rebuilt. My own work as a consultant in the building of City Hall, the Library, and St. Ignatius Church atop Fulton Street on the western edge of San Francisco has been a contribution to that end.

I saw a woman, my wife, die; and I want to see a woman, my daughter, launched into some path of happiness. There are books yet to read, lunches to enjoy at the Bohemian Club—and the Exposition, I must see that through. Day by day I have watched this pastel dream city take form. I am most taken with the Tower of Jewels and the Palace of Fine Arts; indeed, I am most taken with this new San Francisco of ours in general, which surprises me, for I lived so intensely in the old city that the Fire and Earthquake took from us. Mayor Phelan asked me to serve on the Committee for the Adornment and Beautification of San Francisco, and thereby hangs a tale. We are not going to have the Burnham Plan. We are going to have the Exposition instead. I agree with John McLaren, the creator of our Golden Gate Park: the Exposition can be a model for our future city, our future San Francisco.

The future! Yes, I shall have some sort of future. I insist upon it. The very fact that I did not marry until I was forty-five, becoming a father at forty-eight, shows a delayed biological mechanism in my life. Having seen—and resisted on the field of battle—the coming of the twentieth century, I am destined to experience a good deal of its pleasures and pains. God willing, I could survive another ten years or so. Or I could die tonight in my sleep.

It begins to fit into a pattern, this life of mine. The war in Europe has not yet become America's—but I know what it is all about. I fought against the emergence of the abstract, greedy, power-hungry modern state when I wore the uniform of the papal Zouaves, as remote as that episode in my life now seems. John Charles Scannell, Marina's young lawyer friend, talks of our inevitable entrance into the European conflict, but I am not so sure.

I have my health. After churning away for sixty-seven years, my stomach yet digests. My bowels yet evacuate. My breathing is good; my heartbeat, so Dr. Schumate tells me, is regular. I am somewhat given to portliness, but no matter. I walk much about the city, and that seems good for me. I sleep six solid hours a night.

By the sheer fact of my survival, I have become something of a symbolic figure around San Francisco, a tory bohemian Nestor; and that amuses me, in that I spent so many years away from San Francisco in exile, at odds with this provincial town, which I now love, but which—especially after Ralston's drowning off North Beach and the failure of his museum, which he wanted me to direct—I once so vehemently repudiated.

Ah, San Francisco! I knew you in the 1850s when I was a boy, and in the 1860s, the time of my poetic adolescence, shared with Charlie Stoddard and Josie Royce, now of Harvard, and asking for a stroke in the way he's campaigning across the country against the Germans. We both studied in Germany—Royce at Göttingen, I at Heidelberg—so Josie shouldn't be so outraged by what's going on now in Europe. We both encountered the Junkers in our student days, although we knew another Germany as well, the magical kingdom of universities, beer halls, castles, wine, and the roseate promise of scholarship.

San Francisco is the anchor and chain of my collection of *memorabilia,* which I must eventually get into some historical archive or other. Perhaps I'll leave it all to the new Public Library, which we are building on the Civic Center to face City Hall. I could donate my books also, if Marina agrees. There

50

could be a special room housing my books, manuscripts, letters, and *memorabilia*—the Sebastian Collins Room, a monument to high provincial American life, the scattered leavings of an aesthete, a scholar, a would-be expatriate, a local figure in the landscape of emerging San Francisco.

The archivist handling my papers would not have a very difficult task. Marina and I have done most of the work, including arranging and labeling all the material chronologically. "Box One: Early San Francisco" contains a daguerreotype of my parents, Dennis and Mollie Collins, taken in 1848. My father yet wears his sergeant's uniform from Colonel Stevenson's regiment. My mother wears a bonnet and a shawl and appears exactly what she was: an Irish farm girl, somewhat superstitious and shakily literate, but also a quick study when it came to the details of survival in the Gold Rush frontier. At the age of nineteen, after all, she supported herself and me running a boarding house in San Francisco while Father was away at the mines, trying his luck. I yet cherish the letters Mother wrote to me when I was at Harvard. What a painful, loving effort they represent! My mother was physically strong and, in the long run, good-humored. She was resilient, and proud of her position in life as the wife of the man who organized and led for thirty years the fire department of San Francisco.

I have in "Box Three: The 1870s" a photograph of my father in his fire chief's uniform, dated 1876, which would have put him in his mid-fifties, at the height of his powers, just about the time I was leaving Heidelberg for my second sojourn at Rome. I must admit, in fact, that it was my father's friendship with Archbishop Joseph Sadoc Alemany, the Dominican archbishop of San Francisco who lived in a simple shack next to his cathedral at California and Dupont streets, that got the Archbishop to write Silvano Votto, the Cardinal Librarian of the Vatican (a Spanish Dominican also, who had been a fellow novice with Alemany in the 1830s). The Archbishop was kind enough to vouch for my orthodoxy and beseech His Eminence to make available to me a position as *scriptor* in the Library, so that I might finish my Bernini project. The fact that I had served with the Zouaves helped also, as Cardinal Votto was a ferocious anti-Modernist—as was everyone else in Rome in the immediate aftermath of the First Vatican Council. I obscurely participated in that council as a Zouave private in the papal ranks, standing ceremonially on guard outside the bronze doors of the Vatican as cardinals, bishops, abbots, and assorted *monsignori* alighted from their carriages and swept into St. Peter's in a rush of purple and scarlet to save the Church from heresy and proclaim the infallibility of Pius IX, the pope whom General Garibaldi, despite the valor of one Private Sebastian Collins of the St. Patrick's Battalion, had vanquished on the field of battle.

"Box One: Early San Francisco" also contains other items from the 1850s: newspaper clippings of the Vigilance Committee of 1856, which my father always claimed was a Masonic, anti-Irish cabal; my father's letter of appointment from Mayor Ephraim Willard Burr, dated 3 May 1859, commissioning him chief of the fire brigade; my certificates of baptism (1849) and confirmation (1859), both signed by Father Anthony Maraschi, S.J., of the Jesuit church of St. Ignatius on Market Street, the first of five churches to bear that name, the last one now gleaming in alabaster white atop Ignatian Heights; a photograph of myself (1859) when a student at the Lincoln Grammar School at Fifth and Mission streets, where I first met Charlie Stoddard and Josiah Royce, who was then learning what he later termed "the majesty of the community" by getting beat up in the playground; and finally a photograph of the firehouse on Bush Street, between Dupont and Kearny, next to the California Theater. As chief, Father had the entire third floor as his private residence.

"Box Two: The 1860s" is a more varied affair, for I began the decade a boy of twelve in remote San Francisco, spent its middle years as an undergraduate at Harvard, and served from 1867 to 1870 in the army of the Papal States. Box Two, in fact, actually fills three separate cartons. Carton one, Box Two preserves what survives of my years (1861–1865) at the Boys' High School, San Francisco. There are Latin essays, English

52

themes, mathematical books, which Mother carefully kept because she was so proud of the education I was receiving. Josiah Royce's mother did the same thing. There is a sheaf of my boyhood poetry, including one, "Black Point at Twilight," that Mrs. John Charles Fremont liked. I wrote it after an evening at her home, where Charlie Stoddard had brought me. Mrs. Fremont had Ina Coolbrith print it in *The Golden Era;* it thrilled me, not yet twenty, to see my poem and my name in print. I must do justice to Mrs. Fremont in *Memoirs of a San Franciscan Bohemian.* I must have been the youngest *habitué* of the Fremont salon, but she encouraged me to come, remembering, perhaps, how her father Senator Thomas Hart Benton of Missouri let her be about at an even earlier age. Mrs. Fremont brought me to the attention of Mr. Ralston, and Mr. Ralston sent me to Harvard; so I owe much to that marvelous woman, and I am glad I told her so some ten or twelve years ago when I visited her in Los Angeles just before she died, regal to the end, despite a hip injury that kept her confined to a wheelchair.

William Chapman Ralston of the Bank of California was on the lookout for talent, and he thought that I was talented. He stopped his buggy outside the firehouse on Friday in May of 1886 while on his way down the peninsula to his country seat in Belmont. "Send the boy to Harvard. Yes, that's it, send the boy to Harvard," he told my parents after a swift introduction of himself, which was unnecessary, for my father knew who William Chapman Ralston of the Bank of California was—the city's foremost *entrepreneur,* banker, and venture capitalist, the man whose ambition it was to make San Francisco one of the world's great cities in terms of its arts and commerce, a Rome and Florence on the shores of the Pacific. (Ah, vain dream! Yet still alive today in 1915 with the recent completion of the Panama Canal and the imminent opening of the Panama–Pacific International Exposition!) Ralston had a plan, he told my parents, and it included museums and libraries. The city needed scholars, he said. It already had enough lawyers—and too many bankers. He laughed at his joke, but without

53

removing the cigar clamped between his teeth. If I remember correctly, he kept the cigar in his teeth even as he talked.

"Send the boy to Harvard," he went on, as if it were already decided. "I'll pay for it. And then on to Europe. We'll have him trained in library and museum management. He'll be ready in another ten years, just when my plan calls for the San Francisco Atheneum to be built, 1876, the centennial of our great Nation, so recently preserved from rebellion, baptized anew in the martyr's blood of Mr. Lincoln. Yes, we'll send him to Harvard."

He said goodbye, then raced off, cracking his whip in the air above his two sleek black trotters, heading down Bush Street towards the Mission Road. Both my parents regarded me with an element of respect after that. Not that they cared much one way or another about Harvard. They were, however, impressed by Mr. Ralston—especially my father, whose position as fire chief depended in part upon the approval of the city's business community.

Among the other surviving mementos of these early San Francisco years is a printed letter of credit from Emperor Joshua Norton, the wise-fool in military costume who proclaimed himself Emperor of the United States and Protector of Mexico. Royce and I used to play chess with him at the Mechanics' Library, while his two dogs, Bummer and Lazarus, slept outside. Royce and I always felt there was method to Norton's madness, a certain mocking sanity behind his mask. He always beat us at chess.

I also have a letter from Mrs. Fremont dated 18 November 1867, wishing me well at Harvard and expressing her own hopes for San Francisco's future. This is in Carton Two, Box Two—the Harvard carton—along with my letters of transcript: English literary history from Professor Francis Childs; anatomy from Mr. William James (whose niece Alice now lives here in San Francisco, married to Bruce Porter); mathematics from Professor Langdon; and, my favorite Harvard experience, the lectures of Professor Charles Eliot Norton on art history, to which I listened in a golden trance

54

some fifty years ago. Norton's voice, discoursing on Greece and Florence and the Sistine, I can hear to this day if I but shut my eyes. There are receipts for room and board which I paid for by check, drawing upon an account established by Mr. Ralston specifically for that purpose: Gray's Hall, 1867–1868, lodgings $200, commons $275, tailoring $32, miscellaneous expenses (including beer, tobacco, and an Oxford edition of *Lyra Graeca*) $183.

My Harvard effects are stored in one carton (again Marina's idea), although a discontinuity occurs between January 1868, the middle of my sophomore year, and January 1870, when I resumed my education, an older, bronzed junior, age twenty-two. By now I had seen the wars, as had the men–boys I had encountered at Harvard just after the close of the Rebellion, such as former Lieutenant Colonel Oliver Wendell Holmes, Jr., age twenty-four, a law student. My war was in another country, but it left a number of us just as dead as the corpses of Antietam and Chancellorsville. We died despite our picturesque baggy pants, kepis, white-crossed tunics, and the blessings of the Holy Father, the great *Pio Nono* himself, who sent us forth—French, French Canadians, Irish (among them myself), and French-speaking Belgians—to save Rome and the Papal States from red-shirted *liberalismo,* sent us forth to stay the future.

I can partially attribute my sojourn with the Zouaves to Harvard's President Charles Eliot, the most snidely, patronizingly anti-Catholic, anti-Irish fellow I had up to then encountered, although he did have the good sense to appoint his nephew Charles Eliot Norton to the faculty. "Ah, yes, Mr. Collins," President Eliot would say on those few occasions when we spoke, "Mr. Sebastian Collins of San Francisco." He drew out the "San Francisco" with half-bemused distaste and subtle drollery, as one would say Titicaca or Timbuktu or another such nasty place. It all seems amusing to me now, and harmless enough, but Eliot's pinched face (framed in self-indulgent sidewhiskers *à la* Matthew Arnold), his mandarin, nasal, dry Yankee way of speaking, his posture of bemusement before San Francisco, all reinforced my general inability to adjust to Harvard itself. Royce and I have often talked about this. He, after all, went over to Berkeley to the infant University of California, then little more than a rural academy, before braving Europe and the East. Royce had the benefit of a time of transition. I, on the other hand, swept away by Mr. Ralston's enthusiasm and by my own premature success, hurled myself into a vortex of cultural and psychological complexity, and paid the price. It took a war to enable me to take Harvard—a war I got into in the first place as a gesture of anti-Harvardian defiance.

I've always been too obsessively, baroquely if you will, Roman Catholic for my own good—even now, when I should know better. I took the protestantism of Harvard too seriously, more seriously than Harvard itself ever did. In reaction against President Eliot and the others, and because of my resistance to what Ryan Patrice was demanding of me (how naive I was—to react with such emotionalism when I should have laughed the incident off, not fled by train to Quebec; and if I had not been taking confession in the Quebec Cathedral, I would not have witnessed the mustering-in ceremonies for the regiment of Zouaves being raised there for the defense of Rome, and if I had not seen that, in my confused state, I would not have enlisted)—in reaction, in any event, to whatever it was that President Eliot embodied, I fell in among the Ultramontanes of Boston, a group of Catholic intellectuals who met for Sunday evening *soirées* at the house of Ryan Patrice. Patrice was tutor in Provençal, Catalan, Old French, Anglo-Norman, and modern French languages and literature—a gentleman's appointment to be sure; for without some sort of private income, he could not have sustained on a tutor's stipend such a lavish style of living as he pursued in his flat on Follen Street off Cambridge Common. Those Sunday sessions, and the people I met there, were, in effect, my Counter-Harvard, although in retrospect my evenings at Patrice's now seem all of a piece with my Harvard education:

56

all of it melted in the crucible of fifty years on intervening time.

Attired elegantly in his quasi cassock, leaning languidly against a great marble mantelpiece, talking of Fénelon or the Spanish mystics as he stroked his well-trimmed reddish beard, Ryan Patrice yet remains a clear picture in my mind. We never questioned his quasi-ecclesiastical dress, the soutane he wore like a lounging robe, the dark suits that ever so subtly suggested the polished French *abbé*. Patrice's attire seemed appropriate to a flat furnished in moroccan-bound editions of the church fathers, a *Prie-dieu,* and a bejeweled Russian icon-crucifix. Ryan Patrice was then in his mid-thirties, and very much under the influence of the French Catholic Revival of the 1850s—Lacoirdaire, Gounod's *St. Cecelia's Mass,* the final stages of the North African Reconquest—an ambience he managed to summon up in the little provincial protestant college town of Cambridge. When he sauntered past the Puritan graveyard facing the Yard, like a prelate taking the air in the Vatican gardens, I sometimes thought that those venerable Yankee dead might rise up in protest at the insult offered them by the passing of such a blatantly Romanish intruder. Had I later heard that Ryan Patrice had become a curial cardinal, I would not have been surprised, or that he had apostasized and held a chair in philosophy at the *Collège de France* and kept a mistress, for he seemed then to me to be possessed of an essentially secular cunning that, religion or no, would see him through to his wordly goals.

How surprised, then, was I to find him at Grand Chartreuse when I spent four months of 1894 there as a lay oblate, regaining my strength (in every sense of that term) after years of careless living: saw him, not on the high altar, or in the choir stalls with the other white-robed monks, but in the rear of the great abbey church amongst the gardeners, stablers, and other assorted monastery servants, recognizable to me despite the passage of twenty-five years which had left me forty-three years of age and nearly destroyed by debauchery, and him nearing sixty with the face of an El Greco saint. He'd kept his

57

beard, a trace of the old vanity; indeed he'd kept his good looks, only growing grayish and very thin. Dissipation, on the other hand, had thickened me. Since that time, I have been heavy, although I lost weight when Virginia and I worked the Avila Vineyard in Napa County.

The man who had sent me in a panic away from Harvard was now a saint—a missionary, I later found out, to Indo-China, and the *confrère* there of Blessed Theophane Venard, indeed almost Venard's fellow martyr. Elected Superior General of the Paris Foreign Missionary Society, Ryan Patrice had been offered promotion to the episcopacy. He chose instead to enter Grand Chartreuse as an oblate, putting aside his priestly status to work in the monastery fields. He was a saint and I was a sinner who had virtually crawled to Grand Chartreuse for a rest cure, after sitting in the church of St.-Sulpice in Paris one Sunday morning with a hangover and, with the opening of the clouds, being suddenly bathed in radiant sunlight and knowing right then and there that I had to do something about my life, which had become a rather sorry mess.

Carton Three, Box Two is what both Marina and I call the Military Box. Was I ever truly thin enough to fit into the two military tunics I have kept across the years, either that of the French Canadian regiment I joined in Quebec or that of the St. Patrick's Battalion of Irish Zouaves I later transferred to, after General Kanzler reorganized the papal forces? Did I really do combat duty for two years, then stand in the ranks on the morning of 16 September 1870 as the Pope surrendered to Garibaldi and the Papal States came to an end? I did. And in Carton Three, Box Two, I have the souvenirs to prove it.

I suppose that my Bernini book is the most tangible result of my Heidelberg and Vatican Library years. My shelves are also lined with German books acquired during that period. These should also find their way into a research library. I have, most importantly, the letters written to me by Mr. Ralston while I was pursuing my doctorate at Heidelberg. Why do I persist in calling him "Mr." Ralston as if he were still alive, and I yet a twenty-five-year-old doctoral candidate? Because of my military service, it took me seven years to graduate from Harvard. Ralston might have lost interest in my future prospects.

"He what?" Ralston asked my father, when told the news that I had left the college and joined the papal army. "What in God's name did he do that for?"

"Precisely in God's name," my father piously replied.

Ralston's checks resumed when I resumed Harvard. In June of 1873, when I returned to San Francisco after a seven years' absence (this time by the transcontinental railroad completed in 1869), the proud possessor of a Harvard bachelor's degree, Ralston was exuberant.

"You've done it, lad. You've done it!" He laughed as, with me at his side, he raced his horses against the railroad down to Belmont. Ralston was in the habit of doing this to show off his horses. With two of us in the buggy, we couldn't keep up his usual pace and so somewhere around San Mateo he slowed to a reasonable pace and we talked—or rather, I listened.

"I thought that with this pope's army thing, I'd never hear from you," he said; "but now you're back on the track. Heidelberg next, right? Good. Nothing but the best. This city's growing, lad, and we're not that far away from having the Atheneum, another five or six years. Get your doctorate in art history and get some library training. You'll be the best in the country, and San Francisco will have you at the helm, one of our own, born and bred."

That weekend spent at Ralston's Belmont estate was among the most exciting I ever spent in my life. I have written about it extensively in a completed chapter of *Memoirs of a San Franciscan Bohemian*.

John Trask, Art Commissioner for the Panama–Pacific International Exposition, has promised San Francisco an exhibit of painting worthy of Maybeck's Palace of Fine Arts, to include a wing of California painters. There's so much good art around us now—Keith, Martinez, Gray, Peters, Mathews,

McComas, Williams; and good sculpture—Putnam, Calder; and good architecture—Polk, Maybeck, Mullgardt, Brown: not at all like the city I returned to in 1873, a city bereft of indigenous art. Ralston was a man of action, a little naive perhaps in matters of taste. I suppose he half-thought that if I went to Europe to study the old masters, I could somehow do something about bringing the old masters back to San Francisco. Ralston's notion of the Atheneum was compelling, but vague. He envisioned a museum and a research center, located somewhere on Nob Hill, expressive of the translation of high European civilization to the Pacific Coast. The Bancroft Library, the Sutro Library, and Senator Stanford's university in Palo Alto express similar ideas that have succeeded. When it came to dreaming, Ralston always ran ahead of his time.

Reunited that summer in San Francisco, Josie Royce and I planned to travel to Germany together in the autumn. Daniel Coit Gilman, president of the University of California, had persuaded a group of San Francisco businessmen to contribute a purse to send Royce abroad for postgraduate training in philosophy at Göttingen, so that he could return to Berkeley to teach. He and I were both solidly backed local boys, riding the crest of a wave of energy filling the city after the completion of the railroad in 1869.

"How wonderful, Josie," I said to him when I heard the news. We were walking along Folsom Street past the neo-Roman splendor of South Park towards Tenth Street, where the Royces lived in rather embarrassing poverty. I say embarrassing because Mrs. Sarah Royce, a refined English-born woman, was meant for better things than to be the wife of a gold miner turned reluctant grocer. All of us knew that Mr. Royce was a little touched in the head. All was not right with Mrs. Royce either. A streak of meanness now and then broke through the protective demeanor of her piety. She forced Josie, a left-hander, to write with his right hand, for instance. Royce's handwriting as a result is painfully childlike to this day. What agony for Josie—to write his two score books in a painful, unnatural hand, hearing his mother's warnings to stay with it, well into his sixtieth year. I sometimes think that I was fortunate in having a farm girl for a mother. Mother never questioned me and was proud of everything I did.

"Yes, Sebastian," Josie said that summer day in 1873, "we'll be leaving this place, you and I. We'll be going to the great world beyond San Francisco. For me it's Germany, then Johns Hopkins. For you it's Heidelberg."

"Will you return?" I asked.

"I don't know," Josie said with a shake of his slightly megacephalic head. "Rowland Sill says I can rejoin him in the English department at Berkeley when I finish, but when I get to the East I shall call upon William James at Harvard and ask about other opportunities."

I have a Royce correspondence in Box Four; and it continues through the rest of my collection, for we have kept in touch over the years. In his letters, Royce has been candid to a degree he never is in his idealistic philosophy, especially about California, San Francisco, and Harvard. With his permission, I shall reprint a few of the less candid letters in my *Memoirs,* and save the others for posterity. I have just completed going over the Heidelberg sequence for the *Memoirs,* and I must say I am pleased with it, although I have left out the business with Fraulein Gudrun Wessling, for that is nobody's business. After all, by the time I knew Gudrun I had already been five years or so into my activity in that vital department of biological pleasure and moral misadventure. I am, I believe, the only man in San Francisco, America perhaps, who lost his virginity to a Roman whore when serving in the army of the Papal States.

The Gudrun Wessling episode would be interesting, of course, because of the duel that precipitously ended it. I remember the entire affair quite clearly: the subterranean exercise room in the fraternity house just below the *Schloss;* the leaden weight of my sabre after we had fought for ten minutes, myself grateful for the instruction in the sabre Colonel Alhet of the Zouaves had forced upon us in garrison. Clang, crack, clang, crack—two young men (later friends of a sort), an American from San Francisco and an heir to a minor Bavarian title, fighting in the Year of Our Lord 1874 over a lady who had shared her favors with at least one of them, and possibly both. (What favors! My God, what favors! I was a veritable torrent of semen in those days! How many times did Gudrun and I attain bliss on that wild *Fasching* night!) I felt foolish until Karl cut me on the forearm (I grew rather proud of the scar in later years, however), then I felt angry. I cut him on the shoulder with a double-left feint. We both seemed relieved when the umpire announced, "Gentlemen, honor has been satisfied on both sides. Do you wish to desist?"

We both wished to desist. Foolish? Perhaps. But was I not a one-time Zouave, on guard against the *Garibaldisti?* Our founder, the Most Reverend Minister of War, Frederic Ghislain de Merode—general, archbishop, champion of *Pio Nono*—when he heard of the assassination of the Pope's prime minister Pellegrino Rossi, doffed his cassock, strapped on a pair of pistols (laid aside since his days on campaign with the French Foreign Legion in Algeria), and rushed to the defense of the Pope, besieged by fifth-column revolutionaries. Now and then, boldness is appropriate.

Ralston's fall ended my hopes of a speedy and assured return to San Francisco. I have a letter from him, dictated in great haste just a few weeks before the bank's fall and his own—shall I say it?—his own suicide; for why should he not have come back from that swim in North Beach when he had been making the same swim every day for years? Archbishop Alemany got me to Rome, where I completed my Bernini study for publication in 1878, sailing shortly after for home and a position at St. Ignatius College.

Marina's young man is a St. Ignatius boy, the high school; and a Stanford man, the law school. Yes, I like him well enough, and she certainly does. Yet I would be loathe to lose her just yet. Nineteen-fifteen will be a busy year. I've accepted Charles Moore's offer to serve as a deputy commissioner for the

62

Palace of Fine Arts. I have the *Memoirs* to finish. We'll be entertaining old friends who will be coming to San Francisco for the Exposition. I suppose I'm being selfish. I've always been more than a little selfish—a little too greedy at table, a little too porcine in bed, a sensualist. But what of it? I've always loved the baroque. It's difficult to be an old man with a daughter nearly fifty years younger than you are.

I'm glad I didn't burn the Sybil Sanderson Journal, as I call it—the letters, diary entries, notes, telegrams, and the like documenting the madness that came over me in my thirties and possessed me for half a decade. Gertrude Atherton, Sybil's friend, once said that she'd like to put how I behaved into a novel but that nobody would believe it.

"You were like a character, Sebastian, in an opera," Gertrude recently told me at Templeton Crocker's, "—a bad opera by Jules Massenet."

The Massenet was a little bitchy, even for Gertrude. Sybil, of course, was Jules Massenet's mistress and died in his arms from consumption, age thirty-five, just a few years after the premiere in Paris of *Thaïs,* which I attended, freshly released from Grand Chartreuse and once again embarking for the city, San Francisco, that took me when all else had failed. Sybil made a triumphant return to San Francisco just before her death.

Sybil was my daughter Marina's age, nineteen, when I first met her at James Phelan Senior's dinner party out on Valencia Street. Sybil's father, the Supreme Court justice, was there, and Phelan's son, Jimmy Duval, my student at St. Ignatius, and Richard Tobin of the Hibernia Bank. Joseph Duncan was there also, the banker-poet, and his wife. Duncan deserted his wife soon after, leaving her to raise their three children. My favorite of them was Isadora the dancer, who was so droll with me when I visited her recently in Paris, as if I were so innocent, even at my age, of the flesh, and she, only she, was discovering it for the first time in human history.

It was, in short, an evening of the local Irish ascendancy. There I met her—and I lost five years of my life. Had I instead

63

met my wife at that party (Virginia, hear me, I love you—I remember how your upper lip would moist over when we climbed into the Mayacmas hills for a Sunday picnic), had Virginia been there, would I have reacted with the same dionysian ardor, the same headlong *eros?* Perhaps. I was ready for it, having already internalized *eros* within me as a Platonic archetype. I was, after all, the author of a book on Bernini. (Santayana has been so kind in his remarks regarding my chapter on Bernini's *St. Theresa in Ecstasy*.) I was flesh-hungry and incurably romantic—and even thin.

1888: I write the year I met Sybil like a child writing wonderingly on a slate, half-enchanted by the persistent mysticism of numbers. Sybil wore red, which was unusual for fashion in the early eighties, although her dress was conventionally gathered in great folds behind her in the style of the period; and, as was also then fashionable, she wore a black velvet ribbon around her neck, fastened by a cameo. Her hair was piled high, then fell away in long ringlets, cascading down around a baby orchid affixed to her forehead above her left ear. What a recollection of details! What vanity for an old man! It's all in the journals, in any event, the pressed flowers of the past preserved from a time when I felt eternity well braved for a kiss—like Shakespeare's Mark Antony, finding the world well lost for love.

How could I have thrown a decade of my life away? But, then again, what would I have done otherwise? Written a book? Founded a museum in San Francisco? I've yet to do that, although I have helped in seeing to it that the right sort of city hall has been built, and I am doing what I can to insure a good public library for the city. I have also assisted in the planning of the new St. Ignatius Church. My time had to be spent in some way. No use regretting. Best to accept the past, savor the present, look forward to the future.

The future was on our minds in the late nineties when we commissioned Daniel Hudson Burnham to draw up for us a city plan. I've kept the correspondence and the minutes of the committee. Virginia and I lived for our own future and that of

64

the wine industry when we worked Avila Vineyards. And who relished the future more than my bohemian friends of the twilight nineties and early years of this century? All those bright and lovely people who used to gather at Coppa's Restaurant on Montgomery Street: Isabel Fraser, now in Persia, a priestess, I hear, in a Baha'i Temple (how strange, how amusing); Frank Norris—alas, poor Frank, dead at thirty-one from peritonitis, his intestines weakened from South African fever when he went there to cover the Boer War for the *Chronicle*.

I saw Frank two or three days before he died, on Nob Hill at Taylor and California Streets near the Grace Cathedral. He emerged from the nighttime fog, elegant in top hat, evening clothes, and opera cape, but also with a ghastly, frightened look on his face, as if demon death were stalking him through the foggy city like Professor Moriarty after Sherlock Holmes.

"Frank, where are we off to?"

"Sebastian, good evening. Raphael Weill is giving a dinner at the Poodle Dog for Jeanette and me in honor of the *The Octopus*. I hope they'll have the good taste not to serve seafood."

We laughed. Then, *apropos* of nothing whatsoever save the drawn look in his face, Frank said: "I'm frightened, old friend, I'm frightened."

Frank's gone and the others are getting older. Jack London is unwell, drinking a bit too much and all—and he's not yet forty. Jack seemed a little morose, puffy, truculent at the Grove last summer, angry at more than the fact that the reading committee had rejected his Indian play *The Acorn Planter* in favor of *Nec-Natama*, also an Indian pageant. Jack did join us at Esplandian Camp, however, for a memorable late-night discussion. He, myself, Phelan, George Sterling, Royce, and Downey Harvey consumed a prodigious amount of whiskey as we addressed the problem of the ultimate nature of human love with all the enthusiasm and *naiveté* of college sophomores.

"I'd like to see a Grove play about the fall of San Francisco,"

George Sterling said at one point in the evening. "Remember how in 1906 the preachers of the city said that God had destroyed the town because of its wickedness?"

Looking into the log fire that evening in our cozy bohemian camp, whiskey in hand, I remembered the flames of that terrible devastation. Accounts of that tragic week are numerous, but I will include another one in my *Memoirs*. In one way or another I have known the city since the 1850s. My impressions are of some value. At twilight—hard to tell the exact time, soot, smoke, ashes had so blackened the sky—I climbed the bell tower of Sacred Heart Church at Hayes and Fillmore and watched a monster devour our past. Like vultures feeding on a yet-alive Prometheus, the flames ate away at the innards of San Francisco. Down across Hayes Valley, I saw the college buildings on Van Ness Avenue aflame, and the Church of St. Ignatius also. The copperplated statue of St. Ignatius over the entrance glowed in the smoky dusk from the heat, as if a martyr were being sent to the stake. Then it burst into a fireball of oxidized flames some twenty feet into the air, the inner steel frame of the statue visible through the fire like the blackened bones of a cremated corpse. The flames leapt to the very top of the tower, then the entire church was engulfed in a remorseless rage of fire.

The Panama–Pacific International Exposition celebrates our recovery, but the fair also compensates us for what we San Franciscans have lost. I look down upon the Exposition from my study window as I write. I can see the sun setting behind this pastel dream city, this ideal San Francisco. Cinnamon, cinnabar, mauve, yellow, cerulean blue, apricot—the Exposition colors are the Mediterranean colors of my life: apricot especially, from *apricus* in the Latin, meaning "loving the sun," a word I first construed in my Virgil as a boy in high school, but only felt the full meaning of a few months ago when Marina and I drove down to Montalvo, Phelan's estate, by motor car. The apricot orchards of the Santa Clara Valley rioted white in the sun as we were driven down to Saratoga in Phelan's Croxton-Keeton touring car.

66

Apricus, loving the sun; apricot, the fruit; apricot, the color; the Santa Clara Valley; California itself; Italy, Spain, Greece, the South of France—I am a sun-lover, a man of the South, and so is California and San Francisco (or was—these new skyscrapers leave me perplexed), and so is the Exposition, a Mediterranean daydream, a gesture of chromatic longing for the city which the Fire took from us. Lost, lost, lost San Francisco. Lost youth, lost flesh, lost flowers, lost dreams of love and beauty. Lost everything.

No! Not at all! Slip into regret and nostalgia—and I'll be gone in a year. Hold to the present. I learned that when Virginia died and I lived alone in St. Helena, boarding Marina in town, incredulous that after all I had been through, after having found Virginia at the last possible moment, I would have to begin again.

So much to live for. So much to do. Trask wants me to edit the catalog of the Palace of Fine Arts exhibition, and I will. Elder wants the *Memoirs*—now, yesterday! I shall finish them. I shall give the lectures on art in California. I am by no means finished. I have things to do, cartons of new *memorabilia* to acquire.

Sometimes I ask myself whether or not I really want to go on with my life. I could tastefully slip away at the age of seventy or so. Kathleen Norris would write a lovely obituary in the *Examiner,* listing my modest accomplishments. Marina will finish Mills next year, then get her teacher's certificate, or marry her young man.

Father held on until 1905, reaching the age of eighty-eight. Thank God he did not witness the Fire of '06. His *protegé* Fire Chief Dennis Sullivan was mortally wounded by a fall on the morning of the quake. The chimney of the California Theater next door to the firehouse on Bush where my parents lived for so many years collapsed through Mrs. Sullivan's bedroom. The bricks tore out the weakened bedroom floor, and the accumulated debris was enough to gash the floor of the firemen's dormitory below. Hearing his wife's screams, the Chief darted into her room. It was still dark, and the Chief was blinded by

67

mortar dust. He did not see the crevice. He fell two stories into the garage, where a chemical engine was housed. He must have fallen onto the engine's boiler or onto the building's furnace, for in addition to a punctured lung, he sustained severe burns. Sullivan struggled to his feet and for a moment or two walked about in a daze. He then collapsed. He was taken to Southern Pacific Hospital and then to Letterman Hospital, where he died in a coma on 22 April.

The Fire Department was in chaos for the first day. My father would perhaps have taken charge himself, had he been there; and I'm not so sure but that the Department, or Mayor Schmitz, or even General Funston, would have let him do it. His reputation was still that good. I think I'll hold on to eighty-eight like my father. That gives me until 1936.

Presumptuous! Vain! Stupid! Dear God, I am grateful to Thee for the life that I have had. Thou hast been with me through sixty-seven years, my Joy and my Comfort. I ask now that Thou send me Thy peace, that Thou give me the wisdom of Thy Holy Spirit. Do not, O Lord, leave me an old fool—naked, drunken, laughed at by my offspring like Noah. Teach me to accept Thy will. In Thy will is our peace. Through Christ Our Lord. Amen.

Through Christ, Our Lord—Who is this Christ, dogging my footsteps for a lifetime? Shall I, like Alice Tobin, recite "The Hound of Heaven"? God the Son, Second Person of the Holy Trinity, of one substance with the Father, born of the Virgin, suffered and died on the cross for our sins, and on the third day arose again from the dead: I know the Nicean Creed—and I have felt the call of more venturesome speculations. I am, after all, a scholar of the baroque, recognizing the Man of Sorrows in all His variations, the Crucified One especially. Now if Christ is both God (that is, if God exists) and is also man risen from the dead, then I have a problem with the existence, the cosmic disposition if you will, of His Risen Self. What, exactly, is the extension of His risen glorified body? I link Him, the Risen One, imaginatively with creation itself—not pantheistically, but as the final physical

68

reality of the cosmic process. The universe streams toward the Risen Christ as a river to the sea. In the fullness of time, the Body of Christ shall become the totality of creation.

Build up the Body of Christ, St. Paul exhorts the faithful. There is already underway in human history a unification of flesh through marriage, copulation, parenthood, and something more elusive to understand—a growing communal, noetic bond being formed through culture and institutions, including, above all, the city, yes even San Francisco, the city in time, the substance and symbol of our best possible communal self, so Aristotle tells me.

Theologians speculate about the mystical Body of Christ. They describe it as a spiritual community already in existence, linked to the Risen Savior, Who is flesh. They tell us that we are already spiritually bonded to Christ's flesh through this Mystical Body and through the Eucharist. Meanwhile our own flesh does what? Rot? Make ready a feast for worms? Or evolve in some mystical yet truly historical process towards its own ultimate resurrection and glorification, its unification with the Risen Christ, the Lord of History, in some future mystical and physical implosion of Christ, creation, and mankind that will make us One with God Himself and end all history? Is it our work here below to prepare God's own ultimate body? To build up the Body of Christ?

The sky darkens behind the Tower of Jewels, which will be illuminated by a searchlight when the Exposition opens. The sunset, in the interim, suggests what a dazzling spectacle the illuminated tower will soon be. Sunset brings the tower's thousands of jewel-cut glass knobs to multicolored iridescence. Time for a glass of sherry—and dinner.

Chapter 3

T HESE ARE AMAZING," I said.
"They could be useful," Tiny said.
"This sort of thing is not my style."
"You'd be surprised what can become your style when you think your survival is involved."

We sat in silence for a moment. An old bum rummaged through a garbage can. A cute young blonde in tight curls, Jean Harlow makeup, and a thirties-revival dress walked by on platform heels: Nausicaa to my Odysseus, cast up naked on this far Pacific shore. A solitary seagull soared overhead—a loner cut off from his tribe, or just a bird who preferred his own company. Coming to consciousness, Odysseus might well have glimpsed such a bird against the sun-drenched Phaeacian sky.

"Three years ago Soutane experimented with bisexuality," Tiny said. "Whether he was one for real, or was just experimenting, I don't know. You know how he is: willing to try a lot of things if they're part of the new consciousness. He got involved with Stedman Mooner."

"That's Stedman Mooner in the photograph?"

"Yeah, you can't see his face clearly because of his position."

Stedman Mooner is a handsome, blond man of about thirty—openly gay—who writes a satirical column in the same morning paper Harry Shaw's gossip column appears in, *The San Francisco Express*. Mooner arrived in San Francisco from

70

New York about five years ago and took the town by storm. His column is a soap opera using barely disguised local celebrities for characters—the whole thing done with a light, satiric touch. San Franciscans love it. It's considered a mark of distinction to be in one of Mooner's columns, even at the cost of being made fun of. Mooner has been taken up by society. He lives on Russian Hill and gives great parties. I've been to a few of them. Mooner played Noel Coward and Cole Porter on the piano, rather well as I remember. There were plenty of good-looking girls and no outrageous fairies, only a handful of elegant, vaguely homosexual men in their late thirties and early forties, all of them witty and well-mannered. Mooner takes his style, including his homosexual style, from the 1930s—the era of Katharine Hepburn, *Vogue* magazine, and the discreet homosexuality of Noel Coward and Cole Porter— or so I thought until Tiny Roncola showed me these pictures. Their vulgarity, the very fact of their being taken in the first place, doesn't jive with Stedman Mooner's style. But then again, looking at them in Civic Center, contemplating—even for a moment—the use of them for purposes of blackmail, doesn't fit into my style either.

I should have said to Tiny, "Get lost! I wouldn't touch these things with a ten-foot pole." But I let it ride for a minute or two; and thus to his way of thinking—and mine also—I granted the use of these photographs the validity of being a thinkable proposition.

"Look, Jimmy. This is a no-hurry thing and strictly confidential. It's touchy as hell. You could get everybody in trouble, you and me both. We could go to jail. I'm not naive. This sort of stuff rarely works. Besides, it's immoral."

Immoral! I pictured Tiny and myself some twelve years back at St. Patrick's Major Seminary in Menlo Park, wearing black cassocks, walking around the grounds in silence at *angelus* time, saying the rosary.

"Why get involved then," I asked, "if it's both immoral and dangerous?"

"Don't get involved, then," Tiny said. "All I want you to know is that these pictures are available if and when they ever become necessary. All I'm saying is that we both know enough about politics to realize that Carpino starts out behind. Next June he'll still be behind, even further behind, unless something dramatic happens. These pictures could be that dramatic thing."

"Why were they taken in the first place?"

"Mooner did it on the sly, a secret camera. Apparently he collects photographs of himself *in flagrante delicto* with various celebrities. They say you'd be surprised who he's got photographs of."

"How did you get hold of these?"

"I'm not at liberty to say."

I should have felt angry. Tiny was dragging me into a world where I didn't want to be. But some sort of compromise already existed between us: a compromise difficult to define, yet existing nevertheless—a fragile bond of suppressed, but discernible brotherhood. Tiny was wearing a rather loud glen-plaid suit of heavily polyesterated fabric, a solid-colored brown shirt and a bright yellow tie. He looked like someone from Hayward. I was wearing a Brooks Brothers gray pin-stripe, an all-cotton white shirt, French cuffs, a muted blue polka-dot tie held in place by a gold collarpin, F. Scott Fitzgerald style, and black Gucci loafers, crossed by gold clasps. I looked like someone from New York, which is the way I always try to look. Tiny had failed night law school. I'd gone to Harvard. I ran with a fancy set, at least tangentially. I never fooled myself that my relationship to the upper-crust world was anything but tenuous. I made $10,000 more a year than Tiny did at Redevelopment.

Yet Tiny Roncola and I have more in common that I have with the posh, *bon ton* San Francisco I have courted so assiduously for these past four years since I returned home to San Francisco: the world of Stedman Mooner parties, opening night at the Opera, the Captain's Cabin at Trader Vic's, champagne brunches on Sunday morning at the St. Francis Yacht Club; the world evoked each morning in Harry Shaw's column, a world, a vision which, like Gatsby's green light on Long Island Sound, recedes in the night before all aspiring San

Franciscans; a vast, meretricious beauty, an unattainable dream of the good life as it should be lived by all properly aspiring San Franciscans.

I've bought the myth, and I've made some inroads into it—more than Tiny Roncola has at least. I've listened to Peter Mintin play Cole Porter at L'Etoile on Nob Hill, dropping in there for drinks and persiflage after the opera. I drive a Porsche. I rent an apartment on Telegraph Hill decorated by Eleanor Ford although I can barely afford it. I've been up to Cyril Magnin's penthouse at the Mark Hopkins for cocktails, then rushed down to Fournou's Ovens at the Stanford Court for dinner at the last possible moment before the kitchen closed, rushed there, or to L'Orangerie, or the Redwood Room at the Clift, or the St. Pierre on Pacific, in the company of this or that chatty group. I've even been mentioned in Al Morch's column in the *Examiner*.

I know a number of good-looking women, all peripherally. The purely sexual connection soon exhausts itself, or sometimes, more profoundly, sex leads towards depths of feeling and association which frighten me off—as will no doubt turn out to be the case with Deborah Tanner.

Harry Shaw, San Francisco's Wizard of Oz, has given us all an illusion to pursue, a Noel Coward play to act in, a Busby Berkeley musical to dance in—all of us, male, female, gay, straight, lining up side by side, joining arms, kicking our legs high into the air while an orchestra plays a razzmatazz version of "San Francisco."

Tiny Roncola and I, however, share another San Francisco. That's why I was sitting there with him that afternoon in Civic Center. That's why I enjoy our occasional Friday Fisherman's Wharf lunches. Tiny seemed vulnerable to me then, and now he was about to make me vulnerable, make me like him—an incipient blackmailer, a dealer in the worst sort of dirty tricks. Tiny hadn't amounted to much in life, and for all our apparent differences, neither had I. We both shared a common past and baffled present. We'd gone to St. Boniface School together, just down the block from Civic Center, where at St. Anthony's Dining Room the Franciscan fathers daily

73

feed some five thousand indigents. We'd gone to St. Ignatius High School and the University of San Francisco together. We each tried St. Patrick's Seminary for a while after graduation. We are both, to put it briefly, shipwrecked victims cast up on the far shore of Catholic San Francisco, the local Bark of Peter, which fell apart and sank in the hurricane called the 1960s. Tiny and I are only in our mid-thirties, but we are both rapidly becoming marginal men, obsessed by displacement, paralyzed by longing and regret.

Sebastian Collins felt this way at times, I realize; but his association with James Duval Phelan, who held substantive political and fiscal power in San Francisco, helped stave off temptations to utter hopelessness. In Europe, when Sybil Sanderson laughed him away, Sebastian Collins experienced something akin to a nervous breakdown, brought on by the conviction that he had wasted his time, had pursued the wrong goals in life. When Collins returned from the Napa Valley to live in San Francisco after the birth of his daughter and the death of his wife, James Duval Phelan, then mayor, offered Collins the partially true illusion that together they could shape the course of the city, which when you consider it they did.

Perhaps that is why Tiny Roncola and I brought our expectations to Claudio Carpino. We wanted Carpino to find a place for us. We wanted him to assuage our truncated hopes. He was also from our world—Catholic San Francisco—and he held power, dazzling power, or so it then seemed. He was mayor of San Francisco. Tiny and I were parasites on Claudio Carpino's back. He, after all, and not us, had made a fortune as a brilliant attorney. He, not us, had run for and won the mayoralty. We lived off him—Tiny at Redevelopment at $20,000 a year, myself at the Library at $30,000.

"If we can do this, Jimmy," Sebastian Collins had said to his friend Phelan immediately after the earthquake and fire of 1906 had leveled the city, and it looked as if the plan for the rebuilding of San Francisco drawn up by Daniel Hudson Burnham might have a chance to be put into effect, "if we can

74

build the City Beautiful here in San Francisco, then my whole life will have counted for something."

On a lesser level, and without the destruction of San Francisco as a premise, Tiny and I have both made a similar request of Claudio Carpino, the thirty-ninth American mayor of our city. We have brought our fears and failures to him, like a child coming to a parent for comfort. Give us a place, we've asked him. Give us some sense of possession and continuity in San Francisco, some illusion that we belong, that we count, that we can get something of value accomplished. You're one of us writ large. Take some of us neighborhood boys along with you. Take us to San Francisco. Take us home.

"Tiny," I said, "let's leave it alone for a while. Let's see what happens."

I thought of Tiny's failure at night law school and my own present failure at the Library, where I was accomplishing nothing with my time. I thought of Tiny's oddly solitary life, his little apartment out on Dolores Street, his calls to me now and then to join him for lunch at the Wharf, or go to a Forty-Niner game.

"Sure, Jimmy. We'll do that. I'm not proud of this myself, but what will happen to us a year from January if Carpino doesn't get to be governor? There'll be a new mayor. We'll go out with Carpino. I want to survive."

"So did the carrier pigeon and the great auk. I'll be in touch, Tiny. And I'll keep my mouth shut."

At Community and Economic Development in the basement of City Hall, Danny Pappas and Nadia North were enjoying a cup of coffee when I dropped by for a moment to say hello. Danny's office is plastered with posters like a college dormitory room: only instead of Raquel Welch in her skimpy *Two Million B.C.* costume or Farrah Fawcett-Majors, there are charts and graphs aplenty; a graph showing the rising or falling median income of the city, broken down by neighborhoods (Pacific Heights bullish, Hunters Point bearish); a chart depicting the loss of blue-collar jobs in the city since 1955; a

75

chart depicting the rise of the adult single population of the city (over sixty percent of the city's population lives alone); a chart depicting the decline of the city's child population to a meagre 55,000 or so; a chart listing empty commercial real estate properties throughout the city, the Penney's building on Market Street among them, together with such empty downtown department stores as the City of Paris, Ransohoff's, H. Liebes, and the White House, and empty Mission district department stores like Redlick's, Majestic's, and Lachman Brothers. Another chart shows unused industrial properties such as the Hamm's Brewery, the Planter's Peanuts factory, and a score of half-used, half-abandoned properties in the South of Market Area near the empty piers of our very unbusy port.

Danny's office reminds me of a military command post, plastered with situation maps. One sweep of Danny's graphics—Nadia's graphics, rather, for she keeps them up to date—and you have an instant picture of San Francisco's current situation: an inner city losing population (we are down some 150,000 residents from our all-time 1948 high of 840,000); an inner city rapidly becoming a rich/poor place (for "poor" read minorities) devoid of a child-rearing middle class (read, devoid of whites). This has happened all over America—New York, Detroit, Chicago—and now it is happening here. In the past ten years, over a quarter of a million of the white middle class have left San Francisco for the Peninsula, Marin, or the East Bay. During the working day when the commuters come in, the city swells to some 1.5 million people. The commuters who come in by car or BART from the East Bay, by train or car from the Peninsula, or by car or ferry across the bay from Marin, are the very sort we've been losing all these years, the educated white middle class.

Danny's job is to use federal money to stimulate job-producing activity in San Francisco. In the past ten years federal money, administered by the mayor's staff, has increased the staff from about fifteen in the pre-Lyndon Johnson era to its present eighty or so, most of whom are on the federal payroll.

"Danny," I asked recently, "how much federal money has been used in programs aimed at black people in San Francisco?"

"About $300 million."

I knew the answer already and had prepared my response with the help of Perry Bach, the Library's budget officer, who is also a Christian Science practitioner. It kept us amused to work this out on Perry's pocket calculator late one evening as we waited in the chambers of the Finance Committee of the Board of Supervisors to testify on the Library's budget.

"$300 million," I said. "That breaks down to about $89,000 for every black person in the city. You could send them each a check for $89,000 in the mail. The overhead would be next to nothing, just the cost of having the computer write the checks. Think of it—$89,000! Some would gamble it away or spend it on Ripple. But most black people would use their windfall well. They'd buy houses, send kids to school or college, pool it with others and establish businesses. Imagine getting a lump sum like that. Your life would never be the same. If you really want to help black people, if some sort of reparations are in order because of slavery, then give them money—not programs, which collapse anyway, leaving behind a coral reef of bureaucracy, programs which while they're in operation eat up half their funds in overhead. Give them money—and let them make their own choices."

"It doesn't work that way," Danny said.

I get along with Danny Pappas, despite my conservative, commonsense thrusts at his operation. Danny wears corduroy jackets, tattersall shirts, rep ties, khaki pants, and Clark's desert boots. He looks like an associate professor of English, sort of tweedy and humanistic. He's very handsome in a Greek, Victor Mature sort of way. Our ideological wars are essentially a form of banter. Quite frankly, I couldn't care less if this country wants to squander its tax money on ill-conceived bleeding-heart programs that keep the poor poorer and the bureaucracy more entrenched. It's beyond my control. Yet the waste of money I see throughout city government appalls me. We have a civil service in San Francisco of nearly 30,000 employees to serve the needs of 680,000 inhabitants. We have a budget approaching a billion dollars. Yet day by day the city seems to grow seedier; our public buildings, more decrepit; our public servants, more rude and unresponsive. Where in the hell does the billion dollars go?

But there's something else, too, something having to do with the permanent state of dependence minorities are kept in. It's as if government wants them to remain a permanent helotry so that it has an excuse to continue to gorge itself on more taxes and grow in size. The most intelligent and restive of the minority leaders are co-opted with government jobs. They develop a vested interest in keeping their own people government-dependent, so they can keep themselves necessary as a mediating class. Take Danny Parker, the affirmative action officer at the Library. Danny could be a good lawyer. He could get, say, a degree in accounting or engineering. But because he's intelligent and black, he's paid $20,000 a year to hang around the Library in something called affirmative action. From there, he'll probably go over to Public Utilities if he's lucky—not as an engineer, mind you (he's plenty bright enough to be an engineer), or a division manager, but as an affirmative action officer, tinkering with procedures and techniques, never getting down to substance, never launching upon a solid career.

"Danny," I said to Pappas, "the issues study group for the Mayor's campaign hasn't met in over a month."

"Don't hold your breath," Nadia North said over her personalized coffee mug, which says "Nadia North" in Times Roman type across its side. "Scorse has so badmouthed us to the Mayor that I think Carpino is sorry he ever called us into existence."

Nadia is married to the Mayor's nephew, although she doesn't like that fact to get out. It sounds like patronage. Nadia is breezy and intelligent. In the issues study group she

78

concentrated on women's issues and energy. She put together some excellent position papers which will no doubt gather dust in the campaign.

"What's Scorse's point?" I asked. "His overt point, I mean. I understand his contempt for us on a social and psychological level."

"Scorse's point," Nadia said, "is that there should be no point, no issues-oriented campaign. He says that people are tired of being told a lot of statistical stuff they can't understand. California is too big for anyone to understand anyway. Both the primary and the election, Scorse feels, are going to be matters of intuition and influence, not debate."

"It's always that way," I agreed. "But even in terms of pure image we've got to project the Mayor as someone thinking intelligently about the issues."

"The Mayor will do his own thinking," Pappas said. "And I think Scorse will be calling the shots as far as the campaign strategy is concerned."

"The problem is, Soutane is doing both," said Nadia. "He is talking just enough issues to seem intelligent and connected, but not enough to get into trouble. Meanwhile he's beating hell out of us in the image game. Did you see what he did yesterday?"

We all had read about it, but we let Nadia talk anyway. By now, we've each become mutually reinforcing conspirators in our common failure.

"Right down there in Santa Barbara, Soutane gets into scuba gear and swims alongside an offshore drilling rig— diving down to inspect it, he says, for a possible oil leak. God, it was marvelous. The TV guys ate it up. Then holding a press conference on offshore drilling in his wetsuit, the oxygen tank still on his back, his mask up over his forehead. Jesus, he could have been played by Robert Redford!"

"He probably will," Danny Pappas said, "when they do the Governor Andy Soutane Story." Danny got up, signaling that the coffee break was over.

I walked up one floor and ascended the grand staircase under the rotunda, heading for Room 200. In 1912 Mayor Sunny

Jim Rolph asked Sebastian Collins to serve as part of the architectural selection committee for the new City Hall. The old City Hall had taken more than twenty years to build— twenty years of delays, politics, graft-ridden bids, and various forms of kickbacks and payola. The old City Hall collapsed with the first shock of the quake. Burlap sacks were found mixed in with the cement—a good way for crooked contractors to save on construction costs. Mayor Rolph told the architectural commission, which also included James Duval Phelan, to come up with the best, which they did. They commissioned architects John Bakewell, Jr., and Arthur Brown, Jr., who were proposing a magnificent Louis XIV French Baroque palace, dominated by a soaring 308-foot dome—16 feet, 2⅝ inches higher, Mayor Rolph would later proudly say, that the dome on the nation's Capitol. City Hall was dedicated in 1915, the year of the Exposition. There's a photograph of Mayor Rolph, in striped pants and cutaway, giving the dedicatory oration. If you look to the second row left, you can see Sebastian Collins, also in a cutaway and wearing a top hat, resting his weight on a silver-topped cane, upon which he has folded both hands. Collins looks genial and amused as he glances over to the orating Rolph.

I see the outside of City Hall daily and I'm in it three or four times a day. I'm never there, however, but that I feel in the building a quality of daydream and fantasy. Such a massive assertion of Beaux Arts grandeur, thrust into the center of a modern American city, memorializes the daydreams of 1915: the sense of San Francisco that held Collins, Phelan, Mayor Rolph, and, of course, the two architects who translated their vision into Doric colonnades, granite walls, sweeping staircases, and a soaring rotunda higher than that of the nation's Capitol. It was because of Collins's knowledge of Renaissance and baroque architecture that Mayor Rolph asked him to serve on the City Hall commission in the first place. A baroque passion gripped even Sunny Jim Rolph of the Mission, a conception of San Francisco as a grandly orchestrated City Beautiful: a city of formal parks, stately boulevards radiating from a central square lined with massive public buildings, splashing fountains, statues. The opening of the Panama Canal engendered imperial dreams in the San Franciscans of 1913, the year the City Hall plans were selected, dreams of San Francisco rising to imperial greatness as the chief emporium and stock exchange of Pacific Basin trade, sharing that honor in the southern hemisphere with Sydney, Australia.

Like the Italian Renaissance Public Library which faces it across the Civic Center, City Hall supports a teeming life poignantly at odds with the baroque grandeur of its architecture. As I ascended the great central staircase to the Mayor's suite, I passed a group of denim-clad Haight-Ashbury gypsies sprawling on the lower steps. A young black man in a luxuriant Afro and a multicolored dashiki passed to my left, making eye-contact, then breaking it off as if he didn't like who or what he saw. A tired-looking civil servant—gray-haired, stooped, wearing a white short-sleeved shirt and a narrow tie held in place by a much larger clip—meandered across the landing outside the Board of Supervisors' chambers, tracing the late afternoon corridors of municipal employment. I could see his junior-five bungalow in the Sunset, his daughter, some twenty years back, making her first communion at St. Anne's. She's a Mercy High School graduate, most likely, married to a fireman, two children, living in Westlake. I could see the Studebaker he bought in 1949, and I could feel the way the N-Judah streetcar had rattled down Market Street to Civic Center these past twenty-five years on the routine mornings he headed downtown for work.

As usual, Inspector Ted Potelli was talking on the telephone when I walked into the outer office of Room 200. Potelli serves as Carpino's chauffeur-bodyguard. All in all, Inspector Potelli has a soft gig. He drives the limo, sharing that duty with Inspector Owen Kilduff, who plans to run for sheriff against the incumbent Matt Diego a year from November. Potelli accompanies the Mayor on all flights. He runs various errands. In politics, access is everything. Potelli has total access to Carpino, so he himself holds a species of power. He might have to wait outside in the limo when the Mayor is having lunch, or eat with the press and the other flunkies at

81

banquets—thus showing his retainer status; but Potelli can get to the Mayor in a minute.

Potelli is a beefy ethnic, Italian and Spanish Basque by descent, raised in the Mission district. Carpino recruited him off the burglary detail because he's married to a second cousin of one of the Mayor's brothers-in-law. Potelli is a fierce partisan of the Scorse wing of the Carpino corps of retainers— the non-college, anti-doubledome crowd, the Labor Boys. When he isn't driving the Mayor, Potelli sits in the outer office of Room 200 and talks on the telephone. As a cop, Inspector Potelli packs heat, probably a forty-five. You can see the bulge under his jacket. My very presence drives the Inspector up the wall. I epitomize the doubledome crowd, the intellectuals—as Potelli colorfully puts it—"sniffing the bicycle seats of power." Come to think of it, the Inspector has both a point and a very vivid metaphor.

Jimmy Driscoll, on the other hand, the Mayor's executive aide for neighborhood relations—whose desk is in front of Potelli's in the outer foyer, just beneath the oil portrait of Sunny Jim Rolph—tolerates me because I'm of Hayes Valley Irish stock some two generations back. Jimmy was raised in the twenties and thirties next door to relatives of mine on Waller Street in Hayes Valley, Sacred Heart parish. Over the years he's kept in touch with my mother, who now lives out in the Mission at Sixteenth and Dolores. Jimmy's brother Ralph went to the seminary with my mother's brother, the Most Reverend Robert Casey, a missionary bishop in Peru. For years Jimmy ran a bar out in Castro Valley, Most Holy Redeemer parish, a watering hole catering to cops, firemen, blue-collar workers, and minor officials of the Democratic party. The talk there was old-fashioned San Francisco Irish talk: who made sergeant on the force, who's boozin' too much, who's got laid off, who left or entered the seminary, who's got a beef with the union—teamsters, plumbers, marine cooks and stewards, retail clerks, construction workers, whose daughter got married or went bad, who's running for supervisor or assessor or sheriff or treasurer. Jimmy heard all the talk, cultivated the politicos, and made himself something of a power broker in town, capable of delivering up what's left of the neighborhood Irish vote. When Carpino got elected mayor—thanks in part to Jimmy—he asked Jimmy to join him, which Jimmy did. Jimmy had gone on the wagon two years before—doctor's orders. Forty years of whiskey had taken its toll of his liver. Once dry, Jimmy Driscoll found himself bored with tending bar.

"Jimmy boy," Driscoll said. "It's always a pleasure." He was wearing a powder-blue leisure suit, white shoes, and a red bow tie. Behind him, Potelli had his sports coat slightly open, so that you could see part of the strap of his shoulder holster, Dirty Harry style. As I walked in, Potelli hung up the phone and glared.

"Well, well, Mr. Librarian himself. Over here to offer the Mayor some advice? Tell it to me, sweetie, and I'll make your case to his honor."

"Fuck you," I said.

"Kiss my ass, you fruit," Potelli said.

It was hardly an inspiring or even a witty exchange.

"Now, now, gentlemen," Jimmy Driscoll said. "This is no way for two of the Mayor's trusted advisers to behave. How can we beat Andy Soutane and his boys if we fight among ourselves?"

Audrey Yee, the astonishingly beautiful Chinese reception-ist in the outer office, buzzed me into the corridor leading to the Mayor's suite. This particular corridor is lined with photographs of the Spanish, Mexican, and American mayors of San Francisco, from *Alcalde* Francisco de Haro, who ran the town in 1834, to Claudio Carpino himself. Fifty-two portraits and photographs cover both walls of the corridor. Only Carpino's is in full, living color. Mexican *alcaldes,* American military governors during the Mexican War, American *alcaldes* before statehood (1850), and popularly elected American may-ors: the portraits suggest the entire pageant of San Francisco history. Whenever I walk past these portraits, I hear a *March of Time* newsreel in my inner ear, narrated by Lowell Thomas.

I think of the long, slow, sleepy Spanish and Mexican years, presided over by *alcaldes* Francisco de Haro, Francisco Guerrero, and José de Jesus Noe. Naval Lieutenant Washington Bartlett raised the American flag over Yerba Buena ("Good Herb" in Spanish, the city's first name) on 9 July 1846, then administered the captured village as a military governor. Mayors like George Hyde, Thaddeus Leavenworth, John Geary, James Van Ness, and Andrew Bryant guided San Francisco through its early American years: forgotten men today for the most part, with street signs for tombstones, but in their time bluff, hearty, florid pioneers, energized by oysters and champagne, ambitious to build a city, which they did, and get themselves rich in the process, which they did. I walked past their robust, assertive faces, thickened by good living, framed in sidewhiskers or peering above great beards.

The pre-1870s group were no-nonsense merchants of San Francisco's Iron Age—shippers, stockbrokers, railroad men. The Reverend Isaac Smith Kalloch was the first flamboyantly colorful rogue, the previous rogues being prosaic businessmen rogues. A Baptist minister with an eye for the ladies, Kalloch ran for mayor in 1879 with the support of the Workingmen's party. *Chronicle* editor Charles de Young, offended by a Kalloch *riposte,* shot him down with a pistol. Kalloch was elected from his hospital bed. The Mayor's son then shot de Young dead and was acquitted by a sympathetic jury.

Adolph Sutro (mayor 1895–1897) and Sebastian Collins's friend James Duval Phelan (mayor 1897–1902) played vigorous parts, as did Sebastian Collins himself, in the elegant, aesthetic drama of San Francisco's mauve and yellow *fin de siècle*—the lovely era of gaslit San Francisco, the time of High Bohemia. Both Sutro and Phelan were wealthy, cultivated men of impeccable taste.

Born in Prussia of Jewish ancestry, trained in Europe as a mining engineer, Sutro made a fortune in the Comstock silver mines. He sank a five-mile tunnel into Mount Davidson, Nevada, and ventilated the tunnel. In 1879 Sutro sold his interest in the tunnel for $5 million, then returned to San

Francisco to pyramid his fortune through real-estate speculation. At one point, Sutro held title to about one-twelfth of the San Francisco peninsula. He built the Cliff House and a superb gingerbread mansion surrounded with botanical gardens overlooking the Pacific on Land's End. A connoisseur and bibliophile, Sutro traveled frequently to Europe to collect *objets d'art* and books. His library, some 400,000 volumes (300,000 or so of them destroyed by the fire of 1906), was at one time the finest private library in America.

James Duval Phelan, Sebastian Collins's student at St. Ignatius College, inherited his wealth from his father, a Gold Rush merchant and real estate speculator. After elaborate preparation, which included private tutoring by Collins in the classics, law school at Hastings College, and a two-year sojourn in Europe spent studying every aspect of city management from sewerage to police to the running of museums, Phelan was elected mayor at the age of thirty-five. Aristocratic, assured, a reform-minded millionaire like Sutro (Sutro fought the political control of San Francisco by the Southern Pacific Railroad), Phelan prosecuted corruption, gave the city a new charter in 1898, and set in motion the public ownership of utilities. His old tutor Sebastian Collins joined the young Mayor in a number of these projects.

I recognize, in the hold Phelan had upon Sebastian Collins, something of my own ebbing hopes and fantasies towards Mayor Claudio Carpino. Superbly educated, a self-made millionaire, well-traveled, a knowledgeable man of the world: Carpino once gave every promise of surpassing even Sutro and Phelan—and perhaps even Sunny Jim Rolph himself—as a protagonist of San Francisco's development, of becoming a Lorenzo de Medici in our high provincial Florence on the Pacific.

"Hello, dearie," Ursula Iraslav, the Mayor's appointments secretary, brayed when I entered the last and final antechamber to the Mayor's office. She had a round compact out and was applying makeup to her assertively Slavic features. "You can't go in. The Mayor's busy with some people from San Diego. He told me to tell you, however, to be sure to be on the ferry boat tomorrow when the Police Athletic Association opens its fishing program for poor kids."

"How long will the Mayor be tied up?"

"For the rest of the day, dearie."

I felt humiliated, as I always do when I can't get in to see His Honor. Two years ago, even a half year ago, I used to spend a lot of time waiting in the outer office to get in, like a petitioner outside the suite of a Roman cardinal, cooling his heels every day in an antechamber for a year or more, petition in hand, before being granted an audience with this or that scarlet-robed eminence. Lately, I've been saying fuck it and not hanging around. Barry Scorse has total access—even the rarest of privileges, that of announcing himself with a knock while simultaneously opening the door into the chambers of the Sun King himself.

Esmeralda, the Mayor's wife, has decorated the office in dazzling, very expensive Louis XIV: a great rug, tapestries, an antique clock, and a stunning early eighteenth-century writing desk decorated in beaten gold leaf. Carpino sits enthroned in splendor like Louis XIV or, to change the comparison, like a curial cardinal during the reign of Pope Innocent XIII. I've seen visitors, stunned by the office's opulence, catch their breaths when they were ushered into the Mayor's presence. The aggressive, almost blatant Europeanness of the decor says a lot about Claudio Carpino, whom I sometimes think is more Italian than American in his tastes and attitudes.

"Who's in there?" I asked Terry Shane, the Mayor's press secretary. Shane works in an airless, windowless cubicle down from Ursula Iraslav's office. He was pounding out something on his typewriter when I entered, an ever-present Marlboro clenched between his teeth.

"Some people from the fishing fleet at San Pedro," Shane answered, not bothering to look up from his typewriter or even to stop typing when I interrupted him. Shane wasn't being rude. It's just his *Front Page* style. A junior college drop-out who got his education as a police reporter for the *Oakland*

86

Tribune, Terry Shane can't think unless he's typing and smoking Marlboro cigarettes. Shane lives in San Rafael with his wife and three kids. Over the weekends, he's totally redone his patio in brick and put in a swimming pool with a Jacuzzi. He frequently gives lavish barbecues. He and I are friends. We're both Irish. We both spent time in the seminary. Shane went to Vietnam as a combat correspondent for the *Tribune* and, literally, got part of his ass shot off. I kid him about it. Whether or not he finds it funny depends upon his mood at the time.

"What do they want?" I asked.

Reluctantly, Shane stopped typing. I could hear the whir of his IBM Selectric, like the buzzing fly Emily Dickinson heard before she died.

"They want the Mayor to come out in favor of tuna fish, not porpoises. The Feds say too many porpoises are getting caught in the tuna fishermen's nets. They've put restrictions on how deep the tuna fishermen can lower their nets and what kinds of nets they can use. They want the Mayor to come out in favor of easing the restrictions. If so, the San Pedro fleet will get behind him. If not, they'll go Republican. Most Italians are Republicans anyway."

"What's Soutane's position on this?" I asked, knowing full well the answer already; but I always enjoy talking to Shane. Shane rummaged through a stack of clippings, then pulled one out.

"Here, read it yourself."

It was a *Los Angeles Times* Op-Ed guest essay by Andy Soutane, dated last month. Whales, dolphins, and porpoises, Soutane wrote, are highly intelligent creatures, perhaps even conscious creatures with a noetic system equivalent to man's, one based on hearing rather than sight. In the case of the tuna fleets, the unnecessary slaughtering of porpoises is a crime against nature, justifiably stopped by federal regulation. What is needed, Soutane continued, is a new fishing technology, such as that being developed at the Scripps Institution of Oceanography at La Jolla. Each tuna boat should be equipped

87

with a sonic device that could be lowered before the nets are put down. The device lets out a high-frequency noise that scares off the porpoises but cannot be heard by the tuna. Then the nets can be lowered. Most conflicts between jobs and environment are unnecessary conflicts, Soutane concluded. The proper use of technology and the civilized art of political compromise should see such problems through to resolution.

"What will the Mayor say?" I asked Shane, who had resumed typing.

"He'll probably say, 'Fuck the porpoises and hooray for the tuna fishermen!' " Shane shot back over the roar of his keys. "That's what Scorse and cousin Fred want him to say, something like, 'I prefer jobs for people to porpoises. We've got to give the edge to the human element.' "

"Did you see Harry Shaw's column this morning?"

"What do you think I'm doing now? I'm drafting a reply for the Mayor. He's mad as hell."

"*Alcalde* Claudio Carpino"—so Shaw had opened this morning's column— "is fit-to-be-TIED. Esmeralda, it seems, has been offering *mucho* dinero to certain confidential staffers to find out what REALLY goes on behind closed doors. Agitated by the bevy of young lovelies in the front office, Esmeralda, wants to make sure that everything going on in Room 200 is STRICTLY municipal."

"I'll draft this letter of denial," Terry said. "The Mayor will read it, but I doubt if it will ever get sent. Best to leave the matter alone. Harry Shaw, after all, is in the ring every morning."

He sure as hell was. For forty years, since the late thirties, Harry Shaw, a one-time poor boy from Santa Rosa, born Harry Glickfield sixty-odd years ago, but changing his name to the more mellifluous Harry Shaw upon commencing a columnist's career, has run the most powerful gossip column in San Francisco. For the past three years hardly a morning goes by that Harry Shaw doesn't begin the day with an anti-Carpino barrage.

"We used to get along," the Mayor told me one Friday last

year as we were heading in the limo over to Vanessi's on Broadway for lunch. "We'd meet every month or so for lunch or a drink to talk things over. Then after the Top of the Mark incident everything changed."

He stopped to wave out the limo window to a friendly Max Sobel's Liquor truck driver who'd blasted his horn in greeting. People naturally stare at limos, and once you stared at ours it was easy to tell that the mayor of San Francisco was inside. The Mayor is always getting honked at, waved at, yelled at, sometimes cursed at when he rides through the city. Whatever the response, friendly or not, Carpino always waves back and grins. This is called politics.

"We were at the Mark for a reception. Esmeralda got into a conversation with Eva Shaw about where she came from. Eva, you know, comes from Mexico and is Mexican. She likes, however, to think of herself as Spanish. Esmeralda wouldn't let it alone. She kept quizzing Eva. Eva finally admitted she was born in Mexico—but of Spanish parents. She was furious."

I knew there had to be more to Shaw's hatred of Carpino than this incident, but I let it pass. Hatred often needs an excuse for surfacing, and this was as good as any. Toby Wain, who works with Shaw on the *The Express,* has filled me in on the epic of Harry Shaw's marital life. Eva Lopez Shaw is the fourth and perhaps final Mrs. Harry Shaw. The first Mrs. Shaw was a stripper at Sally Rand's Nude Ranch. Shaw met her on the job at Treasure Island in 1939 during the Golden Gate International Exposition. The future Mrs. Shaw was taking off her clothes at the time. Harry was young then, and very horny. The first Mrs. Shaw had platinum blond hair and, so the audience discovered, very big tits.

Harry met the second Mrs. Shaw in New York after the war, during the time he tried—and failed—to become a New York columnist. Anastasia Livingston was a wealthy WASP Radcliffe graduate. The marriage collapsed from insurmountable ethnic differences. Shaw had a bad habit of getting drunk and telling his wife's Harvard and Yale friends to go fuck themselves. Having gone to Santa Rosa Junior College for just

89

a year, and being Jewish, Harry Shaw was sensitive to the ambience of WASP glitter Anastasia Livingston Shaw surrounded herself with. In San Francisco Harry Shaw's lack of background and education never mattered. Besides, after a year or so with the *Tribune,* it was obvious his column wasn't going to make it in New York, so he might as well let it all hang out. Unlike San Francisco, New York couldn't be dominated by a gossip columnist. Whatever vulnerability New York had in this area had already been exploited by Walter Winchell. Shaw returned to San Francisco in 1948 and resumed his local column. He married a daughter of the city's German Jewish establishment, a certain Jessica Voorsanger.

In 1960 Eva Lopez arrived in San Francisco from Los Angeles. She told employers that she was twenty-five. Thirty-five would have been closer to the truth. Eva Lopez got a job selling cosmetics at I. Magnin's. By 1965, her name changed to Eva Maria del Valde, she had advanced to cosmetics buyer for the City of Paris and was surreptitiously sharing a flat on Telegraph Hill with Harry Shaw, usually around noontime. Mrs. Jessica Voorsanger Shaw found out about the flat in 1967, thought it over for a year, then divorced Harry in 1969—the first Voorsanger girl to get a divorce since Jacob Voorsanger, a gold-seeker turned lumber merchant arrived in San Francisco in 1848 and began making a fortune. A year later Harry Shaw made Eva Maria del Valde, *née* Lopez, at once an honest woman and a social celebrity.

By 1972, the year Esmeralda Carpino grilled her about the distinction between being Mexican and being Spanish, Eva Maria del Valde Shaw had consolidated her position as leader in the *beau monde* and was in no mood to be fooled with. She owned a penthouse condominium on Nob Hill and was good friends with Kay and Ray Soulé, San Francisco's most fashionable and wealthy couple. Now in his early forties, Ray Soulé is the son of the late Saul Soulé, the fabulously wealthy Transistor King of California, by a first marriage. Saul Soulé began his career in the 1920s as a wholesaler of radio repair parts, made a killing in Navy contracts in the Second World

90

War, and parlayed that fortune to gigantic proportions in the 1950s when he acquired the marketing rights to the most successful series of second generation transistors. His son Ray Soulé did graduate work in medieval music at Stanford and pursued a quiet, scholarly life. Saul Soulé died in 1970, leaving Ray a yearly income of some umpteen million dollars.

Being rich, hence independent-minded, Ray Soulé would prefer to avoid the limelight but for the fact that his wife Kay Hales Soulé is obsessed with society, not just San Francisco's but New York's as well. She has recently broken into the charmed circle of *Women's Wear Daily,* her picture appearing opposite that of Lee Radziwell and Jackie O. In her mid-twenties some ten years ago, Kay Hales was working as a cocktail waitress in a place just outside Pebble Beach. She snared Ray Soulé the first night he walked into the place. Kay didn't know who Soulé was, but he sure as hell looked rich—which he turned out to be, beyond Kay Hales's wildest expectations.

I love the drama of American will—the way, as F. Scott Fitzgerald says of the Great Gatsby, so many Americans seem to spring from a Platonic conception of themselves. Kay Hales saw her opportunity and grasped it. Ray Soulé, who until then loved only Cluniac chant, found himself headlong in love with a beautiful, leggy young woman who made him feel like a hero. As I said, I respect Kay Soulé's power of will. She's from a small farming town in the Imperial Valley, so Toby Wain tells me, and I can just imagine the dreams she nurtured in those long years of growing up: sturdy, persistent American dreams, beautiful and sad at the same time—of getting away and doing better. San Francisco is filled with people who are living out as much as possible their deepest fantasies. I think I have a walk-on part in the longest-running musical comedy in history. Kay and Ray Soulé have top billing. They have been very good for each other. Kay keeps her husband in minimal dialogue with the world beyond the boundaries of Cluniac chant. She, meanwhile, has discovered the lavishness of the fortune she charmed her way into. It provides her with an inexhaustible source of amusement. Shortly after their marriage, Kay insisted on moving from Palo Alto to San Francisco, which they did in 1968, the year Ray finished his dissertation on the liturgical practices of the medieval Abbey of Cluny. By the way, Donna Stinger, the *Express*'s grandmotherly society columnist, recently reported that Kay Soulé has agreed to serve as one of the honorary co-chairs of the Andy Soutane campaign for governor.

Not having to work for a living, Ray devotes his full energies to editing the *Quarterly of Medieval Music,* which he also subsidizes. Kay Soulé gives parties and talks them over afterwards with Eva del Valde Shaw. Kay likes to have someone like Eva for a friend because Kay wants at least one person around her with whom to share a tacit understanding of how much luck, cunning and feminine charm it took for both of them to get to the top.

I was depressed as I walked down the great staircase at four-thirty to head back to the Library. I was now, incipiently at least, a party to blackmail. Those Soutane pictures could, after all, be carefully leaked—not directly by me, of course, but say, to one of the nervy girlie magazines like *Bachelor* or *Tiger Man.* Or they could be given to one of the militant gay newspapers who might get into a campaign going on to force Soutane out of the closet in order to strengthen the gay movement. That, in fact, would be the best way to handle it. Incite the militant gays. Get the word out through the gay rumor network. It would then seep upwards into broader circles once the campaign heated up. Such a process, of course, could already be under way without our doing a thing. If Tiny Roncola had these pictures, then who knows what else was known in gay circles up and down the state?

Mayor Jimmy Rolph used to love to descend this staircase before an adoring crowd, an orchestra half-hidden behind a screen of potted palms on the upper landing playing "Smiles," his theme song. Across the great rotunda you can see Rolph's name carved into granite above the eastern balcony. The night

92

before City Hall was to be dedicated, Rolph had a team of stone masons come in during the wee hours of the morning to carve "James Rolph Mayor" in huge letters across the eastern wall, so that for as long as this building stood people would know that it was Sunny Jim Rolph of the Mission who built San Francisco's magnificent municipal palace.

James Rolph, Jr., a genial, popular shipping entrepreneur and city booster, was elected the thirtieth mayor of San Francisco at the age of forty-two on 26 September 1911, beating out the incumbent, Irish-born P. H. McCarthy, a labor leader put in the mayor's chair four years previously by the Union Labor Party. Rolph beat McCarthy by some 20,000 votes. Adding insult to injury, Rolph took the labor vote as well. He won re-election four more times, serving as mayor for five terms before being elected governor of California in 1930.

The years 1911–1930 are for San Franciscans the Age of Rolph. Will there someday be an Age of Carpino? I wonder. Or will some more impersonal force be seen in retrospect as dominating the city during our era? The Age of Dissent perhaps, or the Age of Manhattanization, the Age of Intra-County Metropolitanization, the Age of Faction and Bureaucracy? Will one person ever again dominate San Francisco's political stage? There are, after all—so we are constantly being told—no more heroes.

Between 1911 and 1930 Rolph presided over the birth of modern San Francisco. Under his guidance the Civic Center took shape, including a City Hall (1915), an Exposition Auditorium (1915), openings with a lavish masked ball, and our Public Library (1917), where I am presently entombed alive. Two major tunnels were built: the Stockton Street tunnel (1914), connecting downtown with the northern littoral, and the Twin Peaks tunnel (1917), connecting downtown with a vast cismontane area to the south now occupied by the newer neighborhoods of Parkside, Lakeshore, West Portal, St. Francis Wood, Ingleside. Bonds were authorized to build an aqueduct bringing water from the Hetch Hetchy in the Sierra to reservoirs in San Mateo County

93

south of the city. Three municipal museums arose: the North American Hall (1916) and the De Young (1921) in Golden Gate Park, and the Palace of the Legion of Honor (1924) at Land's End. There was also Kezar Stadium (1925); and in the late 1920s the political and economic planning of the War Memorial complex took place. San Francisco's superb War Memorial, dedicated in 1932, included the city's Opera House, Veterans' Auditorium, and San Francisco Museum of Modern Art.

A Republican, Rolph conducted an aggressively bipartisan administration, making himself (he was a great actor) all things to all men. He charmed the Irish by reeling off from memory the names of all the Irish counties. He gave official recognition to Rosh Hashana and Yom Kippur in the city calendar. Out of his own pocket, he redeemed a $1700 mortgage on the city's African Methodist Episcopal Church. He hinted at descent from John Rolfe of Virginia, Pocahontas's husband, thus establishing claim to a dash of Indian blood. He grew Gallic among the French, seeming even more the *boulevardier*. Among the Italians his gestures expanded and his accent ever so subtly mediterraneanized itself. An Episcopalian, he could recite long passages from the Book of Common Prayer. He also knew when to stand and when to kneel at a Catholic mass.

Proud of his Horatio Alger rise to wealth and position, Rolph never lost the common touch. His parents—London-born father, Edinburgh-born mother—migrated to San Francisco in 1868, settling on Minna Street south of Market Street, San Francisco's pre-earthquake working-class quarter. A year later, 1869, Jimmy Rolph was born. Rolph's father held a secure but modest job with William Chapman Ralston's Bank of California, so as a boy Jimmy Rolph had to hustle.

He hustled. He delivered newspapers. He swept out grocery stores. He ran messages for the trading firm of Kittle and Company. In 1898, when he was twenty-nine, he leased two ships and started his own shipping company. By 1908 he owned ten vessels, a shipbuilding yard, and a coal company. He was elected to San Francisco's Valhalla of plutocracy, the Pacific Union Club on Nob Hill.

94

Rolph was, perhaps, the only member of the Pacific Union Club to live in the Mission district, that vast southern quarter of the city where ordinary citizens migrated after the earthquake and fire of '06 destroyed the South of Market area. Rolph built a mansion at San Jose Avenue and Twenty-fifth Street. In 1903 he organized the Mission Bank, with himself as president. In April 1906, after the earthquake, he helped form the Mission Relief Association, which operated out of a barn he owned on San Jose Avenue. At Rolph's request, Sebastian Collins served as secretary to the Association. Thousands were fed and resettled. This relief work, in fact, first brought Rolph into public prominence. He was asked to head the Mission Improvement Association and, in 1909, he was made a director of the Portola Festival that celebrated the rebirth of the city from the ashes of '06.

As mayor, Sunny Jim Rolph of the Mission was showmanship incarnate. He dressed in a cutaway coat, striped pants, hamilton collar, a fresh flower in his lapel—and brightly polished cowboy boots. He had a genius for public events. He donned a motorman's cap to drive the first streetcar through the just completed Twin Peaks tunnel. When there was a question of the steel structure of the second City Hall, then under construction, not being up to standard, Rolph climbed out on the highest, most isolated girder, risking his life to inspect the workmanship. As a shipbuilder, he said when he had clambered down, he knew steel and he found the steelwork of City Hall more than satisfactory. Whenever possible, the municipal orchestra played his theme song "Smiles" for his public appearances. Rolph usually conducted the orchestra himself for a few bars before getting down to the business of dedicating this or that building or greeting this or that dignitary—the king and queen of Belgium, William Howard Taft, Eamon de Valera, tennis star Helen Wills, Queen Marie of Rumania, Woodrow Wilson. At the City Hall dedication, attended by Sebastian Collins among a few thousand others, Rolph finished his oration, entered the building, ascended the great staircase to Room 200, took off his cutaway, rolled up his sleeves and got to work. The best way to dedicate a city hall, Rolph remarked, was to put it to effective use, serving the taxpayer.

Neither a thinker nor an excessively skilled politician in the smoke-filled backroom sense of the term, Rolph dovetailed his personality with that of San Francisco's, thus achieving an expressive or symbolic kind of greatness. He exuded an ambiance of urbane Edwardian tory bohemianism which the city recognized as its own. The mayor's office was a very personal thing in those days. In a pre-civil service era Rolph possessed enormous powers of patronage and unashamedly used them. He tucked away hundreds of worthy supporters into city employment. He also gave away most of his $500-a-month salary to people down on their luck who came to see him in the mayor's office, keeping a bag of $20 gold pieces in his lower-left desk drawer for the purpose. In those days the Mayor himself personally signed every welfare voucher. Hundreds of thousands of such chits, bearing Rolph's signature, are still stacked in the City Hall basement.

Rolph was a lover of good wine and lavish lunches at Maye's Oyster House on Polk Street or, if he were too busy, hot gourmet spreads sent over to his office by taxicab from the Pacific Union Club. He smoked expensive "Lords of England" cigars and was an occasional *habitué* of the city's higher-class bordellos. He once opened the annual Policeman's Ball by escorting in the grand parade the city's leading madam, Tessie Wall. Marriage vows and Rolph's sincere Episcopalianism now and then crumbled before the vagrant urges of the flesh. For a long time, in fact, he was rumored to be keeping a mistress. But no matter. Those were both better-behaved and more tolerant days in the matter of sexual conduct. Discretion covered a multitude of sins.

No wonder, then, that Rolph failed as governor. In Sacramento he was like a violinist trying to play gypsy music on a bass fiddle. San Francisco was concrete, touchable, tastable. Governed from a hick town in the Sacramento Valley, California was an abstraction—not an opening, a parade, a dedication, but a map on the wall, a stack of densely worded legislative bills piled high each morning upon his desk, awaiting his perusal and signature. Rolph lost his geniality. He suffered a series of heart attacks. He was almost driven from office when he made some offhand remarks approving of the lynching of two San Jose kidnappers. On 2 June 1934 Rolph's heart stopped. He was resting at the Riverside Ranch in Santa Clara County, trying to recuperate from his second-to-the-last heart attack. Before the funeral, his body lay in state under the rotunda of the San Francisco City Hall—dressed jauntily in hamilton collar, cutaway coat, striped pants, cowboy boots, a fresh *boutonnière* in his lapel.

"What are you doing over here?"
"I might ask you the same thing. I thought you ran the Library. In case you forgot, the Library is across the street. Now go back there and run it."
"I thought you were running our literacy program."
"You'll find a number of illiterates in City Hall."
"I enjoyed our visit this noon."
"I've forgotten all about it."
"But not about lunch tomorrow."
"No. Twelve-thirty. The San Domenico. I'll show up if I'm hungry."
"Are you busy tonight?"
"Yes."
"How frustrating."
"Read a good book."
"Any recommendations?"
"Try *The Phenomenon of Man*. It's one of my favorites."
"You're not Catholic, are you?"
"I must go. We've got a supplemental appropriation before the Board of Supervisors next week, money for our literacy program. I'm lobbying some of the administrative assistants to persuade the supervisors to vote for it."
"You've got the body of a goddess."
"Just a healthy California girl, Norton."
"Looking for a healthy California man?"
"Perhaps. Know of any?"

Chapter 4

I T WAS SLIGHTLY after seven-thirty in the morning when Marina and I ascended into the sleek black open-air touring car waiting outside our Taylor Street flat. Jimmy Phelan had sent the car over to take us down to Villa Montalvo outside Saratoga for a Saturday luncheon. Robert Poole, Jimmy's chauffeur, told us all about the car as we churned our way along El Camino Real. It was, he hollered over the roar of the engine, a 1910 Croxton-Keeton touring car, manufactured in Massillon, Ohio. It had a chrome vanadium steel gearset, mounted on Timken roller bearings, and was powered by a forty-horsepower Rutenber motor with a four-and-three-quarter-inch bore and a five-inch stroke. I nodded wisely at Robert's enthusiastic description, although I know nothing of motor cars. I do know, however, that the three of us, attired in white smocks, duster hats, and goggles, made the trip down the Peninsula quite comfortably, taking an entire lovely April morning to do so.

Marina refused to wear her duster. She wore instead a dark blue British navy officer's double-breasted bridge coat with gold buttons from Brooks Brothers. She looked, I must say, quite handsome. She would have made a rather attractive recruiting poster for the Royal Navy, were she and the Royal Navy so inclined.

We traveled at an average of thirty-five miles per hour, with stop-offs at San Mateo and Palo Alto. Marina and I usually take the train down to San Jose when we visit Saratoga, and are met at the station; but Robert had to take the Croxton-Keeton into San Francisco for repairs the day before and so we were quite happy to keep him company on the way back down to Villa Montalvo.

As we chugged through the treeless San Bruno Mountains, I could not help but recall earlier trips down to Belmont with Ralston in the early 1870s just after I had returned from Italy and was finishing my studies at Harvard. Quite frankly, Ralston drove his horses at about the same speed maintained by Robert Poole behind the wheel of our touring car. So much for progress! Yet I must admit that the Croxton-Keeton with its four-and-three-quarter-inch bore and its five-inch stroke gives a smoother ride than did Ralston's horse-drawn phaeton.

"Dear Sebastian," Jimmy's note said, "please do come to lunch at Montalvo on Saturday, 12 April 1914, with Marina. Robert will be in the city with the car and will drive you down. We'll see to it that you make the five-thirty train back from San Jose to the city. The weather promises to be perfect. We'll lunch on the veranda, then take a walk in the gardens. I've many new books to show you. I'm calling this my Montalvo–Exposition luncheon because we'll be unofficially inaugurating both my new villa and next year's Fair. Mayor Rolph and Charles Moore, president of the Exposition Company, will be there, along with Herbert Hoover (just back from Europe, where he has been traveling about, encouraging European participation in our Exposition) and his lovely wife Lou Henry. Franklin Delano Roosevelt, President Wilson's most agreeable Assistant Secretary of the Navy, has agreed to come down—and bring along with him the Marine Corps band from Mare Island. Mr. Roosevelt is out here to arrange a visit by the Fleet to San Francisco sometime during the Exposition year. I want you, George Sterling, Mrs. Atherton, and Jack and Charmian London to represent our little city-state of letters. Cora and Fremont Older will come, and David Starr Jordan. Cyril Tobin from the Hibernia Bank is bringing a young colleague to pay attention to Marina, if that young lady wishes any attention paid her. I've asked Polk,

Maybeck, and McLaren to come also, hoping they'll talk brilliantly of the Fair and impress Mr. Roosevelt. We do so much want the Fleet to visit us. My neighbor Paul Masson is dropping by. Downey and Noel are staying with me on weekends. I need their help getting moved into this place. The Senate race goes well."

Jimmy Phelan is the only candidate for the United States Senate who would bother moving into a new house two months before the election, and then give an elaborate luncheon party two weeks later. But then again, this will be the first time we Californians have a chance to elect our senators by direct vote. The Democrats smell victory in the air. I suppose Jimmy will soon be going to Washington to take a seat in the Senate.

The rear seat of the Croxton-Keeton touring car is elevated over the front seat, so we had an almost unobstructed view of the countryside over Robert's head and shoulders. I was initially disconcerted by Robert's habit of turning around to instruct us on this or that point of mechanical nicety in his beloved Croxton-Keeton, but we never left the road—which is more than I can say for my host Mr. Ralston in 1873. Then, as I recall, we went twice into the ditch, once from carelessness and once when a wheel detached itself on a downhill grade, spinning out ahead of us as if in a race to the bottom ravine where we all unceremoniously landed.

"I could complete this here itinerary to Saratoga in a third less the time, Mr. Collins, a third less, but His Honor Mr. Phelan likes me to take it easy-like when I've got distinguished guests like you and the Miss along."

I was glad Mr. Poole was lengthening the trip out by a third. Thirty-five miles per hour is fine with me. Passing through Burlingame, we motored past the stately stands of eucalyptus trees with which John McLaren lined El Camino Real some thirty-five years ago when he had just arrived from Scotland and was working on various Peninsula estates. This was before he became the superintendent of Golden Gate Park.

Marina reached over and held my hand. She was possessed, perhaps, of an intuition that I was thinking of her mother,

100

whom Marina very much resembled this fine April morning. Marina has her mother's thick blondish hair, strong jawline, blue eyes set far apart, smattering of Irish freckles, wide mouth, and no-nonsense demeanor. Marina takes life calmly, in stride, a thing I could never do. I was grateful for Marina's large strong hand in mine, and for her broad shoulders and prepossessing frame as well. Like her mother, Marina is a large woman, generous and assertive in movement and gesture. Her nearness, the sheer dramatic presence of her physical self, fills me with comfort. She is flesh of my flesh; and I have a secret father's knowledge of her heart's pumping, the steadiness of her breathing, the inner rhythms of her blood flow. Marina is so marvelously, so physically alive—and I am more alive because of her. Some of her urgent, compelling health has passed over into her ridiculously over-aged father; and I will live longer because of this shared strength. Virginia died giving Marina life. Marina's gift of life to me is thus also Virginia's gift. I held tightly to my daughter's hand and I remembered Virginia.

San Mateo's main street was stirring with Saturday morning business when we stopped off at the Haven Restaurant for coffee. Farmers drove their heavily laden buckboards and drayage wagons through the streets. There are still many working farms in the San Mateo area, despite the growth of great estates from Burlingame southwards. But I saw city people on the streets as well, and a number of motor cars. Someday, I predict, San Francisco's population will spill southwards and fill up these little Peninsula villages of Burlingame, San Mateo, Belmont, San Carlos, Redwood City.

"Are you having fun, Father?" Marina asked me after we finished our coffee.

We were in the process of re-vesting ourselves in the garments of touring carism. Marina helped me to fasten the latch of my goggles behind my head. I am not sure I understand this new word "fun"—at least as Marina and her friends from the Mills Seminary use it. "Fun" sounds like much too modern a sensation for a bearded portly gentleman in his mid-sixties to experience. I have known pleasure, enjoyment, even intermittent happiness, which Aristotle tells us is the conformity of the will to perfect virtue; but I am not so sure what "fun" is. It sounds like pleasure, only a little more nervous in reverberation. I am nervous enough as it is, and I always have been; but if Marina wants me to have fun, then I shall try to have fun.

"Yes, my dear, I am having fun. What about yourself?"

"I love the ride, Father, and I love Mayor Phelan, but the guest list does sound a little stuffy, doesn't it? All those learned, accomplished gentlemen—I'll hardly know what to say."

"You will manage, my dear. Just speak up. Men like an intelligent, forward young woman, especially when she is pretty like yourself. Watch Mrs. Atherton. She knows how to handle men perfectly—with a mixture of the siren and the bluestocking."

"I'm not pretty, Dr. Collins," Marina shot back in that attitude of drollery and badinage which characterizes much of our discourse. "I'm what is called a handsome woman, not a pretty woman. And I'm just a little bit afraid of Mrs. Atherton."

"Everyone, my dear, is a little bit afraid of Mrs. Atherton, including myself, and has been since she buried poor George in 1888 and went to Europe."

I omitted to mention that Gertrude Atherton left San Francisco on the same train as Sybil Sanderson. The two of them were the closest of friends. In the late 1880s they would walk the streets of San Francisco together, laying plans for their escape to Europe.

"My only worry, Miss Collins," I continued, "is not that you will be bored, but that you will be pestered by Mr. Sterling. As your father, I shall then be forced to challenge his presumption. 'Unhand my daughter, you cad!' I shall say. 'She is innocence and light and you but a satyr bloated with unholy lust.'"

Marina laughed at my sally, then blushed. George Sterling is, after all, a fuckster *par excellence*, as half the women in San Francisco have found out, including the tragically dead (by her own hand—poison) Nora May French. My humor was intended to put Marina slightly on her guard, although, to be perfectly honest, I do not believe that George Sterling is either a cradle-robber or an invader of other men's homes. He is, after all, a fellow Bohemian. His fuckstering occurs within the *demimonde*, and not among the upper classes; for George truly loves his place as the poet laureate of our local establishment and would not endanger it for a casual *amour*; yet it does Marina no harm to be forewarned, hence forearmed.

"Mr. Sterling is not my type, Father. Frankly, I'm bored by impoverished poets with smoldering eyes and Danteesque features. As the daughter of a man of letters, I'm not impressed. I prefer professional men—doctors, lawyers, men of business. I want to have money and a fine home and travel to Europe. I've no ambitions whatsoever for shabby bohemianism."

Truly, Marina is her mother's daughter! I heartily approve of her upper-middle-class ambitions. I only wish that I had been more financially ambitious myself, although Marina cannot complain. I have raised her in solid comfort. To be frank: I have pursued art but not the garret. I have led my life within the context of protecting institutions, most continuously St. Ignatius College where I teach—where, in fact, I shall teach until 1918 when I reach the age of seventy, if the Jesuit Fathers will keep me on that long: which they will, for Jimmy Phelan has endowed a professorship in his father's honor, the James Phelan Professorship of Aesthetics and Art History. I am the chair's first incumbent. The chair has generous retirement provisions, but I prefer to remain teaching as long as possible, lest I degenerate into a seedy old man before the descent into shabby inconsequentiality— checkers, aimless walks in the park, vacant hours spent staring out the window—becomes absolutely necessary.

South of San Carlos, the countryside takes on a more explicitly agricultural appearance. It becomes a Virgilian landscape of orchards and tilled fields reaching an intensity of georgic splendor in the Santa Clara Valley that runs from Mountain View down past San Jose. The poet Bayard Taylor,

John Muir the naturalist, Jack London in *The Call of the Wild*: writer after writer has celebrated the beauty of this garden of the world—this sun-warmed, April-loved Valley of Saint Claire, this American Italy.

The Stanford University campus, which we reached around ten o'clock, is poised against the Coast Range on the Santa Clara Valley's northwest edge. The mid-morning sun was at a perfect angle as we drove past Stanford's buff-stoned, red-tiled quadrangle, designed by the late H. H. Richardson of Boston to suggest an intersection of Franciscan Mission and American Romanesque. Stanford University is a very lovely campus indeed, lovely in a special California way, and never more so than the other mid-morning, when it was warmed by the luminous April sunlight so that its red roof tiles glowed incarnadine and its buff stones took on a shimmering golden haze that blended beautifully with the wheat fields surrounding the quadrangle.

David Starr Jordan, Stanford's president, wants Royce to come out and lecture on philosophy for a year, as did William James in 1906. James's lectures, however, were rudely interrupted by the April Earthquake which eight years ago destroyed much of the Stanford campus. Classes were suspended and James left for Cambridge. Royce could have easily been recruited in '91 when he had not as yet been granted a tenured professorship at Harvard and was, in his ambivalent way, homesick for California; but I doubt if Jordan could now get him back here for even a year. Royce, by the way, is profoundly disturbed by events in Europe. As America's leading German-trained philosopher, he feels personally betrayed by the Kaiser's sabre-rattling.

Such a lovely, dreamy Mediterranean campus, this Stanford—but such a protestant university! More protestant, even, than Royce himself. Jordan is a great man, a builder, but he can be tiresome with all his earnest talk of plain living and high thinking, his mountain climbing and baseball and eugenics, his filling up of the campus with perfect specimens of biological manhood and womanhood. An Emersonian

Oversoul hovers over Stanford like a protective halo, urging one and all onwards and upwards towards the assumption of the white man's burden. Yet I do admire its young men— the Irwin brothers, young Herbert Hoover, already a millionaire—and I must not be bitter over the fact that both Stanford and Berkeley are destined for greater things than my College of St. Ignatius, which has been lodged since the Earthquake in an abandoned shirt factory on Hayes Street.

I am writing this some eight years and eight hours from the initial tremor of 18 April 1906 and the subsequent three-day fire which destroyed the superb buildings of our College at Hayes and Van Ness. St. Ignatius College has not been able to recover its institutional momentum since losing those buildings. Our marvelous library and scientific laboratories were destroyed. When I joined the faculty, St. Ignatius College was on the way to becoming a superb Jesuit college in the European manner, something between a European lyceum and an American college. Now I have no idea what we are. The future of higher education rests, I fear, with Berkeley and Stanford, not with us. Money and vision and creative will animate these institutions, whereas we Catholics of San Francisco seem, since the Fire at least, to have lost our energy when it comes to the matter of philanthropic ideals and a taste for cultural excellence.

Jimmy Phelan studied with us at St. Ignatius, as did another California senator, Stephen Mallory White; but Jimmy has also been a regent at the University of California since 1889, giving a lot of his time and energy to that institution. Mrs. Hearst, he has told me, is determined to outdo Mrs. Stanford's university at Palo Alto. Phoebe Hearst wants California at Berkeley to be a great university: a Harvard or a Heidelberg on the shores of the Pacific. She shall get her wish. Only Jimmy among our Catholic upper class has shown any interest in putting money into St. Ignatius. The Catholic upper class is in the process of moving down to Burlingame and becoming country squires, indifferent to the future of San Francisco.

The scruffy, saloon-ridden town of Mayfield, in any event, mocks David Starr Jordan's teetotalism and Unitarian rectitude. As we motored through Mayfield, I could see a number of swinging-door saloons already busy with customers. Palo Alto, on the other hand, was perfectly genteel, very much the proper college town—like Berkeley.

"I'd like to come down to Stanford for my teaching certificate," Marina remarked as we motored out of Palo Alto.

South of Palo Alto the agricultural richness of the Santa Clara Valley asserts itself in fertile splendor. We drove past acre upon acre of orchards, many of them blooming in plum, peach, almond, apple, cherry, pear, walnut, and chestnut blossoms. Such a profusion of varying tree shapes, leaf textures, and flowering buds! To our right, lion-colored foothills dotted with scattered live oak trees rose westwards towards the Coast Range and the Pacific beyond. On the higher hillside regions, you could see the darker green patches of fig and olive groves. To our left more prosaic fields ran down towards the bay: radishes, leeks, onions, parsley, peas. Here and there a run of wild poppies invaded the domesticated fields with a sortie of bright orange, broken by white cottages or even a mansarded house where farming had brought some prosperity. Brown-and-white dairy cattle lazily drifted but a few feet away as our Croxton-Keeton chugged by, as if they were too content even to be disturbed by the noisy inventions of modern science.

Outside of Mountain View vineyards begin. One particular vine-guarded cottage (it possessed both a mansard roof and a porch) reminded me of our place at Avila Vineyards near St. Helena in Napa County where I lived with Virginia from 1894 to 1895 and where, nearly twenty years ago, I gained the daughter riding beside me and lost the wife now buried in the graveyard of a tiny Napa Valley church. The vines were quietly gaining strength. It was only mid-April. I remembered with gratitude and sadness the one full year Virginia and I shared together.

I remembered our shared Virgilian world of patient nurture

106

and cycle of seasons: April through June, the growing time, from buds, to flowers, to berries; March, when the leafbuds began to swell with their promise of autumnal fruit, each succulent plant so vulnerable to deer and rabbits, or, bursting into fruit, becoming prey to birds and bees. Throughout the long, hot California summer Virginia and I tied canes, thinned foliage, and sprayed the berries with sulphur as they ripened from green to red or white by late summer, tested anxiously by us for sugar and acid, warmed by the sun, cooled by coastal fogs which crept each morning down along the hills. Cabernet Sauvignon, Sauvignon Blanc, Zinfandel, Merlot, Barbera, Chardonnay, Chenin Blanc, Pinot Blanc, Pinot Noir, Semillon: the varietal grapes of California, planted in 1880 by Agoston Haraszthy, from whom we bought the Avila Vineyards—lovely, lovely grapes, waxy and juiceful and noon-loved by flights of drunken bees.

Then in late September came an anxious time, the time of final summer and early fall when an unexpected night's frost can damage a vintage irrevocably; and so, in the dark hours, Virginia and I set out burning pots to assuage an unexpected cold. By day, we cleaned vats and checked our cooperage in expectation of the coming crush. Then the decision, made after testings and intuitive calculation. Harvest time! The time of swift work. Some of the skilled Spanish harvesters we hired were capable of taking in 2,000 pounds of grapes in a single day. The picking began early in order to avoid the heavy heat of late afternoon: the picking itself, the stacking of lugs, the filling of gondola-vats, the rush—towards the end, in mid-October—to avoid an early rain. How proud I was of my ability to perform manual labor, I who had lived such a sedentary life. Shorn of fruit, the vines defied the dying year in riotous hues—yellow, crimson, purple, red—the older the vine, the more blazing the color, as if once more to celebrate the fact that something immemorial has been accomplished.

The crush itself, meanwhile, proceeded apace: skin, pulp and stems sifted out; juices sent to vats; there, over the next three years or so, to be racked from barrel to barrel (sediment

107

left behind) in stone cellars, cool and quiet, before being bottled as vintage wine, a wine Virginia never tasted—the one vintage, 1895, issued by our Avila Vineyards.

We drove past a very quiet Santa Clara County Fruit Exchange. In the summer, hundreds of wagons laden with plums and apricots will descend upon the Exchange every day. I could see the bell tower of Santa Clara College to the east of El Camino Real. The Alameda, now serviced by streetcar, runs from Mission Santa Clara into San Jose, where at Eldorado and First Street is the Phelan Block, an office complex developed by James Phelan, Senior, in the late eighties. We did not turn eastward to San Jose as we often do, but southwestwards towards Saratoga and Villa Montalvo.

You approach Villa Montalvo via the road that leads through Saratoga to another foothill village, Los Gatos, where the Jesuit Fathers maintain their Sacred Heart Novitiate. Saratoga is a picturesque montane town, reminding me of similar villages in Tuscany. New Yorkers settled it in the early 1860s. They came for the mineral waters that bubble up from a number of the local hot springs, naming the place after the New York resort town of Saratoga.

As our Croxton-Keeton chugged up the mountain road leading to the eastern edge of Saratoga, Marina and I looked back to see the flowering orchards on the valley floor below. When we turned around, we could see the creamy walls and red tiled roof of Montalvo rising from a surrounding stand of cypress, pine, and ilex trees. We drove past the sweeping Italian gardens laid out by John McLaren. Jimmy awaited us on the terrace that spreads itself across Montalvo's main entrance. He was dressed in white, and his reddish-gray beard was, as usual, neatly trimmed. He stood next to one of the two marble sphinxes that guard the terrace. Box and Black Prince ran barking towards our car. Save for our Croxton-Keeton, this might have been a scene from the Italian Renaissance, with Jimmy as a rusticated Lorenzo de Medici, greeting some Florentine visitors.

Jimmy bought this 160-acre estate three years ago. We

108

picnicked on the grounds the day he signed the deed, after having spent the morning in San Jose. While Jimmy looked after his banking and real estate interests, I had visited some Jesuit friends at the Santa Clara College. Jimmy's architect William Curlett joined us later for lunch on the grounds of what had become that day the Villa Montalvo Estate. After sandwiches and chablis, we walked about the empty fields, talking of what Jimmy had in mind: nothing less than the finest country house on the Peninsula—not the biggest, but the finest. My mentor William Chapman Ralston began the trend of Peninsula villas more than fifty years ago when he acquired and expanded Count Cipriani's estate in Belmont. Burlingame and Hillsborough now teem with majestic piles. Within the past year, in fact, four new ones have been launched: Rosecourt in Hillsborough, built by the George T. Camerons; Templeton Crocker's Uplands, a Renaissance palace done by Willis Polk; Beaulieu in Cupertino, a burst of Ionic whiteness amidst seventy acres of leafy-green vineyards, also designed by Polk. Harriet Pullman Carolan sent to France to secure the services of the architect E. Saint-Saëns to design her spectacular Hillsborough chateau, as yet unnamed. Jimmy's Montalvo, then, is part of a trend: the rustication of San Francisco's rich into country estates. Jimmy has been coming down here to the lower Santa Clara Valley on business and pleasure for years. He has a passion for the Italianate aspects of the lower Peninsula landscape.

It was mid-August, and very hot, the day of our first visit. We lunched in a redwood grove for the coolness. Curlett, poor man, died before Montalvo was finished; but he did listen well that day, and he caught the spirit of Jimmy's vision as we walked around the estate, landscaped now by McLaren in the Italian manner, but then as untutored by art as the rugged Appenines through which I foraged with my fellow Zouaves some forty-five years ago. Drowsy bees kept us reluctant company as we walked. The afternoon heat seemed too much even for them.

"I'd like," said Jimmy as we walked off the effects of our wine and our sandwiches, "something that expressed this valley's kinship with Italy and Spain, something suggestive of Golden California. Build me a villa expressive of the Mediterranean south but evocative as well of a Californian ideality. I would like Villa Montalvo to rise from that promontory there, serene and assured, as if these hills had been settled for two thousand years. Design me something that a poet might envision as an imaginative symbol of California herself."

"Give him," I said, "a palace of art, a place such as the conquistadors might have dreamed of as they trekked up through the deserts of the Southwest in search of the seven cities of gold."

As we took our aperitifs on the eastern terrace last Saturday, some three years after our initial walk through the bee-buzzed poppy fields, I could see that Jimmy has got his wish. Only Mrs. Phoebe Hearst's estate in Pleasanton, the Ibero-Moorish forty-room extravaganza, Hacienda del Pozo de Verona, approaches Montalvo for sheer charm. Jimmy intends to do a lot of entertaining at Montalvo during the Exposition year—when he is back from Washington, that is.

Young Franklin Roosevelt, President Wilson's Assistant Secretary of the Navy, was treating Jimmy as if he were already a United States senator: sending a Marine band down from Mare Island to play for our luncheon party. The United States Navy will soon have a good friend in the upper chamber of the Congress. There were some twenty Marine musicians, conducted by a middle-aged warrant officer wearing a monocle and a Van Dyke beard. The Marines were very smart indeed in their navy blue coats with gold brass buttons, light blue pants with a red stripe running down each leg, white helmets such as London bobbies wear, and red insignia stripes on their sleeves. Their instruments shone in the sunlight.

General Kansler, incidentally, insisted that we Zouaves have good regimental music. It promoted morale and *esprit de corps*, he believed. I remember one evening in April of 1869 at our barracks adjacent to Castel Sant'Angelo. The regimental band played operatic airs in the courtyard as we prepared our kits for the next day's march. That was the first time I heard the *Casta*

Diva aria from Bellini's *Norma*. I heard it again the next year at Castelgandolfo, the pope's summer residence outside Rome. I stood guard at one of the Pope's *soirées*, and so had an excellent view of the proceedings. *L'Abbé* Liszt played *Casta Diva* on the piano. His Holiness was so moved by Liszt's soulful playing that he walked up to the *Abbé*, put his hand on his shoulder, and hummed the haunting air of Signor Bellini in accompaniment. There were tears in the Pope's eyes. Even Cardinal Antonelli, *Pio Nono's* cynical, lady-loving Neopolitan Secretary of State, seemed touched.

Our Marines, however, did not play Bellini; they played instead some of Mr. Sousa's new marches and the more lively of Stephen Foster's songs. During the luncheon itself, the Marines disappeared into the rear kitchen of Montalvo, where the servants had set out a splendid lunch for the troops. The warrant officer, a certain Mr. Ralph Hooper, remained with us as a seated guest. He flanked Mr. Roosevelt's left throughout the entire affair, like an *aide de camp*. It was all very smart, like an operetta. Just before the dessert, Mr. Hooper excused himself to march his Marines down to the lower garden. They accompanied our coffee and lemon sherbet with the charming music of Sigmund Romberg and Victor Herbert. We took our cognac to the haunting melody of "Ah, sweet mystery of life, at last I've found you."

"I'm glad the Marines have landed," Charles Moore said to Franklin Roosevelt. "Mr. John Philip Sousa, formerly of the Marine Corps, will be with us for the Exposition. We have commissioned the French composer Saint-Saëns to do an Exposition symphony. It's called 'Hail California.' It's scored for a full orchestra, Mr. Sousa's military band, and a choir of three hundred voices."

"Very proper, Mr. Moore, very proper," the Assistant Secretary replied. Roosevelt is barely into his thirties. He has a jaunty demeanor and the broadest possible Harvard accent. They say President Wilson thinks the world of him.

We began our luncheon with what Marina calls "cocktails" on the tiled north loggia. A great lawn bordered in pink

111

geraniums swept down to our right, then a stand of cypress and pine trees, and a silver-green eucalyptus or two. Through an opening in the trees, where the roadway has been cut, we could see the Santa Clara Valley below, April-carpeted in flowering almond, plum, and apricot. I do not like Marina's word "cocktails," by the way. I prefer to think of the sort of drinks we took on the loggia as "aperitifs." "Cocktails" are too nervous, as if alcoholic roosters were strutting about, or worse, spurring each other in a cockpit. We, by contrast, sipped sherry and champagne and nibbled on English biscuits in a most leisurely, well-behaved manner.

I complimented John McLaren upon his design of the grounds. Scotsmen do have a way with growing things! McLaren has worked wonders with Golden Gate Park. He is a gardener, not a landscape architect or a landscape engineer, although his accomplishments in his chosen field (like those of Luther Burbank) soar beyond those of so many colleagues possessed of formal training and university degrees. Johnny McLaren and I share a passion for trees. Above all other trees, I personally favor cypress trees—the trees beloved by Dante, the Florentine who knew that love moves the sun and the stars. In San Francisco cypresses are everywhere. In their Monterey variety, but also in their imported European stocks, they wave their rich green boughs atop windswept hills yet defiant of settlement. They shade residential plazas like Alamo Square, where Marina and I camped out in 1906 when fire devoured the city. They stand sentry along the rocky headlands where California, and America itself, drop precipitously into reluctant completion. Cypresses thrive in San Francisco's mixture of sunshine and wet weather. In sunlight they gesture outward, expansively as if in celebration of San Francisco as a minor memory of southern Europe, a vague but pleasing Italian afterthought. And when at evening the fog sweeps into what George Sterling describes as the cool, gray city of love, the cypresses recede into themselves, becoming secretive and sibylline. They were, after all, the favored trees of the ancients and they keep a long memory of pain and desire.

"My compliments, John," I said as I sipped my sherry. John

112

was drinking Scotch whiskey, neat, in a wine glass. "We could be at the Villa Medici at Careggi outside Florence."

"Aye, that's what Jimmy wanted, something grand and formal and Italian, so that is what I gave him."

Jimmy Phelan overheard my Villa Medici comparison and approached us.

"I presume, Sebastian, that you'll allow me to play Lorenzo," he laughed in that deep rich baritone voice of his. He was obviously pleased with the way his first major luncheon at Montalvo was progressing.

Mrs. Atherton was wearing one of her hats. She was telling a long, and no doubt very droll, story to Cyril Tobin, Marina, and the young man who later turned out to be John Charles Scannell. Marina wore a quite fetching pale-yellow dress which she calls a "shirtwaist." Fun—cocktail—shirtwaist: I am learning a lot of new words from this young daughter of mine. How embarrassing, how delightful, to be a grandfather in chronological age, yet cast by biological fact into a father's role! More men should sire daughters at the advanced age of forty-nine. Marina laughed when Mrs. Atherton's story ended. She and the young man seemed very conscious of one another.

"You already are the Lorenzo of San Francisco, Jimmy," I ventured. "But what roles are there for Johnny McLaren and myself? I'm too old and stout to be Pico della Mirandola, and Johnny drinks too much neat whiskey to be Ficini."

"Yes, but we do have a Savonarola in Fremont Older," Jimmy said, falling into the spirit of the thing. "Fremont has done more than anyone to drive graft and corruption out of San Francisco. Right now I'd say that he is one of the most powerful newspaper editors in America."

Jimmy, of course, was correct. Under the goading of Fremont Older, editor of the *Bulletin*, San Francisco has spent these past seven years cleaning its graft-ridden house.

"We could have used the real Savonarola during the graft trials," McLaren said dourly. "And I'll be thanking you, Sebastian, for your nice words on these gardens. Just as long as Jimmy doesn't want too many statues about."

McLaren cannot abide statues in his beloved Golden Gate

113

Park. Seven years ago, Jimmy commissioned sculptor Douglas Tilden to cast a statue of Junipero Serra to be placed at the entrance of the Music Concourse. Johnny McLaren was furious, but what could he do?

"A few classical items is all we'll be having here, Johnny," Phelan said, "and a bust of Shakespeare for the Shakespeare Garden."

David Starr Jordan, the Hoovers, and Mr. Roosevelt joined us. In my day, one sipped aperitifs in a seated position. These standing cocktail parties have more fluidity. People move about. It is like attending ten different parties simultaneously. Jack and Charmian London saw our group and sauntered over, leaving Mrs. Atherton in charge of the remaining large gathering. The rest of the company broke up into smaller clusters. Charles Moore, the president of the Panama-Pacific Exposition Company, and George Sterling were talking together. George wore a natty blue yachtsman jacket with gold buttons and white duck pants. He seemed very comfortable in an open-necked Byronic collar and a cravat. Moore wore a light pearl-gray suit and a straw boater to shield himself from the sun. I have rarely seen Moore so sporty. The Fremont Olders, Willis Polk, and Bernard Maybeck talked together in one corner of the loggia. Paul Masson talked to Downey Harvey and Noel Sullivan. Mr. Masson, I noted with some satisfaction, is even stouter than either I or Willis Polk.

Mayor Rolph had not yet arrived. Rolph is a Republican, not a tenth as wealthy as Jimmy, flamboyant where Jimmy is every inch the reserved patrician—in public at least. Rolph and Phelan are, however, friends from the Pacific Union Club, and since Rolph was elected mayor in 1911 he has done all that he can to keep the city up to Jimmy's standards.

Jack London, I might add, behaved rather well. Parties like this can be difficult for Jack, he being a socialist and hence feeling compelled to bait the rich. When he is with Charmian, however, Jack tends to be better behaved. I have known Jack to be drunk and disruptive. Not that I really mind. I was drunk and disruptive myself for nearly four years. In my case it

114

was a death wish and I think that is what is at the bottom of Jack's drinking as well. Jack has not been the same since Wolf House burned down. He is beginning to sag around the middle, which is not that disappointing in someone like myself, a sedentary scholar, but rather distressing in the author of stories of outdoor adventure. Phelan is ambivalent to Jack, despising him for his radicalism, worshipping him for the glory he has brought to California letters. Jack wore a rather smart tweed Norfolk jacket, a white shirt, necktie, and collar-pin. I have rarely seen him so smart. His spruceness was in obvious deference to Jimmy, for as Jimmy is ambivalent to Jack, so Jack is ambivalent to Jimmy. As a socialist, Jack is not supposed to like the rich; yet he wanted Wolf House the same way Jimmy wanted Montalvo: as an embodiment of a dream come true. He built it. It was superb, and then someone set it to the torch the night before Jack and Charmian were supposed to move in.

"Can't the President do anything, Mr. Secretary? A war like the one Europe is facing could destroy western civilization."

David Starr Jordan, president of Stanford University, said this to Roosevelt. Jordan is well over six feet tall and features a droopy walrus-like mustache. Roosevelt had to tilt his already tilted chin even higher into the air to catch Jordan's soulful eyes. London barely allowed Jordan time to finish his sentence.

"And drive millions of working people like cattle to the slaughter," London said.

Jordan loathes London, considering him a fake proletarian; yet because Jordan is a pacifist and so also is Jack a pacifist, being a socialist, Jordan accepted London's supporting comments.

"President Wilson is doing all that he can to insure the peace," Mr. Roosevelt said in that clipped sing-song way of his. For someone barely thirty, Franklin Delano Roosevelt is awfully self-assured. He is as patrician as Jimmy, even more so (and so is Wilson in his Princeton-Presbyterian way). Yet they are all Democrats, while Mr. Hoover—who then joined our conversation—is a Republican, in spite of being a poor boy who worked himself up the hard way, as they say. Here we were, then—Democrats, including a Democratic sub-cabinet officer, a Republican (or two Republicans at least; for I presume that Lou Henry Hoover is also a Republican—a charming Republican in a filmy peach-colored dress), a socialist, Jack London, and a pacifist, David Starr Jordan— talking about events, the imminent war in Europe, so far away from Montalvo and so far beyond our ability to affect their course.

"It's always the ordinary people who take it—in the stomach," London said. I am certain that he meant to say "take it in the ass" but did not, out of deference to his distinguished company and proper surroundings.

Had Jack London been my contemporary, he might have joined Garibaldi's Redshirts in the 1860s, which would have balanced off my enlistment in the Zouaves. I might have killed Jack, just as I killed the other one, and it would be Jack's face that would remorsefully return so often to my memory: a look of incredulous bafflement in his eyes as my bayonet struck home and his guts were rent asunder. They will soon be doing this again to one another in Europe, just as we did it to one another at Mentana on 3 November 1867—first with Stutzen carbines that fired twelve rounds per minute, and then with bayonets. We left a thousand Redshirts dead on the field that day, including one whose baffled agony I will remember to my dying day. In the end Garibaldi himself fled the field.

"Courage, courage, boys, long live Italy!" he cried to them.

"You lead us to slaughter!" they cried in return, breaking ranks under our attack. Our wounded and theirs were brought by train to Rome. The American Mrs. Catherine Stone and the Contessa della Torre organized a sanitary service to nurse the sick. The Queen of Naples herself, dressed in a white apron, went among the hospital wards, handing cigars and bonbons out to the wounded soldiers, Redshirts and Zouaves alike.

My unit, the St. Patrick's Battalion, marched into Rome on 6 November, entering by the *Porta Pia*. General Kanzler and his staff led us through the city in triumph, like legionnaires

116

returning from Gaul. We even marched our prisoners behind us (as in *Aïda*), bringing the captured wounded along in small carts. They were a sorry lot, their red shirts in tattered fragments, their heads wrapped in bloody bandages. Jack London is correct: in war, ordinary people are the ones who suffer, who take it in the posterior, and elsewhere.

"Mayor Phelan might corroborate this point," Herbert Hoover said. "I found it difficult to interest European governments in sending missions to the Exposition. All they can think of is the war."

As European commissioner, however, Hoover has done a brilliant job for the Fair, despite his difficulties with war-distracted governments. Like Roosevelt, Hoover is still young, barely forty. He has been a self-made millionaire since his mid-thirties. He and Lou Henry have been living in London of late, producing a joint translation of Agricola's Renaissance mining treatise *De Re Metallica*. David Starr Jordan is very proud of Hoover, who came to Stanford in 1891 on scholarship and who graduated in Stanford's first class.

"You can assure them, Mr. Hoover," Mr. Roosevelt said, "that the United States Navy will guarantee the safety of any treasures sent to San Francisco. I daresay, San Francisco will soon be a safer place for *objets d'art* than either France or Germany."

Just before luncheon was served, Mayor Rolph arrived in the Croxton-Keeton. Robert Poole had picked him up at the train station in San Jose.

"Delighted, delighted," Jimmy Rolph said to all of us in turn as he moved about, shaking hands, apologizing for his lateness. He wore a cutaway coat, striped pants, and cowboy boots, which I find colorful if eccentric. Rolph laughingly addressed Phelan as Senator. Rolph is a Republican, but it does look as if Phelan will be the first Democrat to represent California in the Senate in nearly two decades.

"Sebastian Collins," Rolph said as he shook my hand. "The city of San Francisco eagerly awaits your memoirs. I was talking to Paul Elder about them only the other day. He told me that they promise to be the literary event of the Exposition year."

It is difficult not to like Jimmy Rolph. I melted under the beam of his smile and his flattery. How does he remember so much? My memoirs cannot be much in his line, but he had a reference to them ready when he shook my hand. I am flattered—despite myself—flattered that he remembered them and that he thought they—or I—were worth the effort. Rolph downed three glasses of champagne in quick succession; then Antonio, Phelan's impeccable Spanish butler, announced lunch.

We lunched on the broad east terrace overlooking the gardens. A red, yellow, and green striped awning protected us from the direct rays of the sun. We sat in high-backed straw chairs around tables for seven, covered with floral displays and here and there divided by six-foot-high potted palms. We lunched on California fruit cocktail, followed by a salad plate of olives, celery hearts, and tomatoes. Then came a very delicious *aiguillette* of *sole marguery*. Off to our left, three Mexican cooks in white jackets broiled *filets mignon* over an open coal fire in a waist-high brick oven—barbecues, they are called. A new word—like fun and cocktails. After the fish, Antonio signaled the cooks and they served the *filets* to us, along with fresh green beans and potatoes *au gratin*. An alligator pear salad followed. For dessert, we enjoyed vanilla ice cream and *petits fours*. One young man—Antonio's son, I believe—circled the table continuously, refilling our glasses with chilled white wine, and champagne with the dessert.

We sat down to luncheon at one and had our coffee and cognac at two-thirty. Towards three we took a tour of Montalvo and the gardens, conducted by Phelan himself. Robert the chauffeur drove Marina and me down to San Jose to catch the five-thirty train back to San Francisco. I found the entire affair very interesting. I was not bored for a moment. Charles Moore gave Franklin Roosevelt quite an earful concerning the Panama-Pacific International Exposition: how

118

it cost $50 million to build, how the Pacific Ocean Exposition Company opened in a shack near Union Square just a few months after the Fire of 1906, how $4 million in bonds were sold in one day at auction.

"We've reclaimed an entire portion of the San Francisco peninsula, the Harbor View, from marshland," Moore exclaimed. "Think of what a spectacle it will be when the Pacific fleet of the United States Navy steams through the Golden Gate past the Exposition."

"We'll be there, Mr. Moore. We'll be there—provided we're not at war," said the Assistant Secretary of the Navy, his prominent chin made even more assertive by a vigorous mastication of celery.

Paul Masson tapped his glass, calling us to attention. Masson is a Burgundian by birth, a very large man with a rosy face. He would have made a wonderful character for Balzac, had he been born in an earlier era. Masson epitomizes the provincial wine-maker: full of appetites and lust for life. His champagne—and his crayfish salads—are marvelous.

"Ladies and gentlemen," Masson said. "I came to California from Burgundy as a boy of nineteen in 1878. That was thirty-six years ago. I am now in the prime of life."

We laughed. Who could be more in the prime of life than this flamboyant epicure, this maker of champagne and consumer of crayfish salads? I have heard that he recently gave an actress a bath in a copper tub filled with champagne—and that he hopped into the tub with her. At his age! I approve most heartily.

"Since I made the champagne you are now enjoying, and since I am Mr. Phelan's neighbor, I do not think it out of place if I offer a toast. Let me put it in my own way. I came to California. I made champagne. My champagne won an honorable mention at the Paris Exposition. Now I shall have the honor of being the next-door neighbor of a senator of the United States."

We applauded. Mrs. Atherton stood up.

"California," she said, "could use a gentleman of James

119

Duval Phelan's character in the United States Senate to show what kind of a culture we have out here. I hope young Mr. Roosevelt is taking note of what he sees. I hope he takes the word back to Washington that California has come of age."

"Hear, hear," Phelan's nephew Noel Sullivan said. We all drank our champagne.

"And I hope," continued Noel after we had put our glasses down, "that as senator my uncle can do something for the cause of Irish autonomy. England must allow Ireland home rule."

That subject was dropped immediately. Opinion differs widely among the Irish of San Francisco on this question. I personally favor home rule for Ireland as an affiliated commonwealth of the United Kingdom; but even among otherwise moderate Irish-Americans, there are many fierce republicans who want total independence. I for one am glad that my parents migrated to the United States and that, once in America, they continued on to San Francisco. I think of them frequently, my father and my mother, two young Irish immigrants, my mother not yet out of her teens, finding themselves in New York in 1846, their prospects next to nothing before Father joined the Stevenson Regiment and they sailed for California. The war with Mexico killed many Irish immigrants to this country, especially those of the New York-mustered St. Patrick's Brigade who deserted the American army and fought for the Mexicans because the Mexicans, like the Irish, were a Catholic peasant people being suppressed and usurped by a superior power. One by one, the soldiers of the St. Patrick's units were captured and summarily shot. They were, however, Americans in name only. As was the case in the later Civil War, the Irish were merely available as cannon fodder for Yankee generals to hurl into battle. Colonel Stevenson, on the other hand, saved the lives of the Irish lads he enlisted for service in California. Stevenson wanted colonist-soldiers, as had the Spanish in the eighteenth century. The men brought their wives along with them in troopships around the Horn.

120

"Tell me, Mother," I would say as a boy, "how you and Father sailed into San Francisco Bay." This would be around 1855 when I was about seven. The harbor teemed with the masts of ships. Mother related her and Father's arrival in 1846 as if it were a Homeric saga of voyage and discovery.

"After six months aboard that ship," she would say, "we sailed into this bay right here. Mind you, it was empty. I looked over to those hills there." She pointed across the bay to Marin. "And I saw hundreds of grazing elk just as peaceful as you please, bothering nobody."

Jimmy Phelan also comes from Irish-born parents. "You know that I wanted to be an artist," Jimmy told me recently, "but Father had the business in mind." We were sitting over lunch in Jimmy's office in the Phelan Building, 760 Market, which Jimmy rebuilt right after the Fire, putting a grand bronze bust of his father in the lobby. Frank Boni, Phelan's favorite taxi driver, had brought a hot lunch over from the Bohemian Club kitchen, which Jimmy had his secretary warm and serve out of a little pantry-bar adjacent to his office.

"You're not sorry he insisted you join him in the bank?" I asked over our cutlets.

"It's too late for any regret," Jimmy said, holding his wine glass to the light. "And it has worked out rather well."

Yes, indeed, it has worked out rather well for Jimmy Phelan, master of Montalvo, United States senator-to-be. Not every Irishman found a promised land here, however; that is for sure. Ask those persecuted by the Vigilance Committees in the fifties. Ask the poverty-stricken teamsters who got behind Dennis Kearney in the seventies. Kearney was a demagogue, I agree; but there were too many poverty-stricken Irish in this city for something not to happen, and happen it did. There were the lucky Irish, of course, especially the Silver Kings— McKay, O'Brien, McAvoy, Flood—dirt-poor Irish when they came out here, their daughters married now to European nobility, their grandsons lounging over their newspapers at the Pacific Union Club.

Phelan Senior grew fat in later years; but he was lean and

121

hungry in 1849 when he shipped three cargoes of goods to San Francisco. Only one ship made it. With the profits, Phelan Senior bought Market Street property. By 1869, when he was busy shipping wool and wheat by clipper ship to New York, he was worth some $2 million. He came from Ireland at the age of six, and spent his twenties making money, but he had his eye out all the time for an Anglo-Irish Connecticut girl, Alice Kelly, who came out to marry him in late 1859, escorted here by United States Senator Joseph Lane of Oregon and his wife.

Nothing was too grand for Jimmy, the darling boy of his darling wife. Phelan Senior had his son baptized at Old St. Mary's by Archbishop Alemany, whose sponsorship helped me in Rome in the mid-seventies when Ralston's death ended my San Francisco prospects. Phelan Senior was a heavy, direct man, not coarse as I remember him, but self-made and self-educated. When Jimmy was in the preparatory division of St. Ignatius College, Phelan Senior paid me a rather generous honorarium to come out weekly to the Phelan mansion at Seventeenth and Valencia to tutor Jimmy in the Oxford style.

"Give him the best, Dr. Collins, the very best," Phelan Senior told me. "I'll make it worth your while."

In my early thirties at the time, and needing the money, I was glad for the position and for the social contacts it gave me. In the very library where eight years later I met Sybil Sanderson, I tutored my charge, the future mayor of San Francisco and, as it will no doubt turn out some six weeks hence, the future United States senator. I tried to impart to him what Charles Eliot Norton of Harvard had imparted to me less than a decade earlier: a reverence for the art-past, a conviction of high and sustaining ideals in the Western tradition. We read the classics, Latin and Greek. We studied Renaissance paintings and texts. We browsed together in books of architecture and landscape design. Mrs. Alice Phelan would sometimes stand quietly at the library door as we talked, or sit there with us, absorbed in her son's responses to my donnish observations. Noel Sullivan, the son of Jimmy's

122

sister Alice, reminds me of Jimmy in the early eighties. Jimmy had the manner of the Ascendancy right from birth, as do Noel and Noel's sister, Alice Phelan Sullivan, who has just entered the Carmelites of Santa Clara. Jimmy was bookish and dreamy, yet he also emanated an ambience of confidence when it came to the world of affairs. The Tobin brothers have the same air of confidence, although they are not at all dreamy. The Tobins are, rather, a sporty, horsy country squire variety of Irish-Californian aristocrats. They have taken as their model for living the Anglo-Irish gentry of the old country.

After Jimmy graduated from St. Ignatius College and the Hastings College of Law (Phelan Senior insisted that his son be educated in San Francisco), Jimmy went for a two-year grand tour of Europe. I have a collection of letters from him during this period. He wrote me from Paris, Rome, Vienna, Prague. He observed everything he could about the operations of the great European cities. And a good thing, too. By the time he was thirty-five, he was mayor of San Francisco.

The all-but-senator-elect rose to answer the toasts.

"Thank you, ladies and gentlemen," Phelan said. "But it is not my personal prospects that I wish to comment on, but those of San Francisco and the United States Navy, represented with us here this afternoon by its distinguished Assistant Secretary, Mr. Franklin Delano Roosevelt. San Francisco has rebuilt herself, and to commemorate her phoenix-like resurrection she has invited the world to an Exposition. We want the Navy to come, too, Mr. Secretary. America, as you so well know, is now a Pacific power. We administer the Philippines. We have Hawaii and other islands in the Pacific. The opening of the Panama Canal, which our Panama-Pacific International Exposition commemorates, joins Atlantic America with Pacific America. The Pacific Basin is now on the verge of an era of American influence, provided that we have a strong Navy to cruise these vast waters. The Rising Sun of Japan also casts its rays across this Pacific Basin. Someday, I fear, America and the Japanese must clash. In the meanwhile, Mr. Secretary, guests, we want San Francisco to become the city where the impending *pax Americana* begins to radiate its influence. We want San Francisco to be the queen city of the Pacific. As senator, Mr. Roosevelt, I promise vigorous support of a powerful Navy—the Navy which we entreat President Wilson next year to send steaming into the grand harbor of San Francisco."

As I looked around Phelan's luncheon table, I saw many of the men who played major roles in the rebuilding of San Francisco after the Earthquake. Phelan formed us together in 1901 as the Committee for the Adornment and Beautification of San Francisco. It was basically this group, acting as the Committee of Fifty, that administered the city during and after the Earthquake. Fremont Older, the *Bulletin* editor; Downey Harvey; Charles Moore, now president of the Exposition; myself—so many of us served under Phelan in those soul-stirring days.

Just before the city was destroyed, the Committee for the Adornment and Beautification of San Francisco had commissioned a city plan from the famous city planner Daniel Hudson Burnham, who arrived here fresh from laying out an American capital in Manila, the Philippines. We commissioned Burnham because we wanted a new San Francisco, a City Beautiful, transformed, redeemed, rich with future promise; but we got an earthquake and fire instead. When San Francisco lay in ruins, Burnham rushed here from Paris, thinking that his plan would be put into effect in the rebuilding of the city. There was talk of it for a week or two while we all recovered from the shock.

"Gentlemen, gentlemen, what an opportunity," Burnham told us the evening of his arrival. He had been held up in Oakland for a day, but eventually chartered an oyster boat to cross the Bay. Phelan convened the Committee of Fifty so that it could meet with Burnham at General Funston's house in the Presidio. "Nature, gentlemen," Burnham said, "has erased your mistakes. Now we will have the ideal city, the city on a hill." Some felt it a little presumptuous of Burnham to describe the obliteration of San Francisco as a fortunate correction of some previous planning errors; yet the great planner did manage to communicate a sense of enthusiasm.

Ignoring Burnham's recommendations, however, we rebuilt San Francisco on the lines of the old city: which is to say, we rebuilt it as quickly as possible, taking no time for the horrendous redesign of our geometric street grids that the Burnham Plan would have made necessary. It would have taken years to redistrict the city lot by lot, deed by deed, title by title. Yet many of Burnham's suggestions did take hold: the Civic Center, for instance, which rather successfully attempts to be a public square in the baroque style.

"The Exposition, as I see it," Willis Polk remarked at the Phelan luncheon last Saturday, "is the Burnham Plan realized as a fantasy or a dream. For a year at least we'll have the City Beautiful."

Polk has a thunderous, *ex cathedra* way of saying things. The luncheon table fell silent for a moment. Polk drinks and womanizes (frankly, I am jealous!), but he is a brilliant architect. His bold, innovative plans for a glass and steel skyscraper on Sutter Street point, I feel, towards the architecture of the future. Polk has been very generous to Bernard Maybeck, getting Maybeck the commission for the Palace of Fine Arts, the most thrilling of all the Exposition buildings.

What days those were, the time of the rebuilding! The city regained a sense of pioneer purpose. Even Mayor Schmitz, as Downey Harvey pointed out at the luncheon, even Schmitz— later removed from office (unfairly, I feel) for bribery— behaved well. I stood in the bell tower of Sacred Heart Church and watched the city burn, first the College buildings, then St. Ignatius Church, eventually everything up to Van Ness. I then walked down to the collapsed City Hall. Schmitz was conferring with Frederick Funston, the cocky five-feet-tall bantam rooster general from the Presidio whom I knew as a colonel from Mary Griswold's *soirées* on Telegraph Hill in the nineties before he won his brigadier's star in the Philippines. Eugene Schmitz is over six feet tall. "Handsome Gene" we

125

used to call him in the days when he led the orchestra in the pit of the Columbia Theater, before Abe Ruef made him mayor of San Francisco. I have rarely seen Schmitz so noble, so commanding, as he was that day. Downey Harvey said as much right in front of Phelan at the luncheon, despite the fact that it was Phelan who saw to it some six years ago that Schmitz was removed from office for bribery and that Schmitz's mentor Boss Abe Ruef was sent to San Quentin.

"Schmitz," Downey said, "did well by San Francisco in the Fire. In a time of great crisis he proved himself worthy of the mayor's office. His one mistake was to authorize the military to shoot looters on sight, for by this he effectively put the city under martial law, and that was not really necessary."

I agree with Downey Harvey. Allow me to be frank. I do not feel that much was accomplished by removing Mayor Schmitz from office. Phelan, Rudolph Spreckels, and Fremont Older worked for nearly five years to accomplish this goal—the removal of a political boss and his mayor. Yet they never indicted the more significant corruptors, the Southern Pacific and United Railroad interests who owned city government in San Francisco for years. Ruef went to San Quentin for soliciting a bribe from a French restaurant (our local equivocation for bordello), and Schmitz was convicted on similar charges: charges later overturned, mind you, at the appellate level. But Handsome Gene lost his office anyway while his case was on appeal.

Put all that aside for a moment, however, and remember only that Schmitz acted well in April of 1906. There was a little too much shooting of citizens in the immediate aftermath of the Fire; but I will assent to General Funston's claim that it was the ill-trained militia, not the regulars, who were mainly responsible for an overzealous shooting of looters.

As Schmitz and Funston struggled to reach a working agreement as to how to conduct the city during the emergency, a number of citizens gathered before the crumbled City Hall as if it were an *agora* in ancient Greece and the freemen were assembling for democratic debate. Phelan arrived by

126

automobile. He put aside his distaste for Schmitz, for the moment at least, and recommended that the Mayor appoint a Committee of Fifty to assist him in the governance of our stricken city.

"Very well, Mr. Phelan. I designate you chairman and I give you power of appointment. You shall oversee the evacuation of citizens to the Park. General Funston, you shall exercise police authority in all districts. I shall join the firemen in the downtown."

Schmitz, as I have said, was superb, decisive like a field marshal committing troops to battle. I must do justice to him when I draft my Fire chapter for the *Memoirs*. We lived in shock for a week, like civilians in a city overrun by a barbarian army. Then we commenced the work of rebuilding. Phelan appointed me secretary to the Relief Committee. Not for years have I felt so useful as I did then. The federal government sent us more than $2 million in relief moneys to administer. We housed thousands under army tents in the park and fed twice that number every day. I first met our present mayor, Jimmy Rolph, when I went out to inspect the Mission Relief Association, headquartered in a barn on San Jose Avenue. I handled the Committee's correspondence for the year we were in operation. Rolph asked me to help out his organization as well, so I joined it as corresponding secretary.

I never went so far as to wear the jodhpurs, boots, khaki shirts, and Baden-Powell hats that so many San Franciscans affected in the years of rebuilding; but I did feel the excitement in the air, the return of moral purpose if you will, as we founded San Francisco for the second time. For three years the downtown air was dusty with rubble being cleared away. Businessmen set up offices in tents or shacks as soon as the debris was cleared from their downtown lots. By 1909 San Francisco, like the phoenix, had risen from its ashes.

I am beginning to share Phelan's enthusiasm for the building of a new central Library two blocks up from the Hibernia Bank, on McAllister Street at Polk, across Civic

Center from City Hall. A grand library building would anchor that corner of the Civic Center superbly, and we certainly do need a facility to replace the library destroyed by the Fire. 400,000 volumes lost! The books, the papers, the ephemera of our city's first sixty years—all gone, all destroyed! Phelan wants a dramatic Italian Renaissance building with a capacity for more than a million volumes. As usual, he is correct. Great cities need great libraries. We trustees meet next week to choose a design. Phelan, myself, and Horace Davis favor George Kelham's proposal for a monumental Renaissance building, to include a triumphal central staircase and soaring rotunda. Carnegie has given us $375,000 and a bond issue will provide the rest. Mayor Rolph assures us that a bond issue will pass.

Planning for our new Library, I cannot help recall Ralston's hopes for an Atheneum. Ralston wanted the Atheneum to include both an art museum and a research library. Phelan feels that a library on Civic Center might redeem at least half of Ralston's dream. He offhandedly pointed this out as we sat around a conference table in Rolph's office examining various library designs submitted to the city since we announced the competition. The effect on me of Phelan's suggestion was electric.

Perhaps the library we are building could develop into a truly great institution, something resembling what Ralston had in mind: a center for scholarly enquiry, not sheltered in a suburban university's sylvan glades, but situated in the midst of a dynamic, tumultuous city. I am a little frightened of caring too much about this library, now that it is linked in my mind with Ralston's Atheneum. I devoted my youth to preparing myself to become the sort of curator–librarian Ralston had in mind for his proposed institution: a scholar who had suckled at the breast of Europe's best libraries: Heidelberg, the Vatican, the Louvre, the Bibliothèque Nationale—all those places where I did research or made practical observations as to how libraries were managed—accessions, cataloging, reader services, collection-building—

128

so that when I returned to San Francisco I might exercise the high craft of librarianship in California's Euro-American metropolis on the Pacific.

It never happened. Ralston died. San Francisco never received from his or from any other hand such a grand institution as Ralston dreamed of, but perhaps as an old man of sixty-seven I will be able to help pass Ralston's vision on to a future San Francisco generation. If we build this library grandly enough, if it attracts the proper patronage, then it might develop as the Astor, Lennox, and Tilden libraries of the New York Public are developing in their new building on Forty-second Street—into a city-based research institution of true distinction.

I must thank Phelan for nominating me to the Library Board of Trustees, for giving me this chance to connect my past with the city's future. I love libraries. I am a man of libraries because I am a man seeking order in memory, which is also the institutional task of the library in Western civilization. The new Library could link together San Francisco, the European past, and our assured American future. Phelan wants me to speak around town for the library bond issues. I shall prepare some remarks on this theme. I might even mention Ralston.

I have also brought the matter of a monument to the dead of 1906 up to Mayor Rolph. I suggested that we build and dedicate an official residence for the fire chief in honor of Chief Dennis Sullivan and all other firemen who lost their lives fighting the blaze. I was myself, after all, raised on the third floor of the Bush Street firehouse. We could build a downtown residence that would be both a working firehouse and a memorial, and on its upper floors, the official residence of the fire chief.

"Very fitting, coming from the son of our first fire chief. I like it," Mayor Rolph said. "Get a committee together. You chair it. I'll serve as honorary chairman."

Rolph's energy and optimism amaze me. He is so different from Phelan: a South of Market errand boy for a stock firm who earned a million on his own in shipping and coal. Rolph is neither coarse nor vulgar, but there is a definite vernacular energy to the man, which even Phelan admires. His cowboy boots are a little *outré*, I'll admit; but Rolph does get things done. He is an actor and he is making San Francisco his appreciative audience. I, for one, am happy to applaud on cue as long as Sunny Jim continues to do so well by our city.

I sometimes think that I have spent my life in pursuit of false gods and that because of this a certain shallow venality shows up in me now. I am a man of letters with a solid provincial reputation and—in my Bernini book and my collected essays on theology and literature—something of a reputation in the great world beyond. I am estalished and comfortable. Unlike Ryan Patrice, I have not chosen sainthood.

"It took me years to see beyond culture," Patrice told me one day at the Grand Chartreuse some twenty years ago. "I loved the Church as an institution, as a cause, as a glorious continuity in our history; but I never truly knew the Church as a Spouse of the Risen Christ, calling me to Him, calling me to an austerity of love beyond the comforts of even the Church itself."

This from one who thirty years earlier outgloried even *Pio Nono* himself in ultramontane gorgeousness—not to mention that other side of his nature which hissed forth from the flowerband of his aesthetic religiosity like a viper amidst lilies, sending me to Montreal in disgust and fright. In the spare stone rooms of the oblate dormitory of the Grand Chartreuse where we both were quartered, attired in coarse black smocks, I recalled the pre-Raphaelite luxuriance of Ryan Patrice's Cambridge flat: the morocco-bound edition of the Church Fathers, the *prie-dieu*, the Russian icons and Rossetti paintings (the first, it turns out, to reach America), the suggestion of incense in the air. At the Grand Chartreuse, Patrice lived in a tiny cell, where he slept on a cot. His days were spent at work with the lay brothers, and his nights were consumed in prayer. He could have been living in Paris, a bishop, the Superior General of the Paris Foreign Missionary Society; but out there in Indo-China he had discovered a harsher, more glorious calling: an emptying out of the self and a casting out beyond the safe shores of culturally reinforced religion; sanctity, in short, a condition of surrender that pushed him beyond dependence upon cultural circumstances. In his cell, Patrice allowed himself but one reminder of his former life—a superbly executed portrait of Christ appearing to Margaret Mary Alacoque as the Sacred Heart.

"He shows Himself, dear Sebastian," Patrice said to me, "as the Fire burning at the heart of the Universe. This is the Risen Christ, whose transfigured body has become the Flesh of creation itself. The Risen Christ makes of creation one vast eucharist, an indwelling of divinity in matter. His Heart is that Fire/Love that burned in the void before the ages began and will burn for eternity after the ages are complete. There is pain in His fiery heart. All fire, all love, brings pain with it. But on the other side of the fire, there is the peace that passes understanding, the stillness of God Himself."

Will I, Sebastian Collins, ever know that peace, I who am so enmeshed in the comforts and delusions of the immediate world about me? Even at this age of mine, I rage for sensation and for the world in all its pomp and glory. Have I learned nothing after nearly seventy years? There are times when everything—pictures, books, libraries, San Francisco itself—seems so much foredoomed vanity. All that I have elusively pursued is but the sounding of a cymbal and the tinkling of brass. I once thought that if I were called to sanctity, I would be a Counter Reformation saint, a cardinal like Borromeo perhaps, with a hair shirt under my purple. As it turns out, I have sought the purple but not the hair shirt.

Chapter 5

I WAS ALREADY LOOKING forward to lunch with Deborah Tanner at the San Domenico on lower Pacific Avenue as our boat glided away from the Ferry Building onto the blue-green surface of the bay. Traceries of morning fog yet hovered about the pierside as the flotilla cast off at nine o'clock, as it has every June since 1946 to inaugurate the annual Police Athletic Association's summer fishing program for disadvantaged youngsters. From a mile offshore, San Francisco floated on the bay like Atlantis reborn from the sea: a water-borne, water-loved city, radiant in sunlight, under a sky flecked with white ocean birds.

The PAA program takes disadvantaged youngsters out for fishing trips, kids who might otherwise grow up in San Francisco, a city that faces water on three sides, without ever once getting out on the bay. Our boat, one of the new water-jet ferries, was packed with about a hundred boys and a handful of girls: black kids, Latino kids, white kids, all screaming and hollering and fussing with their fishing gear under the guidance of some patient uniformed cops. It was like a thirties movie about Boys Town, starring Pat O'Brien as the kindly priest and Mickey Rooney as the onetime bad boy gone straight.

Street kids haven't changed their appearance in over forty years. Our boys wore the regulation uniform of sneakers,

132

jeans, T-shirts, warm-up jackets. They reminded me of myself around 1950 or so, age ten, and—to speak sociologically—an underprivileged kid myself, living in the Potrero Hill housing project with my mother, supported by county welfare. I used to fish off Pier 90 under the aegis of this very same PAA program, and to this day I can remember my first offshore glimpses of San Francisco. I had been reading the Oz books at the time, and San Francisco looked like Oz, a magical, illusory city, floating on a watery blue.

The ferry, a multimillion-dollar affair purchased last year by the Golden Gate Bridge Authority to take commuters from Marin County to San Francisco and return, cruised at less than quarter speed. Its turbine engines daily skim thousands of passengers across the bay on the forward edge of a churning hydraulic jet stream—perhaps the most dazzling commute in America. Claudio Carpino was a big backer of the project, even when the water-jet ferries came in from the San Diego shipyards 40 percent over cost. Carpino loves the sleek modernity of these boats, their ambience of good design and technological innovation.

The Mayor looked satisfied, almost vindicated, as he stood on the ferry's prow while we cruised off the northern waterfront. We passed the Ferry Building, then Fishermen's Wharf, then the red-bricked Cannery, a onetime Del Monte plant transformed into a three-story complex of shops, restaurants, and boutiques by Leonard Martin, a Manchurian-born son of White Russian émigrés who looks like a Tsarist cavalry officer. We glided by Ghirardelli Square, a similar development of a former chocolate factory promoted by shipping scion William Matson Roth; then past Fort Mason, from which about a million men embarked for the Pacific theater in World War II; and Black Point, where the Fremonts' home still stands and where Sebastian Collins and Charles Warren Stoddard attended Mrs. Fremont's soirees in the mid-1860s, meeting Herman Melville, Bret Harte, and Thomas Starr King. The Marina Safeway reflected the sunlight back to us like a gigantic mirror. Then came the Marina itself, a riviera row of polychromatic Mediterranean villas—buff, yellow, rose, aquamarine, cinnamon—crowding the shore, bordered off from the bay by the sweep of the Marina Green. Already joggers, volleyball players, sun-worshippers, kite-flyers were using the green. Seen from this distance on a sunny day, the colorful villas of the Marina make San Francisco seem something like Oran, Marseilles, or the port cities of the Dalmatian coast—a sail-filled harbor town of the Mediterranean south, the land of water and sun.

As we cruised past the St. Francis Yacht Club, a stucco-white, red-roof-tiled seaside building in the Spanish style, you could see white-coated waiters laying down silver service for the daily luncheon buffet. As a crew member on Bob Porter's small yacht, I belong to the St. Francis Yacht Club through an associate membership. I thought of how pleasant it would be to sail with Deborah Tanner up the Sacramento Delta to Tinsley Island, the Club's resort in the delta country, the Marches of San Francisco's Rome. I made a mental note to ask her at lunch to come up there with me for the Fourth of July week end.

Mayor Carpino held court on the ferry's prow like a Venetian doge presiding over the annual wedding of Venice to the Adriatic Sea. Chief of Police Don Norris stood at his side, resplendent in blue uniform, three gold stars on either shoulder. Father Bianco, the Salesian pastor of SS. Peter and Paul's Church, the Mayor's boyhood parish, stood to the Mayor's left, making the Venetian comparison complete: the doge accompanied by military and ecclesiastical retainers. Carpino wore a luxuriant blue Brioni suit of crushed silk. Behind us the fire department's tugboat shot billowing arches of seawater into the sky, while three dozen or so other boats, including a Coast Guard cutter, took up escorting positions in the flotilla.

The Mayor motioned me to come over. We were cruising past the Piranesian dome and cinnamon-colored colonnades of the Palace of Fine Arts, the only building to survive the dismantlement of the Panama-Pacific Exposition of 1915. San

134

Francisco preserved the Palace of Fine Arts, first, because it was beautiful, but also because, in the words of its architect Bernard Maybeck, it was "a tragic text"—a gloss on the city's feeling of loss and displacement after San Francisco burned to the ground in 1906. That's how Sebastian Collins envisioned the Palace of Fine Arts: as a symbolic assertion of Old San Francisco amidst the rebuilt skyscraper city. Even in 1915, it seems, San Franciscans had their doubts about highrise buildings.

"This dome," Collins wrote in *Sunset* magazine, "is a massive Aeolian Harp, played on by the winds. Its music is the collective sigh of our lost city."

"James, how's it going over there?" the Mayor asked. By over there, he meant the Library.

"Fine, Mr. Mayor." I always say fine when he asks me about the Library. It's expected of me. "But this Marshall Square thing is heating up. Mabel Storm is revving up the commissioners for a fight when the PAC people go before the Planning Commission to get Marshall Square."

"You people ought to build an annex. You'll never get a new main library," the Mayor said.

He said it, but he'd done nothing about it, nor would he. It took too much time to negotiate a compromise, to get a bond issue under way financing an annex and the refurbishment of the old library building. It would take hundreds of hours of meetings and tedious negotiations with Mabel Storm and the insistent ladies of The Friends of Books to coax them from their present Marshall Square-or-nothing position to a compromise. This is the sort of thing a mayor is supposed to do with his time—negotiate, reconcile, guide; but Claudio Carpino doesn't seem to have time for the humbler tasks of municipal government. Ever since he took office in 1964, he's been running for higher office, first a U.S. Senate seat, then the governorship. The very year I became city librarian, I realized with a feeling of betrayal in the pit of my stomach that Carpino could not care less about the San Francisco Public Library. The first budget he gave me was down $1 million

135

from our already woefully low allotment. It took six months of ceaseless, often reckless lobbying on my part to get about $800,000 of the $1 million put back in. Barry Scorse was furious at my defiance.

"What the fuck are you doing?" he shouted to me one day in the portrait-lined corridor leading to the Mayor's office. "If the Mayor gives you a budget cut, take it and keep quiet about it. We need the money elsewhere."

"A million-dollar cut would destroy the place. We wouldn't be able to buy books for a year."

"Have the people read the books you've been buying for the past fifty years," Scorse said. "Have them read the classics. Have them read Dante and Shakespeare and the Bible."

As usual, Scorse made an excellent point. Scorse always talks common sense. A good percentage of the 40,000 or so new books published every year is junk. The Library buys them at great expense, processes and catalogs them, circulates them for a while; then they gather dust on the shelves or have to be discarded to make way for newer books. There's a dumpster in the basement of the Library, which is constantly filled with the Library's discards—the best sellers of a few years ago and innumerable also-rans. When I pass by the dumpster, I often rummage through the pile of abandoned books, feeling the sadness and futility of it all: the dust jackets bristling with promotional quotes, the photographs of the author, the flapcover copy promising an exciting, transforming experience within, all of it now headed for the paper mulcher or the city dump.

Scorse had a point, but if I had mutely accepted the million-dollar cut, I would have looked too much like the Mayor's flunky; so I fought and won part of the budget back. Carpino gave in gracefully to the lobbying compaign I mounted with the help of the Commission and The Friends of Books. He gave in because he was bored. Cross the Mayor on something he cares about and you're up shit creek without a paddle.

Claudio Carpino has been bored with the mayor's job for

some time now. The Charter of 1932 leaves little room for maneuver for the mayor of San Francisco. A third of the city is run by a chief administrative officer, an appointed civil servant given lifetime tenure. The Board of Supervisors can reject any part of the mayor's budget. Between the mayor and his departments sit supervising commissions. So the job is pretty well circumscribed. It's a job of budgeteering and persuasion. By profession, Claudio Carpino is a trial attorney, not a plodding executive accustomed to motivate and persuade. He's used to winning arguments through forensic brilliance, which is OK for a trial attorney. But a politician who wins too many arguments, like Claudio Carpino, who dazzles by his brilliance, like Carpino, who finishes people's sentences for them, like Carpino, in the long run pisses people off—as Claudio Carpino has done too many times for his own good. The sheer talent of Claudio Carpino creates a wasteland around him. Like Julius Caesar, he puts himself too far above the other senators; and so, like Julius Caesar, Claudio Carpino continually runs the risk of being stabbed in the back.

"James—I want to talk to you about the campaign."

"Yes, sir."

"I'm thinking of how we should get it started. Something with a suggestion of history—a pageant or progress through the state on Declaration Day."

By then the flotilla had passed the Presidio and the montane villas of Sea Cliff, where the Mayor himself lives, and was heading back through the Golden Gate Bridge. A fist fight broke out between two of the disadvantaged youngsters, a black kid with his hair braided into a dozen or so braidlets and a chubby white boy. They were quarreling over who spilled whose box of tackle. An off-duty cop broke up the fight. The adults on the boat looked embarrassed. That wasn't the way disadvantaged youngsters being taken out for a ride on the bay were supposed to behave. They are supposed to be grateful and well behaved like in a Pat O'Brien movie.

"We could begin with Mass at Mission San Diego, then head up the state by jet and helicopter to various other points of historical interest that would also lend themselves to statements on issues. I'd like you to serve on a committee to put the thing together for early October."

He broke off the conversation and went over to the two kids who had been fighting. He made them shake hands, which they did—reluctantly. I have my doubts as to whether the campaign will be opened this way, but the idea does have a certain panache. Besides—I'm flattered to be included for a change.

Tired of playing doge on the prow, Carpino turned on the charm for the crowd. He is, after all, running for office—and his success in that enterprise involves my future as well. He shook a few miscellaneous hands, then chatted with Methodius Newman, the city's leading merchant prince, whom Carpino appointed to the Port Commission. The Mayor and Methodius Newman made an arresting pair: two Mediterranean ethnics, Sicilian and Jewish, arrived at wealth, elegance, and power in the context of semi-Mediterranean San Francisco. Carpino is six feet tall, weighs 190 pounds, and is bald in a Yul Brynnerish sort of way that adds to his magnetism. Methodius Newman is half a foot shorter and sports a lustrous head of wavy white hair.

The Mayor bent down to talk to Methodius Newman over the whine of the ship's turbines, the hollering of the excited kids, the cries of the seabirds, the blasts of the foghorn on the Coast Guard cutter. Duke Francesco Sforza, I thought; an Italian Renaissance prince conferring over finances with a Jewish banker from Genoa: a self-made Sforza duke who fought his way up to a throne from the ranks of the *condottieri* in the ferocious wars between the Italian states of Renaissance Italy, a Francesco Sforza who ruthlessly seized power, then tutored himself to enjoy it. Aristotle Onassis, with whom Carpino dealt in matters relating to shipping rice to European markets, thought that Carpino demeaned himself by becoming a mere mayor. "The Kennedys told me this man one day would be president," Onassis told a *Chronicle* reporter when he was passing through San Francisco shortly after Carpino's lavish first inaugural. "Has he gone *pazzo*, crazy?"

138

I walked over to the Mayor and Methodius Newman to hear what they were saying. In the court ritual of the mayor's office I have just enough status, barely enough, to join a mayoral conversation, provided that it doesn't look too personal.

"James," the Mayor said, "we were just talking about you, more precisely, the Library and Marshall Square. Methodius wouldn't want anything to endanger the Performing Arts Center. His group has spent years raising $25 million, the largest single sum ever raised privately in San Francisco for a cultural project. We can't endanger that, can we?"

I was sorry I had come over. I mumbled something about talking sense to the Commission, then I surprised myself with my boldness.

"Mabel Storm is your appointment, Mr. Mayor. Get to her and the opposition crumbles."

Carpino's eyes hooded for a split second, the lids falling halfway across his irises, then raising back slowly over a glassy stare that, just as quickly and momentarily, replaced the fire usually in his eyes. For the first time in our association, I had just earned the one and only outward sign of displeasure Carpino allows himself.

"I'll talk to her," he said. He put his hand on Methodius's shoulder to steer him over to a group of kids clustered around a uniformed officer who was demonstrating the proper way to trawl for sea bass. The Duke and the Duke's banker were displeased with the Duke's ratty librarian.

For all his public gregariousness—and this, after all, is expected from a mayor—Claudio Carpino has few close friends. In general, he avoids society, although his fortune and intelligence would have long since gained him access to all but the ultra-WASP circles of Hillsborough and the Burlingame Country Club. Carpino prefers to live in splendid isolation in his home perched over the Golden Gate straits, like a Saracen sea lord during the Norman occupation of Sicily, enriched by booty from the straits of Messina. The Sicilian factor, plus the Mayor's fundamental intelligence, most likely accounts for his deliberate isolation from the trivial sectors of the local *beau monde*. San Francisco's brainless, chattering society bores Carpino stiff; but also—Sicilians don't mix. They are more clannish than Jews, and for similar reasons of prejudice and persecution. Overrun by Greeks, Romans, Arabs, Normans, Spaniards—Sicily has been a conquered colony since ancient times. Sicilians have developed into a suspicious, genetically mixed people, with as much of North Africa in their veins as Italian Europe. Claudio Carpino holds a good part of San Francisco's WASP establishment in barely disguised contempt. Most of it votes Republican, anyway, and lives over in Marin County or down the Peninsula. He gets along very well with self-made, energetic Jews like Methodius Newman: that is, other Mediterranean people—but he never runs with the *beau monde*.

Few people ever receive invitations to Carpino's home in Sea Cliff. Esmeralda hasn't been entertaining much lately. A lot of people think she's sulking because she feels she's not receiving her proper due as the city's First Lady. This is true, but it is also true that the Mayor prefers his splendid isolation. It's his form of snobbery.

Although Claudio Carpino isn't buying, social San Francisco is very much up for sale. It takes wealthy newcomers but a year or two to buy their way into café society. They buy, in fact, the same small stock of up-for-sale characters who are willing to be wooed over a year's *rite de passage* of expensive parties and restaurant tabs. Even in the short time I've been back in San Francisco from the East, I've seen social aspirants buy their way to social status. Natasha Pushkin, for instance, the wife of psychiatrist Serge Pushkin (he treats personality disorders through an analysis of pubic hair patterns), has just completed the arduous obstacle course of initiation. She began with a series of discreet dinner parties, at which there was always one out-of-town attraction—Hollywood star Wally McLaine, for instance, whom Serge once treated for clap. Wally almost spoiled the fun that evening by too blatantly casting smoldering glances across the *Contre Filet Rotie*, the Perigourdine and the Pinot Noir in the direction of party girl

140

Tammy McKee, with whom he disappeared shortly after, the two of them not even bothering to stay for dessert.

Natasha Pushkin soon progressed from these smaller evenings to more ambitious affairs. She wangled permission from the local administrator for the Department of the Interior to give a dinner dance in one of the cell blocks on Alcatraz. Chartered fishing boats discreetly brought the Pushkins's guests out to the island from a little-used Third Street pier. They ate dinner off tin trays in the Alcatraz mess hall—beef Wellington, washed down by a superb Chateau Lafitte catered by Dawson's—then danced to a three-piece combo in one of the cell blocks. Toby Wain told me that it was the first time he'd ever gotten laid on a mattressless cot in solitary confinement. Whether or not it was the first such experience for his partner, Tammy McKee, I didn't ask. "I'm not black or famous," Toby told me, "but from Tammy's point of view, I was at least there."

I have visited the Carpino home but once—and that was not by invitation. I delivered some papers to the Mayor at his house. A black Rolls-Royce stood parked in an open garage next to the imposing Italian-style villa on the last settled block on El Camino del Mar, just before that boulevard sweeps up to the Palace of the Legion of Honor and curves along the seabanks of Land's End. Two great stone griffins stand guard on a landing before the main door.

The Mayor himself answered the doorbell. He was wearing a maroon silk smoking jacket (although he doesn't smoke) and was sipping his favorite drink, a Campari over ice with a lemon twist.

"Terry Shane wants you to look over the draft of this speech for the opening of the mayors' conference. It has to be retyped for release to the press tomorrow. There's a rush."

Last year Carpino was elected vice-chairman of the United States Conference of Mayors. The Conference was opening its annual convention the next day in the Grand Ballroom of the St. Francis Hotel with Carpino as host mayor. Terry Shane felt it worthwhile to interrupt the Mayor at home to get his final approval on the welcoming speech he had pounded out on his IBM Selectric. Carpino invited me to come in and wait while he read through the speech, which I would then drive down to Shane at City Hall. Most of a political aide's work is go-for-ism: going for plane tickets, going for take-out lunchtime pastrami sandwiches from Knight's Delicatessen on McAllister Street opposite the Library, going for this or that file in Central Records. Being a go-for can get expensive. A millionaire, Carpino usually travels with about fifty cents in his pocket. He takes it for granted that tickets, hotel reservations, cab fare, and the like have already been arranged by Topai Iraslav. Most of the time, they are. If not, Shane, who travels a lot with him, has to pick up the tab—and wait out the tedious process of being reimbursed through city hall channels, or Democratic party channels if the trip is political. If it is a private trip, then Shane is out of luck, for Shane is too proud to ask for his money back, and Carpino, whose life is a whirlwind of planned travel and activity (a mimeographed master schedule, broken into fifteen-minute increments, is issued each day for the following day's activities), Carpino cannot be expected to remember such petty things as a $20 cab fare, a $45 dinner for two, or $3.75 spent for hot dogs and coffee at the Los Angeles International Airport.

Andy Soutane lives in a prefab cabin in the back country outside Carpinteria, cooks vegetarian meals in a stir-fry, and sleeps on a military cot. Claudio Carpino, however, lives in baroque splendor. I stepped into a foyer-solarium dominated by the musical splashing of a Moorish tile fountain. Assorted plants, some of them flowering tropicals, lined the walls. The plants seemed gorged on the sunlight that streamed through the Tiffany glass skylight dome. To my left was a dining room furnished in authentic seventeenth-century Florentine pieces (Carpino gave me a tour before we went into his study), rich and solid and very old. The drawing room, on the other hand, had been done by Eleanor Ford, San Francisco's enigmatic decorator, into something astonishingly modern without being overly Design Research; even here, however, there was a suggestion of the Renaissance in a great oaken sideboard

(Swedish, from the bedroom of Christina I) and three minor old masters on the far right wall. Carpino's study is to the rear of the house, which literally juts out over the cliffside on steel and concrete piles. When an earthquake swallows our little urban Atlantis into the sea, as someday it must, will the entire Carpino household drop precipitously into the churning waters below? Not to worry—they'll have plenty of company on that final fall.

You can look out of the expansive north window of the study across the Golden Gate to the wild hills of Marin. The bridge itself is a sweep of international orange to the right. A Sealand oil tanker moved slowly into the harbor like a homesick leviathan. While the Mayor reviewed Shane's draft, I browsed among his LPs: Beethoven, Mozart, Scarlatti, Pachelbel; and the books covering one entire wall: Belloc, Chesterton, Newman, *The Federalist Papers*, Dante in the Oxford Italian edition, the Collected Essays of Brother Norbert O'Toole (the Christian Brother who taught Carpino at San Anselmo College), Dominican Father A.D. Sertillanges's *The Intellectual Life, Its Spirit, Method, and Conditions, Kristin Lavransdatter* by Sigrid Undset, and—to my surprise—a half dozen or so books by Sebastian Collins, including *Bernini, Eros and Transcendence; Sybil Sanderson, A California Life; Wine Prospects for California; The Promise of California Literature; Essays in Theology and Literature;* and *Memoirs of a San Franciscan Bohemian.*

"Brother Norbert introduced me to Sebastian Collins," the Mayor said when he saw me thumbing through the Collins books. "Norbert said that Collins represented the best of high provincial California letters. I've got a standing order with Warren Howell at John Howell Books for any of Collins's volumes he comes across, but they are hard to come by. Let me get you a Campari."

He refilled his glass from the bar and brought me some of the delicious bitter drink. We sat for a while, sipping our drinks, talking about Sebastian Collins, and enjoying the Tintoretto gold that usually precedes a late June sunset.

"Collins's colleague Phelan was a great mayor," I ventured,

"perhaps the greatest mayor this city has had—so far." I put the "so far" in for Carpino's sake. He accepted the flattery without bothering to notice it.

"Phelan had a sense of urban culture nourished by the example of the great European cities," Carpino said. "I've often thought that the city should spend some money on a symposium on urban culture. We should invite a scholar like Lewis Mumford out from the East and get local people like Allan Temko. We could hold the symposium at the Convent of the Sacred Heart on Broadway."

Mumford again—Carpino frequently makes such suggestions: an international poetry festival, a symposium for the five-hundredth anniversary of the birth of Copernicus, the sponsorship by the Library of a multi-volumed critical history of the city, written by out-of-work academics on CETA jobs, just like a WPA project in the thirties. He talks of them brilliantly, as if they were already accomplished. As he talks, I believe in these events as if they were already in progress. But then comes the let-down. Like most of us, Claudio Carpino plays with more ideas than he puts into practice—many more. He frequently fails to follow through. One of Carpino's proposed symposiums, dealing with the life and thought of the nineteenth-century landscape architect Frederick Law Olmsted, who did the preliminary layout for Golden Gate Park in the late 1860s, actually materialized, only because Sean Crosby, the assistant director of Parks and Recreation (a Harvard-trained lawyer of about my age who turned to city administration), followed through and got a grant from the National Endowment for the Humanities. Carpino did little but preside over the proceedings, which he did brilliantly by the way, showing a total command of nineteenth-century park design theory. The Olmsted Symposium was held in the Hall of Flowers, and the proceedings were published by the University of California Press under the title *The Founding of Golden Gate Park*. Carpino wrote the preface; or rather, I wrote the preface for him. The Mayor is fond of presenting inscribed copies to official visitors as evidence of just how seriously the finer things are taken in San Francisco.

144

When it comes to his private financial affairs, however, Carpino minds the store. I've sat at lunch with him at his cousin's restaurant in the Marina and watched him make $50,000 in five minutes by promising to file an injunction for Don Arafat. Arafat is a onetime Palestinian refugee now worth millions. He owns a string of shopping center movie theaters up and down the state. Arafat is trying to break the Hollywood practice of blind bidding on motion pictures by theater chains. Arafat wants to see the movies before he orders them. We were enjoying a bouillabaisse while Don Arafat explained his problem.

"I'll get the boys," the Mayor said, by which he meant the three sons who work with him in his law firm. "I'll have them seek an injunction in Los Angeles on a restraint-of-trade motion. We can't win it, but it will frighten the studios to know we're involved. Then the boys and I can plan a long-range strategy if you're really serious."

"How much?" Arafat asked with the deceptive directness of an Arab trader. The Mayor scooped a particularly juicy oyster free of its shell, using a tiny silver fork.

"Fifty thousand dollars for the injunction. A percentage of the suit when we win—to be negotiated."

"You're on," Arafat said, then returned to his own luncheon party on the far side of the restaurant. The whole thing took five minutes.

Claudio Carpino is worth about $20 million, a tidy sum for a self-made man. He made his fortune in real estate, banking (founder and board chairman of the Amerigo Vespucci Stocks and Bonds Association), the dairy industry, and the law. In 1959 the State Dairy Association approached Carpino about the problem of California cheese. California cheese was good cheese, the Association said, but it didn't sell very well outside the state. Wisconsin dominated the market. As president of the California Cheese Export Association, Carpino devised a national marketing and shipping program that raised annual sales in the course of five years from $25 million to $70 million. His real-estate interests consist of a series of choice Nob Hill and Marina flats and apartment houses, managed by

145

Esmeralda from an office across the corridor from the law firm of Claudio Carpino and Associates in the Seeliger Building on Sansome Street.

No wonder Aristotle Onassis thought that Carpino had gone *pazzo* by becoming a mere mayor. Before the election, the Mayor had serenely enjoyed the good life of a San Francisco merchant prince: a box at the ballet, the symphony, the opera, a box for the home games of the Forty-Niners and the Giants; a mansion in Sea Cliff, a Rolls-Royce; a summer home in Napa Valley, near Rutherford; lunches at Villa Toscana; dinner parties at Ernie's, the Blue Fox, Alfred's, Jack's; expensive tailored suits, custom-made shirts, Gucci shoes; European vacations. The Mayor has been to Europe on more than thirty separate occasions. He has stayed in Paris more than twenty times and knows that city intimately. For fifteen years he has maintained an apartment in Rome where he spends the Easter season attending the Holy Week ceremonies at various Roman churches, climaxed by a papal Easter Sunday Mass in St. Peter's and, on two occasions that I've heard of, a private audience with the Pope.

The law affords Claudio Carpino his central professional identity and the basis of his fortune. First and foremost, the Mayor is Claudio Carpino, well-known attorney of the firm Claudio Carpino and Associates (some fifteen associates) in the penthouse suite of the Seeliger Building: a firm that since the early 1950s has won for its clients more than $65 million in damages in cases ranging from personal injury to stock cases, contested inheritance taxes, and patent law.

Andy Soutane is also a lawyer, a Stanford Law School graduate, the founder of a public interest law firm that has raised hell in Santa Barbara, Kern, and Kings counties these past ten years on behalf of farm workers, indigents, unwed mothers, abortion on demand (this from a former Franciscan seminarian), consumer fraud against the Spanish-speaking, discrimination in governmental hiring practices—the whole range of public interest issues that have seized the imagination of reform-minded lawyers coming out of law school since the

146

mid-1960s. Soutane probably makes about $10,000 a year from his public interest practice and another $25,000 a year as a state senator. $35,000 a year, or about $22,000 a year after taxes, is more than enough to maintain a life style built around a Carpinteria hideaway and a studio apartment in Sacramento, located at a two-mile jog from the state capitol and also furnished simply. Soutane drives a 1968 Mustang. He vacations on Sierra Club wilderness expeditions costing next to nothing. In Sacramento he lunches at the state employees' cafeteria, lining up with his tray like everyone else for macaroni and cheese.

Claudio Carpino, on the other hand, belongs to a definite genre: the accomplished, high-living San Francisco attorney. The late Jake Ehrlich and the very much alive Mel Belli are perhaps the greatest examples of this genre, although Mel has a taste for hell-raising that Carpino doesn't share.

Mel Belli, the King of Torts, operates out of flamboyant offices on the 700 block of Montgomery Street. I visited him there a short while back to ask him to serve on a committee in suport of National Library Week. I entered an office cluttered with a phantasmagoria of bric-a-brac. Belli sat behind his desk looking like a Roman senator of the late republic. He let me sit for a while in his antique-and-bric-a-brac-cluttered main office while he wheeled, dealed, took long distance calls, directed the course of a knotty bit of legal research, recited poetry, reminisced, and arranged to fly to Honolulu that evening on business.

"Of course I'll help you out on National Library Week," Belli said, "but for God's sake, don't call me flamboyant in your promotional material. I'm not flamboyant. I'm merely Old San Francisco. The problem with the San Francisco Bar is that it has become sanitized, computerized, and lobotomized. Our local legal eagles have become the running dogs of the Chamber of Commerce. Once a citadel of independent-minded, hard-thinking, hard-living, free-wheeling individualists, the Bar is now dominated by a bunch of time-clock-punching acolytes of the Chamber of Commerce, Standard Oil, and Ma Bell. The San Francisco Bar Association is now nationally famous for its lugubrious, vacuous, sterile pronouncements in the language of innocuous propriety. Take a look at the young lawyers on Montgomery Street, androids in three-piece suits, afraid of having a thought of their own, spending the best years of their lives playing up to some Marin County nincompoop senior partner, in the hope of getting a permanent cubicle in some air-conditioned corridor, there to remain overgrown boys for the rest of their days. Come on. I'll show you the office."

Following my sartorially splendid guide—Brioni suit, white-on-white shirt, a rich maroon cravat, a flamboyantly assertive pocket handkerchief, gleaming black boots—I toured the Belli Building. I have always believed that Mel Belli began the Victorian revival some twenty years ago when he refurbished two buildings on Jackson Square, dating from the late 1840s or early 1850s, and furnished them in the plush nineteenth-century San Francisco style: red velvet, leather, wood, exposed brick, flocked wallpaper, an abundance of ferns, greenery, and blooming plants. Mel took me downstairs. From one ceiling hung hundreds of motel keys he's collected. Another room was teeming with autographed pictures of celebrities—Sammy Davis, Jr., Johnny Carson, Phyllis Diller, Merv Griffin, Edmund G. "Pat" Brown. In the tiled steamroom, where Mel relaxes between cases, was a mosaic of Mel, attired in formal barrister style, riding a horse named Blackstone.

"That's Belli on Blackstone," he told me, "also the title of my soon-to-be-published book of jurisprudential, forensic commentary, which is destined to take its place on the shelves next to my six-volume *Modern Trials* as a legal classic. Be sure the Library buys a dozen copies."

We moved through the library, where a young woman lawyer was hard at work behind a positively Dickensian array of legal tomes. Back in his office, Mel offered me a drink at the giant solid mahogany bar with a brass foot-rail that runs the length of one side of the room. It had been shipped around the Horn during the Gold Rush.

"If it were Christmas, I'd offer you some of my famous Pisco

Punch," Mel observed as he poured out a whiskey. "I went down to the Bolivar Hotel in Lima, Peru, to get the recipe."

It was after five o'clock, so I accepted Mel's hospitality, downing a shot of good booze in one swallow as they used to in the 1850s at the Bank Exchange, or Pisco John's, on this block.

"Here's to Bret Harte," Mel toasted. "He wrote *The Luck of Roaring Camp* next door, at 728 Montgomery.

"Yes," Mel continued, "I have a hell of a time these days finding legal playmates—people like Jake Ehrlich, Johnny Taft, Walter T. McGovern, Les Gillen, Vince Hallinan. Today's judges are efficient but dull.

"Judge Edmund Morgan, for instance, used to like to spend his afternoons in the Olympic Club pool, so he'd adjourn court in memory of someone whose obituary he'd pick out of the morning paper a minute or two earlier. Morgan was bald, except for a two-inch square fertile spot over his left ear. He grew a six-foot queue which he then arranged into a hairpiece. When he swam at the Olympic Club pool, it trailed out behind him like a sea serpent.

"Judge Sylvan Lazarus had a burglar skip bail on Easter twice, the second time when Lazarus, who was of the Jewish faith, let the burglar, a Catholic, out of the pokey to attend Mass. The press ran a shot of Lazarus weeping over an Easter lily.

"Judge Matt Brady once asked the DA what a fair sentence would be for a convicted thief. A guy from the local press came in dressed in a wizard's costume, robes, conical hat, wand, and all, and held up a crystal ball.

" 'I see three years, Your Honor!' the wizard cried out. 'Three years it is!' Brady shouted, pounding down his gavel. The Bar Association raised hell."

As the late afternoon light slanted through the shutters, we talked on: about Lucius Beebe, with whom Mel once crossed the Sierra in Beebe's private railroad car; about Lou Lurie and Jake Ehrlich, whom Mel would meet for lunch at Jack's in the old days.

An inter-office buzzer rang. A cab was waiting to take Belli to the airport for his flight to Honolulu.

"Remember—don't call me flamboyant," Belli admonished me as he sprinted out the door. "I'll help the Library as long as you don't call me flamboyant. I'm not flamboyant. I'm only your oldtime San Francisco attorney—a vanishing species."

What Melvin Belli is to personal injury, the king, Carpino, is to commercial practice, although Carpino's style is a lot more subdued than Mel's. I recently accompanied the Mayor to the Federal Courthouse on Seventh Street at Mission, where in an ornate Beaux Arts chamber, he argued a licensing case before three federal appellate court judges. Carpino was defending the right of a small independent Alaskan feeder airline to compete against a federally subsidized rival. As we drove over to the Courthouse, he told me he was keeping active in this case so that he wouldn't lose touch with the law while mayor. The Mayor didn't mention it at the time (Terry Shane later told me), but he owns a good bit of stock in the plaintiff, Caribou Carrier; and, as far as keeping in touch with the law is concerned, who was he kidding? Carpino runs his law firm through his three sons by phone from the mayor's office. No one, except the screaming rad-libs, expects him to abandon a multimillion-dollar practice just because he's mayor. I'm not a lawyer, thank God. I think we have too many of them already in this country, encouraging citizens to rush to litigation like hungry wolves, bogging our society down in thickets of unnecessary legislation. But even a nonlawyer could appreciate Carpino's forensic brilliance before those three federal judges that day. It was a *tour de force* of persuasion, humor, irony, sarcasm, and legal learning. Carpino did everything but bring his cello into the courtroom and play a concert. He won the case. Caribou Carriers is now beating the pants off Tundra Airways in carrying Alaskan pipeline workers to binges in Juneau or Anchorage, then back into the boondocks when they've sobered up.

The flotilla rounded the far side of Alcatraz, skirted the Bay

150

Bridge, then headed in towards the Ferry Building. It was high time, too. The underprivileged kids were getting bored. Directly opposite us we could see the Golden Gateway development, dominated by John Portman's semipyramidal Hyatt Regency Hotel, the soaring towers of the Levi Strauss Building, and the brown glass and copper-colored structural framework of the Alcoa Building. As the largest single redevelopment project in San Francisco, Golden Gateway is a city within a city—a complex of offices, town houses, apartment towers, restaurants, parks, tennis courts. Twenty years ago the lower Washington Street area, a crowded ghetto of warehouses and rotting tenements, served as the city's produce mart. Mayor Chiro, a tough-minded, practical Greek, born in the South of Market, got behind the drive to redevelop the area into a mixed housing and office complex.

"Just look at it, Jimmy," Carpino said to me as our boat cruised off the Gateway towards our mooring on the western side of the Ferry Building. It was about eleven forty-five. I was to meet Deborah for lunch at the San Domenico at twelve thirty. "Twenty years ago that area was a slum of decrepit warehouses. Now look at it. It's a masterpiece of urban renewal. That's what proper leadership can accomplish."

We landed at noon. Having a little time on my hands, I walked through the Golden Gateway on my way to the San Domenico. Dropping in at the Wine and Cheese Center on Jackson Street, I put an order in with Dick Allen for three cases of Alexander Valley Vineyard's just released '72 Pinot Chardonnay. I know the Alexander Valley winemaster, Bobby Fortier, from the Bohemian Club. He'd mentioned to me the other day at the club bar that his Chardonnay '72 had just that day won a gold medal at the Los Angeles County Fair, which means that there will be a run on the stock. Helen Allen told me that my case of Chateau d'Yquem '67 sauterne had come in. I had them bill me for three cases and promised to be home next Saturday morning for a delivery. I love sauterne, especially with a cigar after dinner.

At the San Domenico I sipped a kir over ice with a lemon

151

twist while I waited for Deborah. When I came to think of it, this was our first date, and I was as excited as a high school kid in a similar situation.

The doors of the San Domenico opened. Sunlight flooded the far end of the restaurant, and Deborah appeared in a burst of radiance, hesitating for a second or two as she adjusted to the new light. She was wearing a long-sleeved, stock-necked white blouse, a burgundy-colored mid-calf skirt, and black suede gaucho boots that disappeared beneath the hemline of her dress. Seeing me at the end of the long, narrow room, she walked in that purposeful, leggy way of hers towards my table. I rose to greet her.

If I were François Truffaut, I would put the camera into half-speed now, so that I could slow Deborah's approach to me, make it a dance-walk outside of time, because time stopped for me as she strode towards my table like Isadora Duncan, like a *fin de siècle* figure from an Arthur Mathews mural, like Queen Calafia herself, the legendary amazonian ruler of the Terrestrial Paradise. I'd have the camera catch the way Deborah's booted legs pushed against her skirt, the subtle pressing of breasts against her white satin blouse, the way her stock added length to her neck, the way the sunlight, already refracted by the leaded glass (installed there in 1860), bathed her rich hair in a chiaroscuro of cascading brown and gold. I'd do a close-up to the look of half-amusement in her eyes, her slightly bumped nose, her wide mouth, parted in a half smile.

Slow it down, Monsieur Truffaut, slow it down even further to a dream-dance. Make this moment of greeting, this shock of recognition last and last and last. Catch the flecks of sunlight in my wine, the impossible yellow of lemon peel. Catch the two rows of snowy-white tablecloths past which she walked as if through a winter field of purifying snow. Cut to the red brick of the wall behind me, against which I steadied myself for a second. Move the camera close now. Focus it on the trickle of spilled wine, knocked over in clumsiness as I rose. Show the fear, the stupefaction on my face, as I wonder why time has stopped, why she is walking, walking, walking—but

152

never coming to me. Stop the camera completely now, just as she reaches the table. Keep us there forever, like the lovers on Keats's Grecian urn, facing each other for eternity across a snowy-white table, set with silver for two, one red rose rising from a slender cinnamon-colored vase, a spilled half-glass of wine, a suggestion of Rachmaninoff in the air.

"How clumsy of me," I said, wiping the wine from my pants. It had stained my crotch. I looked like a boy who'd gone wee-wee in a moment of fright.

"What's wrong," asked Deborah, "don't they have restrooms here?"

"I think I love you."

"You've done more than wet your pants. You've been playing with yourself under the table and are all gooey. How disgusting!" She sat down and picked up the menu.

"I haven't been playing with myself. I've just spilled some wine and said that I think that I love you, which is romantic, isn't it?"

"What's on the menu?" she said, running her eyes up and down it for a second.

"Sail with me to Tinsley Island on the July Fourth weekend."

"You and who else?'

"Just you and me."

"You and I, not you and me—I, nominative case."

"That's what I mean, just you and I."

"Where's Tinsley Island?"

"In the Sacramento Delta."

"What kind of boat do you have?"

"I don't own a boat. I'll borrow one from a friend."

"A sailboat?"

"Yes. Thirty-two feet. Fiberglass."

"Sounds like fun."

We ordered paté served with shredded carrots, cold salmon with cauliflower, a green salad, and a bottle of Mirassou '68 Pinot Blanc. As we ordered, Rachmaninoff, originating somewhere in the back kitchen, unexpectedly became Jacques

153

Brel. The San Domenico was filling up with downtowners in that thank-goodness-it's-Friday mood.

"Don't look now," I said to Deborah, "but Harry Shaw has just come in. We must be at the right place."

For nearly forty years columnist Harry Shaw has lunched lavishly every working day at somebody else's expense. Either he's taken to lunch by someone anxious to get a mention in his column, or else the restaurant itself, eager for one of his make-or-break recommendations, just forgets to send around the tab. Harry has his favorite places, but he'll also occasionally try a new restaurant like the San Domenico. After all, forty years of lunches in a small town like San Francisco (population 700,000) soon puts new luncheon possibilities at a premium.

Shaw came in with his girl Friday, Sheryl Green. He nodded recognition to me from across the room, but, thank God, was seated at the far end of the restaurant, on a sort of raised dais, as was appropriate to his princely status.

"Big deal," said Deborah.

"You're not impressed?"

"Shaw's column is a rip-off," she said. "It talks about a San Francisco that never really existed, or if it exists, exists in a very narrow sector and is corrupt to the core. All you get in his column is café society white trash doing white trashy sorts of things. He's got no feeling at all for ordinary people, and even less empathy for minorities. Besides, he's a fool. He's really too old to be carrying on the way he does."

"You're not looking particularly revolutionary today. You're looking rather smart, in fact."

"I dress well because I'm a doctor's daughter. I can't stand tacky clothes."

"How's your tattoo?"

"Still there. Be a good boy and you may get to see it again."

"I hope that having lunch with me doesn't compromise you with your peer group."

"It is a problem. After all, you are management."

The paté arrived. We ate it on slices of freshly baked French bread along with dabs of sweet butter. Dominic St. Pierre, the

154

owner of the San Domenico, orders his paté from Marcel and Henri on Hyde Street. Ours was delicious. Over the paté, I learned that Deborah was raised in Phoenix, Arizona. Her father, an internist practicing in Paterson, New Jersey, was stationed there during World War II as a Navy medical officer assigned to a recuperating hospital for seriously wounded Navy and Marine Corps personnel. After the war, he couldn't face the prospect of Paterson, New Jersey (William Carlos Williams notwithstanding), so he stayed on in Phoenix and married Deborah's mother, a Mills College girl (class of 1939) who was a lieutenant (jg) in the Waves, assigned as the hospital's registrar.

"My mother went to Mills College before the war. She loved it. She wanted me to come up here for college, so I did."

I am beginning to understand the fact that, despite her tattoo and Medusa hairdo and talk of the streets, Deborah Tanner is a nice, upper-middle-class girl, a doctor's daughter from Phoenix. I must suppress the tendency, not surprising in someone of my blue-collar origins, to rag her about what I consider her posturing leftism. Her blouse must have run at least $50 to $75; her skirt, probably $100; her suede boots, not less than $150, perhaps as much as $200. Add another $75 for lingerie, perfume (something from Halston, if I guessed correctly), and jewelry—gold earrings, a topaz ring of Navajo craftsmanship—and I'll bet that it cost more than $600 just to get her on the street this morning. Quite frankly, it's Deborah's class that attracts me, her Sunbelt class, the way she dresses up. I can't stand hippie-type chicks in long skirts and peasant blouses, or aging co-eds who affect the denim dress-down a decade after graduation. This is San Francisco, after all, my San Francisco, Telegraph Hill San Francisco, not Noe Valley.

"Wasn't Mills College a tame place for you?"

"I liked it. I went over to Berkeley for parties and to do research papers in the Doe Library or the Bancroft, so I had enough big campus atmosphere."

"When did you graduate?"

155

"Nineteen-seventy. I got my library degree at San Jose State just last year."

Over the salmon, I learned that she flew as a stewardess for Hughes Air West for three years while working part-time for her library degree at San Jose State. She shared an apartment with two other stewardesses near the University of Santa Clara. She flew fifteen days a month out of the San Jose airport, the Northern California-Idaho-Wyoming-Montana run, leaving her enough time in between to work on her library degree.

"I did my internship at the Orradre Library of the University of Santa Clara—a beautiful building, with tennis courts and an Olympic-sized swimming pool nearby."

I pictured her tall, tanned, muscular body in tennis whites, returning a serve to some rather handsome guy her own age on the University of Santa Clara tennis courts. He had long, black, curly hair and a mustache and looked like Elliot Gould. I saw her doing laps in the University's Olympic-sized outdoor pool. Deborah has the look of an athlete, that's for sure—in contrast to myself, who am fighting a losing battle against the effects of my sedentary *bon vivantism* with a weekly mile run, steam bath, and half-mile swim at the Olympic Club, which isn't enough. I am thirty-five, after all, and had better start taking care of myself. Maybe I should—or could—learn to play tennis. Kids from my background never learned to play tennis, but I could learn now with Deborah and we could play together. I have always been tantalized by an unattainable dream of athletic California—swimming, surfing, tennis, Sierra Club-ish sorts of things in the outdoors. Deborah is obviously already there. I could follow her—learn to respect my body and, California-style, delight in its sun-tanned vitality.

"Isn't librarianship an odd thing for you to get into?" I asked. "I mean, it's not very glamorous or anything."

"I loved the Bender Rare Book Room at Mills. I used to study there all the time. I decided to become a rare books librarian."

"It's a Maybeck, you know, the Bender Room, the same architect who did the Palace of Fine Arts."

156

"Yes, I loved the vaulted ceilings and all those lovely books collected by Albert Bender."

Albert "Mickey" Bender must surely find his way into my Sebastian Collins biography. He and Collins knew each other for years as fellow members of the Roxburghe Club of book collectors who met monthly for dinner and a lecture on one or another bibliophilic topic. Bender died a year after Collins, in 1941, and for many years was both the patron and the patron saint of the arts in San Francisco. Born in Dublin in 1867, the son of a rabbi, and English-educated, Mickey emigrated to San Francisco in the nineties and rose to the presidency of his own insurance firm. In 1923 his beloved cousin, Anne Bremer, a talented young artist, died. After that, Bender devoted his life and income to sponsoring aspiring artists in her honor. Throughout the 1920s and thirties, Bender's bachelor's flat at 1369 Post resounded at night with the talk and laughter of painters, opera singers, book collectors, sculptors, and other devotees of things aesthetic. Despite his age, Sebastian Collins attended a number of these parties in the 1920s, staying sometimes well past midnight—which is remarkable for a man in his seventies. Yet Collins was fortunate. He kept his health well into the 1930s, not taking to his bed until 1938, two years before his death at the age of ninety-two.

"You're certainly a long way away from being a rare books librarian now," I ventured, knowing that such an opening as this, allowing her to talk about her job, maybe even her social and political ideals, wouldn't seem antagonistic.

"I took a course in public library management at San Jose State. Part of the requirements was to work in a branch library in a Chicano neighborhood. I've spoken Spanish since high school. I loved working with the people in that neighborhood. I read to the kids, got Spanish talking-book records to elderly shut-ins, helped people read contracts and rental leases and the like, all of them in deliberately obscure English so as to screw poor people. I never felt so useful in my life as I did that quarter. It turned me away from wanting to be a rare books librarian to wanting to get into outreach programs among the Spanish-speaking."

Over the green salad and the crackers and *Brie*, I learned that she lived in the Potrero on Alabama Street ("I like to hear a lot of Spanish spoken and to use it as a natural thing") and that she'd been with the San Francisco Public Library system for a year and a half, most of it spent—before she came into the Main—to supervise our special outreach program at the Mission branch. We'd polished off our bottle of pinot blanc by then and were feeling at ease. I love winey lunches. I prefer lunch, in fact, to dinner. San Francisco is a lunch-loving town, I mean a full lunch—*entrée*, salad, fruit, cheese, wine, maybe even a sauterne or a port after filtered coffee. I asked Deborah what she liked to do.

"I like my work. I like my flat, although I get some static from my father about living in a rough neighborhood. Actually, you're safer in a poorer neighborhood where everybody knows you. Pacific Heights has a higher rape and assault rate than the Mission district. I like getting around to some of the smaller neighborhood restaurants. I like foreign films at the Surf. I like shopping on Union Street."

"You also like men?"

"You mean, do I sleep around? The answer is no and none of your business. Has anyone ever told you that you can be very vulgar? You've got a sex thing, haven't you—or is it just class anxiety?"

Deborah had understood my salacious intent and turned it against me, without much overt hostility, but with a slight edge to her voice. Damn it, I thought to myself, I've ruined the mood of lulling sensuosity brought about by lunch and the wine. I'm always ruining things.

"You're a Catholic, aren't you?"

"How did you know?"

"Why else would you have gone to Our Lady of Mercy High School in Phoenix or read Pierre Teilhard de Chardin?"

"My religion is my own business."

I suggested a stinger on the rocks. Deborah agreed. She'd loved her lunch, she said. I like women who like to eat. It betokens a basic generosity.

158

During lunch, I'd managed to keep an eye on Harry Shaw. He and his assistant, a rather good-looking, 1940s-style girl Friday, played by Audrey Totter in the movie, lunched well on the beef *bourguignon* and a bottle of French red wine. From where I sat, the label looked like a Chateau Calon-Segur '68 or '69, but I couldn't tell for sure from the distance. Dominic St. Pierre, the owner of the San Domenico, had chatted amiably with Shaw when he first came in. St. Pierre is a fascinating fellow of about forty, the scion of Burgundian *haut bourgeois* family in the wine business (the novelist François Mauriac was a long-time family friend). A graduate of St.-Cyr, the French military academy, St. Pierre fought in Algeria as a paratrooper lieutenant before emigrating to San Francisco in the mid-sixties. He worked as an administrative vice-president for the Bank of Quebec on Montgomery Street before opening the San Domenico a year ago in order to be able to devote more of his time to reading French philosophy, racing his Alfa-Romeo, dabbling in painting, and entertaining good-looking girls at his hillside hideaway in Sausalito. Bohemian in lifestyle, St. Pierre is on the right politically, as are most Burgundians. I suspect that he might even be a monarchist, although I can't say for sure, having had only a few fragmented conversations with him about politics. In any event, he's very much the St.-Cyr type: a temperamental Gaullist (never mind the break with De Gaulle over Algeria), learned, aloof, aristocratic, tough as nails.

"I was wondering about your tattoo."

"You asked me about that yesterday. I told you, I love the Art Nouveau."

"Do you like Klimt?"

"I find him an extraordinarily erotic painter."

"Maybe I'll get a tattoo, then we'd have something other than the San Francisco Public Library in common. How did you get yours? I mean, it's not in character."

"I was stoned on marijuana, that's how. Do you remember when the French missile-carrier *Jeanne d'Arc* was in town?"

I nodded. I had visited the ship with Mayor Carpino. The

159

French Consul General had presented him with one of the lesser degrees of the *Legion d'Honneur*.

"I went to a party on the *Jeanne d'Arc* given by the junior officers for the local French community, meaning the local French girls, or girls of any sort. One of my roommates knew an Air France stewardess who asked us to come along. I wasn't doing anything, so I said what the hell and went. A group of us blew a lot of dope on the foredeck, enjoying the view of the Trans-Pacific Pyramid from the ship's berth near the Ferry Building. We were also drinking a lot of champagne. I asked one of the officers, a very attentive little sub-lieutenant, whether or not he had a tattoo, since he was a sailor. No, he said, but accompany me and I shall get one. We took a cab up Market Street to a tattoo parlor near the Greyhound Bus Depot on Seventh. The sub-lieutenant was proving very attentive. I was trying to make up my mind whether I liked him or not. Luckily, the ride didn't last too long. When we got to the tattoo parlor we selected a nice French flag for Armand—that was his name—but when the tattooist turned on his electric needle, Armand grew pale and chickened out. Meanwhile, I saw this Art Nouveau rose by Klimt in the pattern display. While Armand was putting on his shirt, I commissioned the rose. It took about half an hour. The tattooist was a perfect gentleman. He gave me a towel to cover all but the tiny patch of skin he was working on."

"Did it hurt?"

"I don't remember. I had been smoking a lot of dope."

"What did you think of it the next day?"

"Not much. I have never regretted it, in any event. And it at least got me out of the clutches of Armand. He folded like a tent when the tattooist got to work on my chest. When it was over, Armand dropped me off at the Southern Pacific station in a cab. He sat as far away from me as he could. I had to take the midnight train down to Santa Clara all by myself."

We finished our coffee. Dominic St. Pierre and Harry Shaw seemed to be arguing about something, or at least St. Pierre was red-faced. Shaw and Sheryl Green left very quickly after Shaw threw some crumpled bills down on the table. It was

160

about two-thirty. Deborah and I and another couple were the only ones left in the restaurant.

"What the hell was that all about?" I asked St. Pierre.

"The son of a bitch!" St. Pierre said in his Louis Jourdan accent. "I don't need the business. I told him I don't need the business."

Harry Shaw, it turns out, had waved the bill aside when it had come to his table. St. Pierre was on his way over to make a big display about tearing the bill in two when he saw Shaw wave the waiter away. Perhaps the Burgundian minor gentry shouldn't go into the restaurant business. Their backbones are too stiff. Anyway, St. Pierre insisted that Shaw pay—probably the first time Harry Shaw has picked up a restaurant tab since the Second World War, in San Francisco anyway.

I drove Deborah back to the Library via Montgomery and Market Streets. I enjoyed the intimacy of the Porsche. It was scandalously past the lunch hour.

"Don't worry," she said, "I'll be working until eight or so this evening back-ordering Spanish language materials, so the City and County of San Francisco won't be out a penny."

"Let me drop you off here," I said when we stopped for a light near the Hibernia Bank at Jones and Market. "I hope you don't mind walking the rest of the way. It wouldn't look good for the two of us to walk in together this late, looking so well-lunched."

"You always look well-lunched, Tubby," she said, slamming the door.

Chapter 6

AFTER LUNCHEON, Jimmy himself conducted a group of us on a tour of Villa Montalvo. The Marine band on the lawn played marches and light operatic music as we walked about, as if Phelan were a regimental colonel in dress whites leading us on parade. We strolled around the outside of Montalvo, admiring the one-hundred-year-old carved Granadan doors that grace the official entry of the villa. The doors are carved with portraits of great figures of Spanish history, beginning with King Ferdinand and Queen Isabella. In front of the villa is an oval pool planted in water lilies. In the rear, on the upper terrace, is a lovely oval plunge. Marina calls it a swimming pool. A pergola supported by white Ionic columns and drenched in violet wistaria surrounds this tiled plunge, which is also graced by bamboo plants and flowering shrubs growing in marble containers. On one side is a statue of Nydia, the blind girl of Bulwer-Lytton's *Last Days of Pompeii*. The whole effect of the plunge is that of a provincial Roman bath, in Tours, say, or Autun in Gallacia or Bath itself in Roman Britain.

Built in the Mediterranean villa style, Montalvo encloses a patio where a Moorish tile fountain splashes. We walked from there through pillared arbors draped in cream-and-violet-colored wistaria down to the Italian gardens that fall away from the east façade. Phelan is rather proud of the three-thousand-year-old Egyptian obelisk he acquired in Alexandria during his art-buying tour of Europe and North Africa last year. The obelisk stands by itself in an open lawn. When we returned from the gardens to see the interior of the villa, we left Marina and John Scannell sitting together on a stone bench that rested on the backs of two portentous griffins.

I find some bittersweet amusement in one of the three busts Phelan has emplaced in the redwood grove that borders the western edge of the Montalvo estate. One is of the poet Edwin Markham, of "Man with a Hoe" fame, whom I can't stand—such a tedious *poseur*, with his beard and stagy, shambling democratic air, as if he were Walt Whitman reborn. Joaquin Miller, the second bust, I don't mind. Joaquin was a *poseur* and a rogue, but a colorful one, energetic, and very amusing with his sombrero hat and jug of corn whiskey. But the bust of John Muir saddens me. Muir passed away only last year—after Phelan had gone to Washington and successfully lobbied the Hetch Hetchy bill through Congress. They say Muir died of a broken heart when he learned that the battle was lost, that the Hetch Hetchy Valley—the little Yosemite as it is called—would be dammed to create a water reservoir for San Francisco. Personally, I share the enthusiasm of Mr. O'Shaughnessy, the city engineer: ours will be an aqueduct system to rival that of imperial Rome. Like Rome, San Francisco must reach out across an entire province to secure water for itself. Los Angeles has done it in the Owens Valley, and so must we. I respect Muir and his Sierra Club friends, but like Phelan, I respect the needs of San Francisco more. In any event, I imagined an accusing look on Muir's face as Phelan walked by the bust, leading us back down to Montalvo.

Montalvo has nineteen rooms. The drawing room is dominated by a great Spanish fireplace and ceiling-high French doors. The library is paneled in Circassian walnut. A stained glass window depicting Cabrillo's vessel, the *San Salvador*, sailing into San Diego Bay in 1542—the first recorded European landing here—soars over the foyer. Classical marbles

163

and bronzes are scattered throughout the house. Phelan has also hung innumerable paintings of California by local artists, including a number of our fellow Bohemians: Virgil Williams, Jules Tavenier, Julian Rix, Charles Rollo Peters, Jules Pages, and Arthur Mathews.

In the library, Jimmy showed us a first edition of the Spanish romance *Sergas de Esplandián* by García Rodríguez Ordóñez de Montalvo, published in 1510. It is truly a beautiful book. Montalvo was the first writer to describe California. He depicted it as an island paradise lying beyond the Indies, inhabited by amazons. The women wear golden armor, Montalvo wrote, and they trap and domesticate wild griffins, which they ride as mounts, feeding them on captive men or on their own male children. They are ruled by Calafia, an especially lovely amazon queen. Queen Calafia leads her Californians into battle on behalf of the sultan of Turkey. She is eventually converted to Christianity, marries a relative of the knight Esplandian, and returns to live with him in California. When Hernando Cortez landed in the peninsula of Baja California in 1535, he named the region after Montalvo's amazon kingdom.

In the interior patio of Villa Montalvo, called the Spanish Court, Jimmy has commissioned a wall fountain and a bronze tablet from artist J. J. Mora. From a griffin head, guarded by amazons, water spouts into a basin supported by the wood nymphs also described in *Sergas de Esplandián*. The water arches past the tablet, which says:

MDXXI
Know
Ordóñez de Montalvo's
Fame
Did He not See
In Fantasy
Our California Grow
Out of Old Spain
Conferred Her Name
Foretold
A Paradise

164

His Dream Come True
For Me and You
MCMXII

After leaving the library, I left the party, then in its penultimate moments, in search of Marina. It was nearly four o'clock. The chauffeur Robert Poole was awaiting us in the Croxton-Keeton near the garage, ready to take us to the train station at Santa Clara to catch the 5:20 to the city. I found Marina and John Charles Scannell near the apricot orchard at the far end of the grounds. They were feeding the tame deer that Phelan keeps in a fenced paddock near the orchard. Young Scannell was wearing a red and blue striped linen blazer, a straw boater hat with a maroon band, a white shirt, blue necktie, and cream-colored trousers. Marina's hair, done in a topknot and chignon, had come partially loose. A strand of her blond hair fell down back behind her neck onto her yellow dress, darker gold against a field of pale wheat. They were feeding the deer bits of bread taken from the luncheon table. The apricot orchard blossomed around them. One of the deer, a young male with its first horns, nibbled appreciatively at Marina's fingers.

The train ride to San Francisco took two hours. Marina did not have much to say. She seemed to prefer to be alone with her thoughts, so I did not bother her. While light remained, I read from Hugh Quigley's *The Irish Race in California* (San Francisco, 1878), which I had borrowed from the Montalvo library. A San Francisco priest, exiled from Ireland by the British for anti-Crown activities, Quigley describes the civilization of California as a triumph of the Celtico-Roman spirit. By this he means that the Irish finished what the Spanish began: the translation of a Mediterranean Celtic civilization to these lovely Pacific shores.

The Celts, Quigley claims, always looked southwards, even in the ages prior to the rise of Roman Christianity. They were, after all, of the same basic Celtic stock as the peoples of the Mediterranean. Around 1000 B.C. the Latin branch of the

165

Celtic family poured southwards over the Alps and settled in Italy. The northern Celts, jealous of their Latin cousins' love affair with the sun, vowed that they also would one day possess Rome. Obsessed by the sunlands, they embarked upon a course of nearly eight hundred years of south-seeking invasions. They sacked Rome in 390 B.C., as if to drive it from their consciousness: as though ravishing a woman who tempts by her beauty but refuses to be possessed. Grown strong, Rome moved northwards to conquer its unruly Celtic cousins. The Romans brought to the Celts the gifts of discipline and order. The Roman Empire also asserted the fact of Mediterranean Celtic unity. When the missionary bishop Patrick landed in Ireland in 432 A.D., it was to reclaim for Rome the last of the non-Mediterraneanized Celts. The Irish accepted conversion instantly. They knew that their destiny was in the south. Spain too, Quigley says, is Celtic in origin. In settling California, the Spanish enacted the final act of a grand drama that had played itself out over three thousand years: the conquest of the southern sunny lands by Celtico-Roman peoples, in this case, California, North America's Mediterranean littoral. Just as the Christian Celts of Ireland reanimated Roman Europe through the learning and piety of Irish missionary monks, so too was it now the destiny of Irish California to finish what Spain had begun: the civilizing of Mediterranean California.

I put the book down. It was growing too dark to read. Besides, the sunset over the Coast Range offered a less ambiguous splendor than Quigley's speculations. How naive Quigley's hopes now seem! How contradicted by solid American fact! Yet when I look back upon my youth, I realize that many of us were similarly motivated by such dazzling, prophetic hopes for California and for ourselves. Dreams such as this motivated me at Heidelberg, toiling away in preparation for my assured San Francisco future. Dreams such as this animated Ralston as he invested in a thousand schemes of social improvement. Hopes such as this motivated Charlie Stoddard, preparing through European travel for his assured

166

career as California's great poet. They solaced Hugh Quigley, chained to his teaching duties, a bitterly disappointed Irish patriot looking for vindication from this far-away land where fate had exiled him. Such California dreams never held Josiah Royce, however. Royce got out of California as soon as he could, preferring to sing California's praises from the vantage point of a Harvard professorship.

The sunset bathed the entire Santa Clara Valley in roseate light. As we stopped at the Palo Alto station, I beheld from my train window a sight that Titian would have envied: the sundown incandescence of the red-tiled roofs and buff-gold stone of the Stanford University quadrangle. Surrounded by wheat fields, approached through palm-lined gardens, Stanford looked like a hillside monastery in northern Tuscany at a similar sunset time. Until reaching Palo Alto, our train had been passing through blossoming apricot groves. They, too, recall the south. The colors of our Panama-Pacific International Exposition, chosen by the artist Jules Guerin, are apricot colors, California colors, colors of the sunny south: flecked travertine, light green, ochre, vermilion, cinnamon, verd antique, cerulean blue—and burnt orange. Burnt orange! I love this color almost as much as I love the color apricot. If the Golden Gate straits are ever spanned by a bridge (and this must some day come to pass), the bridge should be painted in burnt orange. A bridge of burnt orange soaring over our American Bosporus—what a glorious sight! The drama of my imagination plays itself out against an apricot-colored scenery, for I have spent my life in sunny countries and have always remained half-pagan as a result. Santayana understands this. "Collins's grasp of the theological tensions at the core of the baroque style," Santayana wrote of me, "are rare in an American scholar. Sebastian Collins understands the mind and the imagination of the Latin south."

Yes, I do Mediterraneanize well—if not well, then at least constantly. I Mediterraneanized on our train ride home up through the Santa Clara Valley, then through the County of San Mateo, retracing the path of Father Serra's El Camino Real in our steam-spouting iron horse. In the sunset of my life, I have an affinity for sunsets. It was not just the day—the glorious California day—that I saw sink over the Pacific, but my life as well. Someday soon (not too soon, O Lord, not too soon!) I shall sink like the sun over the rim of the world and be borne by Charon, the ferryman of Death, across the River Styx. Unlike Dante, however, I will not need Virgil to convince Charon to take me along; for I shall be most decidedly dead.

"What are you thinking about, Father?"

"Death—and apricots—burnt orange—the sunset—Queen Calafia—griffins."

"Why can't I have a normal father?"

"You'll get a normal husband in recompense, a banker perhaps."

"Don't be cheeky. How's your book?"

"Full of sad dreams. Besides, it's too dark to read. I'd rather enjoy the sunset."

"Who is Queen Calafia?"

"Who is Mr. Scannell?"

"I asked first, but I will answer your questions since it is good taste to respect the elderly. Mr. Scannell is twenty-eight years old. He was born and raised on a ranch near Healdsburg and went to Stanford on a scholarship. He is a lawyer with the Tobin brothers. He is very nice. Now who is Queen Calafia?"

"Queen Calafia was the amazon queen of California. She rode a griffin and went around with her left breast exposed."

"Naughty girl. She'll catch cold. I prefer a Croxton-Keeton to a griffin."

"You would, however, have made a good amazon. You're tall enough, and, shall we say, robust enough."

"I inherit my figure from my father; although, in contrast to him, I have kept mine under control."

"I see that you have your energy back. For a while you seemed lost in dreams."

"I did have a lovely day. I enjoyed the Marine band and all those famous people."

168

"Who were your favorites?"

"Mayor Phelan is a darling, and I simply adore Mayor Rolph. He's such fun. I'm mad about his cowboy boots. The Hoovers are a little stiff, but they have distinction. That's what I want to have—a demeanor of distinction, as if I've been everywhere and seen everything."

"Like Mrs. Atherton?"

"Yes, but without her snobbery."

"Like Charmian London?"

"No. She strains too hard at being the great writer's wife."

"She's Jack's mate-woman. That's what they call each other: mate-man and mate-woman."

"How delightfully explicit. I like her better already."

"London is a bit of a rogue."

"Most men are. Even you, Father. Despite your age, you'd be a bit of a rogue if you thought you could get away with it. You poor dear, you think I'd be scandalized."

"You flatter me."

"I mean it. All men are rogues, even old men like you. It's a fact of nature. We women make you behave."

"You also help us misbehave."

"True—the lucky ones. Most of us are forced into the role of making you behave, however."

"Is that what they teach you at Mills College?"

"They teach us to look at the facts, then make intelligent interpretations."

"I feel that we are drifting into a father-daughter conversation about the facts of life."

"You needn't worry. It's too late for that. I already know all about such things—theoretically, of course."

"Of course. You were educated at the Convent of the Sacred Heart."

"That's the problem. I've had to unlearn a lot of things that the madames taught me—and then relearn some of the lessons I unlearned. But don't worry. I'm still *virgo intacta*."

"Thank heavens. It all sounds like such a complicated procedure."

"It's a necessary procedure. Let me explain. The madames, consecrated virgins, you understand, naturally approach sex from a theological viewpoint. They are, after all, brides of Christ. The madames taught us that consequences of heaven and hell ride upon individual moments of sexual activity."

"The Church teaches that?"

"Hear me out. You know what I'm talking about. Don't be pious with me."

"I should have never sent you to Mills."

"Thank God, you did. Hush and let me continue. The problem lies in the duality of sex. It may have theological consequences, but it can also be—for men especially—just a pleasant tumble in the hay, as in Chaucer or Rabelais."

"You redeem yourself through literary reference. What about Dante?"

"He worshipped Beatrice as theologicized eros, but he also tumbled many a Tuscan lass in the hay without benefit of theological justification, including Mrs. Dante Alighieri, who bore him flocks of children. Take the men at the luncheon this afternoon. So many of them were being seductive—not specifically, but in a generalized way, exuding eros and male self-regard like preening peacocks. You know about Mayor Rolph. We all do. But no one blames him for it. Mr. Roosevelt is a ladies' man. I'll say that just on intuition: a good-humored ladies' man, however, not a stingy lecher."

"There is a Mrs. Roosevelt."

"There is always a Mrs. Roosevelt. There's a Mrs. Willis Polk also, and a Mrs. George Sterling, and a Mrs. Paul Masson. But their husbands are all notorious philanderers. Brilliant, creative men seem also to be highly sexed. Sex is part of a total vitality of appetite. At Mills I've learned to respect the natural forces of life—greed and lust, ambition, power, money, the desire for recognition. Sexual appetite is basic to these drives in one way or another. I want a powerful, successful man in my life—but not as his tavern wench. I'll split the difference between Mills College and the Convent of the Sacred Heart when it comes to sex. There must be a free,

170

frank enjoyment of appetite, but there must also be commitment and mutual respect. It's not always angel voices and harps, but it's not always the barnyard, either."

"Where did you learn all this—and remain, I mean, a *virgo intacta?*"

"I learned it from you, silly, from all the accomplished men you've raised me around—and from common sense."

"You deserve a much younger father, Marina, a much younger father."

"I like the one I have. Here, let me hold your hand."

In October of 1881, when I was tutoring Jimmy Phelan, he sent Prime Minister Gladstone a copy of an essay he had written extolling the PM's virtues. Jimmy's essay advanced the classical notion that learning and virtue are the premises of politics: that politics, in its deepest sense, is the practical aspect of the science of ethics, the art of choosing between goods, or between good and evil. Prime Minister Gladstone, Phelan wrote, embodied those ideals. The PM wrote Jimmy a warm, almost effusive handwritten letter of thanks. He was touched, he said, that a lad in a place so far from England might yet have come so superbly into the possession of such fine sentiments.

Another thread in Phelan's development, one for which I take partial credit: Phelan loves Beauty—Plato's Beauty with a capital B, by turns immanent and ethereal. This has been true of Phelan since his boyhood. The letters he wrote to me from Europe during the grand tour he made after graduating from the Hastings Law School pulsate with aesthetic feeling. This sort of tutored aestheticism is rare among American politicians. Phelan, like me, is something of a bohemian—a tory bohemian if you will. His bohemianism proceeds naturally from his art-loving, aesthetic nature. In the most busy years of his banking and real estate career, the decade of the nineties, Phelan found time for a moderate version of *la vie bohème.*

In the nineties Mary Edith Griswold, later the associate editor of *Sunset* magazine, assembled a coterie (myself among

171

them) that brought together a diverse and talented group of Bay Area personalities. The Griswold group was most active in the years immediately preceding Phelan's election as mayor. We'd meet once a week at Mary's place on Telegraph Hill for wine and a late-night supper. It was, I must say, a truly amusing coterie, cutting across political parties and other such trivial differences. All Mary asked was that you be creatively working in the Bay Area and that you be doing something for California.

"I just can't stand people who won't do something for California," she used to say in the perpetually exasperated upper-class New York accent of hers. "I mean really. It's so beautiful—and everything."

For her own contribution to California, Mary Griswold in time helped raise *Sunset* magazine toward its present level of excellence as a journal of literature and regional living. (The latest issue of *Sunset* contains my appreciative essay on the forthcoming Exposition.) I remember Phelan well from those Griswold evenings on Telegraph Hill. His beard was then quite red. He was already making a name for himself locally—president of the Bohemian Club at the absurdly young age of twenty-five; vice-president of the California Commission for the World's Columbian Exposition in Chicago. Phelan helped bring part of the Chicago Exposition to San Francisco in 1894 as the Midwinter Exposition, developing for this purpose the entire Music Concourse in Golden Gate Park, just as the Panama-Pacific Exposition is reclaiming and developing the Harbor View area of San Francisco. At the Mechanics' Institute Fair of 1896, Phelan delivered an electrifying speech, "The New San Francisco," calling for an end to political corruption in the city. Two years later he was elected mayor on a reform Democratic ticket.

Already, those pre-earthquake days seem in my mind a species of ancient history, an antediluvian Atlantis of aesthetic aspiration. Of an evening at Mary's I encountered so many friends—and respected enemies—brought together by Mary Griswold's admixture of New York, California, and Puccin-

172

iesque *japonaiserie*. Mary's house opened out into a garden overlooking the bay. Japanese lanterns glowed there like gigantic mauve and cinnamon fireflies, and beyond them twinkled the glowworm lights of nocturnal ships passing through the harbor. At this distance in time, all those evenings dissolve together, so I cannot distinguish one from another; but I do remember talking with Robert Louis Stevenson, thin and reedy, a week before he embarked for his final voyage to the South Seas. Charlie Stoddard was there also. It was Charlie, after all, who first set Stevenson to thinking about Samoa. From Mary Griswold's garden, Charlie and I could look west towards the Golden Gate and see the twinkling lights of Black Point, adjacent to where the Exposition now stands. Thirty years earlier, in the 1860s, another hostess, Jessie Benton Fremont, gave *soirées* such as Mary Griswold's. Then, however, Charlie and I were in our precocious teens.

"Now Charlie and Sebastian," Mary would say as she burst out to the garden from her crowded flat, "don't you two be mooning there about old San Francisco. I want you both to enjoy the Gay Nineties." Mary would most likely be wearing a brightly patterned Japanese kimono and would be smoking a Turkish cigarette at the end of a long jade holder. Mary Griswold was the first woman I ever saw smoke a cigarette in public.

Within her home, perched on the side of the hill, one might find Joaquin Miller, who dressed as if the gold rush were still on. Miller swigged liquor from a stone crock, capped with a cork. He could be tiresome, especially when he got drunk and recited his poetry. He always wore a great wide-brimmed hat, even indoors, tilted at a rakish angle. At a London party in the seventies, when he'd joined Ambrose Bierce and Prentice Mulford in English exile, Miller let out a war whoop at the sight of a particularly delectable young lady. Getting down on his hands and knees, Miller crawled over to her across the crowded room. Lifting her skirt, he nibbled appreciatively at her ankles. The English loved it. It was just the sort of behavior they expected from Californians. Joaquin behaved a little better at Mary's—but not much better. Mary adored it when he got drunk and asked her to go to bed with him.

"You naughty man," she would laugh. "Is that how you'd approach a squaw when you lived with the Indians—so directly, with no preliminaries, no *finesse?*"

"Madam," Miller would respond, knowing that Mary loved these semi-salacious encounters, "let us cleave to each other like wanton children of nature, awakening at dawn in our Sierran bower to the music of mountain birds."

Mary adored the theater—and opera. I met San Francisco-born impresario David Belasco at Mary's place when he was back in San Francisco with *The Girl of the Golden West.* For some unaccountable reason, Belasco always wore a clerical collar, although he was not ordained in any church. I also encountered opera impresario Henry Grau, ever in the company of some lovely young dryad from the *corps de ballet.* In retrospect, I envy Grau his sexual vigor. I am sixty-seven, but I would love to make love again—had I the opportunity. Time grows short, and love is life. It is also religion, or a good part of religion, as Bernini and the other artists of the Baroque well knew. I've thought about it, but there seems no way that I, a portly, bearded *litterateur* of sixty-seven, could ever lure a dryad to my bower, although Grau was well past sixty when I first encountered him. Look at Benjamin Franklin, active in this vital area of life well into his seventies—and Joaquin Miller, that roguish *poseur*, bringing women back to his cabin in the Piedmont Hills virtually up to the very day of his death last year. Why should I remain bonded over to celibacy? Virginia has been dead nearly twenty years. I kept discreetly active through my fifties, even my early sixties; but of late my erotic isolation has intensified. I find myself solacing my deprivation with the comforts of memory. I would prefer one of Mr. Grau's dryads.

Perhaps I shall offer a novena to Saint Mary Magdalene, she who washed Christ's feet with her tears, anointed them with oil, then dried them with her hair. Dear Saint Mary

Magdalene, I shall pray, thou understand both the weakness of the flesh—and how flesh brings us, paradoxically, to Christ, the Anointed One. You threw yourself at Him in a rush of love that began with profane desire and ended with a hunger that betrayed you to holiness. Let me also experience, once again, ecstasy of flesh—and that subsequent holiness that so surprised you. Send me a dryad, Saint Mary Magdalene, or perhaps just a nice San Francisco girl; a woman under fifty—under fifty-five for that matter—would do fine. Let me revel with her one last time! Then, Mary Magdalene, like yourself I shall stand ready for the higher love. I'll enter a Carthusian monastery, forswearing the flesh.

The *Examiner* crowd, in any event, packed Mary's parties, some of them proving especially voracious when Mary's buffet supper appeared at midnight. I enjoyed the acerbic conversation of young Lafayette Maynard Dixon, the illustrator who wanted to be an artist. I helped get Maynard Dixon into the Bohemian Club, and Jimmy Phelan bought his paintings and gave him his first show. Ambrose Bierce, another *Examiner* writer, who recently disappeared into Mexico, always seemed so much the *poseur* to me, so haughty about his connection with the Empress Eugénie; but the man does write well, if you can tolerate his misanthropy. A decorated cavalry officer in the Union Army, Bierce carried himself stiffly erect, as if on parade. He could be very uncivil, but he tolerated me because he and I shared an experience of active combat. Besides, I fought on the proper side of the conflict. Bierce is a fierce conservative.

"You Zouaves fought well, Sebastian, especially at Mentana," Bierce once said to me at Mary Griswold's, "but the Redshirts are taking over the world. Anarchy and cowardice and vulgarity rule the roost."

Bierce lived atop a mountain in Suisun, Contra Costa county, like a demigod in exile from Olympus. He claimed that the fog of San Francisco aggravated his asthma. He posted his columns to the *Examiner* by mail. He would, however, occasionally come to the city for one of Mary Griswold's parties. George Sterling followed him around like a cupbearer to a visiting divinity. At the time George worked for his father-in-law selling real estate; but he wanted to be a poet. Colonel Frederick Funston and Ambrose Bierce would talk tactics together. Funston was promoted to brigadier in the Philippines and he became the would-be military consul of San Francisco during the terrible days of 1906. He and Bierce carried on elaborate discussions of Civil War battles, in some of which they both fought. I was reminded of Harvard in my freshman year, 1867, when the talk still returned to Antietam, Spotsylvania, Wilderness, Gettysburg.

Luther Burbank, another Griswoldian, and I both love gardens. What wonderful discussions Burbank, McLaren and I enjoyed there concerning the theory and practice of garden design. McLaren was then in the high fervor of effort in the creation of Golden Gate Park . . . I am losing the thread of my discourse. What I want to suggest is a process in Phelan's development. An aristocrat, possessed of a conception of politics as ethical endeavor, Phelan was also a latent artist. He grew into a highly developed connoisseur who was also a very astute man of business. I am positive that just as I helped nourish in young Phelan a classical conception of the *polis*, the city state, which helped form his lifelong attitude towards San Francisco, so too did Mary Griswold, by those parties of hers, show Phelan the enormous possibilities of astute patronage— patronage based on the simple premises of good people, and good food and drink. Not since my own patron, William Chapman Ralston, has there been such an entertainer as Phelan. As a businessman, Phelan doubled the assets left him by his father, so there was, and is, plenty of money.

I believe that Phelan assumed the mayor's office in 1897 in the spirit of a Renaissance patron, or as Mrs. Atherton put it, a reforming Hamiltonian. Reform the city he did. That, after all, was why Fremont Older of the *Bulletin* put him in office, despite the fact that Phelan was barely thirty-five and had no previous political experience. Older and others—Rudolph Spreckels among them—wanted San Francisco modernized

176

and reformed. In 1898 Phelan got a reform charter voted through. The new charter streamlined the civil service, established our present commission system of government, and brought transportation, electricity, and water under municipal ownership.

"This city," Phelan said to me one day over lunch at the Bohemian Club in the first year of his mayoralty, "is a complex event. It is an act of engineering and a work of art. It is a moral community, and something else too—a collective drama, sometimes even a collective liturgy. I want to serve this, Sebastian, serve it in its grandest dimension of existence and in its humblest detail."

Things rarely work out completely as we plan. Ideals account for some of our best actions—in Jimmy's case, for instance, the reform of the charter—but ideals can also blind us to realities, as happened to Jimmy in the Teamsters' Strike of 1901, one of the most bitterly fought labor struggles in San Francisco's history. It was also a ferocious internecine quarrel among the Irish Catholics of the city. Two Irish Catholic San Franciscos—James Duval Phelan's and Father Peter Yorke's; Nob Hill and the Mission district—clashed head-on. The struggle destroyed James Duval Phelan's desire to continue as mayor. Whether or not he could have been re-elected, had he run, is a moot point.

I have met Peter Christopher Yorke but a few times, but I know his type of Irishman: congenitally pugnacious, loving a fight in a good cause, but also loving a fight for its own sake. Archbishop Riordan has rusticated Yorke to a parish in Oakland, but the man's influence still dominates this city. Yorke has a broad Irish face. His features seem now coarse—like a teamster's; now sensitively refined—like a poet-priest's. He is all of these at once—poet, priest, teamster, politician *par excellence*.

"You have to remember that Yorke is a Maynooth man," my friend Monsignor John Gleeson, rector of St. Mary's Cathedral, explained to me.

Maynooth is an Irish seminary, *the* Irish seminary, a huge sprawling stone fortress of a seminary that sends forth to America every year hundreds of Irish peasant lads turned priests: big-boned, big-knuckled men, formed along the lines of a narrow, militant orthodoxy, working well in America, yet also at odds with the country, resentful of America's protestant establishment and dominant protestant tone.

"I have known Yorke since he was a young curate," Monsignor Gleeson recalled about four years ago, just as the new St. Ignatius Church was being finished. The Jesuit provincial had asked Gleeson to give the address at the dedication of St. Ignatius, and he and I were talking leisurely of the church and of the baroque style—of which St. Ignatius is a masterpiece, even if I, consultant to the architect on points of architectural historicism, say so myself: which I do, for I am proud of this Church of St. Ignatius, proud of the way it dominates the western skyline of our city, a triumphant assertion of the Baroque in our beloved Mediterranean city.

Peter Yorke had a chip on his shoulder the moment he arrived here, Gleeson claimed. The conversation had turned to Yorke because we were talking about oratory, and Yorke is, quite briefly, one of the most brilliant and effective orators— in the heated, florid style—the Asiatic style as the ancients would say—that this city has ever heard.

"Archbishop Riordan paid Yorke's way through St. Mary's Seminary in Baltimore," Gleeson continued, "after Yorke left Maynooth to emigrate to America. When Yorke graduated and was ordained, Riordan brought him into the cathedral. That would be in 1888."

Eighteen eighty-eight: the year I met Sybil at the Phelans' house on Valencia Street. The old cathedral at California and Grant was still in use then by the archdiocese. It's now turned over to the Paulist fathers. I never noticed Yorke, although I did attend services at the cathedral when the old Dominican Alemany yet presided there, just before his retirement to a Catalonian monastery. I suppose that had I looked closely at the high altar during a solemn high mass, I might have

178

noticed the recently arrived twenty-four-year-old priest on the altar, serving as subdeacon. I might have noticed his wild Irish eyes, the expression of perfervid piety on his face as he assisted at the mass—a piety that contained within itself restlessness and discontent as well as devotion. Resentment at what? At injustice? At America? At being a priest in the first place? Irish boys of Yorke's sort, poor Galway boys, had little choice in the matter. It was either be a priest or keep a farm or work on the docks. Maynooth offered a way out, but at a price. Was the world well lost? Who knows? I never lost the world. I clung to it as greedily as I could. I still do.

None of this is to suggest that Peter Christopher Yorke was not a devoted priest. He was. He is. But he nourished a smoldering, undefined resentment deep within his bosom that made—makes—him something else as well. Archbishop Riordan sent Yorke to the Catholic University of America in 1889. (Charlie Stoddard joined the faculty soon after as a professor of English.) It was a brilliant opportunity for Yorke; yet for the first few months (so Stoddard later told me) Yorke went into an unexplainable sulk. Archbishop Riordan himself visited Yorke twice at the university in an effort to cheer him up. The Archbishop wanted Yorke to take a licentiate in sacred theology. Quite frankly, Riordan was grooming Yorke for the purple.

"He's a sorehead," was all that Riordan could say of Yorke's malaise.

Yorke told Riordan that he did not like the food at Catholic University—this from a boy raised on cabbage and potatoes! He changed his attitude, however, just as mercurially as he went into the sulks. He did so brilliantly at Catholic University, Gleeson says, that they asked him to stay on as a theology professor when he completed his licentiate. The rector, Bishop John Keane, personally interceded with Riordan to release Yorke to the university. Riordan refused. He brought Yorke back to San Francisco, installed him in the new cathedral on Van Ness, made him his personal secretary, and appointed him chancellor of the archdiocese and editor of the archdiocesan paper, *The Monitor*—all of this when Yorke was barely thirty.

I was gone from San Francisco during these years, 1888–93. While Yorke prayed and worked, I drank and whored, and sometimes prayed. Charles Moore made some hostile remarks against Yorke at the luncheon party at Montalvo the other Saturday—for Phelan's benefit, I presume. The wound from the spear that Yorke drove into Phelan's side has not yet healed. Perhaps only election to the United States Senate can heal it. Moore, in fact, stands for everything that Yorke detested, that galvanized him into the intemperate partisanship that destroyed his career in the Church: getting him removed from the list of candidates for the episcopacy just before Riordan sent the list to Rome—Riordan, who had advanced Yorke's career in the first place, now ending it with a stroke of his pen, yet loving Yorke all the while (so Gleeson claims) like a father punishing a wayward, rebellious son.

Yes indeed, Charles Moore of the Exposition Company embodies everything that Yorke feared or was jealous of—or was righteously angry against: the owners of San Francisco, the Pacific Union and (yes, I must say it) Bohemian Club crowd of polished protestants whose kidskin gloves conceal an iron fist. Frank Pixley of the *Argonaut* was the worst of that bunch. I shared a membership in the Bohemian Club with him, but avoided Pixley whenever possible. I moved down the bar. For all its polished literary elegance, the *Argonaut* as Frank Pixley ran it was a bigoted Know-Nothing rag.

Archbishop Riordan sent young Yorke into the fray, not knowing that the struggle against anti-Catholic bigotry would release something tumultuous and mysterious in the priest: some seething Irish resentment against the established order, including the established Irish order, that fanned into flame like a forest fire leaping from treetop to treetop. Yorke took on Frank Pixley in the pages of the *Monitor*. He also took on the bigots of the American Protective Association, the most vicious of the anti-Irish, anti-Catholic hate groups. The combat of pulpit and pen keyed Yorke up, made him nervous,

180

feverish. He lived constantly on the frenetic edges of polemic. Yorke was removed from the bishop's list because his controversial temperament, his fiery editorials, his electric speeches were not the sort of thing desired in a prelate charged with the advancement of the Church's temporal welfare.

"By the mid-1890s"—this is the way Monsignor Gleeson put it—"the Archbishop realized that he had created a populist Frankenstein. He sicked Yorke on the bigots, but then Yorke decided to take a bite out of a few others as well, including the fancy Irish Catholics."

Yorke took a very big bite out of James Duval Phelan. He leapt at Phelan's throat like a bull mastiff and stayed there until 1902 when Phelan was driven from public life, badly mangled. The ostensible cause of Yorke's attack was Phelan's renewal of a city contract with the Sailors' Home, which Yorke felt discriminated against Catholics. Renewing the contract, Yorke said, put Mayor Phelan "in the forefront of the ranks of bigotry and intolerance"—a rather severe charge, indeed.

Two or three years apart in age, these two young men were destined to clash, whatever the ostensible cause. Phelan and Yorke represented the divided streams of the Irish Catholic experience in San Francisco. The Phelans, the Tobins of the Hibernia Bank, the Floods, the McKays, the McAvorys, the Fairs of the Comstock silver mines—all these Irish had become grand ladies and gentlemen. At times, it almost seems as if they were not Irish any more. Yorke must have hated Phelan's aristocratic airs and classical notions. The Irish have a way of resenting it when their own get ahead. Yorke threw in with the bulk of our local Irish Catholic population—the teamsters, bricklayers, hodcarriers, longshoremen, firemen, policemen, clerks, washerwomen, the barkeeps and ordinary laborers, the widows and orphans, and poor souls who drank too much but still said their rosary. He threw in with the Irish who ate steak and potatoes off heavy plates placed on tables covered in oilcloth, who went to St. Peter's on Alabama Street in the Potrero on Sundays, their faces and hands yet carrying traces of unscrubbable dirt.

181

Archbishop Riordan serves as house chaplain to the Tobins and the Phelans and the other wealthy Catholics. He dines with them *en famille*. He baptizes their children. He spends long weekends with them at their Hillsborough estates. Yorke frequents circles other than those favored by his mentor, San Francisco's elegant, imperial, Roman-trained (and Irish) archbishop. Yorke visits friends in Hayes Valley and the Mission district. He goes out of love, of course, for he is a good priest, despite his sharp tongue, a priest who loves the poor. But he glories in the poor out of a sort of subtle pride, a defiant contrariness, as well. Even now in 1914 Yorke is—let's be honest—causing trouble in his role as a regent of the University of California. He excoriates the university for discriminating against the admission to its professional schools of the graduates of Catholic colleges—which is true; the university does so discriminate. Yet Yorke's combativeness is overdone, as if he were bending over backwards to assert the equality of Maynooth learning over the learning of the California professors. I am flattered, however, that Yorke has put my name before the regents as the type of Catholic scholar unrepresented on the Berkeley faculty. I wrote Father Yorke just the other day a short note of thanks, expressing both my embarrassment and my gratitude.

In any event, Yorke hated everything that he thought Mayor Phelan embodied: an Irishman who had become too rich, too grand, too full of high-flown, comforting notions of civilization.

"Mayor Phelan," Yorke wrote in one particularly venomous editorial, "forgets that he is Irish, that his father came to this country a penniless immigrant, just like the rest of us. Woe to you, Jimmy Phelan, for forgetting your own. You wear purple garments and you eat with kings. You play the *grand seigneur* of San Francisco. But you have forgotten the sick, the humble, the lowly. You trample on the back of God's poor."

Riordan removed Yorke from all his offices shortly after the appearance of this editorial. I accompanied Phelan the day he called on Riordan at the archbishop's home at 1000 Fulton

182

Street. Phelan was furious. His re-election as mayor was in serious doubt after the Yorke attack.

"The man, Your Excellency, is no gentleman. Am I, a Catholic mayor, to be thus attacked in the Catholic newspaper? I protest it in no uncertain terms. I shall complain to Rome if necessary."

Stripped of his duties, Yorke left for a year's visit to Ireland. He returned impenitent. Riordan refused to assign him to a parish, which little mattered to Yorke as he could—and can—always earn his living as a journalist. Yorke took up with Michael Casey and assisted in the formation of the Brotherhood of Teamsters. Casey was also of Yorke's and Phelan's age, the early thirties, an Irishman who immigrated here in 1889, driving a wagon twelve to fourteen hours a day, six days a week, for fifteen dollars.

I am neither a radical nor a Bolshevik—far from it! I am essentially apolitical, since as a young man I saw men die for empty words. The Teamsters' strike put together by Casey in 1901 destroyed Jimmy Phelan politically, but I cannot say that I could not see the Teamsters' point. The working people of this city worked too long and too hard for too little.

The strike broke out in late July of 1901. The longshoremen joined the Teamsters. Yorke and Casey set up a strike headquarters at Powell and Market, from where they gradually brought the city to a halt. By September more than two thousand ships lay idle in the harbor and 20,000 people were out of work. On four separate occasions Phelan tried to get negotiations started between the Employers' Association and the Teamsters. The Association brought in scabs. There were fistfights and broken skulls. Hearst backed the strike, throwing open the pages of the *Examiner* to Yorke, who defended the Teamsters' refusal to negotiate with a plethora of quotations from the encyclicals of Pope Leo XIII.

At the height of the disorder, I toured the city with Phelan in a closed carriage, escorted by two mounted police officers. A forest of masts spread along the quays, reminding me of photographs of abandoned ships left in the bay during the height of the gold rush. Police were everywhere, and lines of sullen pickets. Streetcar service had been suspended. It was a city under siege—internal siege.

"The Employers want the militia called in," Jimmy said wearily as we rattled along the cobblestoned Embarcadero.

"Hey, Jimmy Phelan," a teamster yelled at us as we drove past the Eagle Cafe at the foot of Powell Street. A group of them huddled around an impromptu field kitchen where soup was being heated and served. "Tell your fancy friends, Jimmy Phelan, to give us a decent wage." His mates jeered in agreement. One young fellow in a flat cap ran after our carriage, shaking his fist.

"The militia and lads such as those pickets would surely come to bloodshed if I allowed soldiers in the city," Jimmy said as our carriage headed down Kearny Street en route to the City Hall. "The Employers' Association accuse me of being soft on my own people, the Irish. The Irish, in turn, accuse me of favoring the wealthy. What does Aristotle say about situations like this, Sebastian?"

"He would advise you to avoid extremes. Machiavelli would advise you to seek a way around Yorke's hatred."

"You mean ask the governor in as a mediator?"

I nodded. "Yorke knows that the longer this strike lasts, the more your authority erodes with both the classes and the masses. He will soon want to deal with the governor, however, because in a very short time he will himself want to get off the back of the tiger he and Casey are riding."

"That makes me look like a fool, doesn't it? Calling in the governor because I cannot handle the situation."

"It depends, Jimmy, upon what kind of deal Governor Gage can hammer out with the strikers."

"I might ask Gage to come in—merely to bring the strike to arbitration; then I'll step in as mayor and myself arbitrate a settlement."

What Jimmy did not know was that both sides were fundamentally tired of the entire mess, but wanted a face-saving way out. The Employers secretly gave Governor

Gage authority to settle the strike. Gage personally called on Casey, Yorke, and the Teamsters' strike committee at their headquarters at Powell and Market. Yorke had the satisfaction of having the governor of California in the name of the Employers' Association of San Francisco grant the Brotherhood of Teamsters everything it demanded. Yorke had won. James Duval Phelan looked like a fool.

"I can no longer serve as mayor of this city."

"Don't be foolish, Jimmy," I urged. "The important thing is that the strike is over."

"It might have been over a lot quicker had I not stood in the way."

I could not in honesty deny Jimmy's point.

The strike committee did not dissolve itself after a settlement was signed. It reconstituted itself as the Union Labor party of San Francisco. The party's candidate, Eugene Schmitz, "Handsome Gene," an orchestra leader from the music pit of the Columbia Theater, succeeded Phelan as mayor of San Francisco. A local lawyer, Abraham Ruef, captured control of the Union Labor party, running it and San Francisco through his front-man, Schmitz. Phelan devoted the next eight years of his life to putting Ruef in San Quentin. Yorke destroyed Phelan (for a while), then Phelan in turn destroyed what Yorke had wrought, the Union Labor party.

Oh Irish! Oh poor quarreling Irish! Oh Irish poor whom I have never served! Perhaps Yorke came closer to the truth—although the compromised nature of his motivation appalls me. Yorke is no Ryan Patrice, a mystic called to a communion beyond the realms of sense. Peter Yorke is very much of this world. The papacy itself would not be honor enough for this man. His pride is better served by remaining a simple parish priest in Oakland.

I must do something with my life—I mean the rest of my life, for I have already had life aplenty. I must do something for the poor. But what? Shall I offer a course of evening lectures on baroque art at the Teamsters' Hall—like Ruskin discoursing on medieval art to English workmen? William

185

Morris believed this sort of thing should be done, but I would feel like a fool. What cares a teamster for Bernini? I sometimes think that the grand drama of my century—the rising of the masses—has utterly eluded me. I have pursued the classes, not the masses. I have spent my life on the fringes of the aristocratic condition. I have spent my life in San Francisco.

Chapter 7

W HEN I GOT BACK to my office from lunch, Don
Goldstein, San Francisco's first Jewish fire chief, was
waiting for me on the phone.

"Where in the hell have you been?" he asked. "It's nearly
three o'clock!"

"A working lunch," I said.

"I'll bet. Listen, I need some help. Tommy Delphine is
going to bring his disgraceful proposal up before the Finance
Committee of the Board of Supervisors next Thursday."

Tommy Delphine, San Francisco's first black supervisor,
wants to kick Don Goldstein, San Francisco's first Jewish fire
chief, out of the official fire chief's residence on Bush Street. In
the early 1920s a committee headed by Sebastian Collins raised
enough money to buy a lot on Bush Street near Taylor and
build an official residence for the fire chief. This was intended
as a living memorial to Chief Dennis Sullivan and all the other
firefighters who died fighting the fire of April 1906. George
Sterling wrote a poem for the occasion, which was engraved on
a bronze tablet affixed to the front of the house. The residence
combines elements of a private home and a fire department
headquarters. A driver is on twenty-four-hour call. The
upstairs bedroom has a fire alarm. In San Francisco the fire
chief is obliged to appear personally at anything above a
two-alarm fire. The fire chief's house constitutes the only

187

official civic residence in San Francisco—or at least it has since 1946 when John McLaren died. McLaren lived in Golden Gate Park, in a lovely stone lodge, done in stone Romanesque by architect Edward Swain in 1891. Neither the mayor, nor the police chief, nor the chief administrative officer has an official residence, only the fire chief.

"Why should the fire chief be any different from other department heads? How come he gets a free ride?" Supervisor Delphine harangued at the supervisors' meeting two Monday afternoons ago. Delphine had had a couple of martinis at lunch and was in a feisty mood. "What kind of elitism is this? I move that we study the possibility of selling the fire chief's house so as to put that property back on the tax rolls."

"Sandra Van Dam sent the motion to the Finance Committee for study," Goldstein told me. "Delphine will testify for it next Thursday."

"What a hell of a way to treat San Francisco's first Jewish fire chief," I said. "What do you want me to do?"

"Lead a counter-attack. Get all of the San Francisco-freaks out to protest. Say things like: 'You cannot bring back the dead, nor can you dissolve the covenant we have with them.'"

"Actually," I said, "that's not a bad defense of your place. It's a quasi shrine and must be covered by laws guaranteeing its invulnerability to sale."

"You bet your sweet ass, it's a good defense," Goldstein said. "I'm not San Francisco's first Jewish fire chief for nothing. This place is a monument, a shrine. It shouldn't be sold. Besides, I like not having to pay rent."

"Think about a compromise," I said. "The fact that you get your house for free makes you vulnerable to Delphine's attack. Say that you'll volunteer to pay the property taxes on the place. That way, Delphine's argument is weakened."

"Ouch!"

"Listen," I said, "who else can live for free like you do? The property taxes will come to no more than $3,000 a year. That's less than $300 a month."

"I think I'll denounce Delphine as an anti-Semite,"

Goldstein said. "He doesn't like me because I'm San Francisco's first Jewish fire chief. Whatever happens, Norton, I expect to hear some thunderous cadences from you in my defense. Think of the history this place represents. Sebastian Collins would roll over in his grave if the city sold the fire chief's place. Jesus, Sunny Jim Rolph himself dedicated it."

"I risk my ass going against Delphine," I said. "Mabel Storm wants me to woo the supervisors, not antagonize them. They pay our bills, you know."

"Do it for me, Norton my boy. Do it for the sake of this city's glorious past. Do it for your old pal, Don Goldstein, San Francisco's first Jewish fire chief."

I spent the rest of the afternoon with the Friends of Books, preparing for our five-thirty audience with His Honor the Mayor on the Marshall Square issue. The Friends trooped into my office at three-thirty and we met until five o'clock. Albert Esau, director of planning, also dropped by—very reluctantly. Mabel Storm had put the pressure on him. Esau sulked throughout the entire meeting, looking frequently at his watch. He left early.

Library Commissioner Mabel Storm looked loaded for bear when she led the Friends into my office. I'm convinced that as we grow older most of us develop a fixed look or ambience depending upon the time in our life when our identities went through their final consolidation. Mabel Storm is late 1940s. She wears her hair in a late-1940s roll. Her hats have a late-1940s rake to them, and the shoulders on her suits are padded, 1940s style. She wears fox furs around her shoulders as they did in the late 1940s.

Mabel Storm would have been in her late twenties in the late 1940s (she's in her late fifties now) when—bingo!—she coalesced as San Francisco's leading clubwoman-activist. When he died in 1948, Mabel's late father, Treadwell Barnes, the boon companion and business associate of the late Lou Lurie, left Mabel loads of money. After Vassar and a childless marriage with Timothy Storm (whom no one ever sees; rumor has it that he spends a lot of time traveling back East and

189

abroad), Mabel Storm came into her inheritance and settled on public service, more precisely the San Francisco Public Library, as her mission in life. In the mid-fifties Mabel organized the Friends of Books, an auxiliary society devoted to raising money for the Library and promoting its best interests through public programs and political support. As president of the Friends and simultaneously president of the Library Commission, standing some six feet in her Andrews Sisters high heels, Mabel Storm runs the Library. That means she runs me—like a top sergeant.

Mabel loathes Claudio Carpino and she loathes me because Carpino has forced me onto the Library Commission as city librarian. She said to my face, no less (you have to say this for Mabel Storm: she speaks her mind), that I was a political hack. I had turned the Library into a political football. She told me that when Carpino gets out of office, I would go out of office. That is why I hope that Claudio Carpino will be elected governor. I'd rather be state librarian than unemployed.

Mabel Storm's twenty-year dream is to build a new library on Marshall Square, on the order of what the Boston Public Library has done on Copley Square. The library Mabel envisions would cost nearly $90 million at today's construction costs. This would make it the most expensive building ever built in San Francisco, public or private. A bond issue would have to be authorized by two-thirds plus one of the city's voters. As Albert Esau says, San Francisco just isn't a library town. There is no way in the world that such a bond issue could ever get to the voters, much less be passed by them. But Mabel Storm dreams on. A new library on Marshall Square is her Emerald City of Oz, or, more correctly, the monument she wishes to construct in order to justify thirty years of meetings, fund-raisers, lobbying efforts, and hearings before the Finance Committee of the Board of Supervisors. Mabel frequently drops broad hints that she'll make a sizable contribution to the bond campaign fund, if and when it gets off the ground.

I am in a delicate position, and I know it. Carpino and Downtown want Marshall Square. Mabel Storm, hence the

Library, wants Marshall Square. I hate working for the rich. I hate the way Mabel Storm is late for every appointment, the way she tediously rambles on and on and on as to how she is working her fingers to the bone for the Library. I despise, but must endure, her less-than-delicate hints that to oppose her is to invoke the wrath of the San Francisco Jewish community.

Esau opposes her, and he's Jewish. He opposed her this afternoon. "I won't be bullied," he bellowed. "It's a stupid idea to hold up a solid project like the Performing Arts Center for a pie-in-the-sky dream that has nothing behind it, neither common sense nor good planning in political juice."

I wish I could be as outspoken as Esau.

"We won't be bullied either," Mabel shot back in that little-girl-going-on-sixty way of hers, "not after we've worked our fingers to the bone."

The meeting was a disaster in terms of turning Esau around. In terms of steaming up the Friends for their meeting with Carpino, it was a resounding success. Around five o'clock we stalked across Civic Center to City Hall. I felt like a Thracian warrior captured by a platoon of angry amazons. I half expected Mabel Storm to take me by the scruff of my neck and march me across the Civic Center.

"Remember, James," she said, "we expect vigorous advocacy from our city librarian. No politics. No backroom deals."

We sat in the outer office of Room 200 under a resplendent oil portrait of Mayor Rolph—myself and about twenty women of early, middle, and late middle age. Jesus, what I don't have to do to make a living! I recalled how Carpino's eyes hooded over earlier this morning on the boat when I reminded him that Mabel Storm had been his appointment to the Commission. Carpino could ask for her resignation any time. I knew he wouldn't: then it would mean he would have to face the wrath of the Jewish community for firing one of its prominent daughters who for thirty years had worked her fingers to the bone, or so Mabel Storm says.

Carpino rose from his Louis XIV desk and beamed a greeting as we all filed in. Even Mabel Storm needed a second or two to recover from the dazzling effect Carpino's splendid office has on visitors. The Mayor's friend, architect Mario Tosi, was there also, standing next to an architectural model. It showed the Main Library, cleverly augmented by a rear annex on Hyde Street. Tosi's design completes the square of the Library's three wings. It makes a lot of sense.

"Delighted, delighted," Carpino beamed. "I've asked Mario Tosi to join us this afternoon. I think he has a way out of this Marshall Square dilemma."

Mario wheeled the model in front of the row of chairs where the ladies of the Friends sat frozen-faced. Mario is an elegant man, near sixty and a wonderful tennis player. His tie and pocket handkerchief were a mustard-colored silk; his suit, light gray. A gold tooth flashed forth from his tanned Adolphe Menjou face as he talked.

"What I propose," he said, "is that we finish the unfinished square of the Library's three wings this way, by building along Hyde Street. The trustees would have done this in 1917, had they not run short of funds. May I quote to you from the trustees' report to Mayor Rolph on this matter, dated 15 June 1917 and signed by Sebastian Collins, president of the trustees." Mario took a typed sheet from his pocket.

" 'Since the second installment of the Carnegie grant has turned out to be less money than originally expected,' Sebastian Collins writes in 1917, 'we shall not be able to finish the Hyde Street wing of the Library. The completion of the Library awaits the industry of a future generation.' "

"It is for us to complete this work," Tosi pleaded with the Friends. "A fourth wing could be built for as little as $15 million, certainly no more than $20 million. Ours is an age of recycling and reuse. Here in San Francisco the reinvigoration of older buildings is an art form. I suggest that the entire Marshall Square controversy is unnecessary. It wastes the very energies that we should be putting behind the logical expansion of the Library on Hyde Street."

"We've worked our fingers to the bone for a new library on Marshall Square," Mabel Storm blurted out, oblivious to the

192

logic of Tosi's presentation. "We won't have it taken from us now."

The Brown Bomber, incidentally, has struck again—this time in the Commission Room. When he opened the room up this morning, Manny Vogel, the commission secretary, found a fecal deposit under the commission table. The Brown Bomber (that's what everybody calls him) has previously left his calling card in the freight elevator, the female employees' locker room, and next to the religious books section of the third-floor stacks. It's obvious that the culprit is someone from the staff. Commissioner Mabel Storm has heard about the latest incident and is raising holy hell. If the Brown Bomber ever gets into Harry Shaw's column, she screams, it will ruin the reputation of the Library.

I spent the evening at home, drinking two Heinekens and going over some folders of material I have collected for my Sebastian Collins biography. I'm determined to keep this project moving despite the pressures of my job. I read a rather long and very detailed account in Collins's journal of a luncheon party given by Phelan at Montalvo in April of 1914, attended by Herbert Hoover and Franklin Roosevelt. Collins makes no mention of Hoover's and Roosevelt's attitudes towards each other. I suppose Hoover felt superior to Roosevelt because Hoover was a self-made man. Roosevelt, the dashing Harvard-accented aristocrat, must have put Hoover on edge. There's no mention of Eleanor Roosevelt at the luncheon; but Collins does mention Lou Henry Hoover, whom Will Irwin, Hoover's classmate at Stanford, once described as an absolutely stunning beauty as a Stanford co-ed in the mid-nineties, when Hoover first met her. Hoover would have been about forty at the time Collins encountered him at Montalvo. He'd made a fortune in Australian mining and had served for a short time as director of mines for the Emperor of China before retiring to London to translate Agricola's *De Re Metallica*. Collins doesn't say it, but Stanford President David

193

Starr Jordan must have beamed down with deep gratification at the Hoovers that day from his six-foot four-inch height. The Hoovers were not just the Gibson Man and the Gibson Girl, California style; they were the Stanford man and Stanford woman of Jordan's fondest eugenic hopes—dashing about the world, making money, meeting the people who counted, carrying the newly unfurled flag of Stanford everywhere they went.

I had no idea that Phelan was such an ardent navy man. It makes sense, however: the American navy bringing a *pax Americana* to the Pacific and using San Francisco as its major port. When he was mayor, Phelan had a monument erected to Admiral Dewey in Union Square. To Phelan's way of thinking, Dewey's conquest of Manila Bay was the first step of San Francisco's rise to imperial status. The second was the opening of the Panama Canal. In discussing the rising power of Japan, Phelan uses a striking metaphor. "California," he says (I quote Collins's journal), "is an American Laocoön, the Trojan priest strangled by serpents that came from the sea. Someday the Japanese will send serpents across the sea in an effort to destroy us." Phelan distrusted the Japanese. He tried to prevent them from immigrating to California, seeing in Japanese immigrants a probable fifth column movement once a Japanese attack were launched. Jack London (so Collins indicates) agreed with Phelan. In 1904, covering the Russo-Japanese War in Manchuria, London saw the Japanese crush the Russians: a stunning victory in Japan's first war against Europeans.

Roosevelt, Collins writes, mentioned the books of Homer Lea, whom David Starr Jordan detested—despite the fact that Lea had gone to Stanford. Lea, a little hunchback from Los Angeles, was a military genius. At Stanford in the nineties he fell in with Sun Yat-sen, then in exile in San Francisco, plotting the overthrow of the dowager Empress Tsi An. Lea fought with Sun Yat-sen in the unsuccessful rebellion of 1900, attaining the rank of lieutenant general. When he returned to Los Angeles he wrote two books—*The Valor of Ignorance* and

194

The Day of the Saxon—warning the United States of the imperial ambitions of the Japanese. Lea even included detailed plans and maps as to how the Japanese might land in California and hold it from counter-attack. Jordon hated Lea because he felt that the Japanese were a peaceful people, given to ritual tea ceremonies and floral arranging. He kept silence, however, when Roosevelt told Jack London that Homer Lea's work was taken very seriously by the navy's leading admirals.

Claudio Carpino could have used some naval support this afternoon when Mabel Storm raked his bow with verbal gunfire. I felt sorry for Carpino. His campaign can't seem to get off the ground. Soutane got great coverage on TV this evening when he served in the food line at St. Anthony's Dining Room here on Jones Street in San Francisco. Soutane put on an apron and scooped out, according to the television reporter Linda Schact, 735 mounds of mashed potatoes, over which he poured 735 ladles full of gravy.

"I'm here," Soutane told Ms. Schact, talking and scooping at the same time, "because Father Lloyd Tetzio and I were fellow novices when I studied for the Franciscan Order. Father Lloyd has asked me to drop by and help out."

Soutane served a generous portion of mashed potatoes to a very elderly man in a tattered overcoat held together by safety pins. The old man piped up in a wheezy but firm voice, so that the microphone picked it up: "God bless you, boy! I hope you're our next governor."

Soutane managed a soulful Franciscan glance.

"I'm also here," he told Ms. Schact, "because I want to emphasize the fact that there's a nutritional crisis among the elderly. The old, living on fixed incomes, aren't eating properly. Cats and dogs are better nourished than are many of our inner-city elderly. I want to do something about this tragedy."

The camera cut to Father Lloyd Tetzio in his brown Franciscan habit.

"Andy Soutane left the Franciscans," Father Lloyd told about a million Bay Area evening news watchers. "But he's still one of us. He's still sensitive to the needs of the poor—like Christ and St. Francis."

And here I was with photographs that showed this latter-day Christ and St. Francis in the throes of an unnatural act with columnist Stedman Mooner. It doesn't hang together; but then again, perhaps it does hang together, perhaps our modern world has evolved a new form of sincerity, media sincerity, which isn't your old-fashioned phoniness of hypocrisy, but rather an ability to live on split, even contradictory levels of experience without being torn apart by the tension. Soutane might very well be capable of being two people at once, a private self and a media self, and not feel anxiety over it because today most of modern America is living this way: living in a deficient private self and a fulfilled media self, a self sustained by a constant process of auto-connoisseurship and fantasy, as if one were continuously watching oneself on television.

I got up from my desk and walked over to my window to enjoy the view that adds about $200 a month to my rent. No wonder I don't mind paying $400 a month for a studio. A constant pageant unfolds before my Telegraph Hill window. Now it was the drama of the nighttime bay: the lights from Treasure Island across the water; the glittery arch of the Bay Bridge; the floodlights of the Oakland piers, loading and unloading on a twenty-four-hours-a-day schedule.

By ten-thirty I had finished some notes on Gertrude Atherton. In his account of the Montalvo luncheon, Collins doesn't say much about Mrs. Atherton except that she was wearing one of her hats. April 1914 would have been just months after Mrs. Atherton's resettlement in California. Leaving San Francisco in 1888, along with her friend Sybil Sanderson, Gertrude Atherton spent nearly thirty years abroad, in London and Munich mostly, supporting herself with a constant stream of novels, many of them set in San Francisco. Collins is right: she did wear outrageous hats, even in an era of outrageous hats. She was sixtyish at the time Collins writes and, I suppose, above sexual scandal. Phelan, in

196

any event, then in his mid-fifties, maintained a room for her at Montalvo where she spent many long week-ends, acting as his hostess. Whether or not there was a sexual connection between her and Phelan is a matter of conjecture; yet over the years Mrs. Atherton had men enough in her life—ever since that day on her porch in Menlo Park when she opened a keg of brandy and discovered she was a widow. Her husband George died on a Chilean man-of-war in the course of a voyage to South America. The Chilean Navy shipped him back to Menlo Park in a brandy barrel to preserve the body. "I opened the keg," Mrs. Atherton would later say, "and there was George."

Phelan loved actresses and opera singers. He paid assiduous court to the actress Margaret Anglin (so spirited as Roxanne in Edmond Rostand's *Cyrano de Bergerac*) and Nellie Melba, the famous coloratura soprano; but whether these connections ever became sexual is difficult to say. When Sybil Sanderson returned in triumph to San Francisco in 1901, Phelan took her and Sebastian Collins to dine in the Cliff House. Collins's journal accounts of Sanderson's return make superb reading. I must say, however, that Collins almost completely eliminates the personal factor from his *Sybil Sanderson, A California Story* (1910), which is a well written and very objective account of the Sacramento-born diva's tumultuous career. In the privacy of his journal, however, Collins is totally honest. I admire his candor, and I envy his frank acknowledgment of thwarted passion and aberrant desire. People seemed to live such grand lives in the nineteenth century. The San Franciscans of Collins's reminiscences all seem so full of appetite for everything of spirit and flesh that life has to offer.

Deborah said that she would be out this evening—with some tennis-playing Elliott Gould bastard no doubt!—but since it was eleven o'clock and a work day tomorrow, she might be just getting home. It took me five minutes to overcome my reluctance to telephone at such a rude hour of the night.

"Have fun?" I said, with some sulk in my voice.

197

"We went to a movie—a French film about erotic obsession."

"Did he like it?"

"She loved it."

I felt relieved.

"I'm thinking of you," I said.

"I feel flattered. I also feel tired."

"Let me come over."

"No."

"Come over here."

"No."

"Don't be difficult."

"Yes."

"I've got a great view."

"So look at it."

"What are you doing?"

"Getting ready for bed."

"I'd like to be there with you."

"That would be both distasteful and immoral."

"Distasteful?"

"Perhaps not distasteful—just tacky. I despise cheap promiscuity. Why should I wake up in the morning with some strange lug in my bed, snoring like a pig, or walking around the house in his jockey shorts, while I fix breakfast as if he owned the place?"

"Immoral?"

"Yes, immoral. It's a good word. Look it up in the dictionary. It means being selfish and dumb and tacky. For elaboration, consult Thomas Aquinas."

"Don't be defensive."

"Don't be so transparently horny. If you're horny, open the *Playboy* centerfold and fiddle with yourself. Don't call me up with the froggy voice."

"Froggy?"

"Yes. Like a bullfrog throaty with lust."

"In this day and age, lust is a blessing."

"Potency is a blessing. Lust is never a blessing."

198

"How do you know about Thomas Aquinas?"

"I'm a librarian, remember. I'm also a Catholic."

"This is getting to sound like a Graham Greene novel."

"I love Graham Greene," she said.

"So do I."

"Then we have that in common. Let's talk about Graham Greene."

"We will, on Sunday, if you're free," I said. "Warner Conrad is giving a luncheon party this Sunday at his place in Palo Alto. Come with me."

"You know Warner Conrad?"

"I know everybody. That's my business."

"I'll come along to meet Warner Conrad. I love his novels."

"I love you."

"You said as much at lunch. Don't be tiresome. It's late. Crawl into your flannel bunny jammies and go night-night."

"Yes, Mother."

"And remember one thing."

"What?"

"Abstinence makes the heart grow fonder."

"I'm growing fonder of you by the minute."

She made a kissing sound over the telephone and then hung up.

If I had had a pair of six-foot bunny jammies in the house, I sure as hell would have put them on in Deborah's honor. I lay awake thinking of her curly head on the pillow. I felt peaceful and secure, like a child. Then I went night-night, hearing the low moan of foghorns as I lost consciousness. At night a foghorn can sometimes sound like a wounded animal crying for its mate.

I needed my rest because my first appointment the next morning was with Leah Mae Hyster.

"You've got a racist staff here," Leah Mae Hyster hissed at me in cold fury. "You've got a racist library in a racist city."

There wasn't much I could say. Miss Hyster was plenty angry. A small, determined woman, light brown in color,

199

Miss Hyster comes from Washington, D.C. Her family has been in federal civil service since Reconstruction. Her grandfather, a Fisk University graduate, served as American Vice Consul to Martinique just before the First World War and was among the first black Americans to reach consular rank in the foreign service. Miss Hyster herself attended Howard University, then went on to the University of Maryland for library school. San Francisco recruited her ten years ago from the Enoch Pratt Free Public Library in Baltimore to serve as our special projects coordinator.

In a constant stream of scattered asides, Miss Hyster lets it be known that she has nothing but contempt for San Francisco, including black San Francisco. In contrast to Washington, she says, San Francisco has next to no black middle or upper middle class—just a bunch of ignorant darkies up from the cotton fields of the South (her phrase, not mine), brought to the Bay Area by Henry J. Kaiser during the Second World War to work in the shipyards.

"The blacks of this city are their own worst enemy," Miss Hyster said to me on one occasion. "They're either shuffling along like Bojangles or jiving it up like Sammy Davis, Jr. But they're not getting into the professions. They're not reading."

Miss Hyster spent the first forty years of her life trying to out-genteel the genteel. Her enunciation is perfect. She dresses like an ad in *Ebony* magazine, with great taste. She is, after all, a good-looking woman. She was in San Francisco only a year when she ended her spinsterhood by marrying the most prominent black mortician in the city, a widower, and moving her books, her lavish wardrobe, her thirty pairs of shoes, her collection of African primitive masks, and her French Creole furniture from Martinique (bequeathed her by her grandfather at his death in 1955) into a new home in St. Francis Wood. The Hysters were the first black family to buy a home in that enclave of white respectability.

I got the item about the thirty pairs of shoes from Sarah Panel, chief of branches, with whom Leah Mae Hyster is ever at war. Sarah Panel herself has but one pair of shoes, to judge

200

from what she wears inevitably to work—a pair of sensible Red Cross shoes.

Miss Hyster's collection of African primitive masks dates from her recent conversion to ethnicity. After forty years of ambivalence, she discovered blackness, or rather, she discovered the political advantages of being black in the highly charged context of social change. She is thus at psychological cross purposes: an upper-middle-class black woman despising the less-than-middle-class black culture of San Francisco, yet thrown into the black camp to advance her career in an age of affirmative action. Result: her latent resentment of white people, suppressed in her family through four generations of federal civil service culminated by the appointment of Marcus Catesby Jones to Martinique in 1912 (they say a portrait of him in full consular regalia hangs over the fireplace in the Hyster's Tudor Gothic home in St. Francis Wood), this latent hostility to whites has surfaced with vengeance. Miss Leah Mae Hyster, special projects coordinator for the San Francisco Public Library, has a score to settle. As a result Miss Leah Mae Hyster is very difficult to get along with.

She threatens my every other administrative decision with an NAACP investigation. Once, when I ordered the transfer of a white librarian to the branch library in Bayview—Hunter's Point, she went to the Human Rights Commission and had me investigated for racism: for trying, she said, to deprive the black children of Hunter's Point of black role models. Actually, I was only trying to separate two black librarians, both working at the branch, who couldn't stand each other and hence fought constantly. Unfortunately, I didn't have another black librarian to replace the one I transferred. The Human Rights Commission investigator, a black man, backed me in my decision, as did Danny Parker, the Library's affirmative action officer; but the whole thing was embarrassing and unpleasant. Like Joe McCarthy tagging you for a communist in the early 1950s, get tagged a racist in San Francisco city government these days and you're screwed good. Jeremiah Jones, for starters, San Francisco's flamboyant, Maserati-

driving black assemblyman, and Supervisor Tommy Delphine, the uncrowned king of Bayview–Hunter's Point, will
nail your hide to the wall. Around San Francisco, blacks have
mastered all the old-fashioned political skills, including
vengeance. They have learned to take care of their own. Piss
enough of them off and you're finished. I saw it happen to our
erstwhile port director, who crossed swords with the black
vice-president of the Longshoremen's Union. For the port
director in question it was very soon bye-bye time. He's now
running a third-rate port in New Guinea. I am therefore
always very careful with Miss Leah Mae Hyster, special
projects coordinator.

"I agree that racism pervades our society, Miss Hyster," I
said piously, "but let's fight it here together in the Library.
Let's fight it as a community."

"Then give me back the senior steno-typist you took out of
my budget," she shot back. Miss Hyster already has one
secretary. Now she wants another one. "I need more clerical
backup to do the administration necessary for my outreach
programs," she continued, her eyes alight with ophidian rage.
I noticed that the bridge of her nose is speckled like a bird's
egg. "If I'm not properly supported, then I can't get the
proper work load out. It's racist not to support black people in
their efforts to help other black people."

"Let's take it to the Administrative Council," I said.

This is a code way of saying, "OK, you can have it. I give
up." Once a request for new personnel gets out in the open
before the Administrative Council, it normally becomes part
of next year's budget. The section chiefs rarely interfere with
the prerogatives of one another. I gave in gracefully. I had no
other choice. Miss Hyster left my office with a look of
satisfaction on her face, as though she had just slapped the face
of the Grand Dragon of the Ku Klux Klan right in the inner
sanctum of Klan headquarters. One of these days I'm going to
learn how to stand up to her. An open confrontation would be
self-defeating. She is, after all, black. Out-maneuvering her
politically seems next to impossible. She's a master strategist

at bureaucratic infighting. Her family has been in civil service for nearly a hundred years. I've only been on the public dole for three years, and I'm not very good at bureaucratic warfare.

I picked up the *Express* and reread Harry Shaw's nasty item in this morning's paper.

"It was almost a TKO at Sunday brunch at the Garden Court of the Palace Hotel," Shaw wrote this morning. "Irate at hizzoner (even lovebirds now and then quarrel!), Madama Mayora herself took a swing at the old boy in full view of the admiring throng. His Eminence Carpino, the Clown Prince of our Bayside Bohemia, beat a hasty retreat before a pursuing barrage of the Palace Court's world-famous raisin toast. Speaking of throwing away your brunch, I felt that way the other nooner at the San Domenico. It was dizzzzzzgusting. Owner Dominic St. Pierre had better go back into the bank business. My beef *bourgignon* tasted like mess call in the French Foreign Legion. Even Corporal Henry Africa would prefer to march or die before assaulting such *bas cuisine*. By the way, guess what bookish City official was at the San Domenico enduring the cuisine along with me? He consoled himself, however, with making goo-goo eyes at a leggy young lovely. They stayed till 2:30. No wonder City government is in such a mess! Nobody does any work any more."

I called Terry Shane. As usual, he sounded harassed.

"It was Esmeralda all right. She was angry with the Mayor over Audrey Yee. Esmeralda thinks Audrey is balling the Mayor, or that the Mayor is balling Audrey, depending on how you look at it, which Audrey isn't, but Esmeralda thinks she is and that's what's important. Esmeralda demanded that the Mayor transfer Audrey out of this office."

I can easily imagine it, a switch play on Jimmy Cagney and the grapefruit: Esmeralda Carpino, her nostrils flaring upwards to match the upward sweep of her henna-red hair, launching a slide of world-famous Palace Hotel raisin toast at the Lord Mayor of San Francisco: the powerful, articulate, cultivated, elegant Claudio Carpino—in full view of assorted brunching tourists and San Franciscans, one of whom snitched to Harry

Shaw. Esmeralda has a temper, that's for sure; most Sicilians do.

Family and money—that's what Sicilians are all about. Claudio Carpino has acquired an overlay of northern Italian culture—an interest in art, books, ideas—but his most basic motivation, I'm certain, revolves around the ties of blood and the lure of the dollar sign. I can only sense this as an outside observer, but I bring to my intuition the reinforcement of historical imagination. Sicily is not Europe, nor is it Africa. It's a little of both. As a family, the Carpinos are close and secretive. As I said before, the Mayor rarely entertains outside of family occasions. The Carpino family speaks the Sicilian dialect at home. The Mayor's sons wear dark suits and kiss their father on the forehead in formal greeting, Sicilian style.

The Mayor has three sons, all of them lawyers, and all of them associated with him in his firm. Carpino is Sicilian—close to his sons. Fierce pride comes into his eyes when they're around. Umberto, the oldest at thirty-three, is quiet and scholarly. He reads Voltaire in French and plays a lot of golf. Carpino is proud of Umberto's gentlemanly attainments: his Stanford undergraduate training, his Yale Law School degree, his restrained Ivy League elegance. Umberto had to be cajoled into the law. He would have preferred to become a professor of French literature. Rocky Carpino is a thirty-year-old bachelor. He drives a big black Cadillac and wears dark suits and Homburg hats. They say Rocky is a piranha fish of a trial attorney who loves the bloody gore of courtroom combat. A graduate of Santa Clara University and the Hastings Law School, Rocky has none of Umberto's gentlemanly pretensions. Rocky likes women and race horses. I've seen him at La Stampa's, a North Beach betting bar, with some incredibly gorgeous broads. I suspect that Rocky is the Mayor's favorite son—or maybe just the Mayor's favorite lawyer among his sons; for Rocky has been handling a lot of the legal business since Carpino became mayor. Terry Shane says that Carpino calls Rocky every morning around ten for a half-hour or so to give him direction on pending cases. The youngest son, Dante Carpino (his nickname is Sonny Grande), plays the stock market. Each of the Carpino sons exaggerates an aspect of his father's personality. Umberto has expanded his father's interest in the arts; Rocky, his interest in courtroom law and good-looking women. Sonny Grande likes money even more than his father likes money, and that's saying something because Claudio Carpino is obsessed by money. Rocky stays close to his father regarding trial strategies. Umberto and the Mayor discuss scholarly points of law. With Sonny Grande, he discusses investments.

It's difficult to say just exactly how the Carpino money is invested. There's a cheese business in San Leandro, a lot of real estate (including a choice corner of Russian Hill), and a pretty extensive portfolio, managed by Sonny Grande. The Carpinos are experts at getting rich using other people's money. "Never gamble on your own dough," is the way Sonny Grande puts it. "And always take your tax advantages." Just last year the Mayor donated a slug of land he owns in lower Santa Clara County to his *alma mater* San Anselmo College. He bought the property about ten years ago for $50,000, paying some $10,000 down. Last year he had a friend of his in the real estate business appraise it at $500,000, then donated the property to his *alma mater* as an income tax deduction of $750,000. Aside from the fact that Carpino paid no income taxes because of the donation, the Archbishop of San Francisco made him a Knight of Malta to boot. Not a bad return on a $10,000 investment.

"The $10,000 was probably borrowed in the first place," says Terry Shane. Terry is a little bitter, having paid for too many of Carpino's taxi fares and hot dogs at the airport.

I'm amazed how a passion for making money has survived through three generations of Carpinos. Rocky and Sonny Grande are as grasping as Sicilian peasants just off the boat, despite the fact that the Carpino family is in the third generation of its American prosperity. I find something deliberately unassimilated, resistant in a Sicilian sort of way, in this compulsive activity on behalf of gain. The Carpinos are already worth $20 million. Isn't that enough? I identify strongly with Umberto, the scholarly son who is my age, although he has rebuffed a few efforts I have made to become friendly. I am, after all, not family. I only share his love of books.

When it comes to the Carpino money, however, I'm probably guilty of sour grapes. I belong to the genre of Irish who seemed doomed to financial failure, the sort who work for wages all their life and for whom a pension, usually a government pension, constitutes a dazzling financial success. My family is fifth-generation American Irish, but not one of us ever had little more than a pot to piss in, and sometimes not even that.

My maternal great-grandfather was a teamster; my maternal grandfather, a fireman. Until his untimely death from a brain tumor at the age of twenty-seven, my father worked in the shipyards at Hunter's Point. His father drove a streetcar for the Market Street Railway, and his grandfather, my paternal great-grandfather, spent forty years atop a horse-drawn hansom cab. I've often speculated that he, James Vincent Norton (after whom I'm named), probably had the pleasure of driving Sebastian Collins home at night when Collins emerged merrily from the Bohemian Club after an evening's entertainment. My great-grandfather Norton (1848–1910) owned his own cab, but he rented his horses. He drove from 1865 to 1905, basing himself at a stand outside the Palace Hotel on Market and Kearny Streets. In any event, neither he, nor his son, my grandfather the streetcar driver (1870–1942), nor my father (1918–1946), nor my maternal great-grandfather the teamster (1847–1930), nor my maternal grandfather the fireman (1870–1925) ever made, or saved, a goddam dime. We—and that includes me—have nothing to show for nearly one hundred and twenty years in San Francisco, while the Carpinos have $20 million to show for slightly more than half that time. And here I am, a Carpino dependent—although it

206

is the taxpayers, not the Carpinos, who are picking up the cost of my upkeep! My genes, no doubt, are those of a client people, the sort of people championed by Father Peter Yorke. Despite my Harvard Ph.D., I seem destined to remain a member of the laboring classes, like three generations of Nortons and O'Hallorans before me.

The fact is: had I even an iota of Carpino's money, I'd most likely spend it—like an Irishman with a winning ticket in the Sweepstakes. I'd buy books. I'd travel. I'd improve my wine cellar. The most prudent thing I could manage—if I could even manage that!—would be to invest in tax-free municipal bonds and live off the interest. At best, in other words, I'd turn the money into a pension, Irish style. I guess that deep down I desire to be in civil service. After graduating from the University of San Francisco, I spent two years studying for the diocesan priesthood at St. Patrick's Seminary in Menlo Park. Had I persevered to ordination, the Archdiocese of San Francisco would have taken care of me for life: a nice apartment in a comfortable rectory, three meals a day, and a couple of hundred dollars a month in spending money. Failing that sinecure, I've landed in civil service; only my appointment as city librarian does not have civil service tenure. I just don't have the instinct for money, for business, for investments. How easy the Carpinos make it seem—getting rich. No one in my ancestral tree grasped, nor do I grasp. My response to the Carpino greed—for greed it must be called: a constant, ever-hungry greed—my response is a mixture of contempt and envy. Like Sebastian Collins, I'll probably go through life with my mind on matters other than making a buck.

Marina Collins Scannell, by the way, Sebastian Collins's daughter and John Charles Scannell's widow, does not live with the Little Sisters of the Poor at St. Anne's Home on Lake Street because she has to. Her son, John Charles Scannell II, president of the Trans-Pacific Corporation, can well afford to take care of her. Mrs. Scannell, so Mrs. Pennyworth of the History Room says, simply prefers to live with the sisters, paying her own way for a small room, and devoting a number of hours every day to helping the sisters out with other, less vigorous residents.

"She's very alert," says Mrs. Pennyworth. "She likes to be useful, and she's a mine of information about old San Francisco."

When I get into high gear on the Sebastian Collins book, I'll ask Mrs. Scannell for an interview. If she has a sense of humor, I'll tell her that I find the fact that her son, the grandson of Sebastian Collins, built the Trans-Pacific Pyramid rather amusing.

In recent years, since the tension started, the Carpinos have gathered for their immemorial Sunday dinners at daughter Barbara's home on Commonwealth Avenue in Jordan Park. Not that I've ever been invited. This is just what I hear from bits and pieces dropped here and there in the course of the Mayor's casual conversation. Claudio Carpino, by the way, has made the down payment on a home for each of his married children. He'll buy Rocky a place if and when Rocky ever settles down. Preferring a country squire's life, Umberto lives in Hillsborough. Sonny Grande has a Moorish style mansion in the Marina. Barbara's Jordan Park townhouse has become the family's neutral ground ever since the Mayor and Esmeralda have been having trouble. By meeting on Sunday nights there, no one has to take sides between his or her father or mother. Barbara graduated from Dominican College in San Rafael and is married to the owner of the Villa Toscana Restaurant on Francisco Street in North Beach. She's in her mid-twenties and seems a nice enough kid, overshadowed perhaps by her brothers, which is common enough, I suppose, in Sicilian families.

I can easily imagine them all together on a Sunday evening at Barbara's these days: the Mayor doing his best to keep Esmeralda in good humor; Umberto in expensive casual clothes and Gucci loafers, flipping idly through the pages of a French classic; his wife Dorothea—a refined, fawn-like creature from

208

Providence, Rhode Island, who was taking a master's degree in Italian at Yale when she met Umberto—fussing over their three children; the children themselves, two boys and a girl, dressed as expensively as possible, running, perhaps, over to where Esmeralda sits on the couch near Rocky, who is watching the last minutes of the football game on television. Barbara is cooking in the kitchen, while her infant daughter, another Esmeralda, sits in a high chair eating strawberry Jello. Sonny Grande and his wife Cecilia—a former secretary in the Carpino law office—play cards with the Mayor in a library alcove off the living room. The bookshelves are filled with humanities paperbacks from Barbara's days at Dominican College. The tension between Esmeralda and the Mayor is suppressed by the rituals of family life; for the Carpinos have been getting together this way on Sunday evenings, one generation or another, ever since the Mayor's father and mother married in 1908.

Claudio Carpino senior came to San Francisco from Sant'Ursula, a fishing village in Sicily, in 1905. He was eighteen at the time. On a far corner wall at the Rainieri Restaurant in North Beach, there's a wedding photograph, taken in 1908, showing Claudio Carpino and his bride, Emelda Scosano, at their wedding dinner. The elder Carpino was evidently doing well by then, for the wedding party looks prosperous enough—the men in frock coats and stiff white shirts, the women in lace dresses. The Mayor's mother wears a Botticellian floral fillet on her head and has a wistful look in her eyes. In this photograph you can see the resemblance between Emelda Scosano and Barbara Carpino.

Claudio Carpino senior met his wife during the evacuation of San Francisco sometime between the eighteenth and twentieth of April 1906. Carpino ferried hundreds of Italians escaping from a burning North Beach across the bay to Sausalito in his fishing boat, accumulating a small fortune in cash in the process. With this money, Claudio Carpino senior went into the wholesale fish business after North Beach was rebuilt. He constructed a packing house at the foot of Hyde

209

Street in the area now known as Fisherman's Wharf. Emelda's family, the Scosanos, also in the fishing business, owned a fleet of about ten vessels. When Claudio Carpino senior went over to the Scosano home on Filbert Street to ask for Emelda's hand in the formal Sicilian fashion, he talked business as well as marriage. Emelda waited expectantly in another room, thinking the talk was all about her—her beauty, how much Claudio loved her, the details of the wedding, the dowry. Actually (so Mayor Carpino now tells the story), the marriage details were worked out in short order. Claudio Carpino senior and Signor Scosano then commenced talking business. The would-be son-in-law made his prospective father-in-law an offer he could not refuse: join the Scosano fleet and the Carpino packing house into one operation, acquire a trucking company, then dominate the catching and the distribution of fresh fish to the markets and restaurants of the Bay Area.

For nearly half a century the firm of Carpino and Scosano has been taking fish and crab from the sea, packing it into boxes of ice at the Hyde Street sheds, then shipping the petrale, rex sole, ling cod, sand dabs, salmon, crabs, oysters and halibut to restaurants and markets from San Jose to Santa Rosa. The Mayor's parents have both been dead for fifteen years now. They died in the same year, Claudio Carpino senior going first. A cousin, Ignazio Scosano, now runs the fish business for Carpino Enterprises. The Mayor is still very fond of the Wharf ambience. Terry Shane likes to capitalize on this whenever he can, playing up the Mayor as a simple Sicilian son of the sea: which is bullshit. Carpino went out in a fishing boat once or twice as a kid to see what it was like. By the time he was born in 1915, however, his father was already a prosperous North Beach *patrone* who owned a home on Telegraph Hill, attended the opera with regularity, and read voraciously in the Harvard Classics to compensate for his interrupted education.

The Carpino family has been gathering on Sunday evenings for some seventy years—first, Claudio Carpino senior and Emelda in their Union Street flat, then, by the 1920s, moving to their splendid villa on Avila Street in the Marina District:

watching with pride as their son Claudio junior attended the Washington Irving grammar school, the Salesian Boys Club, St. Ignatius High School, San Anselmo College, and the University of Santa Clara Law School. They knew it, the two of them, that their only child was going to get somewhere in this world: get to that very point, in fact, at which he arrived in 1969 when as mayor he donated a $10,000 organ out of his own pocket to the parish church of Sant'Ursula in his father's native Sicily—the circle complete, Claudio Carpino's son making a gift to the town from which his father migrated at the beginning of the century. Such a tough, beautiful, paradoxical place, this Sicily, producing men like the Carpinos, father and son: men possessed of an essential toughness; jealous, fierce, grasping men, the Arab pirate existing just beneath the surface of the polished European man of property. One can imagine the Sunday evenings that took place before 1908 in Claudio Carpino senior's boyhood in the Sicilian fishing village of Sant'Ursula: not that different from the evenings at Barbara's in Jordan Park some ninety years later, save for the television set and the electric range in the kitchen.

Then, as now, passions smolder beneath the surface of the age-old domestic rituals: some feared or imagined (or confirmed) adultery; some suspected falsity in the sale of a catch; some quarrel over a net. At recent Sunday dinners, Esmeralda shows more and more signs of imbalance, of hysteria brought about by remorseless, tormenting jealousy. I can easily imagine how Esmeralda looks of an evening. I can see the tortured, incipiently crazy gaze in her eyes. Terry Shane and I have been gathering the evidence constantly, almost against our will—a screaming conversation from the Mayor's inner office at City Hall when Esmeralda bursts in unannounced, a remark let slip accidentally or on purpose by the Mayor as we go about the city in the limousine, all suggesting an acceleration of stress.

Son Umberto is made uneasy by all this raw domestic drama. It's too fierce, too Sicilian for his Stanford- and Yale-educated tastes. Sonny Grande tunes out in front of the

211

television set. It's easier that way. Rocky and Barbara take sides, now one side, now the other. Rocky doesn't care if his father chases a skirt now and then—although he has never known for sure whether or not his mother's suspicions are justified. Rocky, after all, is a man of the world. Barbara grieves deeply over the growing rift. She studied Christian Family Life at Dominican College. Her husband, Ronny Di Salvo, and her father the Mayor are playing chess and sipping Campari. Ronny won his way into the Mayor's heart by being such a good chess player. There were evenings during Ronny's courtship of Barbara when he'd come over to see her, but not take her anywhere, just spend the evening over a chessboard with his prospective father-in-law.

Barbara, incidentally, is a hell of a campaigner. Esmeralda rarely goes anywhere with the Mayor, especially of late; but Barbara can always be counted on. In the second campaign, Barbara tore up the city in an effort to win votes. Riding around on election day in a motorized cable car equipped with a sound system, she covered nearly every square block of the city, blaring out over the loudspeaker what a great guy her dad was and how he should be re-elected mayor of San Francisco.

A threat to Barbara's family last year forestalled a final breach between Esmeralda and the Mayor. A woman later identified as a member of the Bay Area Liberation Coalition went to work for Barbara as a babysitter in what later turned out to be the first stages of an elaborate kidnap plot. Inspector Peter Buoncristiano cracked the plot before it ever had the chance to get off the ground when he pulled the woman in on an accessory-to-a-murder charge. She'd helped bump off a coke dealer in the Haight Ashbury. They even shot the guy's Collie dog—in addition to putting a bullet through the dope dealer's head.

"She seemed like such a nice girl," Barbara later said of the would-be kidnapper. "She baked brownies for the kids."

The scare temporarily brought Claudio and Esmeralda together. For nearly six months, while Inspector Peter

212

Buoncristiano unraveled the strands of the kidnap plot, Esmeralda had something to worry about other than herself.

Barbara is no doubt embarrassed over the weekend incident at the Garden Court, as reported by Harry Shaw: the throwing of the raisin toast. They say that Esmeralda was quite a hell-raiser in the 1930s when she was attending the St. Rose Academy and the San Francisco College for Women on Lone Mountain: whatever hell-raising meant in those days. As the Genovese daughter of the Genovese president of one of two Genovese-owned-and-operated scavenger companies of San Francisco, Esmeralda di Salvo had little maneuvering room for misbehavior. She was raised like the protected daughter of a wealthy Genovese peasant—which is what she was. The Sicilians of San Francisco got into fish. The Genovese got into garbage. Each of San Francisco's two scavenger companies is owned by Genovese families, one of them Esmeralda's. Everyone works. Everyone owns shares. Everyone divides the profits on a quarterly basis. Every garbage man in the city, in short, owns part of the company he works for. That's why our scavenger service is so good—because our sanitation engineers are not disinterested civil servants as they are in other cities. It goes without saying that scavenging is tough, brutal work. The scavenger workday begins about three in the morning and ends about one in the afternoon.

Esmeralda's father, Blaso di Salvo (he died in 1959 at the age of eighty), was a second-generation scavenger who in the course of twenty years of early morning, back-breaking work bought out a number of other shareholders. He then subleased these purchased shares to non-shareholding, non-Genovese scavengers who, in effect, worked for Blaso as scavenger-sharecroppers. Every garbage can they lifted put approximately eight cents in Blaso's pockets. In 1929 Blaso di Salvo bought a five-bedroom house in the Marina and a black Buick automobile, and sent Esmeralda to the Dominican sisters at St. Rose Academy and later to the madames of the Sacred Heart at Lone Mountain for her education.

Esmeralda is more than a little sensitive about her Genovese

213

scavenger background. Harry Shaw makes snide references to it now and then in his column, especially after Esmeralda pried it out of Eva Shaw that night at the Top of the Mark that Eva Shaw was Mexican, not Spanish. I understand why scavengers, in San Francisco and in other cities across the world, organize themselves as a self-subsistent caste, tied together by family. That way, they erect a protective wall around themselves, minimizing the possibilities of hurt. Had Esmeralda remained within her caste, she would have had no trouble. It was she, not her father, who insisted upon the St. Rose Academy and the San Francisco College for Women. Her father allowed it, paid for it, but was ever aware of the dangers of upward mobility for his daughter. Yet he must also bear some of the responsibility. The minute that Blaso di Salvo began to buy up the shares of other scavengers and rent them out to non-Genovese, he set in motion a process that would in the fullness of time install his daughter as the reluctant First Lady of San Francisco.

Esmeralda di Salvo met Claudio Carpino junior in 1938 at a Christmas mixer given by the University of Santa Clara Law School for the girls of the Catholic colleges of the Bay Area. The mixer was held in one of the smaller ballrooms of the Fairmont Hotel. It was a huge success. Hundreds of Irish and Italian girls, dressed in their best frocks, descended upon the Fairmont in hopes of meeting an Irish or Italian law student. Visions of future homes in Sea Cliff or St. Francis Wood danced in their heads as the girls penetrated *en masse* the dimly lit ballroom, appearing to the historically minded to resemble a shipload of prospective brides brought around the Horn to San Francisco during the gold rush. Mr. di Salvo himself drove Esmeralda to the Fairmont in the latest of his black Buicks. (My source for the following: Esmeralda herself, who gave me the details in the course of our one and only conversation. Before her troubles with the Mayor began, she apparently enjoyed telling the story.) Mr. di Salvo only half-approved of this new way of meeting men at mixers. Skeptical, he parked his Buick across from the Fairmont on a side street off the

214

Pacific Union Club and waited for Esmeralda to re-emerge at the end of the dance. When she did, around eleven, she was ecstatic, having danced four dances with Claudio Carpino.

"Claudio Carpino?" her father grunted. "The son of Claudio Carpino of Carpino and Scosano Fish?"

"Yes, Papa. He goes to Santa Clara Law School."

Mr. di Salvo was surprised and somewhat gratified. In the North Beach, Marina scheme of things in the late 1930s, the Carpinos were a class family. Fish had more *éclat* than garbage. Perhaps this mixer system had something to it, after all. Otherwise it would have been next to impossible to bring a di Salvo and a Carpino together across the subtle class barriers that separated the two families. Esmeralda, for her part, sank back into the Buick's soft leather upholstery in a mood of delicious reverie as her father drove down Taylor Street towards the Marina. She rehearsed in her mind every detail of her four dances with Claudio: one fast dance, to "Stompin' at the Savoy," and three dreamy slow dances to "I'm in the Mood for Love," "Time on My Hands," and "You and the Night and the Music." Carpino had worn a houndstooth check sports coat, gray flannel slacks, and a striped knit tie held in place by a gold collar pin.

"He danced beautifully," was all that Esmeralda allowed her father when he questioned her.

Two years later, in 1940, they were married in a lavish solemn high nuptial mass at SS. Peter and Paul's Church on Washington Square, a very young Father Bianco officiating. Having seen Father Bianco the other day on the ferryboat with the Mayor, I can easily imagine a younger version of the Salesian priest some thirty-five years ago at the high altar of SS. Peter and Paul's, standing before a darkly handsome couple about to be joined in holy wedlock. The two years that elapsed between those first dreamy dances at the Fairmont and the procession down the aisle of the rococo Italian church had not been totally idyllic. Emelda Carpino, the future mayor's mother, was furious when she learned that her only boy, her precious Claudio, was seeing a Genovese scavenger's daughter.

215

She didn't care how rich the di Salvos were, she hollered on one occasion, she didn't want her boy tied up with that group. She wanted a doctor's or a lawyer's daughter for him. Claudio Carpino senior countered with the point that since her son was going to be a lawyer himself, it didn't really matter. He would have status enough for both of them. Mama Carpino eventually relented. Esmeralda, whom she met six months into her son's courtship, was such a pretty, winning girl: jet-black hair, olive skin, perfect teeth, and a sort of semi theatrical way with scarves and jewelry. Claudio brought her over for one of the Carpinos' perennial Sunday nights (this being in August of 1939), and an hour or so into the evening Claudio saw signs that his mother was being won over. By six o'clock (they had arrived at five, having spent the afternoon at the Golden Gate Exposition on Treasure Island) both Esmeralda and Emelda were in the kitchen at the stove, busy together with the pasta sauce, chattering in a mixture of Sicilian, Genovese, and English.

A month or so later, the di Salvos invited the Carpinos over for dinner. Mr. di Salvo was, as I have said, a wealthy executive, despite the fact that he now and then hoisted a garbage can over his shoulder to show his *compagnones* that he could still do it. Esmeralda had redone the house for her parents during her sophomore year at Lone Mountain, spending nearly $2,000 at Sloane's and O'Connor Moffitt in the process. Mr. and Mrs. Carpino were impressed by the tasteful home of Mr. and Mrs. di Salvo, who were by then, they admitted, their probable in-laws. There were even bookshelves in the living room, with some of Esmeralda's college text books on them, together with a run of the latest novels.

The young couple facing Father Bianco on that long-lost Saturday in June of 1940 came together, then, with the blessings—and the generous financial backing—of both sets of parents. Both the di Salvos and the Carpinos were heartsick, however, that Claudio and Esmeralda were moving to Washington, D.C., where Claudio had a position with the Commerce

216

Department; yet they were proud of Claudio's good job with the Corporate Division. Three weeks before the wedding, Claudio Carpino senior and Blaso di Salvo had met for lunch at the Fior D' Italia, just across the square from the church where their children were to be married. After lunching on seafood bouillabaisse and pasta, they drank red wine and smoked dark, hard Toscano cigars. By the fourth glass of wine they were admitting to each other that they had worked hard in America and that America had been good to them.

"Two college kids, eh," Blaso di Salvo said. Both he and Claudio Carpino senior started laughing.

Later on in the conversation, Claudio said, "Two college kids," and they laughed again as if hearing it for the first time.

It became a bond between the two of them, fisherman and scavenger, both having made good in San Francisco. Over the fourth glass of *grappa* and the third Toscano cigar, they agreed to settle $10,000 each on their children as a wedding present.

"Two college kids," they laughed.

Graduating from the University of Santa Clara Law School in 1939, Claudio Carpino went to work with the Department of Commerce in Washington, D.C., Corporate Law Division, where he specialized in foreign and domestic cartels. During the war, he served as a staff officer with the Bomber Command in London as an intelligence specialist helping the Army Air Corps and the RAF pinpoint industrial targets in Germany. As an expert in cartels, Carpino had a way of ferreting out camouflaged factories by making estimates from the most recently known pre-war patterns of production and distribution. He'd draw lines of convergence from 1936 or '37 or '38 emplacements and say where he thought current distribution points should be. The Allies would bomb hell out of the site, and sure enough, months later Carpino's intuited points of convergence would turn out to have been an underground warehouse or roundhouse or production plant. Carpino knew how cartels operated. Nazi Germany, he told the generals, was one big cartel. He made lieutenant colonel before he was thirty.

217

Returning to San Francisco in 1946, Carpino opened an office in the Hobart Building on Market Street, taking whatever cases came along, and keeping as active as possible in the courtroom field. He defended a scion of Pacific Heights on draft-dodging charges and lost. The lad went to McNeil Island prison for a year. He fought deportation proceedings against a North Beach grocer who had slipped into San Francisco from Valparaiso, Chile, in the early 1920s without benefit of a visa. The grocer's sister-in-law, who owned half the store with him and was angry in a dispute about sharing profits, had turned him in to the immigration authorities. Carpino brought in half of North Beach, including Father Bianco, to testify before the federal judge as to the grocer's character and high standing in the community. Carpino got the illegal alien off with a $2,000 fine and five years' probation. There wasn't even a whispered mention of deportation proceedings.

In 1952 Carpino represented Georgio "Paisano" Emiliano, the gambling czar of Sonoma County. The State Assembly Committee on Rackets and Organized Crime subpoenaed Emiliano to come over to Sacramento to discuss bookmaking and numbers rackets in the Sebastopol, Calistoga, and Russian River resort area. Emiliano was never indicted. Old newspaper photographs in the Library's History Room show Emiliano before a battery of microphones. A much younger Claudio Carpino is whispering something into Emiliano's ear, about his constitutional rights, no doubt. Both of them are wearing dark, double-breasted suits and look like Richard Conte and George Raft in a forties Warner Brothers movie.

In 1954 Hollywood producer Victor Papadoulos gave Carpino his *entrée* into the big time and the big fees. As an independent producer, Papadoulos wanted to sue the studios for tieing up theater chains with exclusive contracts, which forbade competitive bidding by independent film makers such as himself. No southern California firm would touch the case for fear of losing studio business. Darrell Mannheim, however, a partner in a Beverly Hills firm that Papadoulos had unsuccessfully approached, recommended his old friend from

218

Department of Commerce days, Claudio Carpino of San Francisco. Carpino, Mannheim told Papadoulos, had one of the finest legal minds in the country. Papadoulos flew Carpino down to Palm Springs and they talked. Three weeks later Carpino was in the federal district court with a restraint-of-trade suit against three major studios and two theater chains. Carpino and Papadoulos won their case and were sustained on appeal. The Papadoulos case made Claudio Carpino famous and led to a long-time connection with Hollywood clients.

Claudio Carpino spent a lot of time away from home in those days, mainly in New York, Boston, Chicago, and Palm Beach. He made a lot of money and he might have fooled around a bit. He was in his mid-forties, some twenty years into his marriage to Esmeralda, and needing his batteries recharged. There's a rumor that he kept a mistress during this time—a rather well-known Broadway actress who used to specialize in playing arch but sweet roles in warm-hearted comedies. Claudio Carpino, to put it bluntly and unfashionably, has lots of *machismo*; it is a quality of raw animal energy, not crude, but persistent, like the odor of musk. Women get excited when the Mayor strides into a room—all that semiprimitive Sicilian energy, after all, subsumed and upgraded by breeding, education, political power, citrus cologne, and $20 million in the bank. I've seen him in a room of angry women's libbers who were protesting this or that sexist abuse in city government. The Mayor had them calmed down in no time—had them subconsciously fibrillating, despite their surface anger, to the steady inner humming of his hormonal dynamos. Carpino has his sex appeal under control, and he's never been known to abuse it; but back some twenty years ago, in the first flush of his Hollywood days, it is highly possible that he let it run wild for a while. Who wouldn't? Jealousy over this probably has helped coax Esmeralda into her present condition of anxiety.

Esmeralda has no worries about her next meal, however. Claudio Carpino keeps her in the grand style. As an attorney, the Mayor can't help but make money.

He sues at the drop of a hat and wins when he sues. Over the years, he's made law in a number of fields. He once sued the State of California, Division of Fish and Game for seizing the catches of North Beach sardine fishermen on the grounds that much of the catch was below the legal size. Arguing the case on the basis of the Fourteenth Amendment—deprivation of property without due process of law—Carpino got the impounded catches restored, together with a court-ordered agreement that a certain unavoidable percentage of any given catch of sardines could be under-sized.

Carpino has been able to give Esmeralda everything, including the First Ladyship of San Francisco. Esmeralda dresses in suits by Geoffrey Beene, Samri frocks, Pucci dresses. She goes to Europe at least once a year on buying sprees, running up astronomical bills at Chanel, Pucci, Fabiani. Her black hair, which was beginning to be streaked with gray, turned henna red in the early 1960s after she disappeared for a month to a San Diego fat farm. Her ankle-length fur coats—mink, sable, chinchilla—have remained uninterruptedly luxuriant. I personally have trouble grafting the Esmeralda I and all of San Francisco now know—spoiled, capricious, eccentric—onto the remembered image of the aspiring college kid of the late 1930s: the Lone Mountain girl who read the *Divine Comedy* with studious attention and helped her mother in the kitchen.

There's one way you can read Esmeralda's present state of hysteria: Esmeralda never found an outlet for her talents. She went to college, read a number of Modern Library classics, married Claudio Carpino, then found herself on the shelf. It was, and still is, a pleasant shelf: a mansion in Sea Cliff, a weekend place over at Stinson Beach, expense accounts with leading designers across the world, membership in a number of social auxiliaries (the Symphony Association, the Museum Auxiliary, the board of trustees of the Art Institute). Hers is a recurring idyll of lunches at Trader Vic's, opening nights at the opera (the one "social" event where the Carpinos feel comfortable), shopping sprees, or afternoons spent napping in the be-draped recess of her private boudoir. Take the matter of Esmeralda's membership in the Francesca Club. That alone would satisfy the ambition of many social-climbing San Franciscan women. Esmeralda is one of the few Italians who belong to that citadel of upper-class WASP womanhood. Not bad for the daughter of a man who began his professional career hoisting garbage cans over his shoulder!

For the past five years Esmeralda has owned and operated a book boutique on Union Street called the Athenian Owl, for which she does most of the book selection. This satisfies the blue stocking side of her nature. Esmeralda gives wine and cheese parties at the Athenian Owl for local writers when they publish a book, picking up the tab herself.

"Something is eating away at Esmeralda's gut" is the way Terry Shane put it to me recently over drinks at the lower bar of the Mark Hopkins. "It's got everybody, even the Mayor, baffled."

"She's a little mature for women's lib," I said.

Shane sipped his drink morosely. He catches most of the crap Esmeralda hurls every day at the fan in Room 200.

"Listen, man," he said, "in California suburban grandmothers are kicking husbands of forty years' standing out of the house. In one case I know of, a sixty-year-old pillar of the community has opened up an art gallery in Inverness and is shacking up with a twenty-five-year-old ceramicist. Her daughter is furious. Over in Marin County where I live, they've got a Grandmothers' Round Table. They're reading Masters and Johnson and talking about getting more out of their sex lives."

"The irony is," I said, "that if every woman over fifty who feels she's wasted her life were to vote for Carpino, we'd be swept in by a landslide."

"How could we go public so it wouldn't backfire?"

"Maybe you could get her on a talk show. She could frankly discuss her struggle for identity as a political wife."

"Best to keep the whole thing private."

I have a feeling, however, that it isn't going to stay private.

Something will explode. God, I'm glad I'm not a woman! I've got my identity problems, sure; but women these days are being pressured like crazy to justify their lives in "real world" terms. That's okay for some girl out of college, but a woman of Esmeralda's age is past her major choices. There are times when I'm on Esmeralda's side. The social supports for being a quiet grandmother just aren't there.

As I say, you can see the problem in psychological terms. Esmeralda feels that she's wasted her life, that she hasn't put her talents to use because the proper modes of activity just weren't available to Catholic girls of her generation who married high-powered, successful men. She feels contempt for having allowed her husband to put her on the shelf.

Or could it be a biological, menopausal sort of thing? A woman in her fifties just hasn't the same pep as a man in his fifties. Even women's lib can't change that fact. Women live longer, true; but they also seem to peak earlier. Middle age, which a man can slide into gradually, hits women like a ton of bricks. The Mayor preens about like a peacock. A nimbus of virility surrounds him. Esmeralda has had two face-lifts (this according to Shane), a recoloration of her hair, and makes twice-yearly pilgrimages to southern California fat farms. She still doesn't look as good as the Mayor does. She never can. It's just nature.

Esmeralda is tormented by sexual jealousy. She's convinced that the Mayor is balling every good-looking girl in the office. From her point of view, there's evidence to this effect. When he was first elected, the Mayor made a big point of telling the press that he'd promised his wife that he'd be home every night for dinner at six. These days he's out of the house twenty-five nights a month. It's natural that Esmeralda suspects he's seeing other women. After all, there's plenty of suspicion that he did so in the past, especially during his Hollywood days.

Quite frankly, I doubt that the Mayor is playing around. Shane swears that he isn't, and if anyone would know, it would be Shane, who travels with him constantly. Carpino definitely doesn't want to be home with Esmeralda, however, for whatever reasons; or else he would be there. Carpino cannot be bullied by anyone or anything, including a mayor's schedule. What's gone wrong? Something primitive, something Sicilian? Some anxiety that relates to caste distinctions supposedly laid aside thirty-five years ago? Or something obscure, as in François Mauriac's novel *Vipers' Tangle*: something that has its hidden, odious nourishment in the deepest resentments of the soul?

Chapter 8

IN THIS MARVELOUS YEAR OF 1914, you can drive out to the Cliff House at Ocean Beach from downtown San Francisco in just twenty minutes by motor car. The south side of Fulton Street parallels Golden Gate Park. The sand dunes to the north of Fulton Street are in the process of being subdivided into a residential section to be called the Richmond District. From First Avenue to Forty-eighth Avenue, where Fulton Street runs into the Ocean Beach, you can see hundreds of new homes under construction. When Royce, the late Charlie Stoddard, and I used to tramp out here in the mid-1860s, there was no Golden Gate Park and only a scattered ranch house or two on the sand dunes. Making an entire day of it, we would hike out along the toll road now called Geary Boulevard and eat our sack lunches in sight of the Cliff House. We would then tramp back to the city, arriving at twilight.

My father Dennis Collins (1817-1905), the first fire chief of the City and County of San Francisco, died nine years ago at the age of eighty-eight. My mother Mollie Collins (1830-1906) died of a broken hip a year later, just a month before the Fire and Earthquake. Up until the year 1860, when I turned twelve, my parents and I lived in a cottage in Happy Valley south of Market Street. It was a five-room cottage, built in 1850 and lasting until the late 1870s, when it was torn down to make room for the Wade's Opera House.

224

Raised on a farm in County Kerry, Ireland, my mother married my father when she was seventeen and he was thirty. They were married in early 1847 and left for America the day after the wedding.

"Mother, tell me about the olden days," I used to ask her when I was a boy. We would sit up together in the kitchen, waiting for my father to come home, sometimes from a fire. In those days, San Francisco seemed always to be on fire. The city burned down some six times in the mid-1850s alone.

"The olden days weren't so fine, Sebastian dear," Mother would say. "There was never enough to eat in the Old Country, and the work on the farm was terrible hard indeed. Your father had ambition, and so we left together after getting married and sailed for New York."

Although she was raised on a farm and possessed but a rudimentary education, I cannot honestly describe my mother as a peasant. She read the daily newspaper deliberately, for instance, sounding the words silently on her lips. I shall always remember the first time (I was thirteen or so) that she asked me to read a word for her in the newspaper. It was the word "reconnaissance," used in a dispatch from the East describing the operations of Confederate cavalry outside Washington, D.C.

"What's this word, darling?" Mother asked me simply, without hesitation.

"It's 'reconnaissance,' Mother."

"And what does 'reconnaissance' mean?"

"It means to go out and take a look, to reconnoiter."

"To what?"

"To reconnoiter—to go out and take a look."

"You mean to make a reconnaissance, don't you?"

We laughed. Mother would have been all of thirty-one or thirty-two at the time. A deepening bond formed between us from moments like these. Mother never hesitated to ask me the definition of various words. Some I knew. Some we would look up together in a battered copy of *Webster's Dictionary*, drawn together by our little adventure.

"I'm thanking God that you're too young to be in the East,

225

fighting and dying to no purpose," Mother said at another time when we sat together in the kitchen waiting for my father to return home. As we waited, Mother usually read the *Post* newspaper by the light of an oil lamp on the kitchen table while I did my school work for the next day's recitations at the Boys' High School. Like a lot of the Irish, Mother kept her distance from the Civil War, not saying which side she favored (although I suspect that it was the South). She did allow, however, that she was glad to be a continent away from the fighting. It is a miracle that so many Irish fought so loyally for the Union cause. Barely off the boat, they were herded into federal regiments, then sent against the Confederate guns. Thomas Starr King, the Boston Yankee pastor of the First Unitarian Church here in San Francisco, used to whip the city into a frenzy of pro-Union sentiment. I have never before or since heard a man speak as well as Thomas Starr King did—fiery oratory in the grand manner; but Mother and, to a lesser extent, Father kept their counsel. The Civil War to their way of thinking was a protestant affair and none of their business.

Even if I was asleep in my bed on the back porch, I could hear Father tramp up the front stairs when he came home. Father attended fires wearing great leather boots that went over his knees: "Three Musketeer Boots" I called them after I had read Dumas's novel. Father also carried a large, ornately engraved metal voice-horn, through which he would direct the efforts of the other firemen. Tramp, tramp, tramp, he would enter the house, then fling himself exhausted on his favorite chair. It was my job to pull his boots off. Father would extend one leg at a time. I would face away from him, his leg between my knees. I knew exactly how to loosen the fit of the heel first, then work the leather off around his ankle, before pulling the entire boot off. If I loosened the boot properly, it slipped off with no trouble at all.

Mother always had hot food ready for Father when he returned, and a bucketful of beer to go with his meat and potatoes. I do not recall them conversing much with each other at the table if Father came home particularly exhausted,

226

but I do not recall any angry words between them either. When Father had a "snootful" (his phrase) he stayed out of the house altogether, sometimes for days at a time. He slept over at the fire station, which he was not required to do, being the chief.

"Your father is at the station," was all that Mother would say about it—"at the station" in time becoming Mother's equivalent of Father's "snootful." Father was at the station some three or four times a year for periods never exceeding three or four days. Other than that, he seemed to have his problem in hand—if problem it was. A taste for the grog is, I feel, more in the nature of an Irish disposition than a problem, although it can become a destructive habit. I myself drink more than I should, especially as I grow older. I try to stay with wine, sherry, and beer, although I do love a good whiskey. For Marina's sake (she hates to see me with a "snootful" or "at the station") I woo sobriety, just as Father stayed sober most of the time for the sake of Mother. I drank hardly at all during the brief year with Virginia in Napa County, the two of us living such a healthy outdoor life.

Drink ruined some of the Irish in early San Francisco and it still does, but Father and Mother always struggled to be a cut above the ordinary. My father's father ran a pub on the road to Dublin—the Armagh Chalice it was called—and as a young boy my father, so he later told me, would carefully observe the fine fellows on their way to the city. Ambition meant but one thing in the Ireland of those days: get out of Ireland, or at least get to Dublin. As the younger son of a publican, my father was actually a member of the petty bourgeoisie, such as it was; yet he had no prospects of inheriting the tavern. Besides, he had watched too many people continue down the Dublin road to be content to spend his life pouring drinks out for those who would be moving on. He wanted to move on himself, and this he did when he was just twenty, leaving for Dublin, where he eventually found employment on the Lord Lieutenant's Fire Brigade. My father's family and my mother's family, incidentally, had known each other for years. My mother was just seven years of age when my father left for Dublin.

"He'd come back every few years," Mother once told me of her courtship. "I'd look for an excuse to go down to the Armagh Chalice and see him: so grand in his red coat and striped trousers. A regular British gentleman he was, a member of the Lord Lieutenant's Fire Watch. He never noticed me until I turned thirteen. By the time I was fifteen, he was coming home twice a year and staying for a week at a time, and looking for an excuse to meet me."

To this day, I have no idea of what went on between them—the semi-peasant farm girl of fifteen, sixteen, seventeen, and the semi-bourgeois fire-watchman some thirteen years her senior. I imagine that they courted in the immemorial way of country people. They both were reticent to speak of their personal lives. Those were famine years in Ireland, in any event, and there was little joy of life for anyone. Farm folk died of malnutrition in their very homes. More than a million left for America in a period of a few years.

"It's a good thing that your father was older than I," Mother once remarked. "I would not have had the courage to go to America on my own, and if I stayed behind I might have died before I was thirty, like my two sisters after me. But your father had been to Dublin and knew how to manage. 'Let's marry and go to America,' he said to me one night as we sat outside the Armagh Chalice. 'You don't want to be staying here, do you, and not having enough to eat and working another's land until you're an old woman before your time?' It was like a fairy tale. Your father was a grand man, and I was but a country girl. I aspired to him in the secret places of my heart, but I never dreamed that we'd be marrying and running off to America, using some of the money he'd saved from the Fire Watch to pay our passage to New York. I threw my arms around him and I cried out like a shameless creature: 'O Dennis darling, I'll follow thee to Hell itself, for I love thee with all my heart!'"

"She burst into tears," my father said once, recounting his impressions of their betrothal scene. "She clung to my neck and shook with great choking sobs that seemed to come from

228

the very depths of her being. She had no shoes to wear, and only a coarse linen dress on her, but to me she seemed like a heroine of Old Ireland, ready to brave the sea and an unknown land with her man."

"Rather than lose him, I'd as lief left then, right away, without benefit of clergy," Mother related once in a moment of surprising candor. (I am gathering together the scattered remarks of fifty years, coalescing them for dramatic effect.) "But we arranged for a wedding within the week and left for America the day following."

Mother and Father spent much of the next year and a half at sea: from Ireland to New York, then from New York around Cape Horn to San Francisco, where they arrived in March of 1847 as members of the Seventh Regiment of the New York State Volunteers. The horrors of a voyage from Liverpool to New York on a crowded immigrant ship can best be left to the imagination. Father and Mother, in any event, rarely discussed it, except to say that they were fortunate to survive the voyage without dying of fever or disease. The voyage from New York to San Francisco, by contrast, was remembered by both of them as a pleasant idyll—save for the stormy passage around Cape Horn.

"So Captain Shannon throws Phil Kelly in the guardhouse about a week or so out of Rio de Janeiro." This from my father, some time in the mid-1860s, recalling the old days over beer with some fellow veterans of the Stevenson Regiment. " 'I'll have no damn Irish b'hoy, drunk and disorderly,' says the Captain, fuming over the rum Kelly had snuck aboard ship and passed around. Mrs. Kelly and the little Kelly lass are crying their eyes out because their daddy is in the pokey. So that night a couple of us lads marched over to the foredeck where the brig was kept like an affronting chickencoop or unnecessary outhouse and we smashed it to pieces, pulling the boards right off the frame in true b'hoy style. Phil Kelly's inside, not knowing what the hell is happening. He thinks it's a storm or something. I'll never forget the look on his face when we'd succeeded in stripping the entire guardhouse bare.

229

Only the frame was left. 'Come on out, Kelly! You're free!' we yelled; then started to sing a song we'd made up to the words of 'Old Dan Tucker.' Captain Shannon came out on deck and tried to be angry, but he was too good an Irishman to stay mad. He muttered something about a court martial, but he eventually let us off with just the job of rebuilding the guardhouse, Kelly included."

Laughter all around, and more stories, and myself, a boy of twelve or so, taking it all in, surprised by the free way my mother joined in the men's laughter; but then again, she had served in the Regiment as well, side by side with the men.

To begin at the beginning: my parents arrived in New York in July of 1846. In August of 1846 my father enlisted in Company I of the Seventh Regiment of New York Volunteers, bound for California. My father had nothing against Mexicans; in many ways he had more in common with the Catholic peasants of Mexico than he did with their Yankee aggressors. But he wanted to go to California, and the Seventh Regiment, commanded by Colonel Jonathan Drake Stevenson of New York, was headed for California as an army of occupation and, after the war with Mexico ended, as a source of settlers for California. The Seventh Regiment, you see, was not returned to New York, but discharged in California. Married men such as my father and Private Phillip Kelly were allowed to bring their wives and families along; for women and children were needed in California as well as men.

Why California? I asked my parents this upon a number of occasions. I asked it as a boy and again as a man. I last asked it of my aged parents in 1905, myself a man of fifty-seven, well into middle age, looking for some clue as to how my long, tangled, incomplete relationship with San Francisco ever began in the first place; for had my parents stayed in New York, as did millions of other Irish, my life would have been very much different. My father's answer was elliptical. The more I think about it, however, the more significant it seems.

"I could see some of the same things catching up with the Irish in New York that caught up with them in the Old

230

Country—things like poverty and disease, oppression and self-hatred. I wanted Mollie and me to have a truly fresh beginning, so we joined the Army and sailed off for the other side of America."

Father enlisted in Company I of the Seventh Regiment, Captain William E. Shannon commanding, at Fort Columbus, New York, in August of 1846. A large number of the lads, including Captain Shannon himself, were Irish-born; but there were also Germans, French, Scots, and a score or so of Yankees and New Yorkers. Since the soldiers were destined to be discharged in California as colonists, a better-than-ordinary cadre of enlisted men filled out the ranks. Company I had two lawyers, a druggist, and a medical student serving as ordinary troopers, together with blacksmiths, carpenters, masons, millwrights, a tailor, a barber, a butcher, and (according to my father) a solitary bookbinder: recruited, I suppose, in the event that learning should ever arise in California. Colonel Stevenson himself did not die until 1894, so over the years he was able to preside over intermittent reunions of his colonizing regiment. I attended a number of these with my father.

"Well, Collins," Stevenson once said, "you did all right for a b'hoy—and that was because of that lovely wife of yours."

A b'hoy is an Irish lad out for a good time and perhaps a bit of trouble. Phillip Kelly, for instance, whom Captain Shannon shut up in the guardhouse on the deck of the *Susan Drew*, was a b'hoy, despite the fact that he also had a wife along, and a daughter as well. My father was quite popular with his fellow troopers, but my mother—to judge in retrospect—seems to have been positively adored. Mrs. Stevenson attached Mother to her suite as a companion and domestic attendant to look after her and keep her company on the long voyage out from New York. In the evenings, becalmed off Brazil, the ship's company would fall out for a serenade under the stars by the regimental band, the women gathered around Mrs. Stevenson on the quarterdeck, officers' and enlisted men's wives inter-mingled in the enforced democracy of a crowded ship, but ever mindful of the social distinctions of military rank. Frederick

231

C. Crambs, the chief musician of the regimental band, composed a "California Grand March," in honor of the Volunteers' departure from New York. Years later, I heard it played at the reunions I attended at the Occidental Hotel in San Francisco. It was a brassy Teutonic sort of a march, full of bravado and oompapah on an E-flat tuba.

On the *Susan Drew*, by the way, the enlisted wives worked their passage out to California. Private Kelly's wife worked as a laundress. Mother cooked for the ship's officers and warrant officers, and looked out for Mrs. Stevenson, who had taken a fancy to her.

The *Susan Drew* reached Rio de Janeiro in mid-November, after a voyage of more than two months. It took six weeks of tempestuous sailing to make it around Cape Horn to Valparaiso, Chile, where they arrived in late January of 1847. Mother always remembered the exotic beauty of Rio de Janeiro, but she spoke of Valparaiso as a city where she might have happily spent the rest of her life.

"Some thirty lads deserted the Regiment in Valparaiso," Mother pointed out; "and it was touch-and-go for a while with your father and me. We met a lot of Irish living in Valparaiso when we walked about the city—living grandly, mind you, in haciendas surrounded with roses and lemon trees and speaking Spanish with brogues, and owning their own land and cattle and practicing their Catholic faith with no interference whatsoever. To the likes of us, Valparaiso seemed like paradise."

San Francisco, by contrast, where the *Susan Drew* anchored in March of 1847, was a collection of adobe huts and rickety wooden shacks. California was already eight months past its conquest by the United States Navy, so there was no combat for the Seventh Regiment to plunge into, thank God. It was the United States Army's task, rather, to administer California as a conquered territory, which it did with great success until statehood was granted in 1850. Company I, my father's company, was garrisoned in Monterey; but Mrs. Stevenson, not wishing to lose Mother, arranged that Father be detached

232

from Company I for service at the regimental headquarters in the Presidio of San Francisco.

You might then consider me an army child, for I was conceived, gestated, and brought into this world while Father served as corporal (later sergeant), Headquarters Company, Seventh Regiment, New York State Volunteers, the Presidio of San Francisco, military territory of California, Colonel Jonathan Drake Stevenson commanding. When you come to think of it, my parents had miraculously improved their lot from that time some two short years earlier outside the Armagh Chalice when Father had proposed marriage. Father always had a certain skill in making his way in this world. Going down to Dublin as an inexperienced youth, he managed a billet in the Lord Lieutenant's Fire Watch. Enlisting in Fort Columbus as a private, he ended his army career wearing three gold sergeant's chevrons across his sleeve—his wife and baby boy (your servant Sebastian Collins) ensconced in a serviceable cottage in the noncommissioned officers' quarters to the west of the Presidio parade ground, overlooking the Bay of San Francisco. My father could always manage things, no matter what came up.

As I grow older (and older!) I think of my parents more and more frequently, trying to penetrate the inner reality that hides itself behind familiar detail. I see them at twilight before the Armagh Chalice, Mother staring boldly into Father's face, throwing her arms and her life headlong upon him, with him asking unambiguously for that life and feeling in the immemorial way of men of his coping kind competent enough to protect and cherish his woman, no matter what. I tried to be thus for Virginia—to manage the vineyards, to father a child, to offer support; but Virginia died. I shall never forget the look Virginia cast upon me when I entered her bedroom after Marina's birth, sick with the knowledge that this could very well be the end. It was a far, far different look from the look Mother gave Father in front of the Armagh Chalice.

I think of my parents in their brief sojourn in New York, Father walking off a construction job when the Yankee foreman called him something derogatory—walking briskly off the job, that is, for the foreman was left behind on his knees, stunned by a blow to the jaw; and the people from the brickworks were yelling for the police. Was Father jealous, I ask myself, when the other men wanted to dance with Mother aboard the *Susan Drew*? Or was it understood between Father and his mates that he was extending the right to dance with his wife to them as a courtesy—because they were without their own wives and sweethearts? There was nothing but the uttermost fidelity between them; of that I am certain. In later years, Father had his snootfuls; but there was never a suggestion of other women. When no further children came, Mother did lose a certain self-confidence *vis à vis* my father, fecundity being greatly prized among the Irish pioneers of that time and place; yet he always treated her with the utmost chivalry, even when she and he were at odds, which is sometimes the case with even the happiest of marriages.

"You were born the very month, May 1848, when word reached San Francisco that gold had been discovered the previous January in the Sierra." This from Mother upon the occasion of one of my requests that she tell me about the olden days. "Your father was not discharged until August; but in the last months of his enlistment he was straining at the bit to get to the gold fields, and this, mind you, from a sergeant who supervised more than a few floggings of troopers who deserted and were arrested in the mines by the Army and brought back to the Presidio for punishment. They'd tie the poor fellow to a post and lash him until his back looked like a tiger had clawed it, and your poor father commanding the punishment detail and thinking to himself, 'There but for the grace of God go I'; for no one was more eager to be off to the mines than he."

From August 1848 to early 1851, Father worked in the gold fields, leaving Mother and me behind in San Francisco. Mrs. Stevenson took Mother into service that first year of Father's absence, so in a very real way we never truly left the Army. From 1849 to 1851, Mother ran a boarding house on Sansome Street, financed by a portion of Father's first year

234

earnings. She cooked for no fewer than thirty men twice a day and saw to the housekeeping. San Francisco was a difficult place in those days. The scum of the seven seas flocked to the city in pursuit of the golden fleece. Men outnumbered women ten to one. Mother's lot must have been difficult—left alone at the age of nineteen with an infant son, in a remote, reckless frontier town in the throes of a gold rush, chained to an incessant round of domestic labor. Father made it down to the city from the Mother Lode whenever he could, but that was only every three or four months.

"I thought I was lucky when we came to California and the war was over," Mother once said. "But then the gold rush came, more dangerous to Dennis than any little war with the Mexicans. The killing and the fighting in the gold country was just terrible. Each time he returned, I begged him to stay. With him home, I could make even more money with the boarding house than I was already making, and that was good money; but he had this dream, like the dream of a thousand other lads, of striking it rich; and so he departed again for the mines, leaving you and me to fend for ourselves on Sansome Street."

It was years before I learned why Father decided to leave the Mother Lode and return to San Francisco. My parents simply never discussed this. A memoir appeared in 1880, however: *Early Days in the Diggings* by Albert Casey, a onetime miner with the York State Shamrock Mining Society of Nevada County, California. Interested in the mining era, I perused the volume, especially taken by Casey's account of one year of utterly wasted labor building a flume on the north fork of the American River near Dutch Flat. The flume, Casey wrote, was a juggernaut. It wound around a mountainside for nearly three miles, diverting tons of water in what was intended to be a two-way mining effort: the mining of the exposed riverbed, and the use of the diverted water to wash down a particularly promising hillside. The York State Shamrock Mining Society of Nevada County was a cooperative venture. Each miner who worked on the sluice owned stock in the company, which had been initially capitalized out of the accumulated savings of each of the miners' previous year's work. Since the flume took merely a year to build, towards the end of building it, each man connected with the York State Shamrock Mining Society had two years of his labor and fortune sunk into the venture.

"On the morning of 17 January 1851," Casey writes on page 181, "we twenty miners gathered round the sluice gate for a ceremonial inauguration. Twelve months of backbreaking labor were behind us. Ahead, so we thought, was fame and fortune, the just reward for our Herculean labors: for twelve months of butterless flapjacks, sleeping under canvas on the hard ground, and lonely celibacy. What we had not figured for, however, was the effect of the winter rains. The proper function of our sluice system depended upon our being able to regulate the volume of water going into the flume, water being one of the heaviest elements known to man. Too much water tonnage—and our flume, clinging to the steep hillside like an elongated insect, was done for. One of our lads, Dennis Collins by name, a trained fireman with a knowledge of hydraulics, argued vehemently against the opening of the sluice gate at that particular time. The water was too high behind it, he said; but the rest of the boys, including myself, were anxious to get on with the job. We wanted to start mining for gold. We were sick and tired of coolie labor. So we opened the gates and the water rushed forward with the roar of an angry demon. Had the river flowed in an accommodating, orderly fashion into the flume, we might have diverted it. Engorged, however, with melted snow and Sierran rainfalls, the river leapt ahead over our fragile timbers like an amorous stallion kicking itself free of a corral. Realizing (too late!) the danger, a dozen of us tried to wrestle the sluice gate into a locked position; but the sliding mechanism jammed under the water pressure. Under the weight of this unexpected, swollen torrent, our flume collapsed off the hillside like an overburdened camel. Parts of it sank to its timbered knees, like a camel coming to rest. Other sequences burst asunder, rolling down the mountainside in an avalanche of wooden debris. I shall

236

always remember the look of sarcasm and resignation Dennis Collins cast upon his mates who had overruled him to such disastrous effect. (How prophetic had proven the young fireman's hydraulic predictions! How tragically unheeded!) 'Well, lads,' Collins said as we stood in stunned silence, 'water can be a tricky thing.'"

"When Dennis returned from the Shamrock disaster," Mother remarked after I had read her Casey's account, "I told him that I was sick and tired of the gold rush. I'd rather be back in Ireland than working in San Francisco alone without him, with one or another of the men at the boarding house always pestering me about leaving my husband, or worse, warming their bed for an evening or two—not that I blamed them, poor lads. There were precious few girls in town; but that wasn't my way. I wanted my husband home, and I did not care whether or not he had struck it rich."

At age sixty Mother could afford to be frank. The fact that men would be approaching her while Father was away makes sense in retrospect, she being all of nineteen, twenty, twenty-one at the time. The sexual anxieties of the gold rush must have been very intense, so few of the men having access to women. No wonder that *The Annals of San Francisco* (1855) speaks so approvingly of the city's flourishing houses of prostitution. Such establishments were, in effect, agencies of social service.

Father died nine years ago, in 1905, at the age of eighty-eight, which bodes well for my longevity. Up to the end, he wore the drooping walrus mustache of the late 1850s, the time when he was confirmed in his position as the first chief of a municipally supported fire brigade. Lillie Hitchcock Coit—the fire department's daughter of the regiment—insisted that Father deserved to be chief because he was the handsomest man in the department. Indeed, Father did make an impressive sight in full uniform, all six full feet of him, his mustachios fiercely assertive, an array of gold buttons on his blue tunic, his engraved metal voice-horn carried with the swaggering aplomb of a field marshal's baton. Father died

237

in his great walnut-wood bed like an Old Testament patriarch, attended for the last rites by Father Peter Yorke, who Father always insisted was "one damn fine priest" despite Yorke's rabid support of labor unions. The day of Father's death, he drank a tall, frosty glass of beer, and ate four plump black juicy olives, spitting out the pits neatly into his napkin when he was finished chewing. After his death, Mother often sat quietly in the kitchen, as if awaiting his momentary return from a fire. I often sat with her—a fifty-seven-year-old son, the circle of time encircled, sitting with Mother once again as I had as a boy of twelve in the year of hope and promise, 1860, reading to her, as I often did then, from a Dickens novel.

The bookseller-publisher Paul Elder has encouraged me to expand upon my memories of early San Francisco for *Memoirs of a San Franciscan Bohemian*. Of late, I have been jotting down a time-harvest of random memories, preparatory to drafting the chapter. I remember the terrible days of the Vigilance Committee of 1856, for instance. I was eight years old at the time. Armed volunteers took over the city in the name of law and order. Celebrated so undeservedly in our local folklore, the Vigilance Committee of 1856 was in effect a well-organized insurrection by the Masonic protestant bourgeoisie, aimed at breaking the growing power of the Irish in San Francisco. The two men hanged by the Committee, James P. Casey and Charles Cora, were both Irish Catholics—and the fact that only Irish Catholics were hung, my father insisted at the time and ever after, was not coincidental. Father considered the Vigilance Committee, with all its secret symbols and pass-words and rites, as a species of bigoted Know Nothingism. For nearly a year the Committee ruled the city, drilling its volunteer troops in Portsmouth Plaza like a Cromwellian army of occupation. The Committee brutally hung Cora and Casey out the window of a warehouse, and for some time after that, the Irish lads of the city walked softly.

Despite the fact that it bordered on a wilderness to one side and the Pacific Ocean on the other, San Francisco was a good city to grow up in. For a boy in his native place, after all, Here is always Here. There is never a longed-for, long-lost Somewhere Else, unless the boy has moved a great distance from his home after having attained his teen-age years. The harbor of San Francisco bristled with the sailless spars of anchored tall ships. The denizens of the four corners of the world walked our streets, dressed like Turkish corsairs, jabbering in outlandish tongues. Brass bands blared from within the saloons; and kept women in feathers and silk took the air in open carriages. San Franciscans of the 1850s and 60s lived a good bit of their collective life outdoors on the streets, promenading, or in restaurants or hotel lobbies, chatting together, striking poses. I have already mentioned Emperor Norton, with whom Royce and I played chess at the Mechanics' Institute. The Emperor was one among many street characters. There was also the Great Unknown, for instance, a brooding, Byronic gentleman in opera cape, top hat, and formal dress, his aged, shrunken cheeks brought to life by rouge, and on his bald head a curly wig. The Great Unknown stalked the streets like a dispossessed Parisian boulevardier awaiting a final curtain. George Washington, another street character, promenaded about in a uniform of a Revolutionary War general, complete with a powdered wig.

By 1866, the year I left for Harvard College, San Francisco had grown into a handsome city luxuriant in the amenities of life. In my last year at the Boys' High School, I submitted an essay for composition class entitled "The Strengths, Deficiencies, and Future Prospects of San Francisco." My instructor, Mr. Eugene Strain, forwarded it to the editors of *The Golden Era*, who published what is now item number 1 in my modest bibliography. "And therefore," I perorated in the full flush of my Harvard acceptance, a certificate signed by President Eliot himself, "let us look with confidence to the future of San Francisco. Behind us lies a brief but dramatic history. Before us lies a prospect of infinite possibilities. Fifteen years ago, our streets oozed in mud. Our miscellaneous populace pursued Mammon with orgiastic frenzy. Today, the spires of churches

239

rise triumphantly in our sky; and a refined culture has sunk its taproots into our sandy soil." I soared bombastically on like this for some length, but I did make one point that some fifty years later, I yet find valid: "Let us glory in our isolation," I say, "for it has given us intensity of focus. Because we are so alone, so remote, we San Franciscans cherish civilization all the more. We are like a Greek colony in the Mediterranean—more Greek than the Greeks themselves. To paraphrase the founding Puritans of Massachusetts, we face the grand Pacific like a city on a hill, a New Jerusalem of American hopes." I am described in a headnote to this essay, incidentally, as "among the first American children to be born in San Francisco," which is true. Not only was I born here, moreover, I was also conceived here sometime in September of 1847 in the Presidio of San Francisco: which might account for both my obsession with San Francisco as an imaginative ideal and for the fact that, despite my avoidance of the War Between the States, I backed willy-nilly into the armed conflict between Garibaldi and the pope. Born to an Army sergeant, I seemed destined to wear a uniform.

The Golden Era published another effort of mine, a poem, "Black Point at Twilight," which appeared in June of 1867, the same year that the Poems of my late friend Charles Warren Stoddard appeared. It was Charlie Stoddard who first invited me to Mrs. Fremont's soirées at Black Point.

We feel here power, authority, grace.

I wrote of San Francisco in the year 1867. (But more than San Francisco, I wrote this of myself as well.)

We sense suggestions of another place.
But heed, lest the roar of Pacific rim
Mute California to another hymn,
The twilight toll of a Tuscan tower
Calling to rest at the twilight hour.
Heed, lest the pungent Yerba Buena plant
Dissipate the remembered scent
Of red roses on a sunlit Lisbon wall.

A little precious, I'll admit; but remember that I was only eighteen at the time and full of romantic fancy. This poem constitutes my warning to myself not to forget the European past, despite the fact that I had never been to Europe, or had never been out of California for that matter, and was, when it came down to it, a provincially born, provincially educated lad in his final year at the Boys' High School, San Francisco, his imagination disordered through bouts of reading at the Mechanics' Library, his head slightly turned by William Chapman Ralston's promise of patronage. Mrs. Jessie Benton Fremont made Stoddard and me feel fully capable of doing great things in a literary way for California—which in the final analysis meant doing great things in a literary way for San Francisco.

I knew Charlie Stoddard—Charles Warren Stoddard to be exact—from the C. Beach Bookstore on Sansome Street, where he worked intermittently as a clerk. I say intermittently because, although Charlie showed up for work every day, he spent most of his time at the shop reading books and writing verse which he sent to *The Golden Era* under the preposterous pseudonym of Pip Pepperpod. Some five years older than I, Charlie was in his early twenties at the time, a young man of epicene good looks, by turns shy and grandiloquent, and (so it turned out in the course of his happy-sad life) a sometimes practicing homosexual. Charlie allowed me to browse in the English and European magazines kept in stock at C. Beach's shop, for I was then in the process of applying to Harvard at Mr. Ralston's behest and did not wish to show up in Cambridge (which then seemed as far away as the moon to me) ignorant of current literary and intellectual trends in England and on the Continent. In contrast to myself, who relished academic education and was thrilled by the prospect of Harvard, Charlie Stoddard hated school. Like Royce, Stoddard had an element of nervous instability in his make-up. He literally could not bear the restraints of the classroom, not to mention the incessant bullying of the other boys, who were driven by Charlie's almost girlish good looks and fey way of speaking into constant acts of aggression by which they might assert their threatened adolescent masculinity. The herd instinct demands that boys like Charlie be brutalized in what is almost a communal rite of sexual assertion through the dominance of anyone affected with the disease of feminine traits. Charlie renounced further education at the age of sixteen to go to work in C. Beach's bookstore. Like Samuel Johnson, Charlie completed his education by reading the inventory. Five years or so separated me from Charlie Stoddard, just as four years or so separated me from Josie Royce; yet despite the more than eight-year span between the three of us we became friends, bound together by a certain aesthetic nervousness. I include myself, incidentally, in the condition of incipient neurasthenia characteristic of Stoddard and Royce, although in my case a more aggressive animal nature than possessed by either Royce or Stoddard has mitigated my condition, anchoring my nerves on the solid shore of sensual satisfaction. Both Royce and Stoddard experienced collapses at various points in their lives, whereas I collapsed but once and that was due to unrequited love.

As I said earlier, the three of us—ages fourteen, eighteen, twenty-two—would tramp out to the Ocean Beach together, talking, talking, talking. Royce was so precocious that far from being intimidated by us two older lads, he quite often led the conversation. All three of us had our sights set on the great world beyond San Francisco. I looked forward to Harvard; Josie intended to study philosophy in Europe; and Charlie wanted to travel and write poetry. In one way or another, all three of us made our escape. Charlie and I, however, drifted back to San Francisco in middle life, grateful for the provincial acceptance we had so unconditionally scorned in our youth.

Charles Warren Stoddard was born in Rochester, New York, in 1843 of Yankee Presbyterian stock. He arrived in San Francisco as a boy of twelve. He returned to New York a few years later to live with his grandparents for a while, before returning again in 1859, the year of his first nervous collapse. In 1864 Charlie had another nervous breakdown. Sailing to

Hawaii on a clipper ship, he recovered his strength in the course of a number of happy months spent sunning himself on the beach. Forever after, he worshipped the god *Helios*. I suppose that it was Charlie's bronzed face that I first noticed when I first met him at C. Beach's Bookstore. It was tanned to the color of mahogany.

"I am a heliophile, my boy, an inveterate, impossible sun-worshipper," Stoddard told me soon after, when our friendship had commenced. "I must have the sun or I go positively insane. I literally collapse. The sun is my healing mother. I cannot abide a Presbyterian climate."

When we reached Ocean Beach on our rambles, Stoddard would doff his clothes, save for a pair of lederhosen-like undertrousers which he called his "sun-togs." In the Hawaiian Islands, he told us, he roamed the beaches wearing absolutely nothing at all, "an innocent child of nature"; but one had to be more careful in the Presbyterianized United States. An afternoon of sun soothed Stoddard remarkably. Strung tighter than piano wire at the beginning of the day, he purred like a cat after an afternoon of soaking in the sun off Seal Rock.

"Look at those darling seals," he said once, pointing to a pride of sea lions lazing atop a sun-splashed cluster of rocks offshore from the Cliff House. "Those aquatic beasties correctly divine nature's free gift of heliotherapy. Let us do likewise. Let us bare ourselves to the sun and perhaps we also shall attain the peacefulness of spirit that characterizes our lovely Brother Seal."

Under the spell of Stoddard's persuasion, Royce and I once consented to take off our shirts and burnt to a crisp in reward for our trustfulness. Neither of us had the making of a heliophile. Stoddard, however, merely grew browner and browner. I must say, however, that I have since learned to love the sun as did Charlie—from a more metaphorical point of view, that is. I have never developed a taste for sunbathing.

At the time I first met him, Stoddard was furiously scribbling poetry. The San Francisco bookseller Anton Roman published Stoddard's collected *Poems* in 1867. Francis Bret

Harte of *The Golden Era* wrote the introduction, and the artist Wiliam Keith engraved the illustrations. (Both Harte and Keith, ironically, attained more fame and fortune than Charlie Stoddard ever did.) A superbly produced book, *Poems* featured a green cover stamped in gold leaf, and Franklin Old Style type set beautifully by printer Edward Bosqui on thick linen-rag paper with dramatic rhythms of type and clear space. Retreating to Yosemite at the time of publication, Charlie nervously awaited reviews under the calming influences of daily sunbaths on the shore of the River Merced. Upon his return, he basked in the equally soothing warmth of Mrs. Fremont's approval. Josie Royce, so Stoddard said, was yet too young for Mrs. Fremont's *soirées* at Black Point; but I might tag along if I were so inclined. Now that Mr. Ralston had singled me out for patronage, I could (so Charlie suggested) move among the exalted company at Black Point without feeling too intimidated, my untested youth notwithstanding.

"Ah, yes, Mr. Ralston's fellow," Mrs. Fremont remarked when Stoddard first brought me along to Black Point for an evening of champagne, sandwiches, and conversation. Jessie Benton Fremont was just past forty at the time, 1866. She and her husband, Major General John Charles Fremont—the Conqueror of California and the state's first United States senator, as well as the first presidential candidate (in 1856) of the newly formed Republican party, and the commanding general in the Department of the West in the recent conflict between the states—had just returned to San Francisco, where he hoped to recoup his finances through the astute management of his agricultural properties in central California. From my study window, as I write, I can see Black Point jutting into the bay, adjacent to the about-to-be-opened Panama–Pacific International Exposition. The home built by the Fremonts on Black Point in the mid-1850s still stands. Set in a stand of cypress and eucalyptus trees, it opens out to the bay like a ship under sail. Mrs. Fremont gave many of her parties right on the edge of the Point, overlooking the white-capped currents of the bay. To this day, some fifty years later, I can still recreate in my mind the excitement of my early visits to Black Point—my first faltering steps, as it were, into the great world. On my first visit, I wore a blue frock coat, very new, with brass buttons, doeskin trousers, a high-stocked collar and a generous cravat, which I tied a number of times earlier in the afternoon to attain an appropriately artistic flair.

Mrs. Fremont began her *soirées* with an obligingly splendid sunset beyond the horizon of the Golden Gate, first named by her husband in his *Geographical Memoir on Upper California* (1848)—or by Mrs. Fremont herself, if you accept the notion (many do) that she wrote most of her husband's books. Sandwiches followed. Then talk. Mrs. Fremont was passionately devoted to the artistic future of California.

If it can be said of an eighteen-year-old lad in his first complete set of store-bought clothes that he fell in love with the devoted forty-one-year-old wife of a national hero, then let it be said that I fell instantly in love with Jessie Benton Fremont—not erotic love, mind you, desirous of possession, but a sort of mute worshipping from afar of her total, accomplished femininity. All that I asked of her was a moment's approval and attention, which I received—a hundredfold. Upon being introduced by Stoddard on the lawn behind the house, Mrs. Fremont looked me up and down with something resembling a mother's approval (she was, at the time, some four or five years older than my mother), then took my hand and led me over to a knot of guests. My heart pounding, I thrilled to her handclasp as we walked the short distance across the lawn. I thought for a moment that she had forgotten to drop my hand, but no: on she walked for some fifteen yards with me in tow like a bashful child. It has been, I say, some fifty years since then, but no woman has ever again taken my hand with such electric effect. She led me towards a strikingly handsome man whom I soon recognized to be the General himself. Royce and I have come the closest we ever came to quarreling because of his hostile treatment of General Fremont in his study of early California. Royce was profoundly wrong—more, he has an academic's jealousy of the man of action. Royce sought to prove that Fremont acted viciously when he took up arms against the Spanish Californians in 1846. I disagree. Every inch the hero, Fremont acted as the servant of Manifest Destiny. To paraphrase the Roman adage regarding Carthage: *California delenda est*—California had to be seized. It was the destiny of America to become a continental nation.

"John," Mrs. Fremont said. "Here is that marvelous young man Mr. Ralston has told us about—the Latin and Greek scholar who shall one day direct our Atheneum."

She placed my hand, which she had held for an ecstatic eternity, into the General's hand. He shook it while looking me squarely in the face. The General was as I had imagined him—handsome, commanding. Even in repose, he suggested the clash of sabres and the galloping of horses and treks across an uncharted wilderness. Today, 1914, it is easy to see the truth of Mrs. Fremont's claim for her husband: "From the ashes of his campfires cities have sprung." Then, however, in 1866, the campfires were yet warm; but even so I had no trouble sensing Fremont's greatness. It emanated from him physically. I refuse to quarrel with Royce regarding his negative assessment of Fremont's career. Old friendships should not be subjected to unnecessary stress, but should I ever speak frankly of the matter, I should accuse Royce of envy—the intellectual's envy of the adventurer, the mismarried man's envy of the romantically matched, the plodder's envy of those who attack destiny with a sword thrust or reel about pursuing their fate, in a charge of light cavalry.

"You are welcome, Mr. Collins," General Fremont greeted me. "San Francisco will soon have need of your talents."

"I must study first."

"Well, study you shall—after some sandwiches and champagne."

He signaled a Chinese waiter, who poured me my first glass of champagne—a pleasure I've repeated these past fifty years as frequently as possible. The General wore civilian clothes, but he was unmistakably the Pathfinder. Some twenty years

246

previously, in 1846, Fremont had entered California at the head of a column of trappers, mountain men, and Army topographical engineers who—upon hearing of, or suspecting, the outbreak of war between the United States and Mexico—formed themselves into the Mounted Battalion of California Volunteers, riding down *El Camino Real* in conquest. At the time of my visit to Black Point the General was in his early fifties: no longer a youthful hero, but possessed still of the hope of reconsolidating his fortunes, which had been on the wane since his defeat for the presidency in 1856. Little did we know then that the effort would prove unsuccessful, that Mrs. Fremont—that most literate of women, trained in the French, Spanish, and English classics by her father, Senator Thomas Hart Benton of Missouri—would be forced to turn to her pen for her family's support, which she began to do in the early 1870s. In 1866, however, a mood of recovery was in the air.

Mrs. Fremont talked much of literature that first *soirée*, asking me to join her and Stoddard and Francis Bret Harte and a sad-eyed bearded New York author, Herman Melville, intending a visit to his troubled son who, unfortunately, had already committed suicide (as did so many others out here) some months before his father's arrival. The talk that evening centered upon a proposed literary journal, which Harte, Stoddard, and the poet Ina Coolbrith launched some two years later, when I was in Italy, under the name of *The Overland Monthly*, publishing Harte's short story "The Luck of Roaring Camp" in the first issue, together with Henry George's "What the Railroad Will Bring Us" and Stoddard's Yosemite poem "In the Sierra."

Very much the dandy, Bret Harte wore a cinnamon-colored suit and a black and white checkered vest and canary-yellow gloves. He removed one glove to hold his champagne glass, tucking the glove into his vest pocket, from which it hung like a flag of militant dandyism.

"We do so very much need a journal," said Mrs. Fremont. "Something expressive of our glorious possibilities."

"And of our humor," said Harte.

"And making some money for all of us," said Stoddard, "so that I won't have to work any longer in that nasty bookstore."

Charlie Stoddard, you see, was a Bedouin, a gypsy ever in search of the lands of the sun. In 1870 he sailed to Tahiti. He returned for a second visit to Hawaii in 1872, writing up his South Sea experiences in a series of lush Tintoretto-colored essays which Mr. Howells published in *The Atlantic Monthly*. Charlie brought them out as a book, *South-Sea Idylls*, in 1873, the very year he appeared on my doorstep in Heidelberg after wandering about England for half a year.

Charlie knocked upon the door of my room at approximately three in the morning. To this day, I have no idea how he discovered that I had taken lodgings at Neckarstrasse 182, unless he had been in correspondence with my parents.

"I'm drunk," he said as I opened the door. "I've been drinking with some charming fellows at the Red Oxen. Put me to bed and we'll talk in the morning."

I guided him to a divan in my outer room, which I cleared of books and papers. As I restacked these materials on my eating table, Charlie stood by patiently. Only when I pointed to the cleared sofa did he collapse upon it in instantaneous sleep. When I returned from my morning lectures the next day, I found Charlie sitting bleary-eyed over a cup of coffee. He had slept until noon.

"My dear boy," he said, "you have been busy. All these books. I'm impressed."

Charlie, it turned out, was on his way to the Middle East, to the Holy Land first, then the Arabian peninsula, before going on to Egypt—all of which journeys are familiar to readers of his travel sketches. He had taken the train to Heidelberg the day before, expressly to visit me; but dropping by the Red Oxen for some refreshment, he had fallen in "with some charming fellows in funny hats and dueling scars" and had spent the next ten hours there drinking beer.

As I've pointed out, Charlie was a secret homosexual— although the subject of his sexuality never once came up between us in all the years I knew him: not directly at least.

Now and then I was able to sense that a certain bit of trouble Charlie had gotten himself into had a sexual dimension to it, but Charlie was ever the gentleman about his private life. He sought the comforting protection of older women—Ina Coolbrith above all—and women, in turn, as did Ina, responded wholeheartedly to Charlie's manifest need to be taken care of. In one side of his nature, Charlie yearned for a lost world of innocence. He would, if he could, have remained a boy all his life. The search for such innocence—and the solace of being childishly naked in the sun—returned him again and again to the South Sea Islands. "I'd rather be a South Sea Islander," he once announced in his Rincon Hill eyrie overlooking the Bay of San Francisco, a cottage filled with the art and bric-a-brac of Polynesia; "I'd rather be a South Sea Islander sitting naked in the sun before a grass hut, than be the Pope of Rome."

Both Rome and the South Seas, however, spoke equally to his yearning, imaginative, diffusedly erotic temperament. Charlie spent his life wandering in a labyrinth of aesthetic gesture. Whether he was deliberately lost or not I cannot tell; for I have not as of yet answered the questions of art, religion, beauty, sex, in my own life, much less judge how Charlie conducted his. Naked on a South Sea Island beach, Charlie surrendered the burden of his troubled self to the healing sun. Incense, the chanting of monastic choirs, the splendors of papal Rome offered him a similar release from the torments of self-awareness.

"What a cruel joke for God to have had me born a Presbyterian," Charlie once remarked. "I loathe Presbyterians. I loathe starched collars and silent Sundays. I loathe all those horrible stories in the Bible about murder and incest. When grandmama and grandpapa used to read from Holy Writ on Sundays back at Rochester, New York, I never thought that I could make it to dinnertime. Every hour, as they droned on and on, I grew more feeble of spirit. The very memory of it makes me want a drink."

Taking instruction from no less a personage than Archbish-

249

op Alemany himself, Stoddard was baptized in 1867, the year his *Poems* appeared.

"Listen, dear boy," he said of his conversion to the Roman Catholic Church, which occurred the month before I left for Harvard, "I believe everything His Excellency says before he says it. Incidentally, I love the way they fix the flowers on the altar at St. Mary's Cathedral, don't you? And the incense. I simply adore incense. I never believe in Almighty God more than when I smell incense."

As was frequently the case in his life, Charlie was playing for effect. *A Troubled Heart* (1885), the religious memoir he wrote when he was teaching at Notre Dame University, demonstrates the true imaginative and theological depth of Charlie's conversion—although, while making this point, I cannot deny the theatricality of Charlie's religiosity, or its ambiguous complexity for that matter. Charlie's occasional homosexual indulgences must have weighed upon his conscience, accounting no doubt for the heavy drinking of his later years. The core of Charlie's Catholicism, however, always centered itself upon a Solemn High Mass, with lots of music and incense, and with flowers on the altar.

"Let's go down to Munich and see Joe Strong," Charlie said after he had finished his coffee. We had spent an hour gossiping together in the manner of friends who have not seen each other for a few years: wondering what comes next, wondering if previous understandings still obtained. Joe Strong, a burly San Franciscan who looked more like a drayman than an artist, was studying painting in Munich at the time. It being Friday and my lectures concluded, I agreed to go. Taking the train down to Munich, we spent a wonderful weekend in Joe's studio and all over Munich. Joe began a portrait of Charlie dressed in the brown robes of a Franciscan friar, one hand resting on an open Bible, the other resting on a skull. The portrait today hangs in the Bohemian Club. Joe presented it to the Club in lieu of dues. I never pass the portrait, noticing the *recherché* theatricality of Charlie's monkish masquerade, that I don't think of the festive times we all spent together some thirty-five years ago.

The late seventies and early eighties seem in retrospect a naive, simple time—for San Francisco at least, or, to refine it further, for my San Francisco, for bohemian San Francisco. The whole world was then in its early thirties, full of vigor and appetite, eager to quaff the chalice of life. Joe Strong returned from Munich and married a young beauty, Belle by name, a buxom, giving sort of a female, possessed of Chaucerian warmth that had not the slightest suggestion of vulgarity. I returned from Rome. In between trips to North Africa or to the South Seas, Charlie ensconced himself on the south side of Rincon Hill. Charlie's cottage was a veritable museum of the South Seas. Robert Louis Stevenson, our companion from those days (now gathered to rest), describes Stoddard's cottage in his novel *The Wrecker* (partially set in San Francisco) as a "museum of strange objects—paddles and battle-clubs and baskets, cocoanut bowls, snowy cocoanut palms—evidences of another earth, another climate, another race, and another (if a ruder) culture." We'd meet at Charlie's place, or we'd go over to the studio which Joe Strong shared with the French painter Jules Tavernier in the Montgomery Block.

Tavernier took opium and painted in an eerie, phantasmagorical style which was no doubt influenced by the opiate with which he dosed himself. Strong's wife Belle kept a perennial *ragout* steaming on a coal stove. Legend had it that the *ragout* eventually was transmogrified into an organic being, alive for more than a decade. Belle replenished it with meat and onions and wine every time the *ragout* threatened to give up the ghost. The *ragout* provisioned a decade of impromptu supper parties. Belle Strong was one of those women who genuinely love to have men around her, a lot of men, without in any way compromising her husband's honor. God help anyone so foolish as to dare compromise Joe Strong! One blow from Joe's ham-like fist and any would-be suitor of Belle Strong would join the Seraphim!

"Belle, love Charlie," Stoddard said the first time we piled up the stairs for a supper-party at the Strong-Tavernier studio. Charlie frequently used baby talk or charmingly abbreviated words into his own idiosyncratic prattle. As he spoke, Charlie

251

rested his head upon Belle's ample bosom. Belle ran her fingers through Charlie's thinning hair (Charlie was near forty at the time) and vowed to love him ever after. Joe Strong roared his approval.

"That boy," said the twenty-year-old Belle of the forty-year-old Stoddard, "brings out the mother in me."

Before arriving in San Francisco, Jules Tavernier spent a number of years as a field artist with the United States Cavalry fighting the Sioux on the Great Plains. Jules's portion of the Montgomery Block studio was hung with Indian trophies. Joe decorated his half with German tapestries. A large grand piano divided the two men's respective spaces. About once a month Belle would put out the word among our set that the *ragout* had reached a point of critical growth. It needed devastation. We would converge upon the studio at twilight from our respective places of employment, climbing the high stairs and giving the secret knock demanded by Tavernier because, chronically in debt, he lived in constant fear of bill collectors and court subpoenas. Virgil Williams of the Art Institute would be there, a master of perfect Italian, which he and I spoke together in a corner for the sake of the practice. I remember encountering Henry George, the journalist from the *Post*, resting from the labor of writing an economic treatise, *Progress and Poverty*, for which he also set the type. John Muir would drop by. John—he has been dead now but a year—spent six months of every year in the Sierra and the other six months in San Francisco writing up his wilderness experiences. Fred Somers, editor of *The Argonaut*, could fill a room with roaring laughter.

Most of us belonged to the Bohemian Club. Jules Tavernier and Henry George, in fact, were part of the circle of artists and journalists who founded the Club in 1873. Quite often, we would slip the word to visitors to the Club that if they wanted to experience *la vie bohème* in its pristine form, they should drop by the Tavernier-Strong studio on such and such an evening for wine, sourdough bread, cracked crab, and a plateful of Belle Strong's *ragout*. Oscar Wilde wore a puce velvet suit to one evening—and even Charlie Stoddard

252

confessed himself out-posed by the English aesthete who had, as he put it, wended his weary way to the occidental uttermost of western civilization. Rudyard Kipling spent a good part of one evening *tête à tête* on a couch with a pretty young actress from the California Theater on Bush Street. The actress threw back her head to laugh, revealing a long white throat and some charming *décolletage*. Kipling's thick glasses filmed over with moisture.

We once had a costume party. I wore a red silk robe of a Chinese mandarin. Charlie came as a Bedouin sheik. Many of our evenings ended with recitals by Charlie upon the studio's heroic grand piano. An excellent pianist, Charlie played by the romantic light of a candelabra, *à la* Chopin. He loved to make thundering Lisztian rushes across the keyboard, while casting looks, by turns dreamy or smoldering (depending upon the music), upon the most senior lady present. As I said, Charlie had a way with older women. He often recited poetry by heart, playing softly to accompany the sonorous verse, most of it by Charlie Stoddard.

For a few years Robert Louis Stevenson graced San Francisco with his luminous presence. A tall, reedy young Scotsman, perhaps already infected with the tuberculosis that would carry him off in 1894, Stevenson married a San Francisco divorcee in 1880, Fanny van de Grift Osbourne, whom he had met in the South of France and pursued halfway across the world to San Francisco. Stoddard and RLS (as we all called him) were very close. In *The Wrecker*, Stevenson tells the story of their initial meeting atop Rincon Hill. Living solitarily in a rooming house on Bush Street as he awaited the final decree of Mrs. Osbourne's divorce, Stevenson was wont to wander the foggy, ramshackle streets of San Francisco. One day he climbed Rincon Hill south of Market Street, attracted there by the picturesque cottages clinging to the bay side of the hill. Sitting down to sketch the view of city and bay, RLS met Charlie, then living in one of the cottages. Charlie invited him in for a cup of tea. It was the beginning of an intense friendship. Through Charlie, RLS very rapidly penetrated the center of our local bohemia. We all loved him. He was gentle, kind, ironic. RLS first learned of the magic of the South Seas from Charlie, incidentally—the South Seas where RLS lived and wrote in the final years of his life before succumbing to tuberculosis, having for more than a decade of astonishing creativity outrun the gray ghost of death, from France to California, back to Scotland, then down across the world to Samoa, where the end came at age forty-four.

"I've lost my taste for this town," Charlie told me not long before RLS's departure for Europe. "RLS says he can't see how anyone can work in San Francisco, and I'm beginning to agree. I'm past forty and what have I accomplished? Not much. A few essays, a book of poems, little else. It's all the damn living we're supposed to be doing out here. We feel obligated to burn time like an incense stick of pleasure—just because it's San Francisco and we're so far away from everything and constantly feel a half-despairing impulse to authenticate ourselves through dissipation and exuberance. No wonder Gertrude Atherton and her friend, the young opera singer you are so mad about—what's her name?"

"Sybil Sanderson."

"Yes, Sybil Sanderson, that's her. No wonder those two girls are so anxious to leave for Europe. You don't have to justify Europe. It's already justified. We San Franciscans are always having to justify ourselves. We get so bored and exhausted from asserting our specialness that we drink too much and stay up too late and don't get any work done the next morning."

I felt a little defensive, for I agreed with much of what Charlie was saying. The problem with San Francisco was then, and still is, that it is a remote, provincial city—yet a city touched by larger imperatives, or so I thought then and still halfway do now. In San Francisco it is very, very easy to fall between the two stools of provinciality and the urge for a larger context. The tension can paralyze the will. I must admit, however, that after this florid renunciation I expected Stoddard to cast off for England or the Continent. By the mid-1880s, after all, San Francisco had already been abandoned by hordes of creative souls who agreed with Charlie's diagnosis of San Francisco's disheartening provinciality. If the importance of San Francisco is that it sustains the imperatives of the wider world, they reasoned, why not seek the wider world directly? If the comparative luxuriance of the East, especially Boston, could not hold to an American career the likes of Henry James, John Singer Sargent, Francis Marion Crawford, then what chance had San Francisco to keep its talent? Samuel Clemens, Bret Harte, Henry George, Ambrose Bierce—by the mid-1880s these and others had sought greener pastures. Homegrown talent such as Gertrude Atherton, Sybil Sanderson, Isadora Duncan, David Belasco would soon follow. Think of my surprise, then, when Charlie told me that he was leaving not for Boston, Paris, Rome or Vienna— but for South Bend, Indiana.

"The good fathers of Notre Dame College have offered me a post as professor of literature," Charlie announced. "I shall seek the sylvan glades of academe and there court the muses in an ambiance of pious rusticity. I shall say my prayers and write my books, undistracted by the temptations of this wicked, wicked city."

"You'll be bored to death," I protested, not then realizing that my ultimate fate would also involve the pounding of scholarly rudiments into freckled foreheads, albeit in San Francisco.

"Precisely, Sebastian. Divine boredom—the leisure, the *otium*, to contemplate and to complete some vast literary project, a grand novel, perhaps, or a literary history, or some speculations into the final redemptive effects of beauty upon this too-too-utter vale of tears."

Charlie spent a year at Notre Dame before being called to a better-paying position as professor of literature at the newly founded Catholic University of America in Washington, D.C. I have on hand a letter he wrote me from South Bend.

"The dear boys come to classes," he writes, "tired from playing football, and I deliver my lecture in such a gentle monotone that they sleep peacefully. I am very popular."

255

Stoddard taught at the Catholic University until 1902, lured there by the prospect of a steady income in a congenial urban setting. He moved his books and South Seas bric-a-brac into a suburban cottage which he named St. Anthony's Rest, setting up housekeeping with a young fellow by the name of Kenneth O'Connor, whom Charlie called the Kid. The Kid, however, developed a drinking problem, as did Charlie himself. Homosexuals have a tendency towards heavy drinking, as I have noticed, since they live constantly under a burden of guilt and the threat of social repudiation. Bishop John J. Keane, the rector of Catholic University, fired Charlie after it became obvious that Charlie was missing too many of his classes because of incapacitating hangovers.

"That ends a dream that became a nightmare," Charlie wrote me of his dismissal. "There can be no such thing as a Catholic university that is truly a university, for all Catholic educational institutions are religious fakes and the Catholic University of America is more priest-ridden than Rome itself."

Pushed to the wall, Charlie, for all the vibrancy of his aesthetic Catholicism, still nurtured a Rome-baiting Presbyterian within his soul. He returned to San Francisco in 1905 after spending the previous three years in a drunken haze. A number of times he came close to death—which must be the most horrible death imaginable, death from drinking, I mean: a hangover is bad enough; but to die in despair from alcoholic poisoning ("a severe insult to the brain" the doctors call it) as Charlie almost did, or to rot one's innards so that internal hemorrhaging occurs—how frightening.

In 1905, I found myself fifty-seven years old and a teacher like Charlie Stoddard (albeit an employed teacher), greeting again the once-young man who long ago shared my dreams and rambled with me out to the Ocean Beach, disporting himself there like a pagan divinity; the once-young man who first took me to the Fremonts' *soirées* on Black Point on that breathtaking spring evening in May of 1867, my neck slightly choked from my high starched collar and Byronically tied ascot. Here I was then: helping this very same fellow off the

256

train at the Oakland station, his once epicene features hidden by a snowy white beard, his lithe sun-browned body thickened by age and the excessive nourishment of steady potations of liquor.

"It's a happy homecoming, Sebastian, for all the sadness of it—because you're here and because you are still my friend."

"I am always your friend, Charlie, and San Francisco is always your home."

After a few months it was obvious that Charlie could not adjust to the accelerated pace of modern San Francisco. He managed to ease off on his drinking, however, and recovered something of his old histrionic flair. He spoke incessantly of the San Francisco he had known in the seventies and early eighties, and of his old bohemian friends—Tavernier, Joe Strong, Julian Rix, Virgil Williams—so many of whom were dead and gone. Six months after his arrival in the city, Stoddard announced that he was moving to Monterey. There, he told me, the ambiance of Old California persisted. I knew that moving to Monterey was a good decision because it restored in Charlie some of his old insouciance.

"I hope," he announced to me with something of his former grandiloquence, in such contrast to the monosyllabic booze-dry wispiness of his voice upon his arrival at the train station five months earlier, "I hope to drift down the southern coast and swing into an eddy—a priest's garden and veranda, in an old adobe mission village, where one lisps Spanish, indulges in the siesta; makes worry over the mass-wine. In the legends of the past are the joys of the present. Where the tinkle of guitars—the quivering vibrant rhythm that seems to play upon the heartstrings—and the clack-clack of castanets are heard in the land; and where one at last dies in the odor of sanctity and cigarettes."

"I see that you have recovered your lost grip on reality," I said. It was like old times, hearing him fantasize like that.

We buried Charlie five years later at the Carmel Mission on a morning in late April, Charlie having died in the spring like an old shepherd, solaced by the sportings of one last season.

George Sterling, Jimmy Phelan, myself, and Joaquin Miller and a number of others in the Carmel art colony served as pallbearers at the funeral. Phelan and I took the train down together to Monterey.

"Think of me, dear Sebastian," Charlie had written not long after his arrival in Monterey, "as enjoying the pastoral pleasures of a year-long Bohemian Grove encampment. I live a life of sunshine and contentment. The younger writers of Carmel lionize Joaquin Miller and yours truly for being hoary survivors of California's first bohemia. I, in turn, bestow my apostolic benediction upon their efforts. I do this in utter sincerity; for George Sterling, Jack London, and Mary Austin, the luminaries of the Carmel crowd, are artists of both achievement and further promise. At our abalone roasts, I sit on the beach by a fire drinking dago red and savoring the scent of abalone broiling on the glowing coals. Of an afternoon I take my ease in the garden of Mission San Carlos Borromeo— where soon I shall rest my weary bones—and I savor the scene of Spanish Catholicity. I have become quite good friends with the swallows. The other day, I recalled our audience together in Rome with *Pio Nono* just before His Holiness's death. The Holy Father embraced you with tears in his eyes, calling you his American Zouave. Rollo Peters, whose lovely oil nocturnes of Monterey you so admire, has a balconied home overlooking the Bay of Monterey. I sit with him of an evening, watching the moonlight on the water. 'Rollo,' I said the other night, 'your brooding nocturnes are understated, for the moonlight is possessed of even more iridescent sadness than you put into your seascapes.' I sit also in the rear room of Jules Simoneau's restaurant on the plaza, sipping wine, nibbling on fresh cantaloupe, recalling with old Jules the time RLS and I came down here in 1879. As you can see, I do a lot of sitting—as if I were waiting for something or Someone: Death it is, or the Heavenly Bridegroom, although I must say that it is difficult to think of Death, or even Jesus, when one has at last come into one's long desired Arcadia after so long and erring an exile."

258

Charlie's coffin was lowered into the ground with his head facing the altar of the Mission, in the old medieval manner of churchyard burial. The bones of some ten thousand Indian neophytes bristled beneath the weedy earth like dragons' teeth.

"Where tent you tonight, old Bedouin?" Joaquin Miller asked in a deliberately discernible *sotto voce* after Father Raho finished the Latin prayers of interment. Ina Coolbrith seemed about ready to faint. Charlie loved this old poet above anyone else in the world, and she returned his affection.

"Wherever he tents, Joaquin," Ina said after a moment, "it will be a beautiful place. Charlie had a way of bringing beauty along with him, wherever he went, like a hat or a pair of gloves. When he rushed into *The Overland Monthly* office on Portsmouth Square forty years ago, the room seemed to glow with his presence. I didn't have to see Charlie much after he left San Francisco. The sheer knowledge that he was still on the same planet with me dispelled any possible desperation of loneliness."

The other night when we sat up awaiting Marina's return from the Fairmont Hotel, Royce and I reminisced about our boyhood friend, each of us by turns thumbing through my collection of Stoddard's limited output—the elegant, slender volumes of poetry, travel sketches, memoir, criticism, and fiction which occupy an honored place on my shelf.

"Stoddard was a local colorist," said Royce, "like Washington Irving—a genial appreciator of scene and atmosphere. He perceived life through the haze of the picturesque."

"He was a very tormented man," I said, "troubled by drink, art, sexuality, and religion—which, come to think of it, are rather noble preoccupations."

"He seemed addicted to the minor key," said Royce.

"He hated bombast and was in his own way a rather modest man," I rejoined.

"I miss him, Sebastian."

"So do I."

Farewell, Charlie, gentle shepherd, buried four years ago

with your head resting upon a tile from the Mission altar. Farewell, beloved bohemian friend. Never again shall you knock upon my door as you did that early morning in Heidelberg some forty years ago, stopping by *en route* to the Holy Land. I have your books for remembrance and comfort: your idyll of South Pacific sunshine, the story of your troubled religious heart; your biography of Father Damien the Leper, whom you so admired; your novel of lazy mornings in San Francisco, spent over coffee and Turkish cigarettes and the daily postal harvest of next week's invitations. Never again shall you and I stroll San Francisco's foggy bohemian streets.

Charlie Stoddard, so Royce says, lived in the minor mode, and so also perhaps have I. I am Sebastian Collins, a semiobscure provincial scholar and man of letters. My reputation, like the city's fog, has been burned off by the sun that shines beyond the San Francisco peninsula. Perhaps it is just as well. I have discovered local acceptance and a measure of personal peace in my life. Royce has achieved greatness, but is personally miserable. I have done solid work in scholarship (I have Santayana's assurances of it!), and I have played a role in promoting the culture of San Francisco; but I must be honest—greatness has eluded me. Never mind: God alone is great. Ours is but to serve His greater glory. In His will, as Dante says, is our peace. In His divine glory is our reputation.

My mentor William Chapman Ralston had other ideas—about greatness and glory, I mean. Greatness, the tormenting promise of San Francisco's greatness to be precise, animated Ralston like a possessing fury, driving him to a thousand projects, such as the financing of my education so that I might return to direct an Atheneum. Some of Ralston's projects were reckless, although I like to think that his generosity in subsidizing me to Harvard and to Heidelberg has paid off in some small dividend to the city he loved as one loves an eager mistress.

The transcontinental railroad had two years of construction remaining before completion when I left San Francisco for the

East in the fall of 1867; so I made the journey to Massachusetts by steamer down to Panama City, then across the Isthmus by train to Chagres. I then took ship up through the Caribbean to New Orleans, then sailed on to New York City. Mother and Father put me on the steamer in San Francisco, a sail and paddle-wheel affair, the *Mariposa*, run by the White Star Line.

The night before my departure my parents and I sat together over dinner, talking excitedly at intervals, then falling into sad silences. I had always been a home-loving lad, close to Mother and regarding Father with a mixture of affection and awe. Even then, nearing nineteen, I had passed up both of them in the matter of education, and perhaps even in terms of exposure to the great world—so much as that world was available to me in San Francisco. Yet, as I say, I was still a home-boy, a domestic lad, virginal and very much tied to Mother's apron strings. And why not? In the Old Country, the Irish keep their children home longer than is common in the United States, if they can afford it; indeed, in larger families, one child, usually a daughter, stays home all her adult life to care for her parents when they grow old.

Mother baked ham and sweet potatoes, and Father wore a good suit to the table, as if it were an occasion, which it was, after all, my departure for Harvard after nearly nineteen years of home life. I knew that Mother was treating my departure as a special occasion because she served dinner on her best china, despite the fact that there was no one else at the table save Father and myself. Mother used her best china only at Christmas and Thanksgiving, or upon those infrequent occasions when company came.

When she helped me organize my files, Marina insisted upon pressing between two sheets of waxed paper the news-clipping from the San Francisco *Post* that announced my departure for the East. Marina pressed down on either side of the waxed sheets with a lightly heated clothes iron. The heat of the iron melted the wax, sealing the clipping on both sides.

"You can do the same thing to old leaves," Marina observed as she touched the iron down lightly.

261

"Or to wedding invitations," I observed.

"Or to tickets of admission to the Busybodys' Convention."

I let the matter drop.

Pressed between two sheets of waxed paper, the clipping, some forty-seven years old to begin with, now has an archival life of hundreds of years, should anyone prove interested. Under the caption "S.F. Schoolboy to Harvard," I re-read the article of *bon voyage* that had so excited my parents, they seeing my name in the newspaper for the first time. The years have dimmed the clipping, but the clear bite of good hand-set type has kept the letters discernible.

"Mr. Sebastian Collins," it reads, "the son of Fire Chief Dennis Collins and Mrs. Mollie Collins of 287 Minna Street, the City, departs next week on the *Mariposa* for the East. Mr. Sebastian Collins will matriculate at Harvard College. A graduate of the Boys' High School, Mr. Collins intends to pursue the liberal arts at the famed New England university. Mr. Collins, eighteen, is among the first children of American ancestry to be born in San Francisco. The fact that he makes a voyage back to such a citadel of Atlantic culture as Harvard College, raised and tutored in our city in the classical and modern languages and in every department of current science, casts credit upon our Pacific metropolis. We wish Mr. Collins godspeed and we offer our congratulations to his preceptors at the Boys' High School. So far as it is known, Mr. Collins is San Francisco's first locally educated Harvard scholar, although many graduates of that distinguished institution now make their home on these Pacific Shores."

"I wonder what kind of meals they'll be giving you at Harvard?" Mother said, passing me a tureen of mashed sweet potatoes. "They say fish is good for the brain. I'll allow that they'll be giving you a lot of fish."

"But not on Friday," said Father, biting into a generous forkful of ham. Father ate European style, using his knife in his left hand, and holding his reversed fork in his right. He'd build up the food on his fork, using his knife, then take food directly into his mustachioed mouth. Mother cut her food, then reversed her knife and fork in the American fashion. All my life I've eaten both ways—now one way, now another, for years at a time. I am currently eating in the European manner.

"I'm proud of you, boy," Father said, "but your mother and I hate to lose you."

"I wonder," said Mother, "how they handle the laundry at Harvard, and I'm worried whether your books got there." We had shipped my books out ahead of me, Mr. Ralston arranging for a special price through his shipping connections.

"They'll get there, Mollie, and Sebastian will be having a grand room in the College. Mr. Ralston has seen to that. What's your hall again, lad?"

"Gray's Hall, third floor."

Thirty years later Frank Norris occupied these same rooms when he spent a year at Harvard studying writing under Professor Gates.

"Just think of it, Dr. Collins," Frank Norris said boyishly. (I was always "Dr." to Frank.) "The very same rooms! You and I had the very same rooms at Harvard! That must mean something."

"Take a walk with me, lad," Father said after dinner. We strolled out to North Beach, then a semideveloped section of the city. We passed scattered shacks, many of them with fishing nets drying out front. There was a saloon or two. A band of Chinese in queues and silken shirts clattered past us, filling the evening air with the sing-song of their conversation. A reticent man, Father steeled himself for a Talk. It took about a half an hour for Father to get through it. Redacted, the Talk can be summarized thusly: avoid loose women, but if you feel overwhelmed by the urges of nature, consort only with proper professionals; in no case seduce a decent girl. Study hard and make something of yourself because the Irish are an oppressed people, deprived of such opportunities as a Harvard education; but if the Yankees at Harvard come down on you hard for being Irish, tell them that Ireland was a land of scholars when the English were yet running about in animal skins, painting themselves blue.

"If I ever thought," Father said in the course of one remark that I remember fifty years later because his words touched me deeply at the time and still do. "If your mother and I ever dreamed when we sailed into the Golden Gate twenty years ago, or back before that when we ran off together to America, her barefoot and in a coarse-cloth shift, that in one generation we'd be having a son at Harvard, well then, we'd have not been able to imagine such splendor for ourselves."

We picked our way back through the marsh area, reaching Portsmouth Square, which by the late 1860s was beginning to lose some of its status as the heart of the city, although you wouldn't know it that evening by the press of people on the streets and the blare of brass bands coming from within the saloons. At age forty-seven Father had attained the full vigor of his manhood. He stood six feet tall (at five feet, ten inches I am two inches shorter than Father was) and he weighed some two hundred pounds. His hair and mustache had turned snow-white in the manner of the Irish, and also like many of the Irish he had a ruddy complexion—made even more roseate by his outdoor life as a fireman and by a lifelong love of bracing spirits. I am somewhat heavier than Father, incidentally; but then again, the demands of teaching and writing are less exhausting than those of serving as the busy fire chief of San Francisco. In addition to a mustache that I flatter myself has something of the fullness and sweep of Father's corsair-like lip whiskers, I have worn a short, well-trimmed beard since my forties.

As we walked back to our home on Bush Street, people stopped to greet Father by his Christian name or by the simple sobriquet "Chief." So many people knew who he was, San Francisco being a fire-conscious town. Father, by the way, looked splendid in his full-dress uniform, which he wore for formal civic occasions: a double-breasted, blue frock coat, set off by at least fifty gold buttons, dominated by a large gold star over his right breast pocket that unambiguously said "The Chief."

When we arrived home, Mother had hot chocolate waiting for us, and apple pie, which she had sliced and set out on the table while we were gone.

264

"I wonder," she asked, "if they have hot chocolate at Harvard?"

By the year 1867 there were hundreds of thousands of lads my age who were either dead or maimed for life from the carnage of the Civil War; and there I was—pink and healthy, virginally nineteen, plied with hot chocolate and apple pie. At Harvard I soon learned that Civil War veterans were a caste apart. They were men, while the rest of us were boys. Few such grizzled veterans enrolled with me in the freshman year; but a handful of my classmates in the Class of 1871 did spend the years 1865, 1866, 1867 allowing broken bones to mend or resistant wounds to heal or learning how to walk with a wooden leg before negotiating the treacherous cobblestone streets of Cambridge. My class had one former crewman from the ironclad *Monitor* and an invalided company first sergeant who had made the charge at Gettysburg when he was all of seventeen. Most veterans, however, were by 1867 in their senior year or passed on to the law or medical faculties. Oliver Wendell Holmes, Jr., then in the Law School, strode through the Yard like a Greek hero returned from the Trojan Wars. Promoted to lieutenant colonel of cavalry before he was twenty-three, the son of the Autocrat of the Breakfast Table had fought through some of the most bloody campaigns of the Rebellion. I remember Holmes's clear blue eyes and the air of command that emanated from him as he strolled across the Yard, as if he were reviewing a battalion before some dangerous action.

One of the first things I did upon arrival at Harvard—after unpacking my trunks and arranging my books on my shelves (they arrived safely)—was to walk over to the just completed Memorial Hall on the edge of the Yard and read the names of the Harvard war dead, Union and Confederate, carved on the marble walls of the sanctuary. The places—Antietam, Spottsylvania, Wilderness, Gettysburg; and the names—Lowell, Pickett, Folger, Arundel, summarized the War before my provincial gaze in a roll call carved in stone. While I had had

265

my hot chocolate and apple pie and learned Latin and Greek in far-off San Francisco, these New England boys (and yes, these Virginia and South Carolina and Mississippi boys as well) charged into smoke and steel, and were mown down like wheat before an insatiable scythe.

A soaring red-brick Gothic structure surmounted by a great spire, Memorial Hall can be seen from Boston across the Charles River. Next to Bulfinch's golden dome atop the Massachusetts State House on Beacon Hill, Memorial Hall was the first building on the Boston-Cambridge skyline to catch my attention. It shimmered in the distance like a medieval cathedral.

"That's Harvard," said the driver of my horse-drawn streetcar, next to whom, on the very first seat, I sat as we wended our way up Massachusetts Avenue. "That red tower is Harvard."

My heart pounded as I gazed upon the soaring Gothic tower in the distance, dedicated (I later learned) to the war dead of the university. Jude the Obscure never gazed at the spires of Oxford with a longing equal to mine; unlike Jude, I was destined to enter into possession of those magical Gothic halls that shimmered ahead at the conclusion of the streetcar tracks. I was to enroll at Harvard.

My ship had anchored in New York the day before, and I had wasted no time getting across Manhattan and piling my luggage onto the Boston train. Sitting by myself next to the window, I feasted my eyes on a new American landscape—its variety of trees, its variegated topography of meadow and hill and forest, in such contrast to the bolder confrontations of sea, mountain, and rock that characterize the San Francisco Bay Area where I grew up. I hugged myself with excitement. I was in the East!

Reporting to the dean's office in University Hall, I received my lodging assignment to Gray's Hall from the undergraduate housing clerk, a small, mousy man who operated from behind a wire cage on the first floor like a bank teller. My room impressed me as the epitome of luxury. I admired the

266

fireplace, the built-in walnut bookcases, the washstand (no indoor plumbing, however, but a water pitcher on hand to be filled from the pump downstairs, and jakes in the basement). Mr. Ralston insisted that I have first-class accommodations.

"I want his mind on his studies," Ralston bellowed to my parents, demanding that I be placed on Harvard's A-Schedule: with, that is, complete boarding and laundry facilities, to include a private room.

"I want no resentments, no barriers to academic achievement. I am, you see, myself a self-made man and I can honestly say that many of the hindrances engendered by scarcity are not ennobling, as certain philosophers claim, but distracting; or worse, they are boring. I'll have no resentments and no hindrances. The boy enters Harvard from an A-Schedule city, San Francisco, so order the A-Schedule!"

Mr. Ralston kept his word. I wanted for nothing. Certain of the lads on my floor, in fact, themselves crowded some two or three to a room, called me "the gentleman from San Francisco," or more briefly, "the gentleman" because of the lavishness of my lodgings and equipage. President Eliot, as I have mentioned before, approached me with a certain barely concealed sardonic hostility. As I look back upon it, I must have been the only Irish Catholic in the class of 1871, as well as the only Californian—much less the only San Franciscan. Many of the staff at Harvard—porters, gardeners, cooks, maintenance help—were local Irish, but there were precious few among the student body. Mr. Ralston had made sure that there would be no resentments as to accommodation, but he could not have predicted the more subtle resentments that eventually found their way into my heart.

But that took a year and a half to unfold, and even then the course of it was interrupted in the fall of 1868 when I left the College for two years in Italy. There, like the Harvard veterans of 1861–1865, I learned what it was like to charge into a maelstrom of smoke, steel, and fire. During my first year at the College, I took standard courses: Latin, Greek, mathematics, natural science, ethics, the historical foundations of

Scripture. It was only after I returned to the College in 1871 that I concentrated my reading in the fields of art history and aesthetics.

"Make yourself an educated man," Ralston abjured me upon my departure from San Francisco. "Return to us from Harvard capable of discrimination and complex judgments. Then we'll send you to Europe for professional education. I do not feel that San Francisco needs to import an Atheneum director from the East or from abroad. We shall develop our own cultural leadership from native stocks. But just as Colonel Haraszthy has harvested and shipped to us the shoots of European vineyards for grafting upon our native vines, so too must you also be grafted with the learning of Europe and New England. We'll send you forth to sip the pollen from an older civilization's flower, then we shall make our own Californian honey."

Mr. Ralston frequently spoke that way, in florid hyperbole; but since he was talking about me, since he was opening up for me such startling vistas and prospects, I never minded the orchidaceousness of his rhetoric.

Memories and impressions from my first year and a half at Harvard: a random sampling, or rather, a New England sampler, sewn with the thread of memory. As the *Mariposa* pulled out of the Golden Gate, I saw a herd of elk run across a ridge of the Marin hills. Elk were very rare that near the city, although they had grazed *en masse* on the hillsides some twenty years earlier when Father and Mother first sailed into San Francisco Bay. . . . Point Concepcion off Santa Barbara, with its association with Richard Henry Dana, Jr., and *Two Years Before the Mast*. . . . An ocean sunset off San Diego: a splendor of purple, orange, and gold. . . . The train ride across the Isthmus of Panama: a realization that this must have been hell to cross some twelve years previous before the completion of the trans-Panamanian railroad, to be forced to negotiate an impenetrable tropics by canoe and muleback. As it was, the hot, sticky, steamy-wet train ride was uncomfortable enough. . . . At Chagres: bananas for breakfast, bananas for lunch, bananas for dinner. The southern carpetbagger in the lobby of the steamship depot, who leaned aside for a second in the course of arranging his ticket to San Francisco and sent a horrid bolus of brown tobacco juice from his mouth in an arc of some eight to ten feet, hitting bullseye into a cuspidor. "You're heading the wrong way, son," he later said to me when we were chatting. "The opportunity is on the western edge of the continent." . . . Panama City at twilight: Negroes, roadside fruit stalls, the old Spanish citadel brooding over the city by moonlight, raucous laughter from within the interior patio of a walled home, guitar music from somewhere in the distance, a parrot in my hotel lobby who said, "Good morning, Mr. Lincoln," to anyone who stepped up to the desk clerk. . . . The offshore view of Manhattan, the total confusion of the New York docks: stevedores, porters, customs inspectors in blue uniforms, the sheer gratitude I felt when, secure in the back seat of a hansom cab, my luggage resting atop the rack behind the driver, I followed the clippity-clop, clippity-clop of our horse across Manhattan, headed for the train station. . . . My room in the Parker House of Boston, the steeple of Old North Church visible from my window. Leaving my shoes outside my door that evening (after asking the attendant down the hall why the others had done so), retrieving them the next morning waxed and buffed to a gleam. . . . A smoker at the Hasty Pudding for prospective members of the incoming freshman class: bottled beer, smoked salmon on rye bread, a lot of laughter, and a facetious review in which one boy did a superb imitation of President Eliot, save that his false mutton side-whiskers flared out to absurd lengths, giving him the guise of a giant butterfly in a frock coat. . . . A letter from my mother: "I miss our evenings together over tea, you at your books at the kitchen table, but I comfort myself with the hope that your absence is for the best. Three major fires last month, and your Father in the thick of it all as usual." . . . President's night, Mr. Eliot receiving us stiffly as we passed in line before him. I decided then and there that the Hasty Pudding comedian had been merciful in his caricature.

Something cold and aloof about Eliot, something that epitomized to me the frosty edge of Yankee superiority which got on my nerves—as grateful as I was to be at Harvard. . . . Autumn: the elms in the Yard and the Cambridge streets, a riot of color such as never experienced by a native Californian: russets, yellow, varieties of browns and greens. . . . The Gothic grandeur of Gore Hall Library, where I sat in an alcove warmed by winter sunlight coming through the glass, reading, reading, reading. . . . A fire in my room on a winter's night, with some of my hall-mates in for a bottle of sherry and a great wooden box of California walnuts, sent to me by Mr. Ralston: cracking walnuts, drinking sherry, hearing one of the fellows say, "Well, Collins, you're a bit of a swell, aren't you, but generous with your grog, and that's a good thing. Tell me honestly now, since you're from the West, have you ever copulated with an Indian girl?" As of yet I had copulated with no girl at all, white or Indian. My deflowerment in Rome, city of lost innocence and lost illusions, awaited my enlistment in the Zouaves.

I enlisted in the Zouaves because of Ryan Patrice, affiliated tutor to the College in Romance languages and literature, whom I met in the Christmas of 1867 after midnight Mass at St. Paul's Church off Harvard Square. In the language of contemporary espionage, Ryan Patrice was an undercover agent for the Papal States. I found all this out years later, partly from discussions with him at the Grand Chartreuse, but even before that, from perusing the semisecret agenda of the War Ministry housed in the Vatican archives. I managed this in the late 1870s when I was employed as a *scriptor* in the Vatican Library.

For the Pope to defend the sovereignty of the Papal States from General Garibaldi at the head of the armies of the Italian Kingdom took money, considerable amounts of money, armies having a way of proving expensive. Monsignor Mérode, the minister of war, distrusted Cardinal Antonelli, the secretary of state; Antonelli epitomized to Mérode everything that was

270

cynical and corrupt in the administration of the Papal States. Antonelli, on the other hand, a Neopolitan petty bourgeois (subsequently ennobled) who had climbed up through the ranks of the church bureaucracy without bothering to be ordained a priest, saw in Mérode an atavistic reactionary, an episcopal crusader from the eleventh century bent upon an ultimately self-destructive holy war against Garibaldi. Antonelli advised the Pope to negotiate the political autonomy of Rome within the Italian Kingdom with the Pope given a presiding role as magistrate of the city and its immediate environs. Monsignor Mérode had fought as an officer in the French army in Algeria before embracing holy orders; as much the soldier as he was the priest, he urged armed resistance. *Pio Nono* took Mérode's advice, and many people died as a result.

But I am getting ahead of my story. Suffice it to say that Monsignor Mérode commissioned a dozen or so agents, all of them accomplished clerics like Ryan Patrice, to operate in the Catholic countries of Europe and Latin America, and among the Catholic population of the United States and Canada. These agents were charged with promoting opinion among the Catholic hierarchy and influential lay people favorable to the Church's armed resistance against Garibaldi, and, of equal importance, with raising funds for the papal army. Mérode's agent in Germany, later promoted to the See of Regensburg and given a cardinal's hat, succeeded in getting a shipment of repeating, high-velocity Stutzen carbines into the hands of the pontifical Zouaves, weapons which allowed them to do devastating damage to the Redshirts at the Battle of Mentana. Ryan Patrice had as his mission the fostering of the militant Mérode line among the American hierarchy. At the same time, he handled the technical aspects of raising and transferring large sums of money, contributed by pro-Mérode bishops, directly to the minister of war in Rome. The money came to Monsignor Mérode outside of the regular channels of church finance, these being under the direct supervision of Mérode's rival Cardinal Antonelli, the papal Secretary of State.

As I look back on it, I can see that Ryan Patrice had a

difficult task indeed. A good percentage of the American hierarchy favored the separation of church and state in Italy along the American model. They were embarrassed by the belligerent posture of the papacy, defending itself with live ammunition on the field of battle. It all seemed so—so medieval. Because of such American episcopal opposition, Ryan Patrice did not surface overtly in the prosecution of his mission to the United States. Operating from the cover of his Harvard tutorship in Romance languages and literatures, Patrice established and conducted a network of support for Archbishop Mérode's army of Zouaves that reached into every part of the country. The reports I examined in the Vatican Library, part of a *cache* of Mérode's papers sent over to the Library upon the Archbishop's death in 1874, contained neatly summarized Latin statements in Patrice's precise handwriting, suggesting what support he had managed to promote in the Catholic circles of Boston, New York, Chicago, San Francisco.

In the San Francisco report, which I eagerly read, Patrice wrote that he visited the city in 1865. Upon a confidential interview, he found the ordinary, Archbishop Alemany, a Spanish-born Dominican of militant orthodoxy, very favorable to the cause of the continued independence of the Papal States. Alemany's former secretary, an Irish-born layman currently active in banking circles, Richard Tobin by name, gave a discreet dinner party to which the leading (read, wealthy) Catholic laymen of San Francisco were invited. Utter discretion was observed. The militant protestant press of San Francisco would have liked nothing better than to discover the fact that an agent of the War Ministry of the Papal States was in the city raising money for the maintenance of the very army that kept the Whore of Babylon on her earthly throne and stood in the way of the long-overdue unification of Italy. The Catholic banking and industrial circles of San Francisco, Patrice wrote, being largely Irish-born, were devoted to the Holy See. A sum of $150,000 in gold had been raised, to be transported to Rome through the usual channels. The channels, I later discovered, operated out of Montreal, from

272

which men and money were sent to Europe. Patrice concluded his San Francisco report with a list of contributors. I saw Richard Tobin's name, together with the names of James Phelan senior, Joseph Donohoe (the Union Iron Works), Joseph Sullivan (the Hibernian Savings and Loan Society), and the new names of Flood, O'Brien, Fair, MacKay—the silver kings who were just coming into big money from the Comstock Lode. Each of these men had been born in Ireland, dirt-poor, and was now very, very rich. "I suggest," Patrice concluded in his report, "that appropriate tokens of papal satisfaction be extended to these generous gentlemen of San Francisco. A sprinkling of knighthoods would be in order."

I have never bothered to inquire, but I would not be surprised but that every contributor to Patrice's fund went to his grave swathed in the rich robes of a Knight of St. Gregory, or a Knight of Malta, a Knight of St. John, a Knight of St. Sylvester, or a Knight of the Holy Sepulchre. Admission to these equestrian orders, once staffed by the fierce monk-crusaders of the Latin West, constitutes the highest form of temporal recognition that the Church confers upon the laity. Here in America, the honor is usually reserved for wealthy men who have donated money to the Church.

Ryan Patrice must have been a busy man in the decade 1860-1870, the years of determined papal resistance on the battlefield, the years of his mission to America—the surviving documents of which are now cached away among Monsignor Mérode's papers in the Vatican Archives, sealed off from all but the most discreet view, after having been sorted and cataloged by one Sebastian Collins, *scriptor per* appointment of Cardinal Votto, Library prefect. Had His Eminence known of the personal bond that linked the onetime Vatican agent and the onetime Harvard undergraduate, now one of his scriptorial staff, he might have wisely chosen to assign the task of arranging the Patrice reports to another, less personally involved archival assistant.

"Do you swear under pain of mortal sin and under penalty of excommunication," the Cardinal had asked me when, against the advice of his administrative secretary, he had taken me in, the only such layman so employed, as a *scriptor*, "never to divulge the contents of these archives?"

I did so swear, and I still feel that I have adhered to my oath: not feeling, you see, that the privacy of this journal violates my promise to Cardinal Votto. In any event, I sorted the documentary remnants of Patrice's mission. I saw a report on his Harvard affiliation as a private tutor, accredited to the University for supplemental instruction at private fees. I read an assessment of numerous American bishops from the viewpoint of their stance on the Question of the Patrimony of St. Peter.

Patrice, incidentally, forwarded first-rate reports to the Vatican. In one Latin memorandum, for instance, he reported that European-born bishops in America who had once been members of religious orders tended to favor the continuing independence of the Papal States, since the Italian Kingdom had suppressed a number of religious houses and monasteries. American-born prelates who had come up from the ranks of the diocesan clergy, on the other hand, were indifferent, or frankly hostile to what they considered an anachronism that proved embarrassing in their efforts to harmonize Roman Catholicism with the liberal secular culture of the American Republic. I read a memorandum, dated 23 April 1865, on the recruitment of discharged Confederate officers of Catholic family for the papal Zouaves—especially ex-officers having a knowledge of field artillery. Another memorandum, in French, gave details relevant to the mustering-in of the very battalion I joined in Montreal.

I met Ryan Patrice Christmas Eve, 1867, and shortly after that I joined the circle that gathered on the Sundays Patrice was in Cambridge at his house on Follen Street off the Cambridge Common. Father Kieley, the pastor of St. Paul's Church in Cambridge, introduced us at a *convivium* held in the parish rectory after the celebration of midnight Mass. Catholics at Harvard always identified themselves to each other when the opportunity arose, there being so few of them.

Father Kieley was an amiable parish priest who acted as a semiofficial chaplain to Catholic students at Harvard, of whom there could have been no more than twenty out of a student body of some five hundred. Father Kieley would spot what Harvard boys came to Mass on Sundays (we were clearly distinguishable from the ham-fisted Irish townies comprising the bulk of Father Kieley's congregation); he then took the first opportunity to introduce himself.

I have always loved the magic time of Christmas. The Christmas of 1867 was my first Christmas spent in the snow. I remember how the freshly fallen snow crunched under my feet as I walked down from Gray's Hall to St. Paul's Church for midnight Mass and how my breath created steamy jets in the air. Being so far away from home, I was feeling a little lonely; but the familiarity of the decorated altar—the candles, the ferns, the cherished Christmas hymns—cheered me up with the memory of home things. After Mass, Father Kieley stood outside the church in his vestments wishing everyone a Merry Christmas.

"Come to the rectory for cake and coffee," Father Kieley whispered as I shook his hand. "The Harvard strays will be there."

Something of a snob, Father Kieley—a middle-aged man of some reading—prided himself upon the propinquity of his parish to Harvard. Like most priests of the Archdiocese of Boston, Father Kieley liked to live well. His rectory was furnished with the heavy mahogany and walnut furniture of the period, with shelves and shelves of leather-bound books, and with a half-dozen lavishly framed etchings of European cathedrals gathered by Father Kieley in the mid-1840s when he studied for the priesthood at the Grand Seminary in Montreal, dispatched there by Bishop Cheverus, the French-born ordinary of Boston who wanted as many of his clergy as possible to be educated by the French-speaking Fathers of St. Sulpice. Some twenty of us stood before a great side-table laden with fruit, nuts, cake, hot chocolate, and doughnuts. There were also bottles of Madeira and port, and a plum pudding surrounded by a holly wreath. Being nineteen and hungry, I attacked the plum pudding with gusto and drank two glasses of Madeira. I drank from cut crystal, as I remember, another sign of Father Kieley's taste for the finer things. Outside, the second snowfall of the night began. The wet snow pelted itself gently against the glass—like the tentative tappings of a child against a mysteriously closed door. With the exception of Father Kieley's housekeeper (voluminous in a starched white apron, she appeared intermittently from the kitchen to replenish the provisions on the table), it was an all-male group: a dozen or so undergraduates like myself, too far from home to return for the holidays, a handful of faculty—Catholic bachelors of European descent who tutored in languages, and two or three clerical friends of Father Kieley's.

"Mr. Collins, Mr. Patrice. Mr. Patrice, Mr. Collins," said Father Kieley, refilling my glass with Madeira as I shook the hand of a man more young than old, but not totally young either (Patrice was thirty-five at the time), and not a priest, to judge from his attire, yet not a layman either, to judge also from this same attire, there being something clerical to his well-cut black Prince Albert coat, his starched white collar, and muted cravat.

"Ah, yes, the young man from San Francisco."

Patrice spoke English precisely, but with a faint French accent. He might have been an American raised abroad, or a European who had spent some years in America, moving in the better circles. He was tall and thin and he wore a closely trimmed beard and mustache, auburn in color, which gave to his face a quality one sees frequently in the paintings of El Greco: a sort of luminous elegance of feature, at once sensuous and spiritual, as in the face of El Greco's portrait of Fray Luis de Leon, where the poet-monk's underlying sensuosity of temperament has been subsumed by an imposed asceticism, now become a habit, hence a facial characteristic.

"Yes, San Francisco—some four thousand miles from Gray's Hall, as the crow flies."

276

"Or some ten thousand miles via the Isthmus of Panama."

"You've been there?"

"Briefly."

"It hardly seems worth the effort to be briefly in San Francisco, does it? I mean: it takes such a long time to get there."

"I had some business to attend to, and when the business was over I returned."

"Business? Academic business?"

"I tutor as an avocation. My Harvard connection is fragile and intermittent."

"So is mine," I laughed. "How do you . . ."

"Support myself?"

"That would be rude to ask."

"But you've asked it."

"I apologize."

"You needn't. I sometimes wonder myself. Let's say that I travel for a foreign banking house, on the alert for investment possibilities in the United States. Now that the war is over, Europe is turning its gaze upon the American behemoth. Cattle, railroads, mining—an exciting era of development lies ahead."

I see in retrospect that Ryan Patrice welcomed the opportunity to put forth his cover, even to an insignificant undergraduate. It afforded him an opportunity to rehearse his story. I also noticed, moreover, that when I attempted to make a few remarks about my mentor William Chapman Ralston, cashier of the Bank of California, Ryan Patrice changed the subject.

"Let's not talk about banking," he said. "It's Christmas." So we talked about Harvard instead.

"Are you lonely here?" Patrice asked at one point.

"I'm too busy to be lonely; but yes, I am sometimes lonely." He looked around at the gathering.

"Stay close to the Catholic people of Harvard, and you'll not be lonely."

He brought me around for introductions. I met a third-year

student from Maryland, a little older than I, a very handsome fellow in his mid-twenties, who, it turned out, had served in the Confederate Navy alongside the poet John Bannister Tabb. I was to see Edmund Campion Calvert again at the Battle of Mentana in Italy, when like myself he wore the uniform of a Zouave; yet he wore also the insignia of a staff major of artillery, assigned to the great guns. As my battalion marched past his emplacement, I saw him and I called out "Edmund" from the ranks. He was conferring with a subaltern over a map. Seeing me in the ranks, Edmund smiled and waved in recognition. I crossed my left arm smartly to my rifle in formal salute. Edmund Campion Calvert of St. Michael's, Maryland, was, after all, a commissioned officer of field grade while Sebastian Collins of San Francisco was but a private soldier. Edmund saluted smartly in return and yelled something to me across the noise of our battalion's passage. I could only make out the word "Harvard."

Patrice introduced me to some undergraduates already familiar to me from their attendance at Mass at St. Paul's. One was the son of an army colonel stationed in Arizona; another lived with his parents in Mexico City, where his father worked as a mining engineer. A third was the son of an American rancher in Brazil.

I suppose that all in all I spent some ten evenings at Ryan Patrice's lodgings at 36 Follen Street, before my enlistment at Montreal in October of 1868. Across the years, I have managed to gather together the fragments of Patrice's identity, assembling them in my mind piece by piece as one would a mosaic. Born: 1832. Father: French, the Comte Honoré de Patrice, of the provincial nobility, served as an official in the treasury of the ultra-royalist government of Jules Armand de Polignac, prime minister to Charles X, the last Bourbon king of France. Honoré de Patrice fled to Baltimore, Maryland, in 1830 when the July Revolution placed the Duc d'Orleans on the French throne as Philippe, the Citizen King. Received into the polite Catholic circles of Baltimore, then flooded with French *emigrés*, Honoré de Patrice established

278

himself as a banker. In 1831 he met and married Abigail Seton, the niece of Mother Elizabeth Ann Seton, the widowed socialite from New York, then busy founding the Sisters of Charity in America. Abigail Seton (Ryan Patrice's mother) attended the school for girls established by her aunt, Mother Seton, just outside Baltimore, at Emmitsburg, Maryland.

Born in 1832, Ryan Patrice was raised in Baltimore as part of that city's vigorous French community. To judge from the later course of his life, he must have absorbed much of his father's legitimist sentiment. When Ryan was fifteen, his father sent him to France to complete his education among his cousins of the provincial nobility of Aix-en-Provence, where Honoré de Patrice had himself grown up. Rather abruptly, Ryan Patrice entered the Paris Foreign Mission Society at the age of eighteen, hoping for a career as a missionary priest. After his ordination in 1857, Patrice's superiors sent him to Rome as an assistant procurator for the Society of the Propaganda of the Faith, the Vatican agency charged with supervising the worldwide missionary activities of the Roman Catholic Church. Patrice assisted in the administration of the affairs of his Society before the Curia. At the time, the Paris Foreign Mission Society was in the process of stepping up its proselytization of French Indo-China, the most recent jewél (along with Algeria) in the crown of the reborn French empire. While working at Propaganda in 1858, Ryan Patrice, a Franco-American serving in a French missionary society, personally fluent in French, English, Italian, and German, came to the attention of Monsignor Frederic François Xavier Ghislain de Mérode, a personal friend of Pope Pius IX. Both Mérode and Patrice, it should be noted, were French-speaking ultraroyalists. With Mérode in attendance, Patrice preached a stirring sermon at a departure ceremony held at the Church of Santa Susanna in Rome for a band of missionary priests from the Paris Foreign Mission Society on their way to Indo-China.

Patrice took as his theme the reinvigoration of western civilization through missionary effort. Western culture, he suggested, had always been militantly expansionist. The West had brought to the pagan world the twin gifts of theological orthodoxy and political order. Among the cultures of the West, none prized orthodoxy and order more highly than France, the eldest daughter of the Church. Now—in Algeria, in Indo-China—a new chapter was being written by Catholic missionaries such as these young men standing before the altar, prepared to cast their lives headlong into a demanding ideal: the spiritual conquest of Southeast Asia, the expansion of western civilization.

Sitting at the altar as a representative of the Holy Father, Monsignor Mérode read Patrice's covert message with no ambiguity. Patrice, you see, was clearly suggesting a number of royalist preoccupations—not reactionary royalist preoccupations, mind you, but the sort of orthodox-progressive royalism favored by Monsignor Mérode. The Second Empire, Patrice was suggesting, while not legitimist in the strictest sense (Napoleon III, after all, was not a Bourbon), had nevertheless reorganized France around the twin polarities of monarchy and Catholicism, the foundation stones of European civilization.

Political and theological orthodoxies need not conduct themselves in a tyrannical, obscurantist manner, Patrice argued. The Right, paradoxically, was capable of bringing more benefit to mankind, both in this world and in the next, than either protestantism or protestantism's political equivalent, the liberal democratic secular state.

At the time of his first encounter with Ryan Patrice, Monsignor Mérode was in the process of reforming the penitentiary system of the Papal States: modernizing the prisons themselves, abolishing corporal punishment, drawing up a program of vocational instruction for convicts considered reformable. Mérode fervently believed that an orthodox monarchy, possessed of clarity of purpose and firmness of will, could implement the best notions of modern reform more efficiently and more harmoniously than a turbulent republic. Mérode was many things—a soldier, a civil engineer, a reforming administrator, a mystic, a priest, the sometime minister of war for the Papal States. Born in Brussels in 1820

280

into a noble family, he graduated from the Military Academy of Belgium as a young man with the rank of second lieutenant. His ancestors included the Marquis de Lafayette. One of Mérode's grandfathers had given his life on the field of battle in Belgium's war for independence. At various times Mérode's father had held the portfolios of war, foreign affairs, and finance under King Leopold's prime minister, Rosalie de Grammont. In 1844 the twenty-four-year-old Lieutenant Mérode was attached to the French Foreign Legion on campaign in Algeria. He won the *Legion d'Honneur* for bravery under fire.

"It was the desert that made Mérode religious," Charlie Stoddard observed as he and I reminisced over dinner in the restaurant of the Monterey hotel where Charlie was living in retirement. The conversation had turned to the time thirty-three years earlier, in 1874, that Charlie and I had taken the train from Munich to Rome for a visit. Having been painted by Joe Strong in the robes of a Franciscan friar, Charlie was in a religious mood; so the two of us made a pilgrimage to the Holy City. Quite by accident we had an audience with Pope Pius IX, now living as a virtual prisoner in the Vatican, stripped of his temporal realm. We also stood in an audience of American visitors to the site of the newly excavated, ancient Basilica of St. Petronilla and heard Archbishop Mérode give his last public sermon. He died a month later of acute pneumonia—in the arms of the aged pope he had tried so valiantly to keep on his earthly throne. At the site of the excavation, Mérode spoke of his ancestor the Marquis de Lafayette and of his personal gratitude to American Catholics for their generous support during the vain effort to defend the Patrimony of Peter on the field of battle.

"The desert," Charlie said to me over after-dinner brandy, recalling Mérode and the long-lost year of 1874 when both of us were young, "the desert has a way of bringing one close to God. I experienced this phenomenon myself in Egypt and the Holy Land and wrote of it in my *Mashallah! A Flight into Egypt*. Recreate, Sebastian, this *mise-en-scène*: young Lieutenant

Mérode on campaign in Algeria. First of all, his very soldierly situation, a war of reconquest against the Moslems who had once themselves seized those desert regions from Christians, reminds the impressionable young lieutenant of his Crusader ancestors. The imminent danger of death brings his already religious imagination closer to a conviction of Last Things. Something more, something in the abstract confrontation of sky and sand, the distant vistas, the suggestion of monotheism in the ever-burning sun, stimulates his naturally religious sensibility—and *voilà*! like Christ in the desert, Lieutenant Mérode of the French Foreign Legion returns to the haunts of men with fire in his eyes."

Charlie used to put everything so dramatically; but there must have been much truth to Charlie's intuitions, for Mérode resigned his commission, went to Rome, and entered a seminary. Remaining with the military, he became chaplain to the French garrison at Viterbo, outside Rome, upon his ordination. In November 1848, revolutionaries assassinated Pope Pius IX's liberal prime minister, the layman Pellegrino Rossi. Hearing of this, Mérode tossed aside his cassock and, strapping to his hips a pair of pistols he had kept from his days with the Legion in Algeria, he rushed by horseback to the Vatican to defend the person of the Pope from possible attack. Hearing of the impetuous loyalty of the chaplain, *Pio Nono* attached Mérode to his court when, two years later, the Pope returned from exile in Gaeta after the suppression of the short-lived Roman Republic. The Pope made Mérode a papal chamberlain with the title of Monsignor and brought him into the government. Tall (I suppose he was at least six feet), direct and military in style (to include a military haircut), Monsignor Mérode attended the Pope constantly, like a staff officer on campaign.

"*Pio Nono* just loved to have handsome monsignors about him," Charlie Stoddard observed wickedly in the course of our Monterey dinner. "Mérode must have looked magnificent in the red and the black of a papal chamberlain."

After meeting Mérode, Pius IX rarely went anywhere

without his tall soldier-prelate flanking him as *aide de camp*. *Pio Nono* had a streak of feminine dependence in his personality. At times, he could become almost hysterical. I witnessed this sort of behavior myself as a Zouave on guard in the papal chambers. Mérode brought a needed element of competent masculinity, proved under Algerian fire, to the papal entourage. I would not be surprised but that Monsignor Mérode kept one of his Legion pistols tucked into his scarlet sash. The fear of assassination ever nagged the Pope's immediate circle.

I have never learned exactly how Mérode recruited Ryan Patrice or secured his release from the Paris Foreign Mission Society for undercover work in America. By the time I encountered Ryan Patrice at the Grand Chartreuse, he was long past the discussion of such careerist details. By 1860, in any event, Ryan Patrice was in the United States as Mérode's agent in North America. While slightly accented, Patrice's English was nevertheless perfect; his employment as a private tutor attached to Harvard was totally plausible. Patrice's parents had been carried off by diphtheria in the epidemic of 1850, particularly virulent in the Baltimore area; indeed, their tragic, devastating deaths had precipitated in Patrice the very religious crisis that had pushed him into the priesthood. Only a handful of Patrice's American relatives even knew of his existence, much less his ordination, and so it must not have been too difficult for Patrice to slip back into an American identity that was vague to begin with. French *emigrés* were always returning to France or leaving it, depending upon the political situation.

I myself suspected nothing of Patrice's dual life for some time—but then again, I was a nineteen-year-old undergraduate with limited experience of the world. I did notice, however, that Ryan Patrice was not an ordinary Harvard tutor. He had an entire house to himself at number 36 Follen Street off the Cambridge Common, a three-story affair, elegantly furnished with Persian rugs, books (including a complete set of Abbé Migne's edition of the Greek and Latin fathers), good furniture, and upstairs on the second floor, a small oratory, displaying on one wall a collection of Russian icons. Patrice's Sunday evening *soirées* swarmed with European *émigrés*, a number of them tutors in the College; European-educated clergymen, Roman-educated in the main, and fiercely ultramontane regarding the continued independence of the Papal States; and such select undergraduates as Edmund Campion Calvert of Maryland and Sebastian Collins of San Francisco. In addition to Edmund, a onetime gunnery officer in the southern navy, I met a former Confederate cavalry colonel (Third Virginia Cavalry) traveling north for the first time since the war: a clean-shaven, almost ascetically thin man, *en route*, he told me, to Montreal, where he had associations in an import-export business that also seemed to involve Ryan Patrice.

Merely to recall those days from the perspective of the final months of 1914 is to suggest how much the world has changed these past forty-eight years. The current European war, I fear, will change civilization even more—for the worse. As I peruse the reports from Europe filed in Mr. Hearst's *Examiner*, I realize that an age of barbarism now descends upon us. Reading the atrocity reports dispatched from Belgium, I find it most difficult to comprehend that the Germany I experienced and savored at Heidelberg between 1873 and 1876—a Germany of *kunst, kultur* and *gaudeamus igitur*, of Brahms's *Academic Festival Overture* and a glass of beer in a sunny outdoor cafe enjoyed in the company of one's fellow students—should now play the Hun inflamed by blood-lust: burning, pillaging, raping, destroying such inoffensive, industrious peoples as the Walloons and the Flemings. The carnage I experienced in Italy—as horrible as it was—seems mild in comparison.

When I returned home to San Francisco in June of 1873, after an absence of more than six years, I presented Mr. Ralston with what he had so generously presented me—a bachelor's degree from Harvard College.

"Translate the Latin, if you please," Mr. Ralston said as I

unrolled the document across his desk in his upstairs office in the Bank of California building at California and Sansome Streets. "They didn't teach Latin on the Mississippi riverboat I worked on when I was your age."

I read the Latin as sonorously as possible, then translated the words that admitted me to the company of educated men. Ralston held the document to the window.

"Sheepskin, eh?" he said. "I wonder if they use California hides?"

Ralston also confessed himself somewhat perturbed by the fact that my degree was two years overdue.

"You could have been killed in that comic opera war," he upbraided me. "Your parents and I were worried sick. What would have become of my investment if some Dago had stuck a bayonet into your guts? I'm going to be paying good money to send you to Germany and I don't want to hear that you've up and joined the Kaiser's cavalry. I'll pay for three years— three years, you hear—at the end of which time I want you standing before me in this very room with another fancy degree, no ifs, ands, or buts—and no more damned wars! I want you to learn all about art and how to run a library and a museum. Leave military science to President Grant. And by the way: you're invited down to Belmont this weekend. Be here at noon on Saturday. We'll drive down in the buggy. My trotters always make better time than the train."

He returned to the papers at his desk. I rolled up my Harvard sheepskin and left the room. Ralston was right: I could have been killed. But I wasn't. I survived. I returned to Harvard in January of 1871 and completed my degree. I'll never forget the feeling of lyrical exultation with which I crossed the continent by train in June of 1873, returning home from Harvard and the Italian wars. For one who had made the journey to Massachusetts by sea in 1867, the transcontinental trip of six-and-a-half days seemed a miracle of technological achievement. Great herds of shaggy buffalo grazed impassively on the prairies of the Midwest, through which we passed on the third and fourth days. In eastern Colorado, a tribe of

Cheyenne nomads stared solemnly at us as our train chugged through their ancestral migration path. The entire tribe lined itself up on a bluff above the railway tracks: men, women, naked children, horses, dogs, all together in colorful confusion. I caught glimpses of bare chests, black hair, barbaric jewelry, feathered bonnets, bits of red scarves tied around tawny foreheads. It was as if we were promenading past a band of Albanian gypsies or a tribe of fierce Kurds in the Caucasus Mountains. The Cheyenne aborigines stared at our train in silence as we chugged by; then without warning, the entire tribe broke into a cacophony of murderous, bloodcurdling yells. I distinctly heard the sound of rifle fire. Had I survived the Battle of Mentana, I asked myself, to be butchered by Stone Age barbarians (however picturesque) in some remote steppe east of the Rocky Mountains? Later that year, trains were attacked and passengers killed, but our train was allowed to pass in peace. We made a steady ascent into the Rocky Mountains, a spiral of black engine smoke rising before those of us in the rearward cars like the pillar of fire that led the Israelites of old out from the wilderness.

Aside from this menacing moment with the Cheyenne caravan, I enjoyed throughout the seven-day journey a lavish sense of physical well being. I was twenty-five years of age, in perfect health, a bachelor of arts of Harvard College and a *candidatus* for the doctorate at Heidelberg University. I was heading home for the first time in six years, having survived the slaughter of the Italian civil war. I wore a mustache and a good tweed suit, and I ate excellent meals at the various depots where we stopped along the four-thousand-mile journey. My reading for the trip consisted of the journals of the Lewis and Clark expedition as edited by Nicolas Biddle, Washington Irving's *Astoria*, and Francis Parkman's *The Oregon Trail*: three narratives of transcontinental treks by foot and horseback along the same route I now pursued in such solid comfort.

As my train glided along, I summoned before my imagination all those arduous journeys—by foot, by horseback, by ox-drawn prairie schooner—that had gone into the making of

286

California. I thought of the countless deaths on the trail, of how slowly the landscape must have unfolded before the pioneers' view as they rolled on and on and on for six interminable months across the aboriginal vastness of an unchartered, untamed continent. When our train, augmented by a second engine, began its ascent up the eastern face of the Sierra, I could feel my heartbeat quicken. Beyond Lake Tahoe, somewhere past Truckee, where in 1846 the Donner Party, snowed in for the winter, resorted to cannibalism, our ascent became a descent, and I felt the thrilling physical nearness of impending California. Behind me were the Sierra, the great plateau, the Rockies, the prairies, the domesticated landscapes that begin with the Mississippi, the cities of the East. Behind me was the vast, inutterably lovely and foreboding American mid-continent, yet in the possession of wilderness and desert and Stone Age wanderers. Before me was California, the transmontane Garden of the West, sealed off from the continent by the mighty Sierra as if nature had ordained that she remain an enclosed garden, a *hortus conclusus* for the delight of men, a fabled Terrestrial Paradise as Montalvo wrote of her in the 1540s. When our train passed the town of Grass Valley where Josiah Royce was born, the Sacramento valley came into view. Its vast wheat-rich expanse shimmered in the distance through a golden haze, dotted with clumps of live oak. Our train made Sacramento by nightfall. I spent a restless night in the railroad hotel, thinking of the next day's homecoming. I had left San Francisco as a boy of nineteen—soft-muscled, virginal, circumscribed by his parents' world. I returned a veteran of combat, having seen men killed and having killed once myself to stay alive. In every way possible, I had lost the virginity of youth.

When I held Mother in my arms at the Oakland terminal the next day, I noticed that her hair was graying and that she was wearing glasses. Nearing sixty, Father had not changed a bit since our walk out to North Beach the night before my departure for Harvard. His hair had more gray in it, true; but if anything, he was tanner and more muscular than I remembered him. He embraced me quickly, then held me at arm's length, a hand on either of my shoulders, looking me over with satisfaction.

"That's a nice suit you've got on," he said.

"I had it made in Boston," I said, "at Brooks Brothers."

"You're thinner," my mother said. That was perhaps the last time in my life that anyone has ever felt it truthful to say that I looked thinner.

"He's lost his baby fat," Father said.

"I should hope so," Mother said. "After all, he's twenty-five years old."

By the early 1870s when I returned, San Francisco had grown into the tenth-largest city in the United States. The city I knew in 1867 had yet to it the ambiance of a frontier mining town. Six years of growth had brought quantitative and qualitative differences. San Francisco now spread to the west as far as Van Ness Avenue and out to Mission Dolores in the southern part of the peninsula. An imposing Merchants' Exchange had been built, and what seemed like innumerable churches: St. Patrick's just south of Market off Fourth Street on Mission Road, Trinity Church and St. Dominic's, both on Bush Street, Calvary Presbyterian on Powell, to name but a few. There were new theaters—The New Idea, The Alhambra, The California—and construction was underway on Wade's Opera House, grandiosely intended to be the fourth-largest opera house in the world. Still on the outskirts of the city, Golden Gate Park had been acquired and surveyed by the Board of Supervisors, and the beginnings of planting made in the park panhandle. There were superb public gardens on Folsom Street. Woodward Gardens, a beer garden out on the Mission Road, had added an aquarium to its museum of curios and stuffed animals. A sea wall had been built at the base of Telegraph Hill. It would eventually extend around all the newly reclaimed tidelands off Portsmouth Plaza, preventing erosion and making further fill possible. There seemed more women and children on the streets, and they were better dressed.

288

The Collins family fortunes had likewise improved. Earning an excellent salary as chief of the department, Father also received free quarters on the third floor of the firehouse on Bush Street near the California Theater, owned by Mr. Ralston. Built in the General Grant style, the firehouse was garnished by classical columns carved in wood and was surmounted by a mansard roof. A row of bay windows, built out from the façade in order to catch the sunlight, extended across the third floor.

"You'll be here only for the summer since you're set on going back to Europe," Mother said as we climbed the steps of the new Collins domicile—to be destroyed like everything else by the Fire of April 1906—"but you've got your own two rooms with us on the third floor, a bedroom and a study, and that will be your home no matter where you are."

"My home, Mother," I answered, "is where you and Father are." Little did I know at the time that I would live in these two rooms intermittently for some twenty years, until my marriage in 1894. In a sense, I never really left home until I was in my mid-forties.

At this point I should say something about my mentor, William Chapman Ralston of the Bank of California. Had it not been for Mr. Ralston, I would have had an entirely different career. I would have attended neither Harvard nor Heidelberg, nor would I have fought in the Italian wars. My life would have remained exclusively provincial, whereas it has proved provincial—but touched by the larger world as well.

Born in 1826 in Ohio, Ralston went to work as a clerk on a Mississippi River steamboat after a few years of formal education. After a number of years in Panama City in the steamship business, he moved to San Francisco in 1854 and plunged himself into the world of speculative finance. In 1864 Ralston and a number of associates, including Royce's mentor, the financier D. O. Mills, organized the Bank of California. D. O. Mills served as president and Ralston served as chief cashier. By 1867, the year Ralston sent me off to Harvard, the Bank of California dominated the financial affairs of California and the Far West. The Bank financed the silver mines of Nevada and the wheat ranches of the San Joaquin. It financed much of the commercial life of San Francisco, including the shipping companies that operated out of the city. The Bank maintained agents in New York, London, Hong Kong, and Sydney, Australia. Ralston became president in 1872.

To say that William Chapman Ralston was a banker is to suggest but a small part of his total titanic involvement in the economic affairs of California and Nevada. To my way of thinking, Ralston epitomizes the sort of daring, innovative capitalist who financed the rise of the American West. He invested in everything: railroads, sheep ranches, lumber mills, silver mines, woolen mills, silk farms, shipping companies, real estate. He financed the Palace Hotel, at its opening in 1876 the largest hotel in the world. He built the California Theater on Bush Street, which seated nearly 2,500 people. In his perhaps megalomaniacal way, Ralston considered himself the Lorenzo de Medici of San Francisco. Like the great Florentine merchant prince, moreover, Ralston never held political office. He preferred to rule the city through the power of investment and personal influence. You might say that from 1865 until his death in 1875 William Chapman Ralston governed San Francisco.

Ralston delighted in playing the *grand seigneur*. He entertained constantly at his Nob Hill palace, especially favoring all-night masked balls which began with a champagne supper, continued on through an evening of dancing to a midnight collation, then more dancing until breakfast at five o'clock in the morning. Despite his interrupted education, Ralston revered art and learning. Through the Atheneum, he hoped to make San Francisco an international center of research in the arts. He intended the building and staffing of the Atheneum to be the major project of his later years, and for reasons of his own he associated me with the enterprise.

"You're young, my boy," he said that Saturday, following my presentation of my Harvard diploma in his office at the Bank of California. I had met him as he requested, at noon.

290

We piled into a four-wheeled phaeton, pulled by two jet-black, high-stepping horses from Ralston's Belmont stable. "You're young enough to see the Atheneum through to its maturity. I'll be there, however, to help you get it off the ground. The Palace Hotel will be completed by the time you return from Europe. We'll spend two or three years raising money and having plans designed. Perhaps we'll simply buy up a Nob Hill mansion and start the Atheneum there. In any event, we'll be operating by 1880. I want the Atheneum full of good books and fine art, and I want to read many of the books and study many of the paintings myself under your direction; so study hard at Heidelberg and don't let me down. No more wars! That I insist on—no more joining of armies, understand?"

We drove through the empty fields of the Potrero, once a great Spanish land grant. Acres of orange-gold poppies extended to each side of us, as if a carpet had been laid down in honor of our passage.

"Someday we'll run a boulevard out here from the Palace Hotel," Ralston remarked as we sped along at fifteen miles an hour behind his indomitable pacers. "We'll take the boulevard from Market and Montgomery streets through the eastern edge of the peninsula out to Hunter's Point. That's the logical axis for San Francisco's growth—to the bayside south where the weather is good. The western side of the peninsula is too foggy. Nothing out there but sand dunes."

Our trotters whizzed past Hunter's Point, heading into the San Bruno Mountains. In 1868 Ralston had constructed a million-dollar drydock at Hunter's Point, a small peninsula jutting into the bay. We could see a steamer raised in the drydock for repair as we sped past. The steamer looked forlorn, like a beached whale in the throes of its final agony. I balanced my valise on my lap, filled with a clean shirt and a change of linen.

"Don't worry about your clothes," Ralston said, casting a glance at my battered valise and my by-then dusty Brooks Brothers suit. "I'll have whatever you need down at Belmont."

We ascended *El Camino Real* as it passes through the San Bruno Range. The road was first opened in 1776 by the De Anza Expedition, which settled San Francisco. The Franciscan padres of Mission Dolores improved it as the years passed.

"When you're in Europe," Ralston remarked, the cigar clamped between his teeth barely disturbed by his conversation, "don't just pay attention to books and paintings. I want you to study how things are run over there. See how they manage their museums and their libraries; then we'll up and do them a damn sight better. I'll see to it that you have money to travel around on."

Ralston was neither handsome nor homely. He wore chin whiskers but no mustache. His face had a certain nautical look, like a sea captain's face. He had, in fact, skippered a passenger ship up from Panama to San Francisco in his twenties. With me, Ralston always put on a cheery, optimistic demeanor; but if you peruse some of the photographs taken of him in the 1870s, you can see the strain in his face and the anxiety in his eyes. The pressure he lived under in those final years of his life must have been enormous, especially after he began secretly to reallocate the Bank's resources to cover his overextended investments. His day of reckoning, however, was two-and-a-half years in the future. For the present, he held his reins like Ben Hur in the Roman Colosseum. The energy of his pacers seemed to pass *via* the reins into Ralston's entire body.

To experience a weekend in Ralston's Belmont villa as I did in June of 1873 was to believe that Ralston's finances were inexhaustible, that his reign as the Lorenzo de Medici of San Francisco would go on forever. Approached from *El Camino Real* south of what is now the town of San Mateo, Ralston Hall gleamed before us like a gigantic wedding cake—white and turreted and sparkling atop a hillside with countless diamond-cut windows. Ralston acquired the mansion in 1864 from a certain Count Cipriani, an Italian of whom little is known. By the time of my visit in 1873, architect John Gaynor (he also designed the Palace Hotel) had enlarged

Cipriani's already formidable mansion into a palace of eighty rooms. Ralston Hall was the first of the great peninsula estates, and it was also the most elaborate private mansion in America before the building craze hit Newport, Rhode Island. Walking over the intricately wrought floors of walnut, maple, and mahogany parquet (different patterns for every room, fitted by a shipwright so that neither crack nor nail hole could be discerned), I had the impression that I was walking the water-tight deck of a luxurious antebellum Mississippi steamboat, such as Ralston had worked upon in his youth. My own room had a walnut and maple floor, in diamond patterns, and silver doorknobs and cut-glass windows. Fresh air poured in through a lattice-covered shaft discreetly placed on the ceiling. From my window I could look down across a great sweep of open prairie, dotted here and there by live oak, to the gray-green lower reaches of San Francisco Bay. Across the water I could see the rounded lion-colored hills of the Contra Costa Range. Some of Ralston's forty purebred horses, all of them jet black, grazed in a nearby meadow.

"The other guests will be here by six," Ralston told me as we climbed down from the phaeton. Stable boys were already unharnessing the horses. "Dinner is at seven."

A silent Chinese servant drew me a hot bath sometime after five. I soaked in it luxuriously. When I returned to my bedroom swathed in a great body towel like Rodin's sculpture of Balzac rising from his bath, a full complement of evening clothes—suit, vest, shirt, dickey, cravat, cufflinks, studs— awaited me, laid out neatly on the bed. It took me some minutes, this being my first time in evening dress, but I finally deciphered the mysteries of formal apparel.

Some thirty of us sat down to dinner that evening. Fifteen white-coated Chinese waiters moved silently behind our high-backed chairs, serving and removing courses—fish, salad, oysters, fowl, vegetables, venison, a sherbet to clear the palate, fruit, cake, a custard. They also kept our glasses filled with champagne. Mr. Ralston sat at one end of a vast table ablaze in candelabra and piled high with flowers, and Mrs.

Ralston, a pretty enough woman, but looking rather anxious if I remember correctly, sat at my end, making desultory conversation with a distinguished gentleman, Judge Sanderson of the California Supreme Court, who sat opposite me, to Mrs. Ralston's right. Ralston kept a mistress at the time, and perhaps that accounted for Mrs. Ralston's anxiety. She used to spend months at a time in Europe, taking the children with her. After dinner, an orchestra began to play in the three-story-high ballroom. More guests, another fifty or so, arrived for a ball. The Ralstons watched the dancing from one of the balcony boxes that jutted out over the ballroom floor.

My purpose here is not to dwell overlong upon the splendors of Ralston Hall, however opulent they were and however suggestive of a long-gone era of unthinking, naive luxury. I linger on my Belmont weekend merely to suggest the milieu of almost defiant extravagance in which Mr. Ralston lived. My formal wear, for instance, belonged to a press of such formal attire, in all sizes, kept specifically at Belmont for embarrassed guests such as myself. The servants must have been capable of making discreet fittings by sight alone as a guest soaked in a copper tub of hot water. My unexpected formal wear, furthermore, together with the other accoutrements, including shirt studs and cuff links, was folded neatly in my valise when I left Ralston Hall on Sunday afternoon to catch the train to San Francisco—a gift from Mr. Ralston. I wore this suit, incidentally, throughout the 1870s. By 1880 it had become a little out of date in cut and too tight in fit for proper comfort.

One more incident from the weekend—only because it now seems to me a perfect prophecy, or "providence" as the Pilgrim Fathers called such retrospectively significant events. Sunday morning, after a late breakfast (until noon a buffet table was kept replenished for late risers with rolls, coffee, and chafing dishes of hot breakfast food), I strolled about the estate, enjoying one of Mr. Ralston's fragrant Havana cigars after having restored my strength with liberal lashings of oatmeal porridge, smoked salmon, scrambled eggs, and toast. While leaving the stables, a pony cart driven by young Billie,

294

Ralston's oldest son, then about ten, darted across my path. Like his father, Billie drove his rig at full speed. In a clatter of pony-hooves and a whir of wheels, Billie headed his rig around the far side of the house, disappearing from sight.

"Where is Billie? Where is Billie?" a pretty young girl of Billie's age called to me and to everyone else in particular as she ran up the path from the stables, her white pantaloons flying from beneath her green velvet dress. "He promised me a ride in the pony cart."

"If you stop for a moment," I said, "I'll tell you."

"Tell me quick. Where is he?"

"On the far side of the house."

"He promised me a ride. He'd better not break his promise. My daddy is a judge, you realize, and can send Billie to jail for not keeping his word." With that, she darted off in the direction of the house—Judge Sanderson's daughter Sybil, age eight, bent upon a ride in Billie Ralston's pony cart and whatever else that Sunday morning, or life itself, had to offer.

Chapter 9

Y ESTERDAY was a beautiful Sunday morning, full of
hope and promise as a Sunday can often be. When I
went outside to my carport, I paused for a moment to take in
the view of the peaceful, early morning bay. Only a few
intrepid yachtsmen had launched themselves by eight o'clock,
so the bay was but sparsely flecked with sails. From the
vantage point of Telegraph Hill at least, San Francisco was still
asleep. The spires of SS Peter and Paul's Church down below
on Washington Square glistened more whitely than usual.

I headed the Porsche down the hill, then got on the
Bayshore Freeway at Broadway. On a crystal clear Sunday
morning in June, the advertisements calling attention to the
sex shows on Broadway seemed more sad and dispirited than
obscene. MAN AND WOMAN LOVE ACT screamed one of
them—a photo of a naked man and woman facing each other
in what was supposed to be unbridled lust. There was a
tentativeness, however, to the way the naked male held his
arms out to his companion, as if he had just glimpsed her nude
for the first time and was steadying himself as wonder, desire,
and embarrassment assaulted his senses. Broadway was dirty
with the cigarette butts and paper leavings of last night's
revelry. Trash cans overflowed onto the sidewalk.

I followed the freeway along the eastern edge of the San
Francisco peninsula, then turned off at the Army Street exit,

which puts you down right in the Mission district adjacent to Potrero Hill. This is Peter Yorke country, a onetime Irish ghetto presided over by the fiery Father Peter Yorke, pastor of St. Peter's Parish. Since the war, however, this area has been given over increasingly to San Francisco's ever-growing Spanish-speaking population, Mexicans and Central Americans predominantly. Deborah lives in a three-story Victorian flat dating to sometime in the 1890s when the building of the Mission district was fully under way. I found a parking space near her address, then checked myself in the reflection of the window of a Mom and Pop grocery store. My resortish attire—Gucci loafers, slacks, blue blazer, large-collared Italian shirt (red and white striped)—seemed a little *outré* for the Mission district (I had a momentary thought that I was inviting a mugging), but would be appropriate as soon as I whisked Deborah from her *barrio* hideaway down to Palo Alto.

Climbing three floors, puffing slightly and catching the lingering traces of Mexican cooking in my nostrils, I rang the doorbell which I located just beneath an IMPEACH NIXON decal. I felt nervous—anxious to be accepted, to say the right thing. Deborah opened the door. Swathed in a magenta-colored terry cloth bathrobe, she had obviously just gotten up. She yawned, then leaned over to me, putting her cheek next to mine as she finished the yawn—but also speaking while the yawn was yet incomplete and as I was being momentarily bathed in the sleepy-warm benediction of her breath.

"Sorry, I overslept. Come in. I'll make us some coffee."

Barefooted, she led me down a hallway into the kitchen. As I passed, I caught a glimpse of a book-lined alcove living room and a bedroom dominated by a recently vacated single bed. Though small, the kitchen had a skylight, so the light poured in upon us as I sat at her table (no more than three could sit there comfortably) and watched her brew coffee. She used an electric percolator, which I also use because they remind me of my boyhood in the 1940s when all electrical appliances— percolators, mixmasters, upright vacuum cleaners—seemed so sturdy, designed to last a decade, and suggestive also of domestic stability, which was important to a boy such as me, caught in the middle of my parents' bad divorce.

"While this percolates, I'll get dressed. Take a look at the Sunday *Express* and tell me if there's anything in it."

There is little of value in the Sunday *Express*, or the weekday *Express* for that matter, save the Harry Shaw column. Shaw practically carries the entire newspaper on his back. That is why he's paid so outrageously well. San Franciscans, including myself, are addicted to their daily fix of Harry Shaw gossip. As the smell of freshly brewing coffee filled the kitchen, I sat at the butcher block table beneath a Corita Kent poster and a McCarthy for President dove ("It's a collectors' item," Deborah later told me), and mainlined my daily dose of Harry Shaw. I read about the visit of Lord Bobby Bovere, the playboy peer, to James Fenimore and Livia Imperator's Napa ranch for the weekend. There was a blind item to the effect that a certain insider in the Soutane camp had leaked the information that Kay and Raymond Soulé had offered Andy Soutane the use of the Soulé Lear jet during the campaign. "Watch Kay Soulé emerge as the Pearl Mesta of the Soutane administration," Shaw predicted. "As a bachelor, Governor Soutane will need someone to help him with his parties." I then read a Little Old Lady story. I had already heard of the unfortunate incident, and so had Mabel Storm, who, in her anger, has called an emergency meeting of the Administrative Council next week to deal with the problem of what she terms "the undesirables." Last Wednesday a Little Old Lady disarmed— indeed, nearly dismembered—a flasher at the San Francisco Public Library with her umbrella, thwacking him in a sensitive and exposed portion of his anatomy as he presented her with it *en garde* in the second-floor stack of the Art Department. A leaden feeling came over me as I read on. "The SFPL must be Kink City," Shaw continued. "There are also rumors of a disgruntled patron who, with the swift secrecy of the Viet Cong, is in the habit of leaving about the Library some rather malodorous signs of his displeasure." Now that the story of the Brown Bomber is out, there'll be hell to pay

298

from Mabel Storm. She has already expressed her concern—most forcefully—that the attacks of the Brown Bomber not get into the newspaper. When Deborah came back into the kitchen, I showed her the item. She laughed.

"Everybody on the staff knows about it. Public libraries all over the country attract weird people. That's the special vulnerability we have because we stay close to the public. These days, there are more and more weird people on the streets."

"I think this fellow is an inside man," I said.

"Don't be such a chauvinist. She could also be a woman."

"I doubt it, but let's not talk about it. It's Sunday."

Deborah poured coffee into two heavy crockery mugs that she told me she'd bought at a pottery shop in Mendocino. We took our coffee to her living-room alcove and sat opposite each other in yellow canvas butterfly chairs sipping coffee and listening to Bach's *B Minor Mass,* which Deborah tuned to on the classical station in Palo Alto. The room was simply but beautifully furnished in bookshelves, a Design Research-like couch, the two butterfly chairs we were sitting in, and a number of cleverly matted and framed prints, most of them having something to do with the Southwest—Indians, landscapes—all in very bright Southwestern colors. A few of the books on one shelf still had Mills College bookcovers on them. I felt charmed by our intimacy—and relieved also that Deborah wasn't doing her put-down dialogue this morning. Her snappy patter can be fun if and when I am up to an adequate response, but after all, it was Sunday, a day that should have a relaxed, lazy kind of feel to it.

"How's your coffee?" she asked.

"Excellent."

"It's a special grind, Nicaraguan. I get it down the corner from Mrs. Mendez. She runs the place by herself. Her husband is in jail in Nicaragua—a political prisoner of the Somoza regime."

"Do you know a lot of people in the neighborhood?"

"As many as I can meet. I can't stand the way so many San

299

Franciscans live behind closed doors. In neighborhoods like the Marina and the Richmond and West Portal, you rarely see anyone on the street. In the Mission there's street life. The people live in the Latin manner, publicly, with a certain communal style."

She left for the kitchen and returned a few minutes later with a plate of toast—heavy, five-grain bread, she told me, from a health food store on Valencia.

"White bread is all bleached flour," she said. "Pure carbohydrate and very anxiety producing. Whole grain bread nourishes you. It also calms you down. You should eat properly, then you wouldn't be so fat."

As Deborah gave me a brief disquisition on proper nutrition, upon the evils of salt and refined sugar, I munched my five-grain toast and felt both well nourished and calmed. I also admired her khaki skirt and blue shetland sweater, above which the white wings of a Brooks Brothers button-down shirt graced her neck—a perfect ensemble, by the way, for a Warner Conrad brunch, having to it that tweedy Deep Peninsula look. Deborah advised me to seek a proper balance of protein and carbohydrates and to stay away from too much animal fat. I agreed. I vowed to reform myself under her direction.

"No one can direct you," she said. "You've got to internalize proper nutrition. It's a philosophy of life, a way of respecting your body and keeping it in shape so that you'll have a complete life-cycle."

I agreed. Bach's triumphant *Gloria* filled the tiny room with its evocation of worlds unseen, of overwhelming joy in the Lord God Almighty. We seemed to have forever before us—an eternity nourished on Bach and five-grain toast.

"We all live with contradictions," I said.

"Being fat is not a contradiction."

"Now take you, for instance. You live out here in the Mission and you've got your place decorated in Mendocino Rustic; yet you're dressed like an ad from *Mademoiselle* magazine, very Seven Sisters collegiate."

"You just don't understand Mills College girls," she said. "Mills College is an East Coast/West Coast sort of place. All the best things about California show a certain East Coast cross-over."

"Like me, for instance."

"Perhaps—in the future, when you grow up. Right now you haven't yet assimilated Harvard to your total point of view. You mention it a lot, but only for reasons of status anxiety. I'm not so sure that you even liked the place. What time is the brunch?"

"Eleven-thirty."

"And it takes about an hour to get there, doesn't it? So we've got an hour or so in between, don't we? What do you want to do?"

"Sit here talking," I said.

"Let's go to church instead," she said. "I haven't been to church in ages."

Neither had I as a matter of fact. We walked over to St. Peter's Church, which is only a few blocks from her house, getting there in time for the nine o'clock Mass. The Mass and the sermon were in Spanish, so I couldn't understand a word that was said, although Deborah understood it perfectly. The church was packed with people and a lot of screaming kids. Outside of schoolyards, in fact, I hadn't seen so many kids in one place in San Francisco for ages.

"Latin people are biologically vigorous," Deborah told me as we sped down Highway 280 towards Palo Alto. "They get married and they reproduce and they take care of their own."

"What was the sermon about?"

"About presumption—taking God's grace for granted."

"I'll try not to be presumptuous when next I'm tempted," I said.

"You are by nature presumptuous," she said. "You can't seem to help it."

Highway 280 runs south down the peninsula alongside the San Francisco watershed property, a vast reservation of choice Coastal Range property where the water brought in from the Sierra by the Hetch Hetchy Aqueduct is stored in a series of lake-sized reservoirs. Only parts of Vermont or the Scottish Highlands are as beautiful—at least from what I have seen.

301

We drove past gently-curved mountains in their pristine state and beneath them—great sheets of calm blue water, such as one encounters in the High Sierras. At one point, slightly south of Woodside, a family of deer crossed an open meadow to our right.

I tuned in KKHI-FM on the Porsche's Telefunken radio. We listened to Beverly Sills and Sherrill Milnes in the Angel LP of Massenet's opera *Thaïs* as we sped along. I reveled in the Porsche's intimacy. I thought of the two of us crossing the United States in it, or speeding along the Riviera toward Monte Carlo, as in a scene from *A Man and a Woman*, all sort of French and soft-focus color. The Massenet also reminded me of Sebastian Collins and the account I'd recently read of his thwarted love for Sybil Sanderson. Collins wrote the account in September of 1914, just after returning from the Bohemian Grove.

"Let's get to know each other," I said. We hadn't spoken much on the ride down. The scenery and the Massenet kept us occupied.

"We already do," Deborah said, reaching across to me and grabbing my collar like a teacher seizing a recalcitrant schoolboy. She tugged it gently a few times as she spoke. "It takes time. Don't rush it."

Warner Conrad teaches at Stanford University in the Creative Writing department. He is also a Pulitzer Prize-winning novelist and biographer. Warner is a most Roman man—the Rome of the virtuous republic, that is, not the decadent empire. He and his wife live in Horatian retreat atop a knoll in Palo Alto. During the academic year he drives to Stanford for classes three days a week. The rest of the time he writes—steadily, surely, superbly—five hours a day, from eight until one, followed by a vodka martini, lunch, a nap, and a late afternoon walk through the Coastal Range hills. In the evening he reads. Thirty years of such regularity have added up to a most distinguished literary career. Warner is in his early sixties now, the picture of health—tan, slender, white-haired, like a Roman senator in rustication. His wife is an equally preserved Stanford woman (class of 1940).

The Conrads belie the common assumption that stability and productivity are impossible in California. Both of them have gone the distance. A Stanford graduate (1937), Warner served in the Coast Guard during the war, then went to the Sorbonne on the G.I. Bill along with his friend, poet Lawrence Ferlinghetti. Ferlinghetti, however, has always preferred a bohemian life style whereas the San Mateo-born Warner Conrad has always been, so Ferlinghetti tells me (affectionately, for he's fond of Warner and respects his work), suburban to the core. That's another myth that Warner belies: that nothing good can come from suburbia. Critics frequently make this point, but critics are by and large alienated from American life. Warner Conrad teaches at Stanford. He plays golf and bridge. He and his wife entertain at Sunday brunches. They are both active in the Palo Alto Improvement Association and the Stanford Alumni. They epitomize, in fact, the love affair of the World War II generation with suburbia. Now according to the critics, all this is counter-creative. Creativity, after all, comes only from the East Side, or the ghetto, or some moss-covered antebellum town in the Deep South. Over the years, however, Warner Conrad has managed a steady stream of first-rate books. His novel *Grass Valley*, a saga of the gold rush continuing on through the 1890s, is in my opinion the single finest piece of fiction about California next to Steinbeck's *Grapes of Wrath*. Warner, however, prefers to avoid literary talk. His favorite topic is gardening. He writes a gardening column in *Sunset* magazine which over the years has supplemented his income most satisfactorily.

"How do you know Warner Conrad?" Deborah asked.

"Through the Bohemian Club."

"The Bohemian Club is a chauvinist organization."

"It tries to be," I said.

"Let's talk about Warner Conrad. What's he like?"

"Prosaic on the outside. Inside—to judge from his novels—inside is something else."

"Like you perhaps?"

"I'm chaotic within and without. I'd love to find my center of gravity the way Warner Conrad found his thirty years ago when he was my age. I'd like to have a career that had its source of strength from within and wasn't just dependent upon external circumstances."

"You're not really an administrator, then."

"No."

"Then what are you?"

"I don't know—yet."

"You'd better hurry up and find out, hadn't you?"

"So I tell myself. Thirty-five is the outer limits of adolescence."

We ate barbecued salmon at the Conrads'. Warner had been salmon fishing on the Oregon coast the week previous and had snagged a particularly glorious twenty-pounder, together with three or four smaller fish. He roasted them for us over hot coals in a closed Weber barbecue. Warner wore an apron which said CHEF on it in great letters.

"He doesn't act like I expected him to," Deborah remarked midway through the brunch. "He's like a stockbroker. He's like someone from the Bohemian Club."

"So was Wallace Stevens," I said. "Literature isn't a life style. It's putting words on paper. How you live is your own business." It was a pleasure to have her slightly on the defensive. After all, that's where she frequently keeps me.

"I suppose it's because I'm from Phoenix. I want writers to seem . . ."

"Artistic, wearing a beret?"

Some fifteen or so people filled the Conrad patio. We drank Pimm's Cup before lunch, then sat down at a very long redwood picnic table that seated us all close but comfortably. A great oak tree offered us shade. Warner brought the coal-broiled salmon to the table on a great platter and we all applauded.

"Who'd you talk to?" I asked Deborah as, around four, we drove back to the city on 280.

"Warner Conrad himself. He showed me around the house.

304

I loved seeing the study he built for himself in the garage. It's so serene."

"Did you see any signs of the artist's life?"

"Except for the desk, no. I saw some books and a photograph of Warner and Rhoda that must have been taken sometime during World War II because Warner had on a white Coast Guard lieutenant's uniform. Rhoda had just graduated from Stanford. She's in cap and gown. They're both smiling into the camera."

I shared with Deborah my suspicion that World War II Americans experienced a better time and place than ours.

"You're ignoring all the men who were killed or maimed in the war," Deborah rejoined. "Some three hundred thousand of them. How could it have been a better time? Millions of innocent people perished between 1939 and 1945."

"Forget that for a moment," I said. "No—don't forget it. That's crazy. Let's just focus ourselves on the generation of Americans who fought World War II. When they came back, if they came back, they had more to look forward to than we do. They believed in the essential goodness of American life."

"You sound like the senior senator from my home state."

"I hope so. I voted for him."

"You didn't."

"I did. He'd have made a hell of a better president than Lyndon Johnson. There would have been no Vietnam, that's for sure."

"He would have leveled it."

"Not necessarily. But he would have dealt with the problem realistically."

"I'm spending Sunday with a fascist."

" 'Fascist' is the most overused word in America."

"Tell me more of your World War II theory."

"It's like this. Warner Conrad walked into a Stanford dance when he was a junior and there was Rhoda Fleming, freshman, in a pretty frock, wearing a corsage. Warner still talks about the corsage. Everything was a big deal then, including boy-meets-girl stuff. Then there was the war. Warner was in the Coast Guard, LST Division—the guys who amphibiously landed troops on island assaults. Think of him in his newly-purchased blue uniform, an ensign's gold stripe on his sleeve, taking the train across the country from New London, Connecticut, to San Mateo, sometime in 1942."

"It's like a Warner Brothers movie."

"Exactly. There was a certain unquestioned drama to it all, a heroic scale; and little things counted then as well. Women paid attention to how they looked, and they felt it important to please men. Most women felt this way, even intelligent women like Rhoda Fleming, who ferried fighter airplanes from southern California to Hawaii between 1944 and 1945 as part of the Women's Overseas Transport Auxiliary."

"So that's the meaning of the picture of her on the wing of an airplane, looking like Amelia Earhart."

"Exactly. Rhoda's no clinging vine, yet she always sees to it that Warner's taken care of, even now after more than thirty years of marriage."

Playing a little game between San Mateo and San Francisco, we free-associated images from the generation I claimed had possessed a better America to live their lives in. I made some ordinary suggestions: Lucky Strike, the Cal-Stanford game, the happy hour at the Top of the Mark jammed with uniformed officers *en route* to the Pacific. Deborah countered with a series of perfumes, lipsticks, silk stockings, followed by a seemingly well-rehearsed barrage of Navy lingo.

"My parents, you remember, are part of the generation you're talking about. Mom served as a lieutenant j.g., and Dad was a lieutenant commander in the Navy Medical Corps. They met in the officers' club in Phoenix. I told you all about that at lunch the other day."

"Then you understand what I mean?"

"It's a myth, even you will agree to that, but I'll agree with you that they seemed to question less than we do, judging from my parents and their friends."

"And they enjoyed it more."

"Vietnam did away with the sort of thing you're talking about," Deborah said, "and besides, the party's suddenly over.

306

We've got to play catch-up now. There's too much unfinished business, like poverty."

"Do you think we're wasting our time?"

"Sometimes. But I believe that education is the answer and that public libraries can offer the left-outs and the left-overs the tools of self-help."

"I doubt it," I said, risking her displeasure. "Most people, even the poor, just don't give a damn about the things you and I care about."

"Elitist."

"Realist, you mean."

We drove across San Francisco diagonally from the southwest to the northeast, following 280. By the time we arrived at Deborah's place on Alabama Street it was five o'clock. There was still the evening to go—Sunday evening, which can get to be a rather lonesome time if you're alone, facing a week's work and presiding over the last plaintive gasps of Friday's wonderful weekend possibilities. Sunday night can remind you that one day, maybe soon, your time will be running out.

"What do you do on Sunday nights?" I asked.

"I read or watch the English programs on public television."

"Same here."

I drove up to her flat and hesitated for a split second behind the wheel, fishing for, then receiving her invitation to come in. We sat in her living room, drinking some C.K. Mondavi Chablis. "The best jug wine in America," Deborah called it, transferring a liter of it to a pitcher from the green glass jug in her refrigerator. Acting as if I owned the place, I switched on "Pledger at the Opera" on the FM.

"You're acting as if you own the place," Deborah said.

For an hour we listened to the operatic selections and drank white wine. There's not much of a view from Deborah's front window, merely a row of Victorians on the opposite side of the street, but it was pleasant to watch the late afternoon and early evening light do certain end-of-the-day mutations across the ornate façades of the Victorians. Listening to Pledger's operatic selections, sipping chablis, looking at a darkening sky past the open shutters which Deborah had herself installed, I felt a sense of fading Sunday in San Francisco: a time when the city seemed a little sad and life itself was laced with memory and regret.

"What's this?" I asked.

"It's lentil soup, dummy, thickened with soybean flour for protein."

"I'll have a steak."

"You'll eat lentil soup. Beef wastes the world's resources. It takes eighteen pounds of grain to produce one pound of beef. Read *Diet for a Small Planet*."

The lentil soup was as delicious as lentil soup can be, which isn't very delicious, but I wasn't complaining. We ate it at the butcher block table out of Mendocino crockery bowls, using oversized Basque shepherd spoons designed for communal eating out of an open-fire pot. There was also sourdough French bread.

"I feel ethnic," I said.

"You look ethnic," Deborah replied.

At eight o'clock we watched an episode of British television dealing with the life of George Sand. It depicted the time Sand and Chopin spent on Majorca. Chopin coughed continually. The lovers had gone to Majorca for the climate, hoping that the climate would prove salubrious to Chopin's lungs; but it rained for months on end. Sand and Chopin found themselves facing each other in a dreary, rain-soaked cottage, the love affair of the century reduced to a doomed effort not to get on each other's nerves. Constant, inescapable coughing can take the bloom off anything.

"They're getting on each other's nerves," I said. "Even though she loves him, she ultimately can't forgive him for being a dying man. And he senses her resentment."

"She doesn't resent him for dying, not in a peevish way. She's more enraged that their happiness should be destroyed."

When the program was over, Deborah said, "Good night."

"I didn't know I was going," I said.

308

"You are, now. But also thanks for the day—and for the company."

She leaned toward me and rested her chin on my shoulder for a moment, then whisked her lips across mine, then—the movement was continuous—guided me to the door.

"I get the hint," I said.

I ought to tell Tiny Roncola to go fuck himself. Better yet: I ought to turn him over to the District Attorney for attempted blackmail; only then I'd be an accessory before, during, and after the fact. I couldn't care less what Andy Soutane has done, or hasn't done, in the sack. It's none of my business. I've got my own problems in the sack department.

I can't figure Deborah Tanner out. I'm too old for cat and mouse games. I should be married by now, anyway. I suppose that if I had experienced a normal childhood, whatever that is, I would have been married by now: married to a good Catholic girl whom I would have met at the University of San Francisco: a Lone Mountain girl perhaps, like Sandra Stern, whom my lawyer friend, Charlie Stern, met at USF when she was at Lone Mountain. Charlie and I were walking over to the Bridge Theater on Geary Street one Sunday at sunset in February of 1960. We were passing Lone Mountain on Parker Street when Charlie looks up the side of the hill and sees this girl watching the sunset, her brown-and-white saddle shoes tucked to the side of her skirt the way Natalie Wood would have been sitting in a movie. Without so much as a word, Charlie peels off from me and climbs up the hillside, using the succulent plants for leverage. He starts talking to the girl, Sandra Lorraine, a sophomore, with me waiting down below with egg on my face, not knowing whether to climb up there also, which I didn't do because there was only one girl, or go on to the Bridge and see Alain Delon in *Purple Noon* by myself, which I eventually did, rather miffed at Charlie Stern's unceremonious departure.

Charlie is now a lawyer with a big downtown personal injury firm. He and Sandra were married in his second year at

309

Hastings Law School. They have three boys and a girl. Two of the boys are in the Town School. Charlie makes good money and takes excellent care of his family. They live out on Lake Street near Sea Cliff and have a condominium at the Silverado Country Club in Napa where they spend the summer, Charlie commuting up from the city. They go to Hawaii once a year, and spend every other Thanksgiving at the Ahwahnee Hotel in Yosemite National Park. A self-made guy, Charlie likes to prep his kids out with the latest from Young Man's Fancy. The boys wear matching gray flannel short pants, blazers, white shirts, and red neckties when they all go to St. Ignatius Church on Sundays.

My life is half over. I'm nearly fifteen years into my sex life and what do I have to show for it but the recollection of a few good fucks and a number of bad ones. The very fact that when I was at St. Patrick's Seminary I once contemplated a lifetime of celibacy I find, in retrospect, disturbing to my sexual self-image, although at the time I thought that I was embarking on a grand, spiritual adventure—like St. Francis of Assisi, Bede Jarrett or Ronald Knox. I was going to surrender all earthly love and in return possess the fullness of divine love. What bullshit! All I want now is some corner of my life where I can feel the truth of what Albert Camus's Stranger tells the priest who comes to comfort him in his jail cell on the eve of his execution for a crime he didn't commit: All your certainties, priest, aren't worth the strand of a woman's hair. I want Deborah Tanner. I want a strand of her hair.

Actually, it's a cheap shot to set myself up against the Church. The Church has no responsibility whatsoever for my isolation. Nor is my selfishness the Church's fault. Nor is the blackmail I am incipiently involved in the Church's fault! I do, however, have a sort of Church hang-up. It put me in the seminary for two years, despite the fact that I have no capacity whatsoever for celibacy. My father died of a brain tumor in 1946, and my mother suffered a nervous breakdown. The Church raised me. The first twenty-four years of my life were passed exclusively in Roman Catholic institutions: the Holy

310

Family Day Home at Sixteenth and Dolores, Mission Dolores Grammar School, St. Vincent's Home for Boys in San Raphael, St. Boniface's Grammar School on Golden Gate Avenue, St. Ignatius High School, the University of San Francisco, and St. Patrick's Seminary in Menlo Park; so as you can see, I grew up Catholic.

I never have forgotten this fact, although I realize that my gratitude to the Church for raising me is more than a little unfashionable. America overflows with so-called ex-Catholics who vociferously blame the Church for everything: for Vietnam, for their sex hang-ups, or for the fact that they failed to make the Social Register. Many such complaints arise out of bourgeois anxiety regarding ethnicity. Unable to say that they are ashamed of being Irish, for instance, the upwardly mobile have of late turned against the Church, prime emblem of their repudiated immigrant status.

My Church, however, is not the repudiated Church, made responsible for every failure of nerve or charity. My Church is the Church of art, scholarship and architecture; the Church of Augustine, Abelard and Francois Mauriac; the Church that protected the Irish and the Italians when they came over here—fed them, educated them, got them jobs; the Church of Sebastian Collins, in short: the protector of the poor and the mother of the arts. All of this sounds extreme, but I am being deliberately provocative, for the Church that I knew as a boy and as a younger man has within the past decade been virtually disestablished in a massive act of self-destruction. The Church, which for two thousand years had survived both its own corruptions and the assaults of Moors, Vikings, and Gustavus Adolphus, has of late dismantled itself. Its present life, so far as I can judge, is one of massive confusion, of crumbling and crumbled orthodoxies, of power brought to impotence.

Growing up in San Francisco, I knew the Church in her social, political, and even cultural prime. One identified oneself, not as being from the Richmond district, or the Sunset, or Potrero Hill, but by parish. You were from St. Monica's, or St. Anne's, or St. Theresa's, or, if you had

311

struggled upward to some status, you were from St. Vincent's (Pacific Heights), St. Edward's (Jordan Park), or St. Brendan's (Forest Hill and St. Francis Wood). You attended Mass there on Sunday, daily during Lent. Your children went to the parish grammar school, where they wore uniforms: corduroy pants and sweaters for the boys (blue at St. Boniface, green at St. Patrick's, red at St. Brendan's), a pleated skirt and middy blouse with bow for the girls, who also had their sweaters. You were taught by nuns. They had names like Agnes, Perpetua, Vibiana (come to think of it, many of the names were inspired by virgins who had been tortured to death over matters of steadfast chastity), and they wore medieval or Counter-Reformation habits and veils of various hues: white for Dominicans, brown for Franciscans, blue for Sisters of Charity, black for Sisters of the Presentation. These women were strict and, in the main, very good teachers. If you fooled around in class, they slapped your hand with a ruler. Very few of them were elaborately educated, but they drilled you in the fundamentals: reading, writing, and arithmetic—which you learned, or else. They supervised you at recess and herded you in and out of various religious devotions: Exposition of the Blessed Sacrament, Benediction (I loved the smell of incense, the ringing of the bells, the slow, triumphant passage of the golden monstrance, with its awful burden of the Living God), Forty Hours, Novenas, Litanies, and Retreats.

Boy-girl parties were forbidden in grammar school; but once a week we had folk-dancing. My God! The pleasure of those moments! The rush of erotic hope has rarely been equaled by anything that has happened to me since in that vital department of human activity. To remember that once in 1953 I placed my hands on the hips of Sarah McNeil and did the Bunny-hop is to recall an ecstasy almost beyond toleration.

In any event, it was a complete and encompassing world. I guess the overused epithet "ghetto" could be applied. Athletic life occurred within the context of the Catholic Youth Organization, the CYO. Social life took place at the parish Teen Club, moderated, usually, by a very hip young priest with whom you could have frank talks about sex and who, if you were fortunate, would conduct you, when you were a high school senior, on the perilous pleasures of a ski weekend. For the boys, high school meant Sacred Heart, St. Ignatius, or Riordan, schools conducted respectively by the Christian Brothers, the Jesuits, and the Brothers of Mary. Girls had a much wider selection: St. Rose's, the Convent of the Sacred Heart, Presentation, Mercy, St. Paul's, St. Vincent's, St. John's, Star of the Sea. High schools varied widely in the matter of tone, attitude, and status; for ours was, for all its exterior monolithicity, a subtly variegated culture. St. Ignatius, being conducted by the Jesuits, had the most class, its clientele being middle- and upper-middle-class. The small Catholic aristocracy—and there was one—sent its sons to the Benedictine monks down at Woodside, or to St. Anselm's Priory in Washington, D.C. St. Ignatius teemed with unruly boys bent upon beer-drinking and athletics, but the presence of the Jesuits gave the place a sense of wider purpose. At St. Ignatius you took four years of Latin, three years of Greek, and generous doses of English, science, and mathematics. Much was made of the forensic aspects of education, oratory and debate; and, after four years, you were expected to be able to think and to talk on your feet. Sacred Heart was blue-collar in mood, the guys coming in from the Mission, the Excelsior, and South San Francisco. The Christian Brothers were tough, no-nonsense fellows, who thoroughly understood their clientele. They had no intellectual pretensions whatsoever, but were content literally to beat a few fundamentals of literacy into the thick heads of oily-haired, priapic youngsters more intent upon chopping and channeling a '49 Mercury coupe. Riordan High School expressed the spirit of the Sunset and the Ingleside. For a city school it had a palpably suburban tone, having more in common, for instance, with Sierra High School in San Mateo than with St. Ignatius or Sacred Heart. Riordan fostered a greater number of mavericks than did either St. Ignatius or Sacred Heart, for its traditions were weaker, and its class basis more uncertain.

313

Girls had a wider choice, depending, of course, upon their economic circumstances. Professional people sent their daughters to St. Rose's or to the Convent of the Sacred Heart. Located in the marble grandeur of the Flood mansion on Broadway, the Convent, conducted by the madames of the Sacred Heart, offered a Catholic parallel to the experience of Hamlin's or Miss Burke's. There was an elegance to Convent girls, an atmosphere of caste almost European in mood. They learned French, and on certain religious festivals, they curtsied in formal greeting to the mother superior. The Convent was filled with fine furniture, paintings, and heavy tapestries: as if in recollection, or evocation, of the high European Catholic past, Spanish and French especially—a time of order, elegance, and manners which might somehow be made to instruct the sensibilities of these bourgeois daughters of Forest Hill and St. Francis Wood. St. Rose's girls, as I remember them, had an astonishingly developed level of sophistication. They were chic like the Convent girls, but more light-hearted. Many St. Rose's girls went on to Stanford and to Berkeley, a quite daring thing to do in those days, when upon graduation, you were steered almost invariably to a Catholic college.

My own coming of age took place in this stable, pastoral (in retrospect) world, although my own early years were neither reposeful nor idyllic. Abandoned by divorce, I became desperately dependent on the Church. At the age of four I entered the world of Catholic institutions, in this case, the Holy Family Home, a pioneer institution in the field of day-care. Three years later, after one semester in the first grade at Mission Dolores, I was sent to St. Vincent's Home in San Raphael, a boarding school conducted by the Dominican sisters of Mission San Jose. I stayed there until I was twelve. Above the high altar at St. Vincent's, over the massed choir stalls where every morning the nuns chanted the Divine Office, was a painting done in the lush manner of nineteenth-century religious art, of St. Albert of Cologne, the thirteenth-century Dominican savant, teaching his favorite pupil, another Dominican, the young Thomas Aquinas. Serving Mass in the

314

early morning hours of 1948, 1949, and 1950, I had ample time to explore every detail of that painting: the great tome in Albert's hand (was it physics or theology or alchemy? for Albert was interested in everything), the mood of significant discourse, of quickened intelligence, in the eyes of the two men; the feel of study, of university days: books, manuscripts, quills, scientific instruments. I can see now how significant that painting was as a metaphor for the most compelling aspect of the Church's hold on me. To put it briefly, Roman Catholicism offered a tradition: a condition of sustained and worthwhile effort across a span of centuries. Roman Catholicism offered a way out of personal confusion and social displacement.

All this is not to deny Catholicism's primary existence as a religion, with a central core of doctrine and ascesis dealing with the transcendent. But in a very profound way, Roman Catholicism is the most worldly of Christian faiths, deeply insinuated into the substance of western civilization's art, literature, and struggle for public polity. Kneeling before that portrait of saintly savants in learned discourse, I subconsciously ingested a central Catholic tenet: *fides quaerens intellectum*, faith seeking understanding; or, to put it in other ways: grace seeking nature, religion establishing the premises of culture. Taken at its best, taken the way I, in the following years, chose to take it, Roman Catholicism constituted a hunger for this world as well as for the next. Thus we come to another factor in my own early attraction to the Church: its power and authority. Theoretically and politically, the Church was a state within the state, a city within the city. It offered a career to boys of the various middle classes (in the United States the wealthy rarely enter the clergy), a career that promised education, status, certainty of reward in this world and beyond. Being dispossessed myself and wanting a lot of things—education, place, a use of my talents, a conviction of being worthwhile—I studied for the priesthood for two years upon my graduation from the University of San Francisco in 1962.

315

I studied at St. Patrick's in Menlo Park from 1962 to 1964, when I left the seminary for graduate study at Harvard. Looking back at those days, I consider it in general a happy time of my life. I remember with a good deal of pleasure the great red brick building, lavishly built in the late 1890s, with an eye, so Archbishop Riordan directed, to teaching young lads of immigrant families how to live like gentlemen. My room had an enormously high ceiling. A great oaken wardrobe, designed in the European manner, took up one complete wall. My window overlooked an interior courtyard dominated by a leafy orange tree. My desk banked the window, so as I studied day by day, I watched that orange tree go through a cycle of seasons—the leafy endurance of winter, the blossoms of spring, the fruit of late summer, the stilled branches of fall. We arose early, at five-thirty, awakened by the bell in the chapel tower. By six-fifteen, dressed in a black cassock, I had taken my place in one of the oaken choir stalls that faced each other, monastery fashion, across the chapel, which was decorated in the lush, romantic religiosity of the late nineteenth century. One mural, over the chapel entrance, depicted the ordination of a young priest with the idealized romanticism of pre-Raphaelite religious art. After prayers and Mass, we breakfasted in the long refectory whose high windows soared upwards for a full story-and-a-half, sitting together, some two hundred, at long tables and eating our cornflakes in silence as one of us, chosen that week's lector, read from a book. We kept the *magnum silentium* from after recreation the night before until the end of breakfast—no talking whatsoever, just study, sleep, and prayer. A full morning of classes followed breakfast, except on Thursday, which was a holiday. Before I left in 1964, I managed a full year of Old Testament studies and a year devoted to the study of the gospels in Greek. I also took basic theology, and a number of specialized philosophy courses—metaphysics, epistemology, the philosophy of science—that I had missed as an undergraduate. Lunch was our main meal. The faculty joined us for it, sitting together on a high table, some twenty or so priests of St.-Sulpice, dressed in the same black cassocks and birettas as their more youthful charges. A siesta followed lunch (a vestige of the Roman basis of seminary culture), followed by a period of furious sport. The restraints of the life urged us toward physical release. The seminary was lavishly supplied with tennis, handball, and basketball courts, a football field, a baseball diamond, and a swimming pool. All were used with abandon. Showered and recassocked, we studied or attended a seminar in the late afternoon, then at six walked the exquisite gardens reciting our rosaries. Dinner followed at six-thirty; then we went to our rooms or to the library to prepare for the next day's classroom recitations.

During those two years I managed an enormous amount of reading in St. Patrick's small but carefully selected library. How naive it all seems now—that massive assault I made on the world of books, trying like Thomas Wolfe at Harvard to read them all. I also worked as an assistant to the father librarian and absorbed there, most likely, whatever sense of calling I feel towards my present occupation of librarianship—a sense of vocation that had its full share of idealism once, when I dreamed of working in a first-rate institution. I suppose that St. Patrick's Seminary was my last Catholic boarding school, just as the Holy Family Day Home was my first. As I have said, I became dependent upon the Church as a kid because of my abandoned circumstances. I enjoyed the order and regularity of St. Patrick's, and the atmosphere of study, but by the beginning of my second year there—after a summer spent as a bar waiter in the Mountain Room of Yosemite Lodge—I found myself leafing through the catalogs of university graduate schools. I loved the Church, but I really had no vocation to the celibate priesthood. My summer in Yosemite had convinced me of that. There I had slipped back rather easily into my pre-St. Patrick's pursuit of the fair sex. Some thousand men and women of college age from all over the country work in Yosemite during the summer, giving the place a Fort Lauderdale atmosphere of beer and sex. I knew that by even accepting the job at the Mountain Room I was setting in motion a process that would extricate me from St. Patrick's, but that was what I wanted. I wanted out of the Church and into what I then took to be the great world. My seminarian's *persona* lasted for two days in Yosemite, then I went to my first all-night beach party on the banks of the Merced and got bombed on Coor's. I spent the rest of the summer raising hell in my off-hours and relishing the swinging atmosphere of the Mountain Room during work hours. By August I found myself involved in a summer romance with a senior from Bennington, who advised me to become an Episcopalian so that I could both be a priest and get laid.

I shouldn't have even returned to St. Pat's that fall, but—to be perfectly honest—I had no future prospects except the draft. I spent the fall reviving my conviction that this was what I was cut out for, but the conviction lapsed over the Christmas vacation. I spent the month of December filling out applications for graduate school. Harvard came through with both an acceptance into its American Studies program and—based upon my two years of theological study—the prospect of a teaching fellowship in the undergraduate History of American Religion course.

Andy Soutane had a similar seminary experience with the Franciscans at Mission Santa Barbara, as did Tiny Roncola at St. Pat's—the three of us now linked in a network of sordid possibilities. The Sulpicians asked Tiny to leave midway through 1963. They put it as subtly as they could, but they in effect told him that he didn't have an ecclesiastical personality. Tiny's love of the race track was cited as a case in point. On Thursdays when we were allowed to leave the grounds, Tiny used to catch the train at Menlo Park and get off at Tanforan for a day at the races. He also ran a betting pool among the seminarians—football in the fall, basketball in winter, baseball in spring—allowing himself a generous commission in the process. The Rector heard about it and blew his stack. Clerics are forbidden by canon law from gambling. The last I saw of Tiny before I went east in the fall of 1964, he was tending bar at the Thirsty Shamrock out in the Richmond, making book on the side, and talking about enrolling in the USF night law school.

318

Soutane's involvement with the Church has been more profound than either mine or Tiny's. As students in a seminary for secular priests, Tiny and I remained our own men. Soutane, however, joined an ancient religious order—the Franciscans, founded in the thirteenth century by St. Francis of Assisi—taking solemn vows of poverty, chastity, and obedience in the process. Soutane entered the Franciscans after high school and stayed on for six years—some very formative years, eighteen to twenty-four, in a man's life. It's difficult to bring the three images of Soutane I have in my mind into focus: the brown-robed Franciscan student brother, the charismatic candidate for the governorship of California, and the gentleman in the X-rated photographs shown me by Tiny Roncola. But then again, we all have our secret lives, our hidden moments when we prowl about on all fours in search of distraction and release. Soutane's private life is his own business.

The homosexual angle, however, is interesting. Seminaries used to dread the possibility of its presence. You were never allowed in another student's room. Particular friendships were forbidden. You could never appear in a corridor without a full bathrobe, even on the way to the shower. These were all clumsy rules, originating in the sixteenth-century reform of seminaries organized at the Council of Trent; but they made a symbolic statement regarding a palpable caution in this area. Latent homosexuality, I suppose, has prompted a number of vocations to clerical celibacy. Come to think of it, that is as good a way as any to deal with the problem—sublimating it in the name of religion, assuming an identity that lets one off the hook in the matter of females. Just as long as the latency doesn't blossom into act, as it now and then manages to do—with the usual result, if discovered, of some two or three lads packed off into the secular world in the dead of night, no questions asked, no answers given.

Andy Soutane sure as hell doesn't seem gay. He's single, for sure (so am I); but I always thought that this was because he preferred his career to women, or better, to the responsibilities of one woman. The pursuit of power in the name of reforming idealism, or, to put it another way, the pursuit of reform in the name of power, demands an almost monastic dedication. With women's liberation on the scene, you don't have to be married any more to get laid. Women have now given themselves the freedom to be hustled out the door on the morning after. Staying single, I always thought, Soutane can pursue his advancement with greater concentration. Now I have to admit the possibility that Soutane's bachelorhood has other causes as well. Tiny says that Soutane just went through a period of bisexuality a year or two ago as an experiment. I don't think that you experiment with these things. The impulse is either there or not. Apparently, the impulse is in Andy Soutane.

So what! I won't be a party to what Tiny has in mind. I'm not that desperate anyway. I'd like to think that I'm perfectly capable of making a new beginning in life when Carpino is out of office and I'm on the street. Perhaps it was my historical training that got me involved with Carpino in the first place. Politically speaking, he's as doomed as the dodo bird. Provincial, ethnic San Francisco has next to nothing to say to California at large. Carpino is a walking paradigm of what this town has been until very recently, a provincial capital, an American afterthought, run by arrived ethnics with traditionalist values.

Andy Soutane, on the hand, is the new California, nourished on vegetarian stews and five-grain bread. Soutane is jogging and a ten-speed bike. He's backpacking and the Sierra Club. He's Save the Whales. He's I'm OK, You're OK. He's an est encounter session, hot tubs, rolfing, tai chi, tai quan do, and i chingo. He's dope versus booze, women's lib versus marriage, an army cot versus a Sealy Posturepedic.

Strangely enough, all this is grafted onto a conservative Catholic base. The press loves the fact that Soutane is a former Franciscan friar. It makes him seem a crypto-guru, a sort of swami in the state legislature. The only time I ever met Soutane was at a party at Kay Soulé's house on Pacific Heights. Soutane sat alone on a large curved sofa that dominated the huge living room. I kept expecting him to tuck his feet under

320

his thighs like a yoga master. No one dared to sit on the sofa with Soutane. Rather, they gathered in a half-circle before him like disciples before their master. Soutane, in turn, lectured the multitudes like Christ at the Sermon on the Mount. Kay Soulé's butler served an abundance of sandwiches, however, so there was no need for Soutane to multiply the loaves and fishes. While we munched on crustless ham and cheese sandwiches, Soutane lectured us on California's crucial role in the emergence of a Pacific Basin culture. He then turned his attention to the mating problems of the Koala bears at the San Diego Zoo. Aphorisms and various discursive remarks followed: about the nature of good and evil, about politics as an art form, the noösphere as described by Pierre Teilhard de Chardin, the feminization of American culture, the virtues of vegetarianism, the probity of Cesar Chavez and the greed of the winegrowers, the liberalization of marijuana laws. It was an entirely solitary performance; nor, indeed, did Soutane once stand up and mix among the guests, as I have seen even United States senators deign to do. He spent the evening, rather, in his quasi-lotus position, addressing the multitudes.

Kay Soulé was thrilled to have him there. "I'm on his side. He's a winner," she told me.

Not long after, Kay began flying around the state with Soutane in her Lear jet, getting him in and out of campaign appearances in the smaller towns with a minimum waste of time or energy. Soulé bucks are also pouring into the Soutane campaign, Terry Shane tells me. Raymond Soulé, by the way, spent the entire party upstairs in his study, reading, I imagine. He rarely shows up at his wife's events anyway. I wonder if he's hurt by his wife's becoming a Soutane groupie—albeit a special sort of groupie—in the Soutane campaign? If I were married, I wouldn't want my wife flying all over California with the Robert Redford of state politics. People might get the wrong idea.

The Administrative Council met today in an extraordinary session called by Commissioner Mabel Storm to deal with the problem of the Brown Bomber.

"Do any of you realize the damage done to the reputation of the Library by having this loathsome item appear Sunday in Harry Shaw's column?" Commissioner Storm lamented. "We've already a problem with our reputation because of the derelicts and the sex perverts—now this! Honestly! I want something done."

It is, of course, highly irregular—and slightly illegal—for a commissioner to deal directly with the staff in this manner. It also undermines my authority, such as it is. Were Mabel Storm to play it by the book, she would inform me of her concern and I, in turn, would direct the efforts of the staff: but Mabel Storm doesn't play it by the book. Commissioners are supposed to set policy. Mabel Storm likes to *run* things. She has no qualms about invading this or that department, asking questions and, after half understanding the answers, coming to me with an administrative recommendation that even I can see is half-assed. In any event, here we all were, the senior staff of the Library, gathered together to consider the question of the Brown Bomber, whose surreptitious raids upon various departments of the SFPL had finally made him a celebrity in Harry Shaw's column.

"It's an inside job," said Manny Vogel, the commission secretary, charged with the physical maintenance of the Library. "Nobody except a staff person would have access to so many locked rooms."

"It's a disgrace," exclaimed Mabel Storm. "It's horrible PR. You must do something."

"I've already notified the police," I announced. "The North Station insists that it's a matter for the sex crime detail, but the sex crime detail doesn't want to get involved. They say it's under the category of general nuisance, a misdemeanor; hence it's up to North Station to deal with it. North Station now wants the burglary detail to handle it—from the point of view that while befouling a public place might only be a misdemeanor, breaking and entering is a more serious matter. That's where it is now, with burglary. The inspector at burglary, however, says that he can't give the problem the highest priority."

322

"He has to," said Mabel Storm. "It's a disgrace."

"We should set up some form of entrapment," Manny Vogel suggested.

"Yeah," said Tony Ortega, chief of Main, "we could leave a roll of toilet paper out as bait."

Everyone laughed except Mabel Storm.

"This is no laughing matter," she warned. "This is a disgrace. I want something done."

After some twenty minutes of futile discussion, we agreed to put the library guards on extra alert, which is in itself a sort of joke. Our guards are about as effective as zookeepers on the Serengeti Plain when it comes to securing the Main Library. They just can't cope with the sorts of people who stumble in here. We'd need twice as many guards as we have now even to begin thinking about a surveillance operation.

"Now," said Tony Ortega as we broke up the meeting, "if the Brown Bomber is a member of the Administrative Council, he or she is forewarned. We're on your odorous trail."

Toby Wain has a piece in the *Express* this morning about the mayoral primary in June and the runoff in November. Toby handicaps the contenders. State Senator John Como is the front runner, he says, followed by Supervisor Sandra Van Dam. Toby puts State Senator Mortimer Engles and Superior Court Judge Charles Fessio in a dead heat for third place. The candidacy of Supervisor Al Tarsano has got political observers baffled. A conservative maverick, Al Tarsano is, as Toby writes, "not in first place, but he's not in last place either. Let's just say that Al Tarsano is, as usual, all over the place."

"There's been speculation in a few of Walter Rosenfeld's columns," Toby concludes, "that antitrust attorney Johnboy Turfer and city librarian James Vincent Norton might enter the race as dark horse candidates. Thus far Rosenfeld has failed to create a boomlet. As candidates, Turfer and Norton would fall between serious candidates and the eccentric fringers who run every four years just for the personal publicity. Thus far the mayoral election is shaping up as a John Como shoo-in. As Como put it to me recently: 'I've got the blacks. I've got the

Latinos. I've got the gays. In San Francisco, that means victory.' Como, so far, seems to be telling it like it is."

I called Toby on the phone. He sounded hung-over.

"I'm hung-over," he said.

"You sound like it. Thanks for the plug."

"It was intended to be discouraging."

"I'd feel discouraged if I were thinking about running for mayor. Since I'm not, I feel flattered just to make the lunatic fringe."

"Stick to writing history and running the Library."

"I'm not doing either very well."

"Be sure to read Harry Shaw this morning."

"I already have—with sorrow and regret."

Harry Shaw slipped the Mayor another zinger this morning. Esmeralda, he says, has hired a private detective on unspecified business. "Three guesses," says Shaw, "what's on Madama Mayor's mind."

Strange that Harry Shaw so hates Claudio Carpino. They resemble each other so much. Before Esmeralda badgered Eva Maria about being Mexican, Shaw and Carpino used to meet for lunch once a month, like two sovereign powers willing to negotiate. Now it's attack, attack, attack. Carpino tries to fight back at his press conferences, calling Harry Shaw San Francisco's number one sour lemon. The Mayor makes snide references to Shaw's New York failure—which is ancient history, having nothing to do with Shaw's present San Francisco punch—but to no avail. Terry Shane has told the Mayor a hundred times: "Don't get into a shouting match with someone who's in the ring every morning, with a half-million readers in his corner. You'll get outshouted." But Carpino never listens. He's used to the forensic victories of a court of law. Win the argument in court, and you take home a pile of money. Carpino's anti-Shaw barbs rarely get covered. Shaw, after all, owns his own column and is more than capable of winning the shouting match.

As I said, the two have a lot in common. They're both Mediterranean men with a lot of *amour propre* and a taste for vengeance. I point to the Mediterranean aspects of this

324

vindictiveness because the Shaw-Carpino feud—or rather, Shaw's hatred for Carpino—has to it elements of a fierce vendetta. Shaw shows a pattern in his columns, a cycle of use and discard, commented upon by many, including Toby Wain.

"He'll take someone up," says Toby, "make a city-wide personality out of him. Jesus, the guy will be in the column three times a week. Then: an insult, or an imagined insult, a rebuff, or just plain *ennui*. Then bingo! Out of the blue, the guy is destroyed. If Shaw is feeling merciful, he'll let the rejectee just drop. This, however, is rare. Most of the time, the former friend gets savaged upon his exit from the charmed circle."

Shaw, so Toby says, uses up a set of friends every five years or so. No one who started with him in the late thirties is still a buddy. They're either dead or too old. Shaw abandoned his wartime pals in the mid-fifties, then threw his fifties friends out in the early sixties, and so forth. I'm talking here about the retinue—the girlfriends, the minor characters, the quotable *maître d's*. Shaw has remained constant in his devotion to his social superiors; it's just in his playtime life that he goes through phases. It was booze and pussy just after the war; Jewish respectability in the early fifties; WASP acceptability in the late fifties, a period, incidentally, climaxed by a half-dozen or so invitations to the Burlingame Country Club. In the early sixties Harry Shaw ran with the Hemingway set. He'd head off to Monte Carlo every year for the Grand Prix. He drove a racing Ferrari around town. He'd hang out at Barry Eliot's Manolete Bar and one year did a column about running with the bulls at Pamplona. ("Actually," Toby Wain claims, "he watched from a third-story window.") He fished off the Florida Keys and went after big-horned sheep in the mountain wilderness of Idaho. He spent the mid-sixties with the New Left, writing columns about revolution, rock, Vietnam, the new lifestyle, the oppression of minorities.

In each case, the transition was painful for the circle that formed around Shaw while he was interested in a specific pursuit. Shaw shed these groups like a snake shedding its skin.

325

He couldn't just let a set go, however. He had to pick a quarrel, ruin a reputation, before he moved on. Warren Harcourt gave Shaw his first break when the latter shambled into the office of the *Express* from the Greyhound Bus Depot. In 1949, when Shaw was getting bored by the front-page, stop-the-presses journalistic phase of his life, he ran an item about Harcourt's drinking. He destroyed his friendship with three or four Air Corps pals (they'd formed a PR firm in San Francisco after the war) when he got tired of reliving the booze-and-broads days of war-time London.

Harry Shaw periodically grows ambivalent to the myths he creates. This is an aspect of his superb instincts as a journalist: he moves on with the times. In the late sixties, for instance, during his New Left phase, he was in there swinging with the best of them. He took up with David Harris and Joan Baez. He even demonstrated—just once—against the war in Vietnam: a sedate demonstration on Van Ness Avenue, protesting the appearance of a South Vietnamese ballet troupe at the Opera House.

Since these are the hedonistic seventies, Shaw is now into cocaine and Cuisinarts. He writes a lot about "lifestyle" and gives the latest Mill Valley recipe for veggies. He's also become a wine buff. Some day a social historian will be able to plot the shifts of prejudices, tastes, power groups of San Francisco, 1936-1976, without ever leaving the bound volumes of Harry Shaw's column.

I've already mentioned how cheap Claudio Carpino is, how his press secretary Terry Shane frequently gets caught with even the most minor tab—hot dogs at the airport, cab fare, dinner for two at a hotel when he accompanies the Mayor on a trip. Shaw is even cheaper. They have at least this in common. Obsessed by wealth and conspicuous consumption, Shaw has over the years done all right by himself—despite his heavy alimony payments.

"He never pays for a thing," says Toby Wain. "He got his home from a real-estate developer in exchange for a series of plugs for a new tennis ranch down in Carmel. His Maserati comes from Piedmont Motors in exchange for some colorful Maserati stories. He hasn't picked up a restaurant tab in forty years. Other than the time Dominic St. Pierre made him pay for his lunch at the San Domenico, the only time that I know of that this ever backfired on him was one night at the St. Anselm's School where he's got his kid. He tried to walk past the door into a parents' potluck supper without paying the three-dollar admission fee. The church lady at the gate refused to let him in. Some say there was even a minor scuffle with Shaw coming out the loser."

The ostensible issue over which Harry Shaw has broken with Carpino is development. Carpino wants it. Shaw doesn't. Shaw doesn't feel in control of the emerging San Francisco—the manhattanized city. The very word "manhattanization" recalls his New York defeat. Suppose for a moment that the manhattanization of San Francisco is truly under way, that the city's economic future is as a corporate headquarters: a city of highrises staffed by a suburbanized work force. Such a San Francisco would not be amenable to Harry Shaw's spell. Its eastern-trained, eastern-recruited professional class would find Shaw's mythologizing provincial and slightly pathetic. Harry Shaw is correct when he says that the magic is going out of San Francisco. But the magic is going out of all of urban America as well. We are being networked, as we librarians put it: interrelated more and more with each other through computers, electronic communications, and an interdependent, heated-up socio-economic system. In the face of this, all provincial San Franciscans—Carpino, Shaw, myself, Toby Wain, whoever—are becoming rapidly obsolete. Cities are ceasing to be metaphors, myths, personalities. They are becoming ganglions of electronics, service centers for the business of capital, machines for the consumption of goods and services. The irony, however, is that they are also becoming the refuges of the misfits and the poor. Few of San Francisco's spiffy, educated downtown people live in San Francisco. They live in the East Bay, Marin, the Peninsula. State Senator John Como knows rather clearly that he'll be the next mayor of San

327

Francisco. He's got the votes of the gays and the minority poor: of those, that is, who live here, as opposed to just working here in the downtown highrises.

The item about the private detective in Harry Shaw's column this morning can't help the Mayor politically. Every morning about half a million people read Shaw's column. How can Carpino run the state, they'll ask, if his wife is throwing raisin toast at him in the Garden Court of the Palace Hotel or hiring a private eye to tag his movements? Why in the hell did Esmeralda have to give Eva Shaw the business about being Mexican? Just about every day Shaw is at Carpino's throat like a bull mastiff that won't let go. In one of his journals, Sebastian Collins describes Father Peter Yorke at Mayor Phelan's throat the same way during the Teamsters' strike of 1901.

I remember once at Harvard mentioning Harry Shaw's column in the course of a conversation. "Who's Harry Shaw?" I was asked. The question stunned me. I also found it difficult to answer. How, I mean, do you describe Harry Shaw to non-San Franciscans? Do you say that he is San Francisco's number-one mythologizer: that it is his role in our provincial culture to sustain the illusion that San Francisco is an exciting, magical place? Shaw does that—daily.

The myth he propounds has nothing to do with Sebastian Collins's San Francisco. A Santa Rosa boy, Harry Shaw cares little for the past in the historical sense of the term. His forte is nostalgia, not history—a nostalgia that takes its nourishment from the late 1930s onward—ever since, that is, Harry Shaw arrived in San Francisco. The city began for Harry Shaw when Harry Shaw got here—no sooner, no later. The local gospel according to Harry Shaw is that San Francisco before the Age of Claudio Carpino was a wonder city of enchantment and chic. Everyone had fun and said lots of witty, Noel Cowardish sorts of things over cocktails.

All of us spend our lives in a spiral of experience that ascends in larger circles away from our adolescent self. The circle of experience grows wider and wider, but the point of departure remains the same. Harry Glickfield (later Harry Shaw) grew up a skinny, neglected Jewish kid in Santa Rosa. He read a lot of movie magazines. His father was a school teacher who drank, which is rare—drinking, I mean—with Jews. His mother died when he was ten. Harry dreamed of life in the big city. When he got off the Greyhound bus at Seventh and Mission in 1936 at the age of nineteen and headed over to the *Express* at Third and Mission to ask for a job, he was playing out an immemorial role. He was the poor boy arriving in the big city: Samuel Johnson in London, Benjamin Franklin in Philadelphia, Horatio Alger in New York.

Allow me to quote here from one of Shaw's Sunday nostalgia columns, dated 18 March 1966. Shaw writes his Sunday columns on Tuesday. They are usually not topical, as are his weekday columns, but nostalgia pieces. The Sunday columns, in fact, account for some of Shaw's best writing. They show that he can write, that he might have been a serious writer had he not so early found his niche as a gossip columnist, which over the years has proved a well-paying form of paraliterary imprisonment. All daily journalism is a form of incarceration. Ask my friend Toby Wain.

"I didn't go directly to the *Express*," Harry Shaw writes of his arrival in San Francisco. "No one, in fact, has probably ever been crazy enough to walk from Seventh and Market to Third and Mission, a distance of five blocks, via Nob HIll, Chinatown, North Beach, and the Financial district. It took me three hours of walking to do it; but by the time I arrived at the *Express*, I had calmed my nerves and firmed my resolve to make it here or go back and pick prunes in Santa Rosa. I walked up Taylor Street past the Bohemian Club. A man I later learned was Templeton Crocker, owner of the yacht *Zaca*, was entering Bohemia for lunch. He wore an elegantly tailored pinstripe suit, with a doeskin vest, a homburg hat, and a red carnation in his lapel. I had never seen a man carry a gold-headed cane before, except in the movies. At Huntington Park atop Nob Hill, across from Grace Cathedral, Chinese children were playing exotic, incomprehensible games. I walked down California Street, past the P.U. Club and the Fairmont Hotel, turning left at Old St. Mary's on Grant Avenue into Chinatown. Chinatown in the late thirties still recalled the Chinatown of Arnold Genthe's pre-earthquake photographs. The men wore colored silk pajamas and pigtails. Women hobbled along on bound feet. You emerged from Chinatown into Little Italy, beginning at Filbert Street. I stood outside the window of Molinari's Delicatessen on Columbus, overwhelmed by the profusion of cheeses, salami, dried fish, wine bottles, tins of olive oil. It sure beat the corner grocery store in Santa Rosa. And the girls on Montgomery Street in the Financial district sure beat the farm girls of Santa Rosa High. They all looked like Kate Hepburn—skinny, sassy, well tailored."

Shaw got in to see Warren Harcourt, the twenty-five-year-old boy wonder managing editor of the *Express*. Harcourt liked Shaw and gave him a job in rewrite. Six months later Shaw had a column of his own, covering radio shows and radio gossip. Harcourt insisted, however, that he call himself Harry Shaw. "Harry Glickfield," Harcourt said, "sounds like a furrier." The rest is history—local history.

Throughout the late 1930s and the postwar 1940s Harry Shaw constructed a myth, a fairy tale. San Francisco, in turn, tried to make the fairy tale come true. Like the snake oil salesman from Kansas in L. Frank Baum's story, Harry Shaw became San Francisco's Wizard of Oz. For forty years he has pandered to a dream of his own creation—a vision of San Francisco as the Emerald City at the end of the yellow brick road. San Francisco, Harry Shaw tells us every morning (and we, by and large, believe him), is a city of magic and dreams.

Shaw writes about the way the morning fog refuses to abandon the cypressed headlands to the sun. He writes about the taste of mock turtle soup laced with sherry at Jack's, or the cracked crab, French bread, and chablis served down at the Wharf: a meal that is in and of itself a ceremony of place. He writes about the way seabirds laze overhead at the Music Concourse at Golden Gate Park on a Sunday afternoon while

330

the band plays an overture from Rossini. He writes about Dashiell Hammett's San Francisco, the low-rise, bridgeless city of the twenties, whose foggy streets echo the lonely steps of a trenchcoated Sam Spade. He writes about bars and restaurants, past and present: Izzy Gomez's place on Pacific, its floor covered in sawdust; the lower bar of the Mark Hopkins in the late thirties, where everyone prized bright chatter; Bop City in the Fillmore of the late forties, when the interracial scene was hot; the Manolete on Broadway in the mid-fifties, when the talk was all of Mikonos, the bulls of Pamplona, Dave Brubeck. In and out of Shaw's column like shooting stars have flitted the great, the near-great, the falsely great, and the outright phonies of the city: the characters—Tiny Birdwhistle Armstrong, the Pigeon Lady, the Lavender Man; the hostesses—Pat Atlas, Pat Montandon; the *bons vivants*—Jack Vietor, Sandy Walker; the politicians and civil servants—Harry Ross, Frank McGrath, Dion Holm; the sportsmen—Willie Mays, Joe DiMaggio; the hotels—the Mark, the Fairmont, the Clift; the cablecars; the little old ladies in tennis shoes.

I myself have made Shaw's column a few times and must confess a secret thrill of having done so; for I grew up with the vision of San Francisco as Harry Shaw described it floating before my imagination as the one goal worth striving for—the living of the good life San Francisco-style, Harry Shaw-style.

It was only later in life that I glimpsed the essential falseness of the dream: glimpsed the falseness, but did not cast off the spell; for if I ever did, if San Francisco ever did—cast off the Harry Shaw myth—what would be left? Cleveland with a view? A smallish, remote, rather unaccomplished provincial city, known for little that is first-rate except views and restaurants? Harry Shaw has given four decades of San Franciscans an authenticating self-image to live by. He took them from the severity of the Depression, in which his own family suffered disastrous reversals—his father driven to drink (a rare calamity, as I have said, among Jews), his mother succumbing to diphtheria; he took San Franciscans from this kind of bleakness into the expanded possibilities of the Second World War, in which he himself managed a first lieutenant's commission in the public relations branch of the Army Air Corps Bomber Command in London.

Toby Wain, who occupies a much less formidable niche in the hierarchy of *Express* writers than Shaw, claims that Harry Shaw, born in 1916, is obsessed by the values and aspirations of the Bay Area's World War II, upper-middle-class generation. Harry Shaw, Toby says, is the John O'Hara of San Francisco.

"The bonding device for this group," Toby says, "was to have gone to Stanford before the war. There you joined a fraternity or a sorority, drove a 1938 Mercury convertible roadster, and went up to San Francisco for spring dances at the Palace Hotel, music by Anson Weeks. You also played tennis—an uncommon game in those days—looking very good in your tennis whites. The war caught you in your senior year, or in law school, or just getting started in your father's brokerage firm in San Francisco. You managed a commission in one or another of the services, and married your Stanford girlfriend while on leave in late 1943, just before shipping out overseas. The wedding took place at St. Luke's Episcopal Church, with the reception at your father's club—P.U., Bohemian, Family, or Burlingame Country."

"Let me finish it," I said to Toby. We were lunching at Jack's, where Toby goes at least once a week. Harry Shaw was lunching with Johnboy Turfer over at the other side of the busy restaurant, which was how the conversation got started in the first place.

"After the war, you moved to Atherton or Ross, or if you were especially bohemian, you stayed in Pacific Heights. You had three children. The boy prepped at the Robert Louis Stevenson School in Pebble Beach. The girls went to Miss Burke's or to Miss Hamlin's. You spent your Thursday nights at the Bohemian Club and the month of August on Lake Tahoe."

The fact is: Harry Shaw is not part of this world, and never was, nor will he ever be, although he has coaxed its

332

suggestions into a universalized pattern of the local good life. Harry Glickfield went to Santa Rosa City College for one year, not to Stanford. He arrived in San Francisco on a Greyhound bus, wearing a shiny dark blue gabardine suit, having less than five dollars in his pocket. Sometime in his early years as a columnist, Harry Shaw experienced a simple Cartesian insight: most people go through life with their noses pressed to the restaurant window, looking in at the smart set inside enjoying lunch. Many people crowd the sidewalks at a preview, but only the movie stars walk in for the show. Harry Shaw decided that he would turn his vulnerabilities into strengths through the simple mechanism of reverse compensation. He would play a role and make the role pay. An outsider to San Francisco, he soaked himself in local lore, assuming the stance of an oldtimer remembering when there was a better town. He grafted the image of the better town onto himself. Within a decade, by the time he was thirty-five, Harry Shaw was, for mythological purposes at least, the demiurge of San Francisco.

Obscure, unconnected, he assiduously cultivated the *beau monde*. The local upper crust treated him horribly at first, I'm told by Toby Wain, Harry Shaw's ambivalent Boswell. The WASP elite was especially hard on what they considered an upstart Eastern European, and even the city's German Jewish elite found him a crass *arriviste*. One P.U. Club member, incensed over an item in Shaw's column, once literally knocked Shaw down in the lower bar of the Mark Hopkins Hotel.

I can see the scene now. It is early 1940, so the incensed P.U. Club member's evening clothes have a look of late 1930s elegance; indeed, the velvet-collared overcoat our assailant wears draped over his shoulders only falls slightly askew during the thrashing. Seeing Harry Shaw at the bar, our P.U. stalwart excuses himself for a moment from the company of beminked women and black-tied men with whom he is heading into the Peacock Court. He walks over to Harry Shaw, who at the time is at the bar rolling liars' dice with a few friends from the *Express*. He taps Shaw on the shoulder. Shaw turns. One deft backhand across Shaw's face, followed by an equally efficient jab to the solar plexus. As Shaw bends over, his face is met by a rapidly rising knee.

As Harry Shaw falls to the floor, he notices that his attacker is wearing shiny black patent leather dancing pumps with a grosgrain ribbon bow. At his assailant's feet, trying to shake the ringing from his ears, Harry Shaw remembers the particular item that has no doubt incensed the avenging gentleman: something about a pregnant chorus girl. Shaw's *Express* buddies look sheepishly at each other, more embarrassed than angry. The bartender continues to wipe a glass. It's obvious that no one will even protest the assault, let alone call the cops. Shaw clears his head, then looks up from the floor to the towering figure above him, looks up to an heroic figure of dominant WASP America: square jaw, graying hair at the temples, a face slightly flushed with the redness of good living, but tanned also from yachting and polo. The gentleman in question, a senior partner in a major Montgomery Street investment firm, says nothing for the longest while, but merely smiles as one would to a naughty boy whom one has just spanked but wants to make up with.

"I want nothing else about her in your column. Do you understand?"

Harry Shaw, age twenty-three, nods assent. He understands. The gentleman reaches down and helps Harry to his feet.

"Well then, we understand each other."

He assists Shaw to the bar stool, then says to the bartender: "See to it that Mr. Shaw and his friends drink on my tab for the rest of the evening." He peels off a twenty, puts it down on the bar, then walks into the lobby where his friends await an evening's pleasure.

Class. Real class. For the rest of his life, because of this moment, Harry Shaw has a sense of standards, a way of operating, that modeled itself upon the *modus vivendi* of the chastising gentleman in evening clothes. Twenty years later, in 1960, when the gentleman in question—Justin Geary by

334

name, a descendant of the Geary of Geary Street—shuffled off this mortal coil after six decades of hard work, polo, yachting, chorus girls and champagne, Shaw wrote a full-column eulogy (omitting the incident in the lower bar of the Mark Hopkins) in which he praised Justin Geary for being the epitome of old-time San Francisco class, now on the wane. The evening clothes, the low-keyed Gibson Man demeanor, the professionally delivered punches, the *noblesse oblige* of the twenty-dollar bill thrown on the bar, the sweeping off into the night with the gorgeous girls and other formally dressed gentlemen—no sir, Harry Shaw never forgot that night.

He felt some shame, of course, but admiration overcame his humiliation. He began to realize that there was a world of influence and power that soared safely and serenely beyond the reach of one such as him, an as-of-yet small-time gossip columnist from Santa Rosa. He resolved to learn as much as he could about this world, to adopt its standards and tastes, and perhaps, one glorious day, to be accepted by it.

As Toby Wain pointed out the day of our conversation at Jack's, Harry Shaw served a long, tedious, often humiliating apprenticeship. Marrying a platinum blond stripper with big tits from Sally Rand's Nude Ranch at the Treasure Island World's Fair didn't help matters much; but that was a war-time mistake. A lot of men made them. When Harry tired of crawling all over the first Mrs. Shaw's cotton-candy body, he gave her the old heave-ho. He had learned a valuable lesson in life: you don't have to marry a girl if you want to screw her. Harry's second wife, the New York WASP Radcliffe graduate, helped matters enormously. Although the marriage collapsed along with the end of Harry's fling as a New York columnist, in their brief year-and-a-half together, the second Mrs. Shaw schooled Harry in the rudiments of upper-class life. He learned about food, wines, and tailoring. He learned to play tennis. He met a lot of classy people, whom he assiduously cultivated later, setting them up with parties and girls when they passed through San Francisco, as all of them did at one time or another: pass through San Francisco to admire the view and party it up a bit. San Francisco society whirls around such out-of-towners, here a Connecticut heiress, there a Broadway restaurateur. Bobby Short, for instance, is very popular in San Francisco. The *beau monde* goes absolutely bananas over a title. A defunct Spanish, French, or Italian title will do; but an extant British title works even more wonders. Word must be out in the House of Lords that if you're broke, bored, horny, or all three, scrape up the price of a plane ticket to San Francisco and you'll have the time of your life. Harry Shaw loves to stud his column with references to titled visitors from England, with whom he is on the most palsy of terms.

"For a while," Toby Wain claims, "Shaw became the number one pimp in San Francisco. He was always setting up fancy British, New York, or Hollywood types with classy San Francisco lays. That was up to the mid-fifties or so. After that, it was Harry Shaw who got laid."

Toby then went on to tell me how at a recent stag dinner party he'd attended, given by the city's playboy clothier Ford Booth, Harry Shaw, Booth, and Jeremiah Jones, San Francisco's charismatic black assemblyman, had dessert under the table. Ford Booth arranged the dessert, calling it *bombe orlamente*: which is to say, three hookers came in, crawled under the table, and administered blow jobs to the lucky guests of honor.

"What was Shaw's response?" I asked.

"Aside from the obvious physiological response, including a momentary loss of cool during climax, Shaw carried it off rather well. When it was over, he said: 'Next time I'll try the chocolate pudding.' "

As Toby Wain points out, Harry Shaw's apprenticeship to the haut monde and the beau monde wasn't easy. Skinny Jewish kids with frizzy hair just don't walk into the Burlingame Country Club. The Concordia-Argonaut wasn't much easier. Shaw's third wife, Jessica Voorsanger, got him into the Concordia-Argonaut sometime in the mid-fifties, although even then, married to a Voorsanger, Shaw had a rough time of it. Certain Concordia-Argonauts felt that he was, well, a little too loud and pushy for the club. It took another few years for Shaw to get his first invitation to the Burlingame Country Club. After that, Wain says, he'd drop everything to go down to Hillsborough to play cards with this or that dowager who had taken him up.

If you know Barry Eliot's book *We Like It Here* (Viking, 1959), then you know that by the late 1950s Harry Shaw had made it big in San Francisco. *We Like It Here* features Harry Shaw in about twenty-five percent of its photographs. We see him brunching at Enrico's on a sunny afternoon for that European feeling; dancing in white tie and tails at the Opera Fol de Rol; enjoying a late Scotch and soda at Barry's Manolete Bar on Broadway (Barry is behind the bar, attired in full bullfighter's regalia). We see him Sunday, brunching on a sunny Telegraph Hill deck; taking in the Van Gogh exhibition at the de Young with KSFO disc jockey Don Sherwood; catching the Kingston Trio at the hungry i; chatting amiably in the *entr'acte* at the Opera House with William Matson Roth and the late J. D. Zellerbach, Eisenhower's ambassador to Italy. *We Like It Here* is a very fifties sort of a book—redolent with the hopes and aspirations of the World War II generation in the full noon of its San Francisco enjoyment. This, the apogee of Harry Shaw's arc of influence, was—so Toby Wain describes it—the mauve and yellow noon of provincial contentment.

What was it about those days that makes even me nostalgic? I was in my late teens then, turning into my early twenties, and I must admit that Harry Shaw provided my generation with its initiatory metaphors. I remember dancing at Station J, a marvelous night club on Commercial Street off Montgomery, in the onetime PG&E Power Station J. The San Francisco Symphony Orchestra, or part of it, played there on nonsymphony nights: they played full, resonant, old-fashioned dance music, including a lot of Cole Porter. I remember dancing there one night with an Aer Lingus stewardess I'd met earlier in the evening at a cocktail party given by Gene Fracchia at 1812 Pacific. She was a beauty, the stewardess, as fresh and lovely as the sunrise over the Lakes of Killarney. I held her in my arms and inhaled the scent of heather, shamrocks, and an Irish meadow in the immediate moment after a spring rain. As we danced to "Ain't Misbehavin'," Harry Shaw danced by with one or another of his cafe society friends. They were able to dance and talk at the same time. I was thrilled. This was it: I was really out on the town. I saw him again at the hungry i (Phyllis Diller was making her debut), and again at the Actor's Workshop when Michael Sullivan (he shortly afterwards died of cancer) played King Lear. One night when I was an undergraduate at USF, some friends of mine pulled up alongside Harry at the corner of Post and Taylor—just by accident. Shaw then drove a Jaguar sedan.

"Hey, Harry Shaw!" we yelled.

"You guys should find some girls," Shaw shot back amiably.

We felt like real sports.

As I have pointed out, it wasn't all peaches and cream for Harry Shaw as he climbed to the top. The New York defeat hurt; he had failed in the Big Apple; but it also fused him even more fiercely onto San Francisco circumstances. Literally and symbolically, Harry Shaw began his career by being horse-whipped in the lower bar of the Mark by the very world he had dreamed of as a boy in Santa Rosa, thumbing through copies of movie magazines. The Justin Gearys of San Francisco, moreover, were not finished with him after just one beating.

"Very clever—very Jewish," was the way they most likely put it at the Burlingame Country Club during the long years of Harry's apprenticeship. In dealing with Harry Shaw, you cannot ignore the issue of his Jewishness. Over the years Shaw has himself swung back and forth on a pendulum of ambivalence. He grew up the only Jewish kid in his neighborhood of Santa Rosa. He was one of the few Jewish graduates of Santa Rosa High School. Being Jewish was a liability in the first six or eight years of his San Francisco career. Justin Geary is not known to have uttered anything anti-Semitic during the course of his laconic disciplining of Shaw in the lower bar of the Mark, but something anti-Semitic

338

lurks behind the event. In the second phase of his San Francisco career, just after his New York failure, Shaw threw himself into his Jewishness. He started by marrying Jessica Voorsanger, the heiress of a distinguished high provincial Jewish family. In those years, 1949-1955, Shaw must have looked back upon his beating at the hands of Justin Geary as a local version of the European holocaust. He, too, had felt the fist of the fascist brute.

The problem was, Harry Shaw admired the brute enormously. The brute had class. Even during his aggressively Jewish phase, Shaw sent out constant feelers into the world of protestant privilege. He came near to election to the Bohemian Club in 1956, but was blackballed (so they say around the Club) by none other than Justin Geary himself, then a power on the membership committee. Four years later, Shaw was singing Geary's praises in an elegiac obituary. He praised Geary for his strong lean jaw, his leathery complexion, his John Wayne-like good looks. He praised him for his abundant, virile and varied love life; his prowess as a polo player and a yachtsman; his distinguished war record as a battalion commander of ski troops, Tenth Mountain Division, operating in the Italian Alps.

"Men like Justin Geary made San Francisco into what it is today," Shaw wrote, "a city with a rage for pleasure, a city unafraid of burning the candle at both ends, as long as it's done with style."

"I'm a collector of these incidents," Toby Wain says, "a veritable connoisseur of Harry Shaw-ana. Did you know that Benton Boyd once threw a drink in Shaw's face at the Pacific Union Club?"

"How tacky," I said. "It sounds like some second-rate version of John O'Hara's *Appointment in Samarra*."

"Yes," Toby said, warming to the story, "only there the guy who throws the drink gets depressed. Apparently it was Shaw, the recipient of the unexpected lavation, who went into a depression. This took place in 1954 or thereabouts. De Haro Martin took Shaw up to the P.U. for lunch. It was Shaw's first visit. He veritably swelled like a peacock when he marched into the bar. De Haro Martin, you know, is an *Express* stockholder and the *Express* board of directors was worried at the time about the possibility of Shaw going over to the *Examiner* for more money. Martin wanted to butter Shaw up and he knew how to do it. Unfortunately, Benton Boyd was at the bar that day, half in the bag. Shaw had recently written that Boyd had been asked to resign from the Society of California Pioneers because he could not prove descent from Captain William Richardson, the English-born Marin County ranchero active in the 1830s, as Boyd had claimed in his application. Shaw advised Boyd to search his family tree for evidence of descent from William Leidesdorf, the American Vice Consul to San Francisco in the 1840s. Remember: Leidesdorf was one-quarter black. Shaw meant it as a joke. He's always making racist jokes. Well, Benton Boyd of Kentfield, California, didn't think it was very funny. When he saw Shaw at the P.U. Club Bar, he went bananas—called Shaw a kike and threw a Scotch and soda all over his new glen plaid suit. The men at the bar hustled Boyd out of the club. He was suspended, in fact, for a year. Shaw went into a funk. I guess the assault recalled the Justin Geary incident to his mind—an incident which he hadn't quite worked through."

According to Toby Wain, Harry Shaw's obsession with taste originates in an insecurity that has it roots in Shaw's ambivalence towards his own Jewishness. The fourth Mrs. Shaw, Eva Lopez, also known as Eva Maria del Valde, is a former Catholic. She has, however, converted to the Episcopal faith, becoming active in St. Cyril's, the fashionable Episcopalian parish in Cow Hollow. The Shaws' only child, Juan Carlos Shaw (named in honor of the king of Spain), sings in the St. Cyril's choir. Shaw himself seems to have let the matter of religion lapse, although his column of late has once again become very Jewish. Jewish wits, wags, politicians, attorneys, writers, and the like fill the daily pages, just as their WASP counterparts did two decades ago. As Shaw moves into his sixties, he wishes to be reconciled with the Lord of Israel.

340

As I have said, my Harvard interlocutor had never heard of Harry Shaw. In San Francisco and environs everyone has heard of Harry Shaw. For the past thirty years his ass has been kissed daily by doormen, waiters, restaurateurs, public relations flaks, politicians, aspiring artists, hostesses, and other would-be habitues of his column. A PR acquaintance of mine, Syd Rothschild, tells me that a good mention in a Harry Shaw column can be worth up to $50,000 in PR value.

"Get into Shaw's column," Syd says, "and your phone rings all day."

I've once had a chance to see this flattery at close hand. About two years ago, I was invited by Leonard Bogard, a local novelist, to attend a Round Table luncheon at the restaurant of the Hotel Magellan on Geary Street. The Round Table has met there for a monthly lunch since 1965. The Magellan is supposed to resemble the Algonquin in New York: smallish and literary in a shabby genteel sort of way. Shaw organized the Round Table in 1965 after reading a biography of Alexander Woollcott, one of the Algonquin circle. He thought that San Francisco should have something similar.

"Are you clubbable?" Leonard Bogard asked when he invited me.

"I can be, for an hour or so."

Leonard obviously felt that he was doing me a favor by bringing me among the elect. Leonard wears a beard to make himself look literary and to disguise the fact that his neck is beginning to show signs of the fact that he has passed fifty.

"I'm either San Francisco's oldest young novelist, or its youngest old novelist," Leonard says.

His amusement over his dilemma is one of the best things about him. As the city's acknowledged Doctor of Hip, Leonard Bogard is into everything: hot tubs, vegetarianism, carrot cake, Union Street bars (his latest favorite is the Sun Grove, decorated by Billy Gaylord), body shirts, puka shell necklaces, herbal teas, massage, rolfing, Sufism, nude sun-bathing (in Marin County), *coitus reservatus* (this during a Sanskrit phase), and the Mabel Mercer revival. According to

341

Leonard, he also screws like a mink. To hear Leonard describe the range, variety, and frequency of his couplings makes one want to nominate him to the Harvard Medical School for some kind of award.

"Leonard," I've told him, "you should donate your urogenital system to medical science."

"I will, I will—when I'm finished with it."

Leonard Bogard's novels are usually about getting laid, and so they sell rather well. A lot of girls bag with Leonard in the hopes that they'll someday show up in a novel. Many of them do.

I met Leonard in the lobby of the Magellan. Come to think of it, the Magellan does look like the Algonquin. It has the same dim light, the same array of stuffed chairs in the lobby, and the same adjacent restaurant, catering to the theater crowd.

"You've got a square in two, Oh wise Doctor of Hip," cracked Harry Shaw as Leonard brought me into the corner alcove where the Round Table sits at a round table for its monthly fetes of wine, food, and wit.

Shaw's opening sally didn't seem that funny to me, but everyone laughed heartily. Hah! Hah! Hah!—all over their beaming faces, made even more roseate by the nearly completed bottle of champagne in a silver ice bucket to one side.

Leonard introduced me around. In one way or another, I was familiar with everyone there. I said hello, pleased to meet you, to Joel Berthoff, the University of California professor of English, one of the few Berkeley professors to live in San Francisco. Berthoff drives a Riley and dresses in a sporty, Rex Harrison sort of way. He's the last of the old-style doctrinaire Freudian critics. His latest book, a study of James Fenimore Cooper published by the Cornell University Press, proves that Natty Bumppo, the hero of the Leatherstocking Tales, used his flintlock musket as an extension of his penis; every shot was in reality a sublimated climax.

There was Bart Hopkins, the *Express* daily humorist. The

342

effort to be funny five days a week, Art Buchwald style, keeps Hopkins in a constant state of moroseness. Toby Wain tells me that Hopkins fights depression constantly. Fillmore Du Pleixis, the society novelist, sat to Shaw's right, the place of honor, like the disciple John next to Jesus at the Last Supper. Du Pleixis worships Shaw, and could quite easily have rested his head on Harry's shoulder, as John did to Jesus, without disconcerting the rest of the gathering. Fillmore Du Pleixis squeezes out a Pacific Heights-Tiburon novel once every three years. They are symbolist and obscure, in the manner of John Hawkes. No one reads them, but that doesn't much matter. Fillmore knows enough people to guarantee a sale of 3,500 copies per novel. His publisher breaks even, and everyone seems satisfied. The novels serve to give Fillmore Du Pleixis a conviction of occupation and a rationale for his ceaselessly dining out. He must, after all, follow his *métier*. Enormously rich by inheritance (the Central California Land Company, one of California's largest agribusinesses, founded in the 1870s by Fillmore's great-grandfather, Titian Peale Fillmore), Fillmore Du Pleixis manages his investments with a shrewdness belied by his effeminate, dandified demeanor. He owns considerable stock, for instance, in Murray House, his publisher, and so in a certain sense he can be considered to be self-employed.

"You're putting on weight," composer Tommy Schuyler told me as I unrolled my napkin and unconsciously began to butter a piece of sourdough French bread. I put the bread back on the bread plate. I've never liked Tommy Schuyler since Toby Wain told me that Schuyler had beat up a girlfriend of Wain's who was also balling Schuyler at the time. Schuyler accused her of stealing fifteen dollars from his wallet when she stayed over one evening.

"I can tell you from experience," Toby said, "that even if she did take the money, she's worth more than fifteen dollars in sack time. She's an artist in bed. Schuyler worked her over real bad."

"He writes such gentle, delicate songs," I said.

"Don't bother Norton," Harry Shaw said to Schuyler. "He's

343

got a lot on his mind. He's trying to learn the Dewey decimal system."

"Hah! Hah! Hah!" came from around the table. "Hah! Hah! Hah!"

"Hey, Harry," said J.F. Imperator, the playboy publisher of *Urbane*, the city's local consumerist magazine, "did you hear about the Polish firing squad that formed a circle around the condemned man?"

"No," said Harry, "but they probably all missed."

"Hah! Hah! Hah!" again erupted from the table. Joel Berthoff beamed in self-esteem, as if he were dining at the Mitre Tavern in eighteenth-century London and had just heard a sally from the Great Cham himself, Dr. Samuel Johnson. The woebegone cast dropped from Bart Hopkins's face, and for a moment the incipiently suicidal look left his face. Tommy Schuyler's eyes remained cobralike, but his lips pursed in smile, as if his face was the face of two separate people, negotiating for possession somewhere around the nose. Fillmore Du Pleixis tossed his head back and cackled his best Truman Capote laugh: a naughty-naughty-boy sort of laugh, with more than a faint suggestion of homosexuality.

Mark Yeats, wearing a double-breasted blue blazer with more than thirty gold buttons on display (including four on each cuff for a total of eight) and his Guards regimental tie, entered the festivities. He fed Harry Shaw a line, like a pitcher in a softball game deliberately lobbing an easy one across home plate.

"Harry," he asked, "how can you tell that Norton here is a member of the Carpino administration?"

"You can't. He doesn't have flies circling his head."

"Hah! Hah! Hah!" thundered the Greek chorus.

So it went for two hours, quip after quip. Leonard Bogard, to his credit, seemed annoyed at my being the butt of these opening sallies, but he needn't have concerned himself. I was but the occasion for their warm-up. The Round Table is supposed to be literary, a San Francisco version of the Algonquin Circle, but I can't remember having heard any

344

literary conversation that afternoon, except for a few bitchy remarks by Fillmore Du Pleixis about Jane Janeway's new novel. Jane Janeway and Fillmore are neighbors on Clay Street. They've had a hissy going for years.

"Jane's latest novel smacks of the Cuisinart," Du Pleixis languidly observed in his queenish manner. Du Pleixis can come on straight if he likes, or do an outrageous drag-queen like Flip Wilson playing Geraldine. It all depends on his mood. He can come out of the closet, then go back in, some three or four times in the course of one conversation.

Shaw: "You mean she gives us slices of life?"

"Hah! Hah! Hah!"

As I said, Leonard Bogard needn't have worried about me—or about literature for that matter. Both letters and myself were safe from harm. For more than twelve years the Harry Shaw Round Table has kept itself thoroughly nourished on a diet, not of literature, but of incestuous gossip. These men know everything about each other, and are merciless in their mutual ragging. After the second bottle of Mayacamas Cabernet Sauvignon 1970, they got busy on their monthly orgy of put-downs, one-upsmanship, and *double-entendre* quips. Everyone, however, including J.F. Imperator, who got louder and louder as he got more and more smashed, let Harry Shaw win the game. Harry managed the event like a lion tamer using his whip to keep a squad of big cats sitting on their stools. The cats might roar or strike the air with their lethal paws, but one crack from Harry's whip and they cringed in subservience.

Not being in on all the details, I could only half-follow the conversation. I later repeated some of it to Toby Wain, who loves gossip. Toby provided me annotations, as Leonard Wolfe does in his scholarly edition of Bram Stoker's *Dracula*. Toby, by the way, is clearly bucking to take over from Harry Shaw within the next few years. Harry is sixty-two and can go on for another five years at best. Toby has been assiduously cultivating both Shaw and the Shaw circle. Harry Shaw, Toby says, knows what Toby is up to and is somewhat hostile over the incarnated spectre of his own eventual departure from both this life and his column (the two are synonymous); yet Shaw also finds the prospect of a courteous understudy somewhat flattering. Strange that he can't see that Toby Wain hates his guts. Or maybe he does see it.

"I haven't seen Tania around lately."

This from Tommy Schuyler to Joel Berthoff.

Du Pleixis to everyone: "She's busy with the Foundation."

General laughter. Toby Wain's comment: Tania Berthoff has an intermittent taste for black men. She once disappeared for a week with a black linebacker. When she returned, she told everyone she was in Los Angeles, doing volunteer work for the W.E.B. Du Bois Foundation.

"Have you noticed that glass is getting expensive?"

Imperator to Schuyler. Laughter. Toby Wain footnote: Tommy Schuyler recently threw one of his many girlfriends through a plate glass window. Luckily she wasn't killed, merely cut up a bit. The girl was too frightened to press charges.

"Not as expensive as salad oil." Mark Yeast to Fillmore Du Pleixis.

Toby Wain on this one: "Can't tell for sure. Might refer to something Du Pleixis does with salad oil."

"Read any good books lately?"

Leonard Bogard, novelist, asking Fillmore Du Pleixis, novelist.

Mark Yeast in reply: "I have, Jane Janeway's latest, *Wonderlust*."

Harry Shaw: "She'd better wonder about lust. After all, she was sprung too soon."

General laughter. Annotation by Toby Wain: Joel Berthoff was the butt of this one. He lived with Jane Janeway for a year or so in the late fifties. After they broke up, Jane later went around town saying that Joel Berthoff, the Freudian critic, had a problem with premature ejaculation.

"It wasn't very literary," I said to Leonard Bogard as we walked down Mason Street.

"It was paraliterary," Bogard said.

346

"And rather nasty."

"Most charmed circles get that way."

Tiny Roncola called me today. "What about the material, Jimmy? Shall I send it anonymously to the gay press? Just give the word. It'll be all over the state in twenty-four hours."

"That's what I'm afraid of. This is a tricky business."

"Have you seen the latest polls? Soutane is destroying us. It's two-to-one everywhere except the Bay Area. Here it's two-and-a-half to one."

"This thing could backfire."

"Taking a chance is better than losing because no chances were taken."

"Losing is better than going to jail."

"No one goes to jail for dirty tricks in politics. It's part of the business."

"Nixon might find out differently."

"Nixon will beat the rap. Watergate is a tempest in a teapot."

"Blackmail is immoral."

"This isn't blackmail. It's public education. We're not approaching Soutane or his people directly. Without a threatening approach—no blackmail. Besides, no one could ever trace it to me. I would just send the photos anonymously to the *Advocate*. Then presto—El Stinkeroo."

"It's immoral."

"So is being out of work. So is being a nobody—like we'll be if Carpino is defeated."

"Why haven't you just gone ahead and done it on your own, without asking us about it?"

"What's my percentage that way? I want to be with Claudio Carpino on that day when he comes into his Father's Kingdom, like the Good Thief."

"You'll wind up simply crucified if this thing ever backfires. How do I know the photographs are authentic?"

"Ask Stedman Mooner about them."

"He'd deny it. How'd you get these photos anyway?"

"You asked me that before. Goodbye."

"I live in the Mission but I've never been to Mission Dolores," Deborah said as we entered the two-hundred-year-old Franciscan church on Dolores Street.

"It will be good for your soul and your civic patriotism to attend this," I said. "Besides, you can translate the Spanish hymns for me."

We found seats midway down the aisle. Each year the City of San Francisco celebrates the anniversary of its founding in 1776 by Spanish soldiers and Franciscan padres by having an anniversary Mass in Mission Dolores and a civic luncheon at the Presidio Officers' Club. Both of these buildings, the two oldest edifices in the city, have survived from 1776. As city librarian, I'm expected to attend both events. Yesterday was the third such commemoration I've been through. I asked Deborah along.

"Why not? It's Saturday, and I never really know what to do with Saturday. I usually waste it in errands."

Archbishop McGucken celebrated the Mass, and the Mexican choir from the Mission Dolores school sang a series of lovely Spanish hymns, accompanied by guitar music. Just after the elevation of the host, the ancient Mission bell pealed out and the singing swelled majestically. If I do a Bohemian Grove play about Sebastian Collins—and I've been thinking of working one up—I could open it with some sort of pageant as suggested by yesterday's Mass: a procession, perhaps, of the De Anza expedition arriving on the empty San Francisco peninsula in 1776.

"It's like an opera," Deborah whispered. "Something like *La Forza del Destino*."

"I didn't know you liked opera," I whispered back.

"I love opera."

"Opera is an elitist form, isn't it?" I asked.

"No! In Italy it's a popular form. Please be quiet!"

The last time I saw Franciscan Father Lloyd Tetzio was on the television screen, standing next to Andy Soutane in the serving line at St. Anthony's Dining Room, ladling out gravy over the mashed potatoes Soutane had so artfully scooped on each plate. Present this time in the flesh, Father Tetzio gave a rousing sermon (in English, thank God!) dealing with the foundation of San Francisco some 199 years ago by Spanish priests, soldiers, and colonists.

"We hope and pray," Father Tetzio perorated, standing before the congregation of civic dignitaries in the simple brown robe and sandals of his order, "that something of Spain yet remains in our city—something capable of firm will and disciplined action in the name of high ideals, something incandescent with spiritual fire."

I looked around the congregation to see if there were any possible heroes in attendance. Mayor Claudio Carpino sat in front, his partially bald pate visible to the rest of the congregation like a polished surface of onyx. Esmeralda had consented to show for the celebration, so her piled-high head of henna red curls, covered in a black lace mantilla, broke the monotony of male heads in the front row—hers and that of Supervisor Sandra Van Dam's, whose jet black hair was done in a precisely stylized page boy, suggestive of the 1950s when Sandra Van Dam served as the first female student body president at UC-Berkeley while simultaneously holding down the very prestigious secretaryship at Delta Delta Delta sorority. Next came the head of Dr. Alexander Thurman, president of the San Francisco Historical Society, who parts his hair in the middle, then combs it straight back on either side in two evenly pomaded runs, Rudolph Valentino-style, a mode of hair design that is currently coming back along with wing-tipped Hamilton collars for evening wear. That, after all, was the style of the 1920s when Dr. Thurman was in his twenties and roaring around town in a Stutz Bearcat, the hell-raising scion of the largest pharmaceutical wholesale house in northern California. Retired now from medical practice, Dr. Thurman devotes an enormous amount of his time to historical activities.

I was surprised to see Johnboy Turfer there; yet if Turfer is serious about getting into the mayor's race he'll have to get used to showing up around town at everything from Giants' games to parish bingo bashes in the Sunset. Turfer's houndstooth-check sports coat and yellow elephant-collar shirt stood out dramatically from the row of conservative dark suits in his pew. His head of curly hair cascaded out in what Turfer calls his Polish Afro. Turfer brought along Harry Herma, head of the Ashbury Foundation. The two of them probably haven't been inside a church in years. A pugnacious little Chicano, Herma runs a foundation devoted to the rehabilitation of ex-cons. It operates out of a three-story Victorian on Cole Street. If Herma likes a political candidate, he can field an army of precinct workers, capable of ringing every doorbell in town or slipping a pamphlet under every door in the neighborhoods: which is how elections are won, by direct contact with the voter.

The commandant of the Presidio, an Army colonel in dress blues, sat next to La Favorita in the first pew of the left side of the Mission. Each year, a different female descendant of an early Spanish family is chosen as La Favorita to preside over the birthday ceremonies. This year a De Haro was chosen— Francesca De Haro Brady by name, a sophomore at Dominican College. She wore an eighteenth-century Spanish dress, surmounted by a high lace mantilla—all very picturesque, but not, I'm afraid, true to the style of dress worn by the women who arrived here with the De Anza expedition, having marched north from Tubac, Mexico, over nearly two thousand miles of desert, mountains, and jagged coast. Those first female San Franciscans must have looked like hell when they arrived.

Events like yesterday's commemoration usually attract the political crowd. There exists a genre of politicians' assistants whose task it is merely to show up at such occasions as civic commemorations, weddings, funerals, baptisms, and swearings-in. Tiny Roncola, for instance, partly earns his keep by showing up around town for these affairs, expressing the Mayor's best wishes and His Honor's regrets that the pressing business of the city has kept him from being there. Tiny was at the birthday ceremonies yesterday, just out of habit, I suppose; for the Mayor did make this one, and always has. But so was Cole O'Halloran there, Andy Soutane's local gopher, and that surprised me because Cole's presence definitely represented an encroachment on the Mayor's turf.

Cole O'Halloran spent a few years in the Mission Santa Barbara seminary with Andy Soutane, and I suspect that this relationship will turn out to be the making of Cole, who hasn't got much else going for him. Cole is about my age, loud and brash and red-faced as Irish of a certain type often get. O'Halloran ran for supervisor a few years back, coming in sixth in a contest for five vacancies. When Supervisor Sven Anderson resigned to take a seat on the Superior Bench, O'Halloran stormed into Carpino's office, demanding that he be appointed to the vacant seat because he had placed just beneath Anderson in the election. Carpino ignored O'Halloran's request, appointing instead Ed Chan, San Francisco's first Chinese supervisor. O'Halloran, needless to say, hates Carpino with the special sort of hate that only an already drowning man, denied his last chance at a lifesaver, can feel. Like a lot of us, Cole fears that his life isn't amounting to much. Twenty years ago at St. Ignatius High School, Cole O'Halloran used to be a hell of a good debater. Competing especially in the *ex tempore* debate category, in which the judges threw a topic to you unannounced, such as "Resolved: England should get out of Africa immediately," or "Resolved: Red China should be admitted to the United Nations," O'Halloran always seemed capable of spinning out a web of brilliant debate. In my junior year, O'Halloran got elected president of the senior class. We all knew that Cole was heading places. Cole knew it most of all.

As a reasonably pious kid (who wasn't in those days?), Cole gave the Franciscans a year or two sometime during his undergraduate career at Santa Clara. That's when he met Andy Soutane. The 1960s really distracted O'Halloran. Getting overinvolved in politics, he flunked twice out of the USC law

351

school, first the day division, then night school. He was too distracted to study. Getting a job as Assemblyman Jeremiah Jones's administrative assistant, O'Halloran spent his twenties and early thirties as a political gopher, sustained in his illusion that something was happening to him because there seemed to be a lot of movement around. Like too many administrative assistants to politicians, Cole O'Halloran passed thirty-five without ever launching his own career. Sacramento is a fast town, given to booze and pussy. O'Halloran ran with the legislative assistant crowd who prided themselves upon running the same fast track as their employers—late hours, lots of sauce, poontang from the typing pool. At thirty-seven O'Halloran now has a permanent red flush. At political dinners, to which he is addicted, his face gets almost scarlet after three or four drinks. No matter what the dinner, Cole can be seen making the rounds of the tables, shaking hands, laughing, chatting it up. At first he did this for Jeremiah Jones. Last year, however, O'Halloran transferred over to the Soutane campaign organization as field representative. When Soutane wins—if he wins, I should say out of loyalty to Claudio Carpino—he ought to tuck O'Halloran into some state commission or other, something harmless like the State and County Fairs Administrative Commission, which would be the break of a decade for Cole since he needs some way to get by. Cole, you see, is an unmeltable ethnic. Even before he's forty, he's already too loud and red-faced and impossibly local to cut it in the new San Francisco, much less on a state-wide basis. O'Halloran stands the chance of being dumped because of this. Soutane might not need that many hulking ethnics around once he gets to Sacramento.

After Mass, we all filed out into the adjacent graveyard, filled with headstones from the 1850s: Irish names mostly, including the gravestones of Charles Cora and James P. Casey, two Irishmen hanged by the Vigilance Committee of 1856. "May God Forgive My Persecutors," Casey's headstone reads. In one of his journals Sebastian Collins quotes his father to the effect that the Vigilance Committees were nothing more than

352

Know-Nothing witch hunts aimed at breaking the growing power of the San Francisco Irish. James Sullivan's grave looked especially sad. A pugilist boxing under the name "Yankee Sullivan," the poor bastard committed suicide while under detention by the Vigilance Committee, hanging himself in his cell. Although a suicide, Yankee was allowed burial in consecrated ground because the padre at Mission Dolores ruled that Sullivan had been driven insane by his sudden, unexpected imprisonment.

The Archbishop, Father Tetzio, Mayor Carpino, and Dr. Thurman gathered under the statue of Junipero Serra by Arthur Putnam, the great turn-of-the-century sculptor, at the west end of the cemetery. As they took their places, a lot of the political people in the crowd were rubber-necking around to see who else was there. Turfer and O'Halloran were gawking about like egrets in search of fish. Harry Herma cased the scene in one sweeping look like a con getting the drop on who was where in the exercise yard. When Herma had taken the crowd in with one turn of his neck, he peered straight ahead, again a con, withdrawn into himself amidst the surrounding figures.

"I hope this doesn't take too long," Deborah said.

"It won't. If you're bored, say a prayer for the ten thousand anonymous Indians buried here."

"They died of malaria and VD. They ought to have been left in the hills with their tribes."

I noticed that Deborah was getting a number of check-out stares from some of the men in the crowd, including Cole O'Halloran. Deborah has her library degree, but she still looks more like a stewardess than a librarian. She was wearing one of those Diane von Furstenburg dresses—a green pattern—that hug the form at every turn yet manage also to have a certain crisp, efficient career-girl look. As we were waiting for the ceremonies to begin, Deborah closed her eyes and lifted her face to the sun, seemingly oblivious to her surroundings. Perhaps she's one of those women who go into a sort of primal stupor when they sunbathe. I know the type—literal sun-worshippers whom the sun soothes and keeps minimally neurotic. As she tilted her face upwards, I studied the bump on Deborah's nose and the generous sweep of her wide mouth, the assertiveness of her chin. She's sure as hell a good-looking woman.

Archbishop McGucken blessed the gravestones with holy water. Father Lloyd Tetzio said a prayer for the San Francisco pioneers of both Spain and America who have long ago gone to their eternal rest. Dr. Alexander Thurman made a few remarks about the early days of San Francisco, specifically the Stevenson's Regiment which brought so many New Yorkers to early California. Esmeralda stood dutifully next to the Mayor, the perfect First Lady of San Francisco, as her husband gave one of his totally brilliant, totally compelling *ex tempore* performances.

"I'd like to answer the challenge implicit in Father Lloyd's very fine sermon," the Mayor said. "I don't think that the great days of San Francisco are over, not by a long shot. As world cities go, ours is but an infant despite the nearly two hundred years of gravestones which surround us. Rome wasn't built in a day, nor will San Francisco be. The sources of civic renewal lie within all of us. A great city is a collective moral enterprise. It's a contract, a covenant, between all of us to live up to, generation by generation. We should seek to cherish and embellish what we have inherited, then pass it on, pass San Francisco on, better for the years of our stewardship. Because of those Spanish pioneers, we are here; and because of us here today, San Franciscans of the future will be here to celebrate the 299th anniversary of the city's founding."

"Jesus," Harry Herma muttered semiaudibly behind us, "that guy can sure spin out the shit. What the hell is he talking about? I thought we was here to say Happy Birthday, San Francisco."

That's what the cake in the center of the banquet room at the Presidio Officers' Club said loudly and clearly in red icing: "Happy Birthday, San Francisco!" Some five hundred people packed the luncheon, more than twice the number who had

354

made it to the Mass. A mariachi band played exuberantly. Its blaring, joyous South-of-the-Border music reached the bar where Deborah and I sat drinking chilled Almaden Chablis before lunch. The Presidio Officers' Club has a certain fifty-missions, we-fly-at-dawn atmosphere, as do most good officers' clubs. It was fun to sit there beneath the murals of Spanish California, luxuriating in the wine and the mariachi music.

"Hey, Jim," Cole O'Halloran said, standing over our table. He said "Jim" but he stared at Deborah with porcine hunger in his eyes.

"This is Cole O'Halloran," I said. "He's political."

Deborah said nothing. I couldn't tell if she were interested or not. Cole has a certain IRA-ish magnetism, if a woman goes in for the Irish brute type.

"Your boy Carpino's taking a shellacking in the polls, Jim boy," O'Halloran said, inviting himself to sit down. He managed the maneuver without once taking his greedy pig eyes off Deborah. When Deborah crossed her legs, showing some knee from beneath the folds of her Furstenberg, I thought O'Halloran's eyes would bug out of their sockets. The bastard!

"Carpino's not my boy, Cole. I'm a librarian, remember."

"Cut the shit. You're out on your ass come next November."

"Cole is with Andy Soutane," I said to Deborah. "He's very important."

"I never would have guessed it," she said.

O'Halloran caught the put-down. I had my answer: she wasn't interested. Heartened, I forged a counterattack.

"Cole is a gopher," I said, "a venerable calling. He and Soutane broke bread together in the Franciscans."

"What's a gopher?" Deborah asked.

"Someone who does odd jobs, who goes for things."

"Very cute, Norton, but winning, as Vince Lombardi tells us, isn't the only thing. It's everything. We've got a winner. Carpino's a sinking ship."

355

"What a lot of creepy people you know," Deborah said when O'Halloran shambled off.

"It's a creepy world," I said.

"Not all of it."

"I suppose mine is more creepy than others."

"You ought to get your act together. Find out who and what you are, then act accordingly. Do you really want to spend your best years around these people?"

"Easier said than done."

"But necessary."

I rested my hand for a moment on her knee. I loved the feel of rustling nylon, the suggestion of bone beneath the slight pressure of my hand.

"Your hand is on my knee."

"Do you mind?"

"Keep it there if it encourages you. But we must talk seriously some time about the future."

"What's yours going to be?" I asked, taking the offensive.

"I don't know. I can't tell. I want to try to do something with my life."

"Who doesn't? Steinbeck once wrote that most lives get dribbled away like piss in the dust."

"That's a chauvinist metaphor."

We went to table number 29 where out tickets assigned us. It was the Mayor's staff table. Terry Shane, the press flack, Inspector Ted Potelli, the Mayor's bodyguard, Jimmy Driscoll, his man for neighborhood relations, Barry Scorse, and Tiny Roncola were already busy eating their seafood salads.

"What are you doing with such a gorgeous dame?" Inspector Potelli asked as we sat down. "I thought you was a fruit."

"Miss Deborah Tanner, meet Inspector Ted Potelli," I said. "Don't mind the hair on his inside palms. He's a throwback to an early hominid form."

"There you go again, Norton, using them big words," Potelli said, putting half a French roll into his mouth.

"Are you a real inspector?" Deborah asked.

356

"I try to be," Potelli said, instantly flattered by her attention.

Why is it that grown men act like rams in the rutting season when they get around a good-looking girl? Even with sex out of the question, men will go through the preliminary posturings and gestures of competitive courtship strictly for its own sake. Deborah had the interest of the entire table perked up.

"What do you do for a gig?" Barry Scorse asked Deborah.

"I'm with the Public Library."

"Our library?" Scorse asked.

"The Public Library," Deborah said.

"Jeez," Scorse said, "I ought to spend some time over there."

"You're the head of civil service, aren't you?" Deborah asked.

"Until November anyway," Scorse said with characteristic honesty.

"Then what will you do?" Deborah asked pointedly.

"Go back to the fishing boats, I guess," Scorse said.

The luncheon proceeded rather pleasantly after these preliminary skirmishes. Jimmy Driscoll told us all a very long anecdote about Bobby the Yid, San Francisco's longtime Armenian bookie who used to operate out of a bar out on Silver Avenue. The anecdote concerned Bobby the Yid's successful operation of his business from a cell in the San Bruno jail where he was serving thirty days for nonpayment of alimony. After lunch, the Commandant of the Presidio, the Mayor, and La Favorita cut the Happy Birthday San Francisco cake with the Commandant's dress sword. A round of speeches similar to those delivered in the Mission cemetery followed; then a prayer by Father Tetzio, who invoked the Lord's blessing on all candidates for high office.

"Let's walk around the Presidio," I suggested to Deborah as the luncheon broke up.

"Can I come too?" Inspector Potelli asked.

"Only if you go back and get your leash," I said.

357

"Goodbye, Miss Tanner," Inspector Potelli said. "I admire your charity in trying to straighten out this fruit."

"Nice seeing you again," Cole O'Halloran said as we bumped into each other outside the Club. As previously, O'Halloran stared at Deborah while talking to me. "Let's not be strangers."

"That was a sort of non-event," said Deborah as we walked past a neat row of whitewashed quarters built sometime in the 1870s. Army children were riding bicycles along the quiet street. Stands of eucalyptus trees swayed lazily in the mid-afternoon breeze.

"That was the 199th birthday of San Francisco."

We reached Pershing Street. To my knowledge, no Army buildings from the 1840s survive in the Presidio; but I do suspect that Pershing Street is where the noncommissioned officers' quarters used to be located, so Sebastian Collins would have been born somewhere in the vicinity. I told Deborah what I knew about Sebastian Collins as we walked over past Letterman Hospital, heading toward the Palace of Fine Arts.

"He sounds fascinating," she said. "You really ought to do the biography."

"If I had the time, I'd do it."

"Poor excuse. Make the time, How much of your time are you throwing away in non-events and bullshit?"

"Too much of it."

"I love his pursuit of the opera singer. Give that a lot of attention, and do the nineties well. You fantasize about the post-World War II period. I love the *fin de siècle*. I love the mood and color of the turn of the century. I love the Art Nouveau. How long did Collins spend in Klimt's studio?"

"It's not too certain from the journals, but I'd guess about six months or so in late 1892 and early 1893."

"What did he do there?"

"Screw around."

"Literally or figuratively?"

"Both. It was a confused time of his life."

We emerged from the Presidio and walked down to the

Palace of Fine Arts. Sitting down on a bench, we watched some swans glide to and fro across the lagoon. I told Deborah about Sebastian's very moving meditation before the Palace of Fine Arts, which he wrote up in his journal shortly after the Panama–Pacific Exposition closed. I think that it is the finest thing that Collins ever wrote—better, in my opinion, than anything in his published works.

"Is there a grocery store around here?" Deborah asked.

"We just ate."

"Very funny."

"There's one on Lombard Street."

"Sit here and meditate like Sebastian Collins. I'll be right back."

I meditated upon her retreating form—superb legs, very long and mildly muscular; a very direct way of walking. Lazing in the mid-afternoon sun, I awaited her return. The russet-colored dome and colonnade of the Palace made me think of Rome, a city dominated by the buff, travertine, russet, and cinnamon hues of the Palace of Fine Arts. Maybeck the architect himself suggested that he wanted the Palace to evoke a Roman ruin as sketched by the antiquarian Piranesi in the eighteenth century. Sebastian Collins writes somewhere that the Palace is San Francisco's indirect way of remembering the city lost to the Fire of 1906. It is a metaphor of lost time, of the past most cruelly deprived of even the consolation of ruins and artifacts.

"Hi, I'm back." She was holding a large French roll in her hands. "I'm going to feed the swans."

Uninvited to join her, I kept my place on the bench as Deborah walked down the grassy slope to the lagoon that surrounds the Palace of Fine Arts. Sensing a benefactor, the swans glided toward her as she approached the water's edge. Pulling pieces of crust from the roll, Deborah threw bits of bread to the swans while they were still *en route*. They snapped up the bread bits without interrupting their smooth approach across the water-lilied lagoon. When some five or six of them lined up before her, Deborah threw pellet after pellet in their midst. One swan, a smaller female to judge from its size, fared ill in the free-for-all. It edged to the outside of the group. Deborah moved quickly over to it and, leaning over on bended knee, fed the rest of the roll to the hitherto neglected bird. It nibbled at the quarter roll gracefully, not gulping it in one swallow, but pecking gently three, four, or even five times before the bread was consumed. It was a particularly white swan and its neck arched with exquisite grace as it—or she—moved her head forward to the outstretched bread. Deborah's dress parted as she half-knelt and I could see the clean line of the inside of her left leg as she bent forward to feed the neglected bird. Deborah's leonine mane of curls gave an almost antique cast to her head as she nodded encourage-ment to the nibbling swan. Standing, she bent over and brushed off her dress with both hands, making graceful, feminine, pushing motions down across her legs in the direction of her knees. The swan regarded her for a moment, as if in appreciation, then glided off across the lagoon. Before Deborah even turned toward me, before, that is, she headed up the grassy slope that separated us, her knees showing for flickering moments from between the green folds of her wrap-around dress, I understood what had passed between Deborah and the young female swan. I understood, in a rush of mythic intuition, that Deborah Tanner—Gustav Klimt tattoo notwithstanding—was sexually innocent, perhaps even a virgin.

Chapter 10

ARCH 1867 should have found me ensconced at
Harvard College, digging into the work of my
third semester. I found myself, instead, in Québec City; and
shortly thereafter, I found myself on an Atlantic transport
headed for the Italian wars. Not until January 1870 would I be
able to resume my studies. I fled Harvard for a variety of
reasons: boredom with the routines of undergraduate life,
among them, and a desire to see a bit of the world before
devoting myself fully to a career. But mostly I fled because of
the choice Ryan Patrice was forcing me to make: a choice, a
wholesale surrender, which I had no intention of making then,
nor have I had any intention of making it since, although I
have spent a lifetime keeping company with the implications
of my refusal. Patrice asked too much of me, and so I turned
him down: no, more than merely refuse, I fled by train into the
snowy vastness of upper New England and lower Canada,
pursued all the while by a litany of clackety-clack on the train
tracks that by turns laughed at me, then seemed to implore the
salvation of my very soul.

"You are called," Patrice said to me on that late Sunday
afternoon after a group of us had chanted vespers in the chapel
occupying the second floor of his house on Follen Street in
Cambridge. After vespers, Patrice had asked me to remain
behind for a moment or two while the others went downstairs

for some pre-dinner sherry. A solitary vigil lamp cast a reddish glow through the tiny chapel. Its flickering light almost seemed to animate the Russian icons and sacred pictures that lined the oratory. In the dimly lit late winter chapel, Patrice's ascetic, trim-bearded face resembled an El Greco painting.

"You are called to something higher," he continued after a silence; for I had said nothing, although I was aware of, and dreaded, what was coming. "You are called to labor for the salvation of souls. You are called to the altar. You have been chosen for sanctity."

I suspected what was coming, what then came, because Patrice had been talking to me this way in less and less guarded terms ever since he gave an Ash Wednesday day of recollection to a dozen or so of the Catholic undergraduates. We were all of us stunned, incidentally, when he appeared that morning in the cassock of a priest of the Paris Foreign Mission Society, although a number of us had speculated previously as to Patrice's clerical character. None of us, obviously, suspected the full truth: that Ryan Patrice was working as an undercover agent for Monsignor de Mérode, raising men and money for the pontifical army defending the Papal States. Given the undercover character of Patrice's assignment as an agent of a foreign power, it was, I suppose, a significant act of trust on Patrice's part to reveal his priesthood to us. Harvard, after all, knew him only in his guise as an independently wealthy Franco-Baltimorean adjunct tutor in Romance languages who had excellent connections with various conservative groups in Europe. The dozen of us undergraduates who gathered that morning, however, had been sifted out by nearly two years of association with Patrice as being among the most loyal—and I must say, the most incipiently conspiratorial—of the Romans at Harvard. Patrice knew and trusted us. By revealing his priesthood so dramatically, he bound us to him in the delicious ties of religious conspiracy. The Jesuits and secular priests who worked as secret missionaries in Elizabethan England must have operated in a similar manner: attract, charm, insinuate, reveal—then bind to secrecy.

362

Patrice's Ash Wednesday conferences dealt mainly with the awesome vocation of the priesthood: its status as an *alter Christus,* another Christ, its exalted responsibilities and privileges, its sacramental powers. As Patrice preached, his eyes burned, like the fiery coals that scorched the prophet Isaiah's lips. His black cassock and high white starched clerical collar profoundly changed his presence. In well-cut lay clothes, Ryan Patrice seemed every bit the man of the world, the banker representing French interests, the aristocratic part-time academic, or whatever other guise he presented to the world. Now he was entirely the priest, aflame with an all-consuming fire.

"Who will have the courage to give everything?" he asked at the conclusion of his final conference. As he spoke, he looked at me with special regard, his bituminous eyes burning holes through my broadcloth suit, scorching my flesh, piercing to my very heart itself, inflaming it in fire (a fire soon dead for lack of fuel) as flame surrounds the all-consuming and all-consumed Sacred Heart of the Risen Christ, Lord of Creation. "Who will have the courage, the foolhardy generosity, to cast himself headlong upon the altar of this ideal, embracing the nail-pierced feet of the Divine Master, Christ the High Priest?"

If memory serves me correctly, Patrice did secure one candidate from our little group: a certain Brian Foley, who, as I once gathered from our Harvard Alumni Directory for 1907, is now Father John of St. Thomas, living in a Carmelite monastery outside Providence, Rhode Island.

Patrice had me in mind for his own congregation, the Paris Foreign Mission Society—as I found out that Sunday in March of 1867 when, at his request, I remained behind in the chapel after vespers. He presented me with a neatly folded black garment. Nearly sick with fear, I unraveled it, holding it by the shoulders   a black cassock cut to my size, the Paris Foreign Mission Society crest, a red Chi Rho χρ sewn onto its right breast.

"I am keeping this garment here for you," Patrice said. "When you are ready, I shall invest you in it. As a procurator of my Society, I have the authority to receive you into temporary vows. Once received, you will continue quietly at Harvard, taking your degree. You will then make a formal novitiate in France. After this, you will be sent to Rome for theological studies."

I could not believe what I was hearing. What indication, after all, had I given of such an interest?

"You show every sign of a vocation," Patrice said gently, as if reading my mind. "You are pious. You love the Church. You seek to spend your life in some great cause beyond the ordinary. Follow this disposition. Give yourself to the cause of causes, the love of God and the salvation of souls."

I returned to my room in Gray's Hall that evening in a state of turmoil that prevented sleep. A storm—half rain, half sleet—raged outside my window: the perfect correlative for my stormy state within. Even now, some forty-eight years later, I can recall the conflicting thoughts and emotions that raged within me. Like a helpless moth, I had been drawn towards the consuming fire of Patrice's brilliant personality. Everything about the man had been part of a deliberate, coordinated conspiracy: his personal charisma, the ambiance of aristocratic ultramontane Catholicity that pervaded the Sunday evening gatherings held at his home when he was in town, the subtle suggestion of elite conspiracy that came with his attentions: all of it was designed, so it seemed, to ensnare me, to persuade me to renounce my freedom. Catholicity had provided me with a counter-Harvard, a way of coping with President Eliot's snide remarks and all the deeper, pervasive bigotry that these remarks masked. Even so I had no desire to embrace a life of chastity and obedience, to throw myself into some unknown Void only because Ryan Patrice challenged me to do so. Yet the fascination of the man seemed to fill my room as I tossed and turned sleeplessly. When I finally fell into a fitful sleep at dawn, I dreamed of Patrice staring at me from a gilded picture frame about a baroque altar: as if he himself were the Sacred Heart. I then saw myself, attired in the cassock of the Paris Foreign Mission Society, running down an

364

endless dormitory corridor, knocking frantically at each door as I passed, hoping that one of them would open; but none did. Patrice himself awaited me ominously at the far end of the hallway, his figure silhouetted from behind by the flickering red glow of a sanctuary lamp. He stood quietly, like a statue on a side altar. I pounded and pounded on each unopened door, drawn inexorably towards Patrice out of mingled attraction and fear. Some few doors away from him, I felt a panic that all was lost—then one door opened. Before me stood an aged crone, toothlessly cackling in thorough enjoyment of my obvious distraction. Like Miss Havisham in Charles Dickens's *Great Expectations,* she wore a torn and dingy wedding dress. A male dwarf dressed as a Turkish harem attendant tugged insistently at her skirt.

This next morning I awoke with but one thought: to get away for a while and think things over. I stuffed a change of clothes into a valise, then caught the horse-drawn streetcar heading into Boston. This being Monday, I thought to myself, I shall stay away until Wednesday or Thursday, missing but two or three days of lectures. Some weeks previously, I had enjoyed a lecture on French Canada given by Mr. Francis Parkman at the Boston Atheneum. The lingering effects of Mr. Parkman's discourse must have recurred to me as I arrived at the Boston train station, for I found myself purchasing a ticket for Montreal, Trois Rivières, and Québec City. My train proceeded up through New Hampshire, then over to Montreal, a journey of some sixteen hours. I roamed about Montreal for a day, then caught a late afternoon train for Trois Rivières. On Thursday noon I arrived in Québec. For such a provincial lad as I, the effect of French Canada was that of a visit to Europe. I sauntered about the narrow, winding streets of Québec, ever in sight of Château Frontenac which rises like a medieval fortress in the center of Québec City. Sisters of Charity in white wimples and winged headdresses moved along the streets like flocks of meandering geese. I was charmed by the antiquated French I heard everywhere, and by the closely situated stone-built houses which so dramatically

365

evoked the Europe I longed to see. In Montreal I had spent an hour or so in meditation at the Church of Notre Dame, unsuccessfully trying to sort out all that had happened. At my arrival in Québec, I had not as of yet made sense of it all, so I dropped into the Québec cathedral for further reflection.

I want the world, I thought to myself, not the cloister. I want the life of art, not the formal pursuit of spiritual perfection. How naive, in retrospect, do those disjunctions now seem; for some fifty years of subsequent living have schooled me in the realization that we are not expected to renounce the world for the sake of spirit. Life in the world in and of itself betrays us to things spiritual—merely by so gloriously failing to deliver on its first bright promise. For those who aspire to art and joy, as I did as a young man, life is a conspiracy. Men and women such as myself are constantly being betrayed forward to our adolescent ideals: in my case, a conviction of grandeur, of joy in creation, somehow tied up with the ethos of Mediterranean Catholic culture—a sunny dream of Italy and the South, which I am refueling these days, by the way, by working myself once again through the novels of F. Marion Crawford.

As I sat in the Cathedral of Québec, ruminating over a number of intense questions of youth—grappling, in my case, with a paradoxical determination to possess both religion and art, the spirit and the flesh—I heard the rattle of military drums coming from the public square that fronted the church. This drum music was followed by the sound of marching feet—then the cheers of a crowd. Leaving the dimness of the cathedral, I walked outside to discover that over three hundred people had gathered on the sides of the square. In the center of the open space stood two hundred or so soldiers, wearing what I later discovered were the flamboyant uniforms of pontifical Zouaves: white baggy pants, a blue jacket, and a red Algerian fez, topped by a tassel. Escorted by three Zouave officers, a prelate (Charles-François Baillargeon, Archbishop of Québec, it turned out) was trooping the line, sprinkling the soldiers with holy water. Monsignor Baillargeon followed this blessing

366

with what seemed to me an interminable speech. Instructed at Harvard by Ryan Patrice in the niceties of French pronunciation, I found the Archbishop's accent problematic; but I sensed his meaning. A regiment of volunteers, he said, had been raised throughout French Canada to join the soldiers of Emperor Louis Napoleon now garrisoned in Rome for the protection of the Holy City and the surrounding Patrimony of Peter against seizure by Prime Minister Cavour for the House of Savoy. In a few days, this regiment would sail from Italy, entrusted with its sacred mission. One of the five companies of the regiment was this very one now on parade, composed of sturdy Québecoix, who were returning to the Europe of their ancestors as crusaders for the Catholic faith. The men, Baillargeon orated, together with their splendid officers, took the blessings of all French Canadian bishops with them. At a given signal, the Zouaves dropped to one knee *en masse,* steadying themselves with their rifles which they held in two hands as if they were pilgrim staffs about to blossom forth as in the last act of *Tannhäuser.* The officers smartly drew their sabres and brought the hilts up to their lips. Monsignor Baillargeon intoned a Latin blessing.

The restaurants and cafes of Québec were crowded that evening with exotically uniformed Zouaves celebrating their last night on shore before sailing for a foreign war. I fell in with a number of young privates in a little wineshop down by the river. After the strain of the past week, I welcomed the release of a riotous evening of wine-drinking and song. My boon companions included a farm lad who was at first somewhat hostile to my academic French accent; a former seminarian from the Grand Seminary in Montreal ("on indefinite leave," he said); a graduate in law from Laval, and an apothecary's apprentice, a lad of my own age (both of us being nineteen at the time) who had grown tired of pestles and mortars. Their uniforms—an adaptation of the uniform first worn by a regiment of Berber Zouaves recruited into the French Army in Algeria in the early 1820s—made my somber black and brown broadcloth seem the cloak of insipid,

367

stay-at-home cowardliness, while they, especially as the wine took hold, seemed so many Byronic corsairs, bound for Algerian adventure.

"Join us," Claude Nazaire, the Laval laureate in law, said two-thirds through the evening. "Join us in Rome."

"I cannot," I protested, mumbling something about my studies at Harvard.

"Ridiculous," shouted Octave Signay, the exclaustrated seminarist. "There is time enough for study and career and all those commitments society saddles us with. Join us in Rome. We'll fight for the Holy Father and have one hell of a time to boot."

The landlord threw us out at midnight, which was two hours beyond the time my friends were due back at their temporary quarters at the Friary of the Capuchins. Each religious house in Québec had volunteered to house so many Zouaves during the embarkation process. When we reached the friary, each of my companions embraced me in vinous fellowship—a scene rudely interrupted by the sudden appearance from the porter's lair of my comrades' platoon sergeant, a crusty veteran who (as I think of it now) must have been all of thirty at the time. Two drooping mustachios, however, added enormous authority to his young face. My three companions lost all interest in our farewell. They stiffened to attention. In retrospect, I now understand that Sergeant Girouard relished every detail of the encounter. It allowed him an opportunity to practice his skills as a noncommissioned officer. For the moment, however, I was as terrified of his outburst as if I myself were already wearing the Zouave uniform.

"Disgraceful!" the sergeant hissed, so as not to wake the friars asleep in their cells on the other side of the courtyard. "Two hours without leave—a serious offense. We shall all see the Captain tomorrow morning."

"By your leave, Sergeant," Nazaire the lawyer whispered in the same quiet-loud voice used by Sergeant Girouard. "We were not absent without leave. We were on recruiting duty."

Seeing my silhouette, Sergeant Girouard walked over to me, then picked my features out from the darkness.

"That is correct, Sergeant," I said. "These men only remained in the wineshop because I was asking them about enlistment."

"The pontifical Zouaves of Québec accept only Québecoix," Sergeant Girouard said. "No foreigners are allowed."

"He spoke to us of the possibility of his joining the St. Patrick's Battalion," Octave Signay, the quondam cleric, said. Up until that moment I had never heard of the St. Patrick's Battalion.

"Bring him to the docks tomorrow morning, then," the Sergeant said. "If he appears, I'll know you're telling the truth. If not, the Captain will hear of your tardiness. Now get to bed. We must muster in full kit at six-thirty. We load at nine o'clock for a sailing on the first tide. As for you, Mr. . . ."

"Collins, Sebastian Collins . . . sir."

"A sergeant is not 'sir.' A sergeant is 'Sergeant.' As for you, Mr. Collins, we shall see you tomorrow morning, if these rogues are telling the truth."

I slunk away, perplexed as to how a matter of being a mere two hours late could seem so important. As yet, I did not comprehend the military mind. Back at my room in a small inn near the railroad station, I lay on my bed, recovering my sobriety and thinking of the awful future facing my companions the next morning. Somehow, I could only picture the captain of Zouaves whom they must face on the morrow as a younger and more fearsome President Eliot. In reality, I learned, facing him the next day, Captain Porthos looked more like Emperor Louis Napoleon, to include an elaborate imperial beard and mustache. I had no intention of enlisting, you understand, merely of explaining to Captain Porthos that my four friends had been kept from their quarters only in the interest of recruiting me to the pontifical service. The Captain heard me out from behind a desk in a dockside shack where he was reviewing a list of supplies with the company quartermaster.

"Are you a Catholic?" Captain Porthos asked.

"Yes," I replied.

"Have you ever been convicted of a felony or suffered prolonged periods of insanity?"

"No," I answered.

"Are you infected with a social disease?"

I blushed. As yet, I had not found myself in proximity of a social disease.

"No."

"Can you see, hear, walk?"

"Yes."

"Are you married—supporting an aged parent?"

"No," I replied.

"Is your passport in order?"

"Yes, it is," I said.

"Do you love Holy Mother Church," he asked, "and wish to see the person of the Holy Father, Christ's Vicar on Earth, protected from all harm and the illicit seizure of His Kingdom?"

"Who could say no to that, my Captain?" I asked.

"Very well, then, I offer you passage to Rome as an auxiliary recruit of this regiment. I shall provisionally enlist you in the papal service, intended for the English-speaking battalion of St. Patrick once this unit reaches Rome. Agreed?"

"What time do you sail?" I asked.

"With the tide—around noon."

"I shall return with my answer before then."

I walked back to my inn, paid my bill, then carried my valise to the railroad station, where I sat for an hour or so, my valise resting in my lap. I thought about my parents and their hopes for me. I remembered Mr. Ralston, my benefactor, and his grand dream of an Atheneum for San Francisco. I thought of my room back at Harvard: my books lined against one wall, my box of California walnuts and my secret bottle of sherry hid beneath my bed; my friends awaiting my return at Gray's Hall. But mostly, I thought of Ryan Patrice and what he was so precipitously asking of me. True, I loved the Church: but I did not desire the priesthood. Patrice's presence, however, the force of his personality on mine, seemed to hold me like a trapped rabbit. Fitfully, I pulled at the snares that bound my feet. Was I guilty of the Great Refusal, I asked myself with deep distress—the one sin against the Holy Ghost for which there was no forgiveness? Was I truly called, but rejecting the call? Enlistment in the Zouaves answered my dilemma. I would serve the Church as a crusader, not a cassocked priest. San Francisco had given way to Harvard; and now my embroiled Harvard circumstances suggested Italy, where I had long since yearned to be. Racing ahead of Patrice, I would beat him to Rome. Fighting for the Church, I would prove myself once and for all; then I would be free of his or anyone else's hold on my conscience or imagination. The compelling simplicity of my solution excited me. Some fifteen minutes before sailing time, I reached the chartered Zouave transport, a sail-assisted side-wheel steamer. A great crowd had gathered on the dock: friends and relatives, all cheering goodbye. Panicked that I might be too late, I fought my way through the throng. At the gangplank a Zouave sentry halted me with a rifle extended laterally across my chest. I tried to explain who I was but he found my French incomprehensible.

"Let him pass," Captain Porthos shouted from the upper deck. "The American is one of us."

In April 1867, when I arrived in Rome and was mustered into the Irish battalion of the pontifical army, all Italy was divided into two parts: the kingdom of Italy, ruled over by King Victor Emanuel of the House of Savoy, and the Patrimony of St. Peter, governed by His Holiness Pope Pius IX, the Supreme Pontiff of the Holy Roman Church and the sovereign lord of a shrunken vestige—Rome and its immediate environs—of the once-mighty Papal States. Around 1800 Napoleon Bonaparte dissolved the Papal States in the aftermath of his invasion of Italy. Thanks in great part to the skilled diplomacy of Cardinal Consalvi, then secretary of state, the Congress of Vienna restored these provinces in 1814 (they included a good part of central Italy) to papal rule. The Papal States were lost once again—most of them—in the civil war of 1860-1861, in which General Giuseppe Garibaldi advanced with his thousand Red Shirts north from Naples, and General

Manfredo Fanti led the regulars of Piedmont south from Tuscany in a two-pronged invasion designed to liberate Rome from papal rule and complete the unification of Italy under the crown of Savoy. Only the intervention of French troops on behalf of the beleaguered pontifical army prevented the seizure of the Holy City itself.

On the seventeenth of March, 1861, the Italian Parliament sitting at Turin proclaimed the kingdom of Italy with King Victor Emanuel of Piedmont as monarch. The King's prime minister, Count Camillo Cavour—the patient mastermind of Italian unification—then proceeded to guide another measure through Parliament, proclaiming Rome as the destined, historic capital of the new kingdom of Italy. In September of 1864, the Italian government negotiated an agreement with the Emperor Napoleon III, promising that Italy would not seize Rome if the Emperor removed all French troops from the Eternal City. Put in power by the conservative Right of France, among them the ultramontanes (the fiercely pro-papal Catholic party), Napoleon III could not afford to sacrifice Rome, despite the expense of maintaining a garrison there. The government of King Victor Emanuel, on the other hand, found the presence of French troops on Italian soil a sore point in the matter of Italy's new-found national honor. The so-called September Convention, then, pledged the kingdom of Italy not to seize Rome, despite the fact that the Parliament had already declared the Eternal City to be Italy's destined national capital. It was a situation fraught with tension, a situation that could not last for very long. Without Rome, there could be no Italy. In early 1865, the French garrison left Rome. In June of that year, the capital of Italy was moved from Turin to Florence, within a few days' march of Rome. There matters stood—the Patrimony of St. Peter surrounded by an Italian kingdom desirous of the last consummation of its *Risorgimento*—until the events of late 1867, in which I played a small, but for me, significant part as a private soldier.

To this day, I savor the memory of my first experience of Europe. Closing my eyes, I can recapture each detail of the voyage across the Atlantic in a steamer-sailer crowded with troops—myself among them, temporarily assigned to the resolute supervision of Sergeant Girouard who smoked the most horrible-smelling tobacco in the world (the stench of it clung to his clothes and filled our bunking area with its persistent, malodorous incense). During the long voyage over, Sergeant Girouard, a five-year veteran of the provincial Québec constabulary, took it upon himself to drill me in the rudiments of soldiering: weaponry, the bayonet, close-order drill, the knowledge of rudimentary formations. These lessons helped the Sergeant pass the time; and as he pointed out, they would save some sergeant of the St. Patrick's Battalion the trouble of having to deal with an untutored recruit. Girouard's specialty was the bayonet, the unpretentious but deadly weapon that dominated warfare throughout the entire eighteenth century, including the Napoleonic Wars. I spent a number of hours with the Sergeant on the icy, wind-blasted deck of our ship, mastering various bayonet stances and maneuvers. One drill, a defensive one, the Sergeant was especially proud of.

"In the offense, attack thus," he lectured me, pirouetting through a series of forward thrusts and cross-clubbings. "But in defense, use cunning and your skeletal structure—like this." He dropped to one knee, resting the butt of his musket on the ground, its ominous bayonet poised at a a forty-five-degree angle. "When charged, face your opponent thus, as many points of you as possible anchored to the earth. Hold your bayonet thus, at an angle. Now, your opponent will charge at your settled bulk, his full weight behind his charge. Hold your steel steady. It will determine the line of his attack, although he does not know this, for he is as panicked as you are. Now, when he is some five feet from you, one of two things will happen. If he continues his charge, move thusly upon contact, from left to right, or from right to left, as appropriate, pushing aside his blade. Like thus. Ha! Ha! Ha!"

He barked ferociously, swinging his musket and bayonet swiftly to one side in a lateral motion, like a croupier clearing a roulette wheel.

"Should he pause as he approaches you, on the other hand,

should he shift his position and lose his balance, attack thus. Ha! Ha!" This time, the Sergeant sprang to his feet from the half-kneel and moved forward with his bayonet at the forty-five-degree angle. Some few feet into his attack, he lowered his steel, thrusting it forward toward his imaginary opponent's midsection, crying all the while in a ferocious litany of "Ha! Ha! Ha!" When I had practiced the maneuver to his satisfaction, he said to me: "I have taught you all I know of this weapon, which neither of us, I confess, has used in earnest. Let us see what happens in Italy."

On the seventeenth of April, 1867, I presented myself in Rome to the sentry standing before the Serristori Barracks and was escorted by another young Zouave in the green coat of the St. Patrick's Battalion across a great open courtyard above which the Barracks walls and windows rose with almost prison-like severity. Captain William Stafford of Dublin, Knight of St. Gregory, serving in the papal army since 1860, interviewed me while he stood under one archway, watching a platoon of new recruits being drilled by a noncommissioned officer in the center of the courtyard.

"Why would a Yank want to fight for the pope?" Captain Stafford asked me after I had provided him with but the sketchiest of résumés and discussions of motivation.

"I'm not so sure," I said, thinking of Ryan Patrice.

"You'd bloody well be sure,lad, before you hear the bullets whizzing past your head," Captain Stafford said. He had an unmistakably Irish look to him: pointed features and sandy hair, bright blue eyes, and the flush-red complexion betokening an addiction to steady potations. "But you're Irish anyway, even though you're only a half-caste Yankee Irishman. Where are your people from?"

"Roscommon."

"We are mostly Kerry men, but you look healthy, and you say you'll fight, which remains to be seen; but you say it anyway, which is more than His Holiness's Dago soldiers will say, so we might be trying you out for a few months before we'll be allowing you to take the oath. Join them over there."

"Like this?"

374

"We'll see about uniforms and gear later on in the day. Move smartly, lad."

I trotted to the line of recruits being drilled in the central courtyard by a six-foot-tall sergeant whose bark and ferocity of mien made me long for the tender solicitude of Sergeant Girouard instructing me in the bayonet. At first, I could hardly understand my new instructor because of his brogue; but Platoon Sergeant Sean O'Carroll soon schooled me in the melodic intricacies of his direct and forceful Kerry speech.

The volunteer army I entered that day had been mustered into active service during the invasions of 1860-1861 by Monsignor Frédéric Ghislain de Mérode, minister of war for Pope Pius IX, against the vigorous protests of Cardinal Giacomo Antonelli, the secretary of state, who felt (correctly, it turned out) that the pope could never preserve his sovereignty on the field of battle. A former officer in the French Foreign Legion, Monsignor Mérode was the last—absolutely the last—in a thousand-year line of warrior-priests that included at least one pope, Julius II, who in the early sixteenth century donned armor and personally took to the field to lead his army in defense of the papal patrimony. Cardinal Antonelli, on the other hand, preferred the employment of craft and guile to the clash of arms. Antonelli and Mérode were studies in contrast. Converted in the Algerian desert while on active service, Frédéric Ghislain de Mérode, scion of the Belgian-French nobility, was a priest, a mystic aflame with phophetic fire, and the most conservative sort of ultramontane possible. The bourgeois Antonelli, on the other hand, served as cardinal secretary of state without bothering even to become a priest. He had entered the secular arm of the papal service in 1830, when Pope Gregory XVI ruled over the enormous domain restored to his predecessor, Pius VII, by the Congress of Vienna. Pope Gregory XVI, an obscurantist, reactionary aristocrat who had spent his youth and early manhood locked away in a Carthusian monastery, ruled the Papal States as absolute monarch. The old monk had need of skilled, ambitious men like Antonelli, a banker's son from Naples whom Gregory ennobled and placed in the civil service. Cautious, cunning, adept in the plots and stratagems of diplomacy, Antonelli climbed the bureaucratic ladder step by slippery step: secular prelate, referendary of the superior law court, assessor of the criminal tribunal, minister of the interior (this in 1841), treasurer of the Apostolic Camera (1845). Although Antonelli held degrees in canon and civil law, he refused priestly ordination. When Gregory insisted that he become a canon of St. Peter's Basilica, Antonelli reluctantly accepted the subdeaconate, but would go no further. I personally have always respected Antonelli's honesty in this matter. Why take vows one knows that one is unable to keep? Despite his background as a soldier, Monsignor Mérode was as chaste as the new-fallen snow. As for Cardinal Antonelli—suffice it to say that there were always rumors, well-founded rumors. I later had the opportunity to corroborate at least one of them.

When Monsignor Mérode joined Pius IX's staff in 1850 as a personal chamberlain, there could not have existed a greater antitype to Antonelli in the entire papal court. Tall and imperious, Mérode affected the close-cropped hair of a soldier. Antonelli, by contrast, was small and dark. For many years the Cardinal hid his gnomic face behind a rich black beard, and his hair fell, Shylock-like, in perfumed ringlets about his neck. Pius IX promoted Mérode because he was impressed by the way Mérode had strapped his Algerian service pistols to his hips and rushed to the Pope's defense in November of 1848 after a mob assassinated Pius's lay prime minister Count Pellegrino Rossi and besieged the Pontiff in the Quirinal Palace. The Pope promoted Antonelli because he needed the Neapolitan's cunning and force of will. Pius had more than some suspicion of Antonelli's appetite for certain pleasures of the flesh, and was sorely distressed by the Cardinal's refusal to accept ordination; yet the Pontiff promoted Antonelli anyway: raising him to the College of Cardinals in 1847 and making him premier of the Papal States the next year when Pius was experimenting with a constitutional form of government. Antonelli stepped aside as premier shortly after, to allow a layman to be named head of government. When Count Rossi was stabbed to death, Pius—and Antonelli—fled south to Gaeta in the kingdom of Naples, where they remained in exile for two years. A revolutionary republic, headed by Giuseppe Mazzini as first triumvir, ruled Rome until French troops put Pius IX back on his throne in April of 1850. After that, the Pope turned his back once and for all upon liberalism: no more constitution, no more laymen in government, no more accommodation with progressive sentiment. The Pope turned the reins of secular government over to Antonelli; and for nearly twenty-seven years, until his death in 1876, the harsh-voiced little Neapolitan governed the Papal States.

Mérode, however, proved a constant thorn in Antonelli's side. Foreseeing the inevitable unification of Italy under the House of Savoy, Cardinal Antonelli embarked upon a policy of containment and negotiation. Mérode dreamed of restoring the Papal States to their former authority and grandeur. As interior minister, Mérode worked tirelessly to make the Papal States a model of efficiency, so that the world might learn to respect the Pope as a benevolent temporal sovereign. Mérode built roads and bridges. He reformed the prison system. He initiated a number of projects of social relief.

When Garibaldi invaded Sicily in 1860 at the head of a thousand red-shirted legionnaires, seizing the kingdom of Naples and driving the king and queen into Roman exile, while Piedmont massed its troops on the northern borders of the Papal States, Antonelli urged negotiation. Neither Garibaldi nor Cavour, the Cardinal told the Pope, could afford to risk an all-out war with France. Mérode, on the other hand, urged armed resistance—and Mérode prevailed.

"How could Monsignor de Mérode not have prevailed?" Charlie Stoddard once remarked to me in later years. "What chance did a dark little bourgeois like Antonelli have against a blond and assured aristocrat like the Count de Mérode? I mean really, Sebastian, look at Pius's court: Monsignor De Medici, Count Edward Borromeo, Cardinal Bonaparte, the others—all good-looking nobles, dead set against liberalism. How in God's name could Pius, himself a noble, listen to Antonelli's bourgeois admonitions of caution—Antonelli, that cynical

377

realist with an ambiance of fleshy indiscretions clinging to him—when all those romantically chaste young nobles who surrounded Pius urged military resistance?"

"Don't be naughty, Charlie," I said.

"My dear boy, I'm only being accurate. Pius began his career as a liberal, but the assassination of Rossi turned him into a romantic conservative. The legitimists, yearning for the return of the Bourbons, and the ultramontanes—especially the titled, good-looking boys who comprised his personal court, dreaming of restoring the medieval papacy—egged the poor Pope on in the sweet man's delusion that he could stop the tide of history. Personally, I agree with those handsome dreamers in the papal court. It would have been fun to have kept the Papal States. Just think of it: you and I could be counts! But it was all too late. The modern world—which I loathe, incidentally—was knocking on the gates of Rome. And besides, Sebastian, Mérode's policy almost cost you your life at Mentana, so don't be so forgiving or I'll hate you for it."

In any event, Pius IX did appoint Mérode minister of war—over Antonelli's objections. With characteristic vigor, Mérode set about the organizing of an army. Volunteers poured in from Ireland, England, Switzerland, Germany, Belgium, and France. To serve as commanding general, Mérode appointed his relative, Louis Christophe Leon Lamoricière, the famed commander of the French Foreign Legion in Algeria, then living in Rome, having found religion and also having discovered that he could not abide the imperial pretentions of Louis Napoleon. Lamoricière organized a light infantry corps of some twelve thousand men. He named them Zouaves after the two Berber battalions he had commanded in Algeria some twenty-five years previously. Lamoricière selected a number of noble French legitimist officers opposed to Napoleon III, most notably the Marquis Georges de la Valle de Rarecourt Pimodan, to serve as his field command and general staff.

Begun so bravely, the resistance of 1860 ended in ignominious defeat. On September 18, the pontifical troops suffered a

crushing rout at the hands of the Piedmontese at Castel-
fidardo. Charging the Piedmontese breastworks with fixed
bayonets, General Pimodan's Zouaves were cut down by some
extraordinarily accurate artillery fire. His noble French officers
fell to the earth, crying, *"Viva il Papa! Viva la Francia!"* The
Marquis de Pimodan himself fell to the ground mortally
wounded. General Lamoricière failed to maneuver his reserve
battalions to take up the attack. By late afternoon, the
Pontificals were in retreat. On the twenty-ninth, the papal
fortress of Ancona surrendered after a brief but bitter siege.

The army I joined was reorganized by General Ermanno
Kanzler, a Roman of German descent, from the shattered
remnants of this disastrous (1860-1861) campaign. General
Lamoricière died in 1865, after resigning in disgrace. Mérode
left office in 1865, forced from his ministry by popular
opinion, which was at odds with the Monsignor's aggressive
policies. Pius IX made Mérode archbishop and appointed him
papal almoner to ease the pain of being forced to ask for his
beloved counselor's resignation. As opposed to Mérode's
dreams of reconquest, General Kanzler took a more realistic
attitude towards his Zouaves. Recruiting new troops in Spain
and French Canada, he reorganized his army as a defensive
constabulary of some twelve thousand men, well trained and
well equipped. Our mission: a prudent patrolling of what was
left of the Papal States and the defense of Rome in case of
attack. As I found out some years later when I pored through
the archives of the Vatican library, Mérode kept a discreet
hand in military affairs, assisting through agents such as Ryan
Patrice in the raising of men, money, and material.

My own unit, the St. Patrick's Battalion, began in 1860 as a
volunteer regiment under the command of Major Myles
O'Reilly, a black-bearded patriarchal country gentleman from
county Kerry. In 1862 the Irish battalion passed over into the
Zouaves as a regular unit, with O'Reilly in command (he later
returned home, however, and entered the Irish Parliament).
Along with the Corps of Zouaves military orchestra, the St.

379

Patrick's companies were billed in the Serristori Barracks near the Piazza Colonna: which was where I received my preliminary training under the practiced supervision of Sergeant Sean O'Carroll, also a Kerry man, who had first come to Italy in 1860 as a volunteer with the old St. Patrick's Brigade.

After three months of drill and practice in marching formations, the handling of the Stutzen carbine and the more conventional breechloading rifle, some twenty other recruits and I were sworn into the battalion in mid-July 1867 on an already warm early Roman morning that promised to become a sweltering Roman day. We stood in ranks in the courtyard of our barracks—dressed smartly in our boots, baggy gray trousers, green tunic jackets crossed with white leather webbing, and red service caps that resembled an Algerian fez—and took an oath, administered to us by Chaplain Edward MacLoughlin, also a veteran of 1860, that we would obey our officers and noncommissioned officers and that we would defend, to the death if necessary, the rights of our Holy Father and King, Pius IX, and the Church's prerogatives and patrimony, so help us God. I did so swear and so did my mates, a number of whom would be dead on the field of battle before the year was out.

I spent the summer and early fall of 1867 outside Rome, on patrol against insurrection and brigandage. We marched out of Rome on the Appian Way, which the Roman Legions had taken out of the city in the days of world empire. In Italy, banditry is an ancient and revered art. In the Papal States, banditry and revolutionary sentiment coalesced, unleashing hundreds of scattered thieving bands into the countryside in the name of liberty and a united Italy. For some three months, Captain Stafford led our company from village to village in pursuit of this or that miscreant. In 1867 there was not much left to the Papal States—but it did prove large enough for those of us who marched it in straight lines or in circles, pursuing some red-sashed revolutionary who, in the name of Garibaldi, had relieved a convent of its silver service or a mountain parish's eucharistic monstrance of its precious jewels. I cannot honestly say that the population hated us—although I suspect that our arrivals and departures, even our night marches, were known to every bandit in the vicinity, brought to him on the wings of friendly gossip. In any event, the harvest of our patrolling efforts was scanty: a few of the feeble-minded or criminally insane (delivered up by a village, anxious to be relieved of their perturbing presence); an old blasphemer, in one case, who wanted to be taken directly to the Pope so that he could spit in the Holy Father's face.

All in all, it was a pleasant time in my young life. The frequent outdoor marches toughened me into superb physical condition, and I found ready acceptance among my messmates, despite my lack of a brogue. The Zouaves called me "Yank" and loved to hear details of life in America. Our days were simple: a march in the early morning from one village to another through a landscape of vine-covered hills (I am thinking here of the Frascati region); lunch and a siesta in the early afternoon while Captain Stafford made liaison with the local authorities. Marcello, our company cook, a Roman civilian hired for his skills, did wonderful things with pasta; and there were always local fruits and wine. We would eat our rations from our individual mess gear, but pass the wine from one to another, drinking out of the same bottle, then opening another when that was empty. Sergeant O'Carroll made sure that not too many bottles were passed, else the lads had a tendency to get bumptious. If you were not on picket duty, you could sleep after lunch—until the Captain returned from his own more formal dining with the town magistrate or the parish priest or chief of police, and then we might be up and moving on another half day's march, or told to set up a bivouac for a day to two's stay, which was usually a pleasant prospect indeed: a species, if you will, of extended picnic. Tivoli, Frosinone, Genzano, Latino, Ariccia, Frascati: to this day I can reel off the names of the villages and towns of Latium through which our company passed in our largely futile pursuit of insurrectionaries and brigands.

At Anzio, we camped in sight of the Tyrrhenian Sea; and the Greek and Latin classics overwhelmed me with a power they never possessed in Boys' High School, San Francisco, or even at Harvard College. Looking out over the broad blue expanse of the Mediterranean, I thought of the voyages of Ulysses across Homer's wine-dark sea. I thought of the storm that opens Virgil's *Aeneid,* and the slain stag roasted over the fiery coals of a beach fire upon which the Trojans, on their way to found Rome, feasted themselves when at last blown to safety upon the shores of Carthage.

In early October, rumors of a new invasion reached us at Frascati, where we were billeted quite comfortably in the outbuildings of the former palace of Henry, Cardinal Duke of York, last of the Stuart pretenders, who finished his life in the Church as cardinal and bishop of this lovely mountain town, known for its excellent white wines. Captain Stafford assembled us one late afternoon and announced the news.

"Garibaldi's at it again, lads. He says he'll take Rome on his own, just as he took Sicily—the agreement between the French emperor and the Italian king be damned. The Piedmontese have arrested him, but he's given them the slip, and he's now across the border in Switzerland, calling for all his Red Shirts to join him and march on Rome once and for all. If he tries it, we'll stop him, won't we, lads?"

"Hip, hip, hooray!" Sergeant O'Carroll cried. "Hip, hip, hooray!" We all joined in with lusty accord.

General Kanzler ordered all patrols back to Rome, where the Zouaves were to consolidate and take up a defensive posture. Should the Red Shirts pour across the border in company-sized units and should sympathizers rise up among the populace, isolated units such as ours could be attacked and perhaps decimated. Possessed of a small but good army, Kanzler did not want to lose either mass or maneuver. His strategy, it later turned out, was to allow the Red Shirts to lose their own mass, spreading themselves around the countryside, hence also to lose their maneuvering ability, then hit them with a series of quick, concentrated ambushes. One of the

382

places Kanzler designated for possible ambush was the valley and village of Mentana, a morning's march outside Rome. The Lilliputian kingdom of *Pio Nono* fell into turmoil at the news of Garibaldi's intended invasion. As we marched back to Rome, word reached us of a number of pocket insurrections throughout the countryside. A number of villages fell to the control of revolutionary councils. Unlike the War of 1860 and 1861, however, the Italian kingdom had no hand in these local uprisings. Garibaldi constituted a revolutionary force possessed of its own momentum. The kingdom of Italy, in fact, commissioned a certain clergyman diplomat, Canon Ortalda of Turin, to offer His Holiness the protection of the king's troops against the Red Shirt invasion. Pius IX appealed instead to the French emperor.

My Roman sojourn—indeed, my life itself—might have ended sometime in the early morning hours of 22 October, 1867. During our battalion's absence on partrol duty, radical partisans dug tunnels under the Serristori Barracks, mining the building's foundations with explosives. The companies of the St. Patrick's Battalion were scheduled to reach Rome by the twenty-first of the month. The revolutionaries must have known this through their intelligence network, for they planned in advance to destroy the Serristori Barracks in the early hours of the twenty-second—which they did, partially. At about four in the morning, a deafening roar awoke us in the Barracks. I thought at first that the Red Shirts were shelling the city. The courtyard filled immediately with some two hundred half-dressed or undressed Zouaves, all in a state of confusion. Our sergeants soon ordered us dressed and formed in ranks with no delay. I was ordered to a detail assigned to pick through the rubble of the one wing that was severely damaged by the blast. We recovered the mangled bodies of some twenty-seven musicians attached to corps headquarters—harmless fellows, all Italian, who had provided us all so much pleasure in those evening hours when they would set themselves up under an arcade and solace our garrison evenings with marching music, operatic arias, and traditional

Italian folk melodies. Seeking to blow the Pope's foreign soldiers to Kingdom Come, the Red Shirt irregulars merely succeeded in killing their own people. At Captain Stafford's order, we lay the bodies out in front of our barracks, leaving them there for the entire morning. An angry crowd of Roman citizens formed, cursing Garibaldi and all murderous revolutionaries. History now tells us that a revolt was planned for Rome the moment Garibaldi began his advance; but the grisly spectacle of some twenty-seven dead Italians, killed by their own people, cooled the populace's ardor for revolutionary violence. That morning, we also located the partisans' tunneling. It took a total of three days to remove the explosives packed beneath our foundations. Had the partisans known as much about fusing as they did about tunneling, some hundreds of Zouaves, including yours truly, might have perished. As it was, I never felt secure in the barracks again, thinking that perhaps some cache of gunpowder remained undetected. It was with a sigh of relief that I heard of my transfer to Castel Sant'Angelo—after my return from Mentana.

On the twenty-eighth of October, 1867, a French squadron landed at Civitavecchia. The following day, French troops arrived in Rome. The entire city locked itself behind closed doors and bolted shutters; an eerie silence descended. The sight of French regulars, armed with rapid-firing *chassepots,* convinced even the cynical and dismissive Romans that great and possibly dangerous events were at hand. General DeFailly, the commander of the French expedition, plastered the walls of Rome with posters, one of which I recovered after Mentana and kept as a souvenir of that long ago comic-opera war that ended in such a non-comic hail of bullets and bayonets. "Romans!" General DeFailly proclaimed. (I translate from the Italian.) "The Emperor Napoleon once more sends an Expeditionary Force to Rome to protect the Holy Father and the pontifical throne against the armed attacks of revolutionary bands. You know us well. We come, as before, to fulfill a purely moral and disinterested mission. We will aid you in re-establishing confidence and security. Our soldiers will

384

continue to respect your persons, your customs, and your laws. The past guarantees this."

We Zouaves spent the three days following the arrival of the French in a rush of organization. General DeFailly placed his troops under the over-all command of General Kanzler. From Kanzler's headquarters at Castel Sant'Angelo came the order: all battalions prepare for an offensive march. During those three days of preparation, Captain Stafford must have had us stand inspection at least five times. The Captain personally went through each of our kits, which he directed us to spread before our cots, so that he and the platoon sergeant might take an accurate inventory: ammunition, bayonet, mess kit, sleeping roll, one change of linen, tobacco, authorized personal effects—all arranged geometrically for the Captain's inspection. On the morning of November second, all companies of the St. Patrick's Battalion formed up for a final review. General Kanzler himself and Archbishop Mérode moved through our open ranks, accompanied by Major O'Reilly and Captain Stafford. We usually had music on the occasion of such full-dress inspections, but our Zouave orchestra had been devastated in the sapping of the Serristori Barracks. Mérode blessed the troops as he walked next to Kanzler, who was, as a good general, more interested in our gear and our webbing than in the state of our immortal souls. My soul, incidentally, was possessed of a new stain—one against purity, my first—but I am getting ahead of my story. Upon completion of our inspection, General Kanzler spoke to us in Italian and Archbishop Mérode followed him in English. Kanzler was brief and to the point: something about following orders and fighting well. Mérode told us we were crusaders, Knights Templar, and that, should we fall on the field of battle, we should go immediately to heaven as martyrs for the faith.

The enormity of what I had involved myself in had torn at my bowels with devastating force the moment I helped pull my first corpse from the rubble of the destroyed wing of the Serristori Barracks. I nearly broke into tears as I tugged the corpse of a young lad from the heap of wood and bricks that covered him—one of the flutists, so I recognized him when we

385

washed his face, dead, dead forever, and for no reason that made any sense. Twenty-six of his comrades followed, all equally deprived of our most precious possession, without which there is only the abyss. We stacked them before the Barracks like freshly caught fish. Up until that point (although I had been serving as a Zouave for some six months), I was somewhat unaware, in the deliberately oblivious manner of youth, of the imminent danger of my situation. I had enlisted in the Zouaves out of religious confusion. I was looking for an escape. Life in the Zouaves had thus far proved a comic-opera daydream, something from Donizetti's *La Figlia del Reggimento:* a tramp across the Latian countryside in pursuit of *bel canto* heroines and baritone or basso bandits who had just stepped off the stage of the *Teatro dell'Opera*. With the sapping of the Barracks, however, the comic opera dropped its curtains. This was war, and I found myself a soldier in a foreign army, preparing to do battle unto the death. From that moment on, fear took hold of me, and never left—until a month or more after my company, thinned by death, marched wearily back to Rome from Mentana.

"Dear Mother and Father," I wrote by candlelight in our company's orderly room as I sat there on charge-of-quarters duty two nights before my battalion was scheduled to leave the city. "This letter will be sent to you only in the event of my death. I shall be brief. I love you both, and I wish that I were with you tonight, waiting in the kitchen at Mother's side for Father's return. In a very palpable sense, I wronged you when I so precipitously enlisted in the Pontifical Army; but someday you will perhaps understand what led me to do what I have done. Please know that your son thought of you both with profound feelings of love and gratitude as he faced the prospect of his life coming to an abrupt conclusion. Your son remembered how Father's cheek scratched his own when Father kissed him as a boy, and he remembered the scent of his mother's hair when she sat him in her lap and told him stories of Old Ireland. He now signs himself to both beloved parents, hoping that this letter will never have to be sent."

386

Around midnight, I got off duty when Corporal O'Hare relieved me as charge-of-quarters. I should have returned directly to my bunk in the second floor of the south wing, but I was too agitated by fear to join my comrades in sleep. Picking my way through a breach in one of the damaged walls of the Barracks, I sought the streets of Rome. It was a stupid thing to do. As a despised foreign mercenary, I could have been shot by pro-Garibaldi partisans. I also risked arrest as a deserter, which was not my intention: to desert, I mean, not consciously at least, although I might have made my way out of the city, after securing civilian clothes. My Italian was good enough to get me to the border. I could turn myself over to the American consul in Florence and ask for passage home. I walked the narrow streets of the Trastevere district in great emotional turmoil, keeping out of sight as much as possible. Reaching the Tiber, I stood quietly under a stand of chestnut trees lining the river bank and began to weep in long, dry, choking sobs. It seemed for certain that my world had come to an end, that I would be dead in a matter of days. From where I stood I could see the dome of St. Peter's across the river. It was nearly four o'clock before I returned to my bunk.

My anxieties were soothed the next evening by an unexpected visit to a brothel.

"You're in poor condition, Collins," Sergeant O'Carroll remarked to me the morning after my late night wandering. "You're as fearful as a trapped hare; but no mind—that is normal. You need something else on your mind besides war, like sin perhaps. A guilty conscience can prove a blessing if it takes your mind off your real troubles."

I initially found the Sergeant's remarks a little obscure. He asked me to meet him after sundown, around eight o'clock that evening, in the company orderly room. When I arrived according to his instructions, I found Sergeant O'Carroll seated there, rubbing his bayonet with linseed oil. He rubbed the weapon in long, stroking, caressing motions, blowing on it occasionally to remove a fleck of rag lint.

"Now, Collins," my sergeant said, "I'll not be one to be

interfering with your personal life, but you impress me as a nice religious lad. All of us, of course, have a proper respect for religion or we wouldn't be bearing arms for the Holy Father, now would we, lad?"

"No, Sergeant—I mean, yes, Sergeant."

"That's right, Private Collins. Now I've been analyzing your case of late. You seem peaked, fearful; and it's not because of the war, is it now, because you're a brave lad, as brave as any I know. So I've been asking myself: 'What ails Private Collins?' I and a few of the other noncommissioned officers, with whom I have taken the liberty of discussing your case—begging your pardon—think we have a solution. We feel that your background is, as we put it, incomplete. Oh, we know that you're a university lad, as are some of the others in the ranks, and a very learned man, despite the strange way you have of talking, but we're not speaking here of books, my fellow sergeants and I, all of us so concerned for the welfare of our men. You see, Private Collins, fear is a disease. It can spread from one man to the next like an outburst of plague. We can't be having the only Yank in the company moping about like a whipped puppy, now can we?"

"No, Sergeant."

"You're a quick study, Private Collins, a damned quick study. I'm always bragging about you to the Captain for being one who learns quickly and well. Now as a reward, I'm asking you to join me tonight in a little adventure of a personal nature. Meet me here in an hour and be wearing your civilian clothes."

As a noncommissioned officer, Sergeant O'Carroll had a permanent pass to the city. Rankers were kept more confined to barracks, so as not to fill Rome with too many soldiers at any one time and disturb the populace. The Sergeant got us past the sentry with ease, explaining my presence as "Captain's wishes" or some such phrase. Sergeant O'Carroll showed himself to be an astute psychologist. The activities of that evening completely took my mind off the forthcoming battle. As we marched forth the next day for Mentana, I could barely concentrate on my fears, so filled was I with feelings of both

388

pleasure and remorse at what had transpired in a dark little room on a rather rumpled and soiled bed.

"Good God, lad," Chaplain MacLoughlin brayed early that morning when I insisted that he hear my confession before the troops fell into formation. "The battalion is marching and you'll be stopping me for confession. He pulled me over to an alcove in one of the Barrack's inner arcades. He mumbled some Latin, then said: "Go ahead, lad, what in God's name is it? Make it quick! I'm expected to stand with the other chaplains before the Holy Father's reviewing stand. And you'll be forming up in a moment yourself."

I narrated—briefly—the last night's debauch and I asked God's forgiveness.

"Jesus, lad, I thought you'd killed someone, by the look of you. Say five Our Fathers and five Hail Marys and in the future watch where you'll be poking your pecker on the night before a battle!" He began a rushed recitation of the words of absolution. I crossed myself, just as the Chaplain puffed off across the courtyard and the battalion bugler blew formation call.

"Now, Sebastian, I hope you enjoyed yourself," Sergeant O'Carroll said to me in a fatherly manner as we wended our way through the winding early morning streets of the Trastevere quarter towards the Serristori Barracks. "You're nineteen, I take it, and so it was about time that it happened; but I'll caution you to remain quiet about our little caper. I'm sure that your dear father would understand—and approve—of what has occurred. Don't be worrying about tomorrow, lad. The battalion is well trained and we'll all be sticking together."

At bugle call the next day, I ran to where my platoon was forming up and I found my spot in the first squad.

"Battalion, attention!" bellowed Sergeant Major Henderson. Some three hundred and fifty of us stiffened our bodies in response.

"Color guard, forward!" cried the Sergeant Major. Two standard-bearers and two escorts marched smartly forward, bearing the yellow and white flag of the Papal States and the regimental colors, a white shamrock across a green background. Major O'Reilly received the battalion from the Sergeant Major, the two of them exchanging salutes.

"Guides out," barked Major O'Reilly, and the guide platoon from headquarters company moved out smartly through the arched gateway that faced the Piazza Colonna. It was the guide platoon's responsibility to see that the battalion moved as directly as possible to its destination, as well as to patrol our flanks while we were *en route*.

"Battalion!" Major O'Reilly declaimed.

"Company!" Captain Stafford cried.

"Platoon!" Sergeant O'Carroll bellowed.

"Squad!" Corporal Hennessey barked.

"Forward march," snapped Major O'Reilly, his command repeated down the chain of command as before.

The battalion colors moved forward, directly ahead of Major O'Reilly and the officers of the staff. The battalion drummer and fife-player struck up a lively Kerry marching tune, and out we moved, wending our way through the streets and piazzas of Rome like the colorful paper dragons the Chinese of San Francisco sometimes parade in their New Year's celebrations. Having but slept some two hours the night before, I should have felt exhausted, yet I felt strangely exhilarated to be part of such splendid company on such a splendid day, headed for such a splendid rendezvous with destiny.

General Garibaldi, you see, had overreached himself. In 1860 that leonine tribune of revolution conquered the Kingdom of the Two Sicilies by the sheer bravado of marching upon it with his Thousand. In red shirt and plumed cavalier slouch hat, Garibaldi swept all before him in a wave of triumphant revolutionary fervor. He was now attempting the same maneuver—a march of volunteers, coupled with a popular uprising; yet this time the General moved in opposition to official Italian policy, rather than as the liberating archangel of Italian unification. Indeed, the General had first to escape royal arrest before he made his unauthorized foray into the papal patrimony. As he and his Red Shirts progressed towards Rome, a few uprisings did occur in the countryside, but nothing resembling the events of 1860 when the entire populace welcomed him as Liberator. The subjects of His Holiness were too wary of the French troops to risk a wholesale revolution. Coming within striking distance of the Eternal City, Garibaldi realized that his scattered column was in no shape to place Rome under seige, nor were there signs of any decisive uprising within the city. After defeating a small pontifical detachment at Monterotondo, Garibaldi ordered his Red Shirts to regroup at Tivoli. Intelligence reached Generals Kanzler and DeFailly that Garibaldi's irregulars were in a state of ragged withdrawal, their formation tenuously scattered. The pontifical generals planned an ambush at Mentana, a small village at the crest of a valley whose upper reaches are entangled in concealing shrubbery, vines, and cane. Kanzler's strategy was simple. Drawing his Zouaves up on either side of Mentana Valley, he would conceal them in the underbrush, allowing the Red Shirts to pour down the lower file. At a given signal, the Zouaves and the French would decimate the Red Shirts in a withering cross-fire. The success of this ambush strategy depended upon our rapid and secret deployment: which explains why we were marching from Rome when daylight had barely broken and why we maintained such a rapid rate of march when once we were on the road. By noon we were in position, having outflanked the clumsily maneuvering Red Shirts. My company was emplaced on a ridge just adjacent to the village itself, where the generals established their headquarters.

As a staff major of artillery, Edmund Campion Calvert, whom I had seen on the march out, was personally attached to Kanzler's staff, with responsibility for advising on artillery fire. I had offered Calvert a brisk salute when my company marched past the circle of horses near which he stood, studying a map of the terrain. He smiled and waved to me, hollering something (I recognized only the word "Harvard") above the rattle of a passing battery of horse-drawn guns. Seeing Edmund, I remembered that it was through Ryan Patrice that both Calvert and I now found ourselves involved in a foreign war—my first war, and Calvert's second, for he had served as a gunnery officer in the Confederate Navy during the War Between the States. Outfitted in the gold buttons and epaulettes of the staff, Calvert seemed a very demigod of blond and tan handsomeness. An oil portrait of him in his pontifical uniform now hangs in the senior common room of St. Mary's Seminary, Baltimore. I had the opportunity to view it once in the company of Calvert's boyhood friend and fellow veteran of the Confederate Navy, the poet-priest John Bannister Tabb, to whom I had a letter of introduction from George Sterling, a one-time pupil of Father Tabb's at St. Charles' Minor Seminary in Overbrook Maryland. (Unlike myself, who resisted the temptation, George Sterling spent some six years in pursuit of the priesthood.)

As each Zouave company passed out of Rome through the Campi d'Annibale, incidentally, it paused *en masse* before a hastily constructed pavilion where the Pope and his entourage waited, the Pope himself seated on a portable throne. Drawing before His Holiness, we dropped to one knee at the command of our officers and received the papal blessing: thickly massed contingents of Zouaves attired in the various uniforms of the differing battalions, naked bayonets fixed to our rifles, the lot of us about to be sent on the Church's last military crusade. From where I knelt in the rear ranks, the Pope looked like a tiny doll dressed in white.

My thoughts, however, remained but briefly on *Pio Nono* as I waited in the underbrush above the valley of Mentana for the Red Shirts to fill the floor below. My attention alternated with imaginings of the battle I would soon face and with recollections of my visit to the bordello the night before. I had, obviously, been both embarrassed and intrigued to find myself out of uniform, as it were, in a strange lady's bedroom, my induction into certain mysteries sponsored, and paid for, by my esteemed platoon sergeant, Sean O'Carroll. The lesson was prompt and thorough. My tutoress, a dark-haired woman of about thirty, conducted her instructions with efficiency and dispatch, having been told (I suppose) by Sergeant O'Carroll that this was my maiden venture onto the perilous seas of carnal knowledge. Nervously, I followed her upstairs to a small bedroom. Over the bed, a painted plaster cast of the Madonna and Child was affixed to the wall.

"Take off your clothes," my preceptress instructed me. She, meanwhile, turned her back to me and began to unhitch her own garments. Trembling, I removed my coat, cravat, shoes, stockings, and shirt, folding them neatly in a small pile on a nearby chair. I then removed my trousers and arranged them over the back of the chair. When she turned towards me, a shawl draped carelessly over her shoulders, her unleashed breasts fell before her in a cascade of sumptuous flesh. Walking over to me, she cupped one breast in her hand, as if making an offering of summer fruit. With her other hand, she reached into my yet undiscarded undergarment and took hold of me, her hesitant unicorn. Within a quarter of an hour, I stood on the other side of that particular mystery of human experience, hardly knowing what had happened in the brief time between, save that the process had been a pleasant one, ending—on my part—in unembarrassed abandon as for the first time in my existence seed spilled from me into the womb of life, and I dropped like a spent divinity upon a bosom intended for both a child's nourishment and a man's delight.

"You come back from the battle, American, and we'll do this again," my instructress generously commented upon the completion of our second exchange. She sat near a shuttered window, wrapped in naught save her large Spanish shawl, her dusky features only half-visible in the flickering light of the candle that burned before the plaster cast of the Madonna, providing the narrow room with its only light. As she spoke, she smoked a cigarette that filled the room with the smell of harsh tobacco. "You men are crazy, fighting all the time, and for what—for the Pope or for the King or for Garibaldi—eh! You all wind up dead. Stupid! You stay away from those brutes tomorrow, you hear me. You come back with your white skin in one piece, then we'll do this again."

393

Rising, she threw the shawl from her shoulders and advanced towards me, where I was sitting on the bed, huddled under a military cloak left there, I suspected from the insignia, by a previous patron of at least the rank of sublieutenant. She proceeded to show me what we would do again when I returned safely from the war.

Seated superbly on a great prancing black horse, General Garibaldi himself led the column into the valley of Mentana. Dispirited by their failure to precipitate a popular revolution, the Red Shirts moved carelessly as if they had nothing to lose. They failed to send out the flanking pickets or advance scouts that might have probed and discovered our emplacements. The general's horse pawed nervously at the ground as it picked its way down the valley defile, as if it alone sensed our imminent ambush. General Garibaldi—bearded, long-maned, wearing a wide-brimmed hat tilted at a rakish angle and topped by an ostrich plume and a red shirt devoid of insignia or decoration—advanced before his men like a bronze equestrian brought to life. The Red Shirts marched some three to four abreast, singing revolutionary songs which grew louder and louder as they approached our position. Kanzler had spent the morning emplacing a force of some three thousand pontificals and French on the high ground between Mentana and the village of Monterotondo. Some four thousand Red Shirts now filed along the lower plain, stretched between the two villages. As the last of the irregulars filed through Monterotondo, the pontifical artillery opened fire, sealing off the rear of the column in a wall of explosion and flying steel. Rifle fire crackled from the heights. In the first few minutes of the battle, scores of Red Shirts fell to the ground, picked off like rabbits by the *chassepots* of the French and the Stutzen carbines of the Zouaves. The Red Shirts made for what cover they could find, and there they regrouped themselves, leaving the valley floor littered with hundreds of the dead and the dying. Many bodies lay still where they had fallen, but many twitched in horrible agony. A few of the wounded thrashed about on the ground in terrible convulsions. The pontifical and French

394

artillery continued to cover the valley floor in a hail of explosion and smoke.

After this initial ambush, the second phase of the battle of Mentana began. Riding fearlessly down the valley, Garibaldi rallied his men as best he could. Our withering fire, however, prevented the Red Shirts from leaving their scattered cover and regrouping at any one point into battalion-sized or even company-sized units. They remained pinned down instead in pockets of fifty to a hundred, incapable of mounting a countercharge. The *chassepots* of the French fired twelve rounds per minute and could be reloaded in the breech from the prone position without exposing a soldier to enemy fire. Many of the Red Shirts, however, had antiquated muzzle-loading rifles. Standing or crouching to load, they made easy targets for our sharpshooters. Sensing the rapidly deteriorating situation, Garibaldi grew furious, indeed desperate. He rode from unit to unit trying to coordinate a countercharge.

"Come die with me!" history reports him yelling that day. "Are you afraid to die with me?"

At sixty years of age, Garibaldi had lived a long and full life. He had wandered the world and led revolutions on two continents. He had entered liberated cities in triumph and made love to some of the most beautiful women of his day, and so he was perhaps ready to die. The young men of his hastily organized brigade, however, had their lives before them. They possessed no memories of military honors or parted thighs to take with them charging up the valley hillside against the well-entrenched French and pontificals, as the General was urging them to do.

"Courage, courage, boys, long live Italy!" the General cried above the smoke and gunfire.

"You lead us to slaughter," retorted his rebellious troops.

My company was employed at the Mentana extremity of heights, drawn up in a semicircular perimeter protecting the entrance to Mentana itself. We saw little action in the early stages of the battle, since most of the enemy troops were pinned down midway up the valley. Towards one o'clock, the Lion of Sicily rode down to our end of the fighting, imperturbable to the hail of rifle-fire that chased him in hostile escort.

"He'll be making a charge here, lads," Captain Stafford announced, scuttling down our line in a half-crouch. "He'll be going for a breakthrough to Kanzler's headquarters. Look lively, lads, and prepare for the bayonet!"

Within fifteen minutes, the Captain's predictions came true. Garibaldi rallied a company-sized unit. With fixed bayonets, they were following their general up the slope that led to our position. I suppose some hundred of them made that brave, foolhardy charge, marching into the withering fire of our Stutzen carbines, cut at their flanks as well by *chassepot* fire from the French units to our left and to our right. Why those young men marched with Garibaldi when their compatriots remained pinned beneath cover, I'll never know. They advanced steadily up the hillside, their brethren falling about them, hit by our fire. When they reached a point halfway up the slope without breaking off their assault, I knew then that my life was in danger.

"Prepare to receive bayonet charge," Sergeant O'Carroll called. How one can prepare for something so frightening as a bayonet assault has always eluded me, even when I was doing it, and reaching, at the same time, an intensity of personal panic as Garibaldi's troops continued their march some one hundred yards away, their individual faces now beginning to be distinct as the smoke of rifle and cannon cleared in intermittent lapses of firing. When the attacking Red Shirts began yelling, the noise was terrifying. They yelled like murderous Iroquois falling down upon a hapless prey. I emptied my rifle into the advancing red line, then braced myself for contact.

In seconds they were upon us, running and screaming behind their pointed steel like monstrous insects. I felt instinctively that one charging Red Shirt had singled me out, so I pointed my steel towards his forehead as Sergeant Girouard had instructed me to do some ten months earlier during our Atlantic passage. My opponent was running fast, too fast, and yelling. He broke his gait just before thrusting, as Sergeant Girouard said he might do: shifting his balance and pulling his rifle butt back before swinging into his thrust. I dropped as Sergeant Girouard instructed me to drop: precisely at that moment when he arrested his forward motion; and I came up at him from the ground, pushing my bayonet forward with my right leg. I had nothing against him and he, perhaps, had nothing against me; yet I killed him, thrusting into his stomach lest he kill me. "Thou shalt not kill," the Lord sayeth, but I killed in defense of myself and the right of the Pope to rule a Lilliputian kingdom that should have long since been absorbed into the kingdom of Italy. He looked at me in bewilderment when he found out what I had done to him, death-dealing steel entering his vital parts. I have seen his face again and again in a hundred different nightmares, a face that showed my age at the time: around twenty, darkly handsome, with two rows of gleaming white teeth, broken by one conspicuous gold filling, and a head of curly black hair. I often think of what he would have been like had he lived, had the two of us not been pitted so senselessly against each other. I have imagined him at thirty, taking possession of his father's Tuscan farm; at forty-five, a prosperous, grandfatherly *contadino,* with a taste for radical literature and socialist oratory; at sixty-seven, my age today, a grizzly, white-bearded patriarch, telling stories around a winter fireplace of his days with Garibaldi fifty years before. Once he singled me out as the fated object of his charge, however, only one of us could walk away from our bayonet-embrace. Like insects that couple and die simultaneously, we joined our bodies in a deadly congress of steel.

"Rally, lads, rally," Captain Stafford yelled when the shock of that charge had spent itself. "Reform yourselves!"

To my left Sergeant Sean O'Carroll lay on the ground sightlessly staring at the afternoon sky. Blood ran from a gash in his throat. All of us were so accustomed to his constant stream of orders that we stood about in exhaustion and shock, hovering about O'Carroll's body as if our platoon sergeant

397

would rise from the dead and start giving us orders again. Seeing our indecision, the company first sergeant, Desmond Casey, ran over to our position and got us on the move once more.

"All right, boys, it's reform and withdraw into a tighter perimeter," Casey urged. "We've suffered some losses and some of the enemy have made it through to Mentana."

No sooner had we set up our second perimeter, however, than Captain Stafford moved us out rapidly towards the village. A small band of Red Shirts—not General Garibaldi, who had escaped downhill under a pursuing barrage of bullets once his hastily mounted attack had spent its force—had fought its way into Mentana and was barricaded in a house, from which it was sweeping the Piazza San Nicola with rifle fire. Captain Stafford deployed us around the Piazza, with orders to keep the occupied house under fire until an artillery gun could be brought up to blast the place to Kingdom Come. After some fifteen minutes of our harassing fire, a light cannon was wheeled onto one edge of the Piazza, loaded, then pointed in the direction of the Red Shirts' hasty citadel. Five thunderous blasts reduced the house to rubble—but not before some unnamed Red Shirt, in a defiant, dying gesture, had picked off a staff major of artillery, Edmund Campion Calvert of Baltimore, who had stopped momentarily to observe the crew's handling of the gun.

I could not believe it when I saw Edmund slump over like an overcoat tossed to the ground. Breaking ranks, I rushed across the Piazza and might have fallen to a sharpshooter myself, had the cannon not already done its work. There, on the cobblestones, lay the just-dead corpse of the flower of Maryland chivalry: a Calvert on one side, a Campion on the other, a commissioned officer of the Confederacy, a major in the army of the Papal States, not yet thirty, his blond mustache flecked in the blood that trickled down the side of his face from a solitary hole in his right temple. Edmund seemed at peace—like a medieval knight stretched in cold stone across a vestry sarcophagus. Chaplain MacLoughlin knelt beside Edmund's body and began to administer the last rites.

Dazedly, still in a condition of battle shock, I crossed myself over the body of my dead friend.

I remained on active service until September of 1870, when Rome fell to the army of Italy and the papal Zouaves were disbanded. Siege and surrender, however, were the last things on our minds on 6 November, 1867, when we marched triumphantly back from Mentana into Rome through the Porta Pia. With their staffs in attendance, Generals Kanzler and DeFailly stood on the steps of the Church of Santa Maria della Vittoria (Bernini's *St. Theresa in Ecstasy* decorates a side altar within) while three thousand Zouaves marched by, escorting some seventeen hundred prisoners. Some two hundred wounded enemy were brought in by wagon and by cart. They also passed in review in the manner of an ancient Roman triumph. I almost expected to hear the "Grand March" from *Aïda*. I did not, but as we marched in, the bells of the entire city did peal forth in greeting. While the generals headed towards the Vatican for an audience with the Pope, the St. Patrick's Battalion marched towards the Castel Sant'Angelo, taking some five hundred prisoners with us who were slated for internment there, with ourselves as garrison.

Some one hundred and fifty of Garibaldi's column, incidentally, fell on the field of battle, and about half that number of French and pontificals. By two o'clock on 3 November, it was obvious that the Red Shirts had suffered total defeat. Garibaldi left the field at about that hour. A ragged remnant of his Red Shirts followed. A few days later, the General was arrested by the Italian government outside Florence, charged with fomenting an insurrection.

Ever in search of amusement, Romans were ecstatic over their new situation. Nursing the wounded—Zouave, French, and Red Shirts alike—became all the rage. The exiled queen of Naples herself walked the hospital wards, distributing chocolate bonbons and cigars out of the pockets of a voluminous white apron to recuperating soldiers. Mrs. Catherine Stone, an American, and her friend the Contessa Della Torre organized the upper-class ladies of the city, including the Guelphs or

Black Aristocracy, into a devoted and smartly attired nursing corps. A number of elegant women visited our charges at Castel Sant'Angelo, bringing boxes of clean linen to distribute and arranging floral displays in the dormitories where the wounded prisoners lay. Recuperating Zouaves were especially pampered by these angels of mercy. One lad from my platoon vociferously announced his resentment when he was discharged from hospital and returned to duty.

"She'd come every day," he told us, "a regular countess she was, with big brown eyes like a deer. She'd wipe my forehead off with a cool, damp cloth, just as fancy as you please, and she'd be humming as she smoothed the cloth across my cheeks, smiling like an angel. It was paradise."

I stood guard a few weeks later at the Palazzo Barberini when a civic banquet was held honoring the victorious generals and their staffs. Impressed by the performance of the St. Patrick's Battalion at Mentana, General Kanzler ordered a rotating company of us transferred to the permanent garrison of Castel Sant'Angelo—the ancient fortress fronting the Tiber, connected to the Vatican by an elevated passageway—as a supplementary household guard. I remained garrisoned at Castel Sant'Angelo until the Zouaves surrendered and were disbanded. Assigned frequently to sentry duty in the Vatican itself, I observed great events as they came to me in scattered fragments, snatches of overheard conversation, gestures of ambiguity. In later years, safely back in San Francisco, I filled out my memories through reading. The more complete knowledge of retrospective scholarship, however, must take second place to memories which, while limited to the perspective of a private soldier, are yet soaked in the sensuous imagery of intensely apprehended experience.

I have already described, for instance, the memorable concert given by the Abbé Franz Liszt at Castel Gandolfo in which the Pope was moved to tears by Liszt's playing of the *Casta Diva* aria from Bellini's opera *Norma*. Giovanni Mastai-Ferretti, Pope Pius IX, was, you see, a sensitive, mercurial man, with a deep, almost feminine appreciation of things

400

aesthetic. *Pio Nono* was a nobleman, of course (nearly all the higher clergy were). In his youth he required a dispensation from Pope Leo XII himself in order to be ordained since he was liable to an occasional *grand mal* seizure. Pope Pius IX had wit aplenty, and irony (he loved puns and verbal acrostics), but also a temper that flared forth now and then, sending his court into paroxyms of terror. He was constantly quoting poetry as a strategy of grand gesture. When General Kanzler approached the papal throne after Mentana, for instance, the Pope greeted him with a sonorous declamation of the first octave of Tasso's epic poem *Gerusalemme Liberata*.

In the two years of my Vatican duty, I drew a number of sentry assignments that brought me into the presence of the Holy Father at a number of unguarded moments. I once watched in disbelief as he boxed the ears of a cardinal who had disappointed him in some piece of curial business. His Holiness slapped the poor fellow about the head with a number of abrupt cuffs, screaming all the while that he would break the cardinal in question by reducing him to a simple parish priest assigned to a remote village in the mountains of the Abruzzi. His Holiness frequently grew exasperated with Antonelli, making veiled hints as to the Cardinal's less-than-exemplary personal life.

"How can I replace him?" the Pope lamented upon one occasion when I stood sentry in the council room of the Quirinal Palace, overhearing a cardinal's suggestion to His Holiness that that perhaps a more "clerical" member of the Sacred College be appointed to replace the swarthy Neapolitan subdeacon. "I would obviously prefer that Antonelli possessed the habits of a Carthusian monk," His Holiness lamented, "but I need him where he is and it is there that he shall stay. And in the future I forbid you to carry any more of these rumors to me, do you understand?"

"Yes, Your Holiness."

"Save, that is, in cases of blatant scandal; then I should be notified."

From the vantage point of a sentry's position near the rear

401

exit of the main hall of the Palazzo di San Calisto, Antonelli's winter residence, I saw the very same tattling cardinal at one of the Secretary of State's frequent receptions, enjoying himself enormously, as if there were no finer fellow in the Sacred College of Cardinals than Giacomo Antonelli of Naples. Antonelli loved parties and gave them frequently, when he was not busy mixing in society elsewhere in the city. I stood agape at the lustrous brillance of the women who graced the Cardinal's *soirées*. To me, a young soldier of twenty, they were like angelic creatures dropped from the empyrean. With almost operatic flair, the Cardinal's major-domo, a *castrato* by the name of Cherubino, announced, nay sang, each mellifluous name as various personages and *divas* made their entrances into the Cardinal's ever-crowded reception rooms.

"The Princess Doria . . . the Contessa Pallavicini . . . His Eminence, Cardinal Ugelini . . . The Duchess of Galliera . . . Padre Bigioli, General of the Theatines . . . Monsignor Vincenzio Tizzani, Chaplain-General of the Army of his Holiness . . . the Princess di Teano . . . Michelangelo Caetani, Duke of Sermoneta . . . Cardinal Gaude . . . Colonel Bourbon-Chalus . . . Mrs. Catherine Stone and daughter." Signor Cherubino provided each entrant with a soaring, bell-clear introduction.

Attired in a simple black cassock, with only a scarlet skullcap to suggest his rank, Antonelli moved from guest to guest. I noticed that when he finished kissing a woman's hand, the Cardinal did not release it immediately. If the woman were at all attractive, he held her hand in his for a long moment: rather, he hovered over it as if madame's hand were a fragrant flower to be savored appreciatively through the gently probing instrumentality of His Eminence's great beaked nose. Upon another occasion I walked all-night sentry in the inner courtyard of the Palazzo di San Calisto. Around three or so in the morning, I heard a woman's laughter from the direction of the Cardinal's apartment on the second floor above the garden. Just before dawn, a carriage pulled up to the Palazzo entrance. A caped and hooded figure, obviously female, darted out and was swiftly enveloped behind a rapidly closed carriage door. Milady departed in a screech of wheels and a clattering of hooves. Shortly thereafter, His Eminence himself appeared, wearing knee breeches, silk stockings, buckled shoes, and a frock coat. A scarlet skullcap signaled his cardinalatial condition. The Cardinal spent the hour following sunrise walking in his garden, savoring each petal with the searching attentions of his nose. He seemed especially enraptured of the roses, in which he buried his face with repeated appreciation.

From my limited vantage point, and in my own way, I witnessed the twilight hours of the sovereign papacy. In April of 1868 Rome celebrated a triduum of events: the fiftieth anniversary of the Pope's first mass, the nineteenth anniversary of his return from exile, and the fifteenth anniversary of Pius's deliverance from the very jaws of death when the Church of Saint Agnes collapsed in the course of a papal ceremony, burying the papal court and an audience of seminarians beneath a pile of plaster and rubble. Miraculously, no one was killed.

As if in recognition that its time was limited, Papal Rome adorned itself in splendor. Every piazza was crowded with flags, banners, palm fronds, flowering plants in wooden boxes. The statues, fountains, and obelisks of every piazza were illumined by night with gas jets—the first I had ever seen. A huge cross, also illumined at night by gas, topped Castel Sant'Angelo. On the morning of April 11, the city turned out for a spectacular procession of all classes and conditions: prelates, patricians, the bourgeoisie, the minor clergy, the military, tradesmen, the fire brigade, peasants in from the countryside who paraded with flocks of geese and ducks squawking before them. The composer Gounod, then in Rome with the intention of studying for the priesthood, composed a special oratorio, which a reconstituted Zouave orchestra performed on the steps of St. Peter's for a vast throng gathered in the Piazza San Pietro.

No sooner had this excitement died down than the Pope convened a worldwide Ecumenical Council to address the

403

question of Papal Infallibility. With his loss of secular sovereignty on the horizon, His Holiness demanded consolation in the form of an Infallibility Declaration. The extreme ultramontanes, in fact, talked of demanding that the Council declare both the Infallibility and the doctrine that the pope held the sovereignty of the Papal States by divine right. For the year of the Council, Rome became a vast and lavish pageant, feasting the eye. Cardinals' carriages, attended by uniformed footmen and drawn by gaily caparisoned horses, crossed and recrossed Rome in a fervor of excitement.

In December the Council opened with a procession into Saint Peter's Basilica, before which I stood that day in full dress uniform, saluting the entering prelates with the very same rifle and fixed bayonet with which I had defended myself at Mentana. There were cardinals in scarlet choir dress, archbishops and bishops in robes of magenta, Eastern rite prelates in cassocks of purple and gold, abbots in red and black. The fathers general of the various religious orders proceeded in together—Benedictines, Dominicans, Franciscans, Capuchins, Jesuits, Carmelites, Norbetines, Theatines, Mercedarians, Trinitarians, Augustinians, Servites, Camaldolese, Carthusians, Cistercians—each in the picturesque habit of his order. The superiors of the various clerical congregations and institutes then arrived in procession—Holy Cross Fathers, Oblates of Mary Immaculate, Redemptorists, Crosier Fathers, Passionists, Picpus Fathers, the Paris Foreign Mission Society, the Fathers of the Blessed Sacrament, the Society of Mary, the Society of the Divine Word, the Sacred Heart Fathers, the Salvatorians, the Congregation of the Missions, the Brothers of the Christian Schools, the St. Patrick Brothers, the Alexian Brothers, the Nursing Brothers of St. John of God, the Brothers of Mary—each of these in the differing garbs of their respective congregations. The Noble Guard made a grand entrance, splendid in Napoleonic uniforms, then came the Roman and papal nobility, the men in formal wear, the women in long black dresses and lace veils. Diplomats accredited to the Holy See arrived in every possible

404

style of dress decorated with every possible color of the rainbow. These were followed by the sovereign military orders: the Knights of Malta, the Knights of Rhodes, the Knights of the Holy Sepulcher, the Knights of St. Gregory, the Knights of St. Sylvester, the Knights Templar—and by the various pious societies, too numerous to name. Lastly, His Holiness himself entered: the short, stoutish man for whom this orchidaceous pageant was being played out, the pontiff whose long-since obsolete sovereignty had almost cost me my life. Entering the Basilica, the Pope passed within three feet of me. I caught a whiff of men's cologne in the air.

In retrospect, I realize that I was witnessing the last splendid pageant of some thousand years of Roman Catholic history. Once Rome no longer belonged to the pope, a new era would begin for the church—a more spiritual era no doubt, divorced from the possession of overt secular power. From my sentry's position outside the great bronze doors of St. Peter's, I heard the *Veni Sancte Spiritus* intoned from within, then taken up luminously by the Sistine Choir. Yes, indeed, the Church might very well have been praying for the guidance of the Holy Ghost; for the ultramontanes, backed by Pius himself, were about to force the Doctrine of Infallibility down many an unwilling throat. My adult reading has elaborated my youthful intuition. Men like John Henry Newman, Lord Acton of Cambridge University, Bishop Dupanloup of Orleans, the German theologian Döllinger, even the Bishop of Little Rock, Arkansas, all opposed the Infallibility; but the ultramontanes, the Jesuits, and the conservatives in general prevailed.

It would be dishonest of me, however, to represent myself at age nineteen, twenty, and twenty-one, a mere private of Zouaves, as playing any part in these weighty deliberations, or indeed in paying any excessive attention to them. As a vigorous, lusty young lad in the prime of life—who had, indeed, been returned the gift of life on the battlefield, born again through the death of another—I had my attention taken up with pursuits other than theology. To have been young

405

then, as I was, and also in Rome, was world enough to accumulate a lifetime of memory. Even today, at age sixty-seven, in the extraordinarily perilous year 1914, I can recall the vivid sensations of that time and that place as if they happened yesterday. When I think back on it all, the very music of Hector Berlioz's *Roman Carnival Overture* plays in my brain.

How grand, how splendid, on one's liberty day, to stroll the streets of the city in a freshly turned-out uniform with the Mentana medal awarded our unit by General Kanzler dangling from the left breast of my green tunic, my red fez at an especially jaunty angle. On Sundays I would take a morning coffee in one of the less expensive cafes off the Piazza di Venezia, savoring a Turkish cigarette which I bought singly at a nearby tobacco shop. Refreshed, I would begin my day's adventures. Climbing La Cordonata, a stone ramp built in 1536, I might ascend the Capitoline Hill, the sacred center of Ancient Rome, and enjoy a late morning visit to the museums that sit atop that civic summit; or else, during other free hours, I might stroll through the Borghese Gardens, delighting in the interplay of formal gardens and untutored meadows, ending that stroll amidst the pictures and statues of the seventeenth-century villa built in the midst of the gardens by Cardinal Scipione Borghese, nephew of Pope Paul V. It was at the Villa Borghese, incidentally, that I first learned to admire Bernini, whose *David* and *Rape of Proserpine* overwhelmed me with their theatrical power. I stood riveted beneath the *Proserpine,* intoxicated by the way the flesh of her luxurious thigh yielded to the god of the underworld's greedy grasp. Rome offered me a feast of great art, and I proved a willing gourmand of whatever the galleries, museums, and churches had to offer. I returned to Harvard, then later Heidelberg, possessed once and for all with a cornucopia of internal images, which I have always been able to retrieve from memory, projecting them on the screen of my imagination like a magic lantern show. These images of Europe's high art past, settling within me, took their place alongside remembrances of

406

California; and because Rome intermingled so with California in my deepest self, I became a better San Franciscan, for the San Francisco of my innermost longing has always been an amalgam of both California and Rome.

On certain of those late afternoons of freedom from military duty, I might join the promenade above and below the Spanish Steps—burghers, children, governesses and their charges, soldiers, vendors, hawkers of various wares, foreigners, minor clergy, women of the street, taking the air as the sun crept behind the dome of St. Peter's across the Tiber. I would then stop to think of poor Keats, who died in the Casina Rossa adjacent to the lower staircase; but I would also be on the lookout for a pretty face.

My needs in that direction, however, were professionally serviced; for being young and ramlike, I valued the art itself (once I had discovered it!) more than I valued its emotional or imaginative associations. I loved copulation for copulation's sake, and I was driven to it frequently—in between periods of religious remorse. I asked of *eros* only that it be available on those evenings when an irresistible appetite drove me from my barracks onto the street like a famished wolf. During seasons of reformation and abstinence, I would often awake with my linen stiff from dried seed, expelled in the night as from a fountain that could not be capped. Being young and hence not yet much of a hypocrite, I preferred to sin surreptitiously, and for a fee, with no false words necessary. I learned the location of a number of houses affordable on a private's pay (being impecunious, as well as being religiously remorseful, account-ed for my sojourns of continence) and I would repair to these places, full of urgent demand.

Upon my return from Mentana, I did feel a certain affection and gratitude to the woman who had initiated me and encouraged my safe return; but she had by then married a sergeant in the French army and had moved to Civitavecchia before I could accumulate the surplus capital necessary for a return visit. The mistress of the household thus informed me when I at last reappeared, my pockets and trousers bulging in

407

three directions; so I contented myself with alternative services available from the house. The next day, however, I did not run precipitously to the chaplain and demand forgiveness of sins. Mentana, you see, had alerted me to more awesome evils in this world than copulation outside the bonds of holy matrimony.

When I was repentant and without funds, I found that I enjoyed the churches of Rome much more than the whorehouses. Among my favorite churches to visit were the Gesù (headquarters of the Jesuits), Santa Maria in Aracoeli atop the Capitoline Hill, Santa Sabina atop the Aventine, Santa Maria della Vittoria, with its superb Bernini, and San Silvestro in Capite, the English Church, where I enjoyed the preaching of such visiting English clergy as Newman, Manning, and Wiseman, among others. When remorse faded like the fleecy morning fog of San Francisco, burned off by the ascending sun of lust and replenished capital, I tended to frequent museums much more than I did churches. There, before some of the greatest erotic art in the world, I would fuel the fires of an already raging desire with images of gods and goddesses recumbent on silk-covered couches, or merry country people sporting after the harvest with an unabashed display of rustic female flesh, or the yielding, luxuriant nudity of this or that baroque artist's unveiled mistress, her breasts and thighs rich in roseate flesh tones. Then, in some house of purchased pleasure, I would attempt to make love to Rome herself, heaving over the body of one of her mercenary daughters as if I might be casting my seed into the open womb of the Roman earth itself, already soaked in the blood, bones, and tears of some three thousand years of human travail and ecstatic transport.

Ah, Rome! City of passion and desire! City of my mind and heart! I sought you in your museums and churches, in your cafes, along your narrow winding streets built high on either side with medieval façades. I sought you in the huddled rooms of your bordellos, where I purchased the pleasure of your body. I sought you beneath the sculpted umbrella pines of your promenades and parks. I sought you beneath the soaring dome of St. Peter's and in the silent cloister of St. John Lateran. I sought you at carnival time when the nighttime streets filled with costumed figures, when love might be taken against a Tiber wall from a lascivious, laughing creature bedecked in scarves and gypsy jewelry, who met you in a shared frenzy of abandon, then ran off into the night before you learned her name. I sought you—and you allowed yourself to be found. I found you in greedy kisses and breasts that reshaped themselves beneath my caressing hand. I found you in the suggestion of heroic and insignificant shades wandering your streets—the saints, sinners, emperors, beggars, and pilgrim folk who once, like me, wandered your labyrinthine passageways. I found you on those October evenings when an orange moon hung low in the sky like a planetary fruit, or during the heat of the afternoon when, looking down from the Janiculum Hill above the Vatican, I saw the city—buff, cinnamon, yellow, gold, travertine, red-roofed—sleeping lazily beneath the afternoon sun, lulled by the murmur of the crickets in the cypress trees.

You, Rome, are in all truth the Eternal City. You are the Platonic form, the master archetype, of urban civilization. All cities but participate in what you possess to perfection: the very soul of civilization itself, in all its achievement, glory, compromise, and sordid realism. I have spent a lifetime trying to found a colony for you here in San Francisco, like some ancient *rhetor* sent by the Empire to a distant outpost to teach a newly conquered race Latin, Greek, and the names of the gods worshipped atop the Capitoline Hill. Whatever I love about my native city is whatever there is in San Francisco that has learned the lesson of Rome. In that process of tutelage—first envisioned by Ralston, struggled for in recent times by Phelan—I have played my part of a humble but ardent pedagogue.

Far more than either San Francisco or Boston, Rome was the city of my greedy, appreciative youth—and my young

409

manhood as well, for I returned there for two more years in 1876, after having completed my Heidelberg doctorate.

Once before this quasi-permanent move, however, in June of 1874, Charlie Stoddard and I dashed down from Munich by train for a brief visit. We heard Archbishop Mérode preach, just weeks before his death from pneumonia in the arms of his mentor, *Pio Nono*. Assigned as papal almoner, Mérode had long since abandoned his interest in the things of this world, devoting himself, instead, to work among the poor. After the ceremony—a Mass at the Basilica of St. Petronilla for American pilgrims, in which Mérode spoke of his ancestor, the Marquis de Lafayette—I waited outside the sacristy to introduce myself to the Archbishop as he entered his simple carriage.

"Sebastian Collins, Your Excellency," I said, "late of the St. Patrick's Battalion."

He seemed a very tired man (the exhausted are especially vulnerable to pneumonia), but he remained to chat. I made my request: a letter of introduction to the prefect of the Vatican Library, attesting to my good character. The Archbishop's secretary, a young priest, reached into the pocket of his cassock, took out a notebook and pencil, and jotted down my name and a brief description of my project: to examine the Library's seventeenth-century pamphlet collection for background material on Counter Reformational aesthetics.

"Were you at Mentana?" Mérode asked.

"Yes, Your Excellency."

"We needed a Mentana in 1860. We suffered a Castelfi-dardo and an Ancona instead. After those losses, it was too late. Mentana came too late. I shall send a letter along for you to Cardinal Votto."

Two days later, Charlie and I were taken on a conducted tour of the Vatican Gardens, arranged through the courtesy of Colonel Pallasch, a former officer of the pontifical army, then serving with the household guard. The gardens behind St. Peter's leading towards the Villa Pia are of course magnificent. Our guide, a botanist attached to the Vatican Library, was

410

expostulating on each twig and leaf (so it seemed) when, suddenly, looking over our shoulders as we faced him, our guide fell to one knee and crossed himself. Turning around, Charlie and I beheld *Pio Nono* himself cautiously taking the air in the hesitant gait of an old man; his arm linked to the supporting presence of Archbishop Mérode. Instinctively, Charlie and I both dropped to one knee ourselves. The Pope drew near. Noticing us through his squint, he crossed the air before him in blessing. Mérode recognized me instantly.

"Holy Father," the Archbishop said, "this young man, Sebastian Collins, from San Francisco, fought for you at Mentana."

"He did, you say?" said the Pope. "How sweet of him. They were all such good boys, my Zouaves, such lovely, good boys." He blessed me again, then continued on with his slipper-shuffle for a few more steps. Stopping, he turned around and stood peering at us, as if lost in thought.

"San Francisco, you say. A long way away," he said. "Get up, now, all of you. This is a garden, not a church. I was in Chile as a young priest, you perhaps remember. I loved the Pacific Ocean, so wild, so blue. Do the whales still spout offshore during the migration season?"

"Yes, Holy Father. They are the very same herds we see earlier off San Francisco, heading south."

"I love whales," said the Pope. "And I love bears, also. Animals are so innocent, don't you think?"

"Yes, Holy Father. Animals are very innocent."

"We need a zoological garden in the Vatican. Only the other day, the emperor of Abyssinia offered me a lion, but I have no place to put it. I'm too old now, but I shall leave a memorandum to my successor to build a little zoo back here. Which of you was the Zouave?"

"I was, Holy Father," I said, stepping forward.

"Come over here," the Pope said. "I don't see as well as I used to."

I moved to within a few feet of him. Detaching himself from Mérode's arm, the Pope made his way towards me. I tried

411

to drop to one knee, but he reached both of his arms out and took hold of me by my upper biceps. He studied my face for a moment, and I studied his.

"I lost many fine Zouaves such as you, Mr. Collins. How old are you?"

"Twenty-six, Your Holiness."

He regarded my face for another moment, then pulled me to him in a surprisingly emotional embrace, kissing first one of my cheeks, then the other.

"You shall live a long life," he said. "Pray for my soul as the years ensue. I shall most likely be in Purgatory." Taking Mérode's arm, the Pope walked off without so much as another glance backward. Stoddard and the botanist awefully regarded me as if I were someone over whose head the Holy Ghost had just alighted in the form of a dove.

I saw *Pio Nono* once again in late 1876, at a great outdoor ceremony in St. Peter's Square in which the Pope consecrated the world to the Sacred Heart. Mérode's letter (in it he described me as a personal friend of His Holiness) and the long-standing friendship that existed between Archbishop Alemany of San Francisco and his fellow Dominican, Cardinal Vatto, prefect of the Vatican Library (they made their novitiate together in the same Catalonian monastery), succeeded in getting me more than the mere privileges of the Library. I was made *scriptor,* a paid position with minimal duties. I was expected to devote most of my time to preparing my monograph on Bernini in the context of the theological and aesthetic preoccupations of the Counter Reformation. My routine for those two years was as follows. From eight o'clock until one, I would work at my desk in the Library, then return to my pension for lunch and a siesta. In the late afternoons, I might return to the Library or work at home. In the early evenings, I walked about the city. Two years of such steady application resulted in the elaboration of my Heidelberg thesis into *Bernini, Eros, and the Transcendent,* published in 1878 by the Oxford University Press, my most solid contribution to scholarship, I suppose, as well as being my first book.

Rome, in the years 1876, 1877, 1878, did not have the

charged atmosphere of Rome between 1867 and 1870: which quietude suited me wonderfully, for I was devoted in those years to arduous scholarship. With the death of Ralston in 1875, I knew that I must make my own way in the world without mentor or patronage. At that time, I had hopes that my Bernini monograph, when published, might secure me an appointment to one or another of the eastern universities in the United States. As of then, I was reluctant to return to San Francisco, feeling it too provincial a field of endeavor for my Harvard- and Heidelberg-educated talents.

In the Piazza San Pietro that day in June 1876, as an aged, frail *Pio Nono* consecrated the world (whether the world wanted such a consecration or not) to the Sacred Heart of Jesus, in the crowded piazza, I espied Ryan Patrice before he spotted me. The intervening ten years had changed him dramatically—well beyond the usual transition from thirty-five to forty-five years of age. Patrice had lost about forty pounds, for one thing, and gray streaked his yet-red beard and hair. He stood unpretentiously among a group of priests, all wearing the black cassock and red Chi Rho of the Paris Foreign Mission Society. How could I ever forget that red χρ? At Harvard, Patrice had seared that Chi Rho insignia into my very brain! I walked over and introduced myself. Patrice seemed genuinely pleased to see me again. He invited me, in fact, to come round the next morning to his Society's generalate on the Via Lepanto for further conversation.

Lest Ryan Patrice still have me in mind for the clergy, I invited my landlady to spend that night in my bed (in order to steel myself against temptation!) as I had been accustomed to doing once or twice a week since taking up residence in a pension on the Via Monserrato near Piazza Navona. My landlady, Signora Anna Amari, a widow in her late thirties (her older husband, an official in the Bureau of Agriculture, departed this vale of tears sometime in late 1874), had a very full, very female figure, as I noticed instantly when I presented myself at the pension she had been operating since her husband's death. Anna Amari must have been close to forty, yet her hair was still black, and an element of girlishness played about her face, which was charmingly on the plump side—the result, it turned out, of partaking in her own masterful cooking.

I rented two rooms from her on the topmost floor, a bedroom and a study. I had the entire floor to myself, a fact that assisted our subsequent indiscretions. Our contract called for one main meal, served Roman style, shortly after one o'clock. We all ate together downstairs at a long table, a dozen or so guests—permanent and quasi-transient—including myself, waited on by the Signora's two daughters, two delightful girls in their mid-teens. Signora Anna Amari's cuisine, to speak briefly, was overwhelming. She bought her produce fresh every day at a nearby marketplace. Fish, fowl, veal, pork, lamb, chicken were varied each meal according to market price or freshness. She made her own pasta and baked the day's bread every morning. The Signora presided over her well-laden table herself, seated at its head in a rather good dress, except on Saturdays, when she did not cook. As the widow of a civil servant, and hence knowledgeable of the great world, the Signora expected her guests to provide her with lively conversation. Anyone showing signs of sullen taciturnity was refused the status of permanent resident. Our daily dinners were by and large talkative and enjoyable, as I remember them. Professor Malioni of the Academy of Antiquities discoursed on matters Etruscan, Greek, Cretan, and Roman. Doctor Elto, a hearings officer in the criminal court, provided us with the savory details of the latest crime of passion. Lieutenant Colonel Barbioto, late of the customs service, discoursed on how the evil hand of Sardinia and Corsica accounted for whatever ailed the kingdom of Italy on that particular day.

Life continued on in such an uncomplicated, pastoral vein for a number of months. My relations with Signora Amari were polite and cordial. As a widow—and an older woman!—she held herself slightly in reserve. Her high-necked dresses, I noticed, were often graced with lace at her throat, gathered and held there by some rather fine brooches and cameos. One

414

day after dinner, however, my landlady stopped me at the head of the staircase as I was heading up to my rooms for a siesta. The *fettucini*—done in Signora Amari's special way, with peas, mushrooms and eggs—had been especially good that day, and I had taken a second helping which, along with with the wine I had drunk, urged me upwards towards a restorative nap.

"Signor Collins," my landlady said, "what do you do for the evening meal?" The discussion of food at such a moment of repletion seemed almost sacrilegious, yet I answered to be polite.

"I usually go to a *trattoria*, Signora, or bring bread and cheese up to my room." She grimaced, as if being slapped in the face. A look of mournful pity came into her eyes.

"I shall have something sent up to you," she said.

"Signora," I said, "I must keep my expenses down."

"There will be no extra charge," my landlady said. "It is my pleasure to assist the strength of a hard-working young scholar. My late husband, the subsecretary of agriculture, admired men of learning. At the time of his death, he was gathering notes for a history of husbandry in medieval Tuscany."

That evening around nine, Signora brought up a tray of *gnocchi* (a pasta dumpling), *carciofi alla giudìa* (artichokes deep-fried in olive oil), and a bowl of *stracciatella* (a Parmesan cheese and egg soup). She placed the tray down on my dressing stand, curtsied, then left the room. This ritual went on for over a month. On the evenings I was at home, either the Signora or one of her daughters would bring something up to me around nine o'clock. There was always some form of pasta: *cannelloni, lasagne, ravioli, tortellini, fettucine al burro,* or a local Roman favorite, *spaghetti alla carbonara,* spaghetti, that is, cooked in an egg sauce with pieces of bacon. Italians, of course, understand the vegetable as no other people on earth. I enjoyed *zucchini ripieni* (stuffed zucchini baked in tomato sauce), *cavoli in agrodolce* (cabbage in sweet and sour sauce), *broccoli alla romana* (broccoli cooked in white wine, olive oil, and garlic), and one compelling favorite, *funghi arrostiti*

415

(mushrooms grilled in garlic and oil). Signora Amari made magnificent *minestrone* or *zuppa di pesce* (fish soup), which varied according to the day's catch. Also from the sea came *aragosta con maionese* (Pontine lobster served with an egg mayonnaise), or *scampi alla griglia* (grilled shrimp, garnished with garlic butter). Some nights there would be a country-style omelette, but I also experienced more ambitious entrees as well: chicken in various forms (to this day I can remember her zestful chicken with peppers), *trippa alla fiorentina* (tripe in tomato sauce), *abbacchio* (suckling lamb, flavored with rosemary), or *abbacchio brodettato* (diced lamb cooked in an egg and lemon sauce). Signora Amari prepared her own *mazzafegati* (pig's liver sausage, seasoned with garlic, pepper, and pine nuts), which I loved to eat on chilly winter nights. She also baked her own pastry—*crostata di ricotta* (cheese pie), *stracci* (paper-thin pastry), *zuppa inglese* (rum cake layered in custard)—all of which I devoured without fear of added adiposity. Being young, I burned the excess nourishment off rather easily, often in the service of Signora Amari herself. My landlady's *zabaione,* by the way (custard drenched in marsala), and her *pere ripiene* (pears stuffed with Gorgonzola cheese), are among the finest desserts I have enjoyed in some forty years of devoted dining.

After some five weeks of such delectable nocturnal fare, I made bold to ask Signora Amari to remain for a visit one evening, as she deposited on my desk a tray containing *fettucini* and a fluffy seafood omelette. Signora Amari enforced a strict no-visiting rule in the pension. Male guests, that is, could entertain female visitors only in the lower parlor. I realized this quite clearly when I invited her to remain for a moment, but I felt that since the Signora was the mistress of the house, she possessed the authority to dispense herself and me from her own rules.

"Please, Signora," I said. "Remain only while I eat. I feel so foolish, even barbaric, eating these wonderful meals in my own company—especially when I am so aware whose kindly, and charming, hands prepared the cuisine." I added "charming" in order to be charming myself. My request sent Signora

Amari into great agitation. She fluttered about the room for a moment, one hand held to the cameo at her throat, like a nun in a state of anxiety. She was dressed nunlike in fact, in a silken black dress, with a run of white lace at her throat. Repairing to a little sideboard at one end of my study, I poured two glasses of Madeira wine from a bottle I kept there as an aid to sleep on restless nights.

"Here," I said, handing her a glass. "Sip this and talk with me as I eat."

"Very well, Signor Collins, just this one glass."

She sat on a very heavily stuffed chair—my reading chair—and sipped her Madeira as I uncovered the dish of *fettucini*. We talked of many things: the various boarders in the pension, odds and ends relating to daily life in Rome, some questions about San Francisco. After finishing my seafood omelette, I went over to the sideboard and fetched the Madeira decanter, placing it on the end table next to her chair. Moving my erstwhile dinner chair over to where she sat, I effected something cozily *tête à tête*, the Madeira decanter between us. I poured her a second glass.

"My late husband, the Subsecretary, loved my cooking, as do you, Signor Collins. I used to love to prepare food for him. He died, in fact, at the dinner table, of a heart attack. He was fifty at the time, some fifteen years older than I, but a very strong and vigorous man, despite the sedentary nature of his occupation. He had an enormous zest for life."

"You must miss him terribly."

Signora Amari poured—and downed—a third glass of Madeira before she spoke.

"I do miss him—in many ways."

Under the soft light of a candle shaded in oiled parchment, the years fell from Signora Amari's face. Thirty-eight is to me, at this point of life, the very essence of youth; but when one is twenty-eight oneself, then thirty-eight is the very essence of maturity. From my point of view at that time, Signora Amari was an Older Woman—and in my room, and sipping her fourth glass of Madeira.

"When you first came here, Signor Collins, I noticed an immediate resemblance to my husband, the late Subsecretary. Like you, the Subsecretary was broadly built, strong, but called to a sedentary occupation. Like you, he loved his books—and his wine, and his meals. I have been very lonely, Signor Collins, and—how shall I say—somewhat nervous, since the Subsecretary's death."

"Nervous?" I asked.

"Yes—nervous, lacking calm, shall we say. My husband could always calm me. He had a way of calming . . . my mind . . . and my . . . my body as well. Do I shock you?"

She had shocked me, but I lied. "Certainly not, Signora," I said, mumbling something about what St. Augustine and St. Thomas Aquinas have written on the secondary purposes of the marital act.

"Ah yes, the marital act, Signor Collins." She paused while I poured both of us some more Madeira. "The marital act belongs exclusively to the married, does it not, even though they often take it so for granted, do they not? But what of us who have known its comforts, grew accustomed to them in fact, and are now deprived of their solace?"

"A difficult moral question, Signora, one demanding both insight and charity."

"Then have them both for me, Signor Collins—insight and charity, I mean. Look at my situation. Do you find me attractive? Speak the truth, I am older, of course, and I have grown somewhat heavier with the years, but do you find me attractive?"

"You are as lovely as your cooking, Signora Amari."

"Thank you, Signor Collins," she said. "Now blow out the candle."

I blew out the candle, and within the half hour I discovered the truth of my initially charitable compliment. Signora Anna Amari was as robust, as subtly spiced, and as directly and deeply satisfying as a good Roman meal.

For a young man of my age and needs, the relationship proved extraordinarily convenient. Once, perhaps twice a

418

week, Signora Amari paid me a visit. (After our arrangement began, incidentally, her cuisine flared forth into unprecedented incandescence.) My landlady made known to me some rather straightforward needs, which I did my best to accommodate, since serving her needs served my own as well. A lively affection grew up between us. The Signora loved to chat with me after our calming process had been successfully completed, our two heads side by side on one of her hand-stitched, embroidered pillow cases, which she brought up for my use. I learned all about her two daughters, Amelia and Josefina, and the good dowry the Subsecretary had left for both of them.

"The Subsecretary was a prudent man," Signora Amari said in relation to the dowries. "And he purchased this pension: as income, he said, just in case he should ever leave me a widow."

To speak frankly and with no suggestion of licentiousness: Signora Amari loved what she referred to as the conjugal act. "You are," she once said, "almost as calming as the Subsecretary."

"Almost?" I asked playfully.

"I loved the Subsecretary," she said. "He was my husband. I surrendered myself to him when I was married at fifteen." She cast her eyes about our disheveled bed. "This, what we have, is good, and I am grateful to you for it, especially now that I am older; but nothing can equal the joy of marital love. The Subsecretary taught me that."

Fortunately, Signora Amari remained for a visit on the night following the day that His Holiness Pope Pius IX consecrated the world to the Sacred Heart, which was also the eve of my unexpectedly scheduled call upon Ryan Patrice. I calmed Signora Amari thrice, grateful for the lessons in intimate feminine responses taught me in Heidelberg by Fraulein Gudrun Wessling. Because of Gudrun, I had learned what a man should do.

"Sebastian," Anna said, stroking my cheek. "Even the Subsecretary rarely showed such ardor."

"It must be the *mazzafegati*," I said.

419

"I made it with sage this time. I must use sage more often."

The next morning, sitting in the outer foyer of the general headquarters of the Paris Foreign Mission Society, waiting for the brother porter to fetch Ryan Patrice, I sipped a cup of black coffee which Brother Silvano offered me before disappearing through an oaken door to the cloister within. As Brother swung open the door, I glimpsed an interior patio and garden. A priest in cassock and biretta—a young man about my own age—was walking there, breviary in hand. After a brief wait, one cup of coffee's worth, the door swung open and Ryan Patrice entered the reception room. He also appeared very clerical in cassock and biretta, like the young priest saying his prayers in the garden.

"Sebastian Collins, I am delighted to see you after so many years," Patrice said.

"Nearly a decade. When I returned to Harvard in 1870, you were already gone," I replied.

"I left for France immediately after the fall of Rome, my work in America being finished. The superior general recalled me to Paris."

"You've been in Paris ever since?" I asked.

"No. I've traveled much, especially in the Far East. We are opening new apostolates there. Within a week's time, I myself shall be leaving for Indo-China. Father General has at last given me a missionary assignment. I wanted to leave for the missions as soon as my . . . my political work . . . came to an end; but the General kept me in Paris as his assistant. Now, tell me about yourself."

I told him about myself, and it took about a half hour. A bell rang from within.

"I must be going soon," he said. "We have a community conference at eleven. Are you angry with me, Sebastian?"

"For what?" I asked—deceptively, for I knew exactly what he was talking about.

"For—for my precipitousness regarding your vocation, for the years you lost—for Mentana."

420

"Not at all, Father," I said, not knowing whether or not I meant what I was saying. "I survived the war; and other than Mentana, my years in the Zouaves were a welcomed hiatus before I assumed the burdens of adulthood, and the matter of exactly what I am to do with my life is as of yet undecided, so I cannot hold you responsible for aught save some very good suggestions."

"Thank you, Sebastian. I must confess to you most solemnly that I now believe that we were wrong in the matter of the Sovereignty. The Church's mission is in the realm of spirit, not in the realm of earthly dominion." The cloister bell rang a second time. "You are not chosen to be one of us, Sebastian; but remember us, remember me, kindly, in your prayers. I shall be sailing for the Far East at the end of the week."

"Never forget me, Ryan Patrice," I said. He embraced me warmly for a moment, then looked me full in the face. I saw the old flame glow momentarily in his eyes, and for a moment feared that he might ask me to join him in Southeast Asia.

"You and I are on different paths, Sebastian Collins," he said. "We are both men of imagination and sensate passion— and we both hunger for God. We are also both of us sinners. Go your way. I shall go mine. You will have the world. I shall leave the glory of the world behind. Both of our paths are fraught with danger. There are no guarantees in either of our choices, but we have made those choices, and we are at least ready for our respective journeys." Something compelled me to kiss his hand, as one would kiss the hand of a saint. Despite everything, I loved Ryan Patrice. I loved everything that he stood for.

"I shall never forget you," I said. Patrice opened the great oaken door and vanished into the cloister within.

Walking back to my pension, my mind unaccountably filled with images from the summer of 1870. I remembered how I stood as sentry in St. Peter's Basilica near the tomb of Innocent XI on 18 July, 1870. The basilica teemed with the prelates of the world. Outside, a ferocious thunderstorm raged, darkening the greatest church in Christendom. After the

421

Mass of the Holy Spirit was completed, the voting began. Five hundred and thirty-three of the prelates assembled voted for the Infallibility. Only two voted no. His Holiness, attired in the full regalia of his pontifical office, read aloud the Declaration of Infallibility by the flickering light of a candelabrum placed near his throne. Putting down the text of the Declaration, he intoned the *Te Deum*.

That thunder of Roman skies became a thunder of Italian guns on the morning of 20 September. Called back to France to assist in the disastrous war with Prussia, the imperial French garrison had withdrawn from the Eternal City. The French gone, the Italians attacked. At five-fifteen on the morning of the twentieth, Italian artillery began a five-hour assault on the walls of Rome. By ten that morning, the Porta Pia had been breached. Towards noon, Italian troops entered the city by that devastated gate. General Kanzler signed the terms of surrender at three o'clock in the afternoon. After a thousand years, Papal Rome was no more.

Chapter 11

I T HAS BEEN a very busy summer. Not that the Claudio Carpino gubernatorial campaign is in any better shape at the end of it. It's now early fall and Soutane is even further ahead in the polls. Tiny Roncola keeps pestering me, but I've told him to wait. What he proposes, I tell him, is only a last-minute desperation gesture—one that could backfire. I tell him this time and again.

"The earlier we do it, the better," Tiny insists. "The longer Soutane campaigns around the state, the more he seems Santa Barbara's answer to St. Francis of Assisi. If you try to leak these pictures two months from now, no one will believe you. They'll say they are faked."

"Maybe they are," I said. Tiny said nothing in reply. He merely shrugged his shoulders and left my office.

The pageant committee isn't getting anywhere either, although we have been meeting intermittently over the summer, trying to put something together for next month's formal kick-off of the campaign. We've met in Barry Credish's office over at Public Utilities some three or four times. The first meeting we cut the proposed itinerary down by seventy-five percent. As a retired brigadier general, Credish knows something about logistics. He made it clear right away that you can only get in and out of three, perhaps four, places in one day in California.

"I'll get you out of San Diego by nine and into Los Angeles by ten-thirty or a quarter to eleven. You can make Civic Center San Francisco by one. After that, it's one more place in the afternoon, then Eureka by nightfall. Forget all that business about hitting three or four extra places of historical importance. It can't be done."

"So much for the historical pageant," said Terry Shane. We were sitting at the bar in Raffles down from City Hall at the Fox Plaza, the two of us getting a little smashed on vodka tonics. We'd just emerged from a meeting in which Barry Scorse called the pageant idea a lot of doubledomed bullshit.

"What the hell you got the Mayor up in Grass Valley for?" he asked.

"Josiah Royce was born there," I said feebly.

"Who in the fuck is Josiah Royce?" Scorse asked. "And how many goddamned votes are there in Grass Valley?" Scorse, as usual, had a point.

"Scorse has a point," Terry Shane said over our third vodka tonic. "What would the Mayor be doing up in Grass Valley in his Brioni suit and Gucci shoes?"

"Getting away from Esmeralda," I said.

"Now that makes sense," Terry said. "She called me the other day and right out of the blue says that she knows for sure that we're having orgies in the Mayor's office every afternoon after work. I guess she imagines that we all strip down after work, the Mayor included, and get out the Mazola oil."

"I'll take Ursula Iraslav," I said.

"You won't even be invited if you don't get ahold of this Marshall Square controversy. It's coming down to a hardball situation. Scorse told the Mayor the other day to quit fooling around. He wants the Mayor to get you to give a direct statement to the press coming out against Mabel Storm and The Friends of Books. 'Tell that doubledome Norton to say that the Library should be renovated and expanded to the rear,' Scorse says to the Mayor, 'and that the PAC belongs on Marshall Square. If he doesn't play ball, can his ass.' "

"That would totally alienate me from my constituency," I said. "I'd be the Quisling of the library world."

424

"You're not going to last after Carpino goes anyway," Shane said, "so why not prove yourself loyal to the Mayor?"

"Why hasn't he asked me to do it?"

"That's the decent thing about him, I guess. Scorse would have had your hide nailed to the wall weeks ago."

"Maybe it will be easier in Sacramento," I said.

"Unless something dramatic happens in the next couple of months, there ain't going to be any Sacramento for any of us. The closest we'll be getting to Sacramento will be the long line at the state unemployment office."

"What if Soutane gets caught in a scandal?" I asked.

"Like what?" Shane shot back, draining off his third vodka tonic. "Getting caught in a McDonald's?"

"No, something personal."

"By personal you mean sex."

"Perhaps."

"Listen, Soutane could ball Tara Malone at high noon in front of the Beverly Hills Hotel and it would redound to his credit. Subconsciously, people want their politicans to resemble their movie stars: indulged, I mean, in the matter of sex. It gives people a psychic release—like a spectator sport."

"What if the sex were . . . shall we say unnatural?"

"You mean fruit stuff?"

"Perhaps."

"That could stop him in his tracks. Californians are progressive, but they're not ready for a fruit in the governor's mansion. Do you know anything I could use? Soutane's weird, but he doesn't act like a fruit."

"No, I don't know of anything," I said. "I'm just speculating. You think it could hurt, huh?"

"Yeah, like crazy—if it got out in the right way."

Shane then began to sound very much like Tiny Roncola. "By the right way, I mean that such a drop should not seem like a smear coming from us. You'd have to get the militant gays to challenge Soutane to come out of the closet."

"How would you do that?" I asked disingenuously.

"By slipping the facts of Soutane's fruitery to them on the sly. What's all this, anyway? You know something?"

425

"Not really, just rumors. But if I got ahold of more than rumors, would you use it?"

"I'd sure as hell think about it," Shane said morosely over vodka tonic number four. "We're in shit shape, campaignwise."

Raffles is perhaps the darkest bar in San Franicsco, but not so dark that I didn't recognize Harry Shaw and Albert Esau sitting cozily over drinks at one of the far tables.

"Esau's probably slipping Shaw a lot of anti-Carpino dirt," Shane said when I pointed out the duo.

Harry Shaw is a short man, some five feet five inches tall. He wears a 1930s style Clark Gable mustache and combs whatever is left of his hair straight back across his head. Seeing us, he stood up and called us over to his table.

"Bring the liars' dice along," he said.

Esau seemed as close to sheepish as his innate brashness allowed.

"We don't want to interrupt," Shane said lamely.

"Interrupt hell," Shaw said. "Esau and I were just chatting about city government. I used to do a lot more municipal stuff back in the old days, but I've laid off it lately. Now I'm getting interested again—even to the point of doing my own leg work."

Harry Shaw hasn't done his own leg work in years, so he must have something up his sleeve. Shaw has assistants to run down his items. It's rare to see him out hustling like this. He must have been playing up to Esau for a definite purpose.

We rolled liars' dice and I lost. It cost me eight dollars for a round of drinks. By the time I got home that night I was feeling no pain. The three of us had sat through a long, rambling monologue by Harry Shaw as to how Claudio Carpino was screwing up San Francisco. Many of Shaw's lines sounded as if they had been fed to him by Esau ten minutes before we had come over to their table: a lot of stuff about highrise and zoning laws that destroy the neighborhood feeling of the old town.

"This used to be a hell of a place," Shaw announced, "a real special town. Now look at it—an imitation New York. You used to feel special about living here. Now, forget it. Carpino has given us highrise. He must have a piece of it somewhere, mustn't he? Otherwise, why would he bust his ass so to give every developer what they want, no questions asked? He's a godfather, that one. You see him around town with his sons, the boys casting heavy, ominous looks around as if they were casing the place. It's so Sicilian—all those dark suits and black cars and clannishness. I hear that Esmeralda's gone bonkers."

No comment, obviously, from any of us.

"I hear also that she makes weird phone calls to the Mayor's office."

The three of us, Esau as piously silent as Shane and I, stared at the ice in our drinks. There's never any percentage in talking to Harry Shaw. How can such a ratty little man be read by a half million people a day and a million people on Sunday? How can this Ben Turpin figure with the sketchy pencil mustache divided over the lips be the chief mythologizer for the city that produced Bret Harte, Josiah Royce, Isadora Duncan, Sebastian Collins? Such, I suppose, is the power of the press—or perhaps it is an indication of how thin, false, tensile, and attenuated the civilization of San Francisco has become.

"You don't expect us to talk against our boss, do you?" I asked, made nervous by the silence.

"He'll dump you without a slam-bam, thanks ma'am," Shaw said, grinning. "When his political career is finished next June, he'll walk away from it—and from you people also, and from San Francisco too, without a second thought."

"Who are you supporting for the next mayor?" Shane asked.

"John Como," Shaw said.

That made good sense. State Senator John Como is the sort of good-looking sport Harry Shaw, himself being small and homely, has always admired. A liberal Democratic attorney, John Como runs with the Jeremiah Jones—Ford Booth crowd, which is a pretty fast track. San Francisco's dynamic black assemblyman and his haberdasher pal Ford Booth are San Francisco's leading swingers. Harry Shaw delights in covering their capers—with discreet omissions: the stag parties, the

427

Carmel tennis ranch and Beverly Hills Hotel weekends, the late-night hijinks around Sacramento after a tough bill has been put to bed and it's time to bed down some of the legislative assistants as well. Why is it, anyway, that the left-liberals, who are supposed to pump piss in their hearts for the poor, have the most swinging, affluent lifestyles? Jeremiah Jones is constantly getting the public money—other people's money—spent on poverty programs, while being himself deeply into the pursuit and enjoyment of the perks of decadent capitalism. Jones makes a big deal—or rather Harry Shaw makes a big deal—of his Maserati, his $600 Ford Booth suits, his toothsome and complaisant white chicks, his late-night antics at Dodd's, a chichi downtown disco where the Jeremiah Jones Hustle is the most popular step. I guess Jones is making a complex statement. Number one: he's saying, "I'll play fancy nigger all I want to, and if you don't like it, kiss my ass." His flamboyance, from this point of view, is an act of anti-honky aggression. Secondly, he could be saying: "The system's corrupt, so I'll get mine while the getting's good." Thirdly, of course, he could just be enjoying himself—taking frank advantage of his black constituency's expectation that he be a player, a political Shaft who drives fast cars and balls white chicks in some sociological ritual of asserted equality. Probably all three levels of motivation are pertinent. Jeremiah Jones is one smart dude. He realizes, ultimately, that his affluent white liberal constituency expect to be entertained, whether that entertainment consists of the pleasures of a moderately provoked conscience when Jeremiah Jones tells them how hard black people have it because of honky prejudice, or the more constant entertainment of watching San Francisco's dynamic black assemblyman leading the capering pack of his hangers-on, which, in addition to clothier Ford Booth, included State Senator John Como, who most likely will be the next mayor of San Francisco. Jeremiah Jones is white San Francisco's demiurge, its Merry Andrew, its struttin', prancin' number one minstrel man and jive artist. Como regards Jones with a species of awe, both because of Jones's virtuosity and stamina as a dissipater (one four-day

428

postelection session of chicks and cocaine has already entered local legend), but also because of Jones's ability to rev up the local black population and deliver it to a candidate. With Harry Shaw and Jeremiah Jones in his corner, John Como's got the mayorship cinched.

"I could throw $250,000 of my own money into the race," Johnboy Turfer told me last June when I ran into him at the Presidio Officers' Club during the San Francisco birthday party. "Now that's power."

As Jimmy Driscoll says, you need either a lot of people or a lot of money to win. Johnboy Turfer has got the money, but John Como has got the people. I've been watching something happening these past four years in San Francisco. The city has become a mecca for America's discontented, for those who cannot fit in elsewhere: the gays and the lesbians who couldn't fit into midwestern towns, the young professionals who opted out of the Darwinian competition of the East, the sixties' holdovers who watched the dream of Aquarius die during the Nixon years and headed west to San Francisco where it all started in the first place in hopes of keeping the faith alive, like Christians taking to the catacombs in times of Roman persecution, awaiting a better day. San Franciscans like this, the majority of this town, are by definition liberal, even radical, in their politics. Until the 1960s, most mayors of San Francisco were Republican; but that's all changed now. The culture I came from, blue collar, lower middle class, has scattered to Santa Rosa, Hayward, Burlingame. In its place has grown up a resort city for alienated newcomers. The culture they are creating is based upon consumption, lifestyle, and—in the case of the radicals—political agitation for its own sake. Claudio Carpino is the last mayor to be elected by the now-passing provincial San Francisco.

I sometimes think that I should get my ass out of this town—live in Europe for a while, perhaps Italy. What is best about San Francisco, after all, is its refraction of Mediterranean culture, and that's fast going down the tubes. The envisioned San Francisco of James Phelan's and Sebastian Collins's imaginative aspirations just hasn't happened—or it happened for them only as a dream, a wish fulfillment, and now is no more. The San Franciscans of that era foresaw a new Florence, a new Rome. They cherished the city because of this hope, seeing themselves as citizens of a city-state in dialogue with the great cities of the past. Look how solidly they built everything with such grand assurance: Golden Gate Park, City Hall, the Public Library itself. The Hetch Hetchy Project alone is a marvel of engineering—a dam, aqueduct, and reservoir system rivaling anything in ancient Rome. That's what they were—Phelan, Collins, the rest of them. They were American Romans who had traveled to Europe's Greece, returning with the desire to recreate a Mediterranean city in an American setting. Even when the idea of an Atheneum died, Sebastian Collins kept plugging away. His dreams, his sense of civilization, never abandoned him. The next generation—I'm thinking of men like Jimmy Rolph, and Charles Kendrick who got the Opera House built—kept these dreams alive also. Such high provincial types lasted, in fact, through the time of George Christopher, mayor from 1956 to 1964; but they're dead now or retired—their naive civic idealism replaced by a shallow, hedonistic cynicism that cloaks itself in the mantle of insincere liberal rhetoric. Sebastian Collins took his pleasures where and when he could (my God, didn't he!), yet his moral coherence as a person remained intact. Obsessed by civilization, by the grand manner and the art past, Collins could never degenerate into empty cynicism, no matter how often he failed his best ideals.

John Como, Jeremiah Jones, Harry Shaw, haberdasher Ford Booth, the entire crowd that is on the verge of taking over this town, stands for nothing much beyond the immediate possession of power. If I had the guts to face up to the truth, I suppose that I would have to put Claudio Carpino in the same category as the rest—only Carpino's offense is worse because he knows better. As a boy at the Salesian Boys' Club, Carpino was educated in the Mediterranean ideals of high provincial San Francisco. Yet what has he really done as mayor—anything comparable, I mean, to what Phelan and Rolph accomplished? Carpino strikes the pose, the *bella figura,* in the direction of creative urbanism; but it just isn't there. First of all, he is too distracted by the desire for higher office, wasting his time running for a governorship he hasn't a chance of winning. Secondly, even if he was minding the store, he couldn't get much done: San Francisco has changed too much in its basic population to feel anything remotely resembling the Judeo-Christian, humanistic urges that animated Phelan and Collins. What a stupid fool I was ever to allow myself to come under Carpino's spell! How could someone past thirty be so naive? I sometimes see myself as the last of the high provincials, an accident of time, a nineteenth-century San Franciscan cast miserably on the far shore of the twentieth. It's not Carpino's fault, so why blame him? Had I seen the Mayor right off as just another grasping wheeler-dealer, albeit a brilliant one, I would have saved myself a lot of trouble. But how, then, would I have learned that history is no guide to the labyrinthine present? At least now I know for certain that Sebastian Collins's San Francisco is lost forever. On that score, I'm plenty wised up.

I tried to be a little more optimistic, publicly, at Father Smythe's symposium this August when I gave my lecture "Sebastian Collins and San Francisco's Hopeful *Fin de Siècle.*" Father Smythe set the theme of this year's annual symposium as "Three Literary San Franciscans—Josiah Royce, Charles Warren Stoddard, and Sebastian Collins." He asked James Howell, the director of the California Historical Society, to lecture on Royce and Professor Harold Folger, director of the Bancroft Library in Berkeley, to lecture on Charles Stoddard. Father Smythe has been conducting these symposiums for some ten years now. They consist of three days of lectures, discussions, and dinner parties at various choice locations. I invited Deborah to be my guest for the final evening, which was held at the Palace of the Legion of Honor on Land's End.

Father Desmond Smythe is a most learned bookman and librarian. In the manner of some Jesuits, he is also something of a *bon vivant:* a lover of erudition, fine bindings, good wine, and accomplished company. I can easily say that Desmond

Smythe is perhaps the most totally civilized man I know: developed, that is, spiritually, intellectually, imaginatively—and totally at home in the world. As a young Jesuit scholastic in the late 1930s, teaching at St. Ignatius High School, Smythe knew Sebastian Collins, who was then in his late eighties.

"I consider myself Collins's last pupil," Desmond Smythe once told me. "I'd walk over to his flat on Clayton Street, just down from Fulton. Bedridden, Collins spent his time swathed in blankets on a *chaise longue* which his daughter had moved for him into the sunny back room of the flat. Collins loved the view of the St. Ignatius towers he had through the enormous French windows that swept across one side of the room. He'd doze there much of the time, but he would read also when his strength was up to it—and he loved visitors."

"What would you talk about?" I asked.

"Books, mainly—and the history of San Francisco—and now and then something about religion. 'I suppose it's high time I think about the Last Things,' Collins used to say. 'Time?' I would answer. 'Perhaps—but not high time.' We would both laugh. 'I'll wait until you're ordained,' he once said, 'then I'll be assured of a tolerant confessor for my final shriving.' Collins died long before I was ordained, but not before we enjoyed a number of memorable conversations."

It's no exaggeration to say that I can sense something of the touch of Sebastian Collins in Desmond Smythe: a certain passionate humanism, I mean, together with an omnivorous appetite for learning in all its variety. As a bibliophile, Smythe loves books and libraries; but more than this, he reveres the energies that lie behind the making of books and libraries— the headlong desire, that is, to memorialize experience, to rescue truth and pleasure from the devouring vortex of time.

"Don't be embarrassed of pleasure," Smythe is always saying. "Delight is our primary link with creation. In the end, Aquinas tells us, we shall possess God Himself in pleasure and delight."

Smythe inaugurated the symposia series mainly to please himself, and they do that enormously. They also serve as

432

fund-raisers for the University of San Francisco. Walter Muir Whitehill, the bearded director of the Boston Atheneum, flies out from Boston to serve as moderator. The symposium format consists of a morning lecture, followed by the response of a panel of commentators. After lunch, there is an hour of general discussion—then the evening *soirée.*

"Since next year is the two hundredth anniversary of San Francisco," Father Smythe remarked to Harold Folger, Jim Howell, and me over lunch at the Bohemian Club where we met to discuss our participation, "let's do something concerning turn-of-the-century San Francisco." By the end of the luncheon we had decided upon the triad of Royce, Collins, and Stoddard. Each of these writers was raised in frontier San Francisco and had flourished at the turn of the century. They were, in fact, all three of them friends, having known each other since boyhood.

When it came my turn to speak, I was a little nervous in my initial delivery because Deborah was in the audience. I didn't want her to think of me as a pompous academic. I did manage, however, to make what I consider a number of relevant observations. Stoddard, Royce, and Collins, I pointed out, were each of them high provincials—and each showed a particular pattern of high provincial response. Royce internationalized himself through an intellectual conversion to German philosophical idealism. Psychologically, Royce's theory of loyalty was at bottom a reverse compensation for his disloyalty to his California background, for having, in personal terms, fled the scene of his father's failure. Sebastian Collins, on the other hand, tried to graft a nonsystematic, but reasonably coherent, philosophy of Mediterranean aestheticism on his local circumstances. Royce used German idealism as a mode of symbolic return to his repudiated province. Collins used the Mediterranean metaphor. Collins's books, I pointed out, are concerned either with Italy (or Italy's spiritualization, Roman Catholicism) or with California and San Francisco, which he sees in Italian terms. In some of his work—the little book on California wine, for instance—the two sectors of Collins's imagination coalesce into one setting and place.

433

California is Southern Europe, and Southern Europe is California. Collins embraced the baroque as a field of scholarship, I argued, because the baroque seemed the antithesis of his frontier San Francisco circumstances; paradoxically, however, the baroque provided Collins with the very analogy that made California, more specifically, San Francisco, an arena worthy of his efforts.

Charles Stoddard, on the other hand, was finally defeated by provincial circumstances. Praised too early and too often, Stoddard never internalized Atlantic or European standards. When he did encounter standards beyond California, specifically when he left for Europe in the early 1870s, Stoddard was capable merely of internalizing Europe as a species of the picturesque: a romantic, dreamy *mise en scène* for aesthetic posturing—not Royce's coliseum of philosophical combat, or Collins's museum without walls urging to the systematic study of the art past. Of the three, Charlie Stoddard was the most confirmed hometown boy.

"Is that what you are," Deborah asked me at the Legion of Honor pre-dinner cocktail party, "a hometown boy?"

"It might be what I'm afraid of becoming," I said, astonished at my honesty. "One of those used-to-be promising San Franciscans who now make a career of going to lunch, who are kept alive by an occasional mention in one of Harry Shaw's columns."

The California Palace of the Legion of Honor (an exact replica of the original Palace in Paris) sits on a knoll overlooking the Pacific. The building itself, a temple to European civilization, is as dramatic as the site. We enjoyed our cocktails in the rotunda where original casts of Rodin's *Burghers of Calais* and *Balzac Rising from His Bath,* on loan from the Norton Simon Museum in Pasadena, set the tone of the Legion's largely French collection.

As a personality, Father Smythe attracts the shattered remnants of San Francisco's once mighty Catholic establishment. The symposia (I've been to two of them) can sometimes seem like a London gathering of *ancien régime emigrés* where the talk is all of that horrid beast Napoleon. Mrs. P.D. St.

434

Maurice attended this year's event, as well as her sister the Princess di Capistrano: not the mission, mind you, but the tiny island off Majorca, whence the Prince di Capistrano emigrated to San Francisco in 1947, working his way over—for the experience, he later said—as a stoker of coal in the lower regions of a Marseilles freighter. Some say the Prince's title materialized halfway across the Atlantic, yet as in the case of John Como's automotive adventures, San Francisco is by and large indulgent in the matter of a shaky title, as long as too much is not made of it. A title looks so good, you must remember, on club membership lists or on the rosters of honorary committees sponsoring charity events. Harry Shaw's friend, Mark Yeats, for instance, wears the regimental tie and blazer crest of the Guards regiment with which he is supposed to have fought as a commissioned officer in World War II. There are those, however, who say that Private Mark Yeats sat out the conflict tending an anti-aircraft gun in the Aleutian Islands—but no matter; San Francisco is ever indulgent in such matters. Whether or not Mark Yeats is legally entitled to wear the green kilt and the dress blue tunic piped in white leather of a captain of Border Guards, Yeats does make a smashing appearance each Empire Day when he shows up in this uniform at the British Consul's reception.

Speaking of clothes, Deborah herself wore a graceful *crêpe de Chine* floor-length dress in the Isadora Duncan style, which she was totally entitled to wear by virtue of her neck, her shoulders, her arms, her bosom, her everything, all of this, all of her, I mean, set off by the soft and flowing mauve material that delectably contrasted with the honey-brown of her tanned skin. At least our Tinsley Island sojourn over the Fourth had helped Deborah's tan.

"No chance of your revealing your tattoo this evening?" I had asked when I picked her up at six-thirty, remembering halfway up the stairs that I had left my keys in the Porsche and that there was already a good chance that someone had made off with my car.

"One thing that I like about older men is that they pick you up and take you places. It's like a Tab Hunter, Natalie Wood

435

movie. The answer is: No. The tattoo would prove too much for the kinds of people you've said will be at the Legion of Honor."

"They're not that stuffy," I said.

"You do seem to know a lot of stuffy people. To get back to my point: men my own age, under thirty, never take you anywhere. They meet you places, Dutch treat, or they come over, looking for a free evening. If by chance they do shell out for an evening's entertainment, perhaps even something as lavish as dinner, their assumption is that it will soon be time for beddy-boo."

"I sure as hell have found out differently, haven't I?"

"I find you manageable, that's all."

"To get back to my point, when shall I see your tattoo again?"

"You saw it on Tinsley Island."

I let the matter drop. Besides, I was grateful to find the Porsche where I had left it on Alabama Street.

"What do you think of Balzac?" Deborah asked me a half-hour later as we stood beneath Rodin's heroic statue of the great French novelist, placed in the central rotunda of the Legion of Honor.

"He was fat and he got a lot of ass," I said.

"How vulgar. He also managed to write a lot of excellent novels."

"He was politically an ultra conservative," I said.

"Well then," she said, "I see half a comparison. You're fat. You're also an ultra conservative. But you've only written one book, and you're not getting much ass."

"Not from you at least."

The Princess di Capistrano approached, with Father Smythe in tow, like an attendant *abbé* in a Port-Royal *soirée*. The conversation turned to Father Smythe's plans to spend his sabbatical next year as an honorary choir monk in a Benedictine abbey in the south of France.

"I'll read and I'll pray," he said. "I'll drink the wine of Rabelais country. I'll explore every nook and cranny of the south of France. I'm rereading all of Rabelais and François Mauriac in preparation."

San Francisco's jurist-about-town, Justice Terence O'Brien of the California District Court of Appeals, sauntered by, leading an absolutely ravishing creature by the hand. She followed him like a Sabine woman ecstatic in her sixth month of captivity. At dinner we sat next to Justice O'Brien and his gorgeous Sabine, Monique by name—well, Monica actually, as she admitted halfway through the meal. She changed her name to Monique when she moved north to San Francisco and got into the interior design business. Santa Monica born: Monica from Santa Monica, a luxurious southern California girl, seemingly fey but really rather bright, honey-fleshed and tan all over, laughing appreciatively at the Justice's jokes. At forty-two, O'Brien is the youngest appeals court justice in the state of California. Divorced in some dim time in his late twenties, he has for the past decade been the most sought-after dinner party guest in San Francisco, famous for his droll stories. Seated to his left, Deborah soon came under O'Brien's spell, as did the entire table.

"Why can't you talk like that?" she asked after dinner.

"O'Brien is erudite and witty. He's also got a sixty-thousand-dollar-a-year job for life."

"What has that got to do with it?"

"Everything."

"Nothing, you mean. What's important about him is that he obviously tries to give other people pleasure. You told me he was a coveted guest. I now can see why."

"Pleasure—such as in the case of Monica?"

"Yes—also in her case. Generous people are generous every which way. I find him very attractive, but don't be jealous. You're attractive in your own way as well. Only learn to relax."

Since we had a half-hour before going to the downstairs theater for a chamber music concert, I suggested a walk, even though the fog had long since rolled in over Land's End. Deborah put her coat on—a blue naval officer's greatcoat

437

which she had bought at an army surplus store on Market Street. The bold effect of all those gold buttons against solid blue wool made her look like Ali MacGraw in the movie *Love Story*. Only Deborah Tanner was not going to die.

"You look like your mother in 1943," I said, suppressing the Jenny Cavalieri, Ali MacGraw comparison, "a Wave JG reporting for duty at the Phoenix recuperation hospital, very smart in her privately tailored uniform." We strolled past the cast of Rodin's *The Thinker* that sits in the courtyard of the Palace of the Legion of Honor.

"He must be cold," Deborah said, "sitting out here in the fog with no clothes on. I wonder what he's thinking about?"

"About fate, foreknowledge, and free will," I said. "About the lost meaning of the past, the obscurities of the present, the complete and utter unknowableness of the future."

"It sounds as if he is wasting his time," Deborah said. "He should think of something more practical and not worry himself so much over what he can't figure out. He should get busy and try to think up ways to make the world a better place for his fellow human beings."

"He should go into social work then?"

"No—just make an effort to make his thought useful in a human context. Too much abstract thought dehumanizes."

"Too little thought has its own problems as well."

I put my arm around her shoulders as we walked. Since she was wearing heels, I was forced to reach up some and stretch my arm to reach around her. We walked under an intermittently appearing moon. A river of fog was sweeping in across the Golden Gate. It wasn't too cold, only foggy-chilly in that special San Francisco way. The now-and-then moonlight highlighted the two heroic equestrians that stand guard before the Palace, *El Cid* and *Joan of Arc*.

"Who did those?" Deborah asked.

"A woman—Anna Hyatt Huntington—she's still alive I believe, in her nineties, living in Connecticut."

Strolling across the fog-moistened grass, we stood under the statue of Saint Joan of Arc. The Maid of Orleans's helmeted

438

head, half-lost in a chiaroscuro of intermittent darkness and moonlight, tilted upward in an exaltation of prayerful victory. A slight wind began to push the fog along so that it created the impression that Deborah and I were standing on the bottom of a flowing river of light. The cypress trees that line Land's End faded in and out of the fog at various intervals. When the cypress trees were dark, they seemed like watching prophets. Illumined by moonlight, they shimmered mysteriously, as if on a stage setting for Act One of Bellini's *Norma,* in which the druid priestesses stand beneath the sacred trees ready to offer sacrifice.

"Now there was a woman," said Deborah, walking slowly around the base of the monument.

"They burned her at the stake for her assertiveness."

"But only after she had accomplished what she had set out to do. Better death at the stake than sixty years in a thatched hut, breeding children like a sow."

El Cid stared solemnly in the direction of the twinkling lights of San Francisco. His gaze seemed set upon the illumined towers of St. Ignatius Church as if El Cid were about to lead a charge in an easterly direction to liberate the city from the Infidel.

"Now it's my turn," I said. "El Cid married the woman he loved and he and his wife brought two magnificent daughters into the world, whom El Cid doted over; his marriage, his wife, his children, however, never prevented him from always behaving like the complete hero that he was."

"He was a man, remember. I wonder what Mrs. Cid had to say about it, especially regarding the matter of his frequent absences from home, when he was busy hacking up all those poor Moors."

From the base of the *El Cid* we could look through the stand of cypress trees to our left and see the lights of the Golden Gate Bridge sweeping across to Marin County. Crossing the oval piazza facing the museum, we headed into a grove of cypress trees. Once there, we had a clear view of the bridge, and we could hear the breaking of the surf on the rocks hundreds of feet below us. I turned Deborah towards me and we kissed—not ferociously or greedily, but with a gentle-sad tenderness between the two of us. I buried my face into her hair, awash in her scent and the feel of her Medusa curls on my face. Pressing my lips against her ear, I felt the bones of her skull, marveling at the fragile but sturdy architecture of it all: this skin, this flesh, this engineering of bone and tissue that keeps us alive for a Maytime brief time in an incomprehensibly vast and frightening universe and torments us with desperate dreams of happiness.

"I'm sorry," I said.

"For what?"

"The misunderstanding at Tinsley. For the way I misbehaved."

"Forget it. It was a learning experience for both of us."

"I had no idea," I said, but then I stopped myself, because in truth I did have an idea of her situation. I had sensed it immediately last June when she bent down to feed the swans before the Palace of Fine Arts. I sure as hell bungled Tinsley.

"Let's change the subject," she said, taking my arm and stepping out in that unmistakable way of hers towards the museum. "What time is it?"

"Nine o'clock."

"The concert will be starting any minute now. Let's get back."

"Are you enjoying yourself?"

"You seem to know a lot of older people—but yes, I am."

"I'm on the other side of the divide—by choice, you understand. There are people my age, thirty-five, who run with the younger crowd; but I have little in common with them. I find their music unintelligible and too loud. I'm appalled by their lack of manners or education. I'm bored by parties where everyone sits around smoking pot and staring vacantly at each other, where conversation consists of intermittent monosyllables. I can't abide their naive leftish politics, with Nixon as the guy in the black hat and Woodward and Bernstein wearing white hats; but deeper than this—because

440

I've got no special brief for Nixon—I'm driven up the wall by their total ignorance of the structure and purposes of the American republic, as initially envisioned by men of the caliber of Jefferson, Madison, Adams, and Hamilton, and refounded in the carnage of the Civil War. Too many people think the republic was something cooked up yesterday by Ehrlichman, Haldeman, and Tricky Dick as a conspiracy to thwart the imminent arrival of Woodstock America. So I gravitate to older people, because they at least are capable of complexity and discernment and respect for the mystery of things, politics included."

"Ladies and gentlemen," Deborah said, "our national anthem. By the way, what did you do during Vietnam?"

"I was at Harvard."

"On a draft deferment."

"Yes—a deferment."

"Learning about the finer purposes of the republic while the less privileged were getting shot. Let's not talk about politics. I get depressed—about you, I mean."

Deborah doesn't know how right she is and why—the Soutane pictures, I mean. Even letting the whole mess drift on like this (Tiny called the other day, persistent as usual) ill befits a defender of the American republic as a moral and imaginative enterprise. One can hardly think of John Adams involving himself in such scummy proceedings. I'm a bag of wind, that's for sure.

I'll never forget, incidentally, the way Joan of Arc and El Cid stood so bravely on guard in the moonlight as I returned arm in arm with Deborah to the museum. The two heroes held their swords on high as if in defiant defense of whatever is left of European civilization in San Francisco. We joined everyone in the theater, slipping into our seats just as the Stanford Chamber Music Ensemble came on stage. They played an exhausting but richly rewarding piece by Ravel.

"By the way," Deborah whispered to me during the first intermission, "you've got to stop Mabel Storm from destroying what's left of the Library. Get her to cut a deal with the

441

Performing Arts Center people: Marshall Square in exchange for their backing for a bond issue to improve the Library. That's what all the librarians want."

"I'll tell you the whole sad story on the way home," I said. The chamber music group next played a luminously romantic piece by Schubert. Sentimental slob that I am, I took Deborah's hand into mine midway through the music. I never realized until then what large hands she has.

"You're a fat, horny fascist," Deborah whispered into my ear. "And a chauvinist pig, and you're not taking ahold of your life in the way that you should. And you have no idea of who I really am as a person."

"I love you," I whispered back.

"I love you too," Deborah said, staring straight ahead. "I suppose it's because I'm from Arizona."

"For God's sake, shush!" hissed the Princess de Capistrano.

This summer was my third Bohemian Grove encampment. It was also my most enjoyable. Hearing of my interest in Sebastian Collins, Dr. Al Schumate invited me to stay at Esplandian Camp, where Collins was a member, along with Senator Phelan and Downey Harvey. Esplandian Camp sits perched on stilts midway up the side of Snob Hill, surrounded by redwood trees that soar overhead. On the lower of its two decks are lavatories, sinks, showers, and storage facilities. In Collins's day the camp attendants bunked down there as well. The top deck supports two cabins and a semiopen area between them, covered by an awning, where there is a bar set up. Cushioned benches run around three sides of the top deck. Down one side runs a twenty-five-foot table, cut from one giant pine tree, donated to the camp by one of the members, Al Baxter, who is in the lumber business. In Collins's day there were no permanent cabins on the top deck. Striped tents were put up each year and a rattan rug was laid on the floor. Since Esplandian is named after the knight-errant hero of Montalvo's early sixteenth-century Spanish romance, the motif of the camp is theatrically Spanish. Heraldic shields decorate the walls. Spanish flags fly from the cabin roofs, and

442

green-and-red pennants are draped down the side of the three-story-high construction. The walls delineating the bar area are covered with old photographs. Sebastian Collins is prominently visible in a number of them. One photograph, grainy with age, its frame weatherbeaten, shows Collins at the Grove encampment of August 1914. Collins, Senator Phelan, Josiah Royce, and Downey Harvey are sitting before a luncheon table forested with wine bottles. Jack London sits at one end of the table and George Sterling at the other. Each gentleman is sitting at an angle so as to face the camera. Collins is wearing a Norfolk jacket of rough tweed, a white shirt, and a full cravat—Bohemian Grove apparel being much more formal in 1914 than it is at present. Royce seems slightly ill-at-ease before such a vast array of wine bottles. Collins, however, then sixty-seven years of age, seems the picture of robust good health. He doesn't seem to mind the wine bottles.

In an account Collins wrote of the August 1914 Grove encampment depicted in the photograph, I remember his making reference to a superb nude hung over the bar. The painting survives, having been dubbed the *Archbishop's Daughter* by the present members of Esplandian. The painting depicts a luscious young lady, having just doffed her clothes under a redwood tree, advancing full face—and full everything else—towards the viewer. She is a truly superb creature in her early twenties: the Gibson Girl Revealed, one might say; for the painting was done some time in the late 1890s in the rich, sensuous style of the period. Collins also mentions a brazier that hung from the overhead beams—in front of which he sat one night, whiskey in hand, remembering his late wife and Sybil Sanderson. The open brazier has been replaced by a safer, more convenient Franklin stove.

I joined the Bohemian Club in 1972 as an associate member, a category made available to men who the Club feels can make a special contribution in one or the other art. An associate member is brought in off the regular waiting list at reduced fees, his membership renewable on a year-by-year basis, depending upon his contribution. In my case, the Club needed a trained archivist to work with the more than one-hundred-years' worth of records, correspondence, photographs, and memorabilia accumulated by the Club since its founding in San Francisco in 1872 by a group of convivial artists and journalists accustomed to gathering once a week for discussion and entertainment. Today, the Bohemian Club has a thousand members, drawn mainly from the San Francisco Bay Area. The ambience of the lost California past is what I like best about Bohemia. You hear and read one persistent criticism of the Club: that it has lost contact with its bohemian origins, having become a playground of the rich and the powerful. The criticism is partly true, but exaggerated. The rich and powerful can be found in the Club, true; but the majority of the membership is local and no more than upper-middle-class in income. In the case of associate members such as myself, fees are kept absurdly low.

By the time Sebastian Collins joined the Club in 1894, it was very much as we find it today, although the Club and the city then enjoyed a cordial public relationship. The Bohemian Orchestra gave free public concerts each year, for instance, and had many of its productions reviewed by local newspaper critics. Late nineteenth-century California had the courage to remain vulnerable to Beauty with a capital B, Nature with a capital N, and Art with a capital A. I personally cherish the memory of both Bohemia and San Francisco in those long-lost-turn-of-the-century years when to step inside the Club was to step into the incandescent center of creative San Francisco itself. I think frequently upon those turn-of-the-century Bohemians—so vigorous, so civic-minded, so alive with a passion for art. At times I can almost imagine that I might yet run into them in the Library, browsing in the latest French magazine before luncheon: Ambrose Bierce, master of acerbic wit and the chiseled, marmoreal style, so tall, so bitter behind his fierce military mustache; Bernard Maybeck, dreaming of a new California architecture (he did the Bohemian Grove Chalet down at the end of the River Road), an architecture of organic form and natural materials used directly, but with eclectic references to older European

444

building traditions; Steward Edward White of Burlingame, mining the literary lode of the American Southwest; Professor Henry Morse Stephens of Berkeley, a large, tweedy, bearded don of the old school, book-loving, affirmative, gladly learning, even more gladly teaching, a cigar between his teeth and a tome under his arm as he wended his way down the Grove Canyon now named for him; Will Irwin the journalist, a Stanford man who worked on the *Wave* for a while before going back to New York to write for the *Sun,* where he sat up late at his typewriter the night the news of San Francisco's destruction by fire and earthquake came over the wire and pounded out a ten-thousand-word eulogy, "The City That Was," which remains to this day a *tour de force* of deadline journalism and one of the finest tributes ever written to San Francisco; Bruce Porter, who was nephew-in-law to the great novelist Henry James and joined a blithe circle of *fin de siècle* aesthetes responsible for the humorous review *The Lark* and also turned his hand to stained glass and sculpture (he did the Robert Louis Stevenson monument in Portsmouth Plaza); Ernest Peixotto of the civic-minded Sephardic family, just back from Paris and working on *Romantic California* (1910), one of my favorite books of the period; Frank Norris, at work on *McTeague* or *The Octopus,* two California classics; Xavier Martinez, the painter with whom Sebastian Collins drank one memorable night in Paris, defiantly proud of his Aztec blood, a student of Whistler's who one day at a party across the bay in Oakland rapidly sketched out a portrait of another guest daring to flirt with his wife, tacked the sketch to a tree, pulled out a six-shooter and filled the likeness full of holes, crying out in prudent sublimation: "I keel the son of a beech!"; Jack London, coming down from his Beauty Ranch in Glen Ellen for a day in the city, or engaging in an heroic, monumental drinking bout with his archenemy and fellow Bohemian Ambrose Bierce (London was a socialist, and Bierce, politically speaking, was to the right of Genghis Khan), a bout that Sebastian Collins witnessed and that left both antagonists sleeping it off at the bottom of a Russian River ravine; another

445

friend of Sebastian Collins, George Sterling, San Francisco's uncrowned king of Bohemia, poet laureate of the city, who committed suicide in his Club rooms.

This Bohemian generation was followed by another generation, equally vigorous, although by the early 1900s men of affairs had already begin to outbalance those Bohemians pursuing art or journalism on a full-time basis. Haig Patigian, however, a sculptor, was three times elected president of the Club in its postearthquake years. A certain type of Bohemian, Sebastian Collins among them, carried the best of the nineteenth-century Club into the twentieth. I'm thinking here of men like Collins; James Duval Phelan; *bon vivant* Raphael Weill, president of the White House department store, so genial a man, so alive with Gallic wit and instinctive love of *la vie bohème;* and industrialist Charles Kendrick, president of the Schlage Lock Company, who first joined the Club as a young member of the Chorus and whose greatest civic achievement was expediting the building of the War Memorial complex in the late 1920s after the project had almost collapsed from internecine strife.

"So there," I said to Deborah, having outlined all this to her one night in July when she described the Club as a bastion of capitalist male chauvinist piggery. "That's the real Bohemian Club." We were sitting at David's Delicatessen on Geary, devouring scrambled eggs and pastrami after attending an American Conservatory Theater production of Shakespeare's *Richard the Third.*

"You're deluding yourself as usual, my friend. Whatever the Bohemian Club was in the nineteenth century, this is the twentieth century—a fact you prefer to forget—and the Club is no longer Bohemian with a capital B. You can walk over to North Beach and see the few surviving bohemians who still call San Francisco home—Lawrence Ferlinghetti, for instance, Herb Gold or Richard Miller, or even Kay Boyle who's a sort of hard-boiled lefty bohemian, 1930s style. These people live for one thing only—art. They scramble for it, leaving respectability behind. Now that's bohemian. You and I are by definition and training the *bourgeoisie.* Most of your fellow

446

Bohemian Clubbers are by definition *haute bourgeoisie,* which is basically the same thing, but more of it."

"You admit to being bourgeois, then?"

"I have to face facts. I'm a doctor's daughter, raised in a five-bedroom home with a swimming pool in Phoenix, Arizona."

"Congratulations on your honesty."

"Now you do likewise."

"Do I trust you that much?"

"Try."

"Very well: I'm a lower-middle-class ethnic aspiring towards the *haute bourgeoisie.*"

"More."

"Scrambled eggs—or pastrami?"

"No—more truth. But here, finish these eggs. You look wolfish."

"The effects of enforced celibacy."

"Who's enforcing you? But continue with true confessions."

"I lack, among other things, single-mindedness: the ability to fix upon one thing, one calling, one person, such as yourself—and make a life of it. I keep waiting for something big to happen, but it never does."

"The Bohemian Club also discriminates against women."

"I thought we were talking about me."

"We were, but I got bored."

"Men and women can share many things, but not club life. Men and women can be equals or subordinates, lovers or enemies—but rarely friends."

"Why?"

"Because of the sex factor."

"That's defensive thinking—and a lot of chauvinist self-flattery. What you really mean is that friendship is precluded by men's compulsive sexual aggression, motivated by anxiety over prowess—or even the length of their doodad."

"Their what?"

"Their doodad. Penile anxiety leads men into all sorts of foolishness, including playing up to women they've no intention of really screwing because the energy just isn't there.

447

Once you get a woman in bed these days, you've undertaken a great responsibility. It's no longer slam-bam, thanks, ma'am. You're expected to perform. You're expected to offer satisfaction."

"With your doodad."

"With everything—with your total person, body and soul as the song says. Women now know the difference between a good lay and a bad lay, both in terms of physicality and psychological fulfillment. They want give and take, not just take. They want mutual care and responsibility—not just a doodad pointed in their direction."

"Speaking of which . . ."

"Finish your scrambled eggs."

The central ritual of the Grove encampment is *The Cremation of Care,* an elaborate pageant performed by hundreds of Bohemians to the accompaniment of the club orchestra, in which the corpse of Care is cremated by a phalanx of Bohemians dressed as druid priests before the great Oval Shrine. Dull Care, in any event, dropped from my shoulders each of the three July weekends I headed into the Grove's main gate and surrendered myself to Bohemia's pageant of entertainment and fellowship. Bohemia is an illusion; but so what? So much of life's charm is based upon illusion, upon myth and dream. One of the things I'm constantly experiencing at the Grove is the scattered suggestion of turn-of-the-century California. To see the Campfire Circle illuminated at night by Japanese lanterns first used in the nineties, suffusing the surrounding redwoods in a cinnamon glow, is to experience an uncanny feeling of time past—as I did at Esplandian Camp as well, thinking of Sebastian Collins and realizing that the very bed I was bunking in could have been his. Collins's last Grove encampment was in 1936. He was eighty-eight.

"It was a rather formal camp in those days," Russ Keil, the longtime captain of Esplandian, told me one night. "The men traveled up by train, which ran right into the Grove depot located near Bromley Camp. One night Senator Phelan was in his cabin, dressing for dinner. He was standing before his

448

dressing table in his long underwear. A young man poked his head into the cabin and asked the Senator if he might close the door to his cabin. He had been sent up by the Grove Committee, he said. The light from the Senator's cabin was preventing a dress rehearsal of a nighttime scene on the Grove stage below. 'Very well,' Phelan replied. Later that evening the Senator complained to Downey Harvey about a cheeky servant who had burst into his cabin unannounced. 'That was no servant,' Downey said. 'That was a young member of the Club.' 'Then either he or I must resign,' Phelan said in outrage. 'He saw me as no one gentleman should see another.' It took the collected efforts of Downey and Collins to dissuade Phelan from taking the matter to the membership committee. That must have been around 1918 or thereabouts."

The reading committee, incidentally, sent me a very encouraging note regarding the first draft of my Grove play *San Francisco,* which I am basing on the life of Sebastian Collins. The committee said that it was especially impressed by the Heidelberg dueling scene and the pageantry possibilities evident in the departure of the papal Zouaves from Rome to meet the Redshirts on the field of battle at Mentana. I needed to tighten up my dialogue, however, and to trim the play down by a third before it would be in shape for a Grove production.

Claudio Carpino and Andy Soutane both made the Grove this year, on different weekends. In a gubernatorial year, the major candidates usually make a Grove appearance. It's considered part of the ritual of the campaign. I must say, however, that both candidates, for differing reasons, seem ill-at-ease. Carpino doesn't like the Club because it's dominated by WASP Republicans. Soutane has the same objection, together with the realization that his appearance at the Grove could offend his minority and counter-culture constituencies. Carpino and Soutane each gave Lakeside Talks—noon lectures, that is, by the side of the artificial lagoon that rests in the center of the Grove.

Carpino talked about the role of private enterprise in the

development of the Far West, a paper researched by yours truly with the assistance of Mrs. Marcia Pennyworth of the San Francisco History Room. The Mayor began with the story of the Boston ships of Bryant and Sturgis, who traded with California in the early nineteenth century. He then discussed the careers of James Phelan senior and Samuel Brannan as representative gold rush merchants—followed by the story of the Big Four and the building of the transcontinental railroad. He then discussed the entrepreneurial vision of William Chapman Ralston. All this, Carpino concluded, was an epic of job-creation. Capital put ordinary people to work. Most employment in early California was stimulated by venture capitalists, willing to take a chance with their own money. When the capitalists of California lost their nerve, as they did in the depression of the mid-1870s, unemployment soared because no new ventures were undertaken. What America needed was a new *détente* between government and corporations, a partnership based upon mutual respect and the recognition that neither one side nor the other could escape the consequences of America's social problems. When one considers that most of Carpino's audience were Republicans, the applause might fairly be described as enthusiastic.

Soutane addressed himself to what he called the crisis of capital. The public sector, Soutane admitted, was dangerously overextended. (Applause.) There was too much welfare, too much bureaucracy, too much governmental interference and red tape. (More applause.) If something were not done about this dangerous situation soon, an engorged, overweaning government—federal, state, local—would choke off the vitality of the American people. Self-reliance and individual initiative would go by the board. (Even more generous applause.) The reason all this was happening, however, was that the private sector never seemed able to motivate itself to tackle such social problems as poverty, racial prejudice, decaying inner cities. Government hence stepped in to fill the vacuum. The future of the private enterprise system in America depended upon the ability of capital to create

450

incentive programs to bring the have-nots into some alignment with the haves. Otherwise, a dangerously swollen helotry, a permanently disaffected underclass, would consolidate itself in inner-city America. This class could foment outright rebellion, or it could be manipulated by ambitious politicians and governmental bureaucrats, eager to expand and consolidate their power. (Mixed applause and scattered mutterings.) The future of capitalism, Soutane concluded, is in the hands of capitalists themselves. Did they, or did they not, have a social conscience? (Desultory clapping, with a burst of compensatory applause from a group of woefully outnumbered younger Bohemians. Some Bohemians had already left the Lakeside before the talk was over.)

Carpino stayed at Bromley Camp as a guest of the board of directors. At his invitation—extended to me when I approached him after his Lakeside Talk to offer my congratulations—I joined Carpino at Bromley around four o'clock for a walk. That was probably the second time I've had the opportunity to talk to the Mayor, person to person, without some member of his entourage around. The first time was at Harvard. I doubt if there will be a third time. We walked down past the Civic Center and the Campfire Circle, then headed up Henry Morse Stephen Canyon, catching a trail that circles out to the Russian River atop a redwood-covered ridge. Then we returned to Bromley via the River Road. As a concession to his Bohemian circumstances, Carpino was not wearing a necktie. He was, however, attired in cautious sport clothes. As a totally urban man, Carpino was probably finding the Bohemian Grove a little too rural.

"I'm sorry about Esmeralda's call," the Mayor said.

"Forget it, Mr. Mayor," I said.

Esmeralda had called me a week earlier, at the ungodly hour of five-thirty in the morning. "This is Esmeralda Carpino," she had said. "I know that you and my husband are having a homosexual affair."

For the longest time I couldn't figure out what the hell to say. Only Groucho Marx could have come up with something

451

appropriately surreal in response, and that's who I wished I were—Groucho Marx—as I groggily held onto my bedside telephone, trying to assure myself that the First Lady of San Francisco was truly at the other end of the line, saying what she had just said. After searching for a comeback *à la* Groucho and failing, I thought of the Andy Soutane–Stedman Mooner pictures. I was getting back what I deserved. He who lives by the sword must die by the sword.

"You're mistaken, Mrs. Carpino, and perhaps a little distraught. Let's forget that you called."

Groucho Marx would have managed something much better. I did, however, tell Terry Shane about the call later that morning when I dropped by Room 200, City Hall.

"I'm telling you this for strategic reasons," I said. "Suppose Esmeralda starts pestering the wrong people. She could cause the Mayor real harm." Shane had obviously gone to the Mayor with the story—hence the apology, which must have been difficult for a man of Carpino's age, position, pride, whatever.

"Esmeralda hasn't been herself lately," the Mayor said. "It's probably the change of life. Many women often get troubled as they near sixty."

"If she ever went public with something like this," I said, "she'd destroy you. Slanders of this sort stick like flypaper."

"She won't go public," the Mayor said. "She's loyal to the family."

As a case of poetic justice, I deserve to be tarred with the same brush with which Tiny Roncola, with my possible assistance, plans to tar Andy Soutane—and man, would the tar stick to me! Thirty-five years old, single, a librarian! That's Fruit City, if anything is. Just thinking of it makes me shudder. I'm going to confront Roncola about the entire mess. I'll get those photographs and have them destroyed. The only damage done so far has been to my conscience, which is already covered with scar tissue.

"Are you enjoying the Grove?" I asked the Mayor.

"Not really," he said, "but an appearance here is supposed to be good for the campaign, so I'm told. The redwoods remind me of the Salesian Boys' Club camp down in Felton where I used to go as a youngster."

I had once seen photographs of the Salesian Camp in a story done on the Mayor in *Bay Area* magazine when he won his second term: photographs of earnest-faced Italian youngsters gathered around Angelo Fusco, the director of the Salesian Boys' Club, under a stand of redwood trees sometime in the very early 1930s, the boys in those baggy corduroy trousers that everyone seemed to wear in the 1930s and white shirts left open at the collar to signify that they were being worn as sports clothes. Some of the boys were holding musical instruments, including the Mayor, who sat with a monstrous cello between his knees, very much resembling himself today, save for the full head of hair and whatever it is that forty years of life does to a face without changing its essential continuity.

"I'm not the Bohemian Club type," the mayor of San Francisco said.

We came out on a high bluff where the Russian River skirts the eastern boundary of the Grove. Down river, on the far shore, a half-dozen bikini-clad women were sunning themselves under the sherry-warm Sonoma sun. Mel, the San Francisco fireman who works as the Club lifeguard during the encampment, was paddling an aluminum canoe downstream in their direction. A solid week in the sun had browned Mel to deep mahogany. He looked like a stand-in for Lex Barker as Tarzan. One of the girls was retieing her halter in anticipation of Mel's arrival.

The Mayor and I walked down the River Road, quiet in the late afternoon hour of siesta. Pungent smoke rose from a score of waning luncheon campfires; here and there the sound of laughter, the clicking of dominoes, or subdued piano music drifted out from a camp enclosure. I could tell that the Mayor was bored. He'll stay over for the Grove Play tonight as a courtesy, I thought to myself, but I wouldn't be surprised if Inspector Potelli picked him up outside the Grove Gate at ten o'clock sharp tonight when *Allegory* was over.

"I'm flying up to Eureka tonight," Carpino said, as if to

answer my unasked question. "Potelli is picking me up at ten and we'll be leaving from the Santa Rosa airport. Want to come along?"

"I can't. Esplandian is having its camp luncheon tomorrow."

I knew I was missing a great opportunity. In politics, propinquity to the main man is everything. On the flight up to Eureka, I would have the chance to give the Mayor an earful of my ideas about the campaign. I could urge him, for instance, to detach himself a little bit from the Big Cigar boys in labor and try for a more centrist, less divisive campaign aimed at the unaffiliated majority of Californians. I could ask him to try not to bait in his speeches the Aquarians, the Utopianists, the eco-freaks, the campus activists; it's obvious that they're not his constituency, so why bother? California Democrats who go for the jugular of the harmless far-outs lose the sympathy of centrist party regulars. The essential spirit of California is tolerant, laid back, as long as one's own ox is not being gored.

"We want your input in the campaign," the Mayor said.

Bullshit, I thought to myself; but it was kind of Carpino to try to be nice when he had nothing to gain for being so—except, perhaps, for the fact that he might have been trying to assuage his conscience. I mean: I must look to him like a dumbshit, hulking, academic fool, overfed on great books and Modern Library paperbacks. I'm probably useful in the Library, where people are supposed to care about such things, but in the rough-and-tumble world of municipal and state politics, I require an explanation. The Mayor might have felt a momentary pang of pity for the ineffectual doubledome whom he had extricated from Harvard by force of his persuasive wizardry, but now saw floundering around like a fish out of water. The offer of the Eureka trip could also have been a sop thrown me in reparation for Esmeralda's phone call. Yet here I was: the pitied pitying the pitier. I pitied the fact that his wife was going bananas on him and that his campaign for governor suffered from a fundamental, irreversible handicap. Time had run out. It was too late for Carpino's sort,

454

which is a difficult thing to say about someone in his late fifties (or someone like myself, in his mid-thirties): too late for the New Deal rhetoric, the palling around with the Big Cigar labor boys, the appeals to a provincial ethnicity and a Catholic vote that no longer exists, even in San Francisco—much less California as a whole.

"There's something not quite right with Soutane," the Mayor remarked as we walked past Ye County Gaol Camp, heading back towards Bromley, past Sons of Toil, Sons of Rest, Dragons, and Land's End. "I can't envision the state voting for a bachelor who sleeps on the floor."

The voters, I thought to myself, are more likely to vote for Soutane, military cot and all, than for a married man whose wife throws raisin toast at him in public or hangs out hotel windows threatening suicide. Soutane could win the election on just the single and divorced vote alone. Doesn't the Mayor realize that nobody in California, at least in southern California and the San Francisco Bay Area, is likely to make a vociferous brief for the married state? People under forty just don't have it big for marriage any more. Marriage is too intense, too confining a relationship—too restrictive of sexual freedom; and if there are kids, too devouring of one's disposable income. Soutane's singleness reflects the condition of millions of voters who live alone, and it appeals as well to millions of others who wished that they did. On balance, Esmeralda Carpino seems much more flaky than Andy Soutane to the young and young-middle-aged voters who swing elections in the go-go state.

Still: Carpino is the politician and I'm the hulking humanist, so he must be right—which I don't believe at all, but I'll say it anyway, then back out of the whole mess. It's not my million dollars going down the drain. Let the big shots do what they want with their dough.

That evening's Grove Play—*Allegory,* book and lyrics by Will Parker, music by Carl Eberhard, Peter Arnott, director—was a sumptuous and rewarding production, involving hundreds of actors, singers, and musicians. Set in a science fiction future, *Allegory* was just that—an allegory about a man's need first to find himself before making an offering of his rediscovered self to a woman, who is also—by allegory—grace. Woman is Grace, Parker's allegory states; and Grace is earned through personal pilgrimage, through a seeker's journey.

The hair on the back of my neck bristled and I felt chills go up and down my spine when Erich Stratmann sang the show's show-stopping, big production number, "Journey," for which Carl Eberhard did haunting luminous music:

> Journey, always journey to the stars,
> When you're young and filled with need.
> Always journey at great speed,
> To find your way away.
> For the stars are always wise,
> Dancing high in silent skies,
> Each a spinning soul that speaks to you.
> Journey, you must journey deep inside,
> Take the time you need to find
> What's within your heart and mind.
> And know your truest soul,
> And become your very best,
> Then Grace will grant you rest,
> For you earn it with love.

It was a spectacular moment, no two ways about it. Stratmann stood halfway up the sloping hillside of the Grove stage, against a backdrop of artificial stars. The redwoods on each side of the stage were lit in their upper reaches to an ethereal luminescence. Nature's stars glowed overhead, a galaxy full of them, crystalline and noetic. I thought of the medieval Islamic philosopher Avicenna who speculated that each star was the shining countenance of a subsistent celestial intelligence, an angelic creature revolving in a fixed empyrean, offering constant praise to the Creator in a sublime choir that eluded mortal ears. What a dream: to hear the entire universe aburst in celestial paean to the ineffable Godhead!

"It's a Sumnercraft Thirty-One," I said as we unloaded our

456

gear on the Sausalito dock. "A motor-sailer of fiberglass and wood construction, thirty-one feet in length."

"Is it hard to handle?" Deborah asked.

"Not really," I said, succumbing to the temptation of appearing informed. "It's got double headsails, making it easy for one person to set the sheets. It's also got a hundred-and-eight-horsepower Diesel motor, so we couldn't get stranded even if we tried. The hull has built-in plastic foam flotation, so we won't capsize. It also has a galley and two cabins."

"A cabin for each of us," Deborah said as she tossed her duffel bag onto the floor of the open cockpit with an aplomb that should have made me realize there and then that she had been sailing before.

It was the Fourth of July, 1975, the one-hundred-and-ninety-ninth anniversary of the founding of the American republic: a sunny, clear day—and a sail up through the Delta country to Tinsley Island in the San Joaquin River stretching ahead of us. God, was I glad to be there with Deborah and to have the exclusive use of the Sumnercraft I owned in shares with Robert Porter and Ken Nemzer, whom I'd met at Harvard when he was going through law school. Upon my return to San Francisco, Nemzer had encouraged me to get interested in sailing. Ken owned the Sumnercraft jointly with Bob Porter and a Marine Corps major stationed on Treasure Island who had to sell his share when he was transferred to the Mediterranean Fleet Force operating out of Naples, and when the share opened I bought in: eating up my savings in the process and being forced to borrow the second $5,000 from the Hibernia Bank—but it was worth it, for I've since learned to love sailing, although I remain a tyro. Porter, a regular member of the St. Francis Yacht Club, arranged that Nemzer and I come into the Club as Corinthian Crew members, a lower-priced temporary membership for crew members working a regular member's boat.

I unlocked the cabin. Deborah jumped below, and I began handing our gear down to her: duffel bags, sleeping bags, a couple of boxes of groceries and booze.

"Vodka, tequila, Irish whiskey, wine, champagne—you're planning a Lost Weekend," Deborah said, stowing each bottle safely in a lower locker.

"Be prepared," I said, digging into the box of groceries she had brought along. Each of us had agreed to a fifty-fifty share-and-share-alike provisioning of our expedition. "Nuts, granola, yogurt, five-grain bread, dried apricots, shredded coconut," I said, holding up each item as I removed it from her grocery carton. "We're going to Tinsley Island, not Salt Lake City."

"You've counterbalanced my menu," she said, putting the paté from Marcel and Henri's and the London broil from Petrini's into the food locker. I packed dry ice into the open spaces, making certain that the cheese was properly protected. Deborah went up on deck and I passed the bag containing the two headsails up to her. Without instructions, she got busy helping me connect them to their proper hooks and ties.

"You've done this before?" I asked.

"A number of times."

"When? Where?"

"Let's talk about it when we're under way. We don't want to miss the tide."

I checked the Diesel out and it seemed fine.

"We'll motor down the channel," I said, "then put our sails up once we're out on the open bay."

Deborah jumped down to the dock and untied our lines. I tossed her the key and she stowed the dock line in our berth's utility locker. The other two lines she wrapped neatly, then attached to the proper hooks forward and aft. It took us no more than half an hour from the time of our arrival to get under way. Deborah wore Sperry topsiders, white shorts, and a red-and-white striped French sailor's jersey. She had her hair gathered in a red-and-white bandanna looped behind her neck, and wore an oversized pair of Jackie O sunglasses. I reveled in the length of her tanned legs and the solid strength of her arms. When she stood tiptoe to reach a line, her calves bulged with just the proper degree of muscularity, like a tennis player's legs: tense and muscular, but smooth, without the

458

knots or bulges that joggers' or backpackers' legs sometimes get.

Our route for the day would take us across the San Francisco Bay, through the Carquinez Strait past Crockett and Port Costa into Suisun Bay. Just east of Suisin Bay, the Delta Country begins, so named because here California's two mightiest rivers, the Sacramento and the San Joaquin, converge on their westward flow towards the Pacific. I suppose that there are more than a thousand miles of waterways crisscrossing the Delta Country between Antioch and Stockton. In the 1870s, Chinese laborers reclaimed the region from its condition of total marshland, building up an elaborate system of embankments and dikes. Some twenty years ago, army engineers dredged a deep-water channel all the way up to Stockton, which is now a deep-water port servicing ocean-going freighters. Delta Country consists of rich farmlands, marshy areas, and a labyrinth of interconnecting waterways banked in tule grass. You can think of it as California's bayou country; and like the bayou country of Louisiana, Delta Country possesses an aura of mysterious beauty. Navigating its waterways, you sail past screens of high tule reeds reminiscent of the Nile. Oak and sycamore trees line the banks. Now and then you catch sight of a small farmhouse built in the mid-nineteenth century when the dry land of this region was first farmed: a white frame building reminiscent of New England, or a plantation house suggestive of antebellum South, all of them evoking long-ago hopes for a better life in California.

I used the Diesel to get out onto the open bay. The tide was with us and we had a superb westerly wind. Hoisting sail, we moved across mildly whitecapped waters, heading towards the strait between Tiburon and Angel Island. Past Bluff Point on the northern tip of the Tiburon Peninsula, I planned a westerly tack to San Pablo Strait, followed by a northwesterly move past Pinole Point, then through the Carquinez Strait itself. From there I might go on power, for I am not yet good enough to handle Carquinez Strait on sail. Once into Suisun Bay, I could decide to go back on sail, depending upon the wind and the time available—or I could use the Diesel all the way up to Tinsley to make sure that we arrived there by nine o'clock in the evening.

Once we were on open water, we had a lovely view. Behind us, Sausalito tumbled down the hillside to the water in a cascade of construction like a Mediterranean fishing port. The sourthern side of Belvedere Island was lined with waterside villas sparkling in the early morning sunlight. To our right, Angel Island rose out of the water like a forested island in an Edgar Rice Burroughs adventure novel: some lost Pacific Island upon which Deborah and I would be shipwrecked, forced to elude a hostile tribe while surviving together in the forest, where we would fall into the hands of the Friendly Folk, locked since time immemorial in deadly struggle with the Evil Others—and so forth, and so forth: all of it illustrated by Charles Dana Gibson or James Montgomery Flagg, and run as the cover story in *Scribner's Magazine* some time in the early 1900s.

A herd of seals skimmed along the surface of the waves. Diving for fish, their flippers streamlined to their sides, they tilted upward and shot torpedo-like down into the sea. White ocean birds, including an egret heading toward Bolinas Lagoon, flew overhead. San Francisco receded in the distance like a waterborne Oz, like a mirage of the lost city of Atlantis.

"I'll have a beer," I said. "I ask you for it only because I'm busy at the helm."

"I'll take the helm and you can get your own beer."

Which is what I did: sitting to Deborah's front as she took us across San Pablo Bay. Sipping a half-quart of Budweiser, I admired the way she handled the wheel. The wind blew her French jersey against her body, revealing the tight line of her stomach and the fullness of her upper torso. The cabin FM counterpointed a foreground of aggressive wind and sea sounds with a soft backup of smooth and glassy bossa nova.

"Bossa nova is very early nineteen sixties," Deborah said.

"I'm very early nineteen sixties," I said. "I'm Dave Brubeck, the Modern Jazz Quartet, Cal Tjader, Vince

Guiraldi, John Lewis, Stan Getz, Oscar Peterson. It's been downhill ever since."

"And Peter, Paul and Mary,"

"Yes, they also—singing 'Jet Plane' and 'Blowing on the Wind' and 'Puff the Magic Dragon.'"

"And Pete Seeger."

"Yes, but he survived into the protest years. I'm also the Weavers singing 'Run Come See Jerusalem,' and the Kingston Trio singing 'The Seine, the Seine!' I'm paperback books— Kirkegaard's *Either/Or,* the Penguin editions of Dostoyevsky. I'm button-down shirts and chino pants with a mysterious belt to the rear. Back behind that, I'm Buddy Holly and the Five Satins singing 'In the Still of the Night.'"

"And Pat Boone singing 'April Love.'"

"And the excitement of the first issue of *Evergreen Review,* coming from Sausalito. And Sterling Hayden hanging out at the Seven Seas there and writing *Wanderer.*"

"You need a woman of your own age."

"They're all married—or divorced."

"There's a generation gap between us."

"Ten years—that's all."

"Ten years is a lifetime."

"Why did you give up being a stewardess?"

"I haven't given it up for good. I might still go back."

"Right now you're in your inner-city phase."

"Slightly hostile—but accurate. I liked flying. I could have had the Mexico City run, but I'm enjoying the Library also. Since I got the MLS degree I may as well use it for a while. Stewardessing is tough work: early and late hours, waiting on demanding passengers who are sometimes outrightly abusive, lugging yourself in and out of motels."

"Where did you learn to sail?"

"I had a boyfriend who owned a boat."

"Had a boyfriend?"

"Yes—had. He was killed two years ago in an automobile accident."

"Did you love him?"

461

"I probably still do—at least I still miss him a lot and feel loyal to him in a sort of subconscious way. We grew up together in Phoenix. He went to Berkeley and sailed for the UC team. I'd go with the team on some of their pleasure cruises."

"Were you engaged?"

"Unofficially. We just sort of understood each other. He was killed in a head-on collision on Route 66, heading home to Phoenix. A rented U-Haul van, driven by an inexperienced driver who fell asleep at the wheel, jumped over to the wrong side of the road."

I kept quiet for some time, digesting this new aspect of Deborah's history. It softened my perception of her, making her seem less flip, less self-assured. It conditioned her rather resolute exterior with the suggestion of vulnerability, of having been touched by the essential tragedy of life.

"These are great sandwiches," I said in Honker Bay as we neared Chipps Island. We were running under power and would probably stay that way all the way to Tinsley.

"Avocado, egg, bean sprouts," Deborah said. "And natural mayonnaise."

I poured out some Sonoma Winery Pinot Chardonnay. It was around two o'clock.

"What are you thinking about?" Deborah asked.

"I'm thinking of you," I said. "I'm thinking about you as a kid in Phoenix. I'm picturing you on the campus of Mills. I'm imagining you in your Hughes Airwest stewardess uniform. What's your favorite color?"

"Turquoise blue."

"Your favorite place in the world?"

"Arizona—and New Mexico."

"Your favorite writer?"

"Lawrence Clark Powell."

"The UCLA librarian?"

"The greatest librarian of the twentieth century and a magnificent essayist. I have all his books on the Southwest."

"What would you rather be doing right now? I mean if you had your wish?"

462

"Be right here, dummy. Enjoying this boat and this wine and these sandwiches—and trying to get to know you while you're trying to figure me out."

"I love you," I said.

"We'll see about that."

"I think you're beautiful—and probably good. And you're fun to be with."

"So's Raquel Welch. I need some sun."

Disappearing below for a few minutes, she emerged in a bikini. For the longest time, I forgot to breathe. Spreading a towel on the foredeck, she sat down on it and began to rub herself with suntan oil. The sun—now the hot sun of the interior valley—baked us in healing heat. Let me lie, I ached within myself, with my face pressed to your stomach, feeling your skin salt on my tongue. Let me touch my lips to the heat of your body. My ear to your breast, let me hear the ebb and flow of your blood tides. Let me kiss the toes of your feet: slowly, reverently, an acolyte offering worship. Let me place my body between the smoothness of your thighs, my mouth on your mouth, my tongue to your tongue, my teeth to your teeth. Let me kiss your breasts and the secret places between. Let me rise over you in penetration and enfoldment, the two of us bathed in sunshine like lovers on a Grecian hillside: a long-legged dryad coupled to a feral satyr tamed by her gift of yielding, the two of them half-lost for discretion's sake in a wood of wild olive trees, their love cries intermingled with the encouraging music of cooing doves.

"I'm going to nap for a while," Deborah said. "Be sure to study the chart. The navigation's tricky after Antioch."

After Antioch you must thread your way through a network of waterways. Refreshed by sleep, Deborah helped me out as dusk approached. We read the chart and spotted the markers and sailed from one marker to another along our course.

Once into Delta Country, we joined a Venetian water pageant of sailboats, power boats, houseboats. It was the Fourth of July and the Delta people were out for an evening of fireworks. Each town along the Delta contributes to the Fourth of July display, which begins around eight-thirty when the summer dusk has not yet become night. On a summer nightfall, the Delta sky has a velvety texture—the beginnings of a rich darkness, edged on the western skyscape with lingering reminders of sunset, like black velvet edged in russet. The San Joaquin ran still as we motored through the channelways to Tinsley, our progress acknowledged by stands of high tule grass rustling their tips in the gentle breeze, as if an angel were passing overhead. Then the sky exploded in color. From a half-dozen directions a festive bombardment began: pinwheels, Roman candles, skyrockets bursting into every conceivable configuration as they streaked the dark velvet sky with Titian color. Some fifty square miles of sky rained with falling fire.

"It's like a festival from the eighteenth century," Deborah said, "something from Venice or the Court of Versailles."

She had slipped into a down jacket for warmth. We sat side by side in the cockpit, where I was handling the wheel, guiding us towards Tinsley. I noticed that her knees reached a few inches beyond mine despite the fact that I am two or three inches taller than she. Deborah had brought two mugs of hot tea up from the cabin, which we sipped—made silent by the spectacle of fiery color bursting above us.

"Happy Birthday, America," I said.

She slipped her left arm through my right arm, balancing the tea mug on her knee with her right hand. Steering with my left arm, I linked my other arm through hers. Even under two layers of down-stuffed quilt, I could feel the firm flesh of her biceps. When I sipped my tea, I had to lean towards her to reach the mug in my hand. Upon one such maneuver, our heads touched and we kissed. I thought of Jay Gatsby's solitary breathless kiss with Daisy Buchanan as the two of them— beheld by Nick Carraway who stood in the shadows—danced to distant orchestra music on a patio drenched in moonlight, lost in a world of their own creation. So too did our lips meet for a breathless instant beneath a sky of falling color.

With reluctance, I went to the prow with my flashlight, leaving Deborah at the wheel. Flashing my beam in front of me, I picked out our course, calling directions to her at the helm. For a minute or so of our final passage, I thought that I had perhaps gone up the wrong channel; but then I heard orchestra music and I saw the distant glow of lights, and I knew that around the next clump of tule grass was the waterway that leads to Tinsley.

The St. Francis Yacht Club acquired Tinsley Island some twenty years ago. With earth fill hauled over from the mainland by barge, the Club transformed Tinsley from an unusable marsh to a landscaped park surrounded—and more than half hid from view—by waving willow trees, cypresses, and sycamores. A nineteenth-century wooden lighthouse was towed up the San Joaquin River from San Francisco Bay. Reconditioned, it now guards the south end of the island. A swimming pool was put in, and lawns laid out for bowls, volley ball, croquet. There are also a number of fine tennis courts, a shell-covered pavilion where a dance orchestra plays in the evening, and a long open-air dining area covered in lattice work beneath which more than a hundred club members can be seated at redwood tables, availing themselves of a number of brick barbecues and open stone ovens. To one side of the dining area is a bar that operates from under a rattan shed suggestive of the Hawaiian Islands.

Two sides of Tinsley are devoted to docks and berths, one for power-driven vessels, the other for sail. We secured our Sumnercraft alongside Johnboy Turfer's fifty-foot schooner, *Class Action*. Built of teakwood and mahogany sometime in the early 1930s, the *Class Action* is Turfer's pride and joy, perhaps the most dramatic emblem he has of his rise to fame and fortune as a flamboyant antitrust attorney. When I saw the schooner dockside, its brass metalwork reflecting the beam of my flashlight, I headed for it. The larger the yacht, the less chance there is that it will be moved around over the weekend. Tied up to Turfer, we probably wouldn't have to move for the entire three days of our stay.

We docked at nine. By nine-thirty we were over at the bar with some thirty other club members. The men wore yachting attire that ranged from white ducks and blue blazers to more informal Greek sweaters and Levis. The women were in casual dresses; a few still had their bikinis on, their tan skin yet radiant with the honey warmth of the daytime sun. Deborah drank a vodka tonic and I drank two, then we brought our picnic basket over to a redwood table beneath the lattice work and ate fried chicken and three-bean salad, prepared the previous evening by yours truly. I also opened a bottle of *Clos du Bois* Chardonnay, an excellent wine from a new winery operated by Frank Woods in the Alexander Valley near Healdsburg in Sonoma County. As we ate, a five-piece combo called the Band of Gold played for the dancers who crowded the floor beneath the half-shell pavilion to one side of the island. The Band of Gold played some very smooth and satiny music designed for an older crowd: "My Funny Valentine," "Unforgettable," "In the Still of the Night," "Begin the Beguine," "Night and Day," "That Old Black Magic"— music such as this, led off by a very mellow saxophone and an Oscar Peterson-style piano. After a ten-minute break, Band of Gold resumed, but this time in a jubilant rock idiom, which prompted a younger crowd to mass themselves beneath the half-shell and move wildly to the Dionysian rhythms of the rock beat.

"Come on, big boy, let's dance," Deborah said.

I followed her to the floor and spent the next half hour doing what I could to approximate her dynamite Ann-Margret moves: a dated comparison, I fear, for Ann-Margret is my age; so let's just say her dynamite moves, stylized and ecstatic and replete with sensual feeling. When the slow music began again, I held her in my arms and felt the warm wetness that had dampened her jersey. I also felt her shoulder blades and the hollow made by the small of her back. My mind teemed with images, most of them suggesting sexual intercourse.

"This is midsummer madness," I said.

"Let's not get carried away; but it's very pleasant."

"This is carnival."

"Carnival comes just before Lent."

"You're beautiful."

466

"You could be a decent dancer if you'd shed twenty pounds."

"What was he like?"

"Steady, clean-cut, handsome, and kind. He had red hair, not carrot-red, but sort of auburn. He rode around Berkeley on a motorcycle. He wanted to get a Ph.D. in geology and go to work with the Geological Survey as a field scientist. He'd camped out throughout Arizona and New Mexico as a teenager in one of the Outward Bound programs. He liked to dance and he was a good enough carpenter to make a lot of money at it during the summers."

When we got back to the dock, we had to cross Johnboy Turfer's yacht to get to our own. From the midships portholes of Turfer's schooner came the sounds of below-deck merriment, some half-dozen voices, dominated by Johnboy Turfer's booming baritone.

"Who in the hell is walking across my goddamn boat?" Turfer bellowed, sounding like the troll in *The Three Billygoats Gruff*. He popped his head out of the deck cabin.

"Norton, you bastard, come on down here for a drink."

I had no choice but to head in his direction.

"Who in the hell is this?" Turfer asked, seeing Deborah in the shadows. "The girl from the Mission! You were with Norton at the goddamn Mission! I'll be a sonofabitch! You dog, Norton. How'd a librarian ever meet such a good-looking broad? How the hell are you?" Johnboy grabbed Deborah in a one-armed bear hug. His other hand held a half-full bottle of champagne. At his insistence, we climbed down into the cabin after him. Three downtown attorney types whom I vaguely recognized and their wives filled the main cabin of the *Class Action*. Like Johnboy Turfer, they were drinking champagne: not out of plastic or paper cups as you might expect, but out of proper champagne glasses, the conical sort with no stems on them. A tape deck filled the cabin with middlebrow music, something by Andy Williams if I remember correctly. Like Johnboy Turfer himself, the three men hovered around forty and the women were there also, or slightly younger: good-

467

looking women, to be sure, but possessing also that slightly hard look that characterizes a number of affluent Marin County women I've met who have some time ago said goodbye to thirty.

Everybody, in any event, was celebrating the fact of their early middle-age success. Just as I suspected, they were all lawyers; two of them, in fact, were associates of Turfer. They wore a sort of Edgartown West uniform: La Coste shirts (I counted a total of ten alligators), colored pants *à la* McGeorge Bundy (green, tartan plaid, salmon), loafers or topsiders with no socks. Conversation revealed that two of them were of the genre Transplanted Eastern Attorney (one Harvard, the other Yale), which has taken over the junior and middle ranks of a number of leading San Francisco law firms. Johnboy Turfer went to evening law school in Chicago and slept in his car on his first night in San Francisco, having dined on Ritz crackers and peanut butter purchased from a Mom and Pop grocery store on Lincoln Way adjacent to Golden Gate Park where he had discreetly parked his car; but now he owned this yacht and could fill it with these Ivy Leaguers for the July Fourth weekend at Tinsley. Two of them, in fact, had been lured away by Turfer from Pillsbury, Madison & Sutro through the simple device of doubled salaries and a limited partnership.

"Say hello to everybody," Turfer boomed when we got below.

"Hello, everybody," I said.

"This here is our city librarian, J. V. Norton," Turfer said, "and this gorgeous creature is his girlfriend, D. Tanner."

"Call me D," Deborah said.

"Hello," everyone said in the course of much shaking of hands.

"Claudio Carpino is an asshole," one of the lawyers said.

"I object," I said.

"Objection sustained," said Johnboy Turfer. "I'll have no goddamn talk of politics on this boat unless we're talking about me!"

The women looked at Deborah and saw the image of their

468

lost twenties. Deborah looked back at them in return, seeing perhaps the image of a future that might or might not be hers. Once I ceased to be defensive (rich lawyers always make me defensive), I enjoyed the gathering. We talked sailing and football and the line-up for next year's San Francisco Film Festival. Turfer told a lot of racy, but not gross, jokes.

"Here, doll," he said to Deborah. "I keep this on board in deference to the generation gap." He handed her a marijuana cigarette which he had fetched from a cigar box.

"No thanks, doll—but maybe some other time," Deborah said.

"Then have some more bubbly," Turfer said, refilling her and everyone else's glass.

We left an hour later, with Turfer bellowing goodbye, his body half visible from below deck like a giant groundhog checking for spring. When we got aboard our boat, Deborah went below deck for a minute, then emerged in her bathing suit. Diving off the Sumnercarft, she began to swim away into the darkness towards the far shore of the channel.

"Where in the hell are you going?" I called after her, receiving no response. Hastily undressing, I climbed into my swimming trunks and dove in after her, remembering just in time to take my glasses off and stow them safely in one of my topsiders. The cold water hit me like a shock, contesting— then defeating—the effects of the champagne. Without my glasses, I am nearsighted as hell. Swimming without my glasses in a channel of the San Joaquin River some two hours after midnight, I'm doubly helpless; but I boldly swam out anyway in the direction of Deborah's rhythmic splashing.

"Moby Dick, I'm over here," she called.

Pushing off in the direction of her voice, I found her on the shore of the opposite channel, seated amidst the tule grass.

"Deborah Tanner, I presume?" I said, stumbling up the embankment to the flattened spot she had created amidst the bullrushes. I lay down on my back next to her, the two of us side by side. Without my glasses, I perceived the night as a runny palette of intermingled bright and dark. The stars overhead looked like soggy splotches of milky light, as if the heavens had suddenly gone teary-eyed. From the opposite side of the channel came the muted laughter of some late night revelers watching till dawn in shipborne merriment. The *basso profundo* of a deep-water freighter heading up river to Stockton boomed intermittently in the distance. From where we lay, on an embankment tilted upwards like a lawn chair, Tinsley Island arose out of the water like Avalon, King Arthur's lost isle of the blessed.

"What are you thinking about?" I asked.

"Whether there's really a world out there; whether millions of people actually haven't enough to wear or to eat, or are having their lives crushed by oppressive governments."

"I'm thinking of Alfred Lord Tennyson," I said.

"You would be. What lines?"

Shakily, I recited from memory:

> How sweet it were, hearing the downward stream,
> With half-shut eyes ever to seem
> Falling asleep in a half-dream!
> To dream and dream, like yonder amber light,
> Which will not leave the myrrh-bush on the height;
> To hear each other's whispered speech;
> Eating the Lotos day by day,
> To watch the crisping ripples on the beach,
> And tender curving lines of creamy spray . . .

We lay there for a while until we were fully rested, then we swam back across the channel to the dock, climbed the ladder there and tiptoed across Turfer's deck back to our own boat. As soon as I got aboard, I fetched my glasses from my shoes, dried myself off with a towel, then got redressed. Deborah, meanwhile, went to her cabin. I waited for what seemed an eternity; then, heart racing, a dryness in my throat, I went below. She had crawled into her sleeping bag and was lost to the world, her face turned toward the bulkhead. I listened for a moment to the steady sound of her breathing, then dragged my sleeping bag and foam rubber mattress topside. Stretching

470

them out on the deck, I removed my trousers, then crawled into the sack. For the longest time, I left my glasses on so that I could see the stars overhead.

She handed me a cup of coffee the next morning—after nudging me awake with her foot. I could already feel the day's impending sunshine through my sleeping bag.

"Rise and shine, Captain Bligh," she said.

She was wearing her bikini and an Equal Rights Amendment T-shirt. The sight of her lovely tan legs assaulted my yet groggy mind with a sad conviction of last night's lost possibilities, but as I sipped my coffee I decided to be philosophical about the whole matter. What would happen—if it happened at all—would happen in a natural way, by mutual agreement. Propped up on one elbow, sipping coffee, I regarded the prospect of Deborah's knees.

"You have nice knees," I said.

"Scrambled or over easy?"

"An omelette," I said. "Use some of the Monterey Jack cheese."

"Chauvinist," she said, disappearing below.

We ate our omelettes in the sunshine, which by nine o'clock had increased to more than a suggestion of Sacramento Valley heat. One of the signs of being in love, I imagine, is the endowment of ordinary events with special significance. I must be in love, for I remember each detail of that day—details that will always stand out in memory with fairy-tale precision because I shared them with her. Deborah's presence helped me regain the beauty of the world, to endow ordinary events with magic.

After breakfast, we lay in the sun for two hours on the lawn near the swimming pool, reading our books. Deborah read Sigrid Undset's romance of the Middle Ages, *Kristin Lavransdatter,* which I had recommended to her—while I continued my desultory progress through Henry James's *The Wings of the Dove,* which is about a dying girl's rage to live whatever life remains to her.

"Sigrid Undset certainly makes human love seem a very

471

metaphysical proposition," Deborah said at one point halfway through the morning.

"All Catholic writers do this," I said. "Graham Greene, Evelyn Waugh, François Mauriac, Undset herself: they see the hungers of the flesh as synonymous with the hungers of the soul. Take Kristin Lavransdatter, for instance."

"Don't tell me the plot—I want to experience it slowly."

"Maybe you will," I said.

At noon we joined Turfer and company under the dining pergola. They were playing backgammon. Neither Deborah nor I knew how to play, but Turfer generously provided us with a running commentary, and after an hour or so we both had grasped the basic principles behind this very ancient, and very jet-settish, game. A white-jacketed college boy from Turfer's crew brought up two straw baskets from the ship's galley. They contained a lavish lunch: crab salad in avocado halves, peas and mushrooms vinaigrette, French bread and assorted cheeses, fruit, and blueberry cobbler. Champagne accompanied the backgammon; a Joseph Phelps Riesling introduced the crab salad; and a Chateau St.-Jean Pinot Blanc kept company with the dessert. Everyone was wearing swimming clothes, with most of the women putting some sort of light half-robe over their shoulders. Deborah pushed her Jackie O sunglasses up over her forehead to see better in the shade. One of the women, a blonde on the verge of her Joan Fontaine years, wore a wide-brimmed straw hat raked at an angle: Lady Gainsborough in a bikini. Had the photographer been able to airbrush me from the print, the scene would have made a perfect photograph for *Town and Country,* something captioned: "Californians at play in their Delta St.-Tropez."

The food, the wine, the sun, the proximity of so much sun-kissed flesh, brought me to a pitch of exquisite horniness. I began to experience a certain rushing of the blood under my bathing suit. I had the sudden hope that the lush Mediterranean ambience of Tinsley Island encouraged the Mediterranean custom of the siesta as well. Deborah threw back her head to laugh at one of Johnboy Turfer's jokes and I could see her

472

upper mouth and teeth. I imagined her mouth around me. I remembered a passage in the suppressed portions of one of Sebastian Collins's journals in which a certain redheaded Mrs. Santone of Paris, France, anointed Collins's urgent obelisk with the secret juices of her mouth, urging him towards seminal surrender.

"Let's play lawn bowls!" Johnboy Turfer said, banging his Polish-American fists on the table. "We're all getting groggy sitting here."

"Let's not play bowls on the lawn," I said to Deborah on the sly as everyone was getting up from the table. "Let's go back to the boat."

"How can you play bowls on a boat?" Deborah asked.

When we were below deck on our boat, I took her into my arms and kissed her greedily. Her back was warm to my touch. My aroused manhood was obvious.

"This isn't bowls," Deborah said cautiously, returning my kisses. She moved her head back slightly without disengaging herself from my arms. Looking me full in the face, she announced: "I'm a virgin and, given the time of the month, I'll get pregnant if we do anything. Even virgins can get pregnant."

"You're a virgin?" I said, genuinely taken aback. "No one in the world is a virgin. Virgins don't exist any more, like the great auk or the carrier pigeon. How could you live for a quarter of a century and still be a virgin?"

"Easily—when men wanted to screw me, I said no."

"You're the oldest virgin in the world," I said, sitting down at the galley dining nook, as if hit by a sudden blow to the solar plexus—yet remembering also in an instant Deborah feeding the swans in the lagoon of the Palace of Fine Arts. "You're out of step with the times," was all I could think of to say.

"In this point, I don't like the times. Had Ted lived, I would have long since been sexual with him, perhaps even married. That's where we were heading, Ted and I, without talking much about it. When he died, I lost interest. When I

473

started to fly, I got doubly defensive. One day I kept track of the propositions and come-ons I received. I got two before we landed in Palm Springs. By the time we arrived in Boise, the tally was up to four. If you count the standing offer all female cabin attendants had from the first officer, that made five in one day."

"Lucky girl."

"Perhaps—but how, and for what reasons, does one say yes?"

"Attraction. Desire."

"I guess I got into the habit of saying no."

"You're a tattooed virgin," I said. "I'll put money on it. You're the only tattooed virgin in the United States."

She pulled her bikini top to one side. Amazon-like, her left breast stood revealed to my delighted gaze. It was exquisite: the exposed left breast of Queen Calafia herself, the amazon empress of California, the Terrestrial Paradise; the breast of Raphael's La Fornarina, at once chaste and luxuriant, capable, in time, of nourishing a race of heroes. Stumbling from my naugahyde resting place, I stepped across the cabin. Smitten with desire, I kissed the Gustave Klimt rose which lay in a patch of skin where there was no tan.

"I'll ask you to interpret that as a promise," Deborah said.

"Let the promise be now," I said.

"Not now—perhaps later," she said. Readjusting her halter, she went into the forward cabin and rummaged through her duffel bag. She found what she was looking for: a baggy Mills College sweatshirt, some two or three sizes too large—making for a very chaste overgarment.

"Let's have a serious talk," she said. She opened the palm of her left hand, disclosing three marijuana cigarettes which she had apparently fetched from the duffel bag as well.

"One for you and two for me," she said.

We lit them from the stove, then went topside where we sat together in the cockpit, taking long hits on our Acapulco Gold.

"When Ted got killed, I felt horrible," Deborah said. "I felt

474

hurt and empty and angry about what had happened. I also made up my mind not to throw my life away or to hold myself cheaply."

"Like miscellaneous screwing."

"That—and other things. Like bullshit sentiment, for instance, by which I mean faking it to get by."

"I'm not faking it. I'm crazy about you."

"I believe you are, and I'm growing close to you too, but I don't want to be rushed. You're different, see, from what I expected. Ted was clean-cut and athletic. He was together about where he stood in life and what he wanted to do."

She went down into the galley and lit her second cigarette.

"I take back my 'two for me,'" she said, emerging on deck, a lighted cigarette in her hand; we passed the second joint back and forth as we talked.

"It's a scene from *Reefer Madness*," I said.

"I find that dope helps me to talk," Deborah said.

"Don't smoke too much," I said, "or you'll be heading into Stockton looking for a tattoo parlor."

"Used properly," Deborah said, "dope is a natural sacrament."

"So is wine. So is sexual intercourse."

"To get back to the point: you want to screw me now because I'm here, a closed cabin is available, you feel horny, and you have some affection for me."

"All true."

"But I'm not ready to screw you back."

"All true."

"The longer I went without screwing for the sake of being polite, the more the actual act of love began to mean to me. Let's put it this way: by now I've got a certain psychological investment in my virginity. It's become a measure of my self-worth."

"Tell me what you were like as a little girl," I asked.

She told me, and it took two wonderful hours because I began to tell her about my early life as well. I heard how her father played golf on Saturday afternoons, and how her mother

475

took flying lessons when she was past forty. At Christmas time, she said, they had piñatas in the parochial schools of Phoenix. Blindfolded, you whacked away with a stick at this stuffed paper bird hanging from a hook. If you got it right, you were showered with candy and small presents. When she was in high school, she swam competitively, making All State in her senior year. She also took up golf during summer vacations in college as a way of relating to her father.

"Did you feel abandoned?" she asked me when I told her about my five-year stint at St. Vincent's Home for Boys in San Rafael.

"Sometimes—but it was the only world I really knew. I found it difficult to imagine other possibilities."

"Do you see your mother?"

"Regularly—out of duty, but also out of baffled affection."

"We never fully grow up, do we?"

"In some ways we do, but we can also spend much of our lives rotating in ever expanding concentric circles."

"What's at the center of the circles?" she asked.

"A childhood sense of loss or a never-forgotten adolescent hurt. We circle around it again and again. The circles get farther away from the hurt as we get older, but whatever was consolidated by adolescence remains our essential personality, the fixed point of our compass."

"Is there life after high school, you mean?"

"Something like that—with the Beach Boys in the background singing: 'Wendy,' 'Girl, Don't Tell Me You'll Write,' 'Help Me, Rhonda,' or 'California Girls.' Speaking of which . . ."

Going below, I stuck a Beach Boys cassette into the tape deck.

"You're kidding!" Deborah said. "You're too old for the Beach Boys."

"I'm a Harvard-trained historian, remember? The Beach Boys are all about the California Myth. They sing about an adolescence I wish I had experienced, but didn't, and so feel resentful, as if, like Esau, my heritage had been taken from me."

476

"Must you cerebralize even the Beach Boys?"

"Surfin' Safari" came on. Deborah was perhaps pretty high on pot—I know I was. In any event, she jumped up to the upper deck and began a routine she described as the Surfer Stomp. I reached into the cabin and pulled the portable tape deck topside, turning its volume up considerably. Deborah danced with renewed vigor. Her long legs moved with the grace of a gazelle in flight. She made swimming motions with her arms and threw her face up to the late afternoon sun. For a moment, she seemed the very daughter of the sun itself: a girl-woman from the race's mythic past, dancing across a poppy field splendid in Grecian light.

Let her be mine, I prayed. Let her dance towards me out of the setting sun.

"Far out!" yelled Johnboy Turfer as he clambered aboard the *Class Action*, followed by his entourage. Turfer seemed somewhat blasted from an afternoon of wine drinking. Leaping over to our forward deck, he joined Deborah in a reasonable rendition of the Surfer Stomp. Mrs. Turfer and I watched from the cockpit.

"I didn't know Johnboy could dance," Mrs. Turfer said, "—not like this, anyway."

Chapter 12

I SUBMIT NOW before the high tribunal of scattered memory and lost youth portions of an essay by one Sebastian Collins published in the March 1874 issue of *The Overland Monthly,* entitled "A San Franciscan in Old Heidelberg." This essay, and whatever else I can call to mind from that period of my life with the help of the documents assembled for me by my daughter Marina (not to mention the assistance offered by the act of writing this journal, which has a way of jogging memory), will form the basis of the Heidelberg chapter in my forthcoming *Memoirs.* (I hope, by the way, that Paul Elder will do his usual fine job of design and printing for my memoirs. I hate shabby, ill-made books!) At the time my essay appeared in *The Overland Monthly,* I had already spent six months in Germany and was handling the language with some degree of facility, being totally soaked in it on a day-by-day basis. As I reread this essay, my thoughts led astray by every proper name or concrete reference, I see that a certain Germanism had even at that early date already crept into my English usage.

[From *The Overland Monthly,* March 1875]:

Old Heidelberg is a most romantic place, well worth the seven thousand miles a San Franciscan must travel by land and sea to be able at last to sip a glass of wine beneath the castle of the Counts Palatine. Surrounded by hilly forests, Heidelberg clings to the southern bank of the steep gorge through which the Neckar River rushes for its last twelve miles before its *rendez-vous* with the mighty Rhine on the plain below. The *Hauptstrasse* or Main Street of Heidelberg, crossed by the city's smaller streets, runs parallel to the Neckar, making this charming town of 40,000 a quintessentially riverine city. A solitary eighteenth-century bridge joins the city to the far shore of the Neckar. Although it is called *Alt* or Old, Heidelberg is essentially an eighteenth-century creation. Ruled for centuries by the autonomous Counts (later Electors) Palatine of the Rhine, Heidelberg was burned to the ground in 1689 by the French in their advance into Germany. In 1693, this time in retreat, the French again set the city to the torch. Heidelbergers rebuilt their city in the early 1700s. As the crown jewel of the Grand Duchy of Baden, Heidelberg has since enjoyed more than two centuries of peace.

Rising some three hundred and twenty feet above the Neckar, the red-sandstone *Schloss* (castle), begun in the thirteenth century and added onto ever since, dominates Heidelberg as would a similar edifice constructed atop Telegraph Hill. No matter where you are in Heidelberg, you are aware of the *Schloss,* not only as an architectural presence, but also as a tangible reminder, a chambered nautilus, if you will, of Old Heidelberg's storied past. In pre-Christian times, the *Schloss* was the site of a Celtic fortress. Druid priests encamped annually in the nearby hills, gathering together for their mysterious rites. Long the site of a robber baron fortress in the Dark Ages, the castle emerges into the medieval era as the seat of the Counts Palatine. Nine counts, five emperors, two kings, assorted queens, a duke or two, and an imprisoned pope have all made their homes in the *Schloss,* many of them memorialized in statues that stand in wall niches between the castle's grand windows. The retreating French general Count Melac dynamited the castle in 1693, and so in one sense the *Schloss* is now a ruin. It is, however, a flourishing ruin, visited annually by thousands who enjoy its amalgam of medieval,

479

Renaissance, and baroque architecture, and its view of Heidelberg and the vineyard-clad slopes on the far side of the Neckar River. A 49,000-gallon wine tun, the largest in Europe, is hidden away in the castle's lower reaches.

First and foremost, *Alt* Heidelberg is a university town. Founded in 1386 by Count Rupert I, Heidelberg University is the oldest institution of higher learning in Germany. Staffed by a faculty of forty ordinary professors and a total of sixty-eight professors extraordinary and *Privatdocents* (private tutors), the University currently enrolls some nine hundred students, among whom is your correspondent, Sebastian Collins. Count Rupert founded Heidelberg on the Paris model, with faculties of theology, law, medicine, and philosophy. This fourfold division of the faculty still remains in effect, although the faculty of philosophy has broadened itself out to include most of the liberal arts and the natural sciences. As one of the two universities of Baden (Freiburg is the other), Heidelberg University is by enduring medieval custom a virtually autonomous commonwealth. The ordinary professors annually elect their governing officer, the rector, from their own ranks. The German university, indeed, is built around the ordinary professor, just as the German General Staff centers around the *Junker* officer.

Every ordinary professor has survived a long, arduous climb to the Olympian heights on which he dwells. After taking the doctorate, a neophyte scholar begins his academic career as a *Privatdocent* or unappointed private tutor, lecturing for student fees. (It is, indeed, a sad affair to behold a fledgling *Privatdocent,* newly minted doctorate in hand, lecturing in a grand hall to an audience of some three or four students.) When he reaches his thirties, the *Privatdocent,* if his scholarly publications warrant it, is promoted to professor extraordinary. This exalted rank, however, does not carry with it a living wage. A professor extraordinary, on the other hand, usually attracts a larger number of students than does a *Privatdocent,* and he can also charge them higher fees. The rank of ordinary professor constitutes the summit of academic ambition. Reached in a scholar's late thirties or early forties,

480

the ordinary professorship is a state appointment, in certain cases an imperial appointment from the Kaiser himself, carrying with it a living wage. Unless he has a private income, therefore, a scholar attaining an ordinary professorship reaches his office after nearly twenty years of poverty and arduous labor. Up along this steep, rocky path, scores of scholars drop from exhaustion or settle miserably and marginally into the academic *Lumpenproletariat.* No wonder professors receive such reverence from the German people! They have been tested by a forced march of some twenty years of research and writing. They have deferred the gratifications of marriage and family; indeed, they have endured an almost entire absence of social life. Selected and toughened by such a novitiate, the German professor leads his life in circumscribed but effective circumstances—like a medieval monk.

Student life, on the other hand, is anything but monkish. In comparison to its American counterpart, German student life is an orgy of freedom. Totally indifferent to student attendance at his lectures, the Heidelberg professor lectures on what happens to interest him at the moment. Students sign up for a course of lectures at the commencement of the term, but only a small percentage of them are faithful to daily attendance. The student must, however, present himself for a prescribed series of examinations, should he desire a degree. How and when he reaches that state of preparedness is of no concern to the university; nor is his behavior while at Heidelberg, except for flagrant breaches of the public peace, in which case the student is apprehended by the university police and sent to the *Karzer* or students' prison for a week or so, where his meals and beer are allowed to be sent in. The *graffiti* on the walls of the *Karzer* are supposed to be the wittiest and most erudite in Europe. Heidelberg University does not conduct a residential college in the English or the American sense of the term. Students rent rooms in the city (thereby creating Heidelberg's major industry), and carry on their social life within the various *Vergindungen* or student corps. There are five major student corps at Heidelberg, each with its distinctive sash, insignia, and colored cap. Each corps or fraternity maintains a *Kneipe* or trophy room in a favored restaurant. Here the corps membership lists and archives are kept, together with flags, photographs, silver service, dueling swords, athletic trophies, and beer mugs. The fraternity meets daily for the evening meal, served by the restaurant. A light breakfast is available for those few souls up and about for morning lectures.

Beer drinking and the rituals of beer drinking pervade student life, although after some six months here I have seen but a few cases of the sort of flagrant public drunkenness that is all too often the sad case in San Francisco. Heidelberg abounds in beer gardens which serve a wide variety of delicious brews. The ritualistic *Schmolles* or brotherhood drink is an essential part of fraternity life. I have also witnessed a drinking competition, in which scholars match each other mug for mug, quotation for quotation, joke for joke, far into the night. Drinking songs are elaborate and of great antiquity, some of them originating in the Middle Ages. At the *Kommers* ceremony, students dressed in full fraternity regalia gather to honor a favored professor through an entire evening of drinking, song, and orations. The communal singing during such ceremonies is superb.

As I reread my essay from the vantage point of the year 1914, some forty more years after those golden Heidelberg days, it seems a little too redactive and stiff. It lacks the personal touch. I say nothing, for instance, about my charming third-floor room on the Schurmanstrasse, at Bismarck Platz, right on the Neckar River. My room on the third floor of No. 8 Schurmanstrasse contained a bed, a writing table, bookshelves, and a washstand. An engraving of Napoleon announcing the divorce to the Empress Josephine hung above the fireplace. There was no indoor plumbing. I drew my water from a barrel on the first floor and carried it up three flights of stairs. There was a water-less water closet at the end of the hallway. Tenants' more demanding needs were served by an outhouse in the back yard. (How cold to sit there on a winter's morning, obeying nature's call and studying

482

paradigms of irregular German verbs!) From my room, I had a lovely view of the Platz itself and of the gardens lining the river bank. On warm days I would move my writing table over to the window to enjoy the breeze and the panorama below. When I wished to take a break from my studies, I would browse in the open-air bookstalls facing the river. Sunsets over the Neckar seemed to leap from a Claude Lorraine painting— long, moodily luminous sunsets, punctuated by the lapping of the river against the stone riprap lining the shore and the tolling of the *angelus* bell from the Abbey of Neuberg on the outskirts of the city. In the evening, after hours of study, I would walk in the moonlight along the Neckar, easing my study-tangled nerves amidst the shadowy suggestions of the chestnut trees. On certain festival nights a fireworks display lit up the castle. Great pinwheels and cluster bombs of every color exploded over the gorge, lighting up momentarily the hill forests that loomed over each side of the city. One hill path on the opposite side of the river, called the *Philosophenweg* or Philosopher's Way, wended itself well into the back country, towards the ruins of the ancient church of Michaels-Basilika. On many a Sunday I tramped the *Philosophenweg* or some other hilly trail, or walked upriver to the farming villages where I would see peasants returning from Mass in picturesque sixteenth-century costumes.

In the course of three years, I grew familiar with every street and side-street of Heidelberg: the *Jesuitenkirche,* where I attended Mass, admiring the baroque architecture; the *Heiliggeistkirche* (Holy Ghost Church), built between 1400 and 1436, where over the course of a year so much of the sacred music of Johann Sebastian Bach would be performed by a skilled orchestra and choir. Flush with funds when my monthly stipend from the Bank of California arrived, signed by Mr. Ralston himself (his signature usually accompanied by an encouraging note and a warning to stay out of any and all military organizations), I'd enjoy a joint of roast venison at the Hotel zum Ritter on the *Hauptstrasse,* a Renaissance hostelry that escaped the conflagration of 1693. Goethe, I once read with amusement, fell in love with a serving maid who worked

483

there—and so did I in a manner of speaking, but that is another story. I loved, incidentally, the gigantic liver omelettes served at the *Roter Ochsen* (Red Oxen), gargantuan affairs cooked with lavish generosity by Herr Spengel and served with gusto by one of the voluptuous Spengel daughters, whose ample limbs bore eloquent testimony to the nourishing effects of a lifetime of their father's liver omelettes and buttered macaroni.

We older students unattached to an undergraduate student corps, many of us foreigners, made the Red Oxen our own special place. The Red Oxen was also the headquarters of an undergraduate fraternity, whose back room was covered with etchings, daguerreotypes, and ten years' worth of photographs of graduates. Advanced students such as myself had the privilege of hanging our photographs on the far wall of the front dining room—but only at the invitation of Herr Spengel himself. Having spent a small fortune at the Red Oxen on beer, bread, and liver omelettes, I was so invited by Herr Spengel to present my photograph in 1876, the year I took my doctor's degree. I imagine that it yet hangs there in some far corner: the solemn, starchy-stiff depiction of the young doctor of philosophy in tweed suit and academic gown, standing at the photographer's insistence (he had flags in his studio from every nation) against the backdrop of an artistically arranged American flag.

I remember the thousands of hours I spent in the research seminar of Ordinary Professor Albert Haymart, a remote, learned, terribly troubled man, helpful withal when it came to the instruction of his graduate students. Then in his mid-forties, Haymart had recently published *Die Theologischen Prämissen des Barock,* the fruit of some fifteen years of research, a magisterial study which I possess in the English version translated by Professor Seymour Hamden-Turner of All Souls College, Oxford, as *Theological Premises of the Baroque* (Oxford, at the Clarendon Press, three volumes, 1884). Haymart began his Heidelberg career as a young *Privatdocent* in the late 1850s. He devoted twenty years to the unraveling of the tangled

484

thicket of Counter-Reformational theology as it related to the arts of the baroque era. At the time I studied under Haymart, he had just been made ordinary professor after years of Spartan scholarship. A brand-new ordinary professor's signet ring flashed from his gesturing left hand as he discoursed in lecture hall or seminar. Yet to someone such as myself—someone, that is, who had seen a bit of the world and knew something of that portion of human nature which stands revealed when men march together under fire—something seemed to mar Haymart's happiness. Now and then as he lectured, a certain ambivalence came to the fore. He sometimes made ironic suggestions that perhaps there was more to life than heroic scholarship, that the laurel wreath (and the signet ring) of ordinary professor had not been worth the twenty years of discipline and deprivation. Never do I take Haymart's book off the shelf to verify a reference or to read one of his authoritative interpretations, but that I think that somehow the scholarship so evident in the three volumes of closely printed pages, the exhaustive footnotes and learned appendices, sucked something vital from Haymart like a vampire bat fastened to his throat, draining off his youth and something more precious as well: his ability to regenerate his energies and his appetite for life.

Haymart, incidentally, never published another word for twenty years after his promotion to ordinary professor. In 1896, however, just before his death, Haymart's magisterial *Life of Caesare Cardinal Baronius* (Berlin, two volumes) appeared. In the biography, Haymart delights in every humanizing detail he could uncover in the life of the great Counter-Reformational historian.

Caesare Baronius (1538-1607) spent twenty-five years of research before producing the first volume of his *Annales Ecclesiastici,* a history of Christianity down through the twelfth century. His superior in the Oratory at Rome, Saint Philip Neri, insisted that Baronius do the cooking for the other fathers because, being Neapolitan, Baronius had a gift for good cuisine. Baronius inscribed *Baronius coquus perpetuus*

("Baronius the everlasting cook") over the Oratory stove. Throughout a lifetime of arduous research, Baronius did a daily stint as a parish priest in addition to his cooking duties. Against his will, Pope Clement VIII created him cardinal in 1596, naming him librarian of the Vatican and director of the Vatican press. Amidst a thousand distractions of office, Baronius pushed his history of Christianity forward, ransacking the libraries and archives of Italy in his research.

Baronius found time, however, to write and direct plays (he loved the theater); and once every summer, laying aside his cardinal's robes and insignia, he took a month's ramble in the *Campagna,* sleeping in country inns. In his biography, Haymart accentuates every colorful detail of Baronius's personality—his early poetry, his love of jests, his taste for theatrical performances and concerts of choral music, his ability to cook, and his energetic rambles in the summertime. Haymart plays this side of the Cardinal's personality off against Baronius's exhaustive scholarship, his unassisted life of enquiry and composition, without benefit (before his promotion to the cardinalate) of even a secretary to transcribe a fair copy of his revised first drafts. Marina uses the word "fun" quite frequently. In his own way, despite a lifetime of research in dimly lit libraries and midnight hours of composition in his room, Caesare Cardinal Baronius, the Neapolitan lawyer-poet turned priest of the Oratory, had fun. Haymart's attention to the trifling but revealing details of Baronius's humanity is not typical of Teutonic scholarship. His elaborate analysis of Baronius's sources, however, and the role Baronius played in the larger drama of the Reformation/Counter-Reformation revival of church history is much more typical of German academic biography.

I took two research seminars from Albert Haymart. He directed my doctoral dissertation. He also sat as chairman of the committee that publicly examined my thesis in March 1876. However much it cost him, and however ambivalent he was about paying the necessary price, Albert Haymart was a great academician. I spent thousands of hours in the *Bibliotheca*

Palatina (the University's Palatine Library—a treasure trove of books and manuscripts) reading under his direction in the field of sixteenth- and seventeenth-century philosophy, theology, and art. A Heidelberg doctoral program, incidentally, like the Heidelberg undergraduate experience, was then—and perhaps still is—an unstructured, even casual affair, considered in administrative terms, however exacting it could prove in the actual experience. You presented yourself to an ordinary professor (in my case, Haymart). He accepted you into his seminars. He directed your dissertation. You stood a public defense of your thesis. You were either promoted to the Ph.D. (as I was) or you were asked to do more work on your dissertation. In certain heartbreaking cases, you might be asked to leave the university without a degree.

I stood my defense in the university theater near the *Peterskirche* on a March morning in 1876. A bound copy of my thesis lay before me on a table, like a cadaver awaiting dissection. Haymart and three other ordinary professors sat on a raised dais like judges at a trial for a capital crime. Each examiner had read my dissertation and was well-prepared to spend the next three hours debating the points developed in my research, or arguing with me on any topic they felt relevant to my advancement to the doctorate. A number of my Heidelberg friends, including Karl von Ost and Gudrun Wessling, sat in the audience, together with assorted professors, *Privatdocents,* and aspiring scholars interested in the field of seventeenth-century intellectual history. All in all, I suppose that some twenty onlookers lasted out the entire three-hour session. The examination began in German, crossed over to English (almost every German professor speaks English), and concluded in German.

My dissertation, published in 1878, as *Bernini, Eros and the Transcendant,* was—if I say so myself—a very thorough, very erudite explication of seventeenth-century psychology, theology, and aesthetic theory as it pertains to the work of the great Roman artist, Giovanni Lorenzo Bernini (1598-1680), who painted, sculpted, practiced architecture, and wrote copiously

487

from his sixteenth to his eighty-second year, never failing once in either imagination, inventive power, or courage. In my dissertation, I attempted to explicate seventeenth-century attitudes towards the theoretical disjunction between sacred and profane love, in life itself and as a theme in the arts. I ransacked a rich array of primary sources in an effort to suggest the distinctive relationship between the sacred and the profane cultivated by the creative personalities of the seventeenth century. In the period of high baroque, I argued, naturalism and allegory coalesced. Baroque art was at once dramatically realistic and intensely symbolic. It was fleshy but it was also spiritual. Each detail, furthermore, especially each visual detail, signified an exact theological value with almost mathematical precision. For an artist such as Bernini, alive with the pulsating energies of the baroque, every natural act, every visual surface, allegorized the life of spirit, while remaining co-extant with its own immanent, theatrical sensuosity. To explicate my thesis, I drew upon theological tracts, mystical treatises, the memoirs of saints and sinners, poetry, works of critical theory, Bernini's written statements, and above all other sources, Bernini's triumphant painting, architecture, and sculpture. I tried, in short, to show how Bernini, the exemplar *par excellence* of the consciousness and imagination of the seventeenth century, fused earthly experience and the spiritual analogue into one vital moment, electric with sanctifying grace and sensate ecstasy. In the theory and practice of Bernini and the other masters of the baroque, flesh found radiance in spirit. Spirit, in turn, found in flesh a psychological theater of the ineffable.

I was examined by a theologian, an historian, a literary scholar, and by Albert Haymart, who had mastered all these disciplines. After ten minutes of examination, I could see that my interrogators were baffled, challenged, and a little infuriated by the effrontery of my interdisciplinary effort to suggest the composite sensibility of baroque culture, then to illustrate that collective sensibility through the achievement of Bernini, the dominant, most representative artist of his age.

488

Why did I spend so much time explicating the Sacred Heart devotion, asked the historian, when that particular conception of Christ did not become a significant theme in religious art until the following century? Did Robert Bellarmine truly intend to suggest so much about the physical nature of Jesus Christ, asked the theologian? Was I not exaggerating the bias towards the Incarnation among Jesuit theologians? Did I think, asked the literary scholar, that because I had established parallels between poetry and painting, I had also established necessary causal relationships? Did not the structural, procedural, and teleological differences between poetry, painting, and sculpture preclude any such naive analogies as I had tried to establish?

After an hour of such intense attack, I thought that my dissertation would disintegrate before my very eyes into a pile of disjointed, unrelated fragments, the incoherent gatherings of a scribbling footnote-monger, let loose for three years among the shelves of the *Bibliotheca Palatina*. At this point, Professor Haymart, sensing my stress, led a friendly counter-charge. The best thing that could happen to me, I had been told by a young *Privatdocent* the night before the examination as I calmed my nerves over a stein of beer at the Red Oxen, would be for the professors to launch off into a discussion among themselves, using my examination as the occasion of their conversation. Should the conversation grow acrimonious, however, I could be in another kind of serious trouble. Rivalry and faction among examining professors had sent more than one aspiring candidate back to the library *sans* doctorate, the innocent victim of internecine strife. If the conversation stayed spirited but genial, said the *Privatdocent,* the professors ordinary would thank me for an enjoyable three hours of conversation by passing me on to the doctorate.

Which is what they did at exactly twelve noon, as the *angelus* bell announced the hour from the spire of the nearby *Jesuitenkirche.* How could we blame this young American, Albert Haymart laughed at the beginning of my second hour of examination, if in the course of his German education he falls under the influence of German thought? Ever since Hegel, the best of German thinking had sought the unity of experience; had sought to discern the coalesced trends, the spirit of the age that conferred force and direction upon an otherwise unrelated variety of events. Surely neither philosophy, theology, literature, art, nor psychology existed in isolation—however logical and necessary might be the categorical distinctions we professors make among the various disciplines for the sake of academic enquiry.

For the hour following this rescuing gambit of Haymart's, I was virtually ignored as the professors debated among themselves. Now and then they included me briefly in their conversation. According to the pocket watch I had laid open atop my dissertation to time my answers, it was eleven o'clock before they returned to a vigorous examination of specific points advanced in my dissertation. By then, their attitude towards me had grown friendlier. Yet, they suggested, my scholarship skirted past certain difficulties. I had made some causal connections that should perhaps have been best put forth as suggestive parallels. My erudition, however, was very German, and should be congratulated, as should my ambitious attempt to suggest the unity of an age through the strands of its aesthetic experience. I deserved to be passed, to be named doctor of philosophy at the June commencement, entitled to all the rank, insignia, and privileges accruing thereto. They stood, all four of them, beaming, holding their ringed hands out to shake mine, which was sweaty. They made a few friendly jokes about the United States. One of them slapped me heavily on the back. Karl von Ost approached, clicked his heels, and bowed. Gudrun Wessling stood in a back bench and cast a smile in my direction before she left by a side door.

Elated at passing my oral *examen,* I also felt a sense of sorrow and depression. William Chapman Ralston, who had sent me here, who had dreamed of bringing me back to San Francisco, Heidelberg doctorate in hand, was dead; and with him had died our dream of an Atheneum for San Francisco. My father sent me a bulky envelope of newspaper clippings chronicling

490

the entire affair: the run on the Bank of California by depositors panicked by rumors that Ralston had pushed the bank to the brink of insolvency by overextending its cash reserves; the lines that formed in front of the bank at Sansome and California Streets on the morning of 26 August 1875; the decision later in the afternoon to close the doors; the meeting of the directors that night in the board room; the reckoning, the tally: William Chapman Ralston owed a total of $9,565,907 in debts—some $4,655,973 of it was owed to the Bank of California. As president of the bank, Ralston had borrowed money from the cash reserves to cover some of his many speculative enterprises. The board of directors knew nothing of these loans. Ralston had done it all secretly. As it now stood, the Bank of California, the premier financial institution in the American West, had $4.5 million in liabilities over its assets.

Ralston was forced to sign over everything he owned to the bank. Leaving his office, he walked over to North Beach for his usual swim off the Neptune Beach House at the foot of Larkin Street, acting as if nothing had happened. Some hundred or so yards offshore (so one newspaper speculated), he suffered a stroke. Another newspaper held that Ralston swam deliberately into the treacherous currents that sweep past Alcatraz Island. In either event, he was dead when they laid his body out on the beach. Fifty thousand San Franciscans accompanied Ralston's catafalque out to the Lone Mountain cemetery. Dying in disgrace, Ralston nevertheless received a hero's funeral because, as Mrs. Fremont wrote, consoling me for the collapse of the Atheneum project, "the citizens of San Francisco realized that their uncrowned prince, their Lorenzo de Medici, obsessed with dreams of a new Florence on the shores of the Pacific, was dead, and that only narrow men with mean eyes were left in his place."

I encountered those same narrow men with mean eyes when I tried to revive Ralston's project after I had returned to San Francisco. To a man, they did not wish to hear of Atheneums. Knowing the caliber of San Francisco's *nouveau riche* upper classes, I anticipated their indifference when the news of

Ralston's death first reached me, and I felt it doubly again when I was awarded my doctorate the next year. How I would have loved to present my Heidelberg Ph.D. to Mr. Ralston in his upper office at the bank! How I would have loved once again to race with him down to Belmont behind two fast-trotting, high-stepping thoroughbred black pacers!

I was deeply touched that Gudrun Wessling attended my examination, since the intricacies of baroque civilization exceeded the boundaries of her interests. Herr Graf (Count) Karl von Ost, a Bavarian whom I had faced with sabres some six months previously in a subterranean room below the *Schloss,* sat through it all as well, although, like Gudrun, he had his mind on matters other than the baroque.

Gudrun Wessling worked at the Hotel zum Ritter near the thirteenth-century Gothic *Heiliggeistkirche.* The poet Goethe frequented the Ritter in the early years of the nineteenth century. He fell in love with a serving girl who worked there and wrote some lyrics in her honor. Gudrun was a cut above a mere serving girl, however; she was the account clerk of the entire establishment, responsible for the ordering, billing, and disbursing of funds for both the hotel and the restaurant. Born some twenty-eight years earlier in Lampertheim, a little village on the Rhine south of Mannheim, Fraulein Wessling attended a gymnasium in Worms specializing in business courses. In a graduating class of fifty, she later told, she was the only female. Ever since the 1890s, Fraulein Wessling's type has become common in Europe and America: female stenographers, typists, bookkeepers, clerks—"working girls," Marina calls them—responsible for their own support, living independently of family ties. The retail operation of the American department store is staffed almost entirely by such women. The novelist Kathleen Thompson Norris, for instance, went to work selling gloves at Raphael Weill's White House when both her parents died within the same year. In the Germany of the mid-1870s, however, working girls, other than those in domestic service, were a rarity. Only women of dubious

492

reputation lived independently of family ties. There were barmaids aplenty in Heidelberg, some of them virtuous, some not; but a semiprofessional working girl like Fraulein Wessling, trained in a business skill, was a novelty.

I met Fraulein Wessling at the Hotel zum Ritter in 1875, the second year of my Heidelberg sojourn. I maintained an account at the Ritter, paying it monthly. In this instance, I found myself undercharged in one month's reckoning, so I stepped to the rear of the establishment where the business offices were. Fraulein Wessling sat behind a desk piled high with bills. She wore a striped dress of good quality, high at the neck. She also wore a green eyeshade over her forehead, such as telegraph operators still wear in America.

"*Bitte,*" she said, not looking up from a pile of bills she was perusing at her desk.

"I owe you money," I said.

"A not uncommon characteristic of the English," she said, still arranging her accounts. Because of her eyeshade, I could only see part of her face. She had auburn hair, pulled into a bun, and a rich full mouth—unusual in a bookkeeper.

"I'm American, not English."

She tilted her head to regard me from beneath her eyeshade. I saw that she was about my age and rather pretty.

"You speak German like an Englishman," she said. "Ah yes, now I see: you Americans also speak English, don't you?"

"We try to," I said, noting that she had a slight space between her two front teeth, which the medieval English poet Geoffrey Chaucer says is a sign of sensuality in a woman.

"I once thought of going to America," she said, "but I was told that they treat women worse there than they do here, so I've decided to remain, temporarily at least, in Germany."

"That's all very interesting," I said, "but I am here to tell you that the hotel has undercharged me by a not-overwhelming sum, yet a sum that I imagine you would like to recover."

She took my bill from me, looked it over for a second, then retotaled the account.

"The mistake is here," she said. "He forgot to carry the ten. That is why he is no longer the bookkeeper."

"And why you now are?"

"Precisely. I always carry the ten."

She put her eyeshade back on her head and resumed her paperwork, as if I no longer existed.

"I would like to pay what I owe," I said.

"You look honest enough. We will put it on your next month's bill."

"Allow me to anticipate the revenue," I rejoined, "and buy you dinner here this evening."

She removed her eyeshade and looked me over for a second.

"Very well," she said. "We can eat here this evening. Come back at seven."

At seven I entered the crowded restaurant. Fraulein Wessling was sitting at a table to the rear of the cavernous Renaissance hall, one of the oldest surviving buildings in Heidelberg. She had changed her dress and now wore something dark blue with a run of lace at the throat. You could see a slight crease in her hair left by the eyeshade.

"If we sit here," she said as I sat down, "I can keep an eye on the help. I'm not satisfied as to the efficiency of our operation."

"Meals have been served here since the sixteenth century," I said.

"Three hundred years of inefficiency," she said, "is still inefficiency. In the new Germany we are trying to run things well."

I cannot stress enough how unusual it was in the 1870s—or the 1880s, for that matter—to have the exclusive company of a respectable young woman, such as I immediately understood Fraulein Gudrun Wessling to be. One called upon such women in their homes, or escorted them to chaperoned occasions; but dinner in a restaurant, such as this, and with an employed woman of some education, was a rare event indeed! My daughter Marina, by contrast, flies about San Francisco with her young man Scannell with the freedom of a mountain deer during the mating season.

"You speak German well for a foreigner. Where are you from?"

"San Francisco."

"In California?"

"The last time I looked at a map, Fraulein, it was still there."

"You are making a joke?"

"I am trying to."

"Don't waste your time. It is impossible that I should understand foreign jokes. How old are you?"

"Twenty-seven."

"I am twenty-eight. Are you married?"

"No."

"Good. I detest married men who have affairs."

"Is this an affair, just sitting in a restaurant?"

"We shall see. Herr Ober, over here please. Here's the waiter. Order your food."

I ordered *bratwurst,* potatoes, cabbage, and beer. She ordered veal and carrots. Between us we drank a bottle of Rhine wine.

"Where do you live?" she asked me.

"On Schurmanstrasse, at Bismarck Platz."

"What do you do?"

"I am preparing a doctorate."

"In what?"

"In the history of art."

"Then you must be rich."

"Why do you say that?"

"Only rich people have the time for such things."

"I could be poor, but reconciled to my poverty."

"You wear a good suit. You're well fed. You live in a good place. You study a recondite subject. You are not poor. I know these things. It is my business to know them."

"What do you do here?"

"I keep the books. Someday I shall own the hotel—and others like it."

"You're very pretty."

She seemed annoyed. "I know that I am. Since I have been fourteen, men have been telling me that. But of what use are such statements? Men only wish to sleep with pretty women, within marriage or without. Had I listened to their entreaties when I was younger, I would now be a *Hausfrau* in Lampertheim—fat, intimidated by a slob of a husband, and running after six snot-nosed children."

When we finished our meal, she said: "Let us walk." We walked down to the Neckar River, which is lined with gardens and lawns and an elegant walkway that continues along the river bank. She showed great curiosity about the United States, asking me a hundred questions having to do with the details of day-to-day living in America. I remember making estimates as to how much a number of items cost in the United States—silverware, an overcoat, candles, a comb, a fur coat, a parlor sofa. She seemed dissatisfied with my answers.

"You seem vague," she said after I had confessed to not knowing how much coal cost per ton. "You are a scholar, of course, which means that you are an irresponsible dreamer. What class are you in America?"

"We are not supposed to have classes in America."

"Rubbish. Class in an inevitable fact of life in any society. I, for example, was born into the lower bourgeoisie. My father is an apothecary in Lampertheim."

"My father is the chief of the fire brigade in San Francisco."

"Ah yes, the lower civil service. Then you and I are of a similar class. Good."

"Why is that good?"

"I would deal with you differently were you a member of a higher or lower class than I. I have, for instance, an admirer who is a count, Herr Graf Karl von Ost, the son of a Bavarian landowner."

"And you deal with him how?"

"Deferentially. He says that he loves me, which I believe that he does. He cannot, however, marry me for reasons of class; nor do I at this time wish to become his mistress—not yet at least, for I have not yet explored all the opportunities of

496

my life. I thus treat my young count—he is twenty-four and a candidate in law—deferentially, with the respect he is entitled to; for he is a clean-minded, wholesome young man, who is a credit to his family and to the Fatherland. Take me home now, please, I am tired. I must rise early tomorrow for work. I live at the hotel."

We walked back beneath the chestnut trees that line the Neckar. I admired the clean line of her neck, how her hair massed itself over her commanding brow. From a nearby *Gasthaus* we could hear the noise of a boisterous student song:

> Gaudeamus igitur
> iuvenes dum sumus
> post iucundam iuventutem,
> post molestam senectutem
> nos habebit humus
> nos habebit humus.

"What are they singing about?" she asked.

"About seizing the moment," I said, "about living one's life now—before it is too late. Before you're buried in the ground."

"It must be nice," she said, "to have the time to sing such songs."

"You can have the time," I said, "if you'll but take it."

"Perhaps you will help me," she said.

We walked in silence up the *Hauptstrasse* to the Hotel zum Ritter. She led me to the side entrance, entering the rear portion of the hotel where the upper staff had rooms. At the door she turned to me full-face. Extending her cheek, she pointed to it swiftly in a half-hesitant, yet simply understood gesture.

"You may kiss me here, if you wish, Herr Collins."

I kissed her cheek on the exact spot where she had pointed. She closed her eyes for a brief split second, then vanished into the doorway, leaving behind her the scent of apricot blossoms.

The mention of Herr Graf Karl von Ost involves some

497

discussion of dueling at Heidelberg, in that Karl and I had one very memorable encounter over sabres in a subterranean room of a *Gasthaus* below the *Schloss*. It was not precisely a duel, in the sense of a fight to the death, yet it was dangerous enough, and animated, on Karl's part at least, by the very sort of wounded pride that led men to serious dueling in the nineteenth century. I remember very well, for instance, how in 1858 in San Francisco a justice of the California State Supreme Court shot a United States senator to death on the shores of Lake Merced.

I omitted all discussion of dueling from my *Overland Monthly* article of 1875 because I considered what I knew of this practice to be privileged information. In the 1870s there were some twenty dueling societies at Heidelberg, including the Corps Saxo Borussia, of which I became a *Verkehrsgast* (associate), privileged to attend dueling sessions: which, by the way, were kept quite discreetly from the authorities. *Der Erste* (Captain) of the Corps Saxo Borussia, a young Catholic Westphalian baron, had an older brother who had served in the papal Zouaves on General Kanzler's staff. The fact that I also had served in the Zouaves, albeit in the ranks, came up in what had begun as a rather stiff conversation one evening at Sepp'l, the beer garden favored by the dueling Corps Saxo Borussia. I had been introduced to *Der Erste* by a third party, a fellow seminar student. *Der Erste* at first treated me condescendingly in the usual manner of his class. To retrieve the situation, my friend mentioned my service in the Zouaves, knowing of *Der Erste's* pro-papal family history and of *Der Erste's* brother's service with Kanzler, the German commanding general of the papal forces. Hearing of my service in Italy, *Der Erste* warmed to me immediately, his haughtiness melted by the presence of a brother-in-arms to his own brother—and from such an exotic place as San Francisco to boot. Within the hour I met the two *Dritte Chargierte* (prefects) of the corps and the *Fuchsmajor* (master of freshmen). Within a short time I realized that these younger men looked up to me because of my war experience.

This combat experience, ironically, this memory of smoke and bullets and the cries of the dying on bloody battlefields, prevented me from nurturing a whole-hearted appreciation of the dueling art. The young German noblemen who dominated the dueling corps held dueling in the highest esteem as a ritual of caste and courage. The most avid of them practiced for several hours a day under an experienced dueling master. Dueling sessions between rival corps were held weekly. Each basement or upstairs room of a corps was hung with past trophies. Most duelists, as I have pointed out, were from the noble land-owning class. A number of them intended military careers. For such as these, dueling was a significant preparation for an army career. One flinch, one false backstep, and a captain or a prefect could be summarily removed from office by the other members of the corps, like a disgraced general on the battlefield.

Gradations of rank, customs, and rituals of the dueling fraternities were governed by a rigidly observed code. One began as a novice, charged with learning the mores and lore of the fraternity, then graduated to the condition of *Fuchs* (freshman), instructed in the art of the rapier and sabre. A *Fuchs* might wear the corps cap, but he also had to be available to run errands—fetch beer and the like—for the older members. A *Fuchs* had to use the formal *Sie* when talking to an older fraternity brother. He chose one of these as his *Leibvater* (Body Father): the man, that is, whom he most honored and wished to emulate after his promotion to the rank of *Bursche*, or fully pledged active corps member. After a *Fuchs* fought three duels to his fraternity's satisfaction, the rank of *Bursche* was conferred on him in an elaborate ceremony in which the candidate was invested in the ribbon (worn diagonally from shoulder to hip), insignia, and senior cap of the corps.

Graduates of dueling fraternities dominate the officer corps of the German armies now advancing across Europe. The French and the Russians will find the monocled *Junker,* his face criss-crossed in scars, a formidable foe. Having, as I say, fought in a war and having killed a man in combat, I could

499

never romanticize dueling; yet I understood its Teutonic mystique, its efficacy as a bonding device among fellow members of the same protomilitary caste. Padded at the chest, their throats wrapped in heavy scarves, their eyes protected by slitted iron goggles held tightly in place by a leather strap, the duelists stood face to face before each other, engaged in furious swordplay. Contests ran for three intervals of five minutes each—twenty slashes the first round, fifteen slashes the second, seven slashes the third. An experienced student acted as umpire. Other students, acting as seconds, adjusted throat scarves and tightened belts between rounds, and offered a glass of *Schorle* (wine and mineral water) to the bleeding combatants. The object of the dueling exercise was to slash the cheeks or forehead of the opponent. No flinching or back-stepping was allowed. Attack! Attack! Attack! At the end of round three, students bled profusely from facial cuts. Bits of skin, hair, even bone, clung to the walls or even to the ceiling, flung there by an upward thrust of a rapier. The duelists then marched smartly over to the *Flickarzt* (mending doctor) in attendance, who did the necessary stitching on the spot. Ritual demanded that the stitches be taken without anesthetic and that each student hold the arm of his opponent as he underwent repair. After an evening session, I have seen the washing tubs of a dueling room as thick as red cabbage soup with the blood of duelists.

As I say, I found these rituals comprehensible within the context of German culture, but not my cup of tea. I appreciated the local color, however, taking an especial interest in sabre duels because I had had some training in that weapon. General Kanzler, you see, despised idleness. When we were in barracks, he demanded that we Zouaves drill two hours a day and that all of us, officers and enlisted men alike, receive small-arms instruction. He drilled the ranks in the bayonet (I later saved my life with this gruesome weapon: saved it, but took another's in the process); and he insisted that subalterns and noncommissioned officers become proficient with the sabre. My company commander, Captain William

Stafford (a Dubliner who joined the St. Patrick's Regiment in 1860, passing over to the regular Zouaves in 1862), insisted that I and a few other of the enlisted men learn the sabre also, so that the lieutenants and sergeants would have a ready supply of adversaries to practice upon. While vigorous, our sessions in the barracks courtyard lacked the ritual precision of the Heidelberg sabre duel, as I soon discovered to my distress.

Gudrun Wessling allowed me to call upon her once a week, at times and places of her own choosing. In retrospect, I better understand her now: she was a very early version of the New Woman; but at the time I found her baffling. She needed neither my affection, nor my protection, nor, I suppose, my company. Herr Graf Karl von Ost called upon her once a week and read poetry to her by the river.

"I thought you despised poetry," I said rather meanly. (Jealousy is always a most disedifying emotion. We never act correctly when we are in the throes of sexual envy.)

"I am merely indifferent to poetry, but if Karl likes to read poetry to me, then I shall listen."

Three months into our acquaintance, Gudrun came up to my room for the first time. Suffering from an attack of the flu, I had sent a note around to her by messenger that I was confined to bed and would not be available for our weekly excursion. Around twilight, Gudrun knocked on my door and swept into the room before I could get up from my bed to open the door. She was carrying a basket of fruit, cheese, bread, and a flagon of beer. Sitting on the end of my bed, she spread out a large napkin, on which she arranged the food. At her urging, I began to eat.

"Being sick is horrible," she said. "I hate to be sick."

Outside my window, which overlooked the Neckar from the third floor, another Claude Lorraine sunset was in progress. Gudrun leaned toward me to pour me a glass of beer. I took the bottle from her hand and placed it together with the glass she held on the nightstand. I drew her into my arms. I kissed her on the mouth for the first time in our acquaintanceship, tentatively at first, but then with the greed of an involuntary celibate, age twenty-seven and in excellent health. She kissed me in return, parting her lips so that I could feel the slight gap between her two front teeth on the edge of my tongue.

"Drink your beer," she said, disengaging herself from my embrace. "Beer is good for a fever."

"I have another sort of fever as well."

"Yes," she said, "I felt its symptom under the coverlet." She was referring to my tumescence under the light coverlet, which she had obviously felt when I drew her against me.

"Please don't worry," she said. "I am not offended by what is a perfectly natural response. You are a vigorous young man. When is the last time you experienced sexual intercourse?"

Taken aback by her question, I stammered the truth: "More than a year."

"That is too long for someone of your age. Do you masturbate?"

"As infrequently as possible. It gives me a headache."

"From guilt, no doubt."

"No doubt; but from frustration also. Masturbation is a rather pathetic form of erotic experience."

"But it relieves tension, Herr Collins. That's what you are experiencing now, sexual tension. I am in proximity to you. You already sustain benevolent feelings towards me. I am not unattractive. We are here together on this bed. You have just eaten and drunk, and your fever has abated. What could be more natural than that your thoughts should turn to inter- course and that your body should respond to your thoughts?"

"What of your thoughts?"

"I am thinking that it would be foolish of me to have intercourse with you at this time. I should get pregnant and ruin my life."

She moved up to the end of the bed, near my shoulders. I moved over to make room for her on the edge of the bed between myself and the nightstand.

"I pity your tension, *mein liebster*," she said, putting one of her arms around my shoulder and with the other casting aside the coverlet. I was wearing a flannel nightshirt. My aroused manhood created a distinguishable pyramid below my waist.

"I pity you because I pity myself and I pity the entire human race. We are all such victims of stupid biological forces: eating, drinking, eliminating, sleeping, copulating. Human life can sometimes seem a cruel, stupid joke."

She reached into the picnic basket which she had placed on the nightstand and removed a small crock of butter. Dipping her fingers into the butter, she kneaded her hand, spreading the butter evenly on her palm. When she took hold of me beneath my nightgown, her touch was electric and so was the softly rhythmical movement of her hand.

"Let me serve your convenience," she said. "You really should get a good night's sleep."

She kissed me with a fully opened mouth. Her deft hand increased its pace, faster and faster—until unbearable pleasure came to me in shuddering waves of spasm and release. Rising from the bed, she went to the washstand, poured water into it from a great white pitcher, and washed her hands like a surgeon after an operation.

"Get some sleep now," she said. "Nothing cures the flu like a good night's sleep."

She bent over and kissed my forehead. She tucked the blankets around me like a nanny putting a child to sleep. Sweeping up her picnic basket, she left. I listened to her descend the staircase; then I slept like a baby for ten hours.

Our only other instance of carnal communication occurred some months later at *Fasching,* the German carnival time. All societies (save perhaps the United States!) have a certain part of the year reserved for carnival—for riot and merriment and indulgence of the flesh (*carnis* in the Latin). In southern Germany, carnival time begins on the Feast of the Epiphany (the sixth of January) and continues until Ash Wednesday, when Lent begins. Heidelberg celebrated *Fasching* with a costume parade down the *Hauptstrasse* and with innumerable costume balls. A splendid civic ball was held in the *Rathaus* (City Hall) on the Saturday night before Ash Wednesday. I attended, attired as a California gold miner. I wore denim pants tucked into black boots, a red flannel shirt, and a wide-brimmed sombrero-style hat. Joe Strong came up from

503

Munich for the event. He dressed himself as Pan the goat-god, naked to the waist, his legs wrapped in shaggy sheepskin chaps. He attached two stubby horns to his head by means of a chin-strap. We drank three bottles of Rhine wine in my rooms before donning our costumes, then poured hilariously downstairs. Throngs of Heidelbergers in various stages of intoxication and masquerade swarmed the streets through which we passed on our way to the *Rathaus*. Rather than walk normally, Joe Strong insisted upon performing a goat-dance up the center of the street. He pranced and cavorted like Pan himself sporting among the dryads. At one point, a crowd gathered to witness his drunken gambol. They cheered him lustily as he goat-danced about a young woman dressed in a Grecian costume. A strolling accordionist stopped and provided Joe and the dryad, now dancing herself, with appropriately saturnalian dithyrambs. Exhausted from his capering, Joe drank from a large mug of beer which had been anonymously thrust into his hands. He swilled half the mug, then poured the rest over his head. The crowd cheered lustily as Joe baptized himself in beer.

The assembly room of the *Rathaus* teemed with costumed Heidelbergers, many of them dancing to a brass band playing on a stage. Whole groups of people, their arms locked, swayed to and fro in sweaty companionship, singing lustily. The floor was slippery with spilt beer. As soon as I presented the doorkeeper with the two tickets of admittance presented me by Professor Haymart ("I'll not be attending," he told me), Joe Strong pranced off in the direction of a phalanx of singers. Two girls, one in peasant attire, the other costumed as Marie Antoinette (my supposition), parted arms and Joe locked himself between them. That was the last I saw of Joe that evening.

The Scaramouche who approached me was obviously female, to judge from the full line of her hips and the swell of her bosom. She wore felt boots (green), yellow tights, and a black-and-white checkered domino doublet. Her hair was tucked into her feathered cap and a Scaramouche mask of stiff black silk covered her face.

"Dance with me," the Scaramouche said. I knew at once that it was Fraulein Gudrun Wessling.

"With pleasure," I said, taking her in my arms and joining the other waltzers at the center of the ballroom.

"You dance well for a cowboy."

"Not a cowboy. A California gold miner."

"You dance well for a gold miner."

"And you are a surprising Scaramouche."

"Tonight I am Scaramouche. On Monday I resume my bookkeeping."

I purchased two oversized steins of beer and we drank them off in a half-dozen pulls. Then we danced again. Then we drank more beer. Then we resumed dancing. By midnight the entire hall seemed swept away in a collective frenzy of music, movement, singing, and beer. A young man in monk's robes lay sprawled on the floor near the orchestra, summoned by beer to his pre-Lenten reward: a swinish sleep from which trumpets, drums, and tubas could not rouse him. A *commedia dell'arte* braggadocio, an inflated pig's bladder strapped to his thighs, hollered at the top of his lungs in what I understood to be an obscure Balkan language. A shepherdess in a torn smock showed a shocking amount of cleavage. A man (or was it a woman?) in a gorilla suit did somersaults on the floor. Two policemen (students in costume, or perhaps even wayward members of the Heidelberg constabulary) got into a fistfight, then collapsed tearfully into each other's arms. A live pig ran through the hall, sending a number of women into screams. The pig was followed by a number of drunken young men in farmers' costumes, who tripped again and again on the slippery floor as they pursued their vagrant swine through the throng. Throughout it all, the orchestra played and mugs of beer were passed about from a central dispersing point.

Gudrun and I left the *Fasching* ball at around two, arm in arm, and middling drunk. We walked down the still crowded *Hauptstrasse* towards the Hotel zum Ritter. At Bismarck Platz, Gudrun, still masked, looked down the street to my apartment block.

"I must use your water closet," she said. "I am not able to

505

make it home to the hotel without the immediate use of a water closet."

We turned to the river and walked the remaining block to my building. I fumbled with the key at the front door, my heart pounding, my imagination riotous with remembered images of Gudrun's last visit to my quarters. I scrutinized her body as she climbed the staircase in front of me. The costume she wore revealed her superb female form. When we came to my landing, she entered the water closet at the end of the hallway and banged the door shut. I fumbled for my key, unlocked the door to my room, and entered, leaving the door ajar. A few minutes went by. I sat on the end of my bed, my heart racing. Gudrun entered. Walking over to my bed, she threw back the covers and, without removing a stitch of her Scaramouche costume, threw herself onto the mattress, pulled the covers over herself, and fell asleep. Disappointed, I went over to my stuffed chair and stretched out on it, my feet flung over its matching hassock. Just before I dozed off, I heard some laughter and chords of music from a small, rather disreputable *Gasthaus* down by the Neckar.

An hour or more later (two hours perhaps, I couldn't tell) I awoke when I felt my shoulder being shaken. Gudrun stood before me, attired solely in her Scaramouche mask. She was massaging herself gently with her index finger. Moving close to my chair, she presented herself to me.

"Kiss me here," she said huskily.

I kissed her there.

"Put your tongue there."

I complied.

"Take off your clothes."

Clumsily, I took off my clothes, nervous at this unexpected ending to a long year of involuntary celibacy. She stood before me as I undressed, her index finger back to her pleasure point, circulating deliberately. I took her in my arms, thrilled by the lavish bareness of her back, the feel of her breasts against me, the softness of her derrière, across which I passed my hands as I kissed her. She continued massaging herself as we embraced.

506

When I reached to take off her black masque, she held my arm away.

"It stays," she said. "I am not, strictly speaking, the woman you know from the Hotel. I am partly another person, a *Fasching* changeling. Now kiss my breasts."

I have never in my life been so thoroughly and explicitly instructed *vis à vis* lovemaking as I was that night. As we lay together on the bed, Gudrun Wessling guided my every move. She insisted upon long, slow preliminaries. After some ten minutes of stimulating exercises, I made a move to enter her.

"I am not ready yet," she said. "More of this." She guided my hand down to her secret parts.

"Bring me my purse," she said a little later. Her costume purse, a leather sack, was fastened to her belt, which lay atop her neatly folded costume on a chair next to the dresser. While I was there, I lit the coal-oil lamp, adjusting it to a soft glow. I brought it over to her, maddened by desire—maddened by the intricacies of the past half-hour, maddened by the fall of her breasts as she lay on her back on my bed, by her stomach, so white, by the opening between her thighs which she fingered gently as she awaited my return from my errand. She took the purse from me with her unoccupied hand and placed it on the bed next to her. Reaching in, she drew out some folded tissue and handed it to me. Opening the tissue, I beheld a half-dozen neatly rolled rubber rings.

"They are called condoms," she said. "A Frenchman invented them, I am sure. They prevent pregancies and the spread of disease."

When I saw her the next week, it was as if nothing had happened. She was as cool and crisply efficient as ever. The domino-masked woman who writhed in pleasure in my arms had indeed been a *Fasching* changeling. Yet even in wanton desire Gudrun had been a good, efficient German. She tutored me like a schoolboy. Following the instructions of my Scaramouche lover, I was saved from selfishness or embarrassing mistakes, just as the sheaths she provided for the occasion

507

prevented pregnancy or disease. Having been taught by Gudrun what pleases a woman—having been taught the slow, steady ministrations that lead to female pleasure—I have been saved ever after from abrupt piggishness in bed. Since that nocturnal Heidelberg seminar, I have known that unless a woman pleases herself and is pleased in the way that she wishes to be pleased, there is little pleasure for her partner, save the mechanical satisfaction of release. To confer pleasure on a woman is a great satisfaction for a man. Gudrun's instructions contained behind their clinical surface a tender, loving message. Telling me what she desired on that changeling night—her masked night of forthright hunger—Gudrun shared with me the secret thirsts of her soul.

"Touch me there again," she commanded. I touched her, joyous in the sight of her joy. "Now," she said. Mounted over her body that extended out before me from our loin connection like the soft topography of an earthly paradise, I moved my hips slowly until I saw that her lips parted. I then gently removed the black masquerade from her face. We looked at each other in the lamplight, I seeing her face for the first time as we urged each other to the fullness of what our bodies offered. Our mouths met as final pleasure drew near. Our tongues pressed together and I thought for a moment that she was breathing in my soul. Crying out, I made her a gift of it. With her own cry, she gave me hers in return.

I paid for these passages of delight with a series of sabre slashes across my right forearm, skillfully administered by Herr Graf Karl von Ost in a subterranean room in a *Gasthaus* below the *Schloss*. Not that Karl knew for certain that I had been intimate with Gudrun. As far as I could tell, he did not. Yet he must have suspected as much, for he found me frequently in Gudrun's company at the hotel. What an irony: that this fiercely modern *Fraulein,* with her green eyeshade and lightning arithmetic, her explicit instructions, and her self-supplied prophylactics, should occasion something so feudal as a duel!

508

Karl and I could not help but notice each other when we passed in the narrow hallway of the Hotel zum Ritter leading from the main dining room to the administrative offices where Gudrun worked. We would nod politely as we passed each other. Karl was a handsome young man in his early twenties, blond and possessing the appropriate dueling scars on his aristocratic face. A Bavarian—hence southern, hence Catholic—he nevertheless affected a slightly Prussian style. Intended for the army, a *Junkerische* demeanor would, he knew, stand him in good stead upon his graduation from Heidelberg when he was scheduled to take a commission in a Bavarian regiment of light infantry. Karl did not intend a military career, he later explained to me when we became friends. He was to inherit his family's estates; a few years, however, with a local regiment added the appropriate *éclat* to a feudal landowner's background, just as a law degree aided one in handling the business aspects of the von Ost estates. For reasons of class, Karl never married Gudrun, but he did set her up in Munich with the wherewithal to found an accounting firm. Gudrun Wessling became the first woman in the German Empire to pass a state accountant's examination and to be licensed to practice. Eventually, Karl did take Gudrun as his mistress—but I am getting ahead of my story. Suffice it to say that he loved her and that he was jealous of my attentions. I was Gudrun's age, while Karl was a much younger man. That gave me an advantage. Secondly, I belonged to Gudrun's class, whereas Karl was prevented by the class barrier from offering Gudrun the honorable relationship he would have liked to bestow upon her. How Herr Graf Karl must have smoldered in rage at my bumbling attentions to his *inamorata* in the green eyeshade! That a vulgar American should dare compete with a Bavarian count for a German lady's attentions!

The sabre is the aristocrat of the duel. My affiliate corps, the Saxo Borussia, held those competent in the sabre in the highest esteem. A sabre is at once a crude and a subtle weapon. It can hack and cut, but it can also feint, parry, and slash with lightning rapidity. There are also times when a sabre rivals the surgeon's scalpel for delicate effects. As an onlooker, I enjoyed the sabre duels of the Corps Saxo Borussia, because, as I have said, I had been trained in the weapon by Captain Stafford of the Zouaves. No one, however, was more shocked than I that evening when Karl stepped away from a group of his associates in the Corps Barbarossa, walked across the exercise room where we were all gathered and without warning slapped me across the face with his glove. A collective gasp escaped from the crowd of undergraduates. First of all, there was the unexpectedness of it. No one knew that Karl and I were even acquainted. Secondly, Karl had taken a great risk in crossing the class barrier to insult an American of uncertain antecedents. Thirdly, grudge duels occurred only rarely at Heidelberg. Like everything else, however, they had their ritual. No sooner was I slapped than the *Erste* of my corps, the young Westphalian baron whose brother had served with the Zouaves, stepped to my side and took charge of the proceedings according to established rubric.

"The issue?"

"A personal matter," answered Karl, his handsome, boyish face flushed with anger.

"Your response?" *Der Erste* asked me.

"I have no response. I am baffled by Herr Graf's anger."

"You apologize then?" Karl asked.

"For what?"

"For presumptuousness—and bad manners."

"It is you, Herr Graf, who are ill-mannered."

"Very well," said *Der Erste.* "I declare an impasse. You may choose the weapon, Herr Collins."

"Since tonight was to have been a sabre exercise, I choose sabres," I said, trying then and there to recall my training exercises of five years previously.

"It is the sabre, then," said *Der Erste.* "You shall have three rounds of five minutes each. Goggles and throat bandages allowed. I forbid forward thrusts to the middle body, but cuts to the face, shoulders, and arms and legs are permitted."

Der Erste, in other words, was permitting us the most

510

dangerous mode of dueling available in the Heidelberg repertoire—a form of dueling that was technically against the law and only rarely practiced. Hushed with expectation, the twenty or so students in the room backed off and waited. Even the middle-aged *Flickarzt,* bored by twenty years of stitching up undergraduate scars, seemed interested. Karl removed his frogged student tunic. I removed my coat, tore off my cravat, and rolled up my sleeves. With a piece of chalk, *Der Erste* drew a circle some five feet in diameter in the middle of the room. Karl and I selected sabres from a rack containing some twenty weapons. I chose a sabre of medium weight, stamped with the date, 1854, and the place, Dresden, on its hilt. Karl chose a lighter weapon. Walking to the center of the room, he commenced a series of warm-up exercises which sent a lump into my throat. He whirled his sabre over his head like a charging Uhlan. Slashing forward in attack, he dropped first to one knee, then to the other. He performed a series of knee-bends, one of which would have left me paralyzed on the floor. Attendants strapped iron goggles over our eyes. The world quite suddenly narrowed itself down to two lateral slits from which I must anticipate Karl's moves: avoid them, block them, and, at the same time, launch my own attack. Someone handed me a glass of wine mixed with mineral water. I drank it. Karl sipped his, then poured the rest over his head in the manner of a pugilist cooling himself between rounds.

The entire situation, I thought to myself, was embarrassing. I had no desire to fight this man, certainly not over Fraulein Gudrun Wessling—as much as I had enjoyed our *Fasching* sojourn amidst the delights of Venusberg. I was certain that Gudrun never intended herself to be fought over, that she would laugh if she were here—would lecture us, in fact, about the stupidity, the inefficiency, of such quarrels. Count Karl von Ost, however, seemed every bit in earnest. He had boldly maneuvered me into a situation in which I was liable to certain physical damage—not death, perhaps (people rarely died from these grudge duels), but certainly to a slash or two, or a broken arm, or a severed tendon.

"Gentlemen," *Der Erste* announced, "take your places." *Der Erste* seemed to be enjoying himself enormously; grudge duels were rare events. I have no doubt, in fact, but that I am still talked about in Heidelberg among the Old Boys of the Corps Saxo Borussia and the Corps Barbarossa: remembered at reunions as the American who fought a sabre duel with a look of bewilderment on his face, but fought creditably nevertheless, taking and giving some superb cuts that required a reputable amount of stitches.

We faced each other and offered the traditional salute of touching the sabre hilt to our chins, then extending it forward. Then *Der Erste* called, "Commence the first round!" Having killed a man in combat (reluctantly—only to save my life), I wanted to laugh at all this boyish play-acting, this posturing about with sharpened sabres. Karl's first attack, a downward slash to my left shoulder, made the air whistle. I dropped to my right knee to gain maneuvering room and simultaneously began an upward backhand, left to right, which blocked Karl's opening sally. At the moment our sabres collided, my ambivalence disappeared. Had Karl's swipe connected, my collar bone could have been broken. My upper arm would most certainly have been severely slashed. Still on my knee, I whirled left to right in counterattack. I attempted a circular swipe aimed at his elbow. Karl caught it skillfully at the hilt. Our sabres locked: I used the interval to stand up and step back and regain my guard. The fight was on!

Karl's style with the sabre was elegant, gymnastic, full of surprise and variation. He fought like an officer, with showmanship. I fought like an enlisted man, defensively, husbanding my resources, allowing the officer to take the chances and win the medals. I realized instantly that I could never match the young count's footwork, so I played a cautious game, moving circularly around the chalk diameter in an effort to force him as much as possible to attack me head-on, where my weight and superior strength might be used to advantage. I played in other words, a squat bulldog to his bounding borzoi. By the end of the second round, Karl had sensed my

512

strategy. He began to approach me to the side, holding his body at an angle. In these angled attacks Karl's superior sabreship gave him great advantage. Sidestepping while he simultaneously feigned the beginnings of an obvious diagonal cut, Karl seduced me into an offbalanced attack against empty air. Sensing the ruse, I pulled back, my right forearm exposed. Crack! Karl's sabre cut across my arm, leaving a nasty slash. It was a miracle that a bone was not broken.

I fought round three in agony. My bleeding forearm throbbed with pain. I was breathing heavily. Angrily I tried a double left feint, the one move I could picture with any clarity in my pain-distracted mind, and it connected to Karl's left shoulder, drawing blood. I was totally off balance at the conclusion of my attack and would have provided him an easy target for retaliation. I doubt whether I could have lifted my sabre for another stroke. Mercifully, *Der Erste* announced: "Gentlemen, honor has been satisfied on both sides. Do you wish to desist?" We both wished to desist: I from fatigue, and Karl from satisfied honor.

I held Karl's arm according to custom as the *Flickarzt* stitched his shoulder. Karl expressed satisfaction with the elegant clarity of the wound, a neat cut across his left shoulder. When his stitches were sewn, Karl held my left arm as my right forearm received some two dozen stitches. Strictly speaking, since this was a grudge match, neither of us was obliged to observe the arm-holding part of the ritual, but we did it anyway—spontaneously, I might add; for we had grown to know each other rather well in the previous twenty minutes. I admired Karl's lightness, his elegance and grace. He (as he later told me) admired my persistence, the humility if you will with which I conducted my defense, the lucky desperation of my last double feint.

"You fought like a bear, Sebastian," Karl later told me, "a bear surprised at the entrance to his den."

"Yes, indeed, Karl, a California grizzly bear surprised by a German wolf."

We never talked about the cause of Karl's anger, even when

we later became reasonable friends—not close friends, mind you, but reasonable friends. Noticing that he did not run into me at the Hotel zum Ritter as much as he used to, Karl most likely attributed my absence to the duel we had fought. Actually, I had become involved with a less demanding, more accessible paramour than Fraulein Gudrun Wessling, a barmaid at a small *Gasthaus* in nearby Handschuhsheim. But I did step aside in my own clumsy way. However compromised by caste, Karl and Gudrun did possess something of a future together, whereas between Gudrun and myself there was no future, only a certain unexpressed friendship and the memory of an urgent masquerade embrace.

Karl and Gudrun, as I've already pointed out, came separately to my oral examination. By that time, Karl and I had already spent a few evenings in each other's company over beer: brought together for the first time after the duel by the respective captains of the Corps Barbarossa and the Corps Saxo Borussia at a boisterous dinner in the lower room of the Red Oxen. My *Erste* gave a wonderful, half-drunken speech. In reference to my American nationality, he referred to me facetiously as Old Shatterhand, the plainsman hero of the German Karl May's novels inspired by the Leatherstocking tales of James Fenimore Cooper. He then described the duel in mock heroic terms, quoting copiously from the *Nibelungenlied*. By the end of his account the room was roaring with laughter. Everyone began to sing fellowship and drinking songs, including the entire *Gaudeamus igitur*. Karl and I were brought to the head table and made to shake hands while everyone cheered. The evening ended in a orgy of *gemütlichkeit*, with all of us locking arms as we promenaded down the *Hauptstrasse*, singing at the top of our lungs.

Like myself, Karl is too old for the present war. He must be over sixty now, and Gudrun near seventy—if she is alive at all. I'm certain that Marina would admire her enormously, should they ever meet, which is not likely with a war on, a war into which the United States must eventually be dragged, make no bones about it, and not to fight on the side of the Kaiser either, but against the Germans, who are behaving so bestially in Belgium according to the newspapers. Royce is near-hysterical with anger. As the leading exponent of German philosophical idealism in America, he feels that he has been turned into a huckster by the evil behavior of the Kaiser's armies.

Royce and I remember another Germany: glorious learning, university days filled with song. The German empire contains scores of subcultures and points of view. It was the Germany of the South that I encountered and fell in love with at Heidelberg—a Catholic Germany looking to the Mediterranean, a Germany that two thousand years earlier Julius Caesar had brought into the pale of Rome. Prussian Germany represents another spirit, a harsh, vindictive, fiercely protestant spirit that is now in the ascendancy, a spirit antithetical to the South. The Prussian king has become the German Kaiser, and the Prussian *Junker*—cruel, arrogant, his head shaven, a monocle in his eye—now urges the hitherto suppressed Hun to dominate German behavior. Looking east to Prussia, the Germany of Berlin has betrayed the Mediterranean South, the Germany of Munich and Heidelberg. Germany forgets what its great poet Johann Wolfgang von Goethe learned in Italy: the lessons of liberality, joyousness, the soul expanding in the sunshine, the scent of lemon and roses in a twilit garden. Goethe rediscovered classical Mediterranean civilization as an imaginative ideal for his fellow Germans: a civilization balancing order with justice, urban sophistication with agrarian piety; a culture seeking simplicity, harmony, elegance. Choosing to play the Hun—the barbarian Hun banished from Germany by Christianity, by Renaissance humanism, by Goethe himself—the German Empire turns its back upon Mediterranean clarity and light. It embraces the horrid demons of the Teutonic forest. It howls in concert with the evil wind-spirits of the treeless Prussian steppe.

Perhaps that is why I have been thinking so much of Heidelberg lately—not because I am growing old and hence must live more and more in the past, but because as the lamps

515

of civility go out in Europe before the howling winds of German aggression, I feel the need to summon up to myself the finer Germany I once experienced with such pleasure and remember now with such vividness: summon it up, lest I disbelieve in its very existence and hence lose something precious of my own identity.

Heidelberg survives in me as part of my personal myth, my usable past. Like the rest of my past, Heidelberg is flawed by an element in it of compromised promise, of saddened and saddening unfulfillment. The published research of those years has won me a modest reputation, but not a major professorship. In the long run, I see that I have scattered my intellectual energies too diffusely to attain that obsessive focus demanded by high scholarship in the German manner. Fatally charmed by the exquisite variety of the world, I have written on art, theology, wine, literature, architecture, politics, California. Because I once loved her, I wrote a biography of Sybil Sanderson. I am now using this journal to draft the first version of my memoirs. (I shall, however, not present Mr. Elder with the totally candid recollections of my erotic life which I have allowed myself in this journal!)

All in all, my accomplishment has been solid (so says Santayana), but modest (so say I) in comparison with the heroic dreams that seized me as I devoured book upon book in the Palatine Library. Soaking in the thought and literature of the Counter-Reformation and the baroque, I dreamed of filling entire shelves with the fruits of my scholarship; instead, I have written a mere three books in my field: *Bernini, Eros and the Transcendent; The Art of the Baroque; Theological and Literary Relationships*. My small study *Wine Prospects for California,* my *Call for California Art,* my life of Sybil, and my impending memoirs have all been occasioned by the demands of a particular moment in my life, and not by the transoccasional urges of austere scholarship, which demand that we move beyond the demands of the moment, devoting ourselves to the perspective of the centuries.

And yet I must be honest and say that I never intended to

become a pure scholar. Had Ralston lived, or had he lived and not gone bankrupt, or had he died after securing an endowment, I might have directed the Atheneum of San Francisco, as much a curator and a librarian in my professional functioning as a research scholar. I don't think that there is a major library or museum of Italy, Germany, or France that I did not visit between the years 1873 to 1875 at Mr. Ralston's expense, studying their procedures and administration. I carried with me a letter signed by Mayor William Alvord above a stamped waxen emblem of the official seal of San Francisco. The letter explained that one Sebastian Collins, a citizen in good repute, was preparing for the directorship of a proposed library-museum complex in San Francisco and should be afforded every courtesy in his efforts to study how such institutions were managed in the great cities of Europe. I still possess the letter, together with the notebook into which I meticulously entered my observations on the accessioning and cataloging of books, the care of manuscripts, the restoration of damaged paintings, the design and placement of windows for good lighting, *et cetera, et cetera.* How pathetic this now seems. It is 1914, some forty years after my research, and San Francisco is but beginning to build a library worthy of the city. The Midwinter Exposition of 1894 left us with the beginnings of an art museum, but only the fragile beginnings: the shell of a building and the promise of Michael de Young that he will eventually take an interest in the museum's future. I daresay that at this moment, the third day of September, 1914, there is not a solitary old master in either public or private possession in San Francisco: at least none that I know of; and if anyone would know of the existence of such a painting, I flatter myself that it would be I.

The Art Commission of the Palace of Fine Arts of next year's Panama—Pacific International Exposition is endeavoring to arrange a show of first-rate European painting for the Exposition year, if the hazards of submarine warfare will permit the trans-Atlantic shipment of art treasures. Such an exhibit will serve to elevate local taste.

517

In his dream of an Atheneum, as in so many other dreams he had, William Chapman Ralston overreached himself. Neither he nor San Francisco was up to it. I spent a half-dozen frustrating years in the 1877–1884 period, waiting for someone to pick up the Atheneum torch where Ralston had dropped it, but no one volunteered. Taste, generosity, the civic instinct: all the virtues which characterized Ralston (I say this, acknowledging also that he overextended himself financially and fell into shady banking practices), the virtues necessary to push the Atheneum to reality, seemed to have absented themselves from San Francisco. Millions upon millions of dollars were made here, but precious little of it found its way into philanthropy. Pioneer fortunes were not made by men of taste and refinement, but by semieducated buccaneers loathe to part with a penny for such a useless thing as another one of Billy Ralston's insane schemes. When Governor Stanford's son died so tragically at the age of fifteen in Florence in 1885, and the Governor talked of some great bequest to commemorate his and his wife's grief, I made one last attempt to revive the Atheneum idea. I called upon the Governor at his home atop California Street on Nob Hill. As I sat in the foyer, surveying the wretched copies of even more wretched European paintings hanging about me—academic paintings of the stiffest sort or sentimental paintings of the most trashy sort—I sensed the foredoomed failure of my mission. The Governor cordially heard me out, then told me he had already decided upon an educational institution on his Palo Alto property.

As I slipped into middle age, I less and less felt the compulsion to argue for the Atheneum because it was the idea that had financed my education, and I had to remain faithful to the idea or be guilty of a breach of trust with Ralston. Harvard and Heidelberg had been mine only because of Ralston's desire to found an Atheneum. There was otherwise no way in the world that a fireman's son from San Francisco could have even conceived of so lavish an education, much less pay for it. Yet after a while, I found myself content to let the dead bury the dead. The Atheneum, like Ralston, had met a watery grave off North Beach.

Compromise? Betrayed promise? Bad luck? The immaturity of a provincial civilization? The stinginess of provincial San Francisco? It is impossible to isolate a single cause for the underlying conviction of failure I sometimes feel when I think of myself and my friends and San Francisco. Royce is the most successful of us who chose the academy, but Royce is also a most unhappy man in his personal life. He lives in estranged silence with his wife. The children give him trouble. He sings the praises of the Higher Provincialism of California from the vantage point of his Harvard chair, but he shows no sign of accepting the professorship that Berkeley has kept open for him for nearly a decade. I think back to Royce and Stoddard and myself tramping out to Ocean Beach in the San Francisco of 1866 and I am quietly sad—sad because we survivors are five decades older, and Stoddard is dead, but sad also that the harvest of those five decades has been intermittent and ambiguous.

"Sebastian," Jack London once told me, "I sometimes curse the day I first opened the books. The more you know, the more you torment yourself; the better your chances are of madness or brain fever; and the more vulnerable you become to using booze to bridge the gap between imagination and reality."

Jack is living proof of his own observation. He is drinking too much of late. Charlie Stoddard turned to the bottle in those penultimate years of sorrow and disgrace after his dismissal from Catholic University. San Francisco is filled with people who drink too much. San Francisco often seems a city of people haunted by failure, of dreams that never came true, of better selves and better possibilities that were betrayed in favor of short-term indulgences. I should have become more than I have become, and so should have Charlie Stoddard. The world was all before us in those golden days when Charlie and I ascended the gentle slope leading to Black Point and saw Mrs. Fremont standing before her cottage in a white dress whipped to her still girlish figure by the westerly sea breezes coming in through the Golden Gate. Now the world is all behind us. Charlie and Mrs. Fremont lie in the grave, beyond all dream, delusion or struggle. I visited Mrs. Fremont in her cottage on West 28th Street in Los Angeles in 1901, a year before her death. The women's clubs of Los Angeles presented the home to her shortly after the General died in 1890.

"You're getting stout, Sebastian," she said to me when I entered her bedroom. She had been confined to bed with a broken hip. "You and John Hay have put on weight, and you both have gray in your beards." John Hay, whom Mrs. Fremont had helped when he was a boy, just as she had helped me, was then serving as Mr. McKinley's secretary of state.

"Let's not talk about weight," I said. "Let's talk about books, as we used to do on Black Point."

She reached up and took my hand and I bent over and kissed the leathery, wrinkled skin of her cheek. This fragile old white-haired woman, confined to bed and wheelchair, was the Mother of California. Hers had been one of the great romances of the nineteenth century—that between the spirited, literate sixteen-year-old daughter of Senator Thomas Hart Benton of Missouri and an ambitious, illegitimately born young army lieutenant of the topographical engineers who strode splendidly into her life in dress uniform one marvelous day in 1841 in Washington, D.C. Her wifely energy had helped make California possible, and now her life was reduced to a room. We talked about George Moore's *Esther Waters* and Thomas Hardy's *Tess of the d'Urbervilles,* both of which she was currently reading, but we talked about old books as well, the books of her bluestocking girlhood, still on her shelves. She had lugged these books back and forth across the continent in the service of her husband's career, even down to Arizona when the General served there as territorial governor. She pointed to two ancient leathery volumes on one shelf and asked me to take them down. It was a two-volume French prose translation of *The Odyssey,* printed in Paris in 1819.

"My father would read to me from this book when we rode out on a picnic lunch," she told me. "We would sit under a

520

tree. As I munched on biscuits and apples, he would read to me in his great baritone voice."

Mrs. Fremont died two days after Christmas in 1902. I, however, am still here, fighting an old-age battle for renewal and new meaning. My body retains its strength. My appetites continue to function. I think much lately of my parents in the context of thinking about culture and education—and, strangely enough, I think of Ryan Patrice in the same context. My parents possessed true culture: they knew what they had to know to get by and they were content in that knowledge. They possessed purity of heart and they had clarity of purpose in their lives. I must be careful, however, not to sentimentalize them into two-dimensional caricature. My father had demons that drove him to the bottle occasionally, and my mother had her ambivalences as well. She didn't like protestants, for instance, or anything English, and she was a little narrow in her thinking when it came to "foreigners"—by which she meant anybody who was not Irish. My father's stock-in-trade, his culture, was fire-fighting, and he had mastered it by early middle age. My mother's culture was the domestic life, and she had mastered it by the time she was sixteen.

My parents remained in their appropriate cultures and stations in life. Ryan Patrice cast civilization aside in pursuit of Jesus Christ. Indo-China cured Patrice of a Western-oriented ecclesiasticism. At the Grand Chartreuse where I re-encountered him, I found that nothing remained of Patrice's once elaborate churchliness. He had been burned to the bone by the radiant fires of the Sacred Heart.

I, on the other hand, have never attained either my parents' innate simplicity or Patrice's re-earned purity of heart. I have spent my life wading through a middle-ranged morass of obscured insight and ambiguous sensation. Harvard, Rome, Heidelberg removed me from San Francisco, but not dramatically enough to free me from San Francisco's persistent provincial call. Haunted by an ideal of high civilization, I have passed my time in an obscure city and in obscure circumstances.

521

But enough! I have experienced much of life and I am grateful for it. I rejoice that I did not torture my life in an obsessive pursuit of scholarship, that I did not burn my time away in the annotation of other people's creativity, losing my life in a dream of books. I ingested as much of my own time as I could swallow. I regret nothing. When you choose to live life, then you must pay life's price—which is the recognition that everything, however sorrowful or ecstatic, soon passes, and only memory remains, until the rememberer himself passes, then even memory is no more. Should someone take my few books off the library shelf sixty years hence, I shall not be called forth from the grave. Having long believed this, I accept my decision not to give everything to the production of books. As courageously as my nature allowed, I remembered to live.

"Remember to live. Never make a false god, a brazen idol, of books." Professor Albert Haymart admonished me thus one day in Heidelberg forty years ago, just before I left for the Vatican Library. We had climbed *Königsstuhl,* the King's Seat, together, some two thousand feet above the *Schloss.* From our perch, we looked out over some four hundred square miles of the valley of the Rhine—to the city of Mannheim, to the distant forest of the Vosges and the spires of Speyer Cathedral where eight Holy Roman Emperors lay buried. Through it all flowed Father Rhine himself, a watery mirror of immemorial history.

"This is the first time I have climbed to this peak," Haymart remarked wistfully, "yet I have spent more than twenty years in Heidelberg. I never seem to have had the time."

The sunlight glinted off his heavy spectacles. He suddenly seemed older.

"Thank you for inviting me here," he said.

522

Chapter 13

HAVE YOU EVER CONSIDERED the possibility, Dr. Norton, that you are a racist?"

"Yes, I have, Miss Hyster. It's something we all must struggle with, racist feelings—black and white alike. America is a pretty confused place when it comes to relationships among the races."

Leah Mae Hyster softened visibly at my response. To be frank: I was speaking honestly to her, rather than strategically, which is how I usually handle her—ever aware that I'm dealing with someone who has once before, and would again on the slightest pretext, haul me up before the Human Rights Commission on charges of racism. That morning, however, I had just reviewed Miss Hyster's special projects budget to her satisfaction: by which I mean to say that I had agreed to include every one of her programs in next year's budget and that I had promised her I would fight like hell to get them approved by the mayor's office and the board of supervisors. My complaisance put Miss Hyster into a rare good mood. Serena Tutti, my secretary, brought some coffee in, and Miss Hyster and I, having finished an hour's business in twenty minutes, talked amicably together for the first time since I had arrived at the Library.

"These are good programs," Miss Hyster said, "and I'm glad you're behind them. I'm worried about the minority children of San Francisco. We've got to get them away from the television set, just as we've got to get them off junk food. Television is junk food for the mind, full of cheap carbohydrates. Poor children are addicted to TV. They will not read, just as they reject school lunches in favor of potato chips and Hostess Twinkies."

Miss Hyster has designed a number of programs aimed at getting minority children to read. She has presented to me, and I have approved of, a school visitation program by librarians, together with a plan to stock approved comic books—Classics Illustrated, in the main—in specially set up reading nooks: on the theory that it is better to get kids into the library to read comic books than not to have them come in at all. Miss Hyster has also asked for money to hire some local mimes and children's theater groups to put on performances at the branch libraries. Her most expensive recommendation involves the weeding from our collection of all children's books containing what she describes as racist or sexist stereotypes, and the replacement of up to fifty percent of our children's collection with books written since the civil rights movement, including updated versions of classic fairytales that have been purged of racism, sexism, ageism, colonialism, elitism, and a number of other isms which presently elude me. In the course of our conversation, Miss Hyster and I nearly lost our unexpected amity over her plan to ban the Oz books from the collection on the grounds that L. Frank Baum was a midwestern redneck and that the Oz books are in reality a submerged, subtly realized racist parable: but I prevailed; or rather, Miss Hyster postponed her purge of Dorothy and Toto until another day, in exchange for my promise to back her other programs. So here we were: sipping coffee together in my office, and half getting along.

"You see, Dr. Norton," Miss Hyster continued, "education—even a Harvard Ph.D.—can often just provide a glossy overlay when it comes to racist feelings. Look at the Nazis, for example. At one of the concentration camps, a string quartet played Brahms as the Jews got off the death trains. Now take yourself, for instance. You're from a culture, an ethnic group, that hasn't done much for black people."

"Like John F. Kennedy?" I asked.

"He was an exception. Your ordinary Notre Dame type, on the other hand, or your average American Catholic of Eastern European extraction, hasn't exactly been on our team."

"The Democratic party thinks differently," I said.

"Well, then, let's just agree that a friendly warning is in order, Dr. Norton. You must be on guard against a certain disposition to racism in your background."

"A common American condition, Miss Hyster," I said, finishing my coffee and casting as polite a glance as possible over to the nineteenth-century ship's clock that Miss Marcia Pennyworth loaned my office from the San Francisco History Room. Serena Tutti has rubbed it to a state of pristine finish.

"May I compliment you on your suit," I said. "Is it Magnin's?"

"No. Pucci. I bought it last year in Rome."

Sitting amidst the lingering scent of Chanel Number Five left behind in my office by Miss Leah Mae Hyster, I mused momentarily on our conversation. In her own ambiguous and ambivalent way, the special projects coordinator was trying to tell me something. Watch out, she was saying. Certain residual blue collar attitudes are showing. They could get you into trouble. What Leah Mae Hyster had just said was at once an observation, a warning, and a threat. Maybe it was because it was December, the Christmas season; but I believed that behind the usual black-and-white confrontational bullshit, Miss Hyster was genuinely trying to communicate.

Miss Hyster, in one sense, is correct about my sort of people; but then again, the blue collar, lower middle class has the most to lose from things like affirmative action programs and school busing. The affluent liberals who design these programs and push them through the courts rarely suffer any of the consequences. Their kids are in private schools, and hell will freeze over before enforced affirmative action reaches the professions. I guess Miss Hyster senses that I don't buy the

525

party line that all black people are oppressed and deserve special attention.

Just the other night, for instance, Tim and Gwendolyn Alexander gave their annual Christmas cocktail party, to which I'm invited because Tim and I went to St. Ignatius High School together. Tim has a strong sense of *auld lang syne*. Gwendolyn brought me over to meet Paul Lincoln, the Forty-niner quarterback. Lincoln graduated from Stanford about ten years ago. His father is a prominent black physician in Alameda. Regally handsome and suave in manner, Lincoln has carved a place for himself as the city's first unambiguously social black. Calculatedly cheery and bright-eyed, Gwendolyn foisted me off on Lincoln because she felt that she was doing me a favor. As a city official, however minor, I should know the right people. I chatted with Lincoln for five disconcerting minutes without getting his attention. I tried Stanford, football, some just released *cabernet sauvignons*, even Alameda. Lincoln stared over my shoulder all the while, bored and dismissive. With barely a nod, he left me to join Harry Shaw and Jeremiah Jones, who were creating a charmed circle around themselves in another corner of the room.

Black people, in other words, come in all sizes and conditions. I went downstairs to the janitors' locker room in the basement the other day because I wanted personally to give Cyril Jones the bad news: I had to suspend him for five days for being drunk on duty to the point of incapacitation. Cyril Jones works the night shift. Sometime in the early hours of last Wednesday, Jones passed out in the office of the Friends of Books. Commissioner Mabel Storm came across him around eight-thirty when she let herself into the office. Cyril was lying asleep on the floor, mop in hand. Mabel Storm demanded that I do something about it.

"Hell, man, I don't blame you a bit," Cyril assured me as we sat together in his cubbyhole, decorated in black female nudes from various girlie magazines and a National Geographic cover depicting a Masai warrior in full campaign dress. "I was drunk on my ass. I've been hitting it heavy lately. I always have trouble with the sauce around Christmas time. You just do what you have to do. Five days ain't no big thing." Cyril Jones has salt and pepper gray hair. I've always suspected that he has a lot of Indian blood in him. His cheeks are high and severe, like an Indian's. Creek most likely, or Cherokee, or perhaps even Seminole.

"It's only because Commissioner Storm personally reported you to me and to the personnel officer," I said apologetically. "Otherwise, I could have got you off with just a warning."

"Shit, man," Cyril said. "It was worth it to see the look on that lady's face when I jumped up. She comes in, you see, and I'm out like a light on the floor, hugging my mop for comfort. 'He's dead!' yells the lady. I hear this in my sleep and I jump up swinging my mop, thinking it's a brawl and I'm being messed with; so she goes screaming down the hallway, thinking I'm after her." We laughed, sharing the sudden intimacy of Cyril Jones's basement hideaway.

"Five Christmases ago my wife died," Cyril said. He reached around into his hip pocket, then took a quick pull at a half-pint of Old Granddad. Methodically, he rescrewed the cap, then put the bottle back into his hip pocket. "We been together ever since we was kids in Louisiana. It just ain't Christmas without her."

"I feel like a goddammed heel, suspending you," I said.

"Shit, Doc, you're just doing your job. I'll tell you what. Do me a little favor. Let me add five days vacation time to the five days suspension. That gives me ten days, just enough time for a bus trip down to Louisiana. I'll go stay with some of my wife's people down there. It'll be like having her alive, just to be around the places where we grew up and started messing around together." He pulled his half-pint out again and offered me a swig. It was only ten-thirty in the morning, but I downed a mouthful of burning whiskey.

"Your wife must have been a wonderful woman."

"The best, Doc, the best. That old lady could raise hell with me when she wanted to, but like I say, we've been together since we was kids."

"Cyril," I said, perhaps under the influence of the Old Granddad, "why not take the rest of today off? That'll give you

527

eleven days away from this place." He looked me full in the face. I noticed that signs of old age were beginning to assert themselves across his neck.

"That's damn white of you, Doc." Cyril Jones said. I could think of nothing else to say—except "Merry Christmas"—so I left.

Temptations: reduce Paul Lincoln in my mind to the category Uppity Nigger; see Cyril Jones as Uncle Remus with a drinking problem. By all standards of American achievement, however, Paul Lincoln has earned the right to his snobbery; and Cyril Jones, like Uncle Remus himself, can play the sly fox when he wants to.

"I found out by the time I was thirty that I could only do one thing with my life and that was to write." Larry Seton said this to me recently over lunch at the Hoffman Grill on Market Street. Seton's new novel *Boss Man* has just been sold to Hollywood for a movie starring Sidney Poitier. Seton himself has been creating a mild sensation for some five years now as America's first black writer of Westerns. He made his debut in 1970 with *Half-Caste*. The novel sold only moderately well, but Francis Ford Coppola took out an option on it, thereby putting some $25,000 into Larry's previously nonexistent bank account. *Sidewinder*—completed two years ago and researched right here in the San Francisco Public Library—sold some thirty thousand copies. *Boss Man*, however, has sold more than fifty thousand copies and has been picked up by the Book-of-the-Month Club, in addition to having a huge sale in paperback. And now Sidney Poitier has taken an option on it. *Boss Man* is an enormously ambitious saga of a young black man, Flintlock McCaffrey, who in the 1850s joins Edward Rose, the black trapper and sometime Cree chief, in the Wyoming fur trade and ends up in Lassen County, California, in the early 1900s as a cattle rancher, married to the daughter of a Modoc chief. I helped Seton thread his way through the most relevant secondary material, saving him months (so he tells me) by putting him in touch with the best autobiographies, memoirs, and secondary sources dealing with the times

528

and places he was interested in. I admire Larry Seton because, unlike myself, he has brought clarity and focus to his life.

"I'm in search of something big," Seton told me once after we had gotten on good terms. "I want the West, the great big West, and I want to connect the black man to that epic because he was there, you see, all along, right from the Lewis and Clark expedition down through the Buffalo Soldiers."

The more I know Larry Seton, the more I respect his dedication. Larry is about my age, a graduate of San Francisco State, where he studied creative writing under Mark Harris. He spent some five years as a cowpuncher in Montana and Wyoming before returning to San Francisco and beginning to write. Getting a job as a night sorter at the post office, Seton worked from midnight to eight, then went home to his small studio apartment on Divisadero Street to sleep until two in the afternoon. He spent the late afternoon and early evening writing. It took Larry three years to complete *Half-Caste*, his first novel. On and off, he has been working on *Boss Man* for nearly a decade.

"You've been a great help," Seton said at our celebratory luncheon. "You know a lot about the history of the West."

"And you know a lot about writing about the West," I said, raising my wine glass. "Here's to Flintlock McCaffrey," I said. "Here's to fifty years of good pussy and breaking trail."

Seton raised his glass. "Here's to success," he said. "The thought of Flintlock's life of wild freedom in the outdoors got me through many a night of despair at the post office." Out of Larry's instinctive courtesy, he turned the conversation to my *San Francisco, Ordeal and Transformation*, published last year by Chronicle Books. Seton must sense that I am profoundly ambivalent to accepting fully a librarian's relationship to the world of books. I want to write some books myself, above all a biography of Sebastian Collins. The essence of librarianship is service to others. I am afraid that I am a little too piggy about the possibilities of my own achievement ever to surrender myself completely to that noble calling, although I do love the world of books and I do revere the library as an institution. I am feeling more and more anxious, however, to give some outward expression to my inner life, to see my own name on the dust jacket and the binding. Even as I was helping Larry research *Boss Man*, I envied him his creativity; and envy of writers makes for a lousy librarian.

"With all due respect," Seton said, "you were too nice to the city at the end."

"How so?" I asked.

"You were too facile in asserting that San Francisco would recover the best aspects of its old character and personality," Seton said. "I sometimes think that a time bomb is ticking away in San Francisco, that we are on the verge of some ominous, impending evil event."

"Violence?" I asked.

"Something like that," Larry Seton said. "A new kind of violence, born of the schizoid, dissociated state of consciousness that seems to be taking over this town. Everyone pretends to be mellow, but a lot of the people I know, black and white alike, are pushing it too hard. They're living on the outer edge of something. I can't say exactly what it is that everybody so desperately wants, but they are asking for too much and they're anticipating their eventual disappointment by looking around for someone to blame when the time comes."

"Things were simpler in the days of Flintlock McCaffrey," I said.

"Yeah," said Larry Seton, "then all you had to worry about was getting a bowie knife in your back."

"There are a lot of knives out around this place," Danny Parker, the Library's affirmative action officer, told me a few days after my luncheon with Larry Seton. Parker had come up to my office to discuss the Susan Green case. Ms. Green, a young black woman employed as a library assistant, punched librarian Helen Huskett in the snoot the other day, giving her a black eye. As head of the librarians' guild, Helen Huskett says she's an avowed radical, pledged to the liberation of oppressed minorities, and women everywhere. Now that Susan Green has punched Helen Huskett in the eye, however, Ms.

Huskett is singing another tune. She has got the librarians' guild to pass a resolution demanding that Susan Green be brought up for a dismissal hearing over at City Hall.

"We librarians must be protected from violence," Helen Huskett told me when she brought the resolution to my office. Ms. Huskett was wearing overalls, a denim work shirt, and Earth Shoes. Her hair was pulled back from her head by a red bandana, as if she were a Cuban sugar cane harvester taking a break from bringing in the crop.

"Dismissal," I said, "is a pretty serious penalty."

Huskett pointed to her blackened eye, which protruded like a piece of raw liver adhering to one side of her face.

"I could have been blinded," she said.

"Huskett bugged and bugged the poor girl," Danny Parker argued when he came by my office to persuade me to quash the dismissal proceedings. "Huskett was always telling her how to do everything, point by point, as if the poor girl didn't have any brains at all." Danny, as usual, looked sharp in a well-cut, double-breasted dark blue suit with oversized pinstripes. His Billy Eckstein mustache was perfectly trimmed. "Susan Green is a fine and together young lady, Doc. Since she has been here, she has started taking junior college at night. You realize how uptight these librarians can be about their degrees. A lot of the minority people don't like to be lorded over by white librarians with degrees. Helen Huskett is one of the worst offenders." Susan Green had said as much to me the day before when I asked her to come up to my office and give her side of the case.

"I want to do more than just stamp books out, Dr. Norton," she explained. "I want to be a librarian."

Somewhere in her late teens, Susan Green has stepped off the pages of an advertisement in *Ebony* magazine: beautiful black skin, greenish eyes, a tall, deerlike body, and a glistening Afro that fills the area around her Queen of Sheba face with luxuriant hair like a halo of triumphant negritude. Given the right breaks, this girl can go far—because, to be frank, she is so hauntingly beautiful and, so they tell me, above average in intelligence. Such beauty, of course, can

531

prove a curse in her culture—or any culture for that matter. A constant barrage of seductive attention can at the least preclude her ever having to use her brain, or at the worst, get her left with three kids by the time she is twenty-three. In the ghetto, more than elsewhere, beauty is a fragile and passing flower, quickly crushed beneath the feet.

"I want to get ahead, Dr. Norton. I want to make something of myself. I'm starting City College next semester, then I hope to go to State for my degree. Miss Hyster and Miss Tanner have already talked to me about it. I'd like to go to library school at Berkeley or back east to Howard University or to Tuskegee in Alabama."

"Punching your supervisor in the eye won't look good on your record," I said. Susan Green's gazelle-green eyes welled with tears.

"I'm sorry," she said. "I lost my temper. I was behind the desk, checking out books, when a patron I know, Mrs. Mary Gordon, a retired lady who comes into the North Beach branch a lot, asked me about a certain book. It was out, but I started to talk to her about some of the new books we just got in from Cataloging. Mrs. Gordon likes travel books, so I showed her some new travel books we just got in. She checked two of them out. Later Helen Huskett told me that only librarians are authorized to give advice on books. Library assistants aren't qualified to conduct readers' services, she says, so please don't do it in the future. I lost control of myself. I hauled off and punched her."

"You can't send her over to Civil Service on charges, Doc," Danny Parker told me a day later. "It wouldn't look right for you to be persecuting that cute little black girl. Besides, what has Helen Huskett ever done for you?" I agreed with Danny Parker and I told him so.

"How do I deal with Helen Huskett and the guild?" I asked.

"Put it to them this way: they'll alienate the minority staff if they insist on some punishment. They want to organize the assistants and the techs into a guild, right? Most of the assistants and the techs are minority, right? Most of the librarians are white, OK? Do you realize how impossible it is for minorities working as techs and assistants to make the jump into the professional roles—to get those extra three or four years of college? Some make it, like Mrs. Yamasaki did, by going to evening classes for five years straight, then taking a leave of absence for a year to do a graduate degree; but for most people, becoming a full-fledged, professional librarian is a dream that will never come true. They just don't have enough energy after a day's work to attend classes. Susan Green is young. She might make it by the time she's thirty—if you give her a chance."

"What about the guild?" I said. "You haven't dealt with them." A grin came over Danny Parker's face.

"Now, Doc, I've been noticing that you're kinda friendly with Deborah Tanner, aren't you?"

I must have bristled a bit. I know for certain now that the staff is talking. I have always known that it would only be a matter of time before the word got around that Deborah and I were seeing each other. This will cause some complications. I will no doubt be accused of favoritism, and Deborah will lose her credibility as an activist.

"No offense, Doc," Parker continued. "That's one foxy chick, very together—and well respected in the guild, too. Just ask her to make the case to the guild that it wouldn't look right to be going after Susan Green at this time. After all, Doc, it's Christmas. Give us black folk a break."

I promised Danny that I'd sit on any dismissal papers that John Stickey, the personnel officer, might send over for my signature. I'd also talk to Deborah Tanner, I promised, asking her to get the guild to back off its demand that Susan Green be dismissed.

"You got soul, Doc," Danny Parker said, shaking my hand soul brother-style. "You also got fine taste in women."

Despite the efforts of my superego to resist, I melted under Danny Parker's compliment. I had never been told that before.

I am in need of encouragement, anyway. I feel that my grip on the Library is loosening. The grand jury people hinted as much when they interviewed me last week as part of their every-other-year inspection of the Library. The jurors obviously had been briefed by Mabel Storm beforehand, and by the guild, because they asked some very tough questions.

"Why has your processing rate dropped off by eight percent?"

"Your staff manual is five years old. When do you plan to revise it?"

"Do you have any supplementary appropriations before the board of supervisors? What are they? Why were they not held over for submission in next year's budget?"

"Your overdue notices are behind. When is the last time you reviewed your monitoring procedures?"

"Do you have a systematic program for the training of library pages? Why not?"

"What steps have you taken to insure public input into your book selection policy?"

"Do you meet regularly with the librarians' guild? How would you describe your relations with them?"

"What is the staff's reaction to your plans to open the Main Library on Sundays? What process of consultation did you employ before arriving at your decision?"

After an hour of such precise questions from the three grand jurors—a middle-aged male lawyer; the vice-president of the culinary workers' union (a bossy young dame in a pants suit); and one of Mabel Storm's society friends, a sixtyish and stylish woman, silver-haired and vestigially sexy (like everyone who's gone to Stanford, she told me that she went to Stanford within the first five minutes of our conversation)—I knew that the deck had been stacked. Grand jurors usually give the Library only a perfunctory once-over; but this panel was after blood, and had been well prepped as to what questions to ask. Each of their inquiries directly challenged my abilities as an administrator. I was also cross-examined as to my answers, especially as to my plans to open the Main Library on Sunday.

"I plan to open on Sundays so that working people can use the Library on their day off," I said, looking over to the culinary workers' union official, who had herself worked as a waitress before winning election to her union's board as a reform candidate, backed by the younger waitresses and kitchen workers. I hoped that my pitch regarding working people using the Library would strike a chord of sympathy with her. She didn't seem impressed.

"Where are you going to get the money to pay your staff time-and-a-half for Sunday work?" she asked, throwing me a hard-boiled stare. "Or don't you intend to pay time-and-a-half?"

The guild has been raising holy hell about my plan to open on Sundays and had obviously got to their fellow unionist when they heard she had been named as a grand juror. The onetime waitress then proceeded to cross-examine me on the staffing patterns I planned to use for Sundays. She knew a hell of a lot about staffing patterns. My plan, devised by John Stickney at my insistence (Stickney opposed Sunday hours), involved some rather complicated scheduling of three rotating Sunday shifts, insuring an equal amount of Sunday work over every fourteen-month period. When I tried to explain it to the jurors, the plan sounded awfully complicated, Rube Goldbergish in fact. In mid-explanation, I had the quasi-paranoid thought that perhaps Stickney had set me up with a deliberately defective staffing plan.

Luckily, none of the jurors asked me what I was doing to nab the Brown Bomber. Mabel Storm is so distressed about the Brown Bomber that she wouldn't push that nasty piece of business to further discussion, even to embarrass me, although now that the item has appeared in Harry Shaw's column, it is common knowledge around town. I attended a regional meeting of northern California reference centers recently and a number of the librarians who were there from other systems asked me about the Brown Bomber: had I called in the FBI? was this a new form of terrorism?—sly questions such as this, intended to provoke laughter, but also intended to dismiss the San Francisco Public Library as a rather bizarre place. Just before the Brown Bomber hit my office, incidentally, he struck the boiler room. Ted Bemos, the stationary engineer, was as angry as a hornet. Bemos prides himself on the way he keeps his boiler room in tip-top shape.

"I'll kill the sonofabitch if I ever catch him," Bemos announced. "Right there in the middle of the room when I walked in—disgusting. What the fuck is the world coming to?"

Ted Bemos had my sympathies a few days later when my office endured an attack. I got rid of the deposit myself, using my copy of the *Express*, then washed the rug out with soap and water after opening all the windows in my office. Serena found me on my knees sopping up the soap lather from the rug with a wet towel. I told her what had happened.

"How depressing," she said—which was my reaction as well: depression over the fact that someone on the staff was so sick and tormented that he could strike back against the world only in this disgusting manner. After washing my hands in the hottest water I could endure I returned to my desk, where I discovered a note neatly typed on a three-by-five index card. "In the name of the oppressed peoples of the world," it read, "I salute you. Down with fascism! Power to the people!"

"What has the people to do with this?" asked Serena Tutti.

"Beats me," I said. "Someone among us has devised a new mode of revolutionary warfare."

The phone rang. It was Don Goldstein, San Francisco's first Jewish fire chief. "Norton, my boy," Goldstein said, "you've done it. Tommy Delphine has called off the dogs. They're going to leave the Memorial Fire House alone. I owe it to your editorial."

A few weeks ago, I wrote an editorial on the opinion pages of the *Express*, attacking the plan before the board of supervisors to disestablish the fire chief's residence. I argued that since the firemen who died fighting the 1906 fire could never be brought back to life, the memorial honoring them could never be disestablished. The City and County of San Francisco had, in effect, created a covenant with its honored dead. In my article, I quoted liberally from Mayor Rolph's speech at the time the Fire House was dedicated and from the

536

prospectus drawn up by Sebastian Collins during the subscription campaign.

"That did it, Jimmy," Chief Goldstein said. "Your article tugged at the old heartstrings. Delphine called me about an hour ago and said he was just as good a San Franciscan as the next guy, only as a supervisor he had to be on the lookout for ways to save the city money. I said that I respected his point of view, but felt that the Fire House was a treasured tradition of the city. Delphine said, 'No hard feelings,' and hung up."

"I'm glad to have been of help, Chief," I said.

"Tony Ortega's on the other line," Serena said. My phone has three incoming lines. Sometimes I'm on one of them while the other two are blinking with incoming calls on hold.

"Jimmy," my chief librarian of Main said when I had hung up on Fire Chief Goldstein and punched the flickering button that had him on the other end, "I've got some bad news."

"So what else is new?" I said. Tony Ortega, by the way, is a steady, hard-working guy who made it to the highest possible civil service rank, chief librarian, before anyone told him that he was an oppressed Chicano.

"Someone has destroyed nearly two hundred books," Tony said. "The inner pages of some two hundred books in the literary criticism section have been ripped diagonally across the middle. The guy must have worked quietly over a couple of days' time, taking the books off the shelf, then going someplace where he couldn't be seen and ripping the guts out of the book without breaking the binding. He then put them back on the shelf. Someone brought ten of them to me yesterday morning, all destroyed. I noticed that all the books had the same literary history or literary criticism call number. So I started to spot-check the section. So far, the literature department has found some two hundred destroyed titles."

I felt sick to my stomach. First of all, that's some $20,000 worth of city property destroyed. Secondly, a loss like that wipes out our collection in one entire area. There is no way in the world that our budget has room for the back-ordering and processing of some two hundred titles in one field.

"Keep looking for more destroyed books," I said wearily.

"I'll call the police. Tell the guards to check the literature stacks every twenty minutes until I get back to you."

"I've already done this," Tony said. "An inspector from burglary is supposed to be coming over this afternoon."

I hung up the phone and swiveled my chair to an angle that allowed me to put my feet on my desk. I sat there for the longest time, thinking. Dolefully, I surveyed the cherished artifacts from the city's past that I had borrowed from the History Room: the view of the city in the 1870s, when it bristled with classical façades and church steeples; the oleograph of the Midwinter Fair of 1894, held in Golden Gate Park; the autographed photographs of Frank Norris, Jack London, and Sebastian Collins; Maybeck's proposal for a Grecian temple atop Twin Peaks. My office, I realized, was a fantasy, a daydream of a San Francisco long since past. The reality of San Francisco has more to do with the sick soul who calculatedly destroyed some two hundred works of literary history and criticism. San Francisco, filling up with desperate nuts, is getting to be one big halfway house. You can see the crazy ones on Market Street: the Richard Speck whites, skinny, hunched-shouldered, a Born-To-Lose tattoo on one arm, prowling along in jeans and a white T-shirt, strung out on pills and some free-floating honky-tonk anger; the black dudes with hatred in their eyes; the middle-aged inebriate in an overcoat held together by a beaded Indian belt, hollering words of execration to passers-by. Our streets and streetcars teem with the exhausted, the defeated, clutching in their hands a transfer to nowhere. Our bars fill up too early in the day. There's too much rape and too much murder. Ideological hatred is everywhere. Aging Aquarians from the 1960s have flocked to the city, determined in their paranoid way to find one last Little Big Horn. Faced with this take-over, hard hats, blue collars, the lower middle class have all grown defiantly recalcitrant. Everybody, in short, has a chip on his or her shoulder: race, sexual persuasion, lifestyle, political ideology: you name it—everybody is angry about something! I've seen this process accelerate within the past five years, and it's happening faster every day.

538

Compared to murder or rape, destroying two hundred books isn't a serious crime; but considered as a species of madness, it's even more frightening. "An intellectual hatred is the worst," Yeats writes in one of his poems. That's what we've got here: some desperate sonofabitch with an abstract hatred burning in his gut, but feeling powerless (as we all do), so tearing up books in revenge—a huddled, secretive, nasty gesture of revenge that doesn't even allow itself the gratification of announcing itself to the world. The Bay Area, northern California in fact, teems with such haters: the Ph.D. dropouts who live in lonely rooms; the campus radicals from the East or the Midwest who drifted out to the Bay Area when it began to be over in the East because they thought that they could keep it alive a little longer here where it all started; the sad-eyed grown-up children of suburban affluence who hate their parents; the parents who neglect their children; paranoid racial groups like the Black Panthers; Maoist agitators among the Asians; neo-Nazis among the suburban rednecks,; ecologists who can't abide people; people who hate ecologists; the gays and straights, all at each other's throats.

I can see the poor bastard now: huddled behind the closed door of the first-floor toilet stall, ripping Edmund Wilson apart, ripping W. Jackson Bate apart, ripping Harry Levin apart. Tear! There goes Northrup Frye. Rip! There goes Harold Bloom. Slit! Alfred Kazin, Malcolm Cowley, Van Wyck Brooks—all cut diagonally across their guts, in desperate repayment for an overt failure, or perhaps in payment of naught but an obscure hurt. Thomas Hardy's *Jude the Obscure* savored an exhausted hour with the classics after a day of stonecutting, haltingly broaching the volumes he yearned one day to study at Oxford. In San Francisco, our local Jude the Obscure rips apart what he cannot possess—despite the fact that the books are free for the asking. He could read them if he wanted to, free of charge, at the San Francisco Public Library. I see something symbolic in our local Jude's hatred. San Francisco is filling up with thousands of people beyond the touch of all orthodoxies—no, more than this, hating all orthodoxies, ripping all books apart. The onetime high provincial civilization, the San Francisco of James D. Phelan and Sebastian Collins—reverent, robust, appreciative, derivative but vigorous—has given way to something thin, angry, red-eyed. Yet who am I to pass judgment, or even to point the finger? I'm as fucked up as anyone out here on the land's end of the continent, the place where America and the dream engendered by the inutterable grandeur of the continent peters out into life-style and talk about the latest restaurant. I've got to end the Tiny Roncola thing once and for all. Even as it is, it's gone far enough—too far, in fact.

I spent the rest of the morning preparing myself for an afternoon appearance before the finance committee of the board of supervisors. I knew full well, however, that Susan Bernstein's article on the Library in Sunday's *Express* wouldn't do me any good when it came time to ask the supervisors for money. Bernstein quoted me—correctly—saying some pretty outrageous things. I admit to talking too much. I admit also to being under the influence of the martinis Bernstein plied me with during our luncheon interview at Bardelli's. Susan Bernstein hasn't become the Queen of the Sunday Supplement for nothing. She knows how to extract a story. In my case, it was easy. Bardelli's after all, is a cozy place, dominated by a large pre-Earthquake stained glass window showing a peacock in full strut: which is exactly what I did, strut like a peacock, after two martinis, flattered by Susan's cooing concern over all the problems I was facing at the Library. Susan crossed her legs as we sat at the bar, drinking our martinis and waiting for a table. There is something tremendously sexy about a woman sitting on a bar stool with her legs crossed. Susan wore a wide-brimmed man's fedora and a Marlene Dietrich-style tailored jacket over a white turtle-necked sweater. I guess I have a weakness for modish girl reporters in their mid-twenties who act like they've seen a lot of Katharine Hepburn movies. Under the influence of the martinis, Susan's hat, and her crossed legs, I fell into a line of late-forties Stork Club patter from which I couldn't, or wouldn't, extract myself. For no reason whatsoever, certainly not the immediate prospect of

540

romance (Susan lives in the Marina with Boris Jarvis, painter-in-residence at the Art Institute), I put on a one-man performance, strictly for Susan's benefit. She took it all down on three-by-five index cards, in between appreciative laughs and what I took to be admiring glances through her mauve mascara and false eyelashes.

A month or so later, Susan dished it all back—and then some—in the Sunday supplement article entitled, "All You Wanted to Know about the San Francisco Public Library but Were Afraid to Ask." Taking an essentially comic approach, she depicted the SFPL as a continuous Keystone Comedy. Having graduated from the journalism school at UC-Berkeley, Susan has studied Style. She wrote her article in a blend of New Journalism and Gonzo: casting herself as a wide-eyed Alice being taken on a tour of Wonderland. The effect was devastating. Susan got it all: the entire cast of Library characters: Charlie Chaplin, the Brown Bomber, Little Big Man, the Hot and Cold Flasher, Mr. Peepers, the Little Old Lady with the Portable Television Set, the National Geographic Man, Dirty Old Fan, Born Again, Dirty Face, Handy Andy: all the funny-sad people who have nowhere else to go and whom the SFPL staff, by and large, treats with touching kindness—except, perhaps, for Flasher, Peepers, Dirty Old Fan, and Handy Andy, whose propensities have a way of violating the rights of others, specifically females.

Although I shuddered at the quotes attributed to me, and knew there'd be trouble because of them, I had to admire Bernstein's evocative skill. Among many stories, she related the anecdote (I told her this between the second and the third martini) on how I first encountered Little Big Man. I was taking Steve and Cynthia Van Ness, a socially prominent Fun Couple, on a tour of the Library. The Van Nesses were thinking of putting a fund-raiser together to benefit the History Room. Cynthia had this idea of everybody coming in Victorian costume or else dressed as some famous San Franciscan from the past. The Library hasn't been the recipient of a benefit in living memory, with the exception of the Friends of Books' annual used book sale, so I was pretty excited

541

at the prospect of raising some unrestricted funds and getting the Library into the newspaper as a Fun Place. As I brought Steve and Cynthia back from a tour of the History Room, visions of a dazzling benefit danced in my head like Sugarplum Fairies.

You've got to remember one thing: Little Big Man is not a real Indian. He only dresses up like one, which is why the staff has nicknamed him in honor of the anti-hero of Thomas Berger's novel. Little Big Man is usually harmless, except when he's been drinking with the real Indians who often hold an all-day powwow on the south lawn of the Library. Drifting into San Francisco from all over northern and central California, the Indians get off the bus at the Greyhound Depot on Seventh, then come up to Civic Center, where they congregate. When Little Big Man has been drinking with his Indian buddies, he can get belligerent as hell. The moment I spotted him in the corridor outside my office, I knew that Little Big Man was in an ornery mood. He had lined his face with warpaint, for one thing; and for another, he was weaving drunkenly. Cynthia Van Ness was chatting on about the cost of getting Turk Murphy's jazz band in for the benefit, when Little Big Man let forth a bloodcurdling yell. He ran towards us down the corridor, letting out a series of war whoops. Cynthia Van Ness blanched white with fear. I thought for a second that she would faint. Steve Van Ness stepped out in front of her, prepared, I suppose, to defend his bride to the death against the attacking savage. What with his war paint and his tomahawk haircut and his greasy fringed buckskin shirt and pants, Little Big Man did look frightening. Halting himself a few feet before us, he broke into a shuffling war dance for a moment or two, then raced down the corridor to the staircase leading down to the rotunda.

"Call Tony Ortega," I said to Serena Tutti when I had sat Cynthia Van Ness down on the sofa in my office. "Tell him Little Big Man has gone wild again and to have the guards throw him out."

I fetched some water from the Alhambra cooler in the utility closet. Cynthia Van Ness took the paper cup with trembling

542

hands and drank it gratefully. That was the last I ever heard about the benefit.

"Do I really have killer eyes, Mr. Norton?" Supervisor Dante Foscolo asked me that afternoon at the finance committee meeting. Foscolo stared at me with his killer eyes—about which I had dropped an indiscreet remark to Susan Bernstein, which she had promptly dropped into her article. Foscolo's eyes would do justice to a barracuda, or a mongoose. They are small and steady—and awfully mean. The owner of an insurance company in North Beach, Foscolo won election to the board as a fiscal conservative. His actuarial skills and his small businessman's contempt for civil servants have made him the terror of every department head.

In my brief period in the civil service, I have already won a certain amount of notoriety for the especially vehement hatred I have inspired in Supervisor Dante Foscolo—strictly, so it seems, by the sheer fact of my existence. Mayor Claudio Carpino, for instance, recently encouraged every public employee to take the bus to work on Tuesdays as a way of responding to the oil shortage. It also happens that the Carpinos have a box at the opera for the Tuesday night series. At the Mayor's invitation (Seraphina wasn't feeling well), I met him outside his house in Sea Cliff, and the two of us took the 38 Geary and the 47 Van Ness down to the Opera House, both of us attired in black tie. A couple of TV cameramen tagged along. The next morning, the front page of the *Express* featured a photo of the Mayor and myself in evening clothes, stepping off the 47 Van Ness near the Opera House. After the opera, the Mayor—with me in tow—joined Kurt and Nancy Adler and Beverly Sills at Trader Vic's for dinner. We then took the 1 California home, escorted onto the bus with a television crew. The whole thing, I'm told, drove Dante Foscolo absolutely bananas. The flamboyant insincerity of Carpino's gesture, together with my complicity in it, affronted Foscolo's district merchant's soul with the force of a calculated insult. The entire evening, Foscolo is said to have ranted—opera tickets, dinner at Trader Vic's—probably cost the Mayor three hundred dollars. Who was Carpino trying to fool about fifty cents worth of gasoline?

"No, Supervisor," I said. "You don't have killer eyes. You actually have very nice eyes, and I hope they look kindly this afternoon on my requests for supplemental appropriations for the Library." Dante Foscolo stared at me with his killer eyes. If this were Sicily, the evil eye he sent my way would have laid a curse upon me and my descendants for six generations.

"I read your editorial on the Fire House with interest," Supervisor Saul Quince said. "Such an attack upon the supervisors of this city, coming from a department head of the very same city, is, to say the least, suicidal."

"I was merely trying to argue against disestablishing the Memorial, Supervisor. I meant no offense. My disagreement with the board's plan was stated respectfully."

"The fact that it was stated at all, Mr. Norton, is what amazes me," Supervisor Quince continued. "After all, we supervisors were merely doing our job—trying to save this city money—weren't we?"

"Yes, Supervisor."

"Precisely, Mr. Norton. Now your editorial did not stress that fact, did it? Your editorial merely lambasted us for scrutinizing the tax-free, rent-free status of the fire chief's home, which is a perfectly legitimate, indeed commendable piece of business for this board to be pursuing. Is that not true, Mr. Norton?"

"Yes, Supervisor."

"Well then, the impression is now left in the public's mind that this board doesn't give a damn about this city's glorious past. Isn't that a fact, Mr. Norton?"

"I hope not, Supervisor."

"I think so, Mr. Norton. Lamentably, I think so. May I say, however, that there are no hard feelings on our part. This board, on the other hand, shall this afternoon and in the future extend to you the same courteous scrutiny that you so recently extended to us. Is that understood, Mr. Norton?"

"Yes, Supervisor."

Saul Quince, a brilliant—nay! feared—trial attorney, is a cross between a roadrunner and a piranha fish. Quince ran for the board on the campaign slogan: "Send an S.O.B. to City Hall." The voters complied. In some three years as supervisor, Saul Quince has made good on that campaign promise: an S.O.B. has been sent to City Hall. Quite frankly: despite the fact that Foscolo and Quince loathe me personally, I agree with their conservative attitudes. San Francisco sustains a public payroll of more than thirty thousand employees to serve a population of under seven hundred thousand residents. Our municipal budget is approaching a billion dollars a year. As the right wing of the board, Foscolo and Quince have declared war on municipal spending—which I agree with as a citizen, despite the fact that as city librarian, I'm constantly trying to get the city to spend more taxpayers' money on library programs.

"These are interesting proposals you've brought before us, Mr. Norton," Supervisor Sandra Van Dam, chairperson of the finance committee, said.

When a department head testifies in the supervisors' committee room of City Hall, the supervisors sit on a raised dais, like French judges in a Du Maurier engraving. The testifier stands before the supervisors, in the place of the accused. Sandra Van Dam peered down upon me over her semicircular Ben Franklin glasses. She held my supplementing budget requests in one of her beringed hands, like a written sentence she was about to pronounce on a convicted felon. Sandra Van Dam is a self-made millionaire (restaurant supply business) and one smart cookie. She operates in the hard-boiled, Lauren Bacall style of the late 1940s, the time she was getting her start in a business into which no woman, at least locally, had ever ventured before. Sandra Van Dam smokes Camel cigarettes; in fact, she's the only woman I've ever met who smokes Camel cigarettes. She talks with a raspy voice that betokens thirty years of two packs a day. She is also reputed to be a bourbon drinker; Old Crow, like Camel cigarettes, is a rare taste among females.

"For the life of me," said Supervisor Van Dam, studying the calendar of supplemental appropriations before her, "I can't see how the mayor's office sent these over to us. The city has higher priorities than those items."

"Dr. Norton probably lobbied His Honor at the opera," said Supervisor Foscolo.

"Perhaps these items are of historical significance," observed Supervisor Quince.

"Perhaps Dr. Norton will soon be of historical significance, as far as city government is concerned," Supervisor Van Dam remarked drily over her Ben Franklin glasses.

"Item Seventeen," intoned the clerk of the board, "a supplemental appropriation of $25,000 to establish a series of reading clinics in branch libraries serving significant percentages of non-English-speaking residents."

This, of course, was Deborah's pilot project. She and I had personally worked out the details with Dr. Robert Alioto, the superintendent of schools. Alioto had agreed to assign us a number of remedial reading specialists and experts in teaching English to the foreign-born. They would report to us on a part-time basis for the duration (one semester) of the pilot project. The Library, in turn, was to administer the program, provide the instructional materials, and get the word out to the non-English-speaking that the instruction was available.

"Why should the city and the county be doing the school department's work?" Supervisor Quince asked.

"It's also the Library's work to promote literacy," I said. "A lot of the people who can't speak English cannot be gotten into school. After working all day, they don't have the stamina for a regular course. What we want to do is to set up in conjunction with the school department a network of informal clinics, centered around practical, everyday problems. We'll help non-English-speaking immigrants read rental leases, for instance, or time-payment contracts. The anti-consumer-fraud unit in the district attorney's office likes the program. They say that the non-English-speaking are constantly being ripped off by landlords and loan sharks and various time-payment plans with hidden interest charges."

546

"Sounds like something the state should be doing through the community college system," Supervisor Van Dam said.

"Whoever does it, the school department or the state, will need the Library's cooperation. We're in twenty-seven of the city's neighborhoods. We're able to reach people in a nonthreatening way." I wracked my brain, trying to remember Deborah's arguments and the kinds of expressions she used. "Nonthreatening" was one of them, but there were others also: buzz words with vote-getting implications, buttons to push that might get these supervisors interested. I wanted like hell to get this money for Deborah—which is bad administration, I'll admit, but understandable in human terms. If push came to shove, I'd probably have to admit that Deborah's program was low priority. Immigrants learn English when they're good and ready to—which means when not knowing English is beginning to cost them money.

"Madame Chairperson," Supervisor Foscolo said, "I recommend a vote of deny." Supervisor Quince nodded in agreement.

"Denied," said Sandra Van Dam, bringing down her gavel.

"Item Eighteen," intoned the clerk of the board. "A resolution authorizing the establishment of the civil service category city archivist, to be assigned to the library department."

"Madame Chairperson," Supervisor Saul Quince lectured, "the goal of this board has been to reduce the extant number of civil service classifications, not to expand them."

"Such a position would involve no extra funds," I said. "We would merely reclassify our already authorized position, assigning it to our History Room."

"The valuable time of this committee, Madame Chairperson," said Supervisor Dante Foscolo, turning his killer eyes in my direction, "cannot be taken up with such trivial items."

"Is it trivial, Supervisors," I said, "to attempt to establish some sort of archival program for this city?"

"We've got San Francisco's future to worry about, not its past," said Supervisor Sandra Van Dam. "And besides, it's up to you as city librarian to allocate your personnel in the most effective manner possible. I suggest that you work within the civil service classifications you already have. With my colleagues' permission." She banged her gavel down with discernible force, as if, perhaps, my head or an even more strategic portion of my anatomy were on the mahogany block that received her gavel's thunderous attentions. "Denied," she said. Her two colleagues nodded their agreement.

"Item Nineteen," intoned the clerk. "Seventy-eight thousand dollars to relocate the restroom in the Richmond Branch." The three of them leaped upon me like Siberian wolves snapping at someone who had overturned a sleigh in the dead of winter. I explained the present inconvenience of having the male public walk through the staff room to get to the men's toilet.

"These are austere times, Mr. Norton," said Supervisor Quince. "We can't be laying out $78,000 to please a few city employees."

"Some pretty creepy people walk through that area at night, Supervisor," I argued. "Often there's only one woman alone in a branch. In one case, a library employee was threatened with sexual assault."

"Then assign your pages more effectively, Mr. Norton," Supervisor Van Dam said. Someone, probably her administrative assistant, had obviously briefed her. "I'm sure that you have the administrative ability to get a page into every branch open during the evening hours, do you not?"

"Have the pages?" I asked.

"No. Have the ability," she said, bringing her gavel down for the third and final time.

Leaving the Committee Room, I slumped down the central staircase of City Hall in a state of depression. I was embarrassed to return to the Library, having lost three out of three. Commissioner Mabel Storm is right. I am not the person to lead the San Francisco Public Library to greatness.

"Honestly," Commissioner Storm had fumed at me the Monday morning after Susan Bernstein's article had appeared. "How can you expect the very people you insult in print to authorize your projects, or even to look favorably upon our regular budget requests?" She flung her fox fur even tighter around her neck and adjusted the hat Gene Tierney wore in *Laura* to an even more belligerent angle. "I'm afraid you've made yourself expendable. Carpino leaves office next November. I'd advise you to look for further employment."

Walking across Civic Center, I stamped through a settled flock of seagulls out of pure maliciousness. The seagulls, however, didn't even bother to fly off. Like a flock of stubborn geese, they parted insolently, just enough to let me through, then closing ranks behind me as I passed, they resumed devouring a mound of popcorn tossed on the ground.

"Hey, asshole," yelled an elderly Filipino gentleman sitting on a nearby bench. "That's my popcorn and those are my seagulls, so fuck off."

"Sorry," I said.

"I didn't get the money for the toilets," I told Sarah Panel, chief of branches, by telephone when I returned to my office.

"I didn't get the archivist's position," I told Mrs. Pennyworth at the History Room, hanging up as soon as possible so as to save her the trouble of being nice to me, which she always is, and that is why—in addition to the superb job she does—I wanted to get her the archivist's position in the first place. Since I was seeing Deborah that evening, I postponed telling her about the rejected library program.

It was already four o'clock and I didn't feel like doing any more work, so I told Serena that we could wrap up any remaining dictation tomorrow morning and for her to take the remaining forty-five minutes of the day off as compensatory time.

"You're a doll," Serena said, flinging on a beige polo coat. "I'll do some Christmas shopping."

"Lock the office door," I said. Taking some folders of Sebastian Collins material from the lower right drawer of my desk, I went over to the couch, kicked my loafers off, and spent the next hour-and-a-half sprawled there, reading. Browsing in the Collins collection always takes my mind off

549

my troubles. I read an account by Collins of a leisurely day he spent at the Tobin estate in Burlingame, sometime in the late 1890s. I also browsed through some of his reminiscences of the Grand Chartreuse. It took my mind off my troubles.

The Christmas season has its emotional risks. If you're lonely or generally unhappy, Christmas intensifies your misery. The clash between expectation and reality can become unbearable. I've had some very miserable times at Christmas, trying to fake a warm response, trying to assemble certain incomplete and inconclusive memories from boyhood into a warm and glowy mythic memory of a better time that never really existed: not for me, at least, although I must fight against self-pity in this regard. The sisters at St. Vincent's in San Rafael did beautifully: a decorated tree up in every dormitory and in the game room; an absolutely lavish *crèche* in the chapel; at least two, even three, presents for everyone, donated by this or that philanthropic group. Sister Maritia rehearsed my dormitory through innumerable hymns, which we sang for the entire school on the last day before the vacation began. Many kids had nowhere to go; but Mother always managed to get me back to San Francisco for at least a week—to share her tiny garret apartment on Central Avenue just off Haight Street in a high-turreted Victorian mansion converted into some ten separate rental units. I'd sleep on a canvas cot set up in the kitchen, filled with excitement over being in my own place (not a dormitory) and with my own mother, who unmistakably loved me, despite her inability, once divorced and destroyed in her emotions, to work as a teller at the Crocker Bank on Sixteenth Street and to care for an active boy at the same time. But I did have that Christmas week, and two weeks during the summer, in which to pretend that I was a normal kid, living a normal kind of life.

Christmas comes subtly to San Francisco. Throughout October and early November the city enjoys a warm Indian summer: luscious, opiate days of lingering honey-warmth. Our autumn, in other words, is a second summertime. Our calendar summer, you see, is taken from us by all-day fogs that blanket the city, stabilized here by prevailing westerly winds and a great river of heat flowing in an east-west direction from the sirocco regions of the interior. Then suddenly—you cannot tell exactly when, but it usually happens before Thanksgiving—a winter mood establishes itself. The Italianate opulence of Indian summer recedes from the San Francisco palette. More gray and silver are seen on the morning and late afternoon horizons, and the sunset loses its rubescent splendor. There's even a suggestion of Atlantic chill in the air—not the wet, foggy chill of summer (that is common enough in San Francisco), but a certain dry chill suggestive of mountains and the East.

By the second week in December, signs of Christmas are everywhere: in the massed trees, flowers, and fernery at Podesta Baldocchi's florists; in the Christmas tree lots springing up around the city; in the polychromatic lights strung through the trees of Huntington Park atop Nob Hill. On buses, in elevators, in supermarket lines, people seem a little nicer, a little more patient, with each other. At noon the restaurants are packed with office luncheon parties.

At the Bohemian Club we have our Christmas Jinks in the second week of December: a symphony concert and chorale of Christmas music, and the presentation of the Christmas paper, all of it preceded by a bumptious, jolly dinner. The following week, the week just before Christmas itself, the Bohemian Club gives its Christmas dinner: a lavish event, right out of Washington Irving's *Bracebridge Hall*. It's a jolly Tory English dinner, that is, such as Charles Dickens was already looking back upon by the 1830s as emblematic of a too-quickly vanishing Merry Olde England: sherry, nuts, lobster bisque, stuffed trout, an heroic sirloin brought in on the shoulders of four Bohemians in doublet and hose and dubbed "Sir Loin" by the evening's Sire, who uses a sword to knight the beef, according to the rituals of Bohemia already in existence by Sebastian Collins's time. One of the club's bound volumes of memorabilia, which lies on the great table of the library like

551

an oversized Bible in the Middle Ages, preserves a cartoon from Christmas 1901, showing Collins as Sire, dressed in the flowing robes of a portly Chaucerian franklin, a merry smile spread across his bearded face as he raises his goblet to the camera.

I'll be happy this Christmas because Deborah Tanner will be with me. Throughout the event-filled autumn we have shared each other's company in what is, I hope, shaping up to be a classic courtship: old-style, that is, hesitant, patient, filled with some glimpses of the hoped-for, longed-for poetry of life. At least that's the way I like to think of it.

This year's opera season featured a stunning production of Jules Massenet's *Thaïs*, starring Beverly Sills as Thaïs, the Alexandrian courtesan turned saint, and Sherrill Milnes as Athanael, the monk who tries to save Thaïs's soul but winds up coveting her physical love.

"You look like an overweight *maître d'*," Deborah said as we met downstairs at the Opera House for a snack before curtain time. I was wearing a double-breasted dinner jacket, some forty years old, the sort with very generous, very pointed lapels.

"Town School Clothes Closet," I said, referring to the used goods boutique on Presidio Heights where I had bought the suit. "It only cost me ten dollars. Think of me as a younger Peter Ustinov."

"You were overcharged," Deborah said, "but you do look like Peter Ustinov."

"The money went to a good cause," I said. "They raise money for the school by selling used clothes. I wish I were as witty as Peter Ustinov."

"How did you ever find anything that fit? Someone in San Francisco—not you for sure—has either died or lost a lot of weight."

"He probably did both," I said, "and a long time ago. This jacket is at least forty years old. Look." I opened my jacket and showed her the eagle label of the National Recovery Administration on the inside.

552

"And a Hamilton collar," she said.

"Yes," I said. "Tonight, you and I will bring back the thirties."

"*Thaïs* was first performed in 1894, not the thirties," Deborah said.

"On the sixteenth of March, 1894, to be exact," I said, "at the Grand Opera in Paris, starring California's own Sybil Sanderson in the title role."

"You've been peeking into Milton Cross's *Stories of the Great Operas*," Deborah said.

"That—and into Sebastian Collins's journal. He was there the night *Thaïs* debuted and he wrote about it some twenty years later when he was doing a first draft of his *Memoirs of a San Franciscan Bohemian*."

We bought some soup and sandwiches at the snack counter, then carried our trays over to a table in the middle of the downstairs restaurant. The walls downstairs are filled with innumerable photographs of opera stars who have sung in San Francisco since the Opera House opened in 1932. I ordered a bottle of champagne from the waitress. The restaurant began filling up with men in black tie and women dressed in various degrees of *couture*, from funk, to kicky, to incipient kink, to styles that took themselves a little more seriously. Deborah herself wore something slightly humorous, but also quite smart: it was black and satiny and it suggested a full-length Russian peasant's blouse. It also left no doubt that she was not wearing a brassiere. An overlong string of cultured pearls wound tightly around her neck, choker-style, then fell freely between her breasts in a single-strand loop. Her curly auburn hair was brushed back from the forehead more than usual, to reveal two gold scallop-shaped earrings that clung to her delicious ear lobes as I myself was at that moment desirous of doing. Our champagne arrived. The room grew noisier with the excited chatter of late arrivers, rushing to get a pre-opera drink. I waved hello to *Examiner* opera critic Arthur Bloomfield and his wife Anne, both friends of mine.

Drinking my second glass of champagne, I couldn't believe

my good fortune: to be alive and sitting before this wonderful woman on such a wonderful night, with the luminous music of Massenet in prospect. I felt thoroughly, exultantly, On the Town, the way I had always wanted to be in the side of my nature that will ever remain affixed to a certain adolescent longing for *le beau monde*: for the life of opera and champagne and taxicabs that sped one through the nighttime city toward a place where there will be wine and laughter and dancing to the music of Eddy Duchin's orchestra. The first bell rang, announcing a fifteen-minute curtain call.

"You look beautiful tonight," I said.

"Say it again, Sam," Deborah said.

"You look beautiful."

"That's because I went home and changed after work, then took a taxi down here. It cost me three dollars and seventy-five cents."

"I'm worth it," I said. "I changed in the office."

"Let's talk about *Thaïs*," she said. "What do you think the opera is about?"

"Sacred and profane love," I said, "which is what life is all about—or should be at least, if we didn't keep distracting ourselves."

"You have a sliver of corned beef on your chin," Deborah said.

I removed the sliver of corned beef. We finished our champagne, then walked hand in hand up the staircase to the first floor lobby.

"I've always wanted to sweep down a great marble staircase like Ronald Colman in the last scene of *The Prisoner of Zenda*," I said.

"But now you're sweeping up a staircase instead," Deborah said. "We could turn around and sweep down once or twice if that would calm you."

"I love you," I said, "and besides I'm not dressed for *The Prisoner of Zenda*. I'm dressed for *Thaïs*."

Our seats were excellent: Row R, left center. They belong to Sean Crosby over at Parks and Recreation who takes out a subscription to the entire series. Sean had to be out of town that evening and so he sent me the tickets as a personal favor. Like myself, Sean Crosby loves opera and is an admirer of the great old-time civil servants of San Francisco: figures such as John McLaren who built Golden Gate Park, City Engineer Michael O'Shaughnessy, who built the Hetch Hetchy water system, City Attorney Dion Holm, and all the others from that era when civil servants in positions like Sean's and mine were getting things done, were building up a great American city called San Francisco.

"Tuesday night is supposed to be for rich people; that's what I hear," Deborah said. We were watching the Tuesday-night crowd making their entrance all around us. There were a number of old ladies accompanied by epicene young men of the sort who make their living as escorts for such occasions. A number of late-middle-aged women had starved themselves into fashionability. Mrs. Rebecca Nasion entered behind a mask of makeup. Her great beaked nose gave a pharaonic cast to her face. She might have been Ramses II in drag; indeed, like an Egyptian mummy, she seemed capable of surviving the centuries. In a box to our right, Mr. and Mrs. Harry Shaw chatted animatedly with Ray and Kay Soulé. The Shaws seemed tickled pink to be there. Ray Soulé said something, gesturing. Harry Shaw threw his Ben Turpin face back in appreciative laughter. Eva Maria Shaw squeezed Kay Soulé's arm, like a schoolgirl sharing a naughty joke.

"The Mayor looks worried," Deborah said, looking up at the Carpino box.

Indeed he did—as well he might have. The week before, Carpino had opened his campaign. In my opinion, the opening was a disaster. At some point in early September, Terry Shane tells me, Barry Scorse stormed into the Mayor's office and had it out about the proposal to open the campaign with a day or two of statewide appearances at places of historical significance.

"Our kind of Democrats don't give a damn for that kind of fancy crap," Shane quotes Scorse as saying. "The doubledomes will all vote for Andy Soutane anyway, so why have some artsy-fartsy pageant for people who hate your guts? We're after the working man and the working woman."

Scorse had just taken leave of his job at Civil Service to work full time as the director of the Carpino campaign, so he pretty well called the shots. The Mayor scrapped the historical pageant idea. He opened his campaign instead with appearances over a two-day period in Sacramento, San Diego, Los Angeles, and San Francisco. A half-dozen two-bit movie stars showed up at the L.A. opening, Hollywood already being solidly in the Soutane camp. In San Francisco, the campaign opened with champagne and hot dogs in the Exposition Auditorium at Civic Center. It takes at least a crowd of six thousand to make the Exposition Auditorium seem filled. The free hot dogs and champagne, in addition to the encouragement of city workers by the Mayor's office to go over to the auditorium on their lunch hour, got about two thousand people into the place, which isn't bad as far as political crowds go; yet the auditorium still felt like a morgue. Balconies of banked seats, all empty, looked down upon the proceedings in silent mockery. The crowd on the floor below huddled together for company, leaving great acres of emptiness all around, as lonely as outer space. One of San Francisco's gray and tired dance orchestras played the campaign song commissioned by Scorse: "Carpino's a Real Fine Man" set to the music of "Alexander's Ragtime Band."

"Why the fuck pay good money for a new song?" Scorse had told Terry Shane. "Let's get some music everybody knows."

We milled about from noon to twelve-thirty, listening to the music and some old favorites—including "San Francisco" and "I Left My Heart in San Francisco"—belted out by an unemployed saloon singer who hadn't been working steadily since Bimbo's, the city's last true nightclub, closed down in the late 1950s. Then Carpino came onstage, waving his hands over his head, *Last Hurrah* style. Esmeralda walked behind him, her face a mask of insecurity and torment. About a thousand balloons fell from nets attached to the ceiling, which was a good touch, except that people who had had too much champagne to drink began to stomp the balloons out during Carpino's talk and you couldn't hear half of what he was saying.

Soutane, on the other hand, officially opened his campaign on Labor Day by emerging from a week's solitary trek into the Sierra high country, then holding a press conference at Fallen Leaf Lodge. The television cameras caught Soutane as he descended a steep ridge on the last leg of his seven-day trek, wearing jeans, hiking boots, a flannel shirt, a knitted wool watch cap, and carrying a backpack and sleeping bag on his shoulders. Soutane seemed to walk down out of the Sierran sunset like Leatherstocking in James Fenimore Cooper's *The Prairie*, as played by Robert Redford.

"I've spent a week in God's country," Soutane told the cameras. "I wanted to get out there and be by myself. I wanted to think about the future of California. When you've got a struggle ahead, you can find strength in the wilderness."

Within the next week, the Sierra Club, the Friends of the Earth, the Save the Redwoods League, and the Earth Planet Collective all endorsed Soutane for the nomination.

"Mrs. Carpino doesn't look any too happy, either," Deborah said.

"Maybe that's because she can look across the house and see Harry Shaw in the Soulé box," I said. Indeed, Esmeralda Carpino did seem to be glaring across the house at the Shaws. And no wonder! Shaw has been unmerciful of late—even more than usual, and to be that unmerciful is to be unmerciful indeed!

"Everyone is getting bored by the Claudio and Esmeralda Carpino saga," Deborah said as the lights dimmed.

"Including themselves," I said.

Santiago De Haro and Giovanni St. Peter squeezed themselves into their seats, two rows ahead of us, just as Maestro John Pritchard raised his baton. Even over the applause greeting Pritchard, you could hear the cocaine giggles of De Haro and St. Peter as they stepped over various dowagers in an

557

effort to get to their seats. Although they are hovering on forty, both these scions of San Francisco sustain the look of naughty children out for a prank. De Haro is losing his hair, which can be traumatic for someone accustomed to getting by on his looks, and what is left of it has gone gray; yet his eyes still roll lubriciously about in search of an intrigue. St. Peter, I hear, is given to fits of despondency, up to and including a suicide attempt or two; yet he manages a merry demeanor in public, which you have to give him credit for. San Francisco supports an abundant number of such aging playboys, heirs to this or that early name. Their ancestors dealt in fifty-vara lots. They deal in dominoes. Their ancestors built a city on the forlorn edge of a sand dune, three thousand miles from nowhere. They spend their days intriguing around the pool at the Pacific Union Club on Nob Hill or in the sauna room of the University. Deborah is right. Tuesday night at the opera does belong to the rich, but it would be hypocritical of me to get too worked up about it; for without the rich, there would be no opera at all: no evenings like the one we spent together, side by side, listening to Beverly Sills, Sherrill Milnes, and Nicolai Gedda sing the music of Jules Massenet.

Later, at the Redwood Room of the Clift Hotel, Larry St. Regis played some excellent piano, while Deborah and I sat beneath the Gustav Klimt murals and reviewed our opera programs over a nightcap of brandy and soda (for me) and (for her) Perrier water.

"Why not have some brandy?" I said.

"Liquor might lower my resistance."

"Succumb—play the loose woman for a while—then, like Thaïs, you can become a saint."

"According to the notes here, Thaïs's lover Nicias was young and rich. You are barely one and none of the other. What were you saying about Sebastian Collins at dinner?"

I looked up at the four Gustav Klimt mosaic murals that cover the walls in the Redwood Room—another Sebastian Collins association. Collins and Klimt became good friends when Collins was living in Vienna in the early 1890s. I sometimes think that I should get my finances together, quit the Library, and give the Collins biography the uninterrupted eighteen months that it deserves. Of late, I am finding traces of Collins everywhere.

This November, for instance, Deborah and I went out to the California Historical Society mansion on Jackson Street to see an exhibition celebrating seventy-five years of *Sunset Magazine*. One superb *Sunset* cover on display, done by Maynard Dixon around 1910, depicted the winery of Avila Vineyards at sunset. By 1910, of course, Collins, having buried his wife, had long since returned to San Francisco with his daughter Marina, who would then have been about fifteen. Dixon's cover nevertheless suggested the very same dreamy ideality of California as Vineyard of America that animates Collins's little book *Wine Prospects for California*, first published in 1895. Up from each side of the whitewashed Avila winery ran hillsides of ripening vines. Dixon quite cleverly has one wall of the villa reflecting back some of the color of the sunset. In the distance, the Mayacamus mountains are already half-lost in purple shadow.

"Collins loved Sybil Sanderson, the mistress of Jules Massenet," I said. "He loved her futilely, just as I love you—without hope of satisfaction."

"You're posturing again."

"I know," I said, "but rather well, don't you think?"

"Fair to middling," Deborah said. "I've seen you do better in front of Mabel Storm."

"Perhaps she inspires me more than you do."

"She's more your type, if that's what you mean."

"To return to your original question," I said, launching thereupon into a brief description of Collins's pursuit of Sybil Sanderson.

"It sounds like a novel," Deborah said.

"Will we ever sound like a novel?" I asked. As if by design, Larry St. Regis played Carole King's "Tonight You're Mine."

"They're playing our song," I said.

"But will you still love me tomorrow?" Deborah asked.

"Try me."

"I'm thinking about it."

"Don't sweat it," Deborah said as we climbed the almost perpendicular last block of Taylor Street at just that moment when twilight becomes nightfall. I had parked the Porsche at the garage on Mason and Post. "You tried as hard as you could."

"You solved the Susan Green problem," I said, "and I lost you the literacy program."

"I just suggested to the guild steering committee that they not be naive. Firing a young black woman is no way to organize the library techs. Helen Huskett will just have to offer her black eye up on the altar of unionism."

We surmounted the rim of Nob Hill. The cypress trees of Huntington Park twinkled with the warm colors of a thousand Christmas lights. The great rose window of Grace Cathedral glowed with radiance. The illuminated façade of the Fairmont Hotel—which, like the adjacent Pacific Union Club, survived the devastation of 1906—added its magic to the scene. A California Street cable car clamored by, overflowing with holiday passengers. Crossing California, we ascended the stairs that led into Grace Cathedral. Hundreds like us were streaming into the Gothic pile to hear the annual Christmas concert by the Cathedral Boys' Choir. Just before we entered, Deborah and I turned around and looked across Nob Hill to the magic cityscape that unfolded below. San Francisco seemed reborn, innocent, bathed in radiant light.

"I'm glad I'm here," she said.

"Merry Christmas, Deborah Tanner," I said.

We sat side by side—hip to hip, thigh to thigh, knee to knee—in a crowded pew and heard the singing of Christmas songs, sacred and profane. The singing left one with a certain solemn feeling. After the concert, Julian Bartlett stood in the rear of the cathedral, attired in his dean's robes, greeting people as they filed out.

"Merry Christmas, James," the Dean said as we passed by. I

560

was flattered to be recognized. I introduced Deborah. Dean Bartlett held both her hands in his for a moment, a broad smile across his craggy, handsome face.

"My dear," he said, in that Trollopian manner that Episcopal clergymen of certain standing seem to be able to assume at will. "You're in good company tonight, I trust." He took one of Deborah's hands and placed it in mine. "The peace of Our Lord Jesus Christ be with you both," he said.

We drove over to my place on Telegraph Hill. Christmas—and Deborah—gave my studio apartment the feeling of home. I put some bread and cheese on two plates and sliced some fresh pineapple into two bowls of yogurt. We ate buffet style, facing the nighttime panorama of San Francisco Bay.

"You're improving your eating habits," Deborah said.

"Your benign influence," I said. "I'm also working out at the Olympic Club. I may even take up jogging."

"I'm impressed."

"But I refuse to grow an Elliott Gould mustache."

"That would be out of character. My parents called this morning, by the way. They said they missed me. This has been my first Christmas away from home—ever."

"I'm happy that you stayed."

"I stayed because of you," Deborah said.

"Stay with me now," I said.

"I sometimes become very frightened about all the decisions we have to make," Deborah said.

She cried—not in pleasure, but in pain—when the moment came. Around four o'clock in the morning, I found myself wide awake with no prospect of sleep's return. Getting into my bathrobe, I went out into the living room and sat in my reading chair until the dawn came, overwhelmed by the irreversibility of what had occurred. Anxiety swept through me at intervals, but also a mood of peace touched by a conviction of immanent mystery. I sensed that there might be some vast, lavish, unutterable goodness at the heart of creation, and that the only way any of us could ever get there

561

was through the help of another—but also that once you got there, you would never again be fully alone because the goodness you discovered spoke in a human voice and had a human body and a human face. I resolved never again to lose my way from that goodness, now that I had found it. Thus far, I had lived my life on the surface of things, oblivious to inner meaning. My life, in fact, was already half over; and so much of it had been wasted in distraction, posturing, loneliness. But a new beginning was possible.

I heard the sound of Deborah moving about in the bedroom. She came out wrapped in a blanket, her hair in total—glorious—disarray. She walked over and sat down on my lap, resting her head on my shoulders. I held her in my arms like a drowsy child.

"You brute," she said sleepily. "You deflowered me." She reached out from beneath the blanket and held her hand to the back of my neck. "It had to happen sometime, I suppose. After all, I'm nearly twenty-six."

On the morning of the second Saturday of January in the Bicentennial year 1976, Cole O'Halloran, Andy Soutane's man in San Francisco, telephoned me at my place and said: "Listen, jerk, you're in trouble."

"Cole O'Halloran, I presume," I said.

"Listen, asshole, and listen good. Blackmail isn't your line. Stick to counting books."

"I don't know what you're talking about."

"Well, I do, and it stinks. You're a fucking hypocrite, that's what you are, a pious, fucking hypocrite."

"Cole," I said, "you have a way of repeating yourself."

"Cut the patter, Norton, and realize the trouble you're in. We got an anonymous note over here the other day saying that you are in possession of certain incriminating photographs involving Andy Soutane."

My heart sank. I could feel myself being pulled into quicksand. Tiny Roncola actually had the photographs in his possession; but no matter: the essence of O'Halloran's

562

observation was correct. I had the photographs in my head; and more, I had been agreeing to their continued existence, and—to face the fact of it—I had been one-tenth toying with the idea of their release. In the words of a certain Doonesbury character describing Attorney General John Mitchell, I was guilty, guilty, guilty.

"I'll look into it," I said.

"Right," said O'Halloran. "You look into it—and get back to me, will you?"

"I'll get back to you," I said.

"By Monday morning," O'Halloran insisted.

"By Monday morning," I agreed.

When O'Halloran hung up, I called Tiny Roncola and told him about O'Halloran's call.

"This will force it all out into the open," Tiny said excitedly. "And it's about time. Only something dramatic can help Carpino now. Did you read how Soutane blew his cool at a press conference in San Diego last week? A reporter started to bug him about his being single. Would he live in the governor's mansion, if elected? Who would entertain for him? Why had he never married? Questions like that. Soutane really got sharp with the guy, giving him something about how the governor's job was not a social position and marriage was no sign of virtue, but you could tell the question really bugged him. My guess is that the rumor mill about Soutane being gay is already churning away."

"Tiny," I said, "it's no good. I want you to destroy the pictures."

"You've got to be crazy," Tiny said.

"I am crazy," I said. "Crazy to have let you go this far; crazy to have ever let you talk to me about the possibility of blackmail."

"Seeing to it that the truth gets told isn't blackmail," Tiny said.

"You're sure those pictures are the truth?" I asked.

"You bet they are," Tiny said. He hung up.

"I find it disgusting," Deborah said that night when I told

563

her the whole story—without, of course, mentioning the shade of temptation that had once darkened my soul regarding the use of the pictures. "I wish you had told me before. I might have been of help."

"I was afraid you'd hold it against me."

"I find it strange that you haven't done anything about it," she said.

"What could I have done?"

"Get to the bottom of it," she said. "Find out the truth."

"What if it's true?" I asked.

"So what?" Deborah said. "What people do in bed is their own business. Either the photographs are true or they are fake. In either case, to leak them to the press would be crummy. If the photographs are authentic, they are still incredibly sleazy, and they violate Soutane's rights as a human being. But if they're fake, then Soutane's rights are being doubly violated. He's being set up."

"By whom?" I asked.

"Tell me about Tiny Roncola," she said.

The next morning, at Deborah's suggestion, I telephoned Stedman Mooner through the *Express* switchboard and asked him if I could drop by for a confidential talk.

"It's Sunday, Jimmy, and I'm slightly hung over."

"I'll only be a minute."

"I'm having a bunch of the Rough Riders over for brunch at noon," Mooner said. "You can help me get ready if you want to."

"I had no idea that you were a Republican," I said to Stedman Mooner when he let me into his apartment, located in a neo-Spanish building on the proper side of Russian Hill.

"There's a lot of us closet Republicans in the gay community," Mooner said, leading me into his living room, "and we're only now getting up the nerve to come out of the closet for the second time. Being gay is difficult enough, but being a gay Republican can be downright excruciating. The Rough Riders—that's what we call the San Francisco Gay Republican Coalition, Theodore Roosevelt Chapter—the Rough Riders will be over around noon, so don't think I'm rude if I work while we talk; unless, of course, this is a social visit." Mooner laughed at his witticism. It brought a slight flush to my face.

"Don't be nervous, Norton. I won't bite you. You're too chubby to be my type. Besides, you're a Democrat." He pulled a Hoover vacuum cleaner out of a hall closet, the old-fashioned, upright sort. It must have been thirty years old.

"Mother bought this vacuum cleaner the year I was born, 1944," Mooner said, unwinding the cord. "When I decided to stay out here in San Francisco after Vietnam, she sent it along by Trailways Freight from Vermont. Mother hates a dirty house." He plugged in the cord and the Hoover roared into life like an angry dragon disturbed in its lair.

"Make yourself at home while I spruce up the place," Mooner yelled over the noise. "There's vodka and Bloody Mary mix over at the bar. I'll be right with you."

I had been to Stedman Mooner's place once before, for a party—a heterosexual party, in that it was not a totally gay scene. Mooner had delighted us all by accompanying himself superbly on the piano while ripping through the songs of Noel Coward, the lyrics of which he knows down to the last intricate syllable. Taking Mooner's advice, I mixed myself a Bloody Mary.

One wall of Stedman Mooner's apartment is taken up by a floor-to-ceiling bookshelf. I love to browse through other people's bookshelves, encountering that mélange of strange and familiar titles that show the ways another person's inner landscape resembles my own but is also different. Stedman Mooner is obviously a serious reader: especially in the fields of history and biography. I saw a complete set of Jung, Bollingen edition, and the *Collected Works of Sigmund Freud*, both of which must represent a sizable financial investment on his part. There is nothing artsy-cute to Mooner's apartment, by the way: none of the droll, chichi decorative playfulness that so often characterizes gay domesticity. On one wall I saw a photograph of a younger Mooner in a cadet's uniform, holding a diploma in his hand. Another photograph showed a group of soldiers in jungle fatigues standing together before a helicopter with a cross painted on it. The men had their arms around each other's shoulders.

"I didn't know you went to West Point," I said when Mooner had turned off the vacuum cleaner and was rewinding the cord. Stedman Mooner looks like Tab Hunter used to in the 1950s, except that Mooner has an element of leanness, even hardness, lurking just behind the surface of his boyish face.

"I didn't. I went to Norwich University in Vermont. It's a private military college like the Citadel in South Carolina. You graduate with an A.B. in engineering and an Army commission."

"Is that your unit in Vietnam?" I asked, glancing over at the the picture of the young men in fatigues.

"That was some of the guys from the First Cavalry casualty evacuation unit. I was in the medical service corps in 'Nam. I commanded a medic platoon. Were you in the service?"

"No," I said, feeling uneasy, as I always do with Vietnam veterans.

"Honey, you didn't miss a goddam thing, let me tell you." He went over to the picture and regarded it silently for a moment. "I'm the only one in that picture now alive," he said in a matter-of-fact tone.

"Vietnam is a long way away," I said.

"And a long time ago," Mooner replied. "I much prefer writing a bitchy column to waiting around for Charlie to send us another load of casualties. That photograph shows some guys in my platoon just before they boarded a helicopter for some R and R in Saigon. The helicopter never made it." We went into the kitchen. Mooner began chopping onions.

"I'm doing omelettes for the Rough Riders," he said. "Now, what can I do for you?"

"I wanted to ask if you knew Andy Soutane."

"No. I don't know too many Democrats, and I won't endorse him if that's what you're after—although I thought you were with Carpino." He stopped chopping and wiped his

566

eyes on the sleeve of his collarless shirt: the latest, magenta color, with a white band where the collar should be and white cuffs—Wilkes Bashford, I'd say, retailing for about forty dollars. "Unless, of course, you're switching horses in midstream. Naughty boy. But perhaps prudent. Carpino hasn't a chance."

"So everybody tells me," I said.

Mooner pointed to a wedge of hard Parmesan cheese on the kitchen table. Opening a kitchen drawer, he fumbled among the utensils until he found a cheese slicer. "Make yourself useful," he said. "Keep the slices as thin and as continuous as possible." I followed his instructions.

"Do you know a man named Tiny Roncola?" I asked.

Mooner kept at the onions for a noticeable interval.

"Is this some kind of sexual thing?" he asked.

"It could be," I said.

"Trouble involved?"

"No—not yet at least."

"You can't be any too careful," Mooner said. "I know that this might make me sound like a whining lefty, but I'll say it anyway: gay people, even in this town, are constantly in danger of being hassled. Whom do you represent?"

"I'm trying to represent myself. I'm not looking to hassle anyone. I'm only after information."

"For what purpose?"

"To clarify a relationship."

"Between whom?"

"You and Andy Soutane."

"I never met the posturing phony, but I do know Tiny Roncola." Methodically, he cracked a dozen eggs into an Osterizer. The fact that Stedman Mooner knew Tiny Roncola took me aback. It was like hearing that W. C. Fields knew Pope John XXIII. Their worlds are that different.

"How well do you know Tiny?" I asked.

"Honey, you sound like a cop," Stedman Mooner said.

"Please, it's important."

"Roncola came to one of my—private parties. He's not

567

much to look at, true, but there's no accounting for taste. One of my guests, I forget who, must like the beefy ethnic sort since he brought Tiny along. Tiny told us all that he was straight, but that he often preferred gay company. I thought that he must have been kidding himself, but since he seemed harmless, who cares?"

"Did he come by here often?"

"Two or three times—often enough that I now remember his name. This was some seven or eight months ago, and faces come and go fast on the track I run, especially in this town."

"Did Roncola ever take your picture, or did you ever give him a photograph of yourself?"

"I sense trouble, Norton. Come clean." Mooner dropped his fey Noel Coward demeanor. A certain toughness came into his voice. His Tab Hunter face hardened into a set mask. "What gives?" I told him.

"Son of a bitch," Mooner said. "And with a goddammed Democrat, no less. He could at least have had me getting it on with one of the Republican candidates."

"That wouldn't have been to his advantage."

"Or to yours, either."

"I'm with Carpino, but not with this—nor is Carpino with this."

"How long have you known about these pictures?" Mooner asked.

"Six months—since last June."

"And you did nothing about it?"

"What could I have done?"

"What you're doing now—find out the truth." I had no answer to that one.

"Roncola took a lot of pictures," Mooner said. "He's a camera nut. Didn't you know that?" I didn't. Over the years I was away in the East I'd lost touch with what people were doing.

"Did he ever photograph people in—private positions?"

"Not in my place, he didn't," Mooner said. "I don't go in for that kinky stuff. It gives the movement a bad name.

568

Roncola took a lot of shots at last year's Halloween party, however, if I remember correctly."

"Were you in costume?"

"You might say so. I came in my jock strap—as Apollo."

"Thank you, Stedman," I said. "Please believe me: this entire conversation is confidential."

"I hope so, honey," Stedman Mooner said. "If word ever got back to Mother in Vermont that I was rumored to be hanging around with Democrats, it would break her heart."

As I left, a number of Rough Riders were just coming to the door. They were all wearing spiffy, Sunday brunch ensembles. I didn't recognize any of them; but then, again—I don't know many Republicans.

"I'm sorry it's come down to this, Tiny," I found myself saying an hour or so later as I sat in Tiny's shabby studio apartment on Dolores Street. A disheveled Murphy bed filled the living room. The place needed an airing—badly. It smelled of dirty socks and stale underwear. "I mean, we all thought that we'd come to more than this, didn't we?"

"Cut the pious crap, Jimmy. I've admitted I faked the photos, so let's forget it. I should have sent them in anonymously to a gay newspaper and let things take their course."

"But that would have made you a skilled trickster, Tiny, and you're not. Neither of us is."

"What we are is assholes," Tiny said. He picked up yesterday's socks off the floor and put them on, sitting on the edge of his Murphy bed. Standing up, he took his slacks off a nearby chair and kicked himself into them, leg by leg. "We're the losers, the nobodys, the also-rans."

"Speak for yourself, Tiny."

"I probably am," Tiny said. "What are you going to do?"

"Nothing—except ask you for all copies of those photographs, and the negatives."

"Bedstand drawer. White manila envelope." They were there, just as he said they would be.

"That is all?" I asked.

"Scout's honor," Tiny said.

"Boy Scouts don't commit blackmail," I said.

"Boy Scouts don't have to get by in this frigging world," Tiny said. "Burn those things, will you? I probably never would have had the guts to use them anyway." Tiny walked over to a hot plate resting on top of a battered veneer bureau. There was a single dime store pot on top of it. He filled the pot with water, using the tap in the bathroom sink.

"Coffee?" Tiny asked.

"No, thanks."

"It's only instant, anyway." Going over to the Murphy bed, Tiny gave the rumpled covers a few smoothing passes with his hand. He jerked at one end of the bed. The entire apparatus lifted off the ground and swung into an open closet.

"I love Murphy beds," Tiny said. "I always get a kick out of it when I put mine away."

"So I burned them in my fireplace," I told Deborah that evening. "Right there. You can see the ashes."

"The whole thing is so weird," Deborah said.

It was another Sunday evening, the second of the New Year: a time, like all Sunday evenings, of suggested death and rebirth. In the dying of the week, the eventual running out of all our time is forecast. I die a little bit every Sunday evening, but I also struggle to be reborn, to brace myself for the ensuing week.

"Frankly," she continued, "I'm disappointed in you. You let things drift along, which means that you half accepted the idea." I felt terrible, really embarrassed.

"I feel like a shit," I said.

"Don't be so easy on yourself. How do you think I feel, especially after you and I—got involved?"

570

Chapter 14

T
HE IMMINENT OUTBREAK of war between Germany
and France has cast a pall over the Bohemian Grove
summer encampment. As early as last January, 1914, I invited
Josiah Royce to make the journey out from Cambridge and be
my guest at Camp Esplandian. Royce wrote me in March,
saying that he was too upset over the all-but-certain European
war to consider spending time frivolously at the Grove; I
prevailed upon him, however, to change his mind.

"What happens is now beyond all of us," I argued, "so come
out for the Grove and refresh yourself for the struggle that lies
ahead."

It now turns out that Royce has had a long-standing offer to
teach in the Summer Session at Berkeley from Charles Henry
Rieber, dean of the University of California Summer Session
and a former student of Royce's at Harvard. ("All that will be
remembered of Harvard five hundred years from now," I once
heard Rieber say, "will be that Josiah Royce taught there.")
Royce wrote in late May to say that whereas he could not allow
himself to cross the continent for the sole purpose of attending
a Bohemian Grove encampment, he could allow himself a few
days at the Grove after an arduous stint of teaching at
Berkeley. He would stay with the Riebers during the week, so
as to be near the campus, and spend a weekend or two with
me in the Grove. Royce also promised to accompany me to the

571

dedication of the new St. Ignatius Church, scheduled for 2 August 1914.

"You realize, Sebastian," Josie wrote, "that I am not by temperament a churchgoer. When I was a boy in Grass Valley, I would hide from my parents on Sunday morning so as to avoid religious services. But since you are so proud of your consultant's role to the architect of St. Ignatius; and since we are friends from boyhood; and since I must admit that as a scholar of the baroque you are unsurpassed in this country, and I am therefore a little curious as to what you've helped accomplish in the way of a baroque church on the top of that sandy, bare, windswept hill where you, I, and Charlie Stoddard used to walk (may Charlie find peace in the afterlife, if there is an afterlife!)—considering all these things, dear friend, I shall be glad to break my lifelong habit of liturgical abstinence and go to church, although I must say that even President Eliot is rarely able to get me to attend chapel at Harvard."

Marina and I took the two o'clock ferryboat over to Oakland and met Royce at the train station. As he stepped off the transcontinental express from Chicago, I sensed Royce's underlying anxiety. Nervous by temperament at even the calmest of times, Royce seemed caught in the throes of incipient hysteria, as if the war drums of Europe's marching armies had pursued his train across the American continent from Cambridge. His eyes seemed sunk even further than usual into his overlarge forehead. His manner, absentminded at best, verged on a state of debilitating distraction. I embraced him as he stepped off the train.

"Josie, my friend," I said, "welcome back to California."

"I always love to return to home," Royce said.

Then Marina embraced him. "Uncle Josie," she said, "be good and try to enjoy yourself. I've missed you."

"I've missed you also, Marina. I see that reaching the age of nineteen makes a big difference. You were a girl of fifteen when I left San Francisco. Now you're a woman."

"If I'm a woman, then you'll have to do what I say. Firstly: come over to our house in San Francisco for a few days.

572

Secondly: go to the Grove with Father at the end of the month and cremate Care like a good Bohemian."

"I'm afraid, Marina, that I'm not much of a Bohemian. After all, I'm but an honorary member of the club."

"When in Bohemia, Uncle Josie, do as the Bohemians do. I'll find the porter and arrange for your luggage to be sent over to San Francisco."

We caught the seven o'clock ferry to the city, crossing the bay in that penultimate hour when the first suggestions of the approaching sunset can be seen in the east over the Contra Costa Range. The three of us stood on the stern of the ferry, watching Oakland and Berkeley recede behind us.

"I took my first ferry trip in the other direction in 1871," Josie said. "I crossed over to Oakland to study at the University of California. That was forty-three years ago."

Royce, as usual, was dressed like a parson. He wore a long black frock coat like a parson's and combed his thick mane of white hair back over his head the way a parson combs his hair. Royce has one of those perennially babyish faces, so it was not too difficult for me to remember him as an undergraduate, excited by philosophy and the prospect of postgraduate study in Europe.

Royce comes from a background of nervous instability. His father suffered a nervous breakdown shortly after the family arrived overland by covered wagon in the early 1850s. His mother Sarah dominated the family. I remember visiting Josie in the family home on Folsom Street in the 1860s when I was at the Boys' High School and Josie was at the Lincoln Grammar School. We also used to meet at the chess room of the Mechanics' Institute Library on Post Street, where he and I played chess with Emperor Norton: Joshua Norton to be precise, a Jewish rice merchant, originally from South Africa, who went mad after losing his fortune in an unsuccessful effort to corner the rice market. Emerging from a period of seclusion after his initial breakdown, Norton proclaimed himself Emperor of the United States and Protector of Mexico. He wore a military uniform reminiscent of Emperor Louis Napoleon's and was followed around town by two dogs,

Bummer and Lazarus. Local merchants would honor Norton's script (he printed his own money) so long as he stayed within reasonable limits. Emperor Norton spent many an afternoon over a chessboard at the Mechanics' Library, where they kept—and still do keep—a quiet room reserved for chess players. One day—I was about seventeen at the time—I peeked into the room in search of a casual game and saw Norton in full imperial regalia—a blue frogged frock coat, set off by golden epaulettes, striped trousers, a great cocked hat topped off by an ostrich plume—engrossed in a chess game with young Royce, then about thirteen.

"Come over here and help me out," Norton roared when he saw me. "This lad has got me nearly vanquished!"

To be frank, the game was already lost; Emperor Norton did not have a chance. Royce had already destroyed him in seven moves. Norton and I played valiantly for three or four more moves but were forthwith defeated by the serious young lad with shabby clothes and slightly enlarged head. That would have been around 1865 or 1866. Despite the difference in our ages, five years or so (of no importance now, but a veritable abyss in one's youth), Josiah Royce and I became good friends. We would meet in the chess room of the Mechanics' Institute on Saturday afternoons for a game with Emperor Norton; rather, Norton and I matched wits against Royce, who invariably beat us. Royce and I soon came to know the Emperor rather well—and to suspect that he was not at all as mad as he pretended to be. Playing the fool, we decided, was a shrewd calculation on Joshua Norton's part. Respectably bourgeois by temperament, he had gambled and lost everything. He had seen a decade of remorseless labor burned up in one day like a gathering of dry fennel put to a match. As Emperor Norton, however, San Francisco's beloved madman, he lived off the bemused bounty of the city. He took his meals *gratis* at the best restaurants in town and paid no rent at his better-class hotel.

"Look around you, lads," I remember Norton saying one day as we walked up Sansome Street past a row of banks, including the Bank of California where my future patron, William

Chapman Ralston, was struggling to create a financial empire. "This city is filled with overworked and overworking fools, mad for gold and silver. They will all be dead before their time—dead from exhaustion and too much liquor. I was once even such as these frenzied devotees of Mammon. It nearly destroyed me."

He laughed in anticipation of the joke to come: "Why, it nearly drove me mad!"

Royce and Emperor Norton seemed to have a special bond between them, some intuitive communication that eluded and excluded me. When I later met Royce's father, I began to fathom Royce's relationship with the mad, not-so-mad Emperor of the United States and Protector of Mexico. Royce's father had never recovered from his breakdown. He marginally supported his family peddling fruit from a hand-drawn grocery cart. Like Norton, he had come to California in search of the Golden Fleece and had been broken by his Odyssey. I suspect that even then young Royce knew that he might have inherited something of his father's nervous instability. Emperor Norton offered young Royce an ironic antitype; the madman as a survivor beyond sanity, a hero of parodic coping.

Over the years, my friend Josiah Royce, America's sole systematic philosopher, has suffered a number of breakdowns, most noticeably in the mid-1880s just after he was called to Harvard by President Eliot from his assistant professorship at Berkeley. Like Emperor Norton, however, Royce has coped with his demons through a stylized role. He has become a philosopher, a lover of wisdom; and this is a form of preventive madness, a way of warding off the possibilities of an even greater insantiy through the lesser derangement of systematic thought. I jest—but not completely!

When we approached the San Francisco Ferry Building, our Spanish Renaissance tower that dominates the waterfront, Royce's spirits seemed to improve. Homecoming is always a mixture of sadness and elation. As we drew near to the city, Royce was feeling the elation. San Francisco, after all, is the city where he grew up and where a group of businessmen, encouraged by Daniel Coit Gilman, president of the University of California, put a purse together in 1875 to send him to Germany and to Baltimore for further philosophical study. Royce returned to San Francisco in 1879, possessed of a doctorate from the newly established Johns Hopkins University. He left us again in 1884 for Harvard, called there by his mentor in the philosophy department, William James.

We took a motor taxi from the Ferry Building out to our flat on Taylor Street.

"It's a brand new city," Josie said as we drove up California Street.

"Very little in this part of town survived the Fire of 1906," I said.

I left Royce alone with his thoughts. I have noticed this very same response in other former San Franciscans who departed before 1906 and who return now to the new city. They go through phases of nostalgia for the lost city, hostility towards what we have rebuilt, then a form of bittersweet acceptance of the new cityscape.

"It just isn't the same, Sebastian," remarked Royce as he went through the inevitable phase of hostility. "It lacks the romance of the old city, the stately defiance of its remote existence on the outer edge of the frontier."

We enjoyed a delicious cold supper upon our arrival home: potato salad, sliced ham, sourdough bread, some coleslaw and beer. Marina served, then joined us for the meal.

"Now I'm off," she announced as she cleared away the plates, leaving Royce and me with beer glasses and a number of bottles of lager in an ice bucket.

"I appreciate your announcement, Marina. Will Mr. Scannell be calling on you here?"

"No. He's working late at the office. I'll meet him in the lobby of the Fairmont Hotel. Cyril Tobin is throwing a party for Kathleen and Cigi Norris, who are back from New York, visiting. It's a party for the younger set."

"But of course. Please give my regards to Kathleen and Cigi. I'll wait up for you."

"You needn't."

"I prefer to. Josie and I have much to talk about."

576

Marina hugged me, kissed Josie atop his domeish pate, then swept from the room in that deliberate stride of hers which reminds me so much of her mother. Royce and I sat over the lager, enjoying cigars, like the two students we were in Germany some forty years ago—he at Jena, I at Heidelberg.

"Here, Josie," I said getting up and bringing over the two volumes of his just-published *The Problem of Christianity* from the sideboard where I had placed them earlier this afternoon in anticipation of this moment. "Sign these for me. This is your masterpiece, the fulfillment of all that you have been thinking about and writing about for over thirty years."

"This book," Royce said, "is my attempt to put Christianity into rational perspective. I most likely began its composition in my Grass Valley boyhood when I would sneak away on Sunday mornings so as not to have to go to church. I would sit outside the open window of the church and eavesdrop on the sermon, trying to translate the minister's peroration into equivalencies I could comprehend."

He took one of those newfangled pocket fountain pens from the pocket of his preacher's coat—the kind of pen that miraculously carries its own ink in a tiny rubber vial, filled by suction—then wrote on the inside of Volume One: "For Sebastian Collins, with whom I have shared a lifelong quest. From his friend Josiah Royce. July 20, 1914. San Francisco, where we both were boys together."

"Do you remember the letter you wrote me in Rome, when I was finishing my Bernini study at the Vatican Library?" I asked.

"The one about my first visit to William James? I remember it well."

"I have the letter in my study. Let me fetch it and read it to you."

"You have it so readily available?"

"Marina and I have organized all my papers. I have my whole life available, alphabetically and by date."

"How wonderful. How horrible. Yes, fetch the letter if you please. Better yet, we'll take these bottles of lager up to your study and finish the evening there."

We climbed the stairs to my third-floor study, which looks out over the soon-to-be-opened Panama–Pacific International Exposition. When these pastel buildings are illuminated at night, after the opening of the Fair in February, what a marvelous sight shall greet me from my study window! Even now the Tower of Jewels catches the lights of the city in iridescent refraction. I poked through the third carton of the 1870s sequence as arranged by Marina and rather easily fished out the letters I had saved from the time I spent as a *scriptor* at the Vatican Library under the learned Cardinal Votto. Sure enough: there was Royce's letter, addressed to me at my rooms on the Via Monserrato near the venerable English College and postmarked Baltimore, 8 September 1876.

"Shall you read it, or shall I?" I asked.

"You read it, Sebastian. I'm enjoying the lights of the evening."

"Dear Sebastian," I read, "I'm at the new Johns Hopkins University in Baltimore where Daniel Coit Gilman is now president. Gilman, remember, headed the University of California when I was there and raised the money for my study in Germany. I salute you upon the completion of your doctorate at Heidelberg, but am disappointed that you will not be returning to America. I do, however, sympathize with your being at loose ends after the collapse of Ralston's plan for a San Francisco art museum. If only Ralston had been able to raise some sort of endowment before his death! I am certain, however, that when you return to America you will be able to find a position in one of the museums in the East. California, and that includes San Francisco, is not yet ready for such rarefied things as art museums—or for philosophy, for that matter. I myself am determined upon an eastern career. Last month, upon my return from Germany, I took the train to Cambridge to call upon Professor William James at Harvard. I sought his counsel as to careers in philosophy available in America. There are not many, James advised me when I called upon him in his study in the Harvard Library, but he would see what he could do for me when I finished my preparation at

578

Johns Hopkins. He invited me to come around for dinner that evening at his home on Irving Street. 'We will be dressing, of course,' he said. I found the remark obscure, but I did brush off my best suit at the boarding house before I walked over to Irving Street. I rang the doorbell and to my chagrin stepped into a room of Harvard faculty attired formally in claw-hammers and white tie! I felt every inch the country bumpkin. Noticing my chagrin, Professor James left the room for a short time—then returned in a dark broadcloth suit similar to my own. 'Now then,' he said. 'Royce, is it? Let me introduce you around.' "

We talked Harvard for the remainder of the evening. We talked of Royce's colleague Santayana, although I sensed some ambivalence on Royce's part to his half-Spanish Platonist-skeptic colleague. "The man lacks system," was all that Royce would say, but I could easily guess how much deeper the matter went. Royce embodies the consciousness and con-science of the protestant North—deliberate, systematic, brooding, intoxicated by the absolute. Santayana is Mediterra-nean man personified: passionate, intuitive, by turns skeptical and platonic, but even when most skeptical, most distrusting, ever enamored with the elusive traceries of an unseen loveliness, at once plaintive and fertile, like a Botticellian spring.

We agreed to disagree on Santayana, whom I greatly admire, because we share a common regard for my former teacher who has also been Royce's long-time colleague, Charles Eliot Norton, professor of the history of art at Harvard up until his death in 1908. I owe everything to Harvard, by which I mean that I owe everything to Charles Eliot Norton. Although I completed my professional education at Heidel-berg, I left Harvard with a point of view formed by Charles Eliot Norton that has retained its coherence for more than forty years. As a fourth-year student at Boys' High School here in San Francisco, I read Norton's *Notes of Travel and Study in Italy* (1860). I found myself enamored of Norton's sense of the

579

Mediterranean art-past: classical, medieval, Renaissance. I vowed to embark, as he had done, upon a lifetime of scholarly aesthetic pilgrimage. I determined to give myself to the study of history and philosophy of art. When I returned to Harvard from Italy in 1871, Norton was just beginning his career as professor of the history of art, called to that post by his cousin, President Charles Eliot. Norton's mother, you see, was an Eliot of Boston; his father was Andrews Norton, for years the professor of Sacred Scripture in the Harvard Divinity School. Strange that one of the Eliots, Charles Eliot, that archetypal snob, should alienate me from Harvard during my first attempt at an education there, and another Eliot, Charles Eliot Norton, should so help restore my destroyed idealism when I returned to the College after fighting in the Italian civil war.

Having been through a war in Italy, having seen men kill and be killed, having killed myself, I no longer envisioned Italy as a dreamy never-never land suffused in a smoky-mellow, aesthetic haze. For me it had become a land soaked in blood. In my senior year, 1871-1872, I attended Norton's lectures on art history. I thrilled to Norton's efforts at reconciling realism and ideality. Norton was no cloistered academic popinjay. He had, after all, been in commerce for a number of years following his graduation from Harvard in 1846: the import-export business, making a long voyage out to India as a supercargo. Through travel and through wide social contact, he knew the great world. He knew the Brownings in Florence, Thomas Carlyle in London, Walt Whitman in New York. He defended Whitman, in fact, from the priggish critics who denounced the eroticism in Whitman's poetry—an eroticism, by the way, which I find a delightful compensation for the Good Gray Poet's sometimes tinny ear. I was twenty-three years old at the time, a combat veteran, and no boy at all. I had been through a war, and Norton helped heal me. A conviction of richness and beauty, of the essential goodness of life as revealed through art, returned to me under the influence of Norton's lectures, which poured over my disturbed soul like a soothing balm.

580

"It is the *ethos* of art that is most valuable." I can yet hear Norton lecturing: hear his voice and remember also seeing the stately elm trees in the Yard from the windows of Massachusetts Hall where our class was meeting. "Art is valuable primarily as it reveals the moral and aesthetic preoccupations of a culture at a particular moment of crisis and transformation. As such, art is our most valuable legacy from the past. Art is what is most recoverable because through art the temporal escapes mortality. Art is thus the final harvest of time, the only thing that survives the present moment because art is at once the most material of all things—paint on canvas, a carved piece of stone—and the thing most touched by matter's dynamic opposite, which many call the spirit."

Norton paced as he lectured, filling the room with creative tension. I remember lingering behind after one such lecture to pursue a point Norton had made regarding Ruskin and being invited to walk back with him to his home at Shady Hill, the family estate in Cambridge near the college buildings.

"Yes, you're right, Collins," Norton remarked as we walked. "Ruskin does, finally, give primacy to the social aspects of art history, but only because without art, especially the public art of great architecture, there would be little that is recoverable from the past in the way of social history for us to worry about. Speaking of social history, may I ask where you are from?"

"San Francisco."

"A long way from home, aren't you? And older than our typical student also. Why is that?"

For some reason, I answered Norton in Italian, telling him the story of my sojourn with the Zouaves. We walked down Irving Street towards Shady Hill. It was mid-autumn and the elm trees were riotous in harvest colors. I filled the autumn afternoon, a New England afternoon, with Italian words. I told Norton about William Chapman Ralston, president of the Bank of California, who was paying my expenses to Harvard and, after Harvard, had promised to see me through a period of European study in the hope that I would return to

581

San Francisco at just that point that Ralston would be able to found an art museum and research library in the midst of the city: or rather, overlooking the city; for Ralston had in mind a location atop Nob Hill on California near Mason, a property he was holding undeveloped for this purpose. I told Norton about my Italian experiences, omitting the gore, but Norton was no fool when it came to such things, having himself just taught a generation of Civil War returnees. He read between the lines of my narrative.

"You've been through a lot," he said. "And like the Confederate lads, you were on the doomed side of the dispute. As they did, you fought for the past, for an antiquated social order."

"I fought for the Pope," I said, "and he still sits on his throne, albeit his kingdom has shrunk to a few Vatican acres."

Norton continued on without seeming to hear this. He is, after all, an agnostic and a political liberal, so my defense on the field of battle of an obscurantist, theocratic regime must have struck him as odd, very odd indeed, coming from an American—even an American from San Francisco.

"Yes, you fought for the past, but you did survive, and here you are at Harvard with such wonderful prospects." He questioned me closely about William Chapman Ralston's proposed art museum. "Is there civic support?" he asked. "Will San Francisco rally to Ralston's idea? What he envisions is not yet a reality in either Boston or New York, where—if you don't mind my saying so—the taste for such things is more developed than it is in such a new city as San Francisco."

A number of months later, Norton invited me around to a session of the Dante Society. The Society met monthly at Professor Longfellow's house on Brattle Street. I walked down snowy sidewalks in the early evening, thinking of similar winter walks five years earlier to Ryan Patrice's apartment on Follen Street for Sunday evening gatherings. How much had I been through in the intervening five years! I did not know it then, but as I headed for the coziness of Professor Longfellow's fire, Ryan Patrice, who had once sent me into a panic to Québec when he had demanded that I enter religion, was at that time establishing his first mission in the Mekong Delta region of French Indo-China.

At Professor Norton's suggestion, I submitted a memoir of my Italian experiences to the *Nation*, the New York journal which Norton helped the journalist E.L. Godkin establish. My essay appeared in the *Nation* in the spring of 1872 under the title "Present at the Fall of Rome." I have recently used that 1872 memoir as the basis for my Italian chapter in *Memoirs of a San Francisco Bohemian*.

The night of my visit to Professor Longfellow's home, Norton read excerpts from a work-in-progress, his prose translation of the *Divine Comedy*, which remained unpublished until four years before his death. As a hobby, Norton kept at this translation for more than thirty years. In the course of this time, we corresponded on a number of points of word usage and technical phrases. I shall always remember the way the firelight from Longfellow's hearth fell across Norton's face as he read his translation of the story of Francesco and Paola. "And then they read no more," he laughed, bringing the sequence to an end; only in Dante's poem the reading ceased because the lovemaking began. In our case, it ceased because the hour was late and Longfellow's servant had laid out a spread of doughnuts and hot apple cider on the great oaken table in the parlor.

Through Professor Norton's lectures, I first became aware of John Ruskin and the pre-Raphaelite movement in England. I have enormously enjoyed the recently published two volumes of the letters of John Ruskin to Charles Eliot Norton (1904), which recapitulates their long dialogue. If it ever came down to it, I could easily describe myself as something of a high provincial (Josiah Royce's term) Ruskinian and a high provincial pre-Raphaelite working in an American, or rather a San Franciscan context. At the same time, I sustain, most assuredly, a strong interest in the Roman baroque, which Charles Eliot Norton cherished also: a love that led him to help establish the American Academy in Rome. This institution, incidentally, in its combining of library, museum, and research facilities under one roof, very much resembles what

William Chapman Ralston had in mind for San Francisco. From Ruskin—via Charles Eliot Norton—I first learned to appreciate the points of intersection between mystical religion and flesh.

Since I had served in the Papal States for nearly three years as a trooper, living day by day with the architecture and statuary of the baroque era, an interest in the intersection of spirit and flesh, the hungers of *eros* and the appeasements of *agape*, naturally led me towards an appreciation of Bernini and the baroque. Towards the study of this dramatic, fertile era, I have made what I hope is a solid, albeit minor, contribution. Josiah Royce and I, two provincial San Franciscans in search of the wider world, moved towards our intellectual and imaginative goals in differing directions, which reflected our disparate ethnic and religious backgrounds and temperaments. Royce the English protestant embraced Germany, Hegelian Idealism, the rectitude of high protestant thought. Irish Catholic that I am (for better or for worse!), I embraced Bernini, the baroque, the Mediterranean South that believes in its way yet remains solidly pagan: *paganus* in the Latin, rooted in realities of soil and sun, resigned to the fate, the inevitable pain and wretchedness, of the human condition, and yet all the while defiantly glorying in the occasional, all-too-brief beauties and splendors of art and life and the flesh. Royce sought God through philosophical system. I sought Him through the paradox of my own constant incipient disbelief, my skepticism of mind, and the compelling counterforce of a strong animal faith, a visceral hunger for the transcendant, for light and grace. As in my confession to Rafael Merry del Val in the Church of St.-Sulpice in Paris, flesh has a way of always betraying me to something higher—and yet I dearly love the flesh, even now, when I am old. In his *Problem of Christianity* (now signed for me, and safely on the shelf of my Royce collection that begins with some of the work he did at Berkeley in the early eighties), Royce seeks to equate the mystery of Chrsitianity to certain neo-Hegelian categories of transcendence and atonement through the redemptive community. I, on the other hand, thirst desperately for the Mystical Body of Christ. At this age of mine, I believe (if I believe!) only through my headlong, half-understood dependence upon the Sacred Heart of Jesus, the capstone of Counter-Reformational baroque theology: Jesus Christ as Risen Man, his flesh afire with raging love for material creation; Jesus Christ, the cosmic force, elevating matter to the spiritual by an all-penetrating energy that is both a reality of physics and a reality of divine grace and love.

"What is our plan for the Grove?" Royce asked as we completed each our third bottle of lager and our second cigar. It was around 11:30 and both of us, whether we admitted it or not, were waiting up for Marina.

"We'll go up to the Grove by chartered train on the twenty-fifth. The Cremation of Care is that evening, with Henry Morse Stevens as Sire. The Midsummer Low Jinks will be on the first; and the Grove Play, on the eighth. Senator Phelan is most eager to have you as his guest at Esplandian."

"We'll be making merry in the redwoods while France and Germany are at each other's throats. It's a twilight time for civilization, Sebastian. This war in Europe will destroy the optimistic energy of the nineteenth century. The Europe we knew as young men, the civilization we knew, is committing suicide. How can Germany so betray its best ideals? How can it sink to the bestial level of the ancient Hun?"

Fortunately, Marina came in, and I did not have to answer, for I have no response to the catastrophe that is befalling my beloved Europe. As the leading American exponent of German idealism, Royce feels triply betrayed by the Kaiser's aggression. His onetime schoolmasters have turned into monsters.

"Well, I'm delighted that you two distinguished scholars have found your way up to the library. Shall I fetch some more beer?"

"Not for me, Marina. I'll be off to bed," said Royce.

She walked over to him and kissed his white-maned, slightly megacephalic head for the second time that

585

evening—Royce's great dome of a head, containing a brain that biologically supports a mind that is the finest of its sort in America: a philosophical, speculative, abstract, and abstracting mind that is powerful in its insights and formal procedures, but cursed also by an inherited instability that sometimes obscures its essential luminosity with dark clouds of pessimism and gloom.

"Uncle Josie, I want you to go to the Grove with Papa and have fun—have lots and lots of fun."

"Did you have fun tonight?" I asked. I use the word "fun" quite easily these days, having learned it from Marina. The next step is to have some fun myself.

"Yes, I did. I met John in the lobby. The Norrises rented one of the smaller banquet rooms. There was a tableful of seafood, including caviar, and iced champagne. Kathleen has made barrels of money from her novel *Mother*. Everyone was there."

"Everyone? My dear, not everyone. Josie and I were not there, were we?"

"No, silly. I mean everyone in the younger crowd. A lot of Kathleen's friends from the *Examiner* came—Maynard Dixon the artist, and Adele Rogers St. John, the newspaper reporter. Cigi Norris said that he looked forward to seeing you at the Grove."

"The Grove! You hear that, Josiah? We two old men had best get to bed and rest ourselves for the Grove."

Marina came over to where I was sitting in my overstuffed leather chair. She then did something she hasn't done for years, since she was twelve or so. She sat in my lap, put her arms around me, and buried her face in my neck.

"Papa," she said. "You funny old granddaddy-papa. You smoker of cigars. You devastater of ham, potato salad, and beer. With all the old-fashioned things you care about. I'm telling you something because you're so harmless."

"What is that, you rude daughter?"

"I'm in love. For the first time in my life, I am in love."

I kissed her cheek, scenting in the process a rather good men's cologne that had somehow found its way to her face.

586

On Sunday morning the second of August, 1914, United States Senator-elect James Duval Phelan, myself, and Marina were driven by Mr. Robert Poole in Phelan's Croxton-Keeton touring car to the Ferry Building at the foot of Market Street, where we met Josiah Royce who had taken the ferry over from Berkeley. We motored down Market Street to the Hibernia Bank at Jones and McAllister, where we took a right turn up McAllister, proceeding past the construction site of the new Main Library at Larkin Street, then past the City Hall, and on up Fulton Street to St. Ignatius Church, which now dominates the western skyline of the city. After we passed the Main Library, whose Italian baroque façade is just beginning to suggest what will be its ultimate grandeur, and the City Hall, so splendid in the Sunday morning sunlight, Royce turned to me (he, Phelan and I were in the back seat; Marina sat in front next to Mr. Poole) and said: "Sebastian, you devil! You have rebuilt the new San Francisco almost exclusively in baroque. I see your hand in this!"

"You have the Senator to thank for that, not me."

"Well then, Senator, thank you. I miss the old San Francisco, but this new city—if you keep to the course suggested by the City Hall and the Library—will be perfectly grand."

The Croxton-Keeton took the Fulton Street hill with ease. Phelan and Royce had never met before. The Senator-elect, however, graciously assumed the burden of small talk, sensing perhaps that Josie might very well be a great philosopher but had chosen deliberately to remain socially inept. I say "chosen" advisedly; for at Harvard, Royce is infamous for his smelly cigars, his semi-shabby frock coat, his soft collar and lazy string tie (again the parson's touch). Royce will sit silently through some dinner parties, or, at other times, carry on an autonomous monologue, oblivious to the responses or interest of the other guests. Royce struggled long and hard to win his Harvard professorship. In California, Royce dreamed of Harvard as a Heavenly City, a Brave New World. He married into a socially prominent family, the Head family of San Mateo, in an effort to upgrade himself. God knows that social

587

improvement must have been the reason for the marriage. He and Katharine Head Royce have little in common otherwise. To this day Katharine is contemptuous of her husband in the manner of women who feel that they have married beneath themselves. For a number of years now, there has been what might be called, in the language of the Grand Chartreuse, a *Magnum Silentium* between the two of them. Once appointed to Harvard, Royce began to play the frontier Californian, affecting the very direct, unpretentious style that, when he was stuck out here, seemed the language and idiom of provincial imprisonment.

Not having a great mind like Josie's, and not being rich (for the rich also can do what they want), I have spent my life behaving myself—in most instances. I dress scrupulously. I chat amiably at dinner parties, avoiding either brooding silences or rude monologues.

"In reality, Professor Royce," Phelan remarked as we approached Alamo Square at Fulton and Steiner, "neither Sebastian nor I can take the credit. That belongs to Daniel Hudson Burnham."

We drove past the Mahoney house at 1198 Fulton, facing Alamo Square. Surmounted by an ornate tower, this stick-style Italian villa, built entirely of wood carved to resemble stone, always reminds me of the city lost to fire in April of 1906. Only in old San Francisco did we find such houses: such fantasies made possible by the mechanical jigsaw which is capable of molding wood into a thousand playful shapes. They survive now, these outrageously fantastic houses, mainly in the Western Addition beyond Van Ness Avenue or in the inner Mission district; for the fire destroyed the interior districts of the city, where most of these homes once were—row upon row of them, packed side by side like gingerbread houses in a box.

Phelan mentioned Daniel Hudson Burnham. I had held a copy of Burnham's plan for San Francisco in my hand on 17 April 1906, the day before the earthquake destroyed the city. Printed in booklet form, the Burnham Plan had issued from the press of John Barry that very day.

"You see, Josie," I said, picking up Phelan's hint (we had, after all, to say something; Royce can be difficult!), "just as you have brought system to American philosophy, Burnham tried to bring system to San Francisco through the instrumentality of a grand city plan commissioned by Senator Phelan."

"I'm not a senator until March, Sebastian, but I'll take some credit for the Burnham Plan—as long as you share it with me."

"I'll let both of you take the credit," said Marina, turning around, "as long as we go to the Cliff House for something to eat after the dedication of the new church. Promise me, Father, that it won't take long. I like church services to be short."

"Yes, promise us," said Royce. "I also like brief services."

"No more than an hour and a half," I said. "The dedication will be over by ten-thirty. Then Mr. Poole can take us to the Cliff House for bacon and eggs."

"Good," said Marina. "I'm famished."

We motored past Alamo Square, where refugees from the Fire camped out in April of 1906. At Divisadero Street, St. Ignatius Church came into sight: monumental, white, tower-proud atop a three-hundred-foot rocky promontory overlooking the Pacific. Like City Hall and our Library, St. Ignatius Church is in the baroque style; and as is also the case with those other two baroque assertions of San Francisco's recovery, I've played a minor role in the construction of this edifice.

What is it, this lifelong passion of mine for the baroque? Whatever its origins, I sustain it in common with other citizens of San Francisco, for Mr. Burnham had no trouble in converting all of us members of the Committee for the Adornment and Beautification of San Francisco to the idea of building the City Beautiful here in San Francisco. Sometime in early 1901, Phelan called us together to hear his proposal, and we agreed to it without hesitation. Burnham had a way of inspiring confidence, but he also spoke directly to a metaphor of grandeur that was already lodged deeply within the collective psyche of San Franciscans. It was around March of

1901 when Phelan first had us transported to the top of Twin Peaks by horse-drawn carriages (even Mr. Poole's Croxton-Keeton would have difficulty with Twin Peaks) to meet the famed Daniel Hudson Burnham: the planner of the Columbian World's Fair at Chicago, the man who inspired the revival of L'Enfant's plan for Washington, D.C., the man who had just laid out the new capital city of Manila. Now before us in ample flesh (Burnham and I share a similar physique), he was here to address the gentlemen of the Committee for the Adornment and Beautification of San Francisco, founded in 1891 by young James Duval Phelan, our host the Mayor, who, by the way, had also paid for the carriages. Being so steep, Twin Peaks is an expensive taxi ride! Burnham lectured us about the new San Francisco: the City Beautiful, America's queen city of Pacific Basin empire, which he would build for us just as he had built Chicago, Washington, Manila.

"Gentlemen," Burnham boomed, "I'm here at Mayor Phelan's request to call San Francisco to greatness. Are you ready for it?"

It turned out, of course, that we were not; but for a while, under the pull of Burnham's magnetism, we believed that we were. We spent the morning tramping after Burnham across the bare, windswept heights of Twin Peaks as he delineated his vision with all the certainty of an Old Testament prophet, announcing the city plan of the New Jerusalem.

"There," he boomed, pointing to the old City Hall, crowned by the goddess Athene. "There from our Civic Center will radiate outwards a series of grand boulevards, like rays of sunlight. These will be intersected by a growing rim of concentric boulevards at spaced intervals, the last and final one running adjacent to the water around the entire edge of the San Francisco peninsula. I shall continue the Golden Gate Park Panhandle down Fell Street directly into the heart of the city. Water will cascade down the center of the Panhandle, pulled by gravity into a series of holding pools. Here, atop Twin Peaks, will be a grand sky-park. Water will also fall from here into a series of reflecting pools. There, there, and there"—this said as he pointed to San Francisco's most prominent hills—"we will mass the skyscraper construction of the city, making a virtue of the natural height. This way, we cluster our construction on the heights, leaving the city's plains and valleys available for parks, greenbelts, boulevards, and domestic construction. It is better this way: we thus create rhythms of soaring masses and open spaces, rather than let varying heights of construction clash together discordantly."

San Francisco, as Burnham envisioned it—and as, with the graphical assistance of Willis Polk, he rendered it in the plan printed for the Board of Supervisors the very day before the earthquake—would be like no other city on earth, although it resembled a number of them. There were touches of Rome in Burnham's lavish use of fountains, pools, and moving water; touches of Paris in his use of concentric boulevards and superb massing of public buildings upon open squares. The criss-crossing of the city by parks and greenbelts suggested London. There was something Eastern European, Russian almost, in the way Burnham advised us to mass our skyscrapers onto our hills, thus doubling their soaring effect with a minimum loss of vistas to the rest of the city. As sketched by Willis Polk, these montane congeries of commerce soared like cathedrals of secularity above the plain, five or six of them in all, including a complex devoted to culture and the arts atop Twin Peaks.

Constructed on a rocky promontory some three hundred and fifty feet above sea level, St. Ignatius Church is built on the same principle of using topographical height to reinforce the effect of architectural height. The twin spires and campanile of St. Ignatius, themselves well over two hundred feet in altitude, soar nearly six hundred feet above sea level, visible from innumerable parts of the city, like the inner fortress of a Renaissance walled town.

"Your church seems rather alone out here, Royce remarked as we drove up along Fulton Street towards St. Ignatius.

"The College will catch up to it," I said. "The Jesuits plan to build a new campus adjacent to the church."

591

I certainly do hope money is forthcoming for new collegiate buildings. Since the Earthquake and Fire destroyed our campus, St. Ignatius College has been temporarily housed in a drafty, rickety former shirt factory at Hayes and Shrader streets: such a contrast to our marvelous facilities at the Hayes and Van Ness campus, which were spacious and elegant.

"Off to the shirt factory?" Marina sometimes says to me in the morning as I leave for classes. I walk, incidentally, down Taylor to California, catch a California Street cable car to Van Ness, transfer at Van Ness to a streetcar, then transfer to yet another streetcar at Hayes Street going out to Shrader. The entire journey takes some forty-five minutes. I enjoy the ride. It gives me a chance to relish the daily drama of the city. A number of the motormen recognize me. One of them salutes me as "Doc"; another as "Professor."

"Yes, my dear. I'm off to the shirt factory. Today I'll be doing collars and cuffs."

"I'll take a dozen of them—in Latin, with buttons in Greek."

I am very happy at St. Ignatius College—and well supported by the chair Phelan endowed in my honor. Marina's remark about collars and cuffs in Latin and Greek is to the point. We teach a very classical curriculum at St. Ignatius— Latin, Greek, philosophy, mathematics, modern languages. Father Henry Woods, the prefect of studies, and I both agree that we cannot compete with the diversified curriculum of Berkeley or Stanford. We should, rather, adhere to the *ratio studiorum*, the scheme of studies that has characterized Jesuit education since the sixteenth century. The course of studies at St. Ignatius College proceeds through an initial poetry year, followed by a rhetoric year, followed by two years of solid training in humanities and philosophy. We take in Irish and Italian boys, the first of their families to attempt higher education, and a handful of years later we turn out lawyers, businessmen, politicians capable of a solid, if not brilliant, performance because they have been well educated in the basics of the liberal arts and the sciences.

592

I like our boys. I like their rude energy and good humor, their freckled faces and rawboned physiques. I know exactly what my role as a teacher is: to give them the tools of social improvement, to make gentlemen out of them—gentlemen in the first generation of gentlemanliness. Few of our graduates are as distinguished or as wealthy as James Duval Phelan, who graduated with the class of 1881. He, to speak the truth, might have been expected to go east to Harvard or to Georgetown, the fashionable Jesuit college in Washington, D.C., except that his father insisted that he have a local education in order to understand better the city he would assuredly one day lead. No, our boys are more on the order of Edward O'Day (class of 1900), the journalist, and Michael Buckley (also of the class of 1900), who is in the shipping business: not fancy lads, but quick and capable withal. We bring them in early, at age ten or so, process them through our preparatory departments and our academic department, which leaves off at the twelfth grade. Then we commence collegiate work. I'll match those who take our bachelor's degree with any of the Berkeley or Stanford lads, save in the matter of social polish; but then again, our Berkeley and Stanford lads lack a certain social polish in comparison to the lads of Harvard and Yale. A good number of our St. Ignatius boys are self-supporting, working forty hours a week, leaving them little time for the college shenanigans that David Starr Jordan so encourages down at Stanford.

I run into Jordan occasionally at the Bohemian Club; he never fails to be patronizing about the St. Ignatius College and my employment there. He once suggested that I was underemployed—in light of my scholarship; but he has never offered me a post at Stanford, about which he drones on continuously over nothing stronger than tea, for David Starr Jordan is a teetotaler, which is rare among Bohemians. Nor do I expect that Jordan would ever have offered me a position—even when I was younger and more eligible for a professorship. I am too Roman in my habits of life and my aesthetic tastes—not to mention my religion—for Stanford, which is a quintessentially Protestant place. I would not have been happy among Jordan's teetotaling faculty, so fibrillating with righteous Emersonian sentiment.

Yet in a sense, Jordan is correct. I am underemployed, pounding the essentials of philosophical discourse and art history into well-meaning but resistant lads, intent upon careers in law and business. A number of factors, however, alleviate my situation. First of all, in endowing a chair in philosophy and the history of art, Phelan has seen to it that I am well paid, even to the point of causing a certain amount of jealousy among other members of the lay staff. Secondly, I cherish my associations with the Jesuit Order, which established St. Ignatius College here in San Francisco in 1855. I am, you see, a bit of a secret Jesuit myself; which is to say, I revere the sustaining ideals of the Company of Jesus: its reverence for the traditions of the Latin Christian West, above all else, its passion for the classics and humane learning. I share also the Incarnational worldliness of the Jesuits, for as do they, I love the world in all its sensate variety and beauty; but as they do also, I nurture an awareness that all flesh, all creation, has been transformed by Christ's Incarnation into a triumphant eucharistic hymn. *Ad majorem Dei gloriam* is the Jesuit motto: "To the greater glory of God." My sense of glory is perhaps more secular than that of the Jesuits. I do love the glory of the world, even now as an old man when I should be beginning the process of gracefully letting go of the world; but I also love God's glory. That, after all, is at the core of the baroque style which is also the semi-official style of the Jesuits: glory—the elaboration outwards of an inward light and a radiant energy, as from the sun; only this Sun is the Risen Christ, now the source of energy for all creation. So Ryan Patrice convinced me some twenty years ago at Grand Chartreuse, but so also did I suspect some forty years ago when I first undertook my study of the baroque. The impetus behind the Jesuits and the baroque style is in sum the ambitions of the Counter Reformation: the militant reconquest of Protestant Europe by an embattled Roman Catholic orthodoxy that

594

had reformed itself around an Incarnational nexus of spirit and flesh, transformed by glory and disciplined optimism into something assertive, grand, alive with the radiance of both this world and the transcendent realm of spirit. Flesh, says the baroque (the Jesuit style), needs spirit for radiance; and spirit, in turn, needs flesh for expressive delight.

I get along as well as can be expected with my Jesuit employers. I say "as well as can be expected" because there is always lurking in the celibate Roman clergy a certain begrudging suspicion of us laymen who, they suspect, have known carnal satisfaction—however transitory and however long ago. At the core of the Latin clerical identity is celibacy, a definition involving the rejection of women. Celibacy, in many cases, can be dangerous to the nervous system. Celibacy drives many of the diocesan clergy to drink. The Jesuits upgrade their compulsory celibacy through the psychological reinforcement of solemn religious vows, making something mystical of their enforced bachelorhood; yet the stress of celibacy on normal men, however well-intended, often shows through in the varieties of peevishness, distrust, and suppressed jealousy—a jealousy of *eros*—that so often characterizes the Jesuit relationship to laymen who are in any and all matters pertaining to the Church their subordinates. The Roman Catholic Church has precious few lay saints, and even fewer of these saints might be described as having enjoyed a normal sex life. That is why I shall never be canonized a saint!

Father President John F. Frieden, a scholarly Luxembourger, welcomed me back to St. Ignatius College in 1896, the first year of his presidency and the first year of my bereavement after the death of Virginia. I work smoothly for my Jesuit employers because, as I have said, I am basically in agreement with their ideals. Besides—and here is a point that David Starr Jordan, so enamored of his rural university, forgets—San Francisco, not the College, is the context of my speculative life. I am *homo urbanus*, urban man, to the ultimate degree possible. For me San Francisco itself is a vast, complex work of human speculation: a working-out of elusive myths through the long speculative process that is history. I've spent some sixty-seven years trying to make sense of San Francisco. I have thus far failed to make sense of the place, but that is not entirely my fault.

The great cities of the past all engaged in a work of speculation. They internalized, that is to say, the myths and ideals of their founding time: so much so, that the great cities of world history now seem in retrospect the fully achieved essences of certain stable, discernible civic principles. Beyond all contingency or confusion (for their struggle is over), these cities come to us in memory as metaphors and archetypes of what was in their own epoch the object of flawed but determined quest: Athens, for instance, with its love of rationality and aesthetic balance; Jerusalem, with its jealous passion for the one true God and for the Law; Rome, loving civic virtue and public order; Florence, city of painters and poets; Angkor Wat, temple city; Lhasa, monastery city given to a communal quest for spiritual perfection. There were evil cities also, in which the dominant energies urged to self-destruction. The Hebrew Scriptures are rich in such city-symbols of apocalyptic evil: Babel, city of pride, Babylon, city of arrogant secularity, Sodom and Gomorrah, cities of unholy lust. There will be other evil cities in ages to come. You can be certain of this. Perhaps one of them will be San Francisco. Cities, you see, bear witness to ideals. Their histories—how they work out their destinies—constitute, in effect, meditations upon their founding myths, calculations derived from their original formulae. Even American cities, as new as they are, show signs of this process. Boston's founding Puritanism, for example, survives in the city's passion for learning, its conviction of elitist responsibility for the ongoing work of the intellectual life and the arts.

What, I often ask myself, does San Francisco mean in this context of the city as a dialectical myth? What—if any—are San Francisco's myths and founding premises? I have discovered in more than sixty years of an on-again, off-again relationship to San Francisco that, for better or for worse, San

596

Francisco poses—or imposes—few abstract definitions. It is a city of scattered imperatives and elusive identity. Its founding time was no long meditation upon civic purposes—but a headlong, heedless gold rush, devoid, nearly, of speculative energies. No one elite dominated its early years, grafting its ideals and aspirations onto the taproots of the early city; rather, the pattern of settlement and dominance was cosmopolitan and eclectic, the people of the four corners of the globe and the seven seas coming here and maintaining their ethnic coherence. So many who came to San Francisco had no intention of staying. They made their money (or made and lost their money!) in gold, silver, railroads; then they returned to the East. All of this made San Francisco unstable as to any civic purposes beyond the immediate struggle for cash.

One legacy of this early frontier heedlessness is the virtual absence of philanthropy in nineteenth-century San Francisco. My mentor William Chapman Ralston dreamed great dreams, but he died. With the exception of James Lick's gifts to the Mechanics' Library and the California Academy of Sciences, San Francisco is devoid of significant nineteenth-century endowments. To put it bluntly: the pioneers were tight-fisted. During those years of the 1880s and nineties when in the East great fortunes were founding great institutions—the Metropolitan Museum, the New York Public Library, among others—nothing comparable was occurring in San Francisco, and this despite the fact that the 1890–1906 period, in terms of artistic accomplishment, will, I am certain, turn out to be the highwater mark in our history as a civic culture—and despite the fact that there were fortunes aplenty around town that might have provided endowments.

Had Ralston lived, it might have been different. Ralston planned to do for San Francisco what Senator Leland Stanford did for the university he founded in Palo Alto in honor of his dead son: endow it lavishly, lay the foundations of an assured national future for a local institution. Had Ralston not lost everything and died, I might have avoided finding myself the recipient of David Starr Jordan's pitying patronage and instead

597

found myself, like him, at the helm of a great institution. As it is, I keep school in a small Catholic college housed in a former shirt factory. But such is life.

The very scarcity of high institutions in San Francisco, its thinness of cultural context, makes me cling ever so much more closely to those fragments and suggestions of civilization that we do possess. That, perhaps, is why I am such an ardent Bohemian, cherishing my membership in this organization ostensibly devoted to the arts—in reality devoted to the arts, I should say, although the Club must constantly be put on guard against the encroachments of Philistia, now that it is dominated, not by the bohemian journalists of the 1870s who founded it, but by the Bohemian *grands seigneurs* of the 1910s: the affluent businessmen whose interest and patronage, it must be admitted, keep the Club going. George Sterling, for instance, lives at the Club, his expenses paid for by Barbour Lathrop, a wealthy businessman. Phelan has said to me in so many words that I might move to the Club myself as his permanent guest, if and when Marina marries and moves away. Perhaps I shall spend my declining years there, when the expense and effort of maintaining a household proves too great. In *Blix*, a charming novel of San Francisco in the nineties, Frank Norris has described the dangers of the Bohemian Club for artists most accurately: how the Club, in providing an ambience of the arts, might tempt to the pscyhological substitution of ambience for achievement.

"The Club," Frank once said, "is like San Francisco itself. It can be dangerous to creative effort. The aesthetic glow comes too easily. You think you're living the life of an artist when you're only enjoying a bottle of wine and some chit-chat about writing and painting. The city is filled with old young men who once had promise but whose energy dissipated itself in the course of too many winey lunches."

Frank did his best writing, incidentally, at Harvard and New York, although he wrote most powerfully when he wrote of California and San Francisco. Ironically—for one who so loved the Bohemian Club but was also very suspicious of it—Norris first told me of his *Epic of the Wheat* trilogy in the fall of 1900 one day before lunch when we bumped into each other at the Club library.

"Do as well as you did with *McTeague*," I remember saying, "and you'll be a legend before you are forty."

Frank was all of thirty at the time. The first volume of the trilogy, *The Octopus*, was indeed as good as *McTeague*, but then Frank died on the operating table, in the course of a simple appendicitis operation: dead at thirty-two, the finest young writer this city has ever produced—because you cannot consider Jack London a true San Franciscan. Jack was born in San Francisco but raised in Oakland. He has never truly felt much affection for the city—this city or any city for that matter.

I take San Francisco as I find it, and I try to make it better in my peripheral way. We never got the Burnham Plan, but we do have a City Hall as grand as Burnham envisioned, and we shall soon have a Public Library as grand as our City Hall—in both cases, baroque buildings for a baroque city, a city reaching after grandeur, not quite attaining it, but feeling a quickening of the pulse in the process of overreaching. I am gratified to have served as an architectural advisor on all three projects. In terms of my leaving a permanent legacy to the city, it halfway justifies all the money Ralston spent on me.

"It is superb," said Royce as, driving past Masonic Street, we began our ascent up the Fulton Street hill towards St. Ignatius Church. "It is superb—even for a church."

"It is the largest church west of the Mississippi," said Phelan, a little perplexed by Royce's semi-hostile humor. "It will seat two thousand and it is built on solid rock."

"*Tu es petrus,*" I added, "*et super hanc petram aedificabo ecclesiam meam*: Thou art Peter, the rock; and upon this rock I shall build My church."

"Now stay together," Marina said when we dismounted from the Croxton-Keeton touring car at the corner of Parker and Fulton. "I have our tickets. You need a ticket to get in, even famous gentlemen such as yourselves."

Phelan pulled out his pocket watch. "It is now nine-fifteen," He said. "Mass begins at ten. May I suggest that we walk around the church and see what Charles Devlin and Sebastian Collins have given the good fathers in return for their money."

Three or four hundred other San Franciscans had the same idea. The entire church, so massive, yet so alone on its rocky promontory overlooking the Pacific, was surrounded by promenading crowds: vested clerics awaiting the processional into the church, lay people in their Sunday best taking the air before the hour-and-a-half ceremony, which Marina dreaded because of its length. "Why can't they just bless the place and get it over with?" she asked at one point during the long ceremony. "It's enough to make one an infidel."

"It's like a carnival," Marina observed as we strolled around the church, enjoying the holiday atmosphere created by such a large crowd in such obvious good spirits. "A Renaissance carnival—with jugglers."

"And perhaps an *auto-da-fé*," said Royce, "with a heretic or two burned at the stake."

"For philosophical error," I said dryly. Royce, as I have pointed out, is such a Protestant. Carnivals, especially religious carnivals surrounding the dedication of a church, are not his cup of tea.

"It's an assertion of Rome," said United States Senator-elect Phelan as we paused under the soaring campanile: "an assertion of Mediterranean Rome at the gateway to the Far East."

The bell in the campanile tolled solemnly, announcing the dedicatory mass. Priests in snowy white surplices and violet-colored stoles drifted over to the base of the campanile where the procession escorting Archbishop Riordan into the sacristy was forming. As the bell tolled, a flock of pigeons whirred upward from the plaza adjacent to the church, flecking the skyblue with beating wings of gray-speckled whiteness. The Madeira-warm August sun bathed us in benediction.

"It reminds me of St. Mark's in Venice," said Marina, "although I have never been to Venice. It resembles what I think Venice will look like when I get there."

600

"It's only San Francisco," said Royce.

"That's her point," said Phelan. "It's San Francisco—and Venice and Rome as well."

My friend Charles Devlin, the architect responsible for St. Ignatius Church, has most gloriously given the Jesuit fathers what they wanted: the finest church in the baroque style in North America. Devlin is a scholarly man, knowledgeable in the field of baroque architecture. All that I had to do—at the request of the fathers—was to serve as a sounding board for his ideas.

"Do you think that four stories of colonnades on the façade is too extravagant, Sebastian?" he asked one morning as we pored over sketches in his Sutter Street office. His white eyebrows flared up like doves' wings.

"No. The pediment backs the third and fourth colonnades quite nicely—as in the Gesù at Rome."

Another consultation: Devlin's eyebrows are positively whirring with excitement. "Sebastian, we're running over our costs. We've already spent the allotted three hundred thousand dollars."

"Leave the interior painting undone, Charlie, but don't stint on the dome. Keep the scale of the dome heroic. You must counterpoint the assertion of the towers with a truly grand dome."

"Even if it is a fake dome?" Charlie asked.

"Even if it's a fake dome," I said.

Less than two years ago, on 24 March 1912, Archbishop Riordan laid the cornerstone of St. Ignatius Church. My friend Monsignor Joseph Gleeson, an alumnus of the College, gave the address.

"The building of this structure," he said as the winter winds from the Pacific whipped around us, sending cassocks and surplices in every direction, "will be an aid to bring back the idea that, without faith and without belief, there can be no salvation come to men. The towers of this structure will point ever towards God."

Father Albert Trivelli, the rector and president of St. Ignatius College, then proceeded to read a telegram of

601

congratulations from Rafael Cardinal Merry del Val, the papal secretary of state. I tried to keep my mind on the ceremonies as Archbishop Riordan intoned Latin prayers over the Parker Street cornerstone; but the mention of the name Rafael Merry del Val triggered in me a number of irresistible memories.

With the death of Pope Pius X just this very week, Rafael Cardinal Merry del Val is no longer papal secretary of state, as he has been since 1903 when Giuseppe Sarto, the patriarch of Venice, ascended the papal throne as Pius X. Each pope appoints his own secretary of state. The appointment lapses with the appointing pope's death. Last January, however, the pope appointed Rafael Cardinal Merry del Val to the additional position of Archpriest of St. Peter's Basilica, a post which the Cardinal retains and a post that suits the pious, indeed mystical side of my confessor's nature. After more than a decade of onerous work as the foreign secretary and chief executive officer of the Church, Merry del Val will now have a more priestly, almost monkishly liturgical role to play. The Archpriest of St. Peter's chants the Divine Office daily in choir with the canons of St. Peter's Basilica. The archpriest also heads the chapter of resident canons as their abbot or prior. The archpriest supervises the ceremonies of Catholicism's central place of worship, participating in most of the liturgies. Rafael Merry del Val, then, is now the keeper of the Church's most holy shrine: he is the archdruid in the most sacred grove of sacred oaks, the Levite priest standing guard in the antechamber of the Holy of Holies. The Cardinal's most recent letter to me, in fact, was datelined not from the Borgia Apartments in the Vatican where he lived and worked as secretary of state, but from the archpriest's suite in the rear of St. Peter's where he will now live, ensconced in the very symbolic center of Roman Catholicism itself.

I can see him now in the high choir stall of the canons' chapel, chanting the Divine Office: his dark hair, his beetle brows, his handsome English-Spanish face, the red of his cardinal's cassock. Merry del Val is about fifty now, which is young for a man to put aside worldly power; yet he never lusted after power for its own sake. Power sought him. Merry del Val always wanted to do something more like what he will do now as Archpriest of St. Peter's, something more pointedly otherworldly and priestly.

I call him my confessor, which is rather pretentious on my part: claiming Rafael Cardinal Merry del Val, the Vatican's secretary of state (until two days ago), the current Archpriest of St. Peter's, the sometime papal nuncio to Austria, England, Canada, and Japan as my confessor. I went to confession to him once, in Paris at the Church of St.-Sulpice in late 1892; yet in his typically generous way the Cardinal has kept in touch with me by letter some ten or so times in the intervening twenty-five years. We did see each other once again—indeed, twice more: once in Burlingame and once in San Francisco—in May of 1899, when Merry del Val passed through San Francisco *en route* to Japan.

To begin at the beginning: I spent the years 1889, 1890, and 1891 in a state of collapse. Despair might be a better way of saying it—or drunkenness or debauchery or suicidal dissipation. Whatever it was, it came to an abrupt end one Sunday morning in late 1892 in Paris when, horribly hungover, I tumbled into the Church of St.-Sulpice to hear the music. I was walking by St.-Sulpice on the way to a cafe for a late morning cup of coffee to steady my nerves and ease the pain in my head. I had been awakening this way, headachish and uncertain, for more than three years, ever since Sybil Sanderson laughed at my proposal of marriage. I had been in the habit of wakening with hangovers in Munich, Berlin, Prague, Dresden, back once again in Munich, and finally in Paris for the years prior to my unexpected saunter into St.-Sulpice. The phrase "hangover" is from Marina's set, like "fun" and "cocktail." I rather like this description, finding it perfectly evocative of how one feels the morning after the night before. For some three years I had an intimate, exact knowledge of hangovers. I had awakened alone, a taste of rust in my mouth; or I had awakened with a female companion,

603

with the taste of rust in my mouth laced with the aftersensations of strange kisses, some of them delightful, mind you, but a number of them, the kisses, the aftertaste of kisses, slightly sour—as from cheap brandy, bad teeth, halitosis, or the more subtly acrid aftertaste that comes when we insincerely use another's flesh; when we kiss and copulate greedily, despairingly, like minks intended for the furrier. I awoke alone that Sunday morning, my companion of the evening having arisen from our coarse-sheeted bower of ape-and-angel love to return to her work as tavern mistress downstairs.

"You're a demanding one, *chérie*," I remember Mrs. Santone saying when I insisted that she take off all her clothes. "That could cost you extra." It did cost me extra—and so did my rather fastidious request of preliminaries, which made my partner in lust think of me as romantic as well as lavish. After some tuning of my instrument, I entered her *à derrière* in the manner of the lower mammals. Her position on the bed, mounted on her knees and elbow, her breasts dependent from her body in wanton sway, allowed her, as I could see from the reflection of her face in a cracked mirror across from the bed, to watch with perhaps some degree of droll amusement the stranger heaving away at her buttocks: a wheezing, grunting stranger who had insisted upon an overture of kisses. She had returned my kisses, in fact, and in the returning of them I sensed a generosity that gave me surprise. I felt a quickening of response in her that exceeded the necessities of our contract. Her mouth tasted of wine and cigarettes. We turned to the mirror, I behind her, feeling the excitement of her soft *derrière* against my renascent manhood. She reached both of her arms back behind my neck as I smoothed my hand over her stomach. I sought with my finger the pleasure-point of her downy delta.

"I appreciate the trouble you are taking," she said, as I gently massaged her there. "Men are rarely that patient—or that kind."

As we copulated I could see myself in the mirror across the room: a fumbling satyr, age forty-four, thrusting away at the

604

buttocks of a perfect stranger in search of ecstasy. At the appropriate moment, I bellowed forth like a sea captain on the foredeck of a clipper ship rounding Cape Horn in a storm. She, in turn, signaled her gratification, which I found rather flattering, not doubting for a moment that her moans were sincere. She had carrot-colored hair gathered into a topknot and at the time of our coupling she was wearing naught save black stockings. One of the stockings, the left one, had a hole in its heel. The total effect of the black stockings against her strawberry flesh proved rather encouraging to my middle-aged appetite. After three years of such casual encounters (my erotic pilgrimage was culminated in a three-day marathon at Gustave Klimt's house in Vienna), I was finding myself rather sated, like a horse kept too long with his mouth in an oatbag.

We lay side by side on the bed for a while, resting; then she began to raise and lower her black-stockinged legs into the air slowly, one by one, as if she were embarked upon a course of therapeutic exercise. The dark of her stockings played off against her rosy flesh and the contrasting darkness of her mystic bush. Mrs. Santone was yet young, somewhere in her thirties, I would say, and full of figure. Her large breasts did not lose their shape despite the fact that she was lying on her back; rather they merely settled into montane repose, like snowy Himalayan peaks tipped with rosy sunshine. She did her exercises and sang a lively song about an amorous *curé* and his housekeeper. I pastured for a while upon her Himalayan peaks, the satisfactions of that pleasant occupation rendering me once again *en garde*.

"You marvelous American," she said, noticing the obvious sign of my renewed interest. "This time is free."

She straddled me like a lush sea nymph riding a dolphin in a Bernini fountain, or like Juno mounting Jove in the painting by Annibale Carracci. Reaching above me, I held her breasts in my hands as she made of our already rickety bed a storm-tossed sea. When it was over, I offered to express my gratitude in financial terms for this second most generous encounter, but she insisted upon keeping to the original terms of our

605

agreement, which had been priced at one session. After a third and most extraordinary session, I fell asleep.

When I awoke, she had left. I wore, however, a mark of her regard—a bit of frayed blue ribbon tied around my shrunken manhood. I felt at peace and very grateful to her and glad that she had accepted my offer of an evening's diversion. I also missed her company. The ribbon, I say, was extraordinarily gratifying: not so much as a tribute to my prowess (she had done more than her share of the labor), but because it raised our exchange above the level of sordid commercial encounter. She was so ripe, so rosy, so full of good humor.

I read William Dean Howells's latest novel for a while, then made the mistake of leaving my rooms for a glass of wine at a corner bistro. I fell in with some American art students, including a wild-eyed, utterly charming Mexican lad from San Francisco with a thick black head of Aztec hair that made him look like a walking chrysanthemum, Xavier Martinez by name, in Paris to study under another American, the expatriate James McNeill Whistler. As perhaps happened at the marriage feast at Cana, my one glass of wine turned into two bottles of deadly vintage and I awoke the next morning cursing the noisy bells of a Parisian Sunday.

Thus far I have not suggested a typical conversion story, and this is because I did not experience a typical conversion, or any sort of conversion for that matter. I just found myself ready for the next stage of my life; and as usual, the Church was willing to assist me on my pilgrim journey. I had little conviction of sin. I've always been a little free-thinking when it comes to the urges of flesh. I cannot believe that heaven or hell hangs upon the matter of one copulation more or less, although I do agree that a certain regulation of the sexual instinct is necessary for the sake of civilization. Despite my hangover, I found myself in a pleasantly dreamy, slightly listless mood as I strolled toward a bakery I knew on the Rue de la Joséphine, looking forward to my breakfast of croissants and coffee.

Deeply satisfying copulation such as I had experienced the night before always has a reconciling effect on me. Granted,

606

my encounter with Mrs. Santone began as a commercial transaction. For an hour or so in the early evening I had been watching her work behind the counter pouring drinks for the other customers. Once or twice I caught her looking at me speculatively, and I realized instantly that, while not a professional prostitute, Mrs. Santone was not adverse to keeping an occasional gentleman company to supplement her barmaid's income. She was a widow, she told me between encounters as she did her stockinged exercises on the bed, her husband, a railroad worker, having been killed in a steam boiler explosion. She had a daughter of ten, whom she supported and who she wanted to have a better life than the one her mother was leading. Life for a woman of Mrs. Santone's occupation and class is not easy; yet her physical condition was extraordinary. She was neither stringy nor shrouded in blubber and veins. I was flattered that she found me so amusing. Our second encounter, granted *gratis* and performed so admirably by her in her bold sea nymph manner, totally humanized our relationship. That occurred, if I remember correctly, around eight o'clock; the *fellatio* happened at nine (ah, to be in my forties again, with such remarkable powers of recovery!); so she must have left between nine and ten while I was sleeping the sleep of a depleted Hercules, beribboned by her in touching tribute. I reveled imprudently with the American art students until three or so.

I was, therefore, somewhat shaky and in need of coffee that sunny Sunday midmorning in the autumn of 1892 as I walked past the Church of St.-Sulpice and heard the choir and orchestra performing the "Gloria" from Gounod's *Mass for the Feast of St. Cecilia*. A mild hangover always leaves me in a state of sexual arousal, incidentally, and I was slightly that way, on the edges of tumescence, as I walked to breakfast because I was thinking of the night before.

When Mrs. Santone blew in my ear and suggested that I embark upon the third labor of Hercules, I had protested my exhaustion. Nonsense, she replied, I was an American, a frontier savage, an inexhaustible satisfier of sybaritic squaws.

She wetted the interior of my ears with the lizard-lick of her flickering tongue, then covered me with slow, moist kisses from my neck to my reticent self. Holding my depleted manhood in her hand, she cooed over it as one would coo over a wounded dove, covering it with quick licks and darting kisses until, like a revived bird, it began to flutter. At the first signs of its flight, she received me into the wine and honey warmth of her resuscitating mouth. My wan dove rose on triumphant wings, a veritable eagle, a paraclete of flight and fire. Lord, I said in the words of St. Peter, it is good for me to be here. Her topknot had come disheveled in our previous set-to, when she rode my shaft like a frenzied Valkyrie, so this third time her carrot-red hair spread across my stomach like a field of California poppies. She moved her moist mouth up and down my now-marble shaft in cadenced attention. I stood up and she shifted her position without breaking the fragile bond that joined us. Standing before her as she sat on the edge of the bed, I held her red hair in my hands as, Magdalene-like, she anointed my body with the secret juices of her mouth. She seemed a figure from a Gustave Klimt painting, a creature created solely for moments like these. Bending over, I reached to her private self, which I stroked as deftly as I could, overwhelmed by gratitude, hoping that in the course of this third lovemaking, I could afford her half the pleasure she was affording me. We coupled, her black silk legs draped over my supporting arms. She reached satisfaction before I did, crying out something in a *patois* I could not understand. When my moans began, she deftly pulled away, took me in her mouth, and coaxed from me a third and final surrender of seed, which she swallowed slowly and reverently as if it were a form of eucharist.

Hearing the music from within St.-Sulpice that morning, I walked in. A Solemn High Mass was in progress, with three vested priests at the altar. A choir of surpliced seminarians was singing to the accompaniment of a small chamber orchestra, resonantly backed up by St.-Sulpice's eloquent organ. There are no verbal equivalents for musical statement. Music, after

608

all, is music, possessed of its own irreducible syntax and symbol. Suffice it to say that Gounod's music, splendidly performed, together with the stately rituals of a changed Latin Mass, lulled me into a reverie that very soon became a meditation, then became a moment of renewal and choice.

I am now able to see in retrospect that a woman, Mrs. Santone, my barmaid friend of the night before, through her erotic generosity, had initiated in me a process of healing. Deeply hurt by Sybil's laughter, I had been sulking for three years—although I must not exaggerate my condition. I had been deeply hurt, true. My hurt had led me to drink too much and to haunt the stews, true; but I had also managed to read an enormous amount; to travel extensively (destroying my savings in the bargain); to enjoy hundreds of pictures, buildings, landscapes; and to begin the process of note-taking and cogitation that eventually resulted in the essays published as *Theological and Literary Relationships* (1905). Even when disappointed in love, one must somehow pass the time. You can rise late in the morning and begin your evening's revels at sundown; yet there still remain five or six hours to be occupied with something or other.

I must admit, however, that during those years I, on the whole, led a rather disreputable, bohemian life without discipline or fixed purpose. Later that Sunday afternoon in question, I left my young confessor, Monsignor Rafael Merry del Val, resolved to put my life and my soul into some sort of order. Sybil had laughed at me, true; but a stranger with red hair—a buxom widow, a generous mother—had showered me with unexpected affection. Gustave Klimt, my late Vienna friend, would immediately recognize what I am talking about; for Klimt painted many such moments of healing *eros*. I had put religion aside for a number of years, but it now came flooding back into me—aided by my mood of erotically induced reverie; the receptive languor of a hangover; the shaft of light that poured perpendicularly across St.-Sulpice, entering through a stained-glass window depicting St. Augustine in a pear orchard (deciding upon chastity) and pouring, the light, in a rainbow of sun-borne colors across the altar where priests in golden chasubles were filling the air with melodic Latin chant and intoxicating incense.

Since I am a sensuous man, religion flooded upon me in a rush of sensuous feeling. Gounod's "Credo" recalled for me the march music to which my regiment of Zouaves, the St. Patrick's Regiment, used to form its companies on line for inspection by General Kanzler or Archbishop Mérode, the Pope's minister of war: a handsome, six-foot-tall descendant of the Marquis de Lafayette who yet showed a soldier's stance as he trooped the line in review, escorted by our black-bearded regimental commander, Major Myles O'Reilly. Gounod's *St. Cecilia's Mass* is triumphant, militantly orthodox music. That morning at St.-Sulpice, the music led my thoughts in the direction of considering the prospect of doing something with my life: of marching forward, that is, with faith, instead of marking time as I had been doing the past three years. I found myself kneeling with the offertory bell and bowing my head at the consecration. The celebrant lifted the Host and the golden chalice high over his head for our adoration, and I found myself adoring. Not that I had ever ceased to adore. I had merely ceased to concentrate.

Domine, non sum dignus, ut intres sub tectum meum; sed tantum dic verbo et sanabitur anima mea: Lord, I am not worthy that Thou shouldst enter under my roof; say but the word and my soul shall be healed.

The celebrant stood before us, offering the Eucharist. Hundreds poured to the altar rail to receive. I wanted to communicate, but I held back, for I was impeded by certain technical difficulties. I needed confession. I was in a state of mortal sin. All of a sudden I wanted reconciliation with the Church of my youth, with the splendid faith I was born to. I also began to have thoughts of returning home to San Francisco.

After Mass, the Church of St.-Sulpice emptied. I sought out a confessional box in the rear past a row of side altars. One of the confessionals had a sign on it saying "French, Spanish,

610

German, English." Since I had sinned in all four languages, I slipped past the heavy purple curtain and knelt down in the stuffy darkness. A small wooden slide door was opened, and through the screen I discerned the outline of a man's head, turned to me in profile.

I knelt in silence for a moment, then said: "I am trying to find my way back."

"To God?" the priest asked.

"To Him, yes—and to everything else."

"Then turn your thoughts towards the Sacred Heart of Jesus. There is your only answer, your only way to God."

My confessor spoke perfect English: he had an upper-class English accent, in fact, crossed over with a Spanish accent, as if he were an Englishman who spoke a lot of Spanish or a Spaniard educated at an English public school.

"How long has it been since your last confession?"

I thought for a moment, trying to remember, then said: "Four years." I had last gone to confession around Easter 1887 at St. Ignatius Church on Van Ness Avenue in San Francisco.

"Then you have been away from the sacraments for a long time?"

"Yes, Father, for a very long time. I've been away from many things for such a very long time—my work, my home, my religion."

"What has kept you from them?"

"Myself. My hurt and confusion. My laziness. My piggish sensuality."

"These are common faults. They should not keep you from Christ. He forgives these sins. He heals the sinner."

"I want His healing, Father."

"It seems to me that He has already begun this process."

"You also are helping me."

"God is helping you. I'm but a neophyte priest."

"How old are you?" I asked.

"Thirty."

"That is very young to be sitting in judgment of the sins of the world."

"Our Lord was thirty when He began His public ministry. Besides: I do not sit in judgment. I merely listen—and offer God's forgiveness when it is correctly asked."

"What is necessary for correctness?"

"Repentance—and a firm resolve to sin no more. Do you have sins that you wish to confess?"

"Confess, yes; but the question of repentance is difficult. I confess to fornication, for instance, but fornication has brought me here. I confess to drunkenness, but wine has helped open my imagination to the beauties of the spirit."

"Fornication and drunkenness are but secondary sins in a man of your obvious discernment. What is your real sin?"

"Sloth and despair, arising out of a disappointed love."

"You fell in love and were disappointed?"

"Yes—or at least I used that as an excuse to drift, to put aside the fatigues of pilgrimage."

"That is worse than despair. That is presumption—and the taking of God's forgiveness for granted."

"Then I truly repent of this presumption, Father, and ask Christ's forgiveness."

"What of the other sins, the drunkenness and the fornication?"

"I'll do my best to avoid them, but I can make no promises."

"You're American, aren't you? Hence, you are difficult. Americans can be very difficult. In the technical terms of canon law, I could withhold absolution; for the sins of the flesh are mortal sins, and you seem unclear in your mind as to your repentance of them. Do you, however, promise to return to the sacraments if absolution is granted?"

"Yes, Father. I would ask you, in fact, to communicate me after this confession."

"Then, I'll absolve you, for the sins of the flesh are in and of themselves not major sins, but they do blunt the spirit. They turn one aside from the channels of sanctifying grace. Will you try to avoid the near occasions of such sins, the persons and places that invariably led you to such transgressions?"

612

"Yes—although, as I have said, it was the goodness of a Magdalene that led me here."

"Thank God, then, for Magdalenes," I remember him saying. "Jesus Christ Himself never condemned them as harshly as he excoriated the hypocrites. I am satisfied on the technical points of your remorse. For your penance say the Five Sorrowful Mysteries of the Rosary. Now make an Act of Contrition while I pronounce the words of Christ's forgiveness."

I recited the Act of Contrition while the young priest spoke the Latin words of absolution, although I was yet uncertain just exactly what I was sorry for and to what degree. I decided to leave the question of my guilt or innocence up to God. I merely wanted my life back into some kind of order and I wanted the Church to help me get there.

"Come now," he said when we both had finished the ritual, "I shall give you Holy Communion."

I stepped out of the confessional and allowed my eyes to adjust to the light. A young priest in the black and red cassock of a monsignor stood before me. He wore a black biretta topped by a red tuft. He was dark like a Spaniard, but held himself squarely like the English-trained athlete I later found out that he was. His handsome face was aquiline and aristocratic, sensitive yet humorous also—and forthright.

I followed him to the altar. The pews were scattered with Parisians lingering in prayer. The young monsignor excused himself at the altar rail and entered the sacristy, emerging a few minutes later with a white surplice over his cassock and a red stole over his neck. He genuflected before the tabernacle, removed a golden ciborium from within, then walked down to the altar rail where I knelt.

"*Ecce Agnus Dei,*" he said three times, lifting a white wafer from the ciborium and holding it in front of me like a snowy sunrise, "*ecce qui tollis peccata mundi.*" Behold the Lamb of God, behold Him Who takest away the sins of the world."

He placed the wafer on my tongue.

"*Corpus Domini nostri Jesu Christi custodiat animam tuam in vitam aeternam."* May the Body of Our Lord Jesus Christ preserve your soul for everlasting life.

I swallowed the wafer which the Church teaches is truly the Body and Blood of Christ. The young monsignor returned the ciborium to the tabernacle, then entered the sacristy to devest. I returned to my pew and bowed my head in an effort to make a proper thanksgiving after Communion. It had been more than three years since I had prayed. I became lost in my own thoughts. I thought of Sybil Sanderson and of Mrs. Santone, my friend of last evening: the one bestowing on me what the other lavished on Jules Massenet. I then thought of Gudrun in Heidelberg, who was quick and appreciative like Mrs. Santone—only that was twenty years earlier (forty years earlier from the time I write!) and I hadn't then the capacity for gratitude to Gudrun that I had for Mrs. Santone, being then much younger and hence unaware of just how little satisfaction the flesh affords us in comparison to what we continue to hope from it, and hence how grateful we must be when someone out of generosity, good spirits and frank appetite brings us to a moment of splendor.

But since I was in St.-Sulpice and had just made a general confession and received Holy Communion, I also tried to think of religion as well as sex. As a true devotee of the baroque I am constantly conjoining the two, *eros* and *agape*, sacred and profane love. I thought of Jesus Christ, whom I had just received into my heart; then my thoughts wandered back to San Francisco. I should be getting home soon, I thought, and working for the betterment of my native city. I would find something to do there: not as grand, perhaps, as the Atheneum envisioned by Ralston, but something worthwhile, even if it just meant my teaching at St. Ignatius College (provided that the Jesuits took me back), and writing my essays and books, and some sort of public service connected with the many plans then underway under the guidance of my friend and former pupil James Duval Phelan.

A tap on my shoulder broke my reverie. It was the young monsignor.

614

"You've prayed enough. Don't overtax yourself on your first day back in the fold. Join me for coffee and a light breakfast."

"I'd love to. I'm starved."

"You don't look starved."

I followed him to the rectory adjacent to St.-Sulpice. We sat at a long polished refectory table, eating buttered bread and drinking the strong coffee that an elderly housekeeper poured for us.

"Where are you from?"

"San Francisco."

"I have never been to San Francisco, but I shall visit there one day. I have made myself that promise."

"Are you English, Monsignor?"

"By culture, yes. I was born and raised in England, but I am a Spaniard by nationality. My name is Rafael Merry del Val."

"And I am Sebastian Collins. What brings you to Paris, Monsignor Merry del Val?"

"I am assigned to the Vatican Secretariat of State. I am here temporarily on Vatican business, but let's not talk of me. I wish to talk to you outside the formal constraints of the confessional. I sense that you are a seeker of God as well as a devotee of wine, women, and song. Tell me about yourself."

It took me three cups of coffee and two small loaves of buttered bread to tell my story. Merry del Val listened intently, sipping one cup of black coffee.

"Then we both have experience of Vatican service," he laughed when I finished. "You with the Zouaves and I in the more peaceable role of a diplomat. What will you do next, return to San Francisco?"

"Yes, eventually."

"I would like you to make a retreat first."

"Where?"

"At the Grand Chartreuse. I shall write for you. The Abbot is a classmate of mine from the Ushaw College in England."

"What shall I do on this retreat?"

"Work with the monks. Pray. Meditate on Jesus Christ and what His will for you might be."

615

"You talk as if you were my spiritual director."

"Consider that a fact, Sebastian Collins, until we get you safely back to San Francisco. Remember now: stay away from Magdalenes and too much wine, and make your retreat at the Grand Chartreuse."

It was not until my return to San Francisco, after a six months sojourn at the Grand Chartreuse and after my final attendance upon Sybil Sanderson at the premiere of *Thaïs*, that I filled out the story of Monsignor Rafael Merry del Val.

"He's Spanish nobility, a favorite of the Holy Father's," my friend Father (later Monsignor) John Gleeson told me when I related the story of my "conversion" at St.-Sulpice, omitting, obviously, the story of Mrs. Santone's preconversion ministrations; for John Gleeson, like most of the clergy, does not welcome references to this kind of behavior. It touches upon a sore point, their foregoing of such pleasures. "Leo XIII made him a papal chamberlain with the title Monsignor when he was still a seminarian at the Academy for Ecclesiastical Nobles."

Since my return from Europe I have followed Merry del Val's career with interest and have had the pleasure of a leisurely, intermittent exchange of letters—some ten letters in all from his hand, which Marina has not filed away in a carton but keeps in an open file, for I hope that my most recent letter, dated January of last year, is not my last.

Perhaps I should evoke Merry del Val's career in conjunction with that of the Tobin family; for the only time after my confession in St.-Sulpice that I laid eyes upon the Cardinal ever again (Pius X raised him to the cardinalate in 1903) was at two gatherings in the spring of 1899 hosted by the Tobins for Monsignor del Val when he passed through San Francisco in the course of a diplomatic mission to the Far East.

"I'll be arriving sometime in the last week of May," Merry del Val wrote to me in early May, 1899. "Archbishop Riordan will be my host in San Francisco. My steamer leaves for Yokohama on June first; so there will be time for us to visit and for me to see at last the California you boast so much of."

616

At the time of his visit in May of 1899, Merry del Val had just been named president of the Academy of Ecclesiastical Nobles in Rome and designated for consecration as titular Archbishop of Nicaea, an honor conferred upon him in early 1900 at the Spanish national church in Rome, Our Lady of Montserrat, when he returned from his successful mission to Japan. Pope Leo XIII sent Merry del Val to Japan to negotiate the right of the Church, specifically Jesuit missionaries, to own and operate secondary schools there, something which the conservative faction among the Nipponese emperor's advisors were dead set against. As usual, Merry del Val carried off his diplomatic assignment with great success.

He could, you see, deal with the imperial officials as a social equal. Social class, I have always believed, is the hidden fact of history. The German Karl Marx was absolutely correct about this, although he naively weights the balance in favor of the working class. The Roman Catholic Church—through the nineteenth century at least—has been governed by aristocrats. The late Pius X, Giuseppe Sarto, dead now just two days, was a peasant by birth and hence is an exception to my rule; yet Pius X did have the sense upon his election in 1903 immediately to designate the nobleman Archbishop Rafael Merry del Val as his secretary of state and to run the Church through him.

I have followed the career of my onetime confessor through clippings from the London *Tablet* (I have this superb Catholic review sent to me in San Francisco), through our local Catholic newspaper *The Monitor*, and occasionally, when ecclesiastical events are covered, from stories in the secular press. When Merry del Val was named cardinal secretary of state in 1903, the *Tablet* ran an extensive biography of him, with much emphasis upon the young Cardinal's partially English ancestry and education.

Allow me to repeat myself: ancestry and social class always prevail, especially in European circles, most especially at the Vatican. The popes of the nineteenth century were from the minor nobility. Leo XIII, who promoted Merry del Val to Monsignor when the young seminarian was barely twenty-two

617

and not yet even a priest, had himself experienced trouble authenticating the nobility of the Pecci family when he applied as a young man to the *Accademia dei Nobili*, the pontifical Academy for Ecclesiastical Nobles. Pecci was forced to draw up a genealogy proving his nobility. He never forgot the humiliation. No wonder then, that as Pope Leo XIII, Pecci seized upon Merry del Val as the great diplomatic hope of the Church, placing him instantly in the *Accademia dei Nobili*, where the Church's future archbishops and cardinals of noble blood are trained for the diplomatic service. Merry del Val's lineage was impeccable. (Merry del Val's father, incidentally, the Marquis Rafael del Merry del Val, served at various times as Spanish ambassador to England, Austria-Hungary, and the Holy See.) Immediately upon his ordination in 1888 to the priesthood by Cardinal Parocchi, the Vicar of Rome, Merry del Val was named *Cameriere Segreto Partecipante*, one of the four private chamberlains in attendance to Leo XIII, a post he held while completing his doctorate in theology and canon law at the Gregorian University and taking his diploma in diplomatic studies at the Academy of Ecclesiastical Nobles.

"My duties as a papal chamberlain were uncomplicated but constant," Merry del Val remarked to me of his life as a member of Pope Leo XIII's private suite. It was during his brief visit. The two of us were walking around the grounds of the Richard Tobin estate in Burlingame. Monsignor Merry del Val had just confessed himself charmed by the shingle version of a Norman chateau that Richard Tobin had built for himself. "I merely stood outside the Holy Father's private audience chamber from nine to noon every morning and chatted with those scheduled for an audience. In the afternoon, after His Holiness' siesta, I would join him for a stroll just as we are now enjoying. His Holiness used to love to pay a visit to two enormous lions sent to him by the King of Ethiopia in honor of his name, *Leo*, the lion. They were kept in a cage in the Vatican gardens. The Pope enjoyed watching the lions busy about their luncheon."

"There are no caged lions here in Burlingame," I said,

"although we do have a breed of mountain lion living in our Coastal Range."

"Perhaps I shall encounter some on my ramble through the Coast Range tomorrow with the Tobin brothers and Miss Tobin."

Merry del Val, incidentally, is an accomplished athlete. He plays superb tennis, rides well, loves swimming and mountaineering. No wonder the aged pontiff Leo XIII, then in his seventies, wished to have this handsome, accomplished young clerical aristocrat around him. Leo's predecessor Pius IX, my onetime commander-in-chief, insisted that his immediate staff be recruited exclusively from the ranks of noble clerics—and handsome ones for that matter, but more of this at another time.

We spent the morning in question at the Burlingame Country Club watching Richard Montgomery Tobin and his nephews, Cyril and Joseph, lead the Club's polo team to a near victory over the officers' team from the San Francisco Presidio. The Tobin men have done much to introduce polo to the Bay Area. Now a well-established pastime among the Peninsula set, polo was yet something of a novelty in 1899. Dressed in a Roman collar and a white suit of English cut, Merry del Val moved eagerly among the horses before the polo match. He stroked necks, patted rumps, examined withers and hooves with the eye of an expert in horseflesh, which he was. His English suit and clerical collar, together with his British accent, made him resemble an Anglican country parson out for a shire fair.

"These are excellent horses, Sebastian," he laughed as he joined us under a half-tent from which we were to watch the game. "I would love to play, but think of the scandal it would cause."

"How so, Monsignor?"

"Canon law: Clerics are forbidden to indulge in horse sports. They are considered out of character."

We sat under a great canvas awning and watched the Army successfully fight for its honor against our local civilians.

Colonel John Pershing's men prevailed—the Presidio commandant himself played brilliantly—but not before Richard Montgomery, Cyril, Joseph, Templeton Crocker, and the others gave the officers under Colonel Pershing's command a run for their money. Monsignor Merry del Val watched the maneuvering of the horseflesh, the sweep of mallets, the zigzag darting of the ball with keen interest. Sport brought out the Britisher in him, just as religion brought out his Spanish side. As I watched Merry del Val cheering a particularly brilliant maneuver by Richard Tobin, I had the insight that despite the honors heaped upon him from the time of his entrance into the Church, this attractive young man had made his share of sacrifices when he chose the priesthood. Merry del Val's first boyhood intention had been to seek a commission in either the English or the Spanish army. Having dual citizenship, he was eligible for either service. Like Archbishop Mérode, under whom I served in the Zouaves, Rafael Cardinal Merry del Val would have made a superb soldier.

"A beautiful day, Monsignor," said Agnes Tobin during a lull in the game.

"A charming day, Miss Tobin, in a lovely part of the world. I'm sorry that my visit must be so brief."

Unlike much of the Roman clergy, Merry del Val seemed at ease with women—even hauntingly beautiful pre-Raphaelite women like Agnes Tobin, then in her thirties, with hair like cornsilk and a neck so long and delicate that her friend Alice Meynell nicknamed her Lily, for her face seemed to arch out from her neck like a lily on its stalk. More than merely be at ease with women, Rafael Merry del Val actually seemed to enjoy their company, which is even more unusual in the celibate Catholic clergy. I later learned of his close relationship to his beautiful first cousin, Maria Laura de Zulueta ("Babs"), with whom he was raised in London when his father was the Spanish Ambassador to the Court of St. James's. Babs described the closeness between her cousin and herself in the course of a dinner party at Phelan's city house in late 1910

620

when Mlle. de Zulueta was passing through San Francisco, hence going through the usual round of dinner parties.

"Rafael and I were raised as brother and sister," she said of the Cardinal.

I suppose that I won Babs's confidence when I told her that the Cardinal was once my confessor. Incidentally, it was Maria Laura de Zulueta herself who invited me to call her Babs. I would not have had the courage to have done so on my own.

"I used to be so jealous of him when he received permission to tramp through the Lake Country during school vacations. I wanted to join him and his friends from Ushaw, but I couldn't because I was a girl."

"Your presence might have persuaded some of the Ushaw lads not to continue their studies for the Church," I laughed.

"I suppose so," she sighed. "So many of Rafael's seminarian friends were awkward around me, as if I wanted to bite their heads off; but Rafael was always so sweet with me and with my girl friends, without even once leaving any doubt with us as to his intended ecclesiastical character. Quite simply, he is a delight to be around—cardinal or not."

Merry del Val was thirty-seven at the time of his visit to California, and Agnes Tobin around the same age, give or take a year. Had del Val not been a priest, they might have made a perfect match; the tall, darkly handsome Spanish-English aristocrat and the literary daughter of the first Catholic family of San Francisco. Lord knows that local families with less money and less breeding that the Tobins have made equally distinguished matches with European nobility. Take the Floods, for instance: they began life as semiliterate peasants, and are now connected to some of the best names in Europe.

The Merry del Val family traces its ancestry back to thirteenth-century Spain. The Tobins go back to 1847 when Richard Tobin arrived here from Ireland via Chile and the Sandwich Islands. If we Catholics of San Francisco have produced one distinguished dynasty, it is the Tobins, for James Duval Phelan seems confirmed in his bachelorhood—not in celibacy, mind you, but bachelorhood. Jimmy's love life has always bloomed exotically like a hidden hothouse orchid—but no matter: that is none of my business. Jimmy has by now reached middle age without carrying on the Phelan family name, whereas the Tobins have been prolific.

In 1860 Richard Tobin married Santiago-born Mary Regan, a Chilean of Irish ancestry, in a ceremony at St. Francis Church in the North Beach district of the city presided over by Archbishop Alemany, who also married Phelan's parents that same year. The Tobins had twelve children: nine sons, including Richard Montgomery, and three daughters, including Alice. When Richard Tobin first arrived in California, he found employment as the secretary to Joseph Sadoc Alemany, the Dominican Archbishop of San Francisco. My mentor Ralston's career in banking was meteoric: an Icarian ascent and a plummeting decline. Richard Tobin, by contrast, toiled away for three decades at the Hibernia Savings and Loan Society, patiently building up a solid bank with a solid Irish Catholic clientele, and eventually rising to the presidency of the institution. The Hibernia Bank's main office at Jones and McAllister Streets, designed by Albert Pissis and completed in 1892, survived the Earthquake and Fire of 1906. I never go by its grand Corinthian-columned entrance, or stand under the lovely stained-glass dome arching over its main counting room that I do not think just how long and how hard Richard Tobin labored to build up the Hibernia Bank.

The Tobin story is a common San Francisco story of that time: from Irish peasant to Irish aristocrat in one generation. Richard and Mary Tobin raised two families, for both their oldest son Robert and his wife died early in life, leaving the grandparents to raise the orphaned sons Cyril, Joseph, and Oliver. Richard Montgomery Tobin (who speaks, by the way, of enlisting in the French Army, now that war has broken out in Europe) took over the bank from his father, just as Jimmy Phelan inherited his father's interests. Robert and his nephews Cyril, Joseph, Oliver (they are more like brothers together, than uncle and nephews) were raised as gentry—horsey, headstrong, more than a little spoiled; for the Irish, or at least

622

a certain sort of aspiring Irish, waste no time in assuming the manners and mores of the long remembered Anglo-Irish gentry. The Tobin boys went to Georgetown University in Washington, D.C., then were sent on a tutored grand tour of Europe, much like Jimmy Phelan's. All the Tobin men are, incidentally, mad for polo. They play polo every chance they get. They talk about polo constantly.

It was Richard Montgomery Tobin who gave the lunch for Monsignor Merry del Val in May of 1899. As I have already suggested, the Monsignor and I enjoyed a leisurely walk about the oak and eucalyptus-shaded gardens before luncheon while the boys were showering up from the polo match. I had a strong suspicion that my energetic, sports-loving friend would rather have been back at the Country Club talking over the game than walking in the garden with me. Just before noon Richard Montgomery Tobin joined us. He had played some superb polo in the morning and he now had that exultant, radiant look of a freshly showered athlete who has done well by himself and his mates. Richard and Monsignor Merry del Val were then each about thirty-four: my age in 1882, the age my daughter Marina will be in 1929. How remote, how impossible in futurity, the year 1929 seems: a date I shall live to see only should I live to the age of eighty-one, which is not impossible—not probable perhaps, but not impossible either.

"Monsignor, tomorrow, your schedule permitting, we shall ramble in the hills."

"My schedule permits, Mr. Tobin."

"Call me Richard."

"Very well, provided you call me Rafael. My schedule certainly permits a ramble in the California hills. I have looked forward for a number of years to such a walk."

Like Rafael Merry del Val, Richard Montgomery is tall and handsome. Since that day in May of 1899, R.M., as he is widely known, has developed into a substantial fellow of fifty, an organizer of our nascent opera and symphony, a leading citizen in every respect. Perhaps what I sensed as Raphael Merry del Val, R.M., and I stood at the edge of the lily pad in front of the recreated Norman chateau in Burlingame, California, in the month of May in the year of Our Lord 1899, was that here were two vigorous young men in the first stages of brilliant careers, one in banking, the other in the Church, who sensed a kindred spirit in each other that subtly excluded me. I was fifty-one at the time and already set on the inevitable course of my life. Like a character in a Henry James novel, I could—I can—appreciate life, sense out its subtleties and fragrances, even celebrate them, but rarely do I seem to act. Save for my service in the Zouaves and my year with Virginia managing the Avila Vineyards in Napa, I have not been a very active protagonist in the drama of existence. R.M., by contrast, and this brilliant, handsome Vatican monsignor were both destined to direct events, which they have done. I am not complaining, mind you. I accept the basically vicarious nature of my character and imagination, hence of my life (for we make our own lives)—but I must frankly acknowledge it also and not try to pass myself off as an heroic protagonist, which I am not.

"We shall begin our walk at the Jesuit novitiate at Los Gatos," R.M. was saying. "We shall take an early train there. A long day's tramp through the Coast Range should take us through Saratoga, Los Altos, Woodside, Half Moon Bay. At a point along the way we can be met by our horses for the ride home to Burlingame."

"What lovely names," Merry del Val said. "I shall think I am in the Campagna."

"Parts of our coastal mountains appear that way, Monsignor," said Agnes, appearing from the house to summon us into luncheon. "The flora is similar and so is the sunlight."

My memories of the luncheon are sketchy. First of all I drank too much wine. Secondly, the chablis I drank was my own, the Avila Vineyards vintage of 1894, and so I drank the wine of memory. I do remember, however, that after luncheon R.M., Merry del Val, Cyril, and Joseph all changed into tennis whites and played a number of sets on the estate court, while I spent some time with Agnes Tobin, who was helping me look

624

after little Marina. For a while the three of us watched the tennis match. The tennis court lay adjacent to a stand of great eucalyptus trees. Rafael and Cyril teamed up against R.M. and J.O. (so is Joseph now called—J.O.). R.M. had produced white tennis clothes from the closet for the Monsignor and they seemed to fit perfectly. My daughter Marina was five at the time—a blond, chubby, curly-headed child who simply adored Agnes Tobin. Rafael and Cyril were having the best of the game at just that time that Marina began tugging at Agnes' dress.

"Let's play hide-and-seek," she implored Agnes.

"All right then. You hide in the gardens and I'll follow in five minutes, looking for you."

Marina ran off, overjoyed at the prospect of a game of hide-and-seek with Aunt Agnes.

"She needs a mother," said Agnes as Marina disappeared into a copse of hydrangea bushes, blooming in cerulean blue. You could see the great flowers shake as Marina scrambled beneath the copse, looking for a hiding place.

"She had a marvelous mother," I said, thinking of how much Virginia would have liked this day in Burlingame. Virginia Walsh, my late wife, is my link to the Tobin family, the Tobins having half-adopted Virginia in 1880 after the death of Virginia's father, a widower who served as the assistant chief cashier of the Hibernia Bank. Virginia was twenty at the time, three or four years older than Agnes, and with few prospects in the matter of supporting herself. In the feudal way of the best of the wealthy Irish, Virginia entered the Tobin family as a domestic manager with family privileges—half servant, half adopted daughter, responsible for the internal management of the household.

"Yes, Virginia was marvelous," Agnes replied after a moment's silence. "So loving, so capable. We all adored her. It's difficult to realize that she's been dead nearly five years."

There was laughter from the tennis courts.

"Bravo, Rafael!" Cyril called across the court. "I had no idea you played such good tennis in Rome."

"I learned my tennis at Ushaw. When I play tennis, I play in English. Tomorrow we shall walk in Italian. After this game, I hope to enjoy an American swim."

"You will exhaust them all, Rafael," Agnes said as she rose from her chair to go in search of Marina. Agnes wore a pale apricot-colored dress and a large straw sun-hat, encircled in a floral wreath and raked to one angle as in a Gainsborough painting. I watched her stately form recede down the garden path towards the copse of hydrangeas. I admire women who are full of figure, yet not overly heavy. Today, at nineteen, my daughter Marina enjoys a certain Junoesque presence which I encourage her to be proud of.

"Mr. Scannell must find you an armful," I ventured recently.

"Don't be vulgar, Daddy," Marina said, closing the subject.

Agnes Tobin was a beauty in the spring of 1899, that is certain—and such a bluestocking: with her thrice-weekly trips by train down to Stanford to study classical Greek, adding that intricate language to her existing repertoire of French, Spanish, Italian, and German. In retrospect, I see now that Agnes Tobin, despite the fact that she spent so much time abroad, was part of that brilliant circle of creative young men and women who graced San Francisco in the decade-and-a-half before the Fire. I must admit that linking Agnes Tobin up with the likes of Jack London takes some strength of imagination. Yet there she was: a virginal, pre-Raphaelite, intensely Catholic figure in a landscape—or should I say, a cityscape—that included an astonishing array of diverse artistic talent, much of it bohemian and disbelieving, in contrast to Agnes' almost nunlike demeanor. In *A Call for California Art* (1900) I encouraged all these young people as best I could, arranging my book as a guide to emerging local talent, with a photograph and an essay for each figure and a general introduction. John Barry, my publisher, sold nearly a thousand copies.

Fourteen years later I can turn the pages of *A Call for California Art*, as I sometimes do, and feel comfort in the validity of some of my predictions. I also experience much sadness in seeing the faces of those who betrayed their talents or whose lives ended tragically. Certainly, the architects Willis Polk and Bernard Maybeck, for both of whom I predicted great things, have fulfilled their early promise. Polk's steel and glass office building on Sutter Street is a triumph, pointing the way to the architecture of the future. Maybeck's Palace of Fine Arts, although in the ephemeral idiom of Exposition architecture, says something profound about the collective imagination of San Francisco, so time-drenched and romantically defiant of the paradoxical newness of the post-earthquake city. Maynard Dixon is busy in his Montgomery Street studio, painting scenes of the American West; and Mary Austin writes wonderfully on a hundred different subjects. Before his death less than two years after my book appeared, Frank Norris managed to write a shelfful of novels; and Jack London is well into his fortieth book—although I am worried about Jack, worried about his health since the burning down of Wolf House. Jack is drinking too much and suffering from kidney trouble. In *A Call for California Art*, I predicted that George Sterling, Nora May French, and Agnes Tobin would bring honors to the state, to San Francisco especially, in the field of poetry. Nora wrote some lovely lyrics before her suicide in 1904 on George Sterling's cabin porch in Carmel; and George himself is still with us, having just finished an ode for the opening of the Panama–Pacific International Exposition. Agnes' career, however, has waned since her break with the Meynells. I don't think that she has written a poem in more than five years.

What promise Agnes once possessed! Allow me to quote from my essay of nearly fifteen years ago, illustrated with a photograph showing Agnes one year after the visit of Merry del Val. I am not so sure, incidentally, that Agnes' Secret (I think of Agnes' Secret in capital letters) is, as some claim, that she fell in love with the inaccessible Merry del Val. Agnes was too sophisticated a Catholic to allow something as naive as that to happen. I could, however, be mistaken about this. I myself, after all, spent three years pining over my own inaccessible beloved. Only after marriage and bereavement did I realize

627

what a phantom I had pursued. Agnes' Secret has more to do with Alice Meynell than Rafael Merry del Val. Some cloud, some unnamed threat and repudiation, descended between those two, breaking off their sister-intense relationship.

"Agnes Tobin," I wrote in 1900, "divides her time between London and the place she calls 'my Franciscan city'. Schooled in Latin, Italian, French, and German by the exacting Miss Angier, Miss Tobin is in the process of adding classical Greek to her linguistic repertoire under the tutelage of Professor Foster of Stanford University. Miss Tobin confesses to a love of flowers and children. Her friends call her Lily. Miss Tobin's poetic efforts thus far have been in the area of translation."

For a number of years, Agnes pursued a distinguished career as a translator of classic texts. Her versions of Euripedes, Sophocles, and Dante are among the best translations of these authors that I have ever read. Her versions of Petrarch's sonnets and *canzoni*—published as *Love's Crucifix* (1902), *The Flying Lesson* (1905), and *On the Death of Madonna Laura* (1906)—have insured her a permanent, if minor, place in the American poetic pantheon. At the suggestion of the British actress Mrs. Patrick Campbell, Agnes translated Racine's *Phaedra* into superb Shakespearian blank verse, finishing this just before the Fire of 1906. But since then—almost nothing.

During those years, Agnes' other life was a London life. She and English essayist-poet Alice Meynell formed an extraordinarily close friendship. When Agnes was back home in San Francisco, she wrote Alice Meynell nearly every other day. In 1901 Alice Meynell left her husband in London and came to San Francisco for a year, staying at the Tobin townhouse at Taylor and California Streets. When Alice Meynell and Agnes spoke of their London circle that year (which they did frequently), it seemed to this poor provincial a veritable roll call of literary Olympians: Aubrey Beardsley and Sir Edmund Gosse, Arthur Symons, George Meredith, G. K. Chesterton. On Sunday evenings, the Meynells held dinner parties at 47 Palace Court that were the envy of literary London. I wondered then and I still wonder now (although I have suspicions) what in the world could have induced Alice Meynell to leave her husband for a year, not to mention her brilliant literary circle, and sojourn in far-off San Francisco. In any event, Mrs. Meynell seemed extraordinarily happy that year—like a bride, one might say.

Joseph Conrad, a frequenter of the Meynell circle, was, I am convinced, half in love with Agnes, whom he called Inez because she came from Spanish California. Conrad dedicated his novel *Under Western Eyes* to Agnes. She also formed a close attachment to the poet Francis Thompson, and in the course of trips to Dublin became friendly with the Abbey Theatre circle that included Lady Gregory, William Butler Yeats (who, like Conrad, wrote her long, gossipy letters), and John Millington Synge. No San Franciscan of Agnes' generation had such literary connections. Even Ambrose Bierce (now disappeared into Mexico), who boasted so much of his famous European friends, must be considered an obscure provincial in comparison to Agnes Tobin.

"It is hoped," I wrote in my *Call for California Art*, "that Agnes Tobin's *entrée* into the most distinguished literary circles of London will prove a credit to her native San Francisco, which has sent two other of its artistic daughters, Gertrude Atherton and Sybil Sanderson, to Europe before her. San Francisco looks forward to the unfolding of a career that is touched profoundly by both the mellow culture of the Old World and the young vigor of the New."

"Daddy," Marina said, tugging at my pants leg, "Agnes found me twice."

I picked Marina up and buried my face in her chubby, creased neck. I tasted her sweet perspiration on my lips. I was determined to raise this child well—this gift of God to my old age. I had dressed Marina that morning in a white pinafore, which was now dirt-stained from her crawling beneath the flower bushes. In the aftermath of her game of hide-and-seek with Agnes, Marina was ecstatically happy. We took her into the kitchen and Agnes spooned out a dish of raspberries, which Marina proceeded to drench in cream and sugar. Marina sat on a stool before a pantry work table and deliberately, spoonful by spoonful, ate the raspberries, while also managing to keep an eye on the both of us. At age fifty-one, I could almost have been the father of Agnes and the grandfather of Marina. When Marina finished her raspberries, she lifted the bowl to her face in both hands and drank what was left of the sugared cream, now lined with red streaks of raspberry juice. I watched her little Adam's apple bob gently as she swallowed.

"Do you always allow her to drink out of the bowl?" Agnes asked me.

"I allow her to do just about anything she pleases. That's how you were raised, wasn't it? And Sybil Sanderson as well."

"I want a cookie, please," Marina said.

I took an oatmeal cookie from a jar and gave it to her. She chewed away at it with an air of deliberate concentration. Marina still eats this way as an adult, taking nearly twice the normal time to finish even a routine meal.

"This is an excellent cookie," Marina said.

I felt proud of Marina's vocabulary, "excellent" being a rather ambitious word for a five-year-old.

"I am now going to take a nap," Marina announced when she had finished her oatmeal cookie.

Climbing off the stool, she walked into the dim coolness of the library and stretched herself out on a great leather sofa. Agnes went upstairs, returning with a blanket, which she spread across the already sleeping child, after removing her high-buttoned shoes and taking the great yellow bow from her hair. The bow had come half-undone beneath one or another of the hydrangea bushes. We left the library door slightly ajar, so that Marina could hear voices when she awoke and not be frightened, as children sometimes are when they wake up in a strange place. Crossing the drawing room, Agnes opened the French doors and we sat looking out over the late afternoon stillness. We could hear the laughter of men's voices from the swimming pool on the far end of the property.

"I find it very amusing," Agnes said, "that a future pope may be swimming in our plunge."

630

"Tennis whites might one day give way to the white of the papal cassock—there's a chance of it."

"Perhaps as pope he'll reactivate the Zouaves and you can re-enlist."

"I'm too old for the Zouaves. In any event, they were disbanded nearly thirty years ago. Besides: I have Marina to take care of. Cyril and Joseph can join the Zouaves. They rode superbly this morning."

"What shall I wear tomorrow?"

"Boots, if you have them."

"And a walking skirt—something with a kickpleat. And a Baden-Powell hat for the sun. I'll look wonderful, won't I? Do you think it forward of me to have asked myself along?"

"Not if you can keep up the pace. You'll notice that I didn't invite myself along."

"I mean being a woman."

"My dear, you're adequately escorted—a brother and two nephews, Tobins all. Besides, Rafael seems impervious to scandal. He's from Rome, remember, not from Maynooth. He's quite used to mixed company."

"What sort of work does he do?"

"He is basically a diplomat. The year he was ordained, 1888, Leo XIII assigned him to a papal delegation calling upon Emperor Franz Joseph of Austria-Hungary. He also represented the pope that year at the funeral of Kaiser Wilhelm I of Germany. He has given First Communion instructions to the young King of Spain. He served as the secretary of the papal commission investigating the validity of Anglican orders. He spent last year in Canada as apostolic delegate. In addition to his diplomatic duties, he also serves as president of the diplomatic academy of the Vatican, a post that carries with it the rank of archbishop."

"Why isn't he a snob?"

"Ask him."

"I mean, being the son of a marquis and the like and due to be an archbishop before he's thirty-five."

"I suppose it is the fact that the English public school

631

system, which Ushaw College is modeled upon, beats the snobbery out of a lad."

A week later, back in San Francisco, I received a poem in the mail from Agnes Tobin. It was about two or three days after a most enjoyable dinner party Richard Montgomery Tobin gave for Merry del Val at the Tobin home at California and Taylor in the city. The poem expressed Agnes' ambivalence to the questions of both celibacy and the papal service.

Yellow and white for the Pope—and yellow and white for me;
For wherever the papal colours fly my heart has eyes to see
The sun like gold in the white boughs of a fruit tree in the
    Spring
And the golden censer's slow white trail that mounts like a living
    thing,
A taper bearing tall and straight its bright lancehead of flame,
The face of a carved ivory saint within its gilded frame,
White bread of every day we break, and golden Sauterne wine,
And angels white on Eden's wall in a long shimmering line.
Yellow and white is dear to the Pope—and Oh it is dear to me
Because my true love's golden head is a heavenly thing to see
As he sleeps locked fast to my white white breast. Yellow and white
    for me!

I myself am no stranger to such ambivalence in the matter of eros and religion, nor was Bernini whose *The Ecstasy of St. Theresa* shows religious transport verging on the borderlands of the erotic and *vice versa*. The contradictions of spirit and flesh have always engrossed me as a matter of academic study *vis à vis* the art of the baroque—and as a matter of personal experience in my own fragmented, scattered life. My conversion, after all, began with Mrs. Santone's nocturnal ministrations. Even now, at age sixty-seven, I take solace in the memory of my night with Mrs. Santone and of my weekend at Gustave Klimt's house in Vienna, considering these experiences necessary explorations of the outer boundaries of *eros*. In the case of myself and the young ladies attached to Klimt's studio, *eros* exhausted itself. In the case of Mrs. Santone, *eros* pointed the way back to something more important.

632

What if the forthcoming conclave elects Merry del Val pope? There is some possibility of this, I'm told, although I am certain the Cardinal prefers to remain the Archpriest of St. Peter's rather than ascend the papal throne. I must reread the letters in which he told me that all he ever really wanted to do was to manage a working-class parish in England, as Cardinal Newman did for so many years, or perhaps even to enter the Jesuit Order and serve as a missionary. Should Merry del Val be elected pope, however, he will no doubt be the first pope to play first-rate billiards and excellent piano: that much is certain. I remember him playing billiards down in Burlingame just before dinner, ending an afternoon of games with yet another game, this one in the den where R.M. maintains a lavish billiard table. Marina liked Rafael Merry del Val enormously. She toddled twice into the billiard den, interrupting his game by tugging at the scarlet sash around his waist (he had changed back into his cassock) and insisting upon a moment or two of conversation.

"I'll soon be eating my dinner," she told him on her second sortie into the den.

"After your dinner I'll tell you a story," said Monsignor Merry del Val, papal legate extraordinary to the emperor of Japan. He told Marina a very brief story just before I piled her into the carriage leaving for the Burlingame train station, where we were to catch the 7:00 P.M. train to San Francisco: a very brief story about an elf and a dragon, to which Marina listened with the gravest look of attention on her face, as if she were being presented with the ultimate allegory of creation itself. As we left, Marina insisted that I carry her around to all the Tobins. She embraced everyone deliberately, as if she were concerned that anyone not embraced by her would have his or her feelings hurt. Agnes had retied Marina's hair bow.

Rafael Merry del Val sailed for Japan on the first of June. It was the last night in May that Richard Montgomery Tobin gave him a farewell dinner party at the Tobin home in San Francisco. We foregathered two hours earlier than usual, at

633

five o'clock, in deference to Merry del Val's early morning departure and out of respect for Archbishop Riordan, who does not like late evenings. Both the Archbishop and Merry del Val wore black cassocks with red buttons and piping, set off by red cinctures. Each of the prelates also wore a long red cape. American Catholic prelates usually attend social events in black suits, looking for all the world like undertakers. The Roman fashion, however, which the Archbishop was following in deference to the guest of honor, dictates that cassocks and cape be worn for formal social occasions. Colonel Pershing, commandant of the Presidio, was equally resplendent in formal military dress, all blue and gold, with a spread of campaign ribbons across his chest from our recent sortie into the Philippines. The rest of us—Mayor Phelan, R.M., Cyril, J.O., and myself—stood stiffly about in white tie and tails, until eased by champagne. For some reason or other, I only recall Agnes from among the three or four women who were there that evening. Agnes wore a maroon velvet dress of vaguely medieval cut: that is to say, it was low-waisted and long-sleeved and open at the neck in a way that remained modest while allowing the best possible display of her superb swanlike throat. A thin white decorative ribbon (it seemed all of one piece) skimmed her body at its most feminine contours. In those days Agnes generally wore her hair in a chignon, as was the fashion. That night, however, she had brushed it down around her shoulders. The thickness of Agnes' hair, however, prevented it from lying flat. Her auburn hair, rather, lifted gently out from the sides of her face like the hair of the Blessed Damozel in Rossetti's painting. To me, at least, she seemed to have stepped out of a poem by Tennyson, something about a princess in a tower, seeing life only through reflections in a mirror. Agnes' hair was radiant with light, and radiant also was her face, tanned from the long walk of the day before through the Coast Range.

When the butler poured a third round of champagne, R.M. called for our attention.

"Your Excellency, Your Honor," he said, nodding first to

634

Riordan, then to Phelan. "May I begin the evening with a toast in honor of the visit to our city of Monsignor Merry del Val and to our Supreme Pontiff who has sent him on his mission to Japan, His Holiness Pope Leo XIII."

"Hear, hear," was said all around as we emptied our glasses in honor of a pope who began his career as a reluctant candidate to the priesthood in the old Papal States, the uniform of which I wore in its moments of final agony. As an ambitious official in the Ministry of the Interior, Gioacchino Pecci took on the priesthood only at the insistence of his mentor Cardinal Sala, the prefect of the interior, who demanded that Pecci be ordained in 1837 before he sent him as civil governor to Benevento, a papal city near Naples troubled by bandits and brigands. Taking firm control of the Benevento police constabulary, the newly ordained Pecci stamped out banditry in the area. In 1841 Pope Gregory XVI sent him to administer Perugia, where Pecci successfully suppressed the antipapal revolutionary party. The rulers of the old Papal States were more administrators and politicians than they were priests. *Pio Nono's* secretary of state, the Neapolitan Antonelli, adamantly refused to assume the priesthood, in fact managing a papal career, including promotion to the cardinalate, while remaining in minor orders. Having stood guard as a young Zouave outside Cardinal Antonelli's suite while His Eminence entertained his lady friends, I understand his reluctance to vow himself to priestly celibacy. Why make promises you cannot keep? In later years, in fact, there were a number of younger men promoted to the College of Cardinals who bore a striking resemblance to Leo XIII.

"May I ask Monsignor Merry del Val to respond?" Archbishop Riordan said. Riordan is a Romanist of the first order. You could see in his eyes a certain deference extended to a man nearly half his age and beneath him in ecclesiastical rank—but with superb Vatican connections. In those days, Riordan yet had hopes of winning a cardinal's hat for San Francisco.

"With pleasure, Your Excellency," said Merry del Val in his

totally charming Spanish-British accent. "I extend the Holy Father's best wishes to you all and I thank you for your courtesy to me. As you might know, my first bishop was Cardinal Vaughan of Wesminster. As a missionary to South America in the late 1860s the Cardinal, then a young priest, had the opportunity to visit San Francisco. When he learned that I would be stopping here, His Eminence wrote me from London, offering congratulations. He praised the beauty of the city, indeed of the entire Bay Region in general. May I say that after a week's delightful visit here I agree wholeheartedly with my former Ordinary. You Californians live in a special part of the world."

We sat down to vichyssoise, cucumber salad, and a great Pacific salmon, baked whole and displayed in a massive silver tureen. The Archbishop, seated at the head of the table (Agnes sat at the lower end), offered grace in Latin.

"A mighty *ichthys*, Monsignor," I said of the salmon when grace was finished. *Ichthys* is Greek for fish. The persecuted Christians of early Rome used the Greek word *ichthys* as a secret anagram and password, each letter standing for the first letters of "Jesus Christ Savior of Mankind" in Greek.

"Let's not talk about Greek," said Cyril Tobin. "Let's talk about polo. I want to recongratulate Colonel Pershing on his victory of two days ago."

"I have the feeling," said Colonel Pershing, "that had Monsignor Merry del Val played, we might have lost."

"Perhaps, Colonel, and I thank you for the compliment. I did ride an enormous amount in my teens, when I was contemplating joining the Spanish Army. Had I joined the Spanish cavalry, we might have encountered each other in a more difficult game than polo."

Colonel Pershing seemed slightly flustered, as indeed I believe was Merry del Val's intention. Rafael's British accent makes one forget that he is a subject of Spain. Feelings yet ran high among us about the war of the previous year, and decorations for valor in the recent conflict were strung across Colonel Pershing's blue tunic. To Colonel Pershing's credit, however, he recovered quickly. Rather boldly, as befits a soldier, he tapped his wine glass with his fork and stood. Conversation ceased.

"Ladies and gentlemen," Colonel Pershing said, "may I offer a toast." He paused. We waited. "To the gallantry of Spain."

Pershing knew his audience. Most Catholics in California were dead set against the Spanish-American War, although we patriotically joined in its support once the *Maine* was sunk in Havana harbor. We had no choice. We all drank eagerly to the gallantry of Spain, the Monsignor included.

"I felt the war most unfortunate," Merry del Val said.

"Let's talk about tennis," J.O. Tobin said. "Where did you learn to play so well?"

"I play as frequently as possible at the North American College. The rector, Monsignor William O'Connell, a Bostonian, encourages me to use the College's courts as frequently as I can."

R.M. turned the conversation to cricket. Merry del Val made an attempt to describe its intricacies. I have never met anyone, not even he, who can make sense of that pastime, although the Monsignor was said to be an excellent player, giving it up only when he became an archbishop. After touching upon cricket, swimming, football, then polo for the second or third time, the conversation turned to the day-before-yesterday's ramble through the Coast Range. Sometime later Agnes told me all about the ramble.

"We started at the horrid hour of five in the morning," she related, "catching the five-thirty train to Santa Cruz. We left the train at Los Gatos, arriving at the Sacred Heart Novitiate at seven o'clock in time for Mass. After breakfast there, we climbed up the steep hillside vineyards of the Novitiate until we came upon a trail that continues atop the spine of the Coast Range all the way to Half Moon Bay. We made the Stanford campus in time for a late lunch, then continued on through the foothills until we were met at about sundown by our horses near Woodside. It was nearly ten in the evening before we got back to Burlingame."

"Did you enjoy yourself?" I asked. We were lunching at

Zinkaid's on Powell Street, where I enjoy eating when I am using the Mechanics' Library on Post Street. I had met Agnes at the library that morning and had offered to buy her lunch.

"I never walked so much in my life! The men loved the walking. I enjoyed our *al fresco* lunch under the Palo Alto redwood tree on the San Francisquito Creek above Stanford, and I adored the horseback ride by moonlight from Woodside to Burlingame; but the entire day cost me two blisters. R.M. took some photographs with his Kodak of us all at lunch under the Palo Alto. I'll send you one when they are developed."

In the course of arranging my archives, Marina and I came across the photographs Agnes sent me in June of 1899. Agnes resembles a Jack London heroine in her khaki skirt, Swiss walking boots, plaid shirt, and stiff-brimmed Baden-Powell hat. R.M., J.O., and Cyril Tobin are all in high boots, jodhpurs, and khaki drill shirts—as if they were off to a polo match following their Coast Range ramble. Rafael is wearing an ensemble Tyrolean in effect—a feathered hat, a stalking jacket, and corduroy trousers tucked into boots. One photograph, taken by Agnes, shows the four men side by side in front of the leaning Palo Alto, the very same redwood tree under which De Anza's men camped in 1776, the day before they marched north to discover San Francisco Bay. Another photograph shows Agnes tearing a large loaf of French bread into manageable proportions.

"There were moments," remarked Merry del Val at the dinner party, "when I thought I was back in Italy."

"There were moments," rejoined Agnes, "when I thought that I would collapse. Only the Monsignor's recitations of Virgil, Horace, and Petrarch kept me motivated."

Hearing these names, Phelan led the conversation off in the direction of literature. "Do you think, Monsignor," he asked, "that the arts of California, like California's landscape, might one day also resemble Italy?"

In retrospect, Phelan's inquiry sounds more pretentious than it did then. I now consider the Italian comparison as a gloss on much of the artistic aspiration of California in the 1890–1906 era. I recalled to mind Phelan's question to Merry del Val only three weeks ago as Royce, Phelan, Marina, and I sat through the Solemn High Mass dedicating St. Ignatius Church.

Splendidly baroque in appearance, St. Ignatius Church is actually a Class C building, constructed of wood and stucco. Its superb run of Corinthian columns, its pediments, balustrades, cornices, cartouches, and arches, are not carved in marble and stone as they are in Italian churches, but are faked in cast plaster. In contrast to the prototypes of baroque Italy, the fifth St. Ignatius Church of San Francisco is an illusion, a plaster fantasy, a Class C building aping the antique. Its towers, indeed, recall frontier San Francisco almost as much as they suggest Bernini's Rome: they are wooden frames covered in tin, which is the way San Franciscans roofed their shacks in the 1850s. Even its great dome is a fake, for it is not a true dome at all, merely a wood and plaster blister resting on the roof.

Yet the illusion engendered by this Potemkin basilica on the edge of the American West, some few blocks from the Pacific Ocean, where Asia and the Far East begin, is a compelling illusion, linked to Phelan's question to Rafael Merry del Val across the Tobin dinner table some fourteen years ago. Californians, especially San Franciscans, savored the Mediterranean analogy, even if they secretly knew that they would be able to replicate its motifs only in Class C forms. In the very bravery of its wood and plaster pageantry (a pageantry touched by pathos), St. Ignatius Church gestures in the direction of Europe, and that is what Phelan was asking from the Spanish monsignor about-to-be-archbishop, the multilingual, thirty-five-year-old president of the Roman Academy of Ecclesiastical Nobles. Confirm us in our hope, Monsignor, the mayor of San Francisco was saying: tell us that the dream that obsesses us might one day come true: that San Francisco might attain some grand civic splendor, that it might become another Rome.

"Rome," Monsignor Rafael Merry del Val answered Mayor James Duval Phelan, "Rome wasn't built in a day."

At R.M.'s request, Rafael moved to the piano and

accompanied our coffee with Chopin and Liszt. He played in a direct, vigorous style, devoid of florid romanticism, yet touched by hints of deep feeling. I stole a glance at Agnes as Merry del Val played. She seemed entranced. Years before, standing guard as a Zouave in the papal apartments of Pius IX, I had seen the same look of seraphic exultation on the faces of other equally beautiful women when the Abbé Liszt concertized at the piano. It was a look suggesting that a woman's deepest yearnings were being activated and intensified by music: yearnings that involved both religion and romantic feeling. Women, after all, are the only ones who are fully capable of understanding love, sacred or earthly, or an admixture of both, which is what all true religion and true human passion must be, an amalgam of the sacred and the profane. A woman's sex is delicate, interior, elusive; her satisfactions come slowly, then all in a rush, like an orchid responding to sunlight. How surprised have I been upon occasion these past fifty years to enfold the orchid-flowering of a woman's *eros* in my arms, to witness and perhaps to help along the flaring of smoldering coals into flame. With what delight did I experience such joy with Virginia. Winter rains poured down upon our Napa farmhouse, and the vines outside our bedroom slaked their wine-thirst as Marina was conceived with passion and surprise.

In the course of writing about Bernini's sculpture *The Blessed Ludovica Albertoni*, I once tried to suggest the complex intersection of passions (even in such a moment of extremity as a saint's death) that always animated the art of Bernini. The artist completed this heroic sculpture of a dying nun in 1674, not long before his own death in 1680 at the age of eighty-two.

I first advanced a thesis in my Heidelberg dissertation some forty years ago and expanded upon the argument in *Bernini, Eros, and the Transcendent* (1878). Bernini's depiction of the Blessed Ludovica Albertoni in her death throes, placed over a side altar of the Church of San Francesco a Ripa in Rome (where I first saw it in 1867 as a young Zouave recruit), is

640

Bernini's undoubted masterpiece: an old man's work depicting a saint's death that is both an agony of suffering flesh and an incipient ecstasy resulting from the Heavenly Bridegroom's first touches of beatific possession. The dying Ludovica's posture: her right arm held to her breast, the drawing up of one leg over the other beneath a stunningly realized enfoldment of linen; her facial expression an ambiguous intersection of pain and rapture; the parted lips; the arched back and extended throat—surely only a great woman saint could die like this, a death envied by the very artist who celebrated it in marble while knowing that he himself was drawing near to his own demise.

Death was not on Agnes Tobin's face that night; but passions of the soul surely were, passions which Bernini would have relished: musical passions, and mystical passions, and something else also, something rendered more exquisite by its absolute unattainability, the passion of a rarefied attraction, subsumed and intensified by religious ardor.

"Death even cannot shadow that bright face," Agnes recited, her face catching some of the softly glowing stained-glass reflection of a nearby Tiffany lamp, creating the impression, reinforced by her gown, that she was a medieval lady praying in the subdued backlight of a cathedral choir stall at sunset: or that she were perhaps Laura herself, as Petrarch, worshipping from afar, might have glimpsed her in a Florentine chapel, lit by candlelight. R.M. had asked Agnes to recite one of the Petrarchan sonnets she was currently translating. Agnes obliged, reciting in a lovely, firm voice:

> Death even cannot shadow that bright face,
>   But those bright eyes irradiate his dim crown;
>   What other torchlight need I to go down
> The awful brink of that ambiguous place?
> And who is this that yearns to my embrace,
>   And shows, to try to comfort me, the brown
>   Arms of His Cross—His blood that like a gown
> Masks all His Godhead from the Angelic race?
> His heavenly footfall felled the Tartarus gate;

> Therefore come, Death; thy coming will be dear;
>   Do not hang back, for it is time to go.
> Now she is gone, you know I cannot wait;
>   My soul is in her footprints; they are clear
>   And wind straight downward to the Shades below.

We sat in silence for a moment, soaking in the imagery, hearing the echoes of Agnes' voice.

"If you please, Agnes," Archbishop Riordan broke the silence, "do something by your friend Mr. Thompson."

"I fled Him," Agnes Tobin began, reciting at the Archbishop's request the great poem written by that strange, unhappy man whom the Meynells of London had taken in off the street.

> I fled Him, down the nights and down the days;
>   I fled Him, down the arches of the years;
> I fled Him, down the labyrinthine ways
>   Of my own mind; and in the mist of tears
> I hid from Him, and under running laughter.
>   Up vistaed hopes I sped;
>   And shot, precipitated,
> Adown Titanic glooms of chasmèd fears,
>   From those strong Feet that followed, followed after.

She faltered for a moment, as if in search of a line. Merry del Val took up the recitation, moving the poem along for a few stanzas. Then Agnes took it up, alternating stanzas with Merry del Val, the two of them completing the long poem superbly. At Merry del Val's recitation of

> Naked I wait Thy love's uplifted stroke!
> My harness piece by piece Thou hast hewn from me,
>   And smitten me to my knee;
>   I am defenseless utterly.

I felt an especial pang, for that was exactly how I felt in the years immediately following Virginia's death—stripped of all hope and comfort. Even now, my life can often seem such a vain, wasted thing.

> I shook the pillaring hours
> And pulled my life upon me; grimed with smears,
> I stand amid the dust o' the mounded years—
> My mangled youth lies dead beneath the heap.
> My days have crackled and gone up in smoke,
> Have puffed and burst as sun-starts on a stream.

I yet await the Voice quoted by Francis Thompson in the final stanza of his poem, lines recited that evening, if I remember correctly, by Agnes Tobin.

> Is my gloom, after all,
> Shade of His hand, outstretched caressingly?
> "Ah, fondest, blindest, weakest,
> I am He Whom thou seekest!
> Thou dravest love from thee, who dravest me."

"Lovely, lovely indeed," said Archbishop Riordan, rising. It was ten o'clock. The Archbishop rarely stayed out beyond nine-thirty. The evening was over. We all followed R.M. to the foyer. Mayor Phelan offered the Archbishop, Monsignor Merry del Val, and me the courtesy of his carriage home. We all accepted. Agnes genuflected before Archbishop Riordan and kissed his ring.

"Farewell, Monsignor Merry del Val," she said, taking his hand as she rose from her genuflection. "I trust that you will always think kindly of San Francisco."

I sometimes fear that I have wasted my life in a succession of empty, vain posturings, in a pathetic aping of the grand manner. I am, after all, a fireman's son, the child of a semiliterate Irish peasant woman and a discharged soldier of Colonel Stevenson's colonizing regiment. What right have I to fill the world with grand words, to prattle on about the rise of local literature or the transition from late mannerist to early baroque? My now-dead friend, Charlie Stoddard, like myself a sometime teacher at a small Catholic college, often confessed to me this same horrible feeling of empty pretense and presumption of social class.

643

"My students are, for the most part, knuckleheads," Stoddard once wrote me from Washington. "They come in two varieties: lay knuckleheads and clerical knuckleheads. I do not think that a care for the finer things is a distinguishing trait of the immigrant Irish Church. Were it not for the memory of Rome and my conversion by Archbishop Alemany in San Francisco, I sometimes think that I would have been better off had I remained a Presbyterian." Stoddard was fired shortly after—as much for his disdain of his students, I suspect, as for his homosexuality.

The Irish in their grander phases, on the other hand, tend to forget the poor, their own poor especially. But who am I to judge? When is the last time I visited the sick or the imprisoned, or fed the hungry or consoled the troubled in spirit? What are my memorials to charity? In the time that remains to me I must find some way to help the poor.

"I've had enough of church to last me a lifetime," Marina said as we piled into Phelan's Croxton-Keeton. Mr. Poole the chauffeur drove us down to the Cliff House at Ocean Beach for a late breakfast of bacon and eggs.

Chapter 15

THE ZULU MURDERS have thrown San Francisco into a panic. Within the past three weeks, six white San Franciscans have been shot dead on the streets by young black males who approached them smilingly, then let go with a deadly hail of pistol fire. The police code name for these murders is Zulu; so that's what the newspapers are calling them: the Zulu murders. The attacks have taken place in every sector of the city. A Salvation Army cadet was gunned down on Geary Street. A male nurse got hit in the employees' parking lot outside San Francisco General. A teenager mowing his parents' lawn in the West Portal district was gunned down from a passing automobile. An early morning jogger was felled at the polo field in Golden Gate Park. Another body—that of a retired Air Force colonel—was discovered bound and gagged in the sand dunes of Ocean Beach, just beneath Cliff House. Another elderly man, a vagrant, fell beneath a fusillade of bullets in front of a South of Market warehouse. A photo in the *Express* showed the corpse clinging to a bottle of white port half out of its brown paper bag.

The murders—so random, so vicious—have thrown the city into a state of siege. San Francisco has always been a curiously empty city. You can go for blocks in some of the residential districts without seeing anyone on the streets. Of late, however, even the downtown streets are deserted after nightfall. The tourist trade has fallen off appreciably. Bars and restaurants are reporting a fifty percent drop in business. According to the papers, three major conventions have canceled out, throwing the big hotels into a panic.

"It's bad, really bad," Terry Shane told me when I called the Mayor's office to see what Carpino was planning to do to offset the growing panic gripping the city. San Francisco, to begin with, is a paranoid place—with much justification. The memory of the unsolved Zodiac killings, for instance, is still fresh in everyone's mind. Our homicide rate is at the best of times among the highest in the nation. Hardly a week passes without its harvest (aside from the run-of-the-mill crimes of passion) of bizarre homicides arising out of drug traffic, the sexual underground, or warfare among the various Chinese gangs. There is also a new genre—which police friends of mine are really worried about—the cold-blooded execution of holdup or mugging victims by teenage hoodlums who seem to kill for the sheer nihilistic thrill of it.

"The Mayor is between a rock and a hard place," Shane said. "The Zulu murders are racial in motivation, that's for sure; but Carpino has got to make certain that nothing he does to cope with the situation suggests race—or else the blacks and the civil libertarians will come down on him like gang-busters."

According to Shane, police intelligence attributes the Zulu murders to an underground group calling itself the Exterminating Angels. The Angels are an even more militant offshoot from the Black Brotherhood, a prison organization (San Quentin and Folsom) of militant black cons who found the Black Muslims too tame for their tastes and so broke away and formed their own organization. The Exterminating Angels found the Black Brotherhood too tame, much as the Brotherhood found the Muslims too accommodating.

"These are pretty crazy customers," Shane said. "Police intelligence feels that they are as of yet not really established outside the prison system. These murders could be some sort of initiatory rite for new recruits. Kill a honky, in other words, before you're accepted into the group."

646

"It's a long way from National Brotherhood Week," I said.

"The you-know-what has only just hit the fan," Shane said. "There's a meeting here at three with the chief of police to consider our options. One more thing: the Mayor has asked me to ask around whether any of the staff has heard from Esmeralda lately."

"Not me," I said. "The last time I heard from her was the weird phone call I got this summer. Why? Is something up?"

"You haven't heard from her in the past few days?" Shane persisted.

"Not in the least. I hardly consider myself a member of her intimate circle. To repeat myself: what's up?"

"Nothing," Shane said unconvincingly. "I can't talk any more. Goodbye."

I decided that I would go over to Room 200 for the Zulu meeting, even though, strictly speaking, it was none of my business. I had the feeling that the *coup de grâce* was about to be given to the Claudio Carpino administration; and since its history was also, in part, my own story as well, I wanted to be there for the *Götterdämmerung*, the period of disintegration and collapse, that was surely upon us.

Deborah called. "My parents will be in town next week. They want to meet you."

"Are you sure they want to visit San Francisco now: with the Zulu murders, I mean?"

"Mother did mention something about it, but I said we'd make sure that we were off the street by nightfall."

"Are you sure that you want me to meet them?"

"Of course, why not?"

"You seemed pretty disappointed in me regarding the Roncola pictures."

"That was a month ago, and a lot has happened since."

"I'll meet them on one condition."

"Which is?"

"That you meet my own Aged P."

"This is beginning to get corny."

"Life has a way of getting corny."

647

"Agreed—your Aged P and my Arizonians, at times and places to be determined."

Serena Tutti poked her head into the office. "Commissioner Storm wants to see you," she said.

"Commissioner Storm wants to see me," I said to Deborah by way of explanation as I hung up the telephone.

Mabel Storm always rushes into my office as if the San Andreas fault had just opened up to envelop the San Francisco Public Library and it was somehow my fault. As usual, a fox fur chased itself around Commissioner Storm's shoulders. Today's hat—a winged and feathered affair, blatantly antiecological in spirit—suggested that a seagull had alighted atop Mabel Storm's head as she stalked across Civic Center on the way to the Library and that the poor bird, having become entangled in the Commissioner's Hedy Lamarr upswept hairdo, now beat its wings in a frenzy of panic, trying unsuccessfully to launch itself into the blue. A fox had given its all for the sake of Mabel Storm's neckpiece. Some sort of bird—a dove, most likely—had expired on the altar of her hatmaker's art. An alligator would never again laze upon the sunny banks of the Okefenokee swamp, so that Mabel Storm could clutch and unclutch her handbag; and some sort of hooved creature—a steer, a lamb, a kangaroo, a pig—had gone to its reward so that Mabel Storm might be properly shod. The Commissioner, in other words, wore the pelts of at least four once-living creatures upon her person. I had the feeling, as I always do when dealing with her, that one day she might wear my hide as well.

"I can't stay too long. I'm on my way to the Francesca Club," Commissioner Storm announced in her best downtown clubwoman fashion. "I only want to drop by and see if there's anything you need for next Thursday's Marshall Square hearing. We're all depending on you, you must realize, to put the Library's case forward as effectively as possible."

"I understand the commission's position," I said, "and I'll do my best to represent it."

"Good. It wouldn't do your future in the library world any good for you to lose Marshall Square for us, would it?"

"I'm not aware that I had a future in the library world," I said.

"We'll be able to tell more about that after the hearing," Mabel Storm said. Readjusting her fur piece so that the fox caught his tail somewhere in the vicinity of her left shoulder blade, Mabel Storm left as abruptly as she came, a walking tribute to the arts of slaughtering, tanning, and taxidermy. Her winged headdress and fur made her—for an instant in my imagination—an avenging chieftainess of a savage Teutonic tribe, having just delivered her battle plan against the Roman invaders.

Just before lunch, Cole O'Halloran called.

"I want you to know," he said, "just how delighted we all are with the confidential memorandum you sent us regarding those photographs."

"That's ancient history," I said.

"On the contrary," O'Halloran continued. "You showed real class in tracking it all down and destroying the forgery. We only wish you had indicated who the guilty party was."

"What good would that have done?"

"Nothing for the immediate future," O'Halloran said. "We, of course, wouldn't prosecute or anything. Why beat a dead horse, if you know what I mean? But it would be nice to know just who we have to thank for such a nasty piece of business."

"I presume you're convinced that it wasn't me," I said peevishly.

"Not as convinced as we would be if we know who the true culprit was," O'Halloran said matter-of-factly.

"Someone," I said, "who can cause you no further harm."

"I had a call yesterday from Tiny Roncola," O'Halloran continued. "Tiny volunteered to help us out in San Francisco for the remainder of the campaign."

"A wise move on Tiny's part," I said.

"People like Tiny can always be made useful," O'Halloran said. "His departure from the ranks of Carpino supporters hardly represents a major surrender by the opposition, but it will give us a kick to have Tiny around the office. He's resigning from the Redevelopment Agency and will coordinate our doorbell-ringing effort in the Bay Area."

"Tiny knows the nitty gritty of getting out the vote," I said. "He got a lot of doorbells rung for Carpino in the last mayoral election."

"Precisely," O'Halloran said. "Soutane, at my suggestion, called Tiny personally and welcomed him aboard. Now to demonstrate further that there are no hard feelings, I'm dropping an invitation in the mail to you, inviting you to a little fundraiser cocktail party that Ray and Kay Soulé are giving for Andy some time early next month. We want you there. After all, when the primary is over, everybody has got to pull together behind the candidate, so we can win the governor's chair in November."

You have to admire Tiny Roncola's gall, I thought to myself when O'Halloran had hung up—and Tiny's cunning as well. If Tiny got enough doorbells rung, he'd find himself tucked away for the eight years of two probable Soutane administrations. Tiny has got juice with none of the candidates currently running to replace Claudio Carpino as mayor of San Francisco. Whoever wins the mayorship will need all the patronage jobs at Redevelopment for his or her own people, so Tiny is wise to set his sights Sacramento-wards. In a way, I'm truly touched in Tiny's trust in me. Tiny has every confidence that I haven't blown the whistle on him, nor will I; and he is right. It's fitting, I suppose, that at least one of us gets ahead in politics.

The money, by the way, is on Supervisor Al Tarsano and State Senator John Como to win the mayoral primary in June and face each other in November. The other three candidates are lagging significantly behind. Sandra Van Dam has an excellent reputation in the downtown business world and has been a superb chairperson of the supervisors' finance committee; but she's too hardboiled to make an effective mayoral candidate. As a superior court judge, Charles Fessio has been too long out of the public eye—he lacks name recognition; and State Senator Mortimer Engels is having problems with his health. Tarsano and Como, by contrast, each possess solid constituencies: Tarsano on the right, and Como on the left.

Whichever of them gets the biggest piece of the center will win the election.

Al Tarsano and John Como perfectly embody the present duality of the San Francisco experience; their face-off in November will offer the voters a clear-cut decision about the future direction of government in San Francisco. Al Tarsano—senior vice-president of the El Camino Savings and Loan Association, past president of the Veterans of Foreign Wars, currently serving on the boards of directors of (among other organizations) Catholic Charities, the Hanna Boys Center, the Sierra Club, and the Lighthouse for the Blind—lives in the Excelsior District with his wife and seven children. Tarsano's trademark is a red clip-on bow tie, which he manages to wear constantly. His Christmas card this year (sent to all department heads) showed all four of the Tarsano boys wearing similar ornaments at their respective necks. Tarsano has great support among homeowners in the less fashionable residential areas, from veterans and church groups, the Police Officers Association, and groups such as the Neighborhood Tavern Owners Guild, the Friends of Local Playgrounds, the Greek-American Homeowners League, the South of Market Boys, and the Oldtimers Association. Tarsano's campaign slogan—Save What's Left of San Francisco—says it all. Al Tarsano is the final champion of down-home San Francisco or what can be called the Real City: the block upon block of dreary, crowded houses lining treeless streets, far from the waterside tourist areas or the fashionable districts in the northern tip of the peninsula. This is the San Francisco tourists only see, if they see it at all, momentarily from their cab windows on the way to or coming from the airport: a rather monotonous and desperate cityscape of boxy houses, set one by one next to each other in huddled succession.

"You could call San Francisco Cleveland-with-a-View," Toby Wain once said to me, "except that ninety percent of the houses here don't have a view. They look out on an exact replica of themselves, strung along a treeless street."

"Most urban Americans live that way," I said.

"True," Toby replied, "but most Americans are not

651

constantly being told what a special place they live in. The myth of San Francisco creates a certain tension. Everyone is supposed to be as pleased as punch to be here, even when the facts and circumstances of their lives are as desperate as if they lived in a walk-up cold-water flat in Queens."

State Senator John Como, by contrast, lives in a refurbished Victorian on Fulton Street, facing Alamo Square, in a racially mixed neighborhood. Divorced and remarried to the wealthy socialite, Diana Tempington, John Como began his public career when he took over from Don Sherwood in the early sixties as the morning host on radio station KSFO. Como, however, had ambitions beyond that of succeeding to the laurel wreaths of the city's leading disc jockey. Using his wife's money, Como began buying up a string of marginal radio stations in northern California. He revamped each of them with its own distinctive sound—rock, soul, country and western, mellow, swing—after extensive marketing research into each area. Como Communications now owns some twenty radio stations between Gilroy and Eureka.

In 1970, backed solidly by the city's liberal establishment, Como won his first term as state senator. Possessed of movie-star good looks (at forty-two, he resembles Victor Mature in *Demetrius and the Gladiators*), John Como has provided the city's newspapers with excellent copy. Even San Francisco reporters can remember long enough to copy down Como's glib, disc-jockey one-liners, which are also sensational on the evening television news—where, if a politician can't say it in five to ten words, he or she gets blocked out of prime time coverage. Columnist Harry Shaw salts and peppers his column with Como's quick and quotable *bons mots*, electric with the pithy razzmatazz of the disc jockey's art. Jeremiah Jones, Como, Shaw, and clothier Ford Booth have formed a local version of Frank Sinatra's Rat Pack. Their comings and goings fill Shaw's column: and this, quite frankly, is the basis of Como's political strength. Come November, Harry Shaw will have a mayor of San Francisco to cavort with, and San Francisco will have the first disc jockey mayor in American history.

"Tough, real tough: that's the only way it can be handled," Barry Scorse told the Mayor. "You got to authorize a stop and search by the police of anyone resembling the suspects."

"I disagree," said Terry Shane. "The only description we have is from an eyewitness to the Howard Street killing. A medium-height black male with a mustache: that could fit five-sixths of the black men in San Francisco. Any kind of wholesale stop and search policy will infuriate the black community."

"The Mayor has got killers loose on the streets of his city," Scorse said. "He's got to show California he can handle a tough situation; otherwise, we're left with our tit in a wringer on the law and order issue."

"We'll have both tits in there if we alienate the blacks and the civil libertarians with any sort of Karl Malden 'Streets of San Francisco' crap," Shane retorted. "We signal the voters that it's amateur night here in San Francisco." As press officer, Shane rarely enters into policy decisions, but he was sure as hell making his case to the Mayor now.

"We haven't got the doubledome vote, anyway," Scorse said.

"But we've got a good shot at the black vote up and down the state," Shane retorted. "Black voters, according to what I've been hearing, just can't connect with Soutane. He's too upper middle-class Sierra Club honky, for one thing. And for another thing, they are suspicious of his beat-up Plymouth and his army cot. They expect a main man to live it up with a certain style. We could have some of the black votes, I'm sure, and they count for a lot in the L.A. area—but not if we start acting like the Ku Klux Klan."

Shane and Scorse glared at each other across the rococo opulence of the Mayor's office. Scorse looked like a young and very pissed-off Richard Conte in *A Walk in the Sun*; Shane was played by Richard Egan. Me—I was playing myself: off to one side, in a corner, where I wouldn't get in anyone's way.

"What the fuck are you doing here?" Scorse had asked when I walked into the Mayor's office at three o'clock for the meeting on the Zulu crisis. "This isn't a library matter."

653

"Nor is it a matter for civil service," I said.

"I'm here as the Mayor's campaign manager," Scorse snorted. He did, however, drop his challenge; so I went in. Claudio Carpino has no set order of staffing for taking advice during a crisis. He merely announces a meeting. If you think you've got something to say and have enough juice to get in and say it, then you just show up. If you're challenged, as I was by Scorse, you either leave or hold your own. If you hold your own, you can stay and listen—and even offer advice. This sounds chaotic at first, defiant of the pyramid-shaped staffing pattern beloved by bureaucrats, which narrows the range of reporters and reportees until only five or six people have access to the principal. I've decided, though, that Carpino's habit of taking advice from everyone at once is in reality his very Sicilian way of wielding power. On the one hand, it prevents anyone from becoming the Mayor's chief of staff, much less his prime minister. With no one person dominating the Mayor's flow of advice or information, he gets more variety of input. He is also beholden to no one member of his staff. Everyone has at least the illusion of access to the Mayor, as long as he or she is willing to fight for it. The Mayor, quite frankly, seems to enjoy the Darwinian aspects of his circular staff system. That's the Sicilian part of it. Like a baron of old Sicily, the Mayor keeps his subordinates off balance *vis à vis* him and each other. Barry Scorse dominates us all—as a matter of innate aggressiveness and because of the Mayor's fondness for him; but Scorse doesn't run the staff as he would in a more conventional operation. You can still pull an end run around him, as I did that afternoon. Such a system, furthermore, demands that the principal, in our case Mayor Claudio Carpino, be smarter and more forceful than any single staffer or bloc of staff. Carpino has got that edge on us all by a country mile.

Aside from Police Chief Don Norris, whose proper business this all was, Scorse, Shane, Inspector Ted Potelli, Jimmy Driscoll, and myself were in the room.

"There isn't even a black person in this room," Terry Shane

654

said. "We should get input from the black community before we take any course of action."

"Why embarrass them further?" Jimmy Driscoll asked. "They're already freaked by these Zulu killings—a sort of guilt by association."

"Precisely," Shane said. "That's why we've got to be careful about offering them any insult. They're already very touchy. Rounding up a couple of hundred of black suspects won't calm the situation."

"You've got police morale to consider here, Mr. Mayor," Inspector Ted Potelli said. "The guys on the beat have got to feel that you're giving them the widest possible leeway to nab these killers, and not holding them in so as to avoid offending the black community." Potelli likes to play cop on the beat, although he's had a cushy job in the mayor's office for nearly seven years now.

The Mayor sat silently by as debate crackled back and forth across the office. When everyone had made his point, he said: "I now want two opinions—first, the Chief's. I want that to be strictly a police opinion. After that, I'll ask for some political opinions."

Don Norris shifted his bulky blue-clad frame uneasily from one side to another of the French provincial chairs Esmeralda Carpino selected for the Mayor's office. A total of six stars, three on each shoulder, twinkled beneath the refracted light of the crystal chandelier that Esmeralda insisted the Mayor, out of his own pocket, have installed in place of the fluorescent lighting preferred by the previous administration. When you're chief of police in San Francisco, there is no such thing as a purely police decision. Your star—the stars on your shoulder—rise or fall away with the fate of your boss. Carpino promoted Norris, then a precinct captain, over the heads of a half-dozen senior men, precisely because, he said (or Terry Shane said, through the press release he banged out on his IBM Selectric), "I want a cop's cop behind the chief's desk, someone who hasn't lost touch with the streets." To Norris's credit, he answered the Mayor's question straight. After all, if you're appointed chief because the mayor wants a cop's cop, then it's best to behave like a cop's cop.

"The description we've got so far, Mr. Mayor, is next to useless," Norris said, "if you're talking about a city-wide dragnet. But even if we had a better description of the suspect, we haven't the manpower for a dragnet. If you confine yourself to selected areas, however, the description likewise refines itself. Take black males of medium build with a mustache on a city-wide basis and, like Terry Shane says, you'll be arresting half the adult black males in San Francisco. Each of these murders, however, was committed within two to three blocks of an access ramp to the freeway, or to a major boulevard in the case of the Ocean Beach murder. In one case that we know of, the gunman sped by, firing from a moving car. In two other cases, he approached the victim on foot, fired, then ran for about a block before being picked up by a vehicle. Intelligence and Traffic are currently preparing a map of freeway access points that are also near relatively empty areas, such as parking lots, commercial areas not heavily used by night, and so forth. My rough guess is that there are probably thirty such places in the city. If we confine our dragnet to these areas, it might have some effect. In any event, the probability of a black male resembling the descriptions we now have of being in the vicinity of an empty lot or whatever within a short distance of a freeway access point decreases mathematically. You still risk offending the black community, but the risk is lessened."

"This is a police decision," the Mayor said.

"I'd say do it," Chief Norris said. "It might be weeks before the state attorney general's office or the intelligence unit of the state bureau of prisons can give us any usable leads. We are already working off a list of recently released convicts fitting the description known to be in the Bay Area. We're cross-checking this list with the FBI, looking for any previous history of radical activity. Bureau of Prisons tells us, however, that not too much is known about the Black Brotherhood or its offshoot, the Exterminating Angels. The only inmate who ever showed signs of talking got his throat slit in the shower at Q.

Intelligence work is slow. It may pay off. But the department has got to mount a street response as well, and that means stopping people who fit the description when we find them in crime-probable areas."

"And that means trouble, big trouble, politically," Terry Shane said.

"I'm not a politician," said the Chief. "The Mayor asked me for a police opinion."

"Do what you have to do, Chief," the Mayor said. Don Norris didn't rise from patrolman to captain in ten years for nothing, nor was he promoted to chief because he lacked dramatic flair. Sensing the drama of the occasion, Norris stood up before the Mayor at attention and offered him a salute before about-facing in the military manner and leaving the room.

"May I make a suggestion, Your Honor?" Jimmy Driscoll, hitherto silent, said when the Chief had left the room in a blaze of stars, gold buttons, and gold braid. Jimmy always speaks last—and makes the most sense; that is why Carpino has him on a city salary: to make sense about three or four times a year.

"The chair recognizes the eminent saloon-keeper and diagnostician of *realpolitik*," the Mayor said, smiling. Throughout the entire conversation, Carpino had been paying close attention to the proceedings, but he also showed signs of resigned acceptance. Not a hint of anxiety, much less panic, crossed his face, although the Zulu murders constituted the most ferocious crisis of his time in office.

"What I'd do, Your Honor, is to right now line up some support from good black Democrats. Explain to them that you're between a rock and a hard place. Get a picture in the papers with all of them in your office, showing solidarity." Jimmy Driscoll said this in that flat, nasal, South-of-Market Irish way of speaking that he has along with no more than a thousand other oldtimers in this city. It is an accent that reminds many of Brooklyn, New York, Chicago, because it was the nineteenth-century accent of the urbanized Irish immigrant working class. Harsh, staccato, it has little mellifluousness or grace because it was spoken by a despised class of new Americans, who were up against tough times and finding that the vowel-music of Dublin or the lilting brogues of Cork and Roscommon were inappropriate to a setting of harsh urban encounter.

"Put it together for me, Jimmy, will you?" the Mayor said. He looked around the office in that way he has of ending any meeting—by showing on his face that he is now turning his attention to something else.

"Stay behind for a moment, James," the Mayor said to me as we were all getting up to leave. Scorse threw me a dirty look as he and the others filed out of the room. Big deal, I thought to myself. Do I want to spend the rest of my life in working relationships wherein a nod from the boss, an invitation to remain for a moment after a meeting, constitutes the acme of success? America is the Land of the Free and the Home of the Brave—true; but even we Americans—or, more properly, we Americans of the white-collar class—haven't yet escaped the debasing rituals and obeisances demanded by hierarchical power. If I had a better developed inner self, I could perhaps cope better with all this; but right now, I give away a bit of my soul every time I find myself kissing ass. Smiling when I don't want to, calling nincompoops "Sir," faking attention in my eyes during some interminable anecdote—all of it is done almost instinctively on the basis of my interlocutor's superior status, done in many cases as a social ritual, altruistically you might say, because the superior person receiving my attentions has not, and will never, do me any concrete, palpable good, no matter how much I play the sincere listener, the flatterer even. I sometimes fear that an element of subservience has been implanted in me from birth, the result of some long debasement of my stock in the Old World and its unsuccessful circumstances in the New. Perhaps I come from a race of hat-tippers and forelock-tuggers, shuffling the earth in heavy, crude brogans as the lord of the manor casts a cheery hello on the way to the hunt: not even being mean or dismissive, the lord, but absentmindedly kind, which is the worst insult of all

658

because it signifies the fact that it isn't too important whether you exist at all, just as long as you stay in your place and behave yourself. A criminal gets more attention than a dutiful slob.

All of this I ruminated upon as the Mayor got up from his desk and walked over to one of the French windows that open onto Civic Center, looking east. Harry Shaw likes to compare the Mayor to Mussolini, "Il Duce the Mayor" being one of Shaw's constantly used tags referring to Carpino. Physically, the comparison makes no sense. The Mayor looks more like Anthony Quinn than like Benito Mussolini. Like Quinn (playing Zorba the Greek), the Mayor exudes that abundant masculine power women and men alike—even in this post-Freudian age—find so fascinating, so compelling, especially when there is also a constant suggestion of life force, of theatrical will and arrogant appetite that has resisted viciousness but refuses to be tamed and hence is fraught with danger. Seeing Carpino before the window, gazing out over a vast public plaza, I caught a suggestion—illicit, un-American, unjustified, but a suggestion nevertheless—of roaring crowds and thunderous oratory and the frenzy of collective will: not now, and certainly not expressed by Claudio Carpino (despite Shaw's many digs at *Il Duce*), but someday, long in the future, when the fatigues of our plebiscitary democracy shall have overcome us, when we will have long since surrendered our autonomy to the media and to big government—growing more lonely, more isolated, in the process, and devoid of orthodox sources of strength: religion, family, work—and when an incipiently fascist elite (corporate perhaps, but more likely governmental bureaucrat) will have long since grown bored with according every self-appointed spokesman of this or that self-appointed interest group a polite hearing, enduring the fractured grammar and the self-pitying stares and the indifferent tailoring.

No, not now—and not from an ethnic, big-city lawyer (too clever by a half, as a peer once said of young Winston Churchill) who represents one of the last of his species in a

659

provincial American city; but it very well might come someday. And its first signs—the first symptoms of the collective madness—might very well take their origins here in San Francisco; for as in many cases in the past, the provinces can succumb long before the capital even hears that a revolution has broken out. There is, as Larry Seton says, something massively disordered in San Francisco, some embittered expectation, underpinned by paranoia, that could spread like a cancer through an institution—a church, say, or a political party, or one of these self-help collectives springing up all over the city—blossoming forth like a rotting orchid, sick from too much sunlight, taking countless people down with it, innocent and guilty alike, in some horrible cataclysm.

From what depths of madness, for instance, does this current Zulu insanity originate? Not strictly from racial hatred, certainly, or even from a justified conviction of racial grievance; for if that were the case, America would have long since gone up in flames. The black race has been heroically patient in the face of its tragic American experience. A minority of some twenty-two million American blacks, having decided upon frenzy, could destroy the nation—and itself. Watts showed that, if it showed anything. No, there's more than resentment behind these Zulu killings. There's a quality of disordered imagination, of justified grievance run amuck, that is, potentially, a characteristic of this city. The Zulu killers are most likely bound together in some bizarre cult that nourishes itself on the larger fantasy life of San Francisco: in their cases, it has taken a murderous, paranoid turn; but this also expresses a part of the whole, for paranoia and murderous intent are everywhere.

"This is a very difficult time," I said to the Mayor. His back was still turned to me, as if in rejection.

"It's very different from the way we do things in North Beach," the Mayor said, turning to me. "What do you think is wrong?"

"With San Francisco?" I asked.

"Are these murders San Francisco's fault?"

660

"They are happening here," I said. "Whatever motivates them is in our atmosphere, like a poisonous gas."

"As an attorney, I try to reject metaphysical explanations," the Mayor said. "They have a way of not standing up in court."

"We seem to be in a metaphysical situation," I said. "Killers are gunning people down for metaphysical reasons. They are re-enacting some long-forgotten, horrible myth from the dawn of the race." The eyelid drooped momentarily: the second time I had earned this distinct mark of ducal displeasure.

"I'd like to talk about Marshall Square," the Mayor said.

"The hearing before the board of supervisors is next week," I said.

"That's why I'm bringing it up," the Mayor said. "It's a delicate situation."

The Mayor wasn't exaggerating. For the past six months, the Friends of Books, spurred on by Mabel Storm, have been busy gathering some thirty thousand signatures expressing support for the Library's right to Marshall Square. The Friends of Books have also been lobbying the individual members of the board of supervisors on the Library's behalf. The planning commission voted a month ago to allocate Marshall Square for the Performing Arts Center. That decision, however, has to be ratified by the board. The planning commissioners are appointed by the mayor. The supervisors, however, are individually elected—hence more sensitive to public opinion. Mabel Storm and the Friends of Books have every intention of getting the board to reverse the decision of the planning commission (which it can do) by making that seem the wisest option in terms of popular opinion.

Over the course of the past six months, I've been getting pressure from both sides of the argument. Harold Barrett, the retired vice-chairman of the Bank of Northern California who is heading the Performing Arts Center drive, and Sargeant Mayhew, the chief administrative officer of San Francisco, recently took me to lunch at the Pacific Union Club in a

661

not-so-subtle effort to get me to break publicly with the library commission on the Marshall Square issue. The Pacific Union Club—the old James C. Flood mansion atop Nob Hill—is the Valhalla of our local plutocracy. Both Barrett and Mayhew are members by inheritance (about half the memberships of the club are inherited); and it was part of their strategy of persuasion, I suppose, to bring me there: to flatter a neighborhood boy, that is, with lunch among those whom money has apotheosized.

"The downtown community is most anxious to see the center built," Harold Barrett said over coffee in the club's mahogany-lined library, which looks out onto the noble façade of the Fairmont Hotel. As he talked, I heard a California Street cable car clang by. "Anyone such as yourself, playing a key role, such as you could play, in getting this project complete, would always have a secure place for himself in San Francisco."

"Anyone," said Sargeant Mayhew, "obstructing this effort would have to realize that he held San Francisco back, thwarted her, in the vital area of performing arts development."

The chatty bonhomie over Dubonnet before lunch in the PU Club bar, the lunch itself—interrupted by a number of introductions to passing greats who sailed by our table like Manila galleons, laden with treasure and running before a good wind—this had been the build-up and softening process. Let the local boy see the power and the glory of Valhalla and perhaps he'll do the bidding of the gods. Now, possibilities of reward or vengeance were being suggested. For all their bland assurance, for all the liturgy of caste I had just witnessed them orchestrate throughout the luncheon, Harold Barrett and Sargeant Mayhew—for the first time in their lives perhaps— were experiencing the irrational edge of populist resistance. As an institution, the SFPL was beneath their contempt. Unlike what the elite of New York has done for the New York Public, the elite of San Francisco, bored by books, has let the Library drift into marginal mediocrity. Now it, and I, were standing in their way—momentarily, they thought. It could be

662

handled—only get to James Vincent Norton. Flatter him. Take him to the PU Club. Suggest future security or future peril, depending upon his course of action. Do it all in a gentlemanly manner, over demitasses of coffee in the PU Club library, the walls rich in rising shelves of leather-bound books.

At least they can threaten in a bland manner, I thought to myself, remembering the way that the Librarians' Guild had at our last confrontation howlingly accused me of positioning myself to sell the Library out on the matter of Marshall Square. Even KPIX reporter Linda Schacht, usually friendly to me, implied that I was playing a double game.

"Has the Mayor put any pressure on you to discredit the Library's claim to Marshall Square?" Linda asked me after the planning commission hearing. I blinked at the red light pointed my way by her cameraman and I honestly answered, "No, he hasn't."

I wished that he had, however. That would have boiled it down to a matter of feudal loyalty, which I could handle; but Claudio Carpino is not a man of clear directions. As a matter of descent and temperament, his intentions are circular, ambiguous. So I said that day, having remained behind after the meeting on how best to deal with the Zulu killers: "Yes, Mr. Mayor, it is a delicate situation."

And I couldn't care less, I said silently to myself. I'm bored by the whole thing. I'm bored by the pettiness of my life. I'm tired of having to please so many people at once and doing a half-assed job with everybody I'm involved with. I quit, I resign. I take responsibility for my own life. I'm tired of the myth of this town and I'm exhausted by the reality of it. I'm bored by political ambition, Mr. Mayor, yours and Andy Soutane's and everyone else's.

"I want to share something with you," the Mayor said, turning around from the French window. I hadn't noticed during the meeting how tired his face was. On closer look, you could see the lines of fatigue. "I'm telling you this in utter confidence. I have neither seen nor heard from my wife in ten days. Quite frankly, I do not know where she is."

I knew that it had to be a special call because the phone rang at five-thirty in the morning. The last person to phone me at five-thirty in the morning had been Esmeralda Carpino, who called last August to accuse me of an unnatural relationship to the Mayor. Bumblingly, I groped for my bedside phone. Without my glasses, I'm a basket case.

"Hello, Dr. Norton. This is Esmeralda Carpino," said a cheery voice at the other end of the line.

"Is this some sort of a joke?" I asked.

"Why should it be, Dr. Norton?"

"Mrs. Carpino, you haven't been heard from for about three weeks. Your husband is worried sick. Half the police in the state are looking for you. The FBI has been called in."

"And it's even been on Walter Cronkite," she said.

"Are you all right?" I asked.

"I'm perfectly fine," she said. "I've been traveling around and thinking things over."

As in the case of her last call to me, I couldn't think of anything to say. As before, it was a Marx Brothers' movie: the wife of the mayor of San Francisco, missing for some three weeks, calling me up at five-thirty in the morning and telling me that she has been enjoying a little holiday in her home state. It was all sort of crackers, Animal Crackers in fact, and I wished at that moment that I had Chico's horn to blow into the telephone, two quick hoots, followed by a bird whistle. Instead, I said: "Why are you calling me?"

"I need someone to come down and pick me up, someone from my husband's staff, and I thought of you. A librarian, after all, is a sort of clergyman, isn't he? I like the idea of the city librarian taking me back home. It sounds appropriate, for the evening news, I mean. I own a bookstore, remember?"

"Where are you?" I asked.

"You must first promise not to tell my husband or the police—until we're on the way back to the city. I don't want the police bursting in here, you understand?"

"Yes, ma'am. I promise."

"I'm at the Hacienda Grande Motel, Cabin Five, about two blocks south of Mission San Jose. I'll expect you around ten."

She hung up. I had no choice but to play it her way. Ever since she disappeared, everyone has been playing it her way. I must admit that I wasn't that surprised when the Mayor told me about Esmeralda's disappearance that afternoon in his office. Ever since Christmas, the Carpinos have been skating on thin ice.

"What wife of what prominent politico," Harry Shaw had asked in his December twenty-seventh column, "had to be rushed to the hospital (booze and pills) by her prominent husband? Only Sam Spade knows for sure, and he's keeping mummmm."

"That's right. It's all true," Terry Shane had admitted to me over lunch at the Washington Square Bar and Grill on the last working day of 1975. The place was packed with people playing hooky for the rest of the day. I sometimes think that San Francisco is filled with people playing hooky for the rest of life. Warren Hinckle was at the bar, in black eyepatch and shiny patent leather dancing pumps, declaiming something to Charles McCabe who sat morosely over an ale, like an oversized, angry leprechaun. Both Hinckle and McCabe had out-of-town newspapers tucked under their arms: Hinckle, the *New York Times*, and McCabe, something British, to judge from the thin paper and the close print.

"She's been saucing a little lately and that doesn't go well with all the tranques she's on," Shane said. "The Mayor swept her off the bed like she was a limp rag doll and rushed her to St. Luke's Hospital. He's got a private nurse with her now to make sure she doesn't do anything dangerous."

"She's got a private eye on him because she fears that he's playing around. I'd hate to see their nurse and private eye bills at the end of the month."

"It's total goofiness," Shane said, downing his second Canadian Club and water. "Esmeralda calls Audrey Yee about a month ago and accuses her of having an affair with the Mayor. She tells Audrey that she's put some sort of Sicilian curse on Audrey and her son. Audrey ran into the Mayor's office, hysterical."

As soon as Harry Shaw got wind of Esmeralda's disappearance, he had a field day. It was Shaw, in fact, who first broke the news to the public. "Where is the lovely Esmeralda. Carpino of late?" he asked the very next morning after the Mayor first told me of his wife's disappearance. "It's been nearly two weeks since Madama Mayor has been seen in public."

"News from the Southland!" ran another item. "Police inspectors Ted Potelli and Mike Kilduff have been making the rounds of Southern California fat farms in search of the vanished Esmeralda. Two days ago, thinking that the lovely Esmeralda had hidden herself away within its steamy confines, these two paragons of SFPD acumen kicked in the door to the sauna bath of a San Diego-area spa. Imagine the surprise of the towel-clad matrons within. One moment they are quietly melting away the poundage: then—bang—the door falls flat on the floor, and two gorillas in trench coats stumble in, pistols drawn, looking for Esmeralda. A number of women became hysterical. The San Diego cops took Potelli and Kilduff into custody. It took a call from Chief Norris in San Francisco to get our heroes released. San Diego PD is hopping mad about Carpino's boys going down there with no notice to SDPD and kicking in the door of the sauna bath of one of the Southland's most prestigious fat farms without benefit of a search warrant."

"Potelli thought that Esmeralda might have been being held in the fat farm by abductors," Terry Shane told me.

"In the sauna room?" I asked. "Since when do kidnappers take their victims into a ladies' sauna?"

"Anyway, that's what Potelli told the Mayor," Shane said.

I called in sick to the office, then headed the Porsche down Bayshore Freeway to San Jose. Mission San Jose—founded in 1797, the fourteenth of the California missions—sits on U.S. 50 outside the city of San Jose proper. I'd been there a number of times on field trips when I was a boy. The Dominican sisters of Mission San Jose operate St. Vincent's School in San Rafael; once a year they would bus us down to their motherhouse for a picnic on the grounds adjacent to the three-story brick convent just behind the Mission proper. Despite the goofiness of my

666

situation, the fetching of Esmeralda, I could not help but feel a sense of return to boyhood scenes as I thought of the Mission and the motherhouse and the classical California landscape of lion-colored hills that roll away on every side of the buildings. I remembered the polished order of the convent proper: the waxed hardwood floors, the crucifixes on bare walls, the long tables in the sisters' refectory where we were served milk and cookies before the bus ride back to San Rafael, the gardens next to Mission San Jose itself—orange, lemon, fig, apricot, almond, olive trees, many of them planted by the Franciscan padres a century and a half ago and still (in 1950 at least) bearing fruit. Under these trees, a number of Dominican sisters, wearing the long white robes that date back to the thirteenth century, sat together on ancient benches, perhaps, like the orchard, survivals of the Mission era, as one of their number read from a book. It was a warm sunny day and you could hear the low murmur of bees coming from the convent apiary in the next glen. Swallows darted in and out of the mission belfry like flying crossbows. That is my deepest, most persistent image of California, Sebastian Collins's California: a daydream of Mediterranean Catholic Europe, in total contrast to the sordid urgencies of contemporary San Francisco and the hypocrisies and false gestures of my daily existence.

Take these Zulu killings, for instance. What could be freakier, more remote, from that boyhood memory of the gardens at Mission San Jose, and yet what could be more emblematic as well of those disorders of spirit that hold our civilization in thrall? Even the limited dragnet proposed by the Chief, incidentally, has caused enormous resentment. Assemblyman Jeremiah Jones called a press conference, at which he was joined by a number of prominent leaders from the black community, including my friend Larry Seton. One by one, Jeremiah Jones introduced his friends to the reporters and television cameras present: Larry Seton, novelist; Paul Lincoln, Forty-Niner quarterback; Johnson Hines, surgeon; Hyacinth Pascal, Episcopal priest; LaVal Henderson, blues singer and nightclub entrepreneur. "What do all these

667

gentlemen have in common?" Jeremiah Jones asked in that dynamic, Sammy Davis Jr. way of his. "They fit the vague description we have of the Zulu killers. So, in fact, do I. So do thousands of other black male San Franciscans. Ladies and gentlemen of the press, I submit to you that the current dragnet underway in San Francisco is racist, pure and simple, in both its intent and its execution. I call upon Mayor Claudio Carpino to clarify his position in this matter. I call upon the attorney general of the United States to invoke his extraordinary powers and investigate the Ku Klux Klan situation that we have right here and now in this city."

Built some time in the late thirties and looking for all the world like a setting for a James M. Cain murder mystery, the Hacienda Grande Motel is a cluster of tile-roofed stucco bungalows arranged around a courtyard in the center of which is a beat-up remnant of what forty years ago must have been a rather attractive replica of a Moorish tile fountain. The Hacienda Grande has obviously known better days as a hostelry. I'm sure that it only survives these days as a shack-up joint for San Jose businessmen. The courtyard lawn hadn't been cut in ages. As I passed down the row of cabins towards Number Five, I heard the sound of someone watching daytime television. There's nothing more depressing than a television set turned on at ten in the morning. It betokens a day already over before it has begun. Cabin Five stood at the edge of the motel lot. I stepped up on its scant porch and knocked.

"Is that you?" I heard from within.

"If it's me whom you mean, then yes, it's me," I said. "But if you mean someone else, then the answer is no, it isn't me."

"Don't be smart-alecky," Mrs. Carpino said, opening the door.

Now that Esmeralda has destroyed the Mayor politically on national television, and the Brown Bomber/Book Destroyer (one and the same, it turns out) has been apprehended, and now that Marshall Square has been saved for the Library, and the Zulu killers have been arrested—I should devote some time to thinking about my future.

Irony of ironies, that future could include librarianship, the state librarianship in Sacramento—or so California's probable next governor, Andy Soutane himself, hinted to me in the course of a swift and ambiguous interview at the Soulé fundraiser which Cole O'Halloran got me invited to as a reward for my being a nice boy and taking care of those bothersome photographs. I suppose that I should have felt guilty about showing up at the Soulé event, with the primary not yet over with, and myself a Carpino appointee; yet after Esmeralda's performance ended the Mayor's chances once and for all, an atmosphere of every-man-for-himself has seized staff members and vulnerable department heads such as myself. O'Halloran gave me the opening and I took it, positioning myself strategically in the Soulé drawing room so as to secure an introduction to Andy Soutane. All of this is rather sad, given my fantasies of breaking loose, renting a studio, and cutting it free-lance; but then again, why should I be forced to give up my profession just because Claudio Carpino is going down in smoke and flames? I spent a total of ten years of university education getting four degrees tacked after my name. I am a professional librarian. I can only exercise that profession in a library, so why should I be so quick to dismiss a decade's academic preparation just because I got my professional start under such disastrous circumstances? That, in any event, is how I justified to myself showing up at the Soulé *soirée* while my boss, Claudio Carpino, was still flying up and down the state trying to defeat Andy Soutane. Maybe I'm not doomed, after all, I said to myself. Maybe there's room in the new California for a provincial ethnic retread. Tiny Roncola, after all, has made the transition. Besides, having been with the losers, I wanted to see what the winners looked like. They're rich, for one thing. They live in beautiful houses such as that of Kay and Ray Soulé on Lyon Street, where people drink iced cocktails, as they did that evening, and eat small sandwiches with the crusts cut off.

669

"So glad you could come," Kay Soulé said to me automatically and with the faintest hint of a forced smile when I presented myself at the door. She wasn't putting me down. She just didn't know who I was, or rather, she sensed that I was probably someone not very important. From Kay's point of view, a lot of strange people were there that night. A butler asked me what I wanted to drink, and a maid in a black dress, trimmed in white lace, offered me a crustless sandwich. As honorary chairperson of the Andy Soutane for Governor finance committee, Kay Soulé has personally raised a quarter of a million dollars from social friends across the country. She has gotten Soutane national attention via *Women's Wear Daily*. One rather effective shot in *WWD* showed Soutane sitting between Kay Soulé and Princess Lee Radziwill at a benefit held in Beverly Hills to help the American Indian Film Foundation. The Indian actor Iron Eyes Cody is leaning over from behind, chatting with the Princess and Kay Soulé and Andy Soutane smile on appreciatively. Since that time, Soutane has become hot copy in *Women's Wear Daily, Town and Country*, and a number of syndicated gossip columns. Soutane's good looks, his bachelor status, and his successful drive towards the governorship of California make dynamite copy. Speculation about his love life abounds. Fashion model Tara Malone still holds the lead in the Andy Soutane sweepstakes. A recent AP photograph, for instance, showed the two of them eating ice-cream cones at the beach in Santa Monica; yet a certain tantalizing speculation is beginning to play about the figure of Kay Soulé as well—not in terms of an overtly romantic interest, since Kay Soulé is married and Andy Soutane keeps steady company with Tara Malone, but just as a sort of note of generalized association, bringing Andy Soutane more and more into the force field of Society and the Beautiful People. Donna Stinger, for instance, the social columnist for the *Express*, has had a Soutane–Soulé item nearly every other morning of late: the luncheon party for Soulé attended by, among others, Arthur Schlesinger, Jr., who called Soutane "a fun progressive in the Kennedy mold"; the time that Kay

Soulé left a dinner party she was giving for the Duchesse de Falzenfanz of Luxembourg just after cocktails, rushed down to the airport where her Lear jet was waiting, engines whining in expectation, flew to Madera to pick up Andy Soutane, delivered him to Fresno, then made it back to her home in time for after-dinner coffee.

The fact that the Soulé association hasn't hurt Soutane in the least, but has added to his attractiveness as a candidate, is testimony to two facts: (a) Andy Soutane's ability to have it both ways—to stand up for the Chicano field worker, for instance, just before flying off into the starry California night on the wings of the Soulé Lear jet; and (b) the fact that in America most of the liberal establishment is very rich, and getting richer. Only the also-rans, those incapable of running on a fast track, would dare point out the fact that as his popularity with the people of California grows, Andy Soutane is actually spending less and less time in the company of ordinary citizens. Stardom exempts even elected politicians from the necessities of the common touch.

So there he was now, in Kay Soulé's drawing room, receiving the obeisances of San Francisco's Democratic establishment, which knows a winner when it sees one. Tomorrow, Donna Stinger's social column in the *Express* would be filled with the names of those in attendance; and to the right of the column would perhaps be the photograph taken just after I finished my second bourbon and crustless sandwich: of Kay Soulé, her shock of red hair frizzed out in the new manner (or were her sorrel tresses merely responding to the electricity of political power?), smiling to the camera and holding with one arm her disconcerted husband. Willing to pay for these events as long as he didn't have to attend, Raymond Soulé seemed to want most desperately to be in his upstairs study with his manuscripts of Gregorian chant, or so his body-language said: his torso twisted in a totally different direction than that of his wife's and California's next governor's, his face resembling that of a badger drawn against his will into sunlight. Kay Soulé's other bare arm draped languidly through that of Andy Soutane

671

in just the slightest (and most tasteful) suggestion of possession: not sexual possession perhaps (although there has been talk), but definitely the possession of the kind that major money, combined with an assertive, attractive feminine presence, can exercise over an ambitious, virile (here the benefit of the doubt must be given to Andy Soutane) young candidate for the chief executiveship of the sixth largest (in terms of gross national product) commonwealth in the world. Flash! flash! flash! goes the *Express* camera. Scribble, scribble, scribble goes the grandmotherly Donna Stinger, gathering a harvest of names into her notebook.

These same omnipresent lights, the thuribles of our electronic civilization, had popped, popped, popped in indiscriminate appreciation two nights ago outside the Hall of Justice when the Zulu killers were brought in, all five of them: good-looking, clean-cut young men in business suits and only moderate Afros, not by any means the wild-eyed, pig-tailed bushmen sort you might expect. Two of them, the papers report, are college graduates. One made All City in track in 1966. All are employed, and only one has a prison record of any significance. Whatever else it is as an organization, the Exterminating Angels possesses the bland demeanor of the 1970s. Good grooming, as well as the capacity for random murder, must be a prerequisite for admission. However necessary Chief Norris's spot dragnets might have been, and however harmful they proved politically, they didn't do the trick. The Exterminating Angels were flushed out, in the long run, by information put together by the computer sciences: a license plate, seen and half-remembered by a witness, matching in its first three digits those of a license granted the solitary parolee in the group and those digits then brought into composite symmetry by the computer, along with a third factor—a onetime membership in the Black Brotherhood, a fact fed into the machine five years ago by Sacramento when a profile was done on the gentleman in question prior to his release on parole. Those three facts, brought into coincidence,

672

set lights flashing in the bureau of inspectors: a name! at last there was a name! Three weeks of footwork did the rest, tracing that name through two aliases and six changes of address, until the early morning raid on the basement apartment in Glen Park and—bingo!—just as the application for a search warrant said there might be, evidence of the cult: the *Book of Brotherhood*, an authentic human skull, a painting of the Black Angel of Death—together with two sleeping brothers and a .38 Magnum matching, it later turned out, the requisite ballistics of bullets retrieved from the bodies of the victims.

"Hang around," Cole O'Halloran said, "and I'll introduce you to the next governor."

"Cole," I said "we're both out of our element." Cole's beefy Irish face was redder than usual; but then again, his suit was better than usual as well—a single-breasted pinstripe set off by a white shirt, cuff links, a regimental tie held in place by a collar pin. The Cole O'Halloran I knew usually looked like he had just gotten back from the race track.

"Who's your tailor?" I asked.

"Robert Kirk," Cole said. "I'm getting my wardrobe ready for Sacramento."

"I thought that they wore polyester leisure suits in Sacramento," I said.

"Only the assemblymen," Cole snorted. "The governor's staff will be a little more tasteful—and conservative."

"Don't dress too snappily," I said, "or you'll lose your rapport with the Chicanos."

"Do you see any Chicanos in this room?" O'Halloran asked—rather brutally, I thought, but with a degree of cynicism appropriate to his impending translation to Sacramento.

"Only the maid," I said.

"You're right," O'Halloran said. "Soutane has already chatted with her in Spanish. I'm sure she'll vote for him, come June and November."

673

She sure as hell won't vote for Claudio Carpino, I thought to myself—not after the debacle of Esmeralda's return, in any event. All the way up from Mission San Jose, I had a feeling that it might not go right. I'd called Terry Shane at City Hall from the pay phone at the Hacienda Grande Motel.

"You won't believe this," I said when Shane answered.

"I don't already," he said.

"I'm with Esmeralda Carpino," I said.

"I don't believe you," Shane said.

"You'd better, Terry, because it's true. She called me this morning. I'm driving her up from Mission San Jose."

"What the hell is she doing there?" Shane asked.

"She's been on a tour of the state," I said.

"This conversation cannot be occurring," Shane said. "Is she all right?"

"She's in good physical shape, if that's what you mean."

"Why did she call you?" Shane asked.

"She said that I seemed a neutral party. I've just talked to her and I've got a message for the Mayor."

"The Mayor is home," Shane said. "He didn't come into work today. He's worried sick."

"Mrs. Carpino wants a press conference," I said. "We'll be in the city by noon and she's told me to tell the Mayor that she wants a press conference at their home, noon today."

"Jesus," Shane said. "If they were still fighting in Vietnam, I'd ask for my old job on the *Tribune* back. Noon, you say?"

"Noon," I said, hanging up.

"I've been going around the state by Greyhound bus," Mrs. Carpino told me as I loaded her suitcase behind the seat of my car. "Did you talk to my husband?"

"No, ma'am. I talked to Terry Shane. He'll relay your message to your husband immediately. It's ten-thirty. We'd better get going if we're to make the city by noon."

Esmeralda didn't have much to say on the trip up to San Francisco, but she made up for it at the press conference. Some half-dozen television crew vans were already parked outside the Carpino home as we drove up. Twenty or so cameramen and

674

reporters crowded in front of the Spanish-Moorish facade of the Sea Cliff mansion. Esmeralda got out of the car like a movie star coming down the gangplank of a Cunard liner arriving in New York sometime in the 1930s. She wrapped her fur coat around herself the way movie stars used to do, crossing one arm over another and swathing herself in the fur as she walked into her home, escorted by the popcorn flashing of camera bulbs and questions hollered at her from a half-dozen different directions.

"Mrs. Carpino, where have you been?"

"Mrs. Carpino, is there any truth to the rumor that you've been kidnapped?"

"Mrs. Carpino, have you had any contact with your husband?"

"Mrs. Carpino, will you be asking your husband for a divorce?"

Standing at the door, Terry Shane waited for Esmeralda to enter. When it closed behind him, he said: "Ladies and gentlemen, as soon as the Mayor and Mrs. Carpino have a moment alone, they will be happy to receive the press." Which is what they did some ten minutes later, the Mayor white-faced with fatigue, emotional exhaustion emanating from him in flat waves. Piling in, the press began the rapid, elaborate process of setting up its lights, cameras, microphones, tape recorders, whatever, as the Mayor and Mrs. Carpino sat hand in hand on a settee, awaiting their pleasure.

"Did she give you any hint of what she'll be saying?" Shane asked me *sotto voce.* "The L.A. *Times* and the *New York Times* are here, and two of the major networks."

"Not a word," I said. "She only insisted on the press conference."

"How'd she seem on the ride up?"

"Quiet—as if planning something."

"Thanks a lot, buddy," Shane said.

"We're ready, Mr. Mayor," said one of the network men.

"This is Mrs. Carpino's press conference," the Mayor said. "All I want to say is that my family and I are delighted to have

Mrs. Carpino safely home after her long absence." As if by cue, Barbara, Umberto, Rocky, and Sonny Grande Carpino came into the room. The press conference stopped while the Carpino children embraced Esmeralda and everyone started to chatter away in the Sicilian dialect. Barbara began crying; Umberto looked impassive; Sonny Grande seemed disgusted by the entire spectacle. I was reminded, for a moment, of a scene in a Lina Wertmuller comedy where everyone is talking in Italian and waving their arms in every which direction. The red lights of the TV cameras remained on for the entire performance.

"What you now see before you will be coast to coast this evening," Terry Shane muttered between his teeth.

"It's San Francisco's new version of 'I Remember Mama,'" I said.

"Maybe it will spawn a series," Shane said.

"Mrs. Carpino," asked the man from ABC when things had settled down a bit, "may I ask a simple question? Where have you been?"

Silence. The whir of cameras. The pop of a flash bulb or two. A look of triumph in Esmeralda Carpino's eyes. "I have been examining my life," she said. "I have been up and down the state, revisiting some of the historical sites I enjoyed when I was a girl."

"We've finally got our historical pageant," Terry Shane whispered. "That'll teach Barry Scorse to mess with the doubledomes. The pageant was an idea whose time had come. Esmeralda's on our side." Like myself, Terry Shane will be forced to hit the bricks in search of employment, come November; yet that fact did not blind him to the droll aspects of the entire situation. His attitude was infectious.

"You've finally got the campaign on prime time television," I said.

"Why, Mrs. Carpino, did you go on your trip without notifying your husband or your children?" asked Russ Cone of the *Examiner*.

"Because I was depressed and confused. Because I hate politics and I wish that my husband had never gotten involved

676

in them. Because I was feeling neglected, worthless, cast-off, and I wanted to reassert my self-esteem by disappearing, by dying symbolically, you understand, in an effort to see whether or not I was appreciated." As she spoke, she rubbed the Mayor's bald pate.

"We're either witnessing history—or a farce," Terry Shane said.

"A little of both," I said. "History is often farcical."

"Aside from the fact that I'm embarrassed as hell, I feel sad about it all," Shane said.

"I hear what my wife is saying," the Mayor volunteered, forcing the adrenalin to flow, forcing something resembling the old pep into his words. What a sense of humiliation he must be feeling, I thought to myself: to have worked so hard and come so far, only to be tripped up by the hidden guy wires of a domestic *commedia dell'arte*. "And I am certain that the people of California will understand our situation. I apologize for my neglect and I promise to make it up to Esmeralda."

"Just as I told the Mayor after you called this morning," Terry Shane muttered. "It's intrinsically tasteless, a no-win situation."

"Get out there and do something," I said.

"Ladies and gentlemen," Shane announced, striding in front of the Carpino family, "I'm sure that you'll understand if I say that in my opinion as press secretary, this interview should now end. I trust that you'll all understand." As Shane spoke, Esmeralda Carpino began to sob uncontrollably. Her daughter Barbara led her out of the room. The Mayor remained seated on the settee—like a man deciding whether or not he would ever recover from a just-delivered kick in the groin.

Which was a far cry from the way Andy Soutane sat on the plush Brazilian leather sofa that runs across one wall of the drawing room of the Soulé mansion on Lyon Street. Soutane sat alone, with an admiring semicircle standing before him, as if the occasion were a papal audience—an impression, by the way, heightened by the medieval icons collected by Ray Soulé that ran across the white wall behind the sofa. Some twenty

677

people stood before Soutane in a semicircle, pitching him slow balls which the next governor of California, to no one's surprise, hit out of the park, a home run every time.

"What about the environment?"

"We must protect it."

"What about taxes?"

"They must come down."

"What about the whales?"

"They must be saved."

"The redwoods?"

"A moratorium on lumbering."

"Abortions?"

"A matter of free choice."

"But the poor can't afford them."

"They can if we expand our program of neighborhood health clinics."

"The arts?"

"More support of neighborhood cultural centers."

"Pollution?"

"More authority for smog control districts."

"The courts?"

"More minorities in our judicial system."

"The corporations?"

"New antitrust legislation."

"Women?"

"We need more women in government. I shall appoint a woman to the state supreme court."

The philosopher king, I thought to myself, come at last! The philosopher king for an age of slogans and clichés. Yet nothing, so they say, succeeds like success; and as far as California was concerned, not to mention the gang gathered for cocktails at the house of Kay and Ray Soulé, Andy Soutane was succeeding. Each of his solutions to the problems of the day was received with respectful silence, as if Moses had just come down from Mount Sinai bearing the law on tablets of stone.

"Capital punishment?"

678

"Abolish it."

"The state university?"

"More emphasis on teaching, less on useless research."

"Prisons?"

"They either punish, segregate, or rehabilitate, but not all three at once. The prison system needs clarification."

"Highways?"

"California has too many of them."

The problem for one such as myself, trying hard to be pugnacious, is that Andy Soutane's aphorisms often make a lot of sense. Universities should teach better, and the prison system should be clarified, and we do have too many highways, and why in God's name should such a glorious creature as the whale—possessed of a noetic system equal to our own, a creature symbolic since time immemorial of the lavish generosity of the Almighty in filling the air and sea and land with an infinity of living beings expressive of His exquisite playfulness—be slaughtered for the sake of the Japanese fast-food industry? I sometimes get tired of constantly having to fend off Andy Soutane from my consciousness. He's a phony, of course; all politicians are, but his phoniness does not obscure a certain timeliness—a Californian timeliness—to his message. That's it: I'm tired of feeling the necessity of having to fend off the best possibilities of California.

"Andy Soutane threatens you," is the way Deborah (rather cruelly) put it to me recently after I had bored her overlong by pointing out some of the elements of contradiction and cliché in so many of Soutane's campaign pronouncements.

"Threatens me?" I bristled. "How?" I knew exactly what she meant.

"He symbolizes so much of what you passed up, or never even had a chance at."

"Like what?" I was really asking for it.

"Like feeling free in the Sierra, like playing a good game of tennis, like being at one with your body, like feeling yourself at the outer edge of a new experiment, a new way of perceiving

679

reality and living well—which is what California, in the long run, is all about. You're all inner-city ethnic San Franciscan, and that just isn't California, or at least the one I'm interested in. I like sports and health and the outdoors."

"So you're voting for Andy Soutane?"

"So Andy Soutane likes these things as well, and that involves a political philosophy in addition to everything else: a way of dreaming about a better America and a better world."

I felt jealous. I had the perhaps justified suspicion that had Andy Soutane walked in the room at that moment, all geared up for a Sierra Club expedition into the high country, and fixed his Robert Redford-like gaze on Deborah Tanner, it would be *sayonara* to one James Vincent Norton, M.L.S., Ph.D., sedentary master of useless information. I had a vision of myself climbing desperately up a Sierra glacier, sweat ruining my three-piece suit, while out ahead Deborah Tanner and Andy Soutane moved rapidly across a ridge, silhouetted against an eagle-crowded sky.

There he was, then, the avatar of an impending California, moving graciously now among the guests after his impromptu question-and-answer session. I must admit the truth of much of what Deborah has said about my being threatened by Andy Soutane: a threat doubly compounded, no doubt, by the fact that Soutane—now so quintessentially *au courant* with all the best of the modern Californian sensibility—began his career in an environment so similar to my own. He spent six years in the Franciscans for God's sake!—wearing a brown robe and sandals with no stockings, getting up early in the morning to sing Gregorian chants before the altar at Mission Santa Barbara. Yet he's made the transition to modernity which has so far eluded me. Andy Soutane has found and embraced the new California: has become its guru-in-chief, moreover, he whose erstwhile condition as a Franciscan friar redounds, not to his shame, but to his credit. I mean, for the media it sometimes seems as if St. Francis of Assisi himself were walking on the beach with Tara Malone, eating ice-cream cones, or talking to Iron Eyes Cody in the pages of *Women's Wear Daily*, or nibbling ascetically one of Kay Soulé's crustless sandwiches and drinking Calistoga water with a squeeze of lime. The guy can't lose.

I encountered Harry Shaw. "Have you decided that you'd rather switch than fight?" he asked. I felt crummy for being there, which was no doubt Shaw's intention.

"I'm here in the interests of history," I said weakly.

"Your own?" Shaw quipped.

"No—California's."

"Since when," asked Shaw, "does politics make history?" If Harry Shaw knew what he was talking about, I thought to myself, he had just ventured a rather significant statement. Politics, I have always believed, is the frothy foam of history. At any one moment, something much more important is going on, some subterranean drama of idea and symbol that shapes and determines external event; but that couldn't be what Harry Shaw, gossip columnist, had in mind—could it?

"Does gossip make history?" I asked, risking the great pooh-bah of San Francisco's displeasure.

"Gossip makes me a living," Shaw said. "What makes history is the province of more weightier minds—such as you pretend to have. Now speaking of gossip, what are you doing here?"

"Observing," I said.

"Not choosing?" Shaw asked.

"I have already chosen," I said. "I've chosen not to get involved."

"Then why come here?" Shaw asked—very much to the point, I might add.

"I was invited," I said.

"Do you mind if I give you some advice?" Harry Shaw asked.

"I'd be flattered."

"What I have to say isn't flattering."

"You'll most likely say it anyway."

"Come over here and sit down for a moment," Harry Shaw said. He guided me into a quieter room, a spacious library, in

681

fact, flanked with high shelves of leather-bound books. He seemed eager to talk, which I found somewhat flattering; but then again, I'm easily flattered. As we talked, cocktail party chatter ebbed and flowed in the room, like waves of surf breaking on a nearby shore. As I've mentioned before, Harry Shaw—to paraphrase Alice Roosevelt on Thomas Dewey—comes dangerously close to resembling the man atop the wedding cake. I have also compared him to Ben Turpin, or to a runtier version of Clark Gable, especially the mustache and the hair, which must have been the look in the 1930s when Harry Shaw was spending a lot of time in the movie houses of Santa Rosa and on the lookout for a style.

"I've been watching you, Norton," Harry Shaw said. "I like some of what I see; and I see other things that I don't like."

"Join the club," I said.

"Don't be a wise guy," Shaw said.

"I was trying to be clever."

"You're not the clever type, Norton. You're too—too sincere, if you know what I mean." I knew what he meant; he meant that I was too dumb, too ethnic, to ever be clever.

"I'll take that as a compliment," I said.

"It wasn't meant as a compliment. It was meant as a warning. Now where were we?"

"You were watching me."

"Right, and liking certain things."

"And not liking others."

"Right. It's like Sally Stanford, or was it Tessie Wall, once said to me. 'Harry,' she said, 'I try to manage my girls like they was librarians and this was a library.' You know what Sally meant?"

"I think so," I said.

"Exactly," said Harry Shaw. "You've been doing an OK job at the Library. Like at the Marshall Square hearing the other day. Now people at least know that the Library exists."

"It was a Pyrrhic victory," I said. "All we got was a plot of ground—with no future prospects."

"One thing at a time," cautioned Harry Shaw. "You at least

682

alerted people to the problem—that's a start. Now for what I don't like."

"Can't we just let it go at what you like?" I cracked.

"No—because what I don't like is your boss, Claudio Carpino, and what he's done to this town."

"Politicians and politics are epiphenomenal," I said. "San Francisco is changing because our culture is changing. Carpino is just riding the crest of the wave. That's what most politicians do."

"Then he's one hell of a surfboarder," Harry Shaw said. "This used to be a jewel of a city. People felt good about being here, including myself. Every highrise building that goes up in this town is a nail driven into the coffin of a once charming city. I ought to know. I go way back, forty years back; and it used to be one hell of a town—a fun place, you know what I mean?"

I knew what he meant, and I agreed with him.

"You're sort of a whore, Norton. Don't be offended. I'm an old hooker from way back, but I know just exactly to whom and for what I peddle my ass; whereas you, if you don't mind my saying so—"

"I don't mind your saying so," I said.

"Whereas you are so anxious to connect that you peddle your ass indiscriminately. You peddled it to Carpino, for instance, and that could ruin you in this town."

"Provided the town remembers," I said.

"It'll remember," said Harry Shaw. "Carpino will walk away from this town, come next January. He'll walk away and leave you and everyone else hanging."

"I can take care of myself," I said.

"Good—because you'll have to," Harry Shaw said.

"Why are you so obsessed with Carpino?" I asked.

"Because he's good copy," Shaw said. "When you're in the paper six mornings a week, you need a cast of characters. Carpino makes a good bad guy. Our rivalry is something we both play out to our mutual advantage. We're basically two of a kind, growing old together, you might say."

683

"I guess I've taken the whole thing too seriously," I said.

"You take a lot of things too seriously," Harry Shaw said. "Like San Francisco, for instance. I found your book on San Francisco a little lugubrious, lacking, shall we say, the light touch. You've got to roll with the punches, kid, and never lose the light touch."

"Yet you think that Carpino has helped ruin the town," I ventured.

"I regret the loss of my youth, kid, and now the loss of my middle age. I miss the great times I used to have."

"So you blame the Mayor."

"Right, kid. I make him the symbol of everything that's going wrong. That way I personalize my anxiety—and produce some crackling copy. You see, kid, in the newspaper business you're only as good as today. Yesterday doesn't count. I've had to mix it up around this town for forty years, just to survive. Hell, it's damn tough for a man of my age to be forced to be on the town five nights a week and be bounding all over the right tennis courts on weekends. At my age, I'd like to stay home; but I can't. Go slack for a moment and you're dead—even me, after forty years, no momentum. Six weeks out of the paper and I'd be as forgotten as Jerome Hart or Charlie Caldwell Dobie."

Or Sebastian Collins, I said to myself. This, incidentally, was the nicest side of Harry Shaw I'd ever experienced; and I told him so.

"I'm getting soft," he said, "or I'm just being nice because I'll be zinging you in the next few days for being here." Which he did, the day after the party, saying: "The rats are swimming away from the sinking Carpino ship. City librarian James Vincent Norton, for instance, a mayoral appointee, was very much in evidence the other night at the Soulé *soirée* for Andy Soutane. Soutane, you might remember, will soon be demolishing San Francisco's One and Only at the polls."

"Jesus," Terry Shane said apropos of the item, "I knew it was every man for himself—but don't be so goddam blatant about it."

684

"I went as an observer," I said.

"What did you see?"

"The winners in the odious little game we're playing."

"Did you meet Soutane?"

"Just for a second."

"It happened just after Harry Shaw and I broke off our little *tête à tête*. Kay Soulé came in and insisted that Harry circulate more, he being such a high prestige guest and all. I finished my drink in the library, left there by Kay Soulé and Shaw and thinking to myself that I was getting exhausted by the fatigues of compromised living.

When I re-entered the living room, Andy Soutane— surrounded by that entourage that so many American politicians seem to find so necessary—was in the foyer, getting ready to depart. The Reverend Jimmie Jones of the People's Temple was holding Soutane by the arm and saying something very discreet into his ear: promising his support, no doubt, which counts for a lot in the Bay Area, since the People's Temple membership are known to be great precinct walkers and doorbell ringers when the church gets behind a politician.

"We're with you one hundred percent, Andy," I heard the Reverend Jones say as I walked by.

Cole O'Halloran grabbed my arm as I was opening the door.

"Senator," he said, "meet the Librarian of San Francisco, Dr. James Norton. He's been of some help to us, you'll remember."

"Indeed he has," said Andy Soutane, turning from the Reverend Jimmie Jones and extending his hand. I shook it, feeling a little like Vidkun Quisling; but how can a guy snub Robert Redford, especially when it's his party?

"It was nothing," I said.

"It could have been everything," Soutane said matter-of-factly. "I'll not forget it. California could use a dynamic state librarian." Since we were both leaving, I walked out with him, feeling, uneasily, that I had attached myself to his entourage. At six-three, Andy Soutane towered over the Reverend Jimmie Jones.

685

The Brown Bomber/Book Destroyer got nabbed the very day the Marshall Square issue was heard by the board of supervisors. All of this made for a very busy day. Manny Vogel, Tony Ortega, and Ted Bemos were waiting for me at my office when I got in that morning.

"The commission secretary, the chief of Main, and the head engineer," I said. "It looks like a *coup d'état* is about to happen. Shall I consider myself under arrest?"

"No, boss," said Ted Bemos (Ted calls everyone in authority "boss," then proceeds to do what he damn well pleases), "but you might consider having the Brown Bomber thrown in the slammer."

"I will if we ever catch him," I said.

"We've got him," said Tony Ortega. "Caught him in the act, and his locker is filled with ripped books as well."

"Who is it?" I asked. They told me.

"*Quis custodiet ipsos custodes?*" I said.

"That sounds classy, boss," Ted Bemos said. "What does it mean?"

"Who shall guard the guardians?" I said.

I went before the board of supervisors that afternoon, rather disturbed by my late morning interview with the Brown Bomber/Book Destroyer, whom Ted Bemos, arriving at work an hour-and-a-half early so as to check a faulty steam line in Third East (Ted being afraid that a burst valve might steam our modern biography section into soggy unusability), found in the squatting position, about to make another protest (so he later told me) against the derivative condition of contemporary culture.

"Ladies and gentlemen, who gets Marshall Square is not the issue. The issue before this board is whether or not San Francisco can continue to neglect its library system so shamefully." I orated thusly before the board, having decided to go for broke in the matter of Marshall Square: having decided, that is, to represent the Library to the best of my abilities—knowing all the while, of course, that it was all completely hopeless, that the hopes, say, which James Phelan and Sebastian Collins had for the Library when they were both serving as founding trustees had long since been abandoned by an indifferent San Francisco. The elite of San Francisco lacked an appetite for distinction in its public institutions, or at least its library; and that was that. Deep down, I still believe that we should have cut a deal: Marshall Square in exchange for downtown's backing for a bond issue to refurbish the Main Library, to include a $100,000 grant from the PAC people to the library commission to finance a bond issue campaign. But Mabel Storm submarined that idea. She insists that someday the voters of San Francisco will give us a glorious new $90 million library, rising from Marshall Square like the Alhambra, all shimmering in the sunlight. They never will, of course; but since I'm collecting the librarian's fat salary, I'll go along with Mabel's delusion, because it seems to be the entire Library's delusion as well. Such a course of action, while prudent, is not the most abstractly honorable course—but since when has that bothered me? Had I been born rich, I might have been able to behave more honorably.

"I'm sick. I acknowledge it. I should see a shrink. But I was driven nutty in a good cause." This—from the Brown Bomber/Book Destroyer to me in confidence at my office between eleven and twelve o'clock during the course of our interview. I shan't give his name because I don't think that it would be fair. When told the details of the case, Judge Dillon of the superior court, before whom the security officer was arraigned for the willful destruction of an estimated twenty-five thousand dollars of city property, eased the case immediately into psychiatric channels. The former guard (and even more former graduate student) voluntarily committed himself for treatment, and criminal charges were dropped. There the matter rests: I think it better not to give the name because he may some day be able to return to Berkeley as he said he hoped to do and complete work for the degree.

"Then the note you left in my office about this being a political protest was a blind?"

"Yes. I wanted to throw you off the track. If I had written:

687

'I am doing this to protest the mandarin arrogance of contemporary academic literary scholarship,' you would have thought that I was some kind of crazy—I mean, you might have suspected at once that it was me."

Making no protest, showing, indeed, every sign of calm, he had agreed to wait for the police in my office. Age, his rap-sheet would soon say, 26; height, 5 feet, 11 inches; weight, 135 pounds; race, Caucasian; hair, brown; eyes, blue; occupation, security guard; charge, wanton destruction of public property (books to estimated value $25,000).

"I might have suspected you," I said. "Mr. Vogel has had to discipline you twice for reading books when you were supposed to be on duty patrolling the stacks. We suspected that it was an inside job—the befouling, I mean, not the destruction of the books; that comes as a surprise—so we might have suspected you, were we to suspect that the defecations were literary in intent."

Laughing, he lit up a Pall Mall cigarette, sucking the smoke in greedily. I noticed that the fingers of his right hand were heavily stained with nicotine.

"The Library has been accused of being obstructionist in this matter," I said to the supervisors when it came my turn that afternoon to speak. "And perhaps we are grandstanding just a little bit in order to call some attention to ourselves. The board, however, has noted that some thirty-six thousand signatures of registered voters have been gathered in our support."

"Are you trying to intimidate this board, Dr. Norton?" asked Supervisor Dante Foscolo, fixing me with his killer eyes.

"No, sir," I said, "but I am asking this board to do the logical thing—and that is to assign the unused Commerce High School playing field to the Performing Arts Center, as the library commission has suggested."

"For three years, I read in the Cal library," the Brown Bomber told me, "looking for a thesis topic."

"You don't have to talk to me about any of this," I said. "In fact, since you might be facing criminal charges, it's best that you not talk."

688

"I'm pleading insanity," the Brown Bomber said, "so I won't be going to jail. I'm obviously sick, right?"

"Yes," I said. "I think that you're a troubled person."

"So I'll tell you about it, OK, while we're waiting for the cops. Everybody's been pretty nice to me around here since I came to work, and I feel ashamed of what happened—although I couldn't help myself."

"The defecation was one thing," I said, "destroying all those books was another."

"They almost destroyed me, you see. Libraries, in fact, and the Alexandrian learning associated with libraries almost destroyed me, drove me mad anyway."

"Alexandrian?" I asked.

"Like in ancient Alexandria," he said, "where the Ptolemies built two libraries, containing more than 700,000 scrolls, representing the accumulated wisdom of the ancient world. Great corps of scholars, including Callimachus, the lyric poet who was appointed chief curator around 265 B.C., worked there, sorting, codifying, commenting upon the literature of the past."

"You ought to have become a librarian," I said. He sucked the last centimeter from his Pall Mall.

"I spent a lot of time at the library school in Berkeley," he said. "I audited lectures in the field of library history, just to see if I could discover just when the monkey of derivative learning got upon our culture's back. I eventually decided that it first went wrong with Alexandria. Building the library there meant that creative people had decided that what they were able to do wasn't as good as what had been done in the past. The best response to life, they decided, was to surrender the opportunity for direct living and to comment upon the memorialized experience of those who had gone before them."

I had a sense of unreality throughout the entire conversation. His sentences seemed so—so precise, so rehearsed, academic even. In thinking about the Brown Bomber/Book Destroyer this past year—thinking about catching them, I mean, for I then thought they were two people—I imagined that we'd apprehend some sort of seedy madman, visibly crazy.

The Bomber/Destroyer whom we did catch showed signs of nervousness, to be sure. He's excessively thin; he chain smokes; his hands tremble slightly as he lights one cigarette from the butt end of another; but none of this, in and of itself, betokens a major level of disturbance.

"The public library," I said to the supervisors at the conclusion of my ten-minute plea, "represents a peculiarly American hope: namely, that the riches of the past, the incredible diversity of human culture, might be available to whomsoever is interested, regardless of socioeconomic condition or educational background. The public library is the people's free university, an agency of self-help, self-reliance, and nourishment of mind, imagination, and spirit. That is why we have every hope as we appear before you today that you will not cut off, most abruptly and unfairly, the Library's chances for improvement—to include an eventual expansion into Marshall Square."

"I first started to tear books when I was a graduate student at Berkeley," the Bomber/Destroyer told me, "only it wasn't on the scale of my operation here. I made just a few hits—mainly in the area of myth criticism, although I hit some of the New Critics as well. Towards the end, just before I withdrew from Cal after flunking my orals, I went after some of the literary historians."

"You flunked?" I asked.

"Twice," he answered. "I was in no shape, you see, to get ready. I had this obsession, and when I gave in to it, I loathed myself and was in no shape to study."

"Did you seek any help?" I asked.

"I thought about it, but after I withdrew I wasn't entitled to the use of the university health services, so I just came over here and got a CETA job as a library guard." He lit his third or fourth Pall Mall. I lost track. "I was like a pederast getting a job at a boys' school. I'd patrol the shelves on my daily rounds, passing row after row of books. They drove me crazy, especially the works of critical commentary. You'll notice that I never destroyed a primary source—no critical editions of

690

classics, no anthologies, no original novels or poems. I only went after the stuff that smelled of the lamp, the stuff that made literature seem a kind of gnostic conspiracy, the cabalistic stuff with a lot of abstruse terms and footnotes in fine print."

"The library," I told the board of supervisors, "is civilization's agency of memory. The library orders the creativity of the past, keeping it accessible to present generations. Without libraries, the best of what was thought or said or done in the time before us would be lost irretrievably, or worse, crash on the shores of our consciousness, an unintelligible, cacophonous roar."

"I became obsessed," he told me just before the inspector from the General Works detail arrived at the office to bring him down to the Hall of Justice for a preliminary booking. "I couldn't rid my mind of the notion that libraries were a form of conspiracy. They intimidated us, preventing us from living life at first hand."

"That's crazy," I said.

"The more good literature I read," he said, "the more I became convinced that the people at Berkeley, the people who lived in libraries, were out to kill my mind. For six years, I lived under their domination, scared shitless, forced to wander down this or that labyrinth of murderous pedantry."

"You should have become a park ranger," I said. "You came here, and it cost us a collection."

He slumped down into his chair as if I had hit him with a stunning blow to the solar plexus.

"Then the other thing began," he said softly. "I used to rip up a lot of the books while hiding out on the john, which is what first got me going in that direction, I guess. I convinced myself that I was engaged in an act of existential protest."

After the hearing, Mabel Storm rushed up to me as I was walking down the main staircase of City Hall. "James, you did brilliantly," she said. "I'm so proud of you. The entire commission is proud of you. Imagine! An eight to eleven vote in our favor! It was all so crucial!"

691

Just before a rather bored-looking inspector from General Works came into my office to lay claim to my reluctant interlocutor, I said to him: "I prefer not to talk about this any more. You might be crazy, although you don't sound crazy, just obsessed. Get your head straightened out, if you can. I wish that I could say no hard feelings but I can't, not just yet. You've cost us over twenty thousand dollars and something that can't be duplicated even if we had the money."

"I hope you understand that it wasn't personal," he said. "Everyone here has been so nice. I've just got this thing against derivative literary commentary."

"I won't need the cuffs now, will I, young man?" the Inspector asked.

"No, you won't," he said, lighting the final cigarette from his pack, then crumbling it into a by now teeming ashtray. "I'm not a violent criminal, Inspector. I'm merely the victim of an *idée fixe*."

"Why, you're not at all as fat as Deborah led me to believe," Mrs. Spencer Tanner (Cynthia) remarked as I sat down to drinks at the Top of the Mark with the reunited Tanner family. Cynthia Tanner suggests what Deborah herself might be some thirty years hence. She is attractive in the way that an upper-middle-class lady golfer can be attractive, if you know what I mean: slightly muscular and with a thirty-year tan that gives just a little too much texture to her skin; hair—an unretouched salt and pepper gray—cut short so that an outdoor Arizona life of golf, tennis, swimming, can be led with a minimum of fuss. Mrs. Tanner had dressed for the occasion—drinks at the Mark, followed by dinner at Tadich's Grill (if we could get in)—in something evocative of Neiman Marcus, but Southwestern also in its daring use of color. Like Deborah, she seems to have a fondness for Navajo jewelry.

"He's not very athletic, Mother," Deborah said, "but he voted for Barry Goldwater."

Somewhere in his late fifties, Spencer Tanner, M.D., is played by Gregory Peck. As I shook his hand, the thought

692

crossed my mind: will I look that good in twenty years? The answer is no.

"Barry Goldwater is a personal friend of mine," Dr. Tanner said as we shook hands. "Always glad to meet a supporter of his." His grip was ironlike: deliberately so, I realized as soon as I had extracted myself. My hand ached momentarily with a slight but discernible hint of pain at that point where two of my knuckles had been pressed together at an off angle. Deborah's father wore a double-breasted blue blazer, gray flannel slacks, and black loafers. His maroon necktie, set off by a gleaming white shirt, was decorated in innumerable American eagles, the kind that a naval officer wears on his dress cap. Deborah wore a two-piece suit of midnight blue crushed velvet, set off by a cream-colored, high-necked blouse, the cuffs of which extended themselves from beneath the sleeves of the suit jacket and were turned smartly back, as if in readiness for a few smashes with a tennis racket, were a court available at the Top of the Mark. The three of them looked as if they had just stepped off the pages of a *Town and Country* spread on the good life in Phoenix, Arizona. I felt sort of rumpled and ethnic as I drank my rum martini, straight up with a lemon twist. Dr. Tanner drank Jack Daniel's Black Label. Deborah and her mother drank Campari and soda. Enjoying a drink at sundown at the Top of the Mark reminds me what it must have been like to have crossed the Atlantic by zeppelin in their brief heyday in the thirties. Sitting before the Mark's great windows, you seem to float silently over San Francisco as you watch the evening fog come in through the Golden Gate in great rolling billows, then spread itself, fingerlike, in five different directions across the city.

"I came here once or twice during the war," Dr. Tanner said. "It was one busy place, filled with officers from every branch of the services, many of them *en route* to the Pacific."

"Were you passing through?" I asked, doing my bit to keep the conversation going.

"Yes, the first time—transferred from Brisbane, Australia, to Phoenix, Arizona, if you can believe it. They needed

693

someone at the hospital in Phoenix with experience in tropical diseases."

"That's where we met," Mrs. Tanner said.

I knew all this, but I kept as lively a look of interest on my face as I possibly could. Deborah, after all, had been extraordinarily kind to my mother when we visited her in her tiny studio apartment on Guerrero Street.

"I doubt that you'll understand her," I said as we climbed the stairs to the third floor of an old Victorian mansion, subdivided sometime in the 1920s into a dozen or so one- or two-room apartments. "She's very unusual—'eccentric' would be understating it. Life has run over her like a runaway Mack truck. In her own way, however, she has managed to survive. I first remember her when she was just a few years older than you are now, twenty-seven or twenty-eight; yet as I look back on it now, life was already over for her, even then." I rang the buzzer.

"Hi, doll," Mother said, opening the door. I felt a momentary surge of primal panic, as I always do when I'm around her, as if I were a child again, and hence liable to her mercurial shifts of mood from ungrounded optimism to deeply bitter resentment against whatever it was that had left her, first, a divorcee with a child to raise and, shortly thereafter, a divorced widow deprived of alimony payments.

We entered a room overflowing with memorabilia and bric-a-brac. Mother not only saves everything; she insists upon displaying it. Her crowded apartment is, in effect, a museum of her life—through the Second World War at least. She has clustered a series of framed school pictures into a sort of star-shaped wall display. At the center of the cluster is a photograph of her at about age eight, sitting in a little goat cart, drawn by a real live goat. Mother is wearing a middy blouse and the most enormous floppy bow in her hair and high-buttoned shoes of the sort that lasted into the 1920s. Surrounding this are a photograph of the 1929 eighth-grade class of the Star of the Sea grammar school; an individual photograph of Mother receiving her grammar school diploma

694

from a priest attired in monsignor's robes; a senior prom photograph with the tag "Fairmont Hotel 1934" running across the bottom, showing Mother in a long dress standing next to a gangly young man in a dark suit (Izzy O'Neil, killed on Guadalcanal); and the class portrait of the entire senior class, 1934, standing in front of the Star of the Sea Academy, some fifty girls in all (Mother is second row, center), all in dark blue dresses with white oversized starched collars.

"I went to Star of the Sea," Mother said to Deborah when Deborah looked at the picture. "Where did you go?"

"I grew up in Phoenix," Deborah said.

"Did you have fun in high school?" Mother asked.

"Yes—now that I think of it," Deborah said.

"I've still got all my yearbooks," Mother said.

Another cluster of photographs depicts me at various stages of my spasmodic career. All of them, come to think of it, depict me graduating from one level of school to another, including the final photograph of myself in the crimson robes of Harvard. Mother insisted that I have it taken.

"James has gone to school, wouldn't you say?" Mother remarked when Deborah perused this particular cluster. "I've got a lot of photographs of him in my album, if you'd like to see them."

"I'd love to," Deborah said. I was on edge—yet touched also by her kindness. We spent an uneasy (for me) half hour with various albums of photographs. The spread of the hand-held Kodak camera has allowed the American family the illusion of historicity. Even the most fragmented, scattered, and unhappy of us has a battered family album or two in a drawer or up in an attic, filled with photographs of ancestors standing in antiquated swimgear in front of a Model T Ford at the beach or in a back yard on Sunday (you know it's Sunday because the men are in their suits): all of it in grainy black-and-white or sepia tone, suggesting some continuity in our background, some indisputable proof that it was indeed a specific sexual act between two long-gone great-grandparents that kept the flow of plasm coming down through the centuries so that at last, in one specific womb, as the result of another specific sexual act, it might at last become us, the biological heir to the ages.

"That's my grandfather on top of his cab in front of the Palace Hotel," Mother said. "His name was James Vincent Norton, just the same as Jimmy's name. He died in 1910, seven years before I was born. That's his son, my father, in his fireman's uniform. This was taken around 1920, when I was two. Daddy was killed in a fire in 1925. Would you like a beer?" She went to the refrigerator and fetched three half-quarts of Colt 45, which we drank out of the can.

"The cans keep the beer cold," Mother said as she cracked them open. "And you don't have to wash any glasses." Deborah turned over a photograph of a much younger Mother in a one-piece bathing suit.

"That was taken up at Hoberg's Resort in Lake County in the late thirties," Mother said. "I went to Hoberg's nearly every summer when I was first working—before I got married. That's one of my boyfriends, Izzy O'Neil. His real name was Isadore, but we all called him Izzy. Izzy went to Sacred Heart High and was nuts about me. This shows us at a table at the Palace Hotel, 1938 or so. Izzy loved to dance. His father owned a drugstore, so he studied pharmacy up at UC, but he was killed in the war. Would you two like another beer? It's no trouble."

"One is enough for me at ten-thirty in the morning," Deborah said.

"I'll have another one if you don't mind," Mother said. "I like to watch 'Days of Our Lives' at eleven. It's my favorite show."

We said goodbye just before "Days of Our Lives" came on. "You're a doll," Mother told Deborah as we left. "Come back some time and we'll go through the rest of my collection. We never even got to the yearbooks."

"I didn't see any pictures of your father," Deborah remarked as we drove past Mission Dolores.

"He died a long time ago," I said.

696

Miracle of miracles, the Tanners and I made it into a booth at Tadich's after only a half-hour wait at the bar.

"What's good?" Dr. Tanner asked.

"Grilled salmon steaks," I said. Everyone perused the menu a little longer but said nothing else, so I surmised that their silence implied consent.

"Four seafood cocktails and four grilled salmon steaks," Dr. Tanner told the waiter when he came. "And a bottle of Wente Brothers *Blanc de Blanc*—and another round of drinks while we're waiting." I noticed that Dr. Tanner's patriarchal authority, expressed through the ordering, now included me as well. I took it as a good sign.

"Why is this place so popular?" Mrs. Tanner asked.

"Because the food is good," I said, "and because it has the ambiance of pre-earthquake San Francisco without straining for it. The Hoffman Grill on Market Street is the same sort of a place."

"Isn't being a librarian an odd job for a man?" Cynthia Tanner asked.

"Casanova was a librarian for the last fifteen years of his life—if that's what you mean," I said.

"And so was Pope Pius XI," Deborah said.

"And Colonel John Shaw Billings of the Army Medical Corps," I added pointedly. "He created the National Library of Medicine."

"Still," Mrs. Tanner persisted, "it's not a very aggressive profession, is it?"

"Not in comparison to being a Green Beret," I said, "but it does have its little skirmishes."

"This town seems to have gone crazy," Dr. Tanner said. "First all those killings; then the mayor's wife disappears; then she reappears. Crazy isn't it?"

"I went to Mills College just before the war," Mrs. Tanner said. "The Bay Area in those days was such a dreamy place. As soon as the Bay Bridge was finished, we'd come over to the city on the Key System streetcars. We'd go back after midnight with no worry about safety."

697

"You're ten years older than Deborah, aren't you?" Dr. Tanner remarked over the seafood cocktail.

"Nine years, nine months," I said.

"Pay more attention to your health," Dr. Tanner said. "Our whole family is a bunch of health nuts."

"So I've noticed," I said.

"Swimming, golf, tennis, the whole lot," Dr. Tanner continued. "That's why we like Arizona—plenty of room, good weather, and a wholesome atmosphere."

"But Deborah came to the Bay Area," I said, ill-advisedly it turned out. A look of disappointment crossed both their faces.

"We have our hopes that this is a temporary condition," Cynthia Tanner said. "Deborah understands our position on this."

"I do, Mother, I do," Deborah said.

"We suppose that she's just sowing her wild oats," Spencer Tanner, M.D., said. "Everybody has got to do it at one time or another. Have you sown yours, James?"

"Maybe he's in the process of sowing them," Cynthia Tanner said. I felt I was being warned.

"I guess we're sort of old-fashioned," Dr. Tanner said. "We're old-fashioned people from Barry Goldwater Country."

"You don't look old-fashioned," I ventured. "You look rather sophisticated, in fact."

"Arizona isn't the end of the world," Cynthia Tanner said.

"What we mean by old-fashioned," Dr. Tanner continued, "is that we wouldn't want our daughter to make a mess of her life."

"She's doing fine," I said, meeting his basilisk-like stare (Gregory Peck in *Duel in the Sun*) as steadily as I could. I could have made a more formidable response, I suppose, had I not been chewing a mouthful of salmon at the time.

"So far so good," Dr. Tanner said. "I think we understand each other. Don't eat so fast, by the way, it's bad for you."

Chapter 16

MARINA, myself, and her beau John Charles Scannell visited the Tivoli Opera House last night to enjoy the annual concert of the Bohemian Club Orchestra. Midway through the performance, motion pictures of this year's Grove Play, *Nec-Natama* (an Indian word meaning "comradeship"), were shown on a canvas screen suspended above the orchestra.

While images of J. Wilson Shield's pageant flickered across the screen, the orchestra played selections from Uda Waldrop's Massenet-like score. The plot of *Nec-Natama* centers around an ancient Indian tribe living in a redwood forest much like our own Bohemian Grove. The chief of the tribe is torn between his attraction to two medicine women, the Hate Woman and the Love Woman. Under the spell of the Hate Woman, the Indian leader becomes the Great Hate Chief: brutal and war-like—but also profoundly troubled in spirit. Falling in love with the Maiden of the Gentle People, the Hate Chief decides to submit himself to the instructions of the Love Woman. At the conclusion of the play, the Love Woman, bathed in a pool of radiant light, descends the trail that winds down the high hillside rising behind the Grove stage. The Great Chief and the Maiden of the Gentle People wait side by side on the lower stage as the Love Woman slowly proceeds downward towards them, her hand raised in the benediction of a demigoddess. A chorus of some two hundred Indians and

Spirits of the Forest sing a triumphant welcome. As the Love Woman descends the hillside, the pool of light that surrounds her grows larger and larger in diameter, dispelling the nocturnal gloom. By the time she reaches the two lovers, the entire hillside is ablaze in light. The orchestra and chorus soar triumphantly.

Our Grove Plays are indeed a new California art form: part opera, part outdoor pageant, part liturgy. Written along bold, allegorical lines, involving the triumph of good over evil, the Grove Plays are staged in a great natural amphitheater that rises into a steep hillside surmounted by towering redwoods. Hundreds of Bohemians involve themselves as actors, singers, musicians, stage technicians. The play is performed for one evening only during the midsummer encampment; then partially reprised for the public of San Francisco. After the last swells of Waldrop's music died down, and the flickering images of the Grove Play finale faded from the canvas screen, the Tivoli thundered with applause.

"Did you like it?" I asked Marina. She was wearing a tight-waisted brown suit and a roguish Robin Hood-style hat, pierced diagonally by a great feather, and was looking very grown-up for all her nineteen years and some odd months. I could not help but notice that she and Mr. Scannell entwined their hands together as the lights dimmed in the Tivoli Opera House for the motion pictures.

"I loved the music, Father. But I was hoping to see you prancing on the stage in a loincloth. I didn't recognize you among the warriors."

"You are being forward again, my dear. It becomes your hat, however. My age and girth preclude a warrior's role. Mr. Mathieu, the director, cast me in the less demanding part of Fourth Assistant Priest. I was the fellow who stood in attendance to the Maiden of the Gentle People, making sure that she remained decorous throughout the performance. Having raised you, my dear, I found such devoted guardianship of a young female savage an easy part to enact. When John comes into the club next year, I'll see to it that he

700

receives a role in the Grove Play that demands brevity of attire. Then you shall be satisfied."

Marina reddened slightly at my sally. As she grows older, it becomes more and more difficult to match her badinage. The undoubtedly arresting image of John Charles Scannell in a loincloth seemed, however, to bring her raillery to a momentary lull.

"Next year's play is *Apollo*," I continued as we inched our way with the crowd towards the lobby. "John would make a perfect god of immemorial youth and beauty."

"And you, dear Father, can play Silenus, the large old man with donkey's ears who drinks too much."

"He also tutored the god Dionysus, my dear. He was famous, moreover, for his wonderful stories. He tippled, true; but he also possessed a certain special wisdom bestowed upon him by the gods."

"Let's have a truce, you two," John Charles Scannell said. "You should be more respectful to your father, Marina."

"Only when he deserves it. Besides, I treat him as an equal in a perhaps desperate effort to keep him young. It's not my fault that I have the oldest extant father in San Francisco."

"Yes," I said, again with telling reference, "I should have married early. How old are you, John?"

"Twenty-seven."

"That's a perfect age to get married. Then you'll be yet under fifty when my granddaughter is Marina's age." The reference to John's siring of my granddaughter stopped them both in their tracks. I have, of course, but one daughter for Mr. Scannell to sire that granddaughter upon. We walked in silence for a block or two.

"Let's have some oysters," I said.

We entered the Hoffman Grill on Market Street where Montgomery and Post intersect. Seated in a booth, we each enjoyed a dozen oysters, some garlic bread, green salad, and a schooner of beer.

"How did you guess that we are getting married?" Marina asked as she speared her fourth oyster out of its shell.

701

"My dear, one of the advantages of age is a developed sense of intuition. I merely intuited that you two were in love and were planning to marry."

"Do you approve?" John asked.

"Do you think that I would let you run all over town with my daughter at all hours of the day and night if I did not approve? Of course I approve. You and I are now co-conspirators in the effort to civilize this wild, headstrong woman."

"John and I are equals," Marina said, placing the empty shell of oyster number five back onto its bed of crushed ice. "We both respect the other. I will not be dominated, nor will he."

"However you manage it," I said, "I wish you both well." I shook John's hand over the sum total of thirty-six oyster shells, half of which remained to be eaten.

"I love you, Father," Marina said.

"I know you do, my dear. It's kept me alive to a ripe old age. John, one word of advice."

"Sir?" This solemnly from him, as if the Delphic Oracle were about to speak.

"Do you wish to be happy with Marina?"

"Yes, sir, most assuredly."

"Then treat her as I have treated her for these past nineteen years."

"How is that, sir?"

"Let her do what she damned well pleases."

"That's very good advice, darling," Marina said. "My father is a very wise man."

I do heartily approve of Marina and John's engagement and will confide my approbation to this journal in lieu of a public announcement; for Marina and John wish to keep their engagement secret until Marina finishes her senior year at Mills College. Marina has chosen wisely, if I say so myself. John graduated in law from Stanford and is well situated as an attorney with the firm of Tobin and Tobin. Both Cyril and J.O. think highly of him as a person and as a lawyer. The boy's father is an accountant with the Spring Valley Water

702

Company, which is reasonable enough; and John put himself through Stanford waiting on tables, which shows enterprise. Much of the college boy clings to John's demeanor and personality, but with Marina being older for her age, the two of them seem compatible enough as far as mutual maturity is concerned.

It all seems so easy, so natural—this mating up of two healthy young people, the world all before them as hand in hand with wandering steps and slow, through Eden they take their solitary way. (I must reread *Paradise Lost* one last time before I personally encounter its cast of characters on the other side.) Here they are, then, the two of them, casting themselves headlong upon each other with no true thought for the future—no apprehension at all, let us face it, over what can go wrong between a man and a woman as the years roll on. They held hands in the Tivoli and they rubbed their shanks together in the restaurant booth like two playful colts in a stall, bumping up to each other, and nuzzling, just for the sheer pleasure of touching. Marina and John are so full of things to say to each other that physical contact alone can provide an adequate syntax for their tumultuous communication.

I suppose that I should have a serious talk with John about his prospects and the like, but all that seems well enough in order. His delight in Marina is obvious, and for that reason alone I am happy to take him under my wing as a son-in-law. This is a big house, three stories. It would be easy to divide the foyer into two separate entrances and let them have the top two floors. That way, I wouldn't be losing Marina. I do not wish to lose her. I lost her mother and that was pain enough! Their marriage would be more like my gaining a son than losing a daughter. After all, John already has Marina to himself most of her free time; so if they lived here, there would not have to be that much of a change. We could have meals together occasionally, although I would be careful not to interfere in their lives. Cyril and J.O. have already put him up for the club. We could now and then go up together for Thursday-night Jinks: Sebastian Collins and his son-in-law, the very charming, very presentable John Charles Scannell of the firm

Tobin and Tobin, Attorneys at Law, the two of them together at the bar, enjoying a pre-dinner whiskey and finding enough to talk about despite the forty years separating them. I am positive that Phelan would welcome John into Esplandian Camp at the Grove. What fine times we shall have there, the two of us!

I enjoyed this year's encampment enormously, despite the fact that it took Royce nearly a week to get into the spirit of the Grove—although I am not certain that Josie ever truly did get into the spirit of Bohemia, being, as he is, so upset over the war.

Royce and I caught the ferry to Sausalito early on the morning of July 25th, then boarded the Bohemian Special which the club charters from the North Pacific Railway. Decorated in red, white, and blue bunting, the Bohemian Special flew the Bohemian Club flag from the smokestack. The club chartered five cars this year—three coach cars, a baggage car, and one clubroom car, set up with a bar at the far end, behind which Murph, the white-haired, ruddy-faced barman from our clubhouse in the city, presided with his usual laconic efficiency.

"Mr. Collins, the usual?" Murph asked as I entered the clubroom, after seeing our baggage aboard. By "the usual," Murph means a glass of Irish whiskey, with water, tall, but no ice.

"The usual," I said.

"What about the other gentleman?" asked Murph—by which he meant Josiah Royce, who seemed a little uneasy at the ambience of boisterous merriment that always characterizes the Bohemian Special on its treks to and from the Bohemian Grove. The car was crowded with Bohemians in Grove attire—tweed jackets, jodhpurs, hiking boots, Baden-Powell hats—all exuberant with anticipation of the forthcoming two weeks of midsummer merriment. Fred Myrtle sat in one corner of the club car playing Stephen Foster songs on a very loud banjo.

"I usually don't drink before lunch," Royce said, "but I'd be pleased if the steward would fix me a sherry."

Murph poured us our drinks, which we downed with alacrity. Without asking our opinion of the matter, Murph refilled both of our glasses. Neither of us protested. We were sipping our second drink as the Bohemian Special pulled out of the station, headed north to the Russian River area via Valley Ford, Occidental, Camp Meeker, Tyrone—then finally heading for Monte Rio, adjacent to the Grove. By the time we approached Tomales Bay, the club car was crowded to capacity. Taking Royce in tow, I introduced him around. Jack London was aboard, looking very much the outdoorsman in a white canvas shooting jacket with brown leather piping and brown leather patches. George Sterling wore a Yorkshire suit of Lincoln green. Young Haig Patigian and Charlie Kendrick seemed especially pleased to meet Royce. Above the blare of banjo music, we chatted together as the train skirted the sixteen-mile shore of Tomales Bay. On the far side of the bay rose a series of those rounded hills which are so typical of California. Traceries of morning fog clung to their heights. Herds of black-and-white dairy cattle grazed contentedly on their lower slopes.

"It has," said Royce, "the feeling of the Scottish Highlands."

Jimmy Phelan came in with another Esplandian campmate, Downey Harvey. Downey joined the club in 1881 at the age of twenty-one, just after he returned from Georgetown; so despite the fact that he is barely into his mid-fifties, he is nearing eligibility for the club's Old Guard, those with forty years of membership. Phelan, Downey, Royce, London, Sterling, Haig Patigian, Charlie Kendrick, and I moved back to the bar at Phelan's bequest. Phelan ordered all around on one chit, which he signed with one of the pencils strewing the gleaming mahogany service of the counter.

"My treat, gentlemen," he said. Then, raising his glass of Scotch whiskey, neat: "To the encampment."

"To the Cremation of Care," Haig Patigian added. Haig is a

sculptor—and although young, is already a power in club circles.

The club has been enjoying midsummer encampments since 1878. After gathering at a number of places in the forest country north of San Francisco—Taylorville, Duncan Mills, Cazadero, Camp Meeker—we finally acquired in 1899 a magnificent grove of redwood trees adjacent to the Russian River at Monte Rio in Sonoma County, a place called Meeker's Grove, destined, just as we purchased it, to be logged into oblivion. We encamp there in late July and early August, for some two weeks of ceremonies, plays, concerts, lectures, swimming, hiking, good dining, and the imbibing of alcoholic spirits.

After enjoying our third drink at the bar, we adjourned to our seats in the passenger car where box lunches awaited us: fried chicken, biscuits with butter and honey, an apple and an orange, and white wine poured by Murph who moved up and down the aisle of the train seeing to it that all glasses were forever replenished. The Neapolitan Trio—three Bohemians dressed as street singers—moved from car to car, singing Italian songs. Uda Waldrop, who wrote the music for this year's Grove Play, accompanied the trio on the mandolin. Royce seemed a little embarrassed when the trio came into the car, but he did make an effort to hum along when we all joined the trio in *O Sole Mio*. After they moved on, Bush Finnell, who was sitting some three rows ahead of us, stood up and sang selections from Verdi, Puccini, and Massenet. Charlie Kendrick (he recites beautifully) then read to us from the English Romantic poets.

By the time the Bohemian Special reached Occidental, we were in redwood country. At Monte Rio we switched off onto a track leading into the Bohemian Grove. As the train pulled into Camp Bromley, Bernie Miller led the fife and drum corps of the club band down to greet us. Bernie conducted his musicians with an oversized baton topped by a golden orb, strutting out ahead like a minstrel show cakewalker. Pouring out of the train, we walked to our separate camps to wash up

706

before dinner. Attendants from the Grove staff were already unloading the luggage.

Esplandian Camp—named in honor of the knightly hero of Montalvo's sixteenth-century Spanish romance—sits just behind the Grove stage on a hill to the west of the Campfire Circle sometimes referred to as Snob Hill because the oldest, hence most venerable, camps of the Grove are located here. Perched on a promontory against a spectacular stand of soaring redwoods, the first deck of Esplandian Camp consists of the kitchen and servants' quarters. The second story is a clear deck upon which sit two good-sized canvas tents. Between the tents is a sitting area covered by a striped canvas awning. To the far side of this semi-open foyer is our bar, above which is a most delectable nude—a young lady of perfect proportions who, having cast her clothes onto a bank of ferns, advances through a redwood grove, her eyes liquid with acceptance. Just in front of the bar, a steel brazier hangs suspended from two chains attached to a crossbeam. Some half-dozen sturdy captain's chairs sit before the brazier.

Founded in 1872 by a group of writers, journalists, artists, and other assorted afficionados of the arts, the Bohemian Club has survived to this day as a social and cultural institution of great local vitality. Phelan sponsored me to membership in 1894, and for these past twenty years I have enjoyed both the city club and the Grove upon numerous occasions. I try to lunch at the club at least once a week and attend at least one of our Thursday-night Jinks every month, possibly two if my schedule permits.

This year, as always, we opened the encampment with the Cremation of Care. At the conclusion of dinner on the second night of the encampment, as some five hundred of us sat at long tables beneath the redwood trees, the Sire of the evening called us to silence and announced that by the power of our fellowship, Dull Care was slain. In the distance, a bell tolled and we heard the faint strains of a funeral procession singing Gregorian chant drawing near. The cortege—Bohemians dressed as hooded monks and bearing torches—moved

707

through the dining circle, carrying the corpse of Care on a portable funeral bier. To the music of a muffled drum, the entire club, led by the Old Guard, followed the funeral procession to a pyre piled high with logs. At the pyre, Bohemians costumed as druid priests placed the corpse of Care atop the logs, then lighted the pyre after praying that Dull Care might once again, as it is every year, be banished from the Grove.

"It's a pretty ceremony," said Royce after the Cremation. He, I, Phelan, Downey Harvey, and Charlie Fay sat before the brazier fire on the deck of Esplandian, enjoying a nightcap. "It's charming enough, but the world will not be stopped by it. Care has only just begun to work his mischief upon our troubled civilization."

"Then we must arm ourselves and prepare for our defense," Phelan said. "We must train new divisions and refurbish the fleet."

Phelan leaves for Washington after the first of the year to take his seat in the United States Senate, so we naturally listened closely to his opinion. As an ardent disciple of the late Rear Admiral Alfred Thayer Mahan, Phelan believes that sea power is the key to national survival.

"America has not grown up as a nation," I remember Phelan saying just before we turned in, "until it possesses a great navy and understands the proper strategy for its employment."

It was a good thing that David Starr Jordan, ardent pacifist that he is, was not on the Esplandian deck. Even Royce winced slightly at Phelan's *realpolitik* and aggressive imperialism. I happen to agree with Jimmy, however. The world is catching up to Fortress America. We'll eventually be involved in this European war before it is over. We must become an Atlantic and a Pacific power if we are to meet the challenge of Germany and Japan, and that means a great navy.

I dozed off remembering what a lovely spectacle it was when the Great White Fleet sailed into San Francisco Bay in May of 1908. Teddy Roosevelt, also an ardent student of Mahan, had sent our navy around the world to announce the emergence of the United States as an international naval power. The bay was filled that day with ships of every description—yachts, schooners, tugboats, ferries—as the Great White Fleet steamed in, welcomed by thunderous cannonades from Fort Baker and the Presidio: sixteen battleships, painted white, with ten other ships—cruisers, destroyers, coalers—in attendance, some twenty-six ships in all, anchored offshore like a dazzling floating city of white and gray. We San Franciscans had spent the previous three years rebuilding the city after the Earthquake and Fire, and the arrival of the Fleet seemed to signal to us that the work was done, well done, that San Francisco had been born again into the federation of great maritime cities. We gave a grand ball that night at the Fairmont Hotel for Admiral Evans and the other officers, and the next day some eight thousand bluejackets paraded up Market Street. For the eleven days of the Fleet's stay, hostesses vied with each other for the privilege of seating an admiral, a commodore, a captain, a commander, at their dinner tables— together with a smart young ensign or lieutenant in dazzling dress whites to keep the young women interested.

Phelan is correct: we need a powerful navy. San Francisco especially has much at stake in this matter; for the United States is poised on the verge of an era of expansion into the Pacific. In certain cases, we shall acquire actual possessions, such as we now have in the Philippines. In other cases, we shall content ourselves with spheres of influence, trade relationships, perhaps even the eventual affiliation of Pacific Basin commonwealths into an overseas American confederation, a United States of the Pacific, rivaling the maritime empires of Portugal, Spain, and Great Britain. Hawaii, the Philippines, Samoa, the Carolines, the Marshall Islands—a string of American confederates might one day stretch across the Pacific Basin. San Francisco could become the queen city of such a Pacific empire. We could share spheres of trade and influence with Tokyo, Hong Kong, and Sydney. That is why it was important that we build a grand City Hall in excess of our local needs. We have it in our power to become a maritime capital of the Pacific, not just an oversized California town.

And that is why I am thrilled by the superb Public Library

we are building on Civic Center. A library is an act of intellectual imperialism. A library is an empire of books. Like an empire, a great library brings scattered realms into its possession and confers upon them the gifts of discipline and order. Assyria, Greece, Rome, Great Britain, and now the United States—all great empires have founded great libraries and museums to celebrate the expansion of the mother culture and to memorialize the central authority of the imperial city-state. William Chapman Ralston well understood this connection between library, museum, and empire. He envisioned the Atheneum I was to direct as an essential expression of the cultural and political maturity of San Francisco, its dominance over the Far West and the Pacific Basin. Perhaps the Library we are building on Civic Center may somehow develop into a truly great institution on the order of Ralston's dream, which was also the dream of my own youth as well. We shall see.

During the Grove encampment, Royce and I enjoyed a number of pleasant rambles under the redwoods. The Russian River was high this year, and so the younger members of the club spent a good deal of their time swimming. I bathed in the river upon two occasions. Every night there was a campfire show, and we enjoyed excellent meals in our open-air dining room. Royce and I spent mornings on the deck of Camp Esplandian—he reading, I working on some early drafts of the *Memoirs*. We ate lunch in camp, then took a siesta, followed by an afternoon walk. The redwoods had a calming effect upon both of us. At night, before the fire, Royce spoke of his boyhood in Grass Valley—how his mother kept her family together after failure in the gold rush drove Royce Senior into instability.

"The West is an epic of women," Royce said. "Women nurtured the frontier. I grew up in a world of women. Women saw to it that Grass Valley developed beyond the savage frontier stage. As I was growing up, it often seemed to me that only the women of Grass Valley cared about the things I cared about. My mother packed a portable organ into the prairie schooner that brought her west. She would play it every night after the wagons had been drawn into a circle and the evening meal and chores were done. I like to think of the melodies of those simple hymns she used to play drifting out beyond the campfire light into the primordial darkness beyond: 'Rock of Ages,' 'A Mighty Fortress is Our God,' heard by bewildered Indians and uncomprehending coyotes. What a feeble—and yet what a mighty—sound it must have been: this announcement through portable organ music of my mother's presence in the wilderness and the arrival with her of all that she stood for."

I was relieved that Royce was off at another camp when Ambrose Bierce and Jack London had their already legendary alcoholic tournament. Royce says that he has drunk more at the Grove than he has drunk in his total life—and that is hardly anything at all. In any event, he might have been repelled by the London-Bierce drinking bout. I witnessed only the first part of it. Bierce and London, while both Bohemians, loathe each other; or at least they pretend to loathe each other—for professional purposes. An ultraconservative politically, Bierce despises Jack's socialism; so do I, for that matter, although I understand how Jack, after the poverty of his youth, has become a theoretical socialist out of the psychological necessity of remaining loyal to his class. Bierce also derides Jack's prose style, which he finds incorrect and undisciplined. Jack, in turn, says that Bierce is a *poseur* (which he is); that Bierce is decadent, effete—a Midwestern yokel from Ohio posing as the Last Great Gentleman. The antagonism serves their respective purposes, offering each of them a way of defining his own worth in contrast to the other. Although Bierce now and then has been heard to mutter something about calling London out with pistols, I suspect that the antagonism is not a true hatred. I was strolling up the River Road, in any event, when Sterling called me into one of the camps to witness the long-promised drinking-and-insult bout between London and Bierce. Somehow, the two had been maneuvered into the same camp at the same time by certain

711

mischievous souls and here found themselves with no choice but to fulfill their contemporaries' expectations. London and Bierce sat across a bottle of bourbon on a small table, trading drinks and insults by the hour. I remained for but a half-hour of the tournament, or, to put it another way, for some three shots and fifteen insults worth; but, as is now so well known, the contest continued through lunch, an afternoon canoe ride (when the contest became nautical), through supper and the evening into the wee hours of the morn, until both contestants had vented their spleens and rendered themselves incoherent and, ultimately, unconscious.

Jack seemed subdued, even exhausted, by his debauch when he and George Sterling joined Phelan, Royce, Downey Harvey and myself after the Grove Play for a nightcap by the fire at Esplandian. The redwoods, their heights lost in the nighttime darkness, glowed in their lower regions with the flickering light of numerous campfires throughout the Grove. Glimpsed through scattered openings between the redwood trees, the stars shone crystal-clear overhead. From where we sat, we could hear the distant music of the orchestra playing a reprise of *Nec-Natama* at the Campfire Circle, joined by the mellow tenor of Harold Baxter, who sang the role of the Maiden of the Gentle People. The music came to us in snatches, while the evening breeze made a sighing aeolian harp of the redwood trees. "By a shady tree and a running brook," Harold Baxter sang,

> A Love Woman gave me birth.
> And I drank strong love from her full, rich breasts,
> As brown as the breasts of earth

"Well, gentlemen," said Phelan, when our glasses were filled by the camp attendant and the orchestra, off in the distance, had concluded its music, "it is a perfect evening."

"It is a beauteous evening," Downey Harvey recited,

> . . . calm and free,
> The holy time is quiet as a nun
> Breathless with adoration.

712

"In such a night," I countered,

> Troilus methinks mounted the Trojan walls,
> And sigh'd his soul toward the Grecian tents,
> Where Cressid lay that night.

"In such a night," George Sterling continued,

> Stood Dido with a willow in her hand
> Upon the wild-sea banks, and waft her love
> To come again to Carthage.

"Thanks to Shakespeare," said Phelan, "we have progressed from Downey's nun in adoration, to Sebastian's longing lover, to George's heroine of erotic sorrow; the abandoned and doomed Dido, bearing Aeneas's child in her womb."

"Better to remain a nun," said Downey, "and avoid any unpleasantness." Downey Harvey is a small imp of a man, with a fey-facetious manner and a look of Irish deviltry in his face. His favorite drink is a gin rickey, and his sagest observation is: "Never let them put you behind a desk." Thanks to a fortunate marriage, Downey can practice what he preaches.

"Better to love and lose," said Sterling, "than not to have known love at all."

"Better to act and not to think too much about it," said Jack London. "It's easier that way."

"Gentlemen," said Phelan, "I declare an impasse. Downey advocates that we soar above the flesh. Jack says that we should do what we please and not think about it. George says that we should embrace both pleasure and pain in their due course."

"I presume," I said, "that we are all talking about the sex instinct."

"I thought we were talking about nuns," said Downey.

"An excellent pun, Downey," Sterling said.

"A pun?" Downey asked.

"In Elizabethan parlance," said Sterling, "a nun was a whore."

"But not breathless with adoration," Phelan said.

713

"Yes," said London. "Breathless—and adoring: with the manner of worship known solely to her species. Downey has made a nun pun."

"I only wanted to quote Wordsworth," said Downey, "because it's so peaceful and pleasant up here on the deck of Esplandian Camp."

"Let Royce decide," I said. "He is a philosopher."

"Decide what?" Royce asked. "I cannot determine the question."

"That," I said, "is because it has not been properly formulated. To wit: is *eros,* sometimes called sex, sometimes called love, worth all the trouble?"

"Speak for yourself," said London. "I find it no trouble at all."

"I find it superb trouble," said Sterling.

"Being a nun," said Downey, "I'm not allowed a sex life."

"Being a philosopher," said Royce, "I long ago learned that the human heart is an impenetrable mystery."

"As the mother superior of this convent," said Downey, "I order you all to drink another round."

"As captain of this camp," Phelan said, "I hereby declare rules of procedure, lest the conversation become too suggestive of bourbon and Lewis Carroll. All of us, including myself, shall define the nature of love. We shall then adjourn in silence to ponder each other's definitions, for the hour is late."

"I love parlor games," said Downey Harvey.

"Then we'll begin with you," said Phelan.

"Love," Downey said, "is the final scene of tonight's Grove Play. There's an orchestra and everything is lit up beautifully and you wish it could be like this forever."

"Love," George Sterling said, "is the pursuit of Beauty in its human manifestation. Love is the natural poetry of life."

"Love," said Jack London, "is a biological urge which we fuss over to keep ourselves from getting bored. Love is strictly prose. Its proper activity is copulation, and its purpose in the scheme of things is to keep biological life going on this planet."

714

"Love," said Jimmy Phelan, "is the drama of the soul. All love is ultimately in the nature of a religious quest."

"Yes," said Royce. "Love is the desire and pursuit of the whole. It is our struggle to regain the lost Absolute."

"Love," I said, "is everything that you gentlemen have said that it is. In my case, it has also proven a hunger of the imagination: an urge to possess the fullness of the other and through her to possess creation itself. Through love, I have defied time and kept at bay the temptation to suspect that life may turn out to be a stupid joke, that the universe may be empty of meaning, after all."

"The universe is empty," said London. "Life is a joke."

"Only if we let it be," said Royce. "Only if we refuse the promptings of conscience and mind, emanations of the Absolute."

"If creation is a joke," said Sterling, "then it is a beautiful joke, not a cruel one."

"I think it's cruel to keep the barman up so late," said Downey. "As long as we're speaking of love, let me say that I would love to go to bed, which is where I'm going. Good night."

Phelan, Downey, and Royce all retired to their tent, while Jack, George, and I had an inexcusable last drink before the fire. We did not talk much; rather, we stared quietly into the coals as if each of us were seeing there a fiery Rosetta Stone with which to decipher the compulsions, the obscure, ill-understood hungers that characterize all erotic experience.

Jack London and George Sterling are very close friends. Jack calls George "Greek," and George calls Jack "Wolf." George is past forty, and Jack is approaching it. I know George much better than I know Jack because George is so much a part of the San Francisco scene. You might say that I know George Sterling too well, in fact; for San Francisco is a small town and I know most of the Coppans—the group of bohemians and *demi-mondaines* gathered around George (whom they call the uncrowned King of Bohemia), eating together often at Papa Coppa's restaurant on Montgomery Street, where they have decorated the walls with an astonishing array of impromptu murals, including Nora May French's graffito (written in reverse lettering) which states that she, Nora May French, has the suspicion that they, the bohemians of San Francisco, including herself, may very well in the long run be all damned. To have sat at the table of Coppa's—the old Coppa's, the pre-earthquake restaurant, not the rebuilt place with its *fin de siècle* ambience vanished—was certainly to have sensed, if not damnation, then at least the currents and cross-currents of a surging erotic tide. George Sterling is a great hunter of rabbits and birds, which he shoots by the sackful: an odd avocation, I've always felt, in a poet who is constantly singing the praises of Beauty with capital B, ethereal and Platonic. George is a great hunter of female flesh as well, a compulsive seducer who has driven his beautiful wife Caroline to the edges of insanity. The cries of birds and rabbits reflect perhaps the cries of another destruction, that of the Little Death. Not that I think that George is cruel in his embracements—only intensely narcissistic. He copulates first and foremost in celebration of his own considerable male beauty.

I happened to be at Coppa's the evening Nora May French scrawled her message of damnation on the wall, and so were Jack and Jimmy Hopper, Porter Garnett, Gelett Burgess, Isabel Fraser, Mary Austin, and some three or four other actors in the minor drama of aesthetic San Francisco, Sterling's cool, gray city of love. Nora had slept with perhaps three-quarters, certainly half, of the men gathered at the artists' table. Climbing the stairs to George's studio in the Montgomery block one earlier afternoon, I, pausing to knock, heard from within what I at first took to be the cries of some suffering animal—a wounded deer perhaps, lying in a thicket, or a rabbit mangled in a snare. These were, however, Nora's love cries; realizing this in the second instant of my perception, the animal imagery having sped from the forefront of my consciousness, I arrested my knock and retreated down the staircase in some embarrassment at having stumbled into such an intimate occasion. There was ecstasy in those whimperings (George is no doubt a skilled lover), but there was something

716

else also, as I have suggested: the desperation of a trapped animal capable of gnawing away a paw in order to escape the clenched teeth of an iron trap. Nora's trap, her tragic flaw, was that she was a slave to Venus, going to bed with too many men out of a certain excess of appetite, to be sure, but out of a certain naive devotion to her Muse, as well, feeling, as she did, that giving herself away so heedlessly was a prerequisite of the complete poetic act. I have it on good account that she endured five abortions and was pregnant again on that foggy early morning some five years ago in Carmel when, on the porch of George's rustic cabin, she took cyanide of potassium and ended horribly, writhing in agony, her lovely lips frothed in blood-specked foam. George and Jimmy Hopper fought with each other at the funeral, each of them tugging at the silver urn containing Nora's ashes, claiming the right to be the one to scatter them to the winds that sweep across Point Lobos.

Nora May French was a woman of rounded lines, possessed of a rounded body and the rounded eyes of an inquisitive deer: the perfect prey for men of George's type—angular men, thin men, enamored of their handsomeness. Mary Austin calls all of George's women the Committee. Taken collectively, they are all of the Nora May French type: sensitive aspirants to the life of art, ready to offer up their milk-white young flesh on the altar of aesthetic creation: their own in certain cases—such as with Nora—but the penetrating poet's upon most occasions; for the double-backed beast, George Sterling tells the young lady, rolling her deftly back upon the couch, deciphering the resistant points among her undergarments, deciding upon an angle of entrance, the double-backed beast is the faithful steed that pulls forward the fiery chariot of art.

Jack London, on the other hand, eschews the acolyte sort in favor of two very opposite varieties of womanhood—primitives and Gibson Girls—whom he pursues with two very differing patterns of behavior. Jack likes the whorehouses of Chinatown, the same way he likes boxing matches or any other celebration of the violent, the Darwinian. "A good steak, bloody rare," he says, "then a visit to a Chinese whorehouse. Now that's a

717

perfect evening on the town in 'Frisco." Jack's stories are filled with suggestions of accommodating primitives—and of Gibson Girls shamed, brought down to size, or throwing aside the restraints of social caste to play the wanton like the girls on the Barbary Coast.

"She got on the train in Oakland," he said of one event, favoring us with this narration after we had sat before the Esplandian fire in silence for fifteen minutes or so. "She was a beauty, and very proper. I spied her at the station and made up my mind then and there that it would happen or I'd never again sign myself Wolf. My estimate of her was correct, as I found out in the dining car that evening—a home in the Western Addition, membership in the Browning Society, the California Club, the works. We hardly left my sleeper between Denver and New York, except to sneak separately into the dining car for meals. She wanted me to compare her to an Indian girl or to a Yukon dame. I'd tell her that they weren't half so wild, which was a fact. She was something else, biting and scratching and hollering so loud that the porter knocked on the door and asked if anything was wrong. She wanted me to tell her about the mating of wolves, which I did—and that set her going again. A lawyer's wife, I swear, off to New York to meet him there at the conclusion of some convention. This is about 1909 or thereabouts, just before I sailed for Hawaii in the *Snark*. Called me Wolf and left marks in my shoulders and scratches up and down my back a mile wide. The morning we pulled into New York, she was as cool as a cucumber. Barely had the time of day for me, but pecked her husband ever so nicely on the cheek when he met her at the train station."

"A very improper story, Jack," Sterling said. "Inappropriate to a gentleman's club, and especially inappropriate to Esplandian Camp which is made up of proper Catholic gentlemen such as Collins here."

"But a true story," Jack said, "and necessary to offset some of the fancy talk we heard earlier this evening. Besides—she hurt my feelings. She only wanted me physically. She hadn't even read any of my books!"

"George is right," I said. "No graphic stories are permitted

718

here. Esplandian Camp is devoted to general principles of an elevated nature, not intimate narratives, no matter how well told and by what distinguished author."

"This author is tired," said Jack, "and will be off to his own camp."

"But not," said Sterling, "before summarizing the evening's question, as all three of us shall do."

"I'm tired of debate," said Jack. "Bierce drank me under the table yesterday and I haven't yet recovered."

"Gentlemen," I said, "I call a halt to these proceedings."

Jack and George wobbled down the hill, their arms over each other's shoulder. I watched them go, then returned to my captain's chair before the brazier. The fire, now a heap of glowing coals, had, so I estimated, a half-hour's warmth left to it; so against my better judgment I poured a half-whiskey and sat before its dying glow, thinking of Sybil and Virginia, thinking of Gustav Klimt, Ryan Patrice, and Merry del Val, thinking of the love—of every sort—that had come my way.

In mid-November of 1901, some dozen years after she had shaken the sand of San Francisco from her feet, Sybil Sanderson, the celebrated dramatic soprano of the Paris Opera, returned to the city of her girlhood to appear in a sumptuous production of Massenet's *Manon,* brought here by the Maurice Grau Opera Company of New York and performed on Saturday evening, the sixteenth of November, at the Grand Opera House at Third and Mission streets before a packed and enthusiastic house. Two nights later, Sybil sang the lead in Gounod's *Romeo et Juliette* to an equally demonstrative reception.

"I cannot get over the flowers," Sybil remarked as she, myself, Mayor Phelan, and a half-dozen other guests— including a married banker of some local prominence with whom Sybil had formed an instantaneous connection— lunched together at the Cliff House on Jimmy's largesse: His Honor, our young bachelor mayor, seeming quite taken by the returning *diva,* but also sensing a rival in the gentleman whom Sybil had brought along *sans* spouse. "They thrust roses at me when I detrained in Oakland. They practically smothered me in lilacs and lilies when I got off the ferryboat in San Francisco. My suite at the hotel is banked in mimosa and chrysanthemums. And your darling Bohemian Club sent me a positively gigantic floral wreath for my dressing room—violets, carnations, red and white roses, and the most divine ceramic owl sitting on top. Why, you'd think that I was already dead—and returning to California for my funeral!"

Sybil was due to sing *Manon* that evening. "Dear Sebastian," she had written on a card brought to my home early that morning by hotel messenger (a card crested, incidentally, by something suggestive of the Romanoff double-headed eagle), "I want only you, old friend, with me tonight before I go on stage. Do come by my dressing suite at seven and we shall talk of old times. That will calm my nerves. I shall leave word with the stage-door porter personally to escort you to my suite. Sybil."

Upon my introduction of myself to the porter that evening, the worthy gentleman escorted me to Dressing Room Number One down at the end of a corridor filled with smaller open make-up rooms. Attired in top hat, opera cape, evening dress, a white silk scarf trailing behind my neck, I felt quite the *boulevardier* as I strolled past the open cubicles furnished with electric lights and oversized mirrors, before which sat nubile members of the female chorus and *corps de ballet*, adjusting their wigs and make-up and, in one delightful case, pulling a stocking over a last expanse of rosy-pink thigh, her eye catching mine as she completed that final adjustment and— the delightful minx! a true daughter of the ballet!—extending in my direction a full *révérence* as I stopped to gape, her tutu ruffling out most fetchingly as she folded to the ground like a nesting swan, her arms extended forward and crossed at the wrists, her bottom peeping out most charmingly, as I could detect in the mirror behind her, as she balanced upon one leg stretched delightfully behind her. Such a maneuver, a full *révérence,* would have put me into orthopedic traction for the ensuing six weeks.

"A most charming *révérence,*" I said.

"I enjoy the practice," she said.

An ingratiating rejoinder was forming itself in my mind, reinforced by the image of the unknown dancer and myself supping together after Manon breathed her last on the stage of the Grand, when Manon herself, in the person of Sybil, threw open her dressing room door at the porter's knock and, seeing me midway down the corner, having dropped well behind my guide, called forth: "Sebastian, you naughty man, leave that poor girl alone and come in here. Will you never cease? Such attentions, my dear young lady, positively drove me from San Francisco twelve years ago. I caution you. Beware!"

"You left of your own free will, Sybil. You left for art—for the opera. You left as a girl of nineteen and you've returned a goddess."

Turning from my charming swan (with some regret), walking down the corridor, removing my hat, cape, and gloves, bowing low to kiss Sybil's extended hand, I made the above speech all the while with what I took to be the amount of dash appropriate to a gentleman of fifty-three calling upon an internationally famous opera star.

"It's been seven years since *Thaïs*," Sybil said. "I meant to tell you this at luncheon: you haven't changed. You look wonderful."

"You're being too kind," I said. I did not insult her, however, with a return of the compliment. Sybil appeared drawn and tired behind her make-up. I entered a comfortably furnished sitting room dominated by a large dressing table. A high powdered wig stood at the ready atop a hatter's dummy. A colored woman of Sybil's age, dressed in a black-and-white maid's costume, entered from the second room of the suite. As she opened the door, I glimpsed a large copper-colored bathtub within.

"Anything else, Miss Sibby?" the woman asked.

"Just the wig, Sybil. That will be all. This is Mr. Sebastian Collins of San Francisco."

The second Sybil dropped a less exacting curtsy than my pink-thighed ballerina in the corridor beyond, but her smile was most genuine.

721

"Sybil and I have the same name," Sybil Sanderson remarked, "and we were both born in Sacramento within the same month. Sybil's father was Judge Sanderson's lifelong companion. Sybil and I grew up together."

As a young woman, Sybil Sanderson possessed the thickest, most luxuriant chestnut-colored hair. Arriving in San Francisco as a woman of thirty-one, she presented a bright red coiffure to her girlhood city. I naturally suspected a henna rinse, harmless enough, even necessary, in an about-to-be middle-aged woman pursuing a theatrical career. With no warning at all, the attendant Sybil took hold of her mistress's red locks over either ear. With a peeling motion horrible to behold (it was as if Sybil were being scalped in my presence), the ebony Sybil removed a limp red wig from her mistress's head. Sybil's own hair was scanty—and totally white. The red wig hung in the ebony maid's hand like the bloodied pelt of a slaughtered creature. With her wispy white hair and heavily painted face—garish lips, shadowed eyes, an oversized artificial beauty mark clinging to her lower chin like a glob of black soot—Sybil seemed the very figure of Death from a medieval mystery play, a ghastly skull behind rouge and powder. I must have shown the emotions of horror and pity seething within me, for Sybil laughed bravely as her maid lowered the white powdered wig on her nearly bald head, completing her mistress's transformation into Manon.

"Don't be shocked, dear Sebastian. My hair went completely white when my husband died and I can't be bothered with keeping what's left of it hennaed, so I wear a red wig. Fooled you, didn't I?"

Yes, indeed, she had fooled me, and others besides. In the days that followed, I scrutinized her by daylight to discern the reoccurrence of the Death's Skull I had glimpsed for a second in the reflected face beneath the scraggly white hair, but I sought such a harbinger of doom in vain. Sybil's bright locks, flushed cheeks, flashing violet eyes, radiated animal magnetism as from a primal source. Laughing, which she often did, she lifted her chin to expose an unlined throat. Her ample

722

bosom, luxuriant arms, rounded hips and thighs—seen in outline through silk dresses tailored tightly in the Parisian manner—emanated Junoesque voluptuousness and unchecked female strength. (The girls of Marina's generation, by the way, are much too thin. The women of Sybil's era prized a certain commanding amplitude of figure. Today, American girls all seem to be starving themselves in atonement for nature's gift of rounded femininity.) Sybil's white hair remained a secret, and perhaps she kept another secret also: a secret suspected by Sybil alone, discovered then, or soon after, when red flecks began to spot her handkerchief or when she noticed that a certain warmness never left her brow save after the coldest of baths. Her secret safe for the moment, Sybil dazzled and scandalized San Francisco, tweaking the city that once threatened to preclude her forever from the stage, from the bohemian life of art.

"San Francisco is still as pokey as ever, dear Sebastian," Sybil said as the black Sybil adjusted her powdered white wig. "I don't know how you stand it."

"I stand it because I must, because I am somewhat pokey myself, living here after being born here. A glittering audience of four thousand will soon greet you. This room overflows with bouquets and cards. San Francisco, my lovely woman, is trying to do its best."

"I know, dear fellow, but I just can't help myself. Coming home brings out the rebellious girl in me—despite my white hair."

In the fortnight she spent in the city, Sybil went out of her way to pique our provincial sensibilities. The Crockers, for instance, invited her to one of their receptions. Sybil refused on the grounds of having a headache, but *Town Topics* reported seeing her that very same night at a minstrel show, laughing lustily, escorted by the very same banker who invited himself along to Phelan's luncheon at the Cliff House. Attending another reception, this at the De Youngs', she wore a black sheath dress, its severity broken only by a corsage of violets. In Paris, a black sheath and a violet corsage is the official costume

723

of a *demi-mondaine,* a woman of pleasure. Informed of the significance of Sybil's garb, the De Youngs were understandably incensed. Mrs. Boardman gave a *soirée* for Sybil, which a number of San Franciscans refused to attend on the grounds of Sybil's defiant bohemianism—no matter that she was the daughter of Justice Silas Sanderson, late of the State Supreme Court, an internationally feted singer, received everywhere in the best society of Europe, including royalty.

"I'm bored, dear Sebastian, by everyone telling me that they remember me as a child."

"My dear, I remember you as a child—a girl of nine or ten, frolicking about Billy Ralston's Belmont estate."

"But you are different, darling. You're like family. You're like a dear older brother."

"You have said it all, dear Sybil. Had I recognized that fact earlier than I did, I might have saved my liver from unnecessary abuse."

"Don't blame me for those years, you horrid darling. I was just a girl. You were merely looking for an excuse for your dissipation, that's all, and I happened to be convenient."

As Sybil spoke, she affixed two glassy diamond pendants to her ears. I walked over to where she sat and, standing behind her, I put my hand on her bare shoulder. She turned towards me and kissed my hand, her fake diamond earring dropping across my fingers.

"Sebastian," she said, "my dear, dear friend. We have both paid our debts, have we not? Of everyone in this city, even Gertrude, I wanted only you here with me tonight because I knew that you would understand how much strain this causes me, my coming back."

"Returning in triumph," I said.

"I do have a reputation, that's true, but I also come back to discover the ghost of my girlhood on these streets and to realize what a mess I've made of my life in the years in between."

"You are an artist," I said. "You are not expected to have a tidy life. You could have remained in San Francisco if you

724

wanted the stability of an *haute bourgeoise* existence. You have loved greatly, and it shows in your singing."

"And in my face, and on top of my head. May it show tonight, dear friend. I shall try not to play the spoiled *débutante bohèmienne*. I shall do something nice for San Francisco."

"Just be Manon," I said. "The rest will take care of itself."

Walking backstage on my way to rejoin Gertrude Atherton and the Tobins in the box that R.M. had taken especially for Sybil's homecoming, I encountered my young ballerina friend by herself in a rehearsal area off to one side of the backstage area, putting herself through the most charming series of preparatory exercises. Somewhere in her early twenties (so I judged), she had a rounded Gallic face and dark brown hair and a perfect dancer's body: lithe and tense with unexpected strength. Noticing that I was watching her, she continued her maneuvers, elaborating them, in fact, rushing back and forth upon her upraised feet, her arms making winglike motions: and all for my benefit. When she finished, I applauded and called, "Bravo! Bravo!" She repeated the full *révérence* I had witnessed in the dressing room.

"You must," I said, "be exhausted and famished after an evening's dancing."

"Oui, monsieur," she replied in American-accented but very correct French, better than I could muster in reply. "We dance on an empty stomach and are positively ravenous when the evening is complete."

"Perhaps, my dear, a light collation might be in order after the performance?"

"I should have to seek the permission of Mr. Grau," she said. "We are supposed to be back at the hotel after the performance, unless we have special permission."

"I am a friend of your *impresario,* Mr. Maurice Grau. I knew him before he moved to New York. Your name, my dear, is?"

"Iris, monsieur, as in the flower."

"Well, Iris, my name is Sebastian Collins, as in the appreciator of flowers, and I would be most pleased if you should talk to Mr. Grau at some point after the performance, giving him my name, and seek his permission for you to join me for supper this evening at the Poodle Dog. I shall wait for you in a hansom cab outside the stage door after the performance."

"Monsieur is very kind."

"Not at all, Iris, the pleasure is all mine. Even the possibility of such company flatters an old man."

"Monsieur is not at all old. I shall dance especially for you this evening. *Au revoir.*" Raising herself to her toes, Iris fluttered off to where the *corps de ballet* was assembling at the far side of the backstage area. As she sped along, her feet barely touching the ground, she made graceful winglike motions with her bare arms.

"The whole town has turned out," Gertrude Atherton said when I joined her in the Tobin box. "I haven't seen so many diamonds since President McKinley came to town."

"You are not doing so bad yourself," I said, apropos of the opulent ruby dangling by a gold chain just above the splendid cleavage of Gertrude's black velvet dress. The ruby moved as Gertrude moved, seemingly tossed to and fro by the splendid shiftings of its possessor's formidable frontage. Then forty-five, Mrs. Atherton was in the full flush of her imperious, full-figured handsomeness.

"It's a fake," Gertrude said. "I had it made in Munich about ten years ago when poverty forced me to sell the real one. Poor George gave it to me on our first anniversary. I lived three years on the proceeds of the sale, writing three novels which all sold well."

"I promise not to tell a soul," I said.

"I wouldn't overly mind if you did. Half the diamonds you see in the house tonight are fake. San Francisco is at once a deceiving and a deceived town. Sybil and I used to discuss endlessly the city's passion for fakery when we were plotting our escape."

Authentic or fake, the lavish display of jewelry added much to the glitter of the audience, now settling into its seats in the final moments before the curtain was to rise on *Manon.* Formal

726

attire pervaded even the upper balconies, testifying to the specialness of the evening. Either holders of less expensive tickets had bothered with formal wear that night or the *haute bourgeoisie* had pushed the lower ranges of the middle classes out of the Opera House altogether. The Tobins came into the box: R.M., Cyril, and J.O. looking like oversized penguins, Agnes Tobin perfectly splendid in pale green and wearing her hair up high on her head, gathered into a chignon. When Jimmy Phelan entered Box Number One, the house broke into applause for its dashing young mayor. Jimmy acknowledged the clapping graciously, waving back with one French-cuffed hand. I must admit that I found it all rather splendid: Jimmy Phelan, my tutee and friend, Mayor of San Francisco, being honored by a smartly turned-out assemblage upon the occasion of the city's most famous daughter's return. When Sybil stepped from the coach taking Manon Lescaut to a convent school in the first act, the house broke into such thunderous welcome that the performance stopped dead in its tracks while Sybil acknowledged the applause. She looked quite dramatic in her hooded traveling cape; and from a distance her heavy make-up masked all blemish or fatigue, making her seem the glorious perfection of womanhood. With each hand, Sybil blew kisses to the approving crowd.

"The darling hypocrite," Gertrude Atherton whispered to me. "She's pretending to love her hometown."

"And part of her hometown are pretending to love her," I said. "It's a case of mutual deception."

"All art is a matter of deception," Gertrude Atherton said. "And all love as well. Sybil has given herself with equal enthusiasm to both pursuits."

"She is Manon," I said, "fickle, deceptive, loving pleasure."

"And Thais also," Gertrude said, "loving love for love's sake."

"And Esclarmonde," I said, "the enchanting daughter of the upper classes, possessed of supernal powers."

"Jules Massenet has done well by his mistress," Gertrude said, "but it took that funny little man—God, is he excitable!—three operas merely to begin the exploration of Sybil's personality."

Act One went perfectly. Sybil sang with feeling and, most importantly, with a degree of technical rigor American critics have more than occasionally accused her of neglecting. One New York critic, in fact, went so far as to say that Sybil Sanderson, a woman of independent fortune, was more *dilettante* than thoroughgoing professional; that her training at the Paris Conservatoire had been hasty; and that an enamored Massenet had pushed the young Californian too precipitously into major roles. Sybil's voice (and this sent Massenet into near-hysteric rapture when he first heard her sing) ranges a full three octaves, from G below to G above high C: a capacity exploited to the full in every opera Massenet wrote for her. Sybil's high G won her the sobriquet "The Eiffel Sol." As an actress, Sybil projects a full-bodied, full-blooded directness that I like to consider California's contribution to her stage career. Had she never sung a word, she could very well have won fame as an actress. When Sybil made her Paris debut in a performance of *Manon,* the French thrilled to Sybil's unself-conscious projection of temperament: passionate, mercurial, like Manon—and totally Californian, the French might have been informed. Sybil belongs to a generation of women who were cherished because there were so few girls in California at the time, indulged shamelessly, in fact, but also treated with a certain equality. Much was expected of them. They were not corseted or shut in, either physically or emotionally, and hence they grew up like spirited, cherished mares unbroken by checks of spur or bit.

I noticed this quality of temperament, of stage presence, if you will, the very first moment I encountered Sybil Sanderson in the late eighties at James Phelan Senior's dinner party. I fell in love with her capacity for passionate directness as much as I did with her devastating beauty. Not that her beauty eluded me: it swept me away, in fact, with the force of an unexpected kick from a horse. Greedily, I devoured the details of Sybil's face and figure: violet eyes, chestnut hair, the baby orchid that rested on the left side of her head, its delicate petals in delectable counterpoint to the flesh-sculpture of her ear, the black velvet band, affixed by a cameo, that encircled her milk-white neck; the suggestion, even then, of fullness, of generous arms and bosom, beneath her daring red dress. I stood with mouth nearly agape, wonderstruck by this young goddess, for whom, it seemed to me, all the women of my life had unwittingly served as a cumulative novitiate. Here she is, I said to myself, heart racing as from a quick swallow of brandy: the great love, the grand drama, of my mature manhood!

As difficult as Sybil could be—and many men found this out on a more intimate basis than myself—she was never a snob. Her rejection of me as a lover was purely on personal grounds, and had nothing to do with the fact, I am convinced, that she was wealthy and I was a scholar of ordinary means.

"My ambition, my obsession you might say, is to study voice in Paris and then to become an opera singer."

This from Sybil to me, some five minutes into our first conversation. Were I not so taken with her, I might have listened more closely to what she was saying and possibly recognized then and there that the passion for art overrides all other desires beyond the basic desires of physical survival. Realizing this, I might have bid Miss Sanderson *adieu,* saving myself some four or five wasted years. But I did not listen closely enough to her, and I hardly heard the ensuing remark of Joseph Duncan, the banker-poet, a friend of Phelan Senior's, who, upon hearing Sybil's declaration, said: "My daughter Isadora, barely ten, says the same thing. 'Daddy,' she says, 'when I am twenty I shall go to Europe and become a dancer.' " Isadora, age ten, Sybil, age nineteen, and Gertrude Atherton, age thirty, all felt that San Francisco offered no hope for the life of art, as they wished to lead it. My provincial ambitions and commitments blinded me to the reality of their desperation.

"What about marriage?" I asked, emboldened by her forthright directness.

729

"Don't be ridiculous!" she said. "I rejected that notion three years ago."

"When you were sixteen?"

"Yes—just barely. It happened at the Hotel Del Monte in Monterey, where Daddy likes us to spend a month every summer. Willie Hearst—he was then eighteen—and I fell in love. Willie proposed and I accepted. We announced our engagement to our parents. Senator and Mrs. Hearst were stunned, and so were my parents. Willie and I talked the matter over. We decided on second thought that Willie much preferred starting Harvard in the fall and I would rather go to Paris."

Less than a year after I met Sybil, her father Justice Silas Sanderson died, leaving his wife and four daughters a considerable fortune. After a proper period of mourning, Mrs. Sanderson closed down the family's San Francisco house and moved to Paris, where Sybil entered the Conservatoire.

"Wasn't she just marvelous!" Agnes Tobin exclaimed as the curtain fell on Act Two.

"And so thinks our distinguished young mayor," said J.O.

"And the president of the Merchants' Bank," said R.M.

"And the Tsar of All the Russias," said Cyril.

"And Sebastian Collins," said Gertrude—with malevolence, I might add.

J.O.'s reference to Jimmy Phelan's obvious infatuation with Sybil put Gertrude a little on edge. Their relationship, Gertrude and the Mayor's, is platonic, I am certain, but it is nevertheless proprietary on Mrs. Atherton's part. She loves playing the dowager countess of the administration. Jimmy, on his part, has always favored opera singers; and here was one from his own city and his own class, with whom, moreover, he grew up as a boy. In later years, I discovered (or rather, Jimmy himself told me) that the families Phelan and Sanderson would have wished nothing so much but that their son and daughter, of like age and fortune, should fall in love and marry. Sybil and he, Jimmy told me, were frequently brought together at events such as that dinner where I first met

730

her, the hope being that youthful ardor, compounded by affinity, would ignite the necessary spark. Could there have been something between Sybil and Jimmy that I was too obtuse to recognize: some physical attraction, reinforced by social caste and a mutual reverence for the arts, that might have proved, had it been acted upon, a firm foundation for a successful union? Had they married, and should Sybil have survived until 1914, she would be about fifty today and a United States senator's wife, playing a lively part as a patroness of the arts who occasionally, and only among friends, sang to piano accompaniment after dinner in a luminous, albeit untrained, soprano voice with (so an expert might detect) a three-octave range suggesting the road not taken.

"Sybil was never—nor am I, incidentally—capable of monogamy," Isadora Duncan told me some two years ago in the course of my calling upon her in Paris. "Monogamy stifles the creative instinct. Sybil and I were artists. I still am. Sybil, poor dear, is dead. The sails of our art needed wind from a number of quarters. In a sudden fit of virtue, Sybil did marry one of her lovers, Antonio Terry, a wealthy Cuban living in Paris. She genuinely loved the man. He died, alas, within the year. Sybil then got sick and died herself. So much for artists marrying."

What was this power Sybil Sanderson held over so many men, myself included, driving them to distraction? It was physical, of course, the biological attraction of sex; but it was something above the physical also—not the spiritual, for sure; Sybil did not have a religious bone in her body. She sang Thaïs as courtesan, for instance, so much more convincingly than she sang Thaïs as a reformed sinner. Sybil possessed a certain energy that, while not spiritual, was like an elixir of eros, a power of erotic hunger that emanated from her like waves of electrical energy, bringing all men into the force field of her feminine self, like moths drawn to a flame.

I, for instance, fell into a species of obsession, madness even, because of Sybil, and so did Jules Massenet. In the months following our meeting, I pestered her incessantly with

731

my unwanted attentions. I took every opportunity to secure social invitations to affairs where I knew she would be; and once there, I spent as much time in her company as possible. It took Sybil a month of such persistence on my part to realize that her friend Jimmy Phelan's tutor, a gentleman some twenty years her senior, was doing his very best to pay court. Justice and Mrs. Sanderson must have regarded me as a species of fortune-hunter, a penniless don laying siege to the city's most eligible heiress; yet because I remained polite (save in one painful instance), because I was closely connected to their friends the Phelans, and because (so I now understand) Sybil must have told them that I was harmless, they indulged in no open hostility towards me or my suit.

I, on my part, grew more and more agitated as my passion fed on itself. I fretted. I wrote poetry. I even lost weight. I behaved, in short, as a love-smitten man might be expected to behave in his early twenties, but not after having reached his late thirties certainly. I remember penning a long, rambling letter to Charlie Stoddard, then at Notre Dame, declaring my passion. I yet have Charlie's reply.

"I have burned your letter, old fellow, lest it be subpoenaed and used in your commitment proceedings. You have gone positively mad, Sebastian, and at your age! And with your experience, shall we say, of the physiology of the sexual attraction! Does not the lady in question (I shall speak frankly here in my capacity as your spiritual director), does not the divine Sybil have hair, eyes, nose, throat, mammary glands, private parts, a uro-excretory system, similar to that of the rest of her species? Was she not born? Will she not die? Does she not fill in the time between in the variety of biological functions we share with the lower mammals? She may, dear boy, snore in her sleep and now and then be guilty of an indiscreet passage of gas. The Church teaches us that only the Virgin Mary has been bodily assumed into the celestial spheres, but you, dear Sebastian, acting on your own authority and with the total taint of heresy to your actions, have placed *la divina Sybilla* next to the Genetrix herself. What blasphemy!

Hyperdulia, so Mother Church says, belongs only to the Virgin Mary. Your letter, however, reeks of the incense you've been offering hourly on the altar of a heterodox passion."

At a Christmas party given by the Phelans, dancing with Sybil in my arms, I steered her to a glass-encased solarium off to the left side of the ballroom. A bank of potted palm trees shaded us from view. Emboldened by mulled wine, made desperate by passion, I pulled the young woman to me and drank greedily of her rich, full mouth.

"I love you!" I said, kissing her on her brow, eyelids, cheeks, mouth (again), hair, ears. "I adore you! You are a goddess!"

Even to recall the scene a quarter of a century later makes me shudder with embarrassment. In the course of my life, I have been selfish, carnal, piggish even, with women for whom such behavior constituted an acceptable mode of mutual enjoyment. I have also been most tender and considerate, when such a response brought pleasure. But only once, in the Phelan solarium, behind the potted palms and beneath the colored glass, was I ever so *gauche*, so sentimental and clumsy.

"You weren't clumsy at all, dear friend," Sybil said to me in her dressing room at the Grand Opera when the subject of that Christmas season for some mysterious reason asserted itself into our discourse. "But you did scare me half to death. I thought I was about to be taken then and there beneath the palm trees like some half-clothed Polynesian being set upon by a forecastleman from *H.M.S. Bounty*. Previous to your ferocious assault, the only other male who had ever kissed me in a romantic way had been Willie Hearst, with whom I had shared a few most gentle nudgings one night behind the tennis court at the Hotel Del Monte. You, however, embraced me like a greedy octopus! I must say that in later years I would have known how to respond to such ardor."

"You flatter me, dear Sybil," I said.

"Not at all, dear Sebastian. I have made love to many men and forgotten most of them. Of late, I have been thinking of an earlier, more innocent time, and the men I refused, or

733

merely passed by, in those days. I feel a certain closeness to these men, yourself included. There are not too many of them, alas!"

"Mr. Collins," Sybil had said in shocked tones that evening, breaking away from me and drawing herself up to her full—and very statuesque—height, her violet eyes flashing near-purple with annoyance. "Mr. Collins. Now really! This is most unexpected. Shall I call for my father?"

"No, please," I said. "Do nothing! I apologize most sincerely."

She smoothed her hair with one hand, a fan dangling from a cord around her wrist. "I should hope so!" she said. "And this from a man nearly twice my age!"

Filling her lungs with air, she blew her cheeks into balloons as she expelled her deep breath in one long exhalation, looking me straight in the eye, meanwhile, for a rather long moment as if thinking something over. The music of a waltz reached us from the ballroom beyond. Then suddenly, with no warning, a smile played across her face. She began laughing and for some reason I joined her, the two of us guffawing uproariously. Sybil all the while was tapping me on the shoulder with her fan, as if I were being dubbed Sir Sebastian Quixote, Knight of the Soulful Countenance.

"Give me your handkerchief," she said at last. I handed it to her. She wiped the tears from her eyes and blew her nose triumphantly into the bleached white linen. Folding it neatly, she returned the handkerchief to me, then laughed a little more.

"You silly man," she said. "A goddess, you say." She embarked upon a series of suppressed chuckles which made her cheeks flush and her eyes sparkle and well up again with moisture. "Here's for you," she said, pulling my head down by my left ear as if I were a recalcitrant schoolboy and giving me a cool, moist kiss on the forehead. "Now dance me back to the buffet," she said. "I am utterly famished."

A letter from Sybil arrived two days after the Christmas party, written in a bold, dramatic hand that left room for but a dozen words per page. "Dear Mr. Sebastian Collins," the letter read. "While I have every regard for you as a person and while I respect the sincere, if over-forward nature of your affection, I must discourage you for a number of reasons. The most pressing of these reasons is that I am not interested in you or anyone else and never could be, although I find you a perfect gentleman (the other night notwithstanding) and an excellent conversationalist. Do not be hurt. I am interested in no man at this time. I wish only to study voice in Paris. Certainly you should understand this ambition, you who have spoken to me so encouragingly in the past concerning the life of art. On this level, Mr. Collins, and from this point of view—a shared fondness for art—I remain your rather shaken, but determined friend. Miss S. Sanderson."

Some two years later, the widowed Mrs. Sanderson encountered the famous composer Jules Massenet at a *soirée* given by the American ambassador in Paris.

"You are Jules Massenet," Mrs. Sanderson said with the assurance of wealth and the directness of California. "My daughter Sybil is at the Conservatoire. She sings. Would you like to hear her?"

"Assuredly, madame," said Massenet, then in his mid-forties and at the height of his fame, "at some time perhaps—"

"Why not now, Monsieur Massenet? Here she is and here is a piano."

Mrs. Sanderson fetched Sybil from the crowd. Taken by her beauty, and sensing at once the air of *autorité* that gave Sybil such a commanding stage presence during her brief career, Massenet sat down at the ambassador's piano. He asked the young Californian what she would like to sing. By her own choice, Sybil sang the extraordinarily intricate Queen of the Night aria from Mozart's *Magic Flute*. Devastated by Sybil's beauty, her demeanor, her upper G—so he admits in his memoirs—Massenet ran the next morning to his publisher and secured the rights for a new opera, *Esclarmonde*, to be written expressly for Sybil Sanderson for presentation at the Opéra Comique during the Universal Exhibition of 1889. Sybil sang *Esclarmonde* some hundred times, including at St. Petersburg, where she became unofficially related to the Tsar.

In *Manon*, the *corps de ballet* dances at the end of Scene One, Act Three: an outdoor festival, set in the promenade of Cours la Reine, Paris—just prior to the scene in which Manon seeks out her former lover, the Chevalier des Grieux, now an abbé in the Seminary of St.-Sulpice, convincing him to leave the Church and resume their life together. As she had promised me backstage, Iris danced especially in my honor, although only Iris and I were aware of her dedication. I made no mention to my colleagues in the box that the delightful ballerina third from the left, the one with the most rounded thighs and most pert manner, would, Maurice Grau permitting, be rendezvousing in a discreet upper room of the Poodle Dog with one Sebastian Collins, age fifty-three, after the undeserved death of Manon. I envisioned no seduction, mind you—not of such a charming child; yet I did yearn for the rendezvous as a species of symbolic farewell to the past. Iris was older than Sybil herself was when I first encountered her in the Phelan dining room; and now so quickly, a little more than a decade, Sybil and I, staring on in morbid fascination, could see a death mask staring back at her from the mirror—as might Iris herself in time, and myself, rounding the corner of middle age, the soonest of all to catch a glimpse of the grim reaper. No, I envisioned no seduction. And yet—in the course of the evening—if eyes or lips should meet, why should not an incipiently old man take solace before the impending abyss in that discreet upper room where a *chaise longue* stands to one side of the table and the door locks from within?

My passion for Sybil died during my brief marriage when I fell most truly in love with the mother of Marina. The sight of Sybil's white hair, moreover, replaced friendly regret with friendship touched by compassion. Although it had died on the altar of unrequitedness, my love for Sybil Sanderson had been an ennobling experience. It led me—with a circular motion, to be sure—to Europe and, four years later, to Merry del Val, and the Grand Chartreuse, and Ryan Patrice; and this in turn led me home to the Napa Valley and to Virginia. Because of this, I was most grateful to the statuesque chanteuse of 1888 who all too quickly, too cruelly, became the red-wigged notoriety of 1901 and, even more suddenly, the consumption-wasted corpse of 1903: that once electric body placed in a bier ever so pathetically carried by, among other pallbearers, a grieving Massenet, then sixty-one and very ill himself (although destined to recover).

That night at the Grand, when Sybil as Manon expired so touchingly on the stage at the completion of Act Five, did I have some ghastly presentiment (reinforced by the ineradicable image of her white hair and the red wig that sat so obscenely atop the hatter's dummy) that what was played out on the stage—the premature death by disease of an adored woman of pleasure—would all too soon come so terribly true for the star of the evening? I remember having such a presentiment and I remember stifling it with the sweet image of the pink flesh atop Iris's stocking and her swanlike descent to the floor in my honor. Shall I be blamed for putting the thought of death out of my mind? Sybil did so, preferring to watch with droll amusement the spirited contest between the mayor and the banker. ("Sebastian," Sybil whispered to me at the Cliff House in the course of the sherbet, "they're jealous. Isn't it divine! What a perfect homecoming!") We all think of life as long as we possibly can, postponing our regrets for the last possible moment, taking what comfort we can before the long darkness descends. Sybil had Jimmy Phelan and the banker, and I had the sweet possibility of Iris.

When the applause broke like a spent wave on the rock of Sybil's eighth curtain call, I politely begged off the Tobins' invitation for a post-opera buffet at their town house on the grounds of general fatigue and hurried outside to the line of waiting horses and taxicabs. As luck would have it, my favorite cabbie, James Norton, a robust, beefy-faced Irishman with whom I shared the adventures of the Fire of April, 1906, was at the ready outside the Grand, the first in line of the available hansoms.

"Eh, Dr. Collins, what will it be—a ride home?"

"To the stage door, Mr. Norton, if you please," I said,

entering the leathery mustiness of the hack. "We shall wait there for a while."

"I detect a night on the town, Dr. Collins, a veritable night on the town. I am yours to command—for the entire evening if necessary."

"We shall see, Mr. Norton. For the time being, a vigil before the stage door is all that is required."

A large crowd soon gathered, awaiting Sybil's departure. She made her exit flanked by both Mayor Phelan and the persistent banker. The crowd cheered and applauded as Sybil was swept into a hansom by her two competing gallants, who sat to either side of her in the cab. The hansom driver cracked his whip and his rig wheeled away towards the bright lights of Market Street. Supporting singers and members of the chorus, divested of their eighteenth-century garb, streamed forth from the stage door, attended by departing musicians in evening clothes, many of them carrying their instruments in leather cases. Searching the crowd of departees for Iris, I finally caught a glimpse of her amidst a group of some half dozen young women. Iris's turban, dominated by a trimmed peacock feather held in place by a jeweled brooch, made her seem surprisingly sophisticated and somewhat older than her twenty-odd years. Stepping out of the carriage, I waved and caught her attention. She and her five companions filed together through the crowd as if they were yet dancing on stage. As if by prior choreography, a way was cleared for them to pass.

"Oh, Mr. Collins, I am so happy to see you," Iris beamed. Her gamine companions stood behind her as we talked, the one more pretty than the other. Some of the younger musicians offered us—or rather, them—speculative glances as they passed by, toting their tubas, French horns, violins. "Mr. Grau has given me a note. It is for you." She handed me a piece of foolscap folded in two. For an exquisite second, I felt Iris's moist warm hand in the palm of my own. By the light of a streetlamp, I read Grau's missive.

"Sebastian," it read, "there's no fool like a fool past fifty.

738

When Iris's parents—Belgian immigrants, now farming in upstate New York—entrusted her to my company, I explicitly assured them that I would be on guard against such as yourself, wolves in evening dress. Although I recognize you as such, I do not condemn you, old friend. I am myself your age and I am feeling, as you are, the regrets inescapable to our time of life. I am, my friend, like a father to these girls; and thus, with a father's sternness, I make the following injunctions. You may dine with Iris, provided that you bring along her five companions. I shall expect all six of them returned safe and sound to the Palace Hotel no later than one-thirty. The company wardrobe mistress, Mrs. Featherstone, a capable virago of some sixty summers, will await the return of my dancers in the hotel lobby. Please accept the best wishes of your old friend, together with his sincere gratitude for your genorosity in feeding these hungry women whose appetites threaten to drive me into bankruptcy. Maurice Grau, Impresario."

"How sweet of you to take us to a restaurant, Mr. Collins," Iris said after I had finished the letter. "As you yourself noted, we dancers get so hungry after a performance." Laughingly, the six young dryads, led by Iris, piled into the cab, three to either seat. I tried to squeeze into the seat, but it soon became evident that such a tight fit was awkward and uncomfortable. Iris solved the problem by sitting on my lap. She smelt of rose petals and lemon water, and made a most delicious burden as she balanced her weight on my thighs, one arm held innocently around my neck.

"To the Poodle Dog, Mr. Norton," I bellowed.

"At once, governor," the redoubtable taxi man cried, and off we sped in a clattering of hooves and a rattle of wheels, the leathery mustiness of our taxi interior totally dispelled by the life-warm human scents and subtle perfume accompaniments—lavender, verbena, lemon, rose—of six young ballerinas whose clothes came from sachet-scented trunks and whose young bodies, lingeringly moist from the evening's dance, filled our cab with the most delectably ethereal vapor. By luck,

739

an upper room at the Poodle Dog had just been vacated by a party of early diners. The seven of us—Iris and I, together with the other five, whose names were those either of classical nymphs or of flowers—were soon sitting merrily around a candle-lit table, freshly set with excellent china and silver and covered in a resplendent linen tablecloth and nun-white napery.

I have never seen young women eat so! Oysters, lobster *bisque*, filet of sole, meat dishes (they each ordered something different and nibbled experimentally off each other's plates, comparing the relative merits of their orders), green salad, cheese, fruit, ice cream, sourdough bread, a respectable amount of wine, and a box of chocolates sent up *gratis* by a captivated *maître d'*: our repast took until one in the morning to complete. I heard all the gossip of the Grau Company: how Mr. Grau was not such a stern puritan as he presented himself in his letter to me (a few droll anecdotes to that effect, told by Iris, Daisy, and Daphne); how Miss Sanderson nearly stormed out of a rehearsal when one of the *corps de ballet* tittered as the diva's gown became enmeshed in the spokes of the carriage taking Manon to the convent in Act One; how Mrs. Featherstone's brandy bottle broke in her trunk *en route* to Chicago, forcing that worthy woman to rewash her entire spirit-saturated wardrobe. Iris seemed the natural leader of the merry band. The tip of the peacock feather atop her turban waved over all of us like a feathered fan used to cool the harem of the Grand Turk. Throughout the evening, incidentally, our room suffered no dearth of waiters or busboys. The *maître d'* himself made some three trips up from the lower restaurant to ensure that everything was satisfactory.

The bill paid (I was initially stunned but did my best not to reveal my inner turmoil over the cost of the evening's proceedings), we regained Mr. Norton's taxicab, waiting for us on Post Street by previous agreement. Walking through the restaurant, my six dancers were spontaneously applauded by some two dozen late diners who perhaps recognized them from the opera or were merely charmed by the spectacle of six such

740

glorious girls passing in pageant, escorted by a foiled roué in top hat, opera cape, and evening dress. Passing among the tables, the girls blew kisses to their applauding admirers. One girl, Antiope (named for the Theban maiden who bore Zeus two sons after he seduced her in the form of a satyr), had perhaps drunk more than the rest. In any event, Antiope executed the most vigorous *pirouette* just before her exit through the restaurant entrance: rising to tiptoe and moving her arms in the most graceful patterns as she danced in a tight circle, her feet whirring like hummingbirds' wings.

After a hilarious ride through the North Beach area, the girls calling from the cab to various passersby in three or four European languages, I returned the ballerinas to the redoubtable Mrs. Featherstone, who was asleep in a chair in the lobby. While the wardrobe mistress yet slept, each girl embraced me, one by one, thanking me for the wonderful evening. I was bathed in perspiration and perfumes. A number of them kissed me on the cheek. Iris was the last to embrace me, and to this day I do not know whether or not the awakening Mrs. Featherstone noticed the fact that Iris brushed her lips across mine as she said thank you, good night.

"I have a horror of the void, Sebastian. I am terrified by emptiness. Eros is the life force, pure and simple, defying the abyss, holding at bay the long dark death that threatens every living creature with extinction."

"But you're barely into your thirties," I said, rather taken by the irony that the superb specimen of manliness sitting before me, filling the studio so with his radiant manhood— this young, promising Viennese painter Gustav Klimt— should be so fearful of nothingness.

"My fear has nothing to do with age or time," Klimt said. "It's a matter of temperament, or heredity perhaps. Eros is my religion, and art is my sacrament."

"Then you are dressed most appropriately," I said. Klimt was wearing a flowing blue monk's robe, such as Balzac favored; nor did the comparison cease there, although Klimt, while stocky, never ran to flesh to the degree that Balzac did. Like Balzac, Gustav Klimt was a bohemian with ferociously exacting work habits, living in, through, and for art alone. Like Balzac also, Klimt needed a half-dozen sexual intrigues, together with one sincere affair of the heart, proceeding simultaneously, to fuel the raging fires of his art. As I knew him in Vienna in the early 1890s, Gustav Klimt bristled with physical well-being and energy, his blond hair and full beard exploding from his tan face like a sunburst. His white teeth flashed from behind the beard as Klimt smiled or laughed, which he did frequently. Klimt's muscular neck measured seventeen-and-a-half inches in circumference, and his biceps were massive and as hard as iron. As a convert to the Arts and Crafts movement, Gustav relished the difficult manual labor sometimes necessary for the completion of a work of art. When such effort was not enough to exhaust his enormous energy, he rowed by the hour the heavy longboat he kept on a small lake outside Vienna.

Or he copulated. In season and out, Gustav Klimt pursued woman. Most of the time, he caught them. Klimt and his lifelong mistress Emilie Flöge—an Art Nouveau dressmaker whose shop, Casa Piccola, enjoyed the patronage of the *avante garde* elite of Vienna—had an open, flexible agreement between them, allowing adjacent distractions, so long as such diversions were kept discreet from each other and not allowed to become matters of the heart. I myself adored Emilie—her height, her elongated voluptuousness, those oversized eyes, that wide, hungry mouth, the auburn ringlets that burst from her head like a tangled thicket abloom in wildflowers. For three weeks my admiration achieved an intermittent intimacy before Emilie broke our dalliance off on the grounds that my ardor was showing sings of sincerity.

"I must make love or die," Gustav Klimt exclaimed to me once. "Women are agents of death-defiance; their bodies, vessels of immortality. Female beauty lures us to cross the void of nothingness, carrying our precious burden of life-plasm, which we surrender in ecstasy so that a tenuous, fragile

742

rope-walk of fertile seed might remain strung out over the abyss."

Not an avid reader of books, Klimt lived directly through the flesh and through visual images; yet as I think back on his statements, made to me during my sojourn in the capital city of the Austro-Hungarian Empire—Vienna, city of dreams—the more do Klimt's intuitions seem to resemble modern scientific and philosophical notions. Like a pre-Socratic poet, Gustav Klimt used metaphors and animate images to race out ahead of abstract thought.

"Biology is the miracle of creation," I remember him once observing. "Between the chemistry of creation and the biology of creation exists an impassable gulf. No amount of chemistry, however intricate, can transform itself into the biological. A single living cell is more precious than the most radiant and fiery star because the cell exists on the other side, the biological side, the life side, of the void. The star will one day cool and die. The cell can reproduce itself. The cell possesses immortality."

Vienna in those days, the latter part of 1893, was a most charming place to be. I found my way to the city by the Danube after some three years of vagabonding around Europe. A letter now in my possession, written to me by Charlie Stoddard, sums up those years pretty well. The letter reached me in Vienna under six layers of envelopes, as one landlord or landlady after another sent it along to forwarding addresses in London, Madrid, Florence, Munich, Prague, Dresden, Vienna.

"*En route* to Tahiti, I returned to San Francisco for a brief visit," Charlie had written, "and I found the whole City, our circle at least, yet speculating about your abrupt resignation from the College and expatriation to Europe. I secured this Madrid address from your mother, who looks well by the way. I was delighted to find the Chief, your *pater*, as Roman as ever. Will that man never grow old? He is nearing or past seventy, and I, a boy in my late forties, can barely mount a full flight of stairs while the Chief takes the steps two at a time. Except for

743

the gray in his hair, the Chief hasn't changed since the 1860s when you and I were lads. Such are the rewards of clean living. I must try it—clean living—sometime soon."

In January 1890, resigning from St. Ignatius College, I transferred my life's savings from the Hibernia Bank (the sum of $8,973) to a London bank doing business on the continent. I closed down my affairs in San Francisco and left for Europe. I was a few months short of forty-two and thoroughly sick of my San Francisco existence.

"I am getting nowhere, doing nothing," so I summed up my situation to my closest friend at the time, a young woman in her late twenties, Virginia Walsh, who was managing the Tobins' domestic affairs in San Francisco, living at the Tobin town house at Taylor and California streets. Virginia and I enjoyed a friendship based on strong affinities. We were both children of the lesser Irish *bourgeoisie*, dependent, to a considerable extent, upon the patronage of the great. Like my parents, Virginia's father and mother came to California during the gold rush directly from Ireland via New York. Her father joined the Hibernia Bank in the early sixties, rising to the position of assistant chief cashier before his death in 1880. Virginia's mother died of pneumonia in 1876. The Tobins took Virginia into their household as a governess, a companion, a supervising housekeeper—it would be hard to describe her role. She possessed family status, yet she was also expected to serve the family by keeping it running. While not exactly a mistreated Cinderella, Virginia was expected to pay her way through work. And work she did, from her mid-teen years when she entered the Tobin household, to her departure for Napa County as my bride in 1894. Virginia and I got along famously. Her parents and my parents had been friends since the 1850s. Virginia had a handsome, suitably strong Irish face: brunette hair, a wide forehead, blue-green eyes, a prominent nose, and the most wonderful mouth across which a half-smile always danced. She also had the most refreshingly unpretentious manner.

"Now tell me what books to read, Sebastian, you with your grand education and I having barely finished grammar school.

744

Agnes suggests that you tutor me, and I'm most willing to have you do so."

Virginia had Saturdays completely to herself, so we fell into the habit of walking and talking about the city on Saturday afternoons. I would recommend a book, then we would discuss it on the following Saturday. We once walked, I remember, through the Panhandle of Golden Gate Park out to the glass conservatory of flowers, modeled upon the Crystal Palace of the 1855 London Exhibition. Another time, we took the train out to Land's End and picked our way along the path that skirts the headlands over the sea, finishing our afternoon with tea at the Cliff House, watching the sea lions on Seal Rock. Once, we hiked as far as Hunter's Point, where Ralston built a gigantic drydock in the late 1860s.

"Now why does Matthew Arnold feel such despair in 'Dover Beach'?" Virginia would ask. Or: "Is Mr. Gibbons's depiction of Christianity flawed by irreligious sentiment?" Or: "Do you agree with Newman's definition of literature, Sebastian, and what does he mean by 'notional assent' anyway? I find the concept difficult to fathom." Virginia had a way of going to the heart of the matter, unbothered by erudition, precedent, or received opinion.

"I think Mr. Coleridge is needlessly obscure, hence boring," she once said. "Why write criticism if you're not going to make your opinions clear?" Or: "You might be right about *Moby Dick*. It might very well be a great classic, but the plot collapses. It seems four or five different books enjambed into one."

"Enjambed?" I asked.

"A new word. I learned it yesterday. Walter Pater uses it in one of his essays." Like my mother, Virginia Walsh enjoyed learning new words. For her birthday, I bought her an excellent edition of *Webster's Dictionary*.

"Now you'll never be at a loss for new words," I said.

"My thoughts and emotions are rather basic," she replied. "But now I'll be able to follow your erudite discourse."

By 1890 it had long since become clear to me that no art museum had a ghost of a chance of being founded in San

Francisco, much less anything as elaborate as Mr. Ralston's dreamed-of research institution. As I rounded forty, and faced the rush of years that would soon bring me to fifty, I grew depressed. My futile enamorment with Sybil Sanderson and her departure for Paris dramatized to me in no uncertain terms that I was no longer young, physically attractive, or emanative of the promise of career. Returning to San Francisco from Rome in 1878, I had arrived triumphantly on the scene a young man of thirty, the author of a just-published monograph on Bernini. How could a mere dozen years so totally dispel the hope of that homecoming? By 1890, in any event, I found myself a provincial schoolmaster in a forgotten corner of the world, past forty, putting on weight, and with few prospects before me.

"Why are you running away?" Virginia asked in the course of one of our last Saturday walks about the city as we discussed my intention to expatriate myself.

"I am not running away," I insisted. "I am merely returning to Europe so I can turn over new material to write about. I am by training an art historian. I have published my dissertation and a series of general essays, but for five years now I've done nothing. One can live only so long off the fruits of one's youthful research. I am going to Europe to gather new wheat into my barn."

"Stay home and write about California instead," Virginia said. We were sitting just across from the park carousel on a sunny park bench adjacent to the handsome buff-stoned Romanesque hostelry donated by Senator Sharon to the city for the convenience of mothers with small children. Parents and children stood patiently in line at the entrance to the dome-covered carousel, awaiting their turn to ride on one or another of the life-sized wooden animals. To our left, children were being taken on donkeys by uniformed attendants. On a grassy knoll to our right, families with small children were picnicking on blankets spread across the grass. An Italian organ grinder, with a small monkey leashed to his instrument, moved from family to family, his hand-cranked music in tinny counterpoint to the bellowing organ, crashing cymbal, and booming drum of the carousel music machine.

"How can I write about California?" I asked. "Painting is yet in its infancy here."

"Write about something other than painting," Virginia said. "Write a history of San Francisco. Write a novel. Write anything, Sebastian, but stay in your home city. There's plenty to do here and many who depend upon you."

"Such as who?" I asked with a certain self-indulgent bitterness. I subsequently learned a very important lesson: make yourself agreeable; even better, make yourself useful, and you'll never lack for a circle of friends.

"Such as your students at the College."

"They'll find other teachers."

"Your parents."

"My dear, I am forty-two. It's high time I moved away from home."

"Your friends."

"They have other friends."

"Me, then. I shall miss you—terribly."

"You?"

"Yes me—or am I not to count?"

"Of course you count. You know how fond I am of you."

"Well then—me. I shall miss you."

I cannot recall my reply, but I do remember that it was intended to deflect Virginia's declaration. I also remember taking another look at her as she spoke so generously and at such risk to her personal pride. I saw, as if for the first time, the even line of her white teeth, the curl of her mouth, the adequacy of her breasts.

"You fool, Sebastian," Virginia made clear to me a number of years later as we sat before the fire of our snug cottage outside St. Helena in the Napa Valley, discussing the event. "I threw myself at you shamelessly. I virtually begged you not to leave. But you were so self-absorbed. Honestly, a man of forty-two, pouting like a child!"

"I am now forty-seven, my dear, and I shall pout once again

if you do not come over here instantly and sit on my lap."
Virginia complied, throwing her arms around my neck. Even
in the country, where we both worked so hard tending the
vines, she always had a fresh clean scent to her, as if a linen
closet had been opened and the smell of lavender and lemon
soap were flooding the room.

Virginia had stated the matter correctly, however: at
forty-two I was pouting because some of my dreams had not
come true. Yet my situation was not that blindly self-
indulgent. I did, please remember, gather the material for two
books during my second European sojourn: *Theological and
Literary Relationships* (1905) and *Sybil Sanderson, A California
Story* (1910), both written and published long after my return
from Europe in 1894 but dependent upon the observations,
researches and most intense experiences of those years. Pouting
aside, by 1890 my San Francisco well had truly run dry. I
found myself bored by the assumptions, gossip, and above all,
the self-satisfied stability of my provincial capital. Having
been found wanting by a younger woman eager for a larger
stage of life, I took a second look at myself, discovering that I
had long since passed the midpoint of my life without
accomplishing a fraction of what I had set out to do. I had long
since surrendered all hope for the Atheneum—but not for
further accomplishment in the world of scholarship.
Paradoxically—because research involves discipline and
restriction—I also yearned for movement, for new scenes, for a
greater variety of people in my life.

Europe both answered and failed to answer these needs. In
the course of four years there, I saw many fine pictures and
noble buildings, and I managed—however intermittently—to
do much good research. I also, alas, developed something of a
drinking problem and lived a highly irregular life sexually.
Upon wider observation, I have decided that the mid-forties
are a most dangerous time in a man's life: a long lonely walk
on the far shore of regret. Haunted by opportunities missed,
by a stymied career, by a great love rejected, I solaced myself
overmuch with wine and sporadic bouts of illicit, loveless

748

copulation. As a younger man in Heidelberg and Rome, such pleasures of sense had seemed of the very essence of life itself. Each glass, each kiss, was soaked in futurity—the advance suggestion of an impending lifetime of such pleasures. There would be grapes and caresses aplenty—each sip, each disengagement of garment, each revealed splendor of breast and thigh, told me. That same glass, however, and similar kisses (before I experienced the healing ministrations of Mrs. Santone) communicated the opposite message when I sought them again in middle age in Europe. Abed, time mocked my every effort to stay its menacing flight through carnal frenzy. I felt the Death Skull behind the moist mouth. I tasted decay at the downy entrance to the womb. The womb of life seemed at so many times a portal to darkness, to extinction. Under my caress, jewel-nippled breasts became the horrible dugs, loathsome and pendulant, of an aged crone from Dürer, some menacing prophetess of plague and death and ancient eld. Smiling teeth turned without warning into the snaggled fangs of a mocking laughter; the sigh of rapture became a snake hiss. Lovemaking degenerated into an ape-dance, an obscene humping over the already dug grave of decaying flesh.

I have always loved the pleasures of food and drink. As a Californian, moreover, and a former winegrower, I have sustained a special interest in good wines. As in all fine pleasures, I find in wine a dramatic instance of the abiding mystery of things. From its first fermentation to its final consumption, wine is alive in an infinity of bacteriological processes. The ancient equation of wine with life is thus actual as well as symbolic. Wine is a pathway between the animate and the inanimate. Wine arouses in mankind the suspicion that there is at the heart of things some utter and ineffable goodness awaiting man's use. Wine reconciles man to his sojourn amidst mystery. Wine helps allay the terror of existence, the suspicion that conscious life is accidental and to no purpose. No wonder then that the classical and the Judeo-Christian traditions consider wine a natural sacrament; for wine cannot help but suggest the transcendent. In the eucharist, Orthodox and Catholic Christianity make of wine the very blood of divinity, shed for the remission of sins.

The abuse of wine, therefore, is the violation of a natural sacrament. Habitual drunkenness is a special sort of breach of promise with nature. For the past twenty years, I have been a bottle-a-day man, which I consider a moderate level of consumption for San Francisco. During the years 1890–1894, however, I confess to heavy drinking and to a number of instances of outright intoxication to the point of illness and the loss of my ability to work. As in the case of eros, wine the life-enhancer became the harbinger of death. The draught of vintage

> Cooled a long age in the deep-delved earth,
> Tasting of Flora and the country green,
> Dance, and Provençal song, and sunburnt mirth

taken to excess, filled my stomach with nausea and engendered in my brain fantasies of beasts, demons, horrible creatures from some loathsome netherworld which, toadlike, clung to the side of my bedroom wall or left a trail of green slime across my bedsheet.

As bad as it got, however, I was never the complete *debauché*. I investigated the analogies between the paintings of El Greco and the mystical theology of St. John of the Cross. I compared the *Spiritual Exercises* of St. Ignatius and the architecture of the Church of the Gesù. I researched the sources and analogues, sacred and secular, behind the dramaturgical structure of the Tridentine mass. I sought out pre-Counter-Reformation depictions of the Sacred Heart in church windows and in prayer books and hymnals. I took notes for these and the other essays later published as *Theological and Literary Relationships*: "The Catholic Career of John Donne," "Francis de Sales and Jane Frances de Chantal: The Confessor as Courtier of the Soul," "Quietism and Port Royal," "The Sulpician Aesthetic," "St. Paul of the Cross and the Passionist Practice of Incarnational Prayer," "Ruskin, Newman, and the Oxford Movement," "Dante and the Americans," "Longfellow's Spanish Sojourn." All this was researched amidst whoring and hangovers, and restless movement from Madrid to Prague. From this point of view, then, my second European sojourn proved a success. I gathered a rich harvest into the empty granary of my notebooks and my imagination.

I arrived in Vienna in late 1892, ambitious for an essay (a general periodical effort, not a scholarly investigation) on the emerging decorative and painterly style known as Art Nouveau. My capital sorely depleted, I wrote Mr. Howells at the *Atlantic Monthly* regarding the possibility of his buying an essay on new art trends in Vienna. I received an affirmative reply and the offer of two hundred dollars upon acceptance, a very generous fee indeed. At my request, Charles Eliot Norton, my old professor at Harvard, had spoken to his fellow Cantabridgian Howells on my behalf. In his letter of commission, Mr. Howells encouraged me to develop as much local color as I could—artists' lives especially—as well as laying down the theoretical premises of the Art Nouveau movement. "Give us," Mr. Howells said, "the talk of coffee house and garret, the specifics of studio life, concentrating, if possible, upon one painter or at least one circle of painters working in Art Nouveau."

My *Atlantic Monthly* essay "Gustav Klimt, Young Painter of the New Art in Old Vienna" (June 1893) represents a distillation of the months I spent as a captivated habitué of the Klimt circle. So much of Klimt's best work, I realize, has been done since that time. My essay, however, possesses the special charm of catching an emerging artist in the penultimate phases of his apprenticeship—and an emerging style, the Art Nouveau, in the earliest phases of its practice. Ever since that time, I have been possessed of a special fondness for the Art Nouveau: its riot of pastel and floral color; its decorative skein of crowded organic patterns and luxuriant organic imagery— flowers, vines, leaves, shoots and tendrils of such variety; the almost Oriental, certainly Byzantine, flatness of perspective and formality of composition; the siren eros playing just beneath the stylized surface; the women, Klimt's women, red

751

of hair, luxuriant of bare breast, their eyes and mouths possessed of an immemorial wisdom, their hips promising appeasement for those eternal hungers which the Art Nouveau suggested through masculine and feminine imagery drawn from nature; a Shakespearean riot of phallic and uterine images leaping out from garden plant and floral wreath.

"Decoration and color are not incidental to art," I remember Klimt booming to me as, in a paint-spattered blue monk's robe, he worked at his canvas—in this case, the depiction of a nude girl, redheaded, asleep atop an astonishing violet drapery rich in Mycenean motifs, one thigh drawn high in an expanse of flesh that begged caress, one rose-red rose-white breast peeping from beneath a cascade of riotous red hair. "Decoration and color are art. Nothing, you see, has substance. I suspect that the most elementary particles of matter itself are unstable phantasms. All creation, everything that we see, spreads before us like an organic film on the edge of that fearsome abyss which is the stage of life. My canvas is blank, like the void itself. We fill it like this, with a defiance of patterned abundance." He attacked the canvas while I took notes for my essay for Mr. Howells.

Klimt, incidentally, refused to prune or even cut the teeming garden he planted outside his suburban, wall-enclosed studio. The more flower crowded flower, the more vine clung to tree, or bush warred with vine and grasses—the more Klimt delighted in his horticultural handiwork.

"Look at it, Sebastian," he once said. "See how much of life manages to crowd itself into this closed space. Such is all organic life on this planet, ourselves included, a huddled skein, a jumbled frame of crowded beasts and flowers hung on the infinitely empty wall of the universe." As a joke (I had asked him for a self-portrait for my *Atlantic* essay), Klimt once rapidly sketched out a portrait of himself as an ambulatory set of male genitalia.

"This is hardly suitable for the *Atlantic*," I laughed, but I kept the sketch anyway, for it said much about the Don Juanism of the artist for whom woman, single and collectively,

752

was everything. Klimt banished the male of the human species from his canvas, as if the phallic presence of the pestles and lily pods and spear-stalked plants in the backgrounds of his portraits of women sufficed to suggest certain seed-bearing, seed-transferring necessities. Klimt's signature sign, an octopus with human (indeed Klimtian) eyes and caressing tentacles that ended in something suggestive of the male anatomy, expressed the artist's conception of himself as a creature born like Venus from the sea, his phallic possibilities multiplied eightfold.

"Gustav is both tortured and entranced by variety," Emilie Flöge once remarked, somewhat sadly I noticed, despite the open, bohemian agreement she and Klimt had come to (the benefits of which I myself experienced in the course of a brief exposure to Emilie's caresses, abruptly begun and just as abruptly broken off), all women in their heart of hearts being monogamous because procreation, however thwarted, is yet the formal end, the final cause, of copulation: nature needing us, not for our happiness, but primarily to carry on the species. "Gustav must have many women because he is afraid."

"Afraid?" I asked. "He seems so buoyant. His energy fills the space around him like a physical force."

"He is afraid of death," Emilie replied, her hand on her hip, her self-designed sea-blue dress alive with floral and seaweed patterns, as if she herself had just walked forth from the life-teeming brine, a sea-storm of brown curls edging the shoreline of her brow.

"We are all afraid of death," I said.

"But Gustav is afraid of death in a special way. He is, you see, tempted by the worship of death. He loathes, yet is enamored of, the final extinction. Have you noticed how many of the women he paints are *femmes fatales*? Their embrace is both life-giving ecstasy, and death as well."

"Vienna is a strange city," I remarked. "Some half-acknowledged subliminal drama seems at work here. There is so much life, so much exuberance; yet so much talk of longing, suppression, and death as well."

753

"You are an American," Emilie said. "You must have everything so simple. But everything is not simple. Now kiss me."

I kissed her, almost against my will, and then we made love, myself having for an instant the image of Klimt, in some other secret room in some other portion of this dream-city, kissing some other face—then rising, like myself, uneasily from the bed of miscellaneous eros, half-hearing the hissing of a snake from behind a trampled bed of flowers.

Sailing across the Atlantic in March 1894, I would stand alone on the steamer deck by night under the yet-wintry stars protected by a greatcoat and a muffler against the evening winds. Within me, matching the surging of the sea, I could hear the music of *Thaïs*. My time as a lay oblate at the Grand Chartreuse, working outdoors every day in a score of manual occupations—cutting wood, hauling hay, removing stones from Alpine fields—had toughened me to the point that I actually relished my evening encounters with the stinging winds of the second class deck. If it were stormy, I loved to lean my body into the howling wind, Thaïs's death-scene playing in my mind; or, if it were calm, I would pace quietly to and fro, hearing the violin solo of the Meditation from Act Two in which the Alexandrian courtesan Thaïs paces away the restless night, her soul on the verge of conversion to a purer love. I would think, then, of the letter to Virginia, posted in Paris two weeks before my departure and hence moving ahead of me halfway across the civilized world. I had written this letter in my cell at Chartreuse (a room I shared with six other oblates), sitting on the edge of my cot and trying to make my crude pencil stub and the rough tablet balanced on my knee serve to record the complex thoughts and emotions welling within me. The letter, containing my proposal of marriage, would reach San Francisco at least ten days before I did.

The monastery of *La Grande Chartreuse*, mother house of the ancient order of Carthusian monks, was founded by St. Bruno—a noble ecclesiastic who renounced a Church career

754

and fled the world—in the latter part of the eleventh century. Totally rebuilt in the late seventeenth century in the fortress style of the period, Grand Chartreuse sits in the high, desolate, wild Alpine valley of Dauphiné, some fourteen miles north of Grenoble. Ever since St. Bruno established himself and his followers there in 1084, *La Grande Chartreuse* has been a constant hive of monastic life. The Carthusian Rule calls for solitary meditation, manual labor, and communal prayer. The monks live separately in individual apartments, where they pray and read and pursue various manual crafts. They come together, however, for liturgical worship, for certain meals, and for intermittent recreation, usually long walks in the countryside. Carthusians do not starve themselves, nor do they keep total silence like the Trappist Cistercians, yet the Carthusian Order is among the strictest in the Roman Church, having produced over the past eight hundred years a distinguished array of mystics and saints, including the late Ryan Patrice who died at *La Grande Chartreuse* in the year 1900 in the odor of sanctity in the fifth year of his profession as a choir monk, having transferred to the Carthusians from the Paris Foreign Missionary Society in 1890 after nearly fifteen years as a missionary in French Indo-China. The Carthusian Order consists of professed choir monks who are ordained priests; lay brothers, who are not priests but who do take vows; and lay auxiliaries or oblates, such as I was for four months, who help out with the general work of the monastery in exchange for room and board. Despite the fact that Patrice was an ordained priest and had once refused to accept election as superior general of his Society (a post that automatically carried with it the rank of titular bishop), the former missionary and before that, former secret agent of the Papal States, was working in the fields as an ordinary oblate when I encountered him—eighteen years after saying farewell in Rome. In 1895, a year after I left *La Grande Chartreuse*, the prior encouraged Patrice to transfer to the ranks of choir monks. Ryan Patrice died wearing the white robes of a professed Carthusian.

You approach *La Grande Chartreuse* through an Alpine landscape that grows bleaker and bleaker the higher you rise. The monastery itself sits above the level of four thousand feet in an open pasture surrounded by forest and beyond that by the barren ridges of the Grandson. In 1676 an energetic prior, Innocent Le Masson, began the reconstruction of Chartreuse on a formidable scale. Upon first glance, in fact, the monastery seems a stone fortress—dominated by a score of pointed roofs—set there by Vauban in the time of Louis XIV to thwart the invasion of France from the south.

Upon the occasion of my precipitous confession to Monsignor Merry del Val in the Church of St.-Sulpice in Paris, my confessor advised me to go to the Grand Chartreuse for a long retreat. I remained there some four months, quartered with the oblates, among them Ryan Patrice. I shall never forget that happy time of my life: the rows of white-robed monks chanting in tiered choir stalls by early morning candlelight before the austere high altar of the monastery church; the rough work of the fields—the cutting, stacking, hauling, draying; the exacting duties of the kitchen, helping the brother cook to prepare nourishing meals for two hundred— cheese, eggs, fresh vegetables in season, sturdy dark bread, heavy country soups—in great stone ovens and copper vats, then bringing the food around by pushcart to the various hermitages of those monks living an eremetical life of solitude or serving the lay brothers and oblates *en masse* at sweeping wooden tables lined up under the vaulted stone ceiling of the refectory adjacent to the *grand cloître*. Yes indeed, I earned my way; yet I received more than I gave. Working six hours a day, I sweated away some of the effects of my over-bibulous living. Walking alone along the mountain paths

> Through Alpine meadows soft-suffused
> With rain, where thick the crocus blows,
> Past the dark forges long disused . . .
> Through forest, up the mountainside

(so Matthew Arnold describes the landscape in "Stanzas from

756

the Grand Chartreuse"), I recovered concentration of mind, and I rediscovered the life of the soul, a process aided by my attendance at daily mass and by a number of fortuitous conferences with Ryan Patrice.

"You need to make certain decisions," my young confessor Merry del Val had told me in Paris in the course of describing what he thought I should do while on retreat. "You must decide, for instance, about chastity. You are in your mid-forties, yet what do you have to show as the result of your God-given sexual energies? A wife? Children? No—nothing. The sexual drive is a compelling, precious energy. My priesthood in no way blinds me to its power and charm. Carnal love has been given to mankind for a purpose—mutual delight, procreation, and the sanctification of the soul. Sexual power is not to be squandered, like Onan casting his seed to the ground. You are obviously not called to celibacy." Here a wry grin spread across Merry del Val's handsome Spanish face. "Yet you have never married. Go to the Grand Chartreuse and ask yourself why you have never sanctified your sexual instinct, why you have never allowed your hunger for love to serve the divine purpose."

I pondered Merry del Val's admonition a number of times in a number of different parts of the monastery, as I prayed, walked, or fulfilled my manual duties under the demanding direction of the lay brother in charge. The more I thought on the problem, the more Virginia came to mind. I found myself wishing that she were at my side as I enjoyed a half-day of freedom from work, hiking along the paths leading to the Grandson, or lying at my ease with a book in some flower-strewn Alpine meadow. I recollected the steadiness of her gaze, the accepting manner with which she faced life, the smell of lavendered white linen that seemed ever about her. Walking up to the communion rail to receive the Eucharist from a chasubled Carthusian monk, his head shaven save for a run of hair above his ears (the medieval-style tonsure), I remembered how Virginia and I, the prospect of a Sunday sail by ferryboat across the bay to Marin before us, followed by a ramble and a picnic on the slopes of Mt. Tamalpais, would go to mass together at Old St. Mary's, approaching the communion rail together like (it struck me even then) an already married couple.

Contemplating my haphazard sexual pilgrimage, I felt very little guilt regarding my conduct, having always, I suppose, been deficient in that regard—even today at sixty-seven. I have always believed that Irish Catholicism, forced into puritanical molds by the Jansenist heresy, could stand a moderate return to Gaelic joyousness in the flesh. Our celibate clergy, it seems to me, frequently cultivates a morbid, guilt-ridden preoccupation with sex, which it imposes upon lay people. Even in my quasi-Carthusian state, however, I regretted nothing. Whatever had happened was God's will, and I owed a debt of gratitude to those women who had shared their bodies and their souls (to greater or lesser extents) with me. I remembered them all as a rescented fragrance, a re-heard poem, a yet echoing song: the raven-haired woman in Rome who on the eve of battle led me, hesitating, to the bed; Signora Anna Amari stepping from her chemise, as embarrassed and delighted as a bride on her wedding night; Gudrun's sly glance at me from beneath her green eyeshade when I first called upon her at the Hotel Zum Ritter in Heidelberg after our night of carnival passion; the nervous, frenetic kisses of Emilie Flöge, like the beat of a bird's wing across my mouth; the long, languorous kisses of Mrs. Santone, threatening to suck from me my very soul, exhaled in a breath of ecstatic surrender.

The Church, I had to admit, would see an element of sin in these relationships. Well then, I'll let the Church worry about it! I am no theologian, yet I can comprehend the one great paradox of my faith: we find God only in love, even when love involves error. Such a paradox was discovered by the courtesan Thaïs. By the time I attended the premiere of Massenet's masterpiece at the Paris Opera on the night of 16 March 1894, I had already probed the central message of the Thaïs legend—the razor's edge of love, the irremedial interpenetration of sacred and profane urges—through my meditations at

758

La Grande Chartreuse. Ryan Patrice proved most helpful in assisting me to sort my way through the labyrinth of unrepented error in which I wandered.

"Forget your sins, if sins they be," he urged me. "Cast yourself headlong upon God's love, begging His grace to assist you in reaching the perfection of your nature. Long ago, I sought to make you a priest. I was in error. Your nature would have been destroyed by the priesthood. But you must, within the conditions and possibilities of your God-given character, seek perfection in the time remaining to you on this earth. How shall you do this?"

"Through marriage," I said almost without thinking. "I shall ask Virginia Walsh of San Francisco to be my wife."

"And I shall seek perfection here, Sebastian, in the silence of this cloister. Both of us have made different decisions because we both possess different natures. Both of us, however, are loved by God and called to His perfection."

"The perfection of God is frightening to contemplate," I said.

"Not if you look for it in its most obvious manifestation: the nature God has endowed you with. Marry, procreate," Ryan Patrice said—how Indo-China had humanized him! "To love deeply, to bring an immortal soul into the world, is to imitate the creative work of Almighty God Himself."

Arriving back in Paris in mid-March 1894 *en route* to San Francisco, I secured a ticket for the premiere of *Thaïs*, having seen attractive posters about the city announcing the event. I played momentarily with the idea of calling upon Sybil at the rehearsals under way at the Opera House, but decided against it. My decision not to call upon her was a complex one; the very moment I made it, I walked from my hotel to the post office and posted the long letter I had written to Virginia in my dormitory cell at the Grand Chartreuse. The day after the premiere, I began my journey back to San Francisco, having written a note of congratulations to Sybil and leaving it in the care of the Opera House *concierge*.

"Why didn't you tell me you were in town?" Sybil

admonished me in the course of her return visit to San Francisco. "I was in a perfect fright about *Thaïs* and could have used some hometown support. Jules got so nervous that he ran off to Dieppe the day before. I had to go on stage all alone. And then—the accident. Darling, it was dreadful!"

By "the accident," Sybil was referring to the fact that early in the opera, a clasp broke upon her already daring courtesan's costume, exposing her naked to the waist. A gasp went up from the audience as Sybil turned her dazzling milk-white, pink-crested frontage first in one direction, then in another, reaching behind her all the while for the fallen upper garment. The effect was that of a deliberately provocative mime, rather in keeping with the operatic heroine's yet unreformed character. Trouper that she was, Sybil hardly missed a note as she recovered her fallen tunic. On balance, in fact, the accident added immensely to the evening. Sybil's involuntary nudity dramatized beyond Massenet's wildest dreams the sexual intensity of the opera, making more dramatic, if possible, Thaïs's conversion to Christianity and the monk Athanael's conversion to eros. The audience became, in effect, eye-witnesses to Sybil's sexual magnetism and hence could very well sympathize with Athanael's suppressed, then raging, desire. Because Sybil had been so frankly revealed in her gender, moreover, her portrayal of Thaïs the saint avoided a condition of one-dimensional piety. The audience was ever aware of the woman beneath the nun's habit.

"Dear Virginia," I had written at the Grand Chartreuse (the letter, ten pages in all, took me three sessions to compose; I but excerpt it here), "I write to you in sorrow and hope: sorrow for not having recognized the worth of what was happening between us; hope, that all is not lost. Is it ridiculous for me to say that at age forty-five I have at last reached maturity? Such retarded development! I have been blind, Virginia, but now I can see. I see you, in fact, right before me now, emerging laughingly from one of the lovely Alpine meadows covered in wildflowers which one encounters a thousand feet below this high mountain valley where I have passed months in physical

760

work, reflection, and prayer: thinking of you all the while, I might add, and wondering why I fled you so precipitously nearly four years ago. By now, you have perhaps given your heart to another. If that is the case, I accept my fate. I deserve to lose you. But if there be any hope, then I shall seize desperately upon it, asking you to entertain here and now this clumsily written proposal of marriage, which I shall repeat to you in person—even more clumsily perhaps—when I reach San Francisco."

Staring out onto the white-flecked Atlantic, surging with the awesome power of untamed nature herself, I heard in my mind the music of *Thaïs* and I thought of my homecoming, and I thought of Virginia. Like Thaïs, I had been betrayed by sensuous love to something finer; but like her also, I could not, would not, ever repudiate the sensuous manner of my loving. Despite my maleness, I belong to the race of Magdalenes and Thaïses who began their pilgrimage in wayward surrender. I have never been tempted by the cenobite monk Athanael's rage for abstract virtue, for the transcendent Godhead directly perceived beyond the realm of sense; hence, I have never felt compelled to abandon God because He refused to reveal Himself directly to me. I sought Him, rather, in the beauties and the delights of His creation—in painting, landscape, food and wine, the light in a woman's face, the swanlike arch of her neck—and I sought Him in the flaming love of His Son Jesus Christ, revealed as the Sacred Heart: at Whose feet I threw myself in desperate longing, kissing the wounds left there by the cruel nails, rising to my knees to kiss the pierced hands, then in a rush of fear and shuddering delight feeling the brush of that bearded cheek against my forehead and knowing that all would be well, that the crucifixion of the flesh was past and the time of the resurrection at hand.

Chapter 17

I FIND IT STUPID, outrageous. How could anyone so healthy possibly contract anything that serious?

"Breast cancer can afflict even the healthiest of women," the doctor told me when I asked for an explanation in the corridor outside Deborah's ward at the University of California Hospital ("No, doctor, I'm not a relative, just a good friend").

"At the moment, we don't know what it is, do we? Just lumps, which we'll remove the day after tomorrow and take a look at before we start using the word 'cancer.' Breast tumors are a common enough occurrence and in the majority of cases, there's nothing to worry about." The doctor was younger than I. He had a laid-back Marin County style, complete with a frizzy Afro-Hebro and a mustache. He also sounded as if he knew what he was talking about.

"Her parents are coming in from Arizona tomorrow," the doctor said, "and Dr. Cy Karlin, professor of oncology here, a friend of Dr. Tanner's from medical school, is coming in on the case as a consultant. So it's all in good hands. Removing the tumors and examining them are routine procedures; so—if I might be frank—don't hover around her with such a goddam worried look on your face. That does no one any good, especially the patient. Her good spirits are important to us here. Know her long?"

"About a year."

"She's a dynamite girl. She spent all day yesterday in the terminally ill children's ward, reading to them, telling stories, organizing games."

"She's trained to do that sort of thing," I said.

"So she told me, but I'm impressed anyway. So many women in her situation get hysterical. They become convinced of the worst and have to be calmed down with medication. It's nice to deal with such an easy patient—someone who insists upon contributing."

"When will we know?" I asked.

"By the late afternoon following the morning operation. A biopsy is a pretty simple procedure."

"I know it's after hours," I said, "but can I duck in for a moment?"

"Suit yourself, man, but only if you go in there with a more positive attitude."

"What's there to be positive about?"

"Her, man, her—the chick herself!"

"I heard your voice outside the door," Deborah said when I entered the room. She was propped up comfortably on two pillows. There were three other beds in the room, two of them empty. A young black woman was asleep in a bed near the window. The room had a spectacular view of San Francisco.

"His name is Saul Sternberg," Deborah said. "He's a resident in oncology from New York. He lives in Sausalito and he's Jewish."

"So I gathered," I said. "He's a nice guy."

"Dreamy," Deborah said. "His brother is an assistant professor of law at Yale."

I sat down on the single chair next to Deborah's bed. Leaning over, I rested my head in her lap, as if I were a child seeking a mother's comfort. Deborah grabbed the hair on the back of my neck and tugged it.

"Hey, Bozo, I'm the one who's supposed to be sick."

"I was just resting," I said.

"Well, rest some more," she said. Reaching across her body to embrace her hips, I buried my face in her stomach, inhaling the scent of fresh sheets and hearing a soft, gurgling noise against my ear. Don't be sick, Deborah, don't be sick, I prayed, my face pushed now into her lap, my arms around her legs. No, no, no, no—don't be sick. I thought of her long suntanned legs as I remembered them from Tinsley Island, and I felt their firmness beneath the white, antiseptic smelling sheets. I thought of her tattooed rose, in such contrast, that touch of Klimt, to the Sunbelt side of her nature, and now pointing out the spot, this very same flesh rose, where something firm, some thickening of tissue, extended itself towards the surface of her skin in ominous suggestion of that disorder which all women fear, and so many women must cope with. We found it together, this hideous intruder, in the course of my being there, above the rose, with hand and mouth and tongue. Later, as we lay side by side, I made mention of it, and she said that, yes, she also, had made its acquaintance a week ago and would be going to the doctor the very next day in fact; and then: "I'm frightened." Just that, no tears, no hysterics, no visible emotion; just the stated fact of fear, but no further mention of the fear, even on that day before yesterday when I drove her up to Parnassus Heights, she holding a small overnight bag in her hand as if the two of us were on our way up to Mendocino for the weekend, instead of heading towards the vast hospital complex that sits atop the city's highest inhabitable mountaintop as if to warn all below of our final mortality and the possibilities of true pain in the time in between.

"Mother and Father will be coming up," Deborah told me as she entered the elevator that would zoom her up some ten stories to her ward, an elevator into which the nurse escorting her insisted that I could not enter. "I called them last night. I asked them to get in touch with you when they get here." The nurse pressed a button and the elevator doors closed. Deborah stood facing me as those steel jaws shut on her, her back to the elevator wall, her overnight bag held in both hands, her face whiter than I'd ever seen it before. I stood before the closed doors, looking up at the numerals above the elevator entrance:

764

two glowed red, then three, then four. Ten lighted up and stayed that way as Deborah and the nurse stepped out onto the ward. Ten, ten, ten—the word for routine surgery; for, thus far, that's what Deborah is, a routine case of exploratory surgery, tumor removal and biopsy. I kept her company in my mind's eye as I drove back downtown on Haight Street: seeing her now in her white hospital gown, lying straight, almost like a figure on the lid of a sarcophagus, on her bed, awaiting the day after tomorrow. I was dead wrong, of course, as I later found out from Saul Sternberg, M.D.; for what she really did was not get in bed at all but, after her preliminary checkups, go over to the ward where the seriously sick children were and volunteer to do some reading and storytelling to children battling—many without hope—that dreaded corrupter which now makes its preliminary feints and parries in Deborah's direction. So: *Peter Rabbit* and *The Chronicles of Narnia* or *Are You There, God? It's Me, Margaret,* or *Little Women,* or *The Great Brain,* read to kids with life, triumphant life in their eyes, listening the way kids listen, with their whole bodies, as if creation itself were being reconstrued (so the race itself listened in the dawn-time of our storytelling)—but kids also with an undeserved sentence of death handed out to them by whoever or whatever it is ordering such things: luck, fate, God, whatever. Who cares, anyway, when the sentence is such a hideously unjust one?

Such as Deborah's might be, I thought to myself, holding her around the lower torso and resting my head over her knees. But that can't be. You can't swim, play tennis, eat five-grain bread and drink all those varieties of herbal teas that line one shelf in her tiny kitchen and still get sick, get bitten by that vampire who, I always thought, prefers tissue stained with tobacco smoke or soaked in carcinogens knowingly or unknowingly consumed. Yet the kids two floors below didn't smoke and hadn't sojourned more than a decade in our carcinogenic civilization; yet the vampire had gotten to them, hadn't it? So why couldn't it get a health freak from Phoenix, Arizona, especially in that part of her body where it might be

765

getting her, God forbid, there where all women must be concerned, regardless of their general health?

"What are you two up to? Honestly, some folks have got no shame!"

"Go back to sleep, Erma," Deborah said. "You need your beauty rest."

"How can I sleep with you two carrying on so hot and heavy?" the young woman at the end of the room laughed. "I didn't think white folks ever got so emotional."

I stood up, embarrassed. Erma, as I could see (for she was getting out of bed and swathing herself in a blue bathrobe) is a tall, statuesque black woman of about thirty, or a little younger—or maybe even a little older.

"Erma, meet James. James, meet Erma," Deborah said.

"I'm on my way to the powder room," Erma said, sweeping by like Leontyne Price playing Aïda.

"She's here for the same thing I am," Deborah said when Erma had left the room. "We're both going into surgery the day after tomorrow."

"She's very pretty," I said.

"She's a sales rep with the phone company," Deborah said. Erma half-opened the door and poked her head in. "Can I come in?" she asked. "Or is it still passion time?"

"Don't worry, Erma," Deborah said. "He's harmless."

"You look kinda harmless," Erma said. "You look like the librarian Debby was talking about this morning."

From Parnassus Heights you look northwards across San Francisco at the city's magnificent east-west skyline: across the Haight-Ashbury, the Golden Gate Park Panhandle, the spires of St. Ignatius Church, the Spanish Renaissance tower of Lone Mountain College, the Byzantine dome of Temple Emanu-El, the soaring spires of the Golden Gate Bridge extending themselves above the eucalyptus and cypress treeline of the Presidio. At night, each of these landmarks presents itself in a changed manner, its daytime outline still recognizable, however, through a proscenium arch of moonlight, fog, and electricity. Walking over to the window, I drew a bead on the illuminated towers of St. Ignatius as Deborah went to her closet for her bathrobe. I remembered how we had seen those same bright towers one night last August as we looked east across the city from Land's End.

"Erma and I have our little rituals," Deborah said.

"You've only been here a day and a half."

"That's enough time for rituals. Things happen fast in a hospital. What time is it, Erma?"

Erma reached into her nightstand drawer and extracted a wristwatch. "Eight-fifteen," she said.

"Time to get ready," Deborah said. She was lying atop her bed, wrapped in a yellow terry cloth bathrobe. Erma was similarly deployed atop her own bed.

"Tonight," Deborah said, "we'll have room service. Jimmy, what do you see atop my bedstand?"

"A box of See's candy."

"Now carefully remove the first layer of chocolate," Deborah said, "making sure that you don't spill any of it." I went around to the candy box and did what she asked.

"Now remove the tissue covering the bottom layer," she said. I did so.

"What do you see?"

"Marijuana cigarettes," I said. "Further evidence of your reefer madness."

"Good boy," Deborah said. "Now take one over to Erma and slide this chair over against the door on your way back and sit there, if you please."

I did what I was told. Erma lit her cigarette with a red Zippo lighter, which she then tossed across the room to Deborah, who caught it adroitly, lit her own cigarette, then tossed the lighter over to me. I fumbled the catch, but the Zippo fell into my lap so I was spared the embarrassment of having to get up to retrieve it. I lit up a superbly rolled specimen of Deborah Tanner's favorite plant.

"You're going to turn me into a pothead," I said.

"A pothead," Deborah said, "is preferable to a potbelly."

"What's next on your ritual?" I asked.

767

"A serious discussion, followed by the nine o'clock movie on Channel 44," Deborah said, "followed by beddy-bye at eleven."

"Tonight's discussion," Erma said, "is about what's the first thing we are going to do when we get out of here."

"We discuss a different topic every night," Deborah said. "Last night we discussed our mothers."

"As for myself," Erma said, "I'm going to buy a low-cut evening gown the moment I get out of here, something that shows my gorgeous body to its true advantage."

"Erma has a gorgeous body," Deborah said.

"I can tell," I said.

"Honey, you haven't seen a thing until you've seen me in something slinky," Erma said. "I drive the little boys wild." She took another toke on her cigarette. "What will you do when you get out of here, Debbie?" she asked after exhaling.

"Forget it all as quickly as possible," Deborah said. Someone tried to open the door against which I was sitting.

"Why can't I open this door?" a man's voice asked.

"It's Dr. Sternberg," Erma said. "Let him in." I got up and slid the chair away. Saul Sternberg, M.D., entered. Erma and Deborah cupped their cigarettes and dropped their arms down the far side of their beds. I held mine behind my back.

"I smell the fragrant embers of *Cannabis sativa*," Dr. Sternberg said. "I drop innocently by to get Romeo here on his way, and I walk into a pot party. What time is it, anyway?" Erma went back to the bedstand drawer.

"Nine-ten," she said.

"I'm ten minutes off duty," Saul Sternberg said, "so I shall overlook this little indiscretion on you ladies' part." We all brought our cigarettes out in the open. "The *cannabis* plant," Dr. Sternberg continued, "is not without its medicinal properties, so many scientists tell us." He walked over to Erma's bedside. Erma handed him what was left of her cigarette. Deftly, Saul Sternberg, M.D., extracted the last of the cigarette's essence.

"There is one respected school of thought, moreover," he continued, "which points to wide empirical evidence of the

768

fact that the *cannabis* plant, when ignited and its smoke inhaled, can lead to a feeling of well being, even euphoria."

Deborah handed him the final moments of her cigarette, and it too expired. "Such a state of euphoria is prized by those who have experienced it," he said just before inhaling. The smoke seemed to stay forever in his lungs before he exhaled and spoke at the same moment. "I for one," he said, "accept the findings of this school of thought." I handed him my roach. He looked with some distaste at its soggy end; nevertheless he finished it off, tossing the remnants into the sink with the miniscule debris of the other two roaches. Turning on the tap water, he washed the evidence of our debauch down the drain. "Now, then," he said, "I invite our learned guest to leave as it is nearly nine-thirty, and I bid both of you charming ladies good night."

"That was big of you, Doctor," I said as we stood by the elevator. "I mean, finishing our cigarettes for us."

"I don't know what you're talking about," Saul Sternberg said. "Let's keep our fingers crossed about Deborah. I just got word that her X rays fall into the less dangerous side of the spectrum."

"What about Erma?" I asked. I suddenly felt part of Erma's family also—although I had forgotten to learn her last name and although, strictly speaking, I had no relationship to Deborah Tanner whatsoever.

"Not so good," Saul Sternberg said. "The X rays show the possibilities of something serious. She delayed getting herself to a doctor. We'll be doing what we can, however."

My door bell rang just after six the following evening. I had been waiting for it to ring for at least half an hour. As I expected, it was Dr. and Mrs. Tanner. I had invited them by telephone to come over after they had visited Deborah at UC Hospital. I felt it best that I not try to be there at the same time. The Tanners, like myself, looked subdued by what was happening. Opening the door, I had an instant impression of what a handsome couple the Tanners were, how emanative, even in their troubled condition, of a certain American

769

attractiveness and energy. A definite physical presence—an ambience of achieved well-being, such as I remember people possessing in the illustrations of short stories in *Collier's* or *The Saturday Evening Post*—seems to characterize Sunbelt people above a certain class level. I brought the Tanners into my living room-study.

"May I fix you a drink?" I asked.

"Bourbon," Dr. Tanner said, "not too much water."

"A vodka martini on the rocks," Cynthia Tanner said.

I was grateful for the busyness of fixing drinks. It provided a certain easing off between seeing the Tanners again and talking about why they were here. I fixed myself an Irish whiskey and water. Dr. Tanner sat in my overstuffed reading chair, one knee drawn up, the other leg extended infinitely in front of him. Cynthia Tanner sat on the sofa, her slender legs crossed beneath the pleated skirt of her conservatively tailored beige wool suit. The Tanners, I thought to myself, are a long-legged family.

"Cheers," I said. We all drained our drinks by at least a third, then sat silently for what seemed an eternity.

"How's Deborah?" I finally asked, hating myself for my banality, but being unable to think of anything else to say.

"She's fine," Dr. Tanner said. "She told us you'd called her late this afternoon just before we arrived and that you were by to see her last night. I left her with Cy Karlin, a friend of mine from medical school and the Navy Reserve. Cy made Rear Admiral last year. He teaches oncology at the UCSF medical school. Cy's known Deborah since she was a kid."

"In their time at the University of Pennsylvania medical school, Cy Karlin and my husband were legends of pituitary stamina," Cynthia Tanner said. "It's a wonder neither of them went into gynecology. They had such extensive clinical experience. Fix me another martini, will you, dear?" I fixed all of us another drink.

"Where are you staying?" I asked.

"The Clift," Cynthia Tanner said, sipping her martini. "We always stay at the Clift when we're in town."

"How long have you known my daughter?" Dr. Tanner

asked. He'd asked me the same question that last time he had been in town, but under the circumstances I could not fault him for forgetting.

"Almost a year," I said.

"One hell of a kid," Dr. Tanner said. "She's one hell of a kid. Has a mind of her own, always has. Take coming up here to live in San Francisco, for instance. I didn't mind her not going to the University of Arizona because her mother went to Mills College and she had a boyfriend at Berkeley—he later died, automobile crash—but I was hopping mad about her coming up here to live permanently after she'd left Hughes Airwest. I was hoping she'd get stationed out of Los Angeles or Phoenix—the Mexico City run, which had been offered to her; but she resigns and moves up here and goes to work for the Library."

"Spencer is worried about all the crime," Cynthia Tanner said.

"And the homosexuals," Dr. Tanner said. "Not that I have anything against them either as a group or as individuals, but there are so many of them flocking to San Francisco these days that it sort of tips the scale in their favor, doesn't it? I mean, if you're thinking about a young girl meeting a variety of eligible men."

"Spencer has very old-fashioned ideas," Cynthia Tanner said.

"Not really," he said, "but I like to see younger people have the same sort of fun, if you know what I mean, as Cynthia and I had. I didn't want Deborah sitting in her flat up here in San Francisco, feeling neglected, or taking up with a lot of homosexual men just to have some company."

"There was—isn't—much danger of that," I said. My inadvertent use of the past tense sent a spasm of regret through me. "If there were only one eligible and healthy man left in San Francisco, he'd find your daughter."

"Are you such a fellow, Mr. Norton?" Cynthia Tanner asked. "You're so much older, I mean, and you've never married. Thirty-five and single is a rare category, isn't it?"

"Especially with a heterosexual," Dr. Tanner said.

771

"We'll soon be having a governor who's past thirty-five and single," I said. "And I hope you're not being hostile."

"Not hostile, just curious," Dr. Tanner said.

"I've been asked the same question before," I said, "not the least by my mother. Let's just say that I'm following the venerable Irish custom of not rushing into marriage."

"Have you asked our daughter to marry you?" Mrs. Tanner asked.

"I've lost track of the times," I said. "I've asked her at least a hundred times. I love Deborah very much. I'm nuts about her, in fact."

"You have good taste in women," Dr. Tanner said.

"Would you like to stay for dinner?" I asked.

"We'd love to," Cynthia Tanner said, "on one condition."

"And that is?" I asked.

"One more martini," she said.

"Same here," said Spencer Tanner, M.D.

"Just what the doctor ordered," I said.

I fixed a tossed green salad and boiled some water for *fettucini*. When the *fettucini* was cooked, I diced some leftover ham into it and then blended in the egg sauce I learned to make from the Time-Life Italian cookbook. We ate together at the small table I have against my living room window. As we ate, I remembered all the times Deborah and I had eaten there. I remembered especially our breakfast after we had spent the night together for the first time.

"I feel sore," Deborah had said.

"Pass the Wheaties, please."

"You brute."

"It's the breakfast of champions."

"Some honeymoon," Deborah said.

"We'll do better on our real honeymoon," I said. "We'll go to a wonderful hotel."

"In today's world, James, you don't have to marry a girl just because you've deflowered her."

"Where would you like to be married?" I asked, plunging into my Wheaties. Ever since I've been a kid, I've loved

772

crunchy breakfast food. "Here or in Phoenix? We could go down to Carmel, I suppose." Deborah was wearing one of my pajama tops. Sitting at an angle with her legs crossed, she desultorily ate her breakfast cereal. A stream of sunlight, coming through the window, bathed her crossed legs in bright benediction. The sunlight set the fine hairs of her thighs to glinting like flecks of gold. Upon impulse, I stood up and knelt before her. Taking one of her bare feet in my hands, I kissed it with a rush of desire and reverence.

"Martinis always make me ravenous," Mrs. Tanner said after we had eaten. That was good *fettucini*. Deborah, as you probably know, is an excellent cook—when she's not too much into health food."

"These things are tricky," Dr. Tanner said out of the blue. "Cy Karlin says there's always more than a break-even chance that there's nothing seriously wrong." Mrs. Tanner's eyes welled up with tears.

"It's rotten luck, that's what it is, rotten luck. She's barely twenty-six," she said.

"We were together on her birthday, April 19," I said. "It was a Sunday. She and I went over to St. Anne's Home on Lake Street and visited the daughter of a man whose biography I'm writing. The three of us took a long walk in the Presidio."

"The Sebastian Collins biography?" Dr. Tanner asked. "Deborah has told us about it."

"We spent the afternoon with Marina Scannell," I said. "She's about eighty and a very delightful woman. She and Deborah got along beautifully."

"Deborah has a way with people," Cynthia Tanner said. "She did beautifully as a stewardess. I was surprised that she gave up flying for library work." I opened a second bottle of Freemark Abbey 1970 Cabernet Sauvignon and I listened to their stories of Deborah, solaced by the suffusion of family feeling that was coming in my direction. For a dreadful second, the thought crossed my mind that our conversation resembled in part the sort that can be heard at an old-fashioned wake.

Over wine, in any event, and then over coffee, I heard the details of an ordinary Arizona girlhood rendered extraordinary, in the opinion of the three of us, anyway, by the extraordinary result: a tall, leggy, triumphant young woman, alive with energy and a radiant ambition for living—but lying in a hospital bed for the moment across the city on Parnassus Heights, awaiting the surgeon's morning scalpel. I heard about Campfire Girls, summer camps, braces, bicycle lessons, the country club swim team, the learning of golf from her father (an unusual pursuit among young women, but done to please him), and the young man who shared all this with her and died one evening while coming home.

Intellectuals of various persuasions have a grudge against upper-middle-class America. They find this sector of our society lacking the Fitzgeraldian splendor of the upper classes or the plaintive virtue of the oppressed proletariat and huddled ghetto masses. Such folks, indeed, might perhaps have found the Tanners' recitation of their daughter's coming of age banal. Eastern intellectuals, furthermore (and all intellectuals in America tend to be eastern, no matter where they are living), are basically baffled by girls from Texas, New Mexico, Arizona, and southern California. Banality is often a failing in the Sunbelt, true; and a certain meanness of spirit crops frequently to the surface of its otherwise affirming exterior, especially in the matter of rigid prejudice; but can one honestly say that the rest of the nation is unambiguously better off when it comes to rendering an account in this area of social behavior?

Yet the positive side is there as well. The Sunbelt prizes an old-fashioned (by two decades) range of American values, which some, growing up there, find stifling (Deborah, after all, did leave); even when they do depart, however, they take with them this slightly antiquated heritage that keeps ex-Sunbelt women dressed with more tailored femininity than that of their liberated sisters, and keeps them less cynical in the matter of romance. I, for one, have always yearned for such wholesome American beauty as I have found in Deborah

774

Tanner of Phoenix, Arizona. I like her clear eyes and straightened teeth and her tall muscular body. I cherish the details of her suburban Sunbelt girlhood amidst bicycles and swimming pools. I do not find her banal at all; on the contrary, I often find myself tongue-tied in her presence, even after what happened over Christmas and has happened some few times since, although not as the result of cohabitation or even with any degree of predictability.

Once we began this new phase of our relationship, we began it as equals; and both of us, being Catholics, have carried on our affair with a discernible degree of—if not outright guilt—then at least a mutual refusal to grant full approval to what we were doing together: not because the Church was on record as disapproving of sex outside wedlock (in America, at least, the Church has lost its entire right to speak on these matters), but because what we were doing together demanded some as-of-yet-ungranted recognition of its final, lyrical seriousness, lest it degenerate into just another exploitative relationship, eventually consuming itself in its own ashes, as is so often the case in our wasteland of modern eros.

"We should get married," I would say.

"Why—because we've gone to bed?"

"No—because we're in love."

"How do you know we're in love?" she would ask.

"Because we've gone to bed," I'd say.

"I find your logic circular."

"I find that you're avoiding marriage."

"I'm too young to get married."

"And I'm almost too old; so we'll split the difference."

"That puts us each around thirty," she said.

"A perfect age for marriage," I said. "Besides, we now know we are sexually compatible."

"You sound like Dr. Kinsey."

"But not Havelock Ellis, thank God."

"The question before the house," she continued, "is love. What is it?"

"Partly a biological urge," I said.

775

"I understand that," she said, "but suppose we married, what would we find to talk about for the next forty years?"

"The things that happen day by day," I said. "The sorts of things we talk about now, only more of them."

"How do I know what kind of person you'll turn out to be?" she asked. "You could turn out to be an alcoholic, or a wife-beater, or both."

"You could turn out to be a dyke or a member of the John Birch Society."

"Fat chance."

"If you were in love, you'd have faith," I said.

"I am in love, you know that—sort of; but it seems an awfully crummy world to sustain such dreams as marriage, children, living happily ever after, not getting bored, not running out of things to say."

"I wish that I could inspire confidence in you," I said.

"It's not your fault, believe me. It's the world we live in."

"Why should we look for excuses for our own failure of nerve?" I asked. "Or are you experiencing a failure of appetite?"

"If you're insecure," she said, "turn yourself into Masters and Johnson for treatment. No, you're fine, believe me. It's just that there's so much else involved."

"Now you're sounding thirty-five," I said.

Deborah is correct, of course: there is so much more involved. There's the infinity of adjustments that must be made to make marriage work. There's the fact that modern urban America is a virtual conspiracy against sexual commitment. Marina Scannell said as much when we visited her at St. Anne's on Deborah's birthday, the three of us sitting in the garden behind the great red-brick Georgian pile on Lake Street.

"I thought that my generation was modern," Sebastian Collins's survivor said, "but in comparison to what I see around me today we had childlike hopes for happiness. You young people must face the death of all dreams."

"Were your hopes fulfilled?" Deborah asked.

"Yes—and no," Marina Collins Scannell said, "but that's a long story."

"Do tell it please, Mrs. Scannell," Deborah said. "We have all afternoon."

Encouraged by what I heard that day—some of Marina's own life story and the narrative of the last decades of her father's long life—I have since made excellent progress on the Sebastian Collins biography: up until last week, that is, when the discovery was made that put Deborah in the hospital and her parents here in my living room, calming their fears—but intensifying them also—with one drink too many, and stories of their daughter's girlhood.

"She got serious about books at Mills," her father said. "Before that it was sports, sports, sports."

"Ted's death made her more serious," Cynthia Tanner said. "After that, she began to read much more—and to go to church every other Sunday or so."

"The sisters threatened to throw her out of high school for resisting compulsory Mass on holy days of obligation," Dr. Tanner said. "That would be about her sophomore year. I tried to reason with her, but she said she'd rather go to public high school anyway. They had a better sports program in the public schools, she pointed out."

"I shrieked when I first saw that dreadful tattoo," Cynthia Tanner said. "She came out into our backyard pool in her bikini. She took her top off since only I was there with her, and then I saw it. I could have fainted. I thought she'd become a Hell's Angel groupie or something. 'Your father will be furious,' I said. 'Then please tell him when I'm back in San Francisco,' she said, as calmly as you please. 'I can't stand scenes.'"

"I never made a scene at all," Dr. Tanner said. "I merely remarked that I was relieved that she hadn't had it done on her forehead, or on her hand."

"'That's an excellent idea, daddyboo,' she said. 'I could pick up extra money as the Marlboro Girl.'"

The telephone rang. It was Dr. Cy Karlin, asking for Dr. Spencer Tanner. Dr. Karlin did most of the talking, to judge from the fact that Spencer Tanner listened, not saying much, giving them an occasional hum of assent.

777

"She's asleep," Deborah's father said when he hung up. "Cy's given her something to relax her. She goes into surgery tomorrow morning at nine. Cy's pretty confident he'll be able to make a working diagnosis almost immediately. The lab should come through by the late afternoon."

The Tanners moved into each other's arms. "Oh, Spencer, it's all so frightening," Cynthia Tanner said. I left the room for the kitchen, where I started to clean up. Between the rushings of the tap water, I could hear the sound of Mrs. Tanner's weeping.

Marina Collins Scannell met Deborah and me in the reception foyer of St. Anne's Home. She was already waiting for us when we arrived: a tall (as tall as Deborah, who is five feet ten), handsome woman, commanding even, just past eighty, but still clear of eye and not that wrinkled of skin. Mrs. Scannell's white hair was piled thickly atop her head and held in place by a silver clasp. She wore a smock-type plaid dress, gathered at the waist with a belt, and very sensible shoes, which were the only old-ladyish things about her. Marina Scannell has one of those faces that wears well. She was not, most likely, a raving beauty as a young woman, albeit handsome enough. By thirty, around 1925 or so, she must have begun to gather momentum as the cream-puff good looks of her contemporaries softened into saggy flesh. By age fifty, 1945 or thereabouts, her facial structure—the essential harmony, the nobility even, of her skeletal self—must have revealed itself triumphantly as her peers rushed headlong into lumpen middle age.

The woman who greeted us seemed to step partly out of an old *Scribner's* or *Century* illustration by Dana, Flagg, or Gibson; yet her demeanor was not that of the *grande dame,* despite the fact that her son, John Charles Scannell II, president and chairman of the board of the Trans-Pacific Corporation, is among the most powerful men in northern California. Far from being the *grande dame*—a demeanor testifying to a life of social pursuit and social success—Marina Scannell impresses me more as (just to make a suggestion) the retired first female professor at Berkeley or, say, the retired president of a Seven Sisters women's college. There's a directness about her, I mean to say, an assumption of command that is not at all bossy, but rather pleasant, as if one had suddenly encountered one of Jack London's heroines surviving into the 1970s.

For some ten years now, Marina Collins Scannell has lived in a small apartment at St. Anne's Home, combining the roles of benefactress, resident, and volunteer staff. Her son has settled a considerable sum on St. Anne's Home in his mother's honor. At St. Anne's Home the Little Sisters of the Poor, a worldwide order of nuns founded in Brittany in the early nineteenth century to care for the elderly, provide a retirement home for some two hundred residents. Marina Scannell holds the title Director of Recreation and Programs.

"I'll take you on a little tour first," she said after Deborah and I had introduced ourselves. We saw the chapel, the dining room, and some of the residence floors. Everything was waxy bright and polished, as are all institutions run by Catholic nuns. Old age, of course, possesses in and of itself a certain sadness, a suggestion of earlier, more robust selves surviving in shrunken and palsied bodies. Peeking into one ward, I saw that one gentleman resident ("Warrant Officer Crawford," Mrs. Scannell informed us. "He insists upon his title") had made his bed in the military fashion, with blankets so tautly tucked beneath the mattress that you could bounce a coin off them. At the foot of the bed was a footlocker with "Frederick Crawford, W.O.3, U.S. Army" stenciled in black letters. A stiff brush, with a comb inserted parallel to its handle, stood neatly on the bedstand, the brush arranged exactly parallel to the line of the tabletop. An autographed photograph of Lieutenant General James Gavin stood at a right angle to the comb, and opposite that, also at a right angle, was a photograph—taken some time in the 1940s I would suppose—of Mr. Crawford in uniform, the partially colored gold bar of a Warrant Officer Two conspicuous on his shoulder. Mrs. Scannell took us to the bedridden ward, which was hospital-like; yet those parts of the building where the ambulatory residents lived showed every sign of normal activity, including a beauty salon.

"Mother Superior is especially proud of the beauty parlor," Mrs. Scannell remarked as we peeked into the room where some half-dozen elderly women sat under hair-drying machines. A professional beautician, dressed in white, was rubbing one lady's scant locks in a lathery shampoo. "It keeps the morale of the lady residents up."

In the recreation lounge, a number of elderly men, dressed neatly in dark business suits, were playing checkers. A black, brown, and white dog of quasi-collie lineage sat snoozing at the foot of one man's chair. To one side of the room, a circle of six ladies clustered around a large patchwork quilt, partially complete, which they were tufting and tying with short lengths of red yarn. Marina Scannell led us out into the garden—a large, spacious area, behind the Home and adjacent, on the northern side, to the Presidio, and on the east, to Presidio Terrace, an array of cream-colored Mediterranean villas, dominated by the soaring neo-Byzantine massiveness of Temple Emanu-El. Some few yards from a large shrine dedicated to Our Lady of Lourdes, we sat on a sunny park bench, beneath cypress and palm trees, and there I conducted my interview.

"Do you mind if I use this tape recorder?" I asked.

"Not in the least," Marina said. "I own stock in the company that manufactures that model you're using."

"What I'm interested in, Mrs. Scannell—"

"Call me Marina. My husband died nearly thirty-five years ago."

"What I'm interested in, Marina, is the story of your father's life after 1915."

"You mean after the publication of *Memoirs of a San Francisco Bohemian?*"

"Yes—after the journals begin to give out."

"Father never truly kept a journal, strictly speaking. What you have read are drafts, which he prepared prefatory to writing the *Memoirs*."

780

"He left a lot out of the *Memoirs* that he put into the journals," I said.

"Young man, that's the understatement of the year. And we both know what you mean, don't we? We don't mean all the details of his life in 1914, 1915, do we? In retrospect, however, I wish that Father had left some of that indiscreet material in the *Memoirs*—if, that is, Paul Elder would have published it in that form, which I doubt. Father might then have gone down in history as an American Frank Harris, and an Irish Catholic to boot. Where were we?"

"Talking about your father's life after 1915."

"Oh, yes. Is your machine on?"

"It's on."

"How long do you want me to talk?"

"As long as it takes. I've brought two hours of cassettes along."

She used up the entire two hours' worth of tape. I have since made a transcription of the interview, running to more than fifty typewritten pages. I've sent a Xerox copy out to Marina and given another photocopy to Mrs. Pennyworth at the History Room for inclusion in the Sebastian Collins papers. Mrs. Pennyworth has slugged it in the index file: "Collins, Sebastian (1848–1940), details regarding later life, 1915–1940."

"Let's take a walk," Marina announced after the interview was complete. "It's three-thirty. I usually take a walk around this time." Deborah and I waited for her on Lake Street while she went to her room to fetch a coat. By four o'clock, she pointed out, the evening fog brings a chill to the Richmond district. She emerged in a blue double-breasted bridge coat with gold buttons and a French beret of the same color. A scarf in alternating maroon and white encircled her neck and fell behind her.

"You look ready for the Cal-Stanford Game," I said.

"This sort of coat was fashionable in my days at Mills College," she said. "Over the years I've worn out some six of them, one for every decade since I left school."

"I graduated from Mills, also," Deborah said. "In 1970."

"I'm Class of 1916," Marina said.

Walking up Arguello, we entered the Presidio Gate. From there we headed over to a knoll, from which we had an unobstructed view of the city, the bay, and the Palace of Fine Arts.

"There's a nice trail just below here," Marina said. "It takes us down to the parade ground. Are you up to it?" We hiked down to the trail, which wended its way through some eucalyptus groves and clusters of Army dependent housing.

"You look like a Mills girl," Marina said as we walked. "Mills, Wellesley, Smith—some such place where they don't destroy a girl's grooming in the name of higher education. Are you bookish?"

"I'm a librarian," Deborah said.

"But are you bookish?" Marina persisted.

"I love books," Deborah said.

"In my day Mills girls were hopelessly bluestocking," Marina said. "That's changed somewhat, like everything else, but now and then one runs into an old-fashioned Mills girl such as you, and it's heartening."

"What sort of work did you do?" Deborah asked.

"I finished my teaching certificate at Stanford in 1917, just as the war broke out. I was also married that year and had a baby in 1918 when my husband was away with the 363rd Infantry Regiment in France. It was 1920 before I finally secured a part-time position at the Hamlin School. I taught there twenty years, starting full time in 1925 when Johnny entered school and I had more time to myself. It was around that time also that I began my Sunday book column for the *Express*. I kept the column until after the Second World War, when I began to work with my son in his business."

"When did you write your book of Pacific travel?" I asked.

"I started drafting the material in the late 1930s, but the book was delayed by my husband's death and then by the war itself. It finally came out in 1947."

"I haven't read it yet," I confessed, "but I'm looking forward to it."

782

"*On Pacific Shores* is out of date," Marina Collins said, "but you can catch in it some suggestion of the way the Pacific Basin used to be. My husband and I made our first Pacific trip in 1922, to Australia *via* the Fiji Islands. We made some ten trips all together, nine of them with Johnny along. That's how my son got interested in the Pacific Basin."

Marina Collins Scannell describes herself as a wife, a mother, a schoolteacher who also dashed off a weekly Reviewer's Choice column in the Sunday *Express*: all of which she was, but not exclusively, as anyone knowledgeable concerning the rise of the Trans-Pacific Corporation so well knows. Mother-son teams are rare in the annals of American business; but there are those who feel that Marina Scannell must take at least some of the credit for the rise of Trans-Pacific, a holding company for a number of enterprises—hotels, import/export, charter airlines—involved with travel and trade in the Pacific Basin, from Australia to the Philippines. Marina, in any event, sits as a director of Trans-Pacific and has done so ever since the late 1940s.

"As far as I can tell," Marina said as we walked past the Presidio playground, "Father was born somewhere in this vicinity, within a block or two anyway. And my husband died over there at Letterman Hospital in 1941. He was severely gassed in the First World War and left the Army on disability, entitling him to the attentions of the U.S. Army Medical Corps throughout his life. My husband survived gassing. Twenty-three years later, however, he succumbed to lung cancer."

Passing Letterman Hospital, we ascended the Lyon Street hill on our way back to St. Anne's Home. Marina took the incline with no difficulty, which is more than I can say for myself.

"Did your father keep in touch with Cardinal Rafael Merry del Val after 1915?" I asked. "I forgot to ask in the interview."

"You were most likely taken aback by the scandalous things I related," Marina said. "Many people are. They feel that sexual feeling should discreetly disappear as one grows older—and certainly by age seventy-two, when Father commenced his last—to my knowledge at least!—escapade."

"I have heard rumors," I said, "but until this afternoon I've had no corroboration."

"Well, I've given you corroboration aplenty," Marina said, "but to get back to your question, the answer is yes. In 1920, at the personal request of Merry del Val, Father returned to Rome to testify at the proceedings convened by the Congregation of the Saints to consider the opening of Ryan Patrice's cause for canonization. The Paris Foreign Missionary Society and the Carthusians (Patrice had belonged to both orders) asked the Cardinal, then Archpriest of St. Peter's, to serve as the postulator of Patrice's cause. Merry del Val agreed to do so, having become aware of Patrice's reputation in Southeast Asia when the Cardinal was serving as papal secretary of state. Patrice was declared Venerable in 1922, and there the matter has rested for fifty-three years. I imagine that his cause for canonization will languish for at least another hundred years. The Church, like all of us, has to get by in these changing times. The story of European missionaries in Indo-China is not the most popular item on today's Vatican agenda. The Church prefers to remember her Third World converts, not the blue-eyed missionaries who baptized them."

"How ironic," I said, "that your father's trip to Rome to testify on behalf of the cause of Ryan Patrice's canonization should have proved the occasion of his last erotic adventure."

"Rome had a way of stirring Father's juices," Marina Collins Scannell observed. "Rome quickened his appetites, sacred and otherwise. As far as I know, the young lady in question is still alive, although she's no longer young. She must be past seventy, in fact. She ended up marrying a grape-grower in Santa Rosa."

Circles within circles, I thought to myself: Merry del Val acting as Ryan Patrice's postulator, Sebastian Collins testifying on Patrice's behalf; and now Merry del Val's own cause is being opened at Rome. In the course of these hearings, the Cardinal's correspondence with both Sebastian Collins and

784

Agnes Tobin will be brought forward for examination by the Curia. Merry del Val died in Rome in 1930. Agnes Tobin lived on until 1939, a quasi recluse, closeted in her apartment in the Fairmont Hotel, suffering lengthy bouts of distraction. Sebastian Collins himself succumbed in 1940, the year of my birth. I sometimes wonder whether San Francisco doesn't really have a coherent mythical past, after all—a discernible pattern of collective experience comprised from lives such as these, that someone, perhaps even myself, might one day weave together into a formalized myth. Such a mythic pattern might offset the superficial image our city now possesses in the collective consciousness of the country at large. And yet, what is the true burden of these local lives, gone now for well over a quarter of a century? What is truly useful in the record of their existences? They are neither great, as the world holds greatness, nor oppressed, as the world reveres the symbols of oppression, seeing in that condition an intrinsic claim to virtue. They were merely provincial Americans, Californians of the *fin de siècle*, pursuing their pilgrimages amidst San Franciscan circumstances.

"How old are you, dear?" Marina asked Deborah as we headed down Sacramento Street, past boutiques teeming with fashionable merchandise.

"I'm twenty-six today," Deborah said.

"My dear, you shouldn't waste your birthday walking with an old lady, or worse, sitting in the garden of an old people's home."

"On the contrary, I've enjoyed myself immensely and you're not an old lady at all, are you really?"

"The time has gone by fast. It seems like a dream. I'm eighty and should be concentrating on death, I suppose, but I find life more and more interesting as each day passes, and I've resolved not to worry. Worry, for instance, killed Josiah Royce off at sixty-one. He fretted so much over what Germany was doing in the war that he had a stroke and died in 1916."

We reached St. Anne's Home at about five o'clock. Marina shook our hands vigorously as we said goodbye.

"You'll have a transcript of our interview as soon as it's typed out," I promised.

"Perhaps the next time we get together I shall interview you," Marina said. "I'll ask some hard questions."

"Clue us as to what they'll be," Deborah said, "so we can come prepared."

"They'll be about the two of you," Marina said. "Specifically, they'll be about what your plans are for each other. I envy the two of you—so young, so sturdy, with so much before you. You mustn't waste any of it, you realize; and above all else, you mustn't waste each other's time. I see too much of that these days: men and women taking big bites out of each other's lives without so much as a second thought. If you've found something between you, then build on it. If not, I'd advise each of you to look elsewhere."

Shortly before eleven o'clock, I joined Spencer and Cynthia Tanner in the waiting room outside Surgery. The Tanners were wearing the same clothes they had worn the night before. They looked, in fact, the two of them, as if they hadn't been to bed, but had merely dozed off in their clothes when they returned to the Clift Hotel from my place well after midnight. Mrs. Tanner's eyes were puffy from crying and her husband's face seemed haggard. I wasn't in any great shape myself, having slept but an hour or two the night before. Finding myself wide awake at around three in the morning, I had said the rosary for the first time in nearly ten years. I had trouble remembering the names and the sequence of the five Sorrowful Mysteries, and I couldn't remember whether one begins or ends the rosary with the Apostles' Creed, so I said it twice—forgetting a sentence or two in passing. I haven't really prayed more than a half-dozen times since my mid-twenties, and I was rusty regarding the set prayers I memorized in my youth, but I had no trouble begging God that everything might turn out all right. At five o'clock I shaved and showered and dressed, and went down to Washington Square for the six o'clock mass at SS Peter and Paul's. I went to Communion and

I prayed some more. With the help of my St. Andrew's missal, I read through the Litany of the Sacred Heart, and I recited the Votive Collect for the Sick: "Almighty, everlasting God, the eternal salvation of those who believe, hear us on behalf of Thy servant Deborah who is sick, from whom we humbly crave the help of Thy mercy, that, being restored to health, she may render thanks to Thee in Thy church. Through Christ Our Lord. Amen."

Cy Karlin, M.D., is a tall man, well over six foot three. He seemed as tired as the rest of us as he entered the waiting room, attired in a green surgical smock and cap, a discarded white facial mask dangling down over his throat.

"Spencer," he said, "I haven't seen you look so bad since we celebrated the completion of internship." Hearing this, I sensed good news; otherwise, humor, even between old friends, would be out of place. "She'll be groggy as hell until this afternoon," he continued. "The lab reports should come in by no later than four, but I'll say right now that it looks hopeful—nasty as hell, however, although most likely benign. It had an unusual tubular shape. I had to go in deeper than I planned to get it all out, but no tissue was lost, except for some unavoidable scarring on the surface, which we can patch up later on with cosmetic surgery."

Cynthia Tanner embraced her husband, then Dr. Karlin. Dr. Karlin and Spencer Tanner shook hands silently, shy smiles spread across both their faces. Dr. Tanner then shook my hand. Mrs. Tanner put her cheek next to mine in a gesture I remembered Deborah having used the first time I called upon her at her flat on Alabama Street.

"You've been great," Cynthia Tanner said, "—like one of the family."

Deborah was weeping when I entered her room early the next morning. It was the first time I had ever seen Deborah Tanner cry. I never imagined, in fact, that I would ever see her this way. She was like another person. Despite her pale and drawn face, she seemed much younger, almost girl-like as she wept. Through the open neck of her gown, I could see the

787

bandages swathing her chest. Saul Sternberg, M.D., was standing by her bedside.

"Erma just went back into surgery," he told me. "She has to have a partial mastectomy."

"It's not fair," Deborah wept. "She had such a gorgeous figure: much better than mine, really. All I lost was that stupid tattoo. I was tired of it, anyway."

Chapter 18

T WO MONTHS AGO, San Francisco's Dream City
opened to the world. On 20 February 1915, Mayor
Sunny Jim Rolph led a crowd of some one hundred and fifty
thousand San Franciscans through the gate beneath the Tower
of Jewels, inaugurating the Panama-Pacific International
Exposition, which will run for a year in honor of the opening
of the great canal through the Isthmus of Panama. Having
watched from my study window the classical courts and
palaces of the exposition rise to their present polychromatic
splendor alongside the bay, I relished the opportunity at long
last to wander on foot through the Enchanted City. The
painter Jules Guerin, who serves as the exposition's Director of
Color, has given us a dazzling oversized palette of harmonized
hues. An artificial travertine substance, made from gypsum
and hemp fiber, covers each of the exposition palaces. Against
this tonal base of buff brown (I remember this as the base color
of Rome), Guerin has orchestrated a symphony of Mediterranean tincture. He has had the garden lattices, the flower
containers, the lawn curbs, and all exterior woodwork painted
a lovely French green, playing this subtle color off against the
much darker oxidized copper-green with which he has covered
the ten large palace domes, except for the dome of the Court of
the Universe, which is yellow. Varieties of red abound:
orange-pink for the flagpoles; pinkish-red, running from terra
cotta to russet, across all colonnade backgrounds; rosette on all

ceilings and vaulted recesses. My own favorite color, burnt orange, covers the smaller domes and most external mouldings. Guerin has highlighted much of the architectural decoration with blue-green flecks. The larger urns and vases (some of them over six feet in height) are done in verd antique, a blend of copper-green and gray, faintly lined in yellow and black. Every aspect of the exposition harmonizes with this color scheme. Murals, for example, are confined to five colors: yellow ocher, burnt orange, vermillion, cerulean blue, and white. John McLaren, the Landscape Engineer, has selected all flowering plants so that they conform in color. McLaren has even gone so far as to fire the sand used in the pathways in a brick kiln until it attained a cinnamon color harmonious with Guerin's overall palette. The guards themselves wear a buff uniform set off by yellow tabbing and red puttees. The total effect of all this color and all this classical architecture is one of Mediterranean fantasy. The exposition is a Piranesian daydream, a pastel city that never was, nor ever could be, save only in San Francisco's collective imagination.

There is nothing fantastic, however, about the automobiles being manufactured by Mr. Ford at the Palace of Transportation, a complete motor car rolling from the assembly line every ten minutes, or the great electric turbines and diesel engines on view in the Palace of Machinery, or the aeroplanes that loop and dance in the sky overhead. The theme of the exposition is Progress, and decorative motifs suggesting Progress pervade the exposition's architecture. Louis Christian Mullgardt's Court of Ages provides the central statement of Progress. The newspapers have dubbed it "the cathedral of the exposition", "the holy of holies", "the place of prayer." Like a medieval cathedral, Mullgardt's Court of Ages sets forth the story of creation. Decorative motifs begin with sea plants and crustacean life and ascend through the animal kingdom upwards along the Tower of Ages until reaching Albert Weinert's sculptures of prehistoric man and woman, which surmount the entrance to the Tower. Statues by Chester A. Beach and Robert Aitken carry this prehistoric couple through various

790

stages of civilization until the apex of the Tower where sits "The Present Age," a mother with her children. Lest the direction of all this evolutionary movement be forgotten, the Adventurous Bowman atop the Column of Progress looses his arrow westbound. Above the arch of the Tower of Jewels stand the four types who brought Progress to western America: the adventurer, the priest, the philosopher, and the soldier. Above the Arch of the Setting Sun are representations of the various racial stocks that peopled the trans-Mississippi West. Together, they guide a prairie schooner in which sit a pioneer girl and two smaller boys: the Future of California.

Having arrived here in a covered wagon, these children would be about my age today. Like myself, they would be the elder generation, baffled by diesel engines, mass-produced Ford motor cars, and acrobatic aeronauts looping and turning above San Francisco Bay. I must not, however, make myself sound overly alienated; for I actually relish these signs of the future—Marina's future, I must mention, and that of her fiancé John Charles Scannell. Nineteen-fifteen, the year of the Panama-Pacific International Exposition, is their time of youthful idyll, their interlude of courtship and romance. Marina and John are growing in knowledge of one another against a backdrop of exposition events: picnicking on the cliffs of Land's End as the Great White Fleet steamed into the Golden Gate; rushing off on a Sunday afternoon to the Court of Ages to hear Saint-Saëns's specially commissioned symphony, "Hail, California!", scored for orchestra, chorus, and Mr. Sousa's military band; walking hand in hand in the enormous art gallery at the Palace of Fine Arts, where I espied them unawares from a discreet distance, myself there to enjoy the California painters. May they find happiness together such as Marina's mother and I so briefly found!

"John and I have determined never to argue," Marina announced one recent morning apropos, I suspect, of the fact that, in a slightly testy mood, I had made a few waspish comments to Marina regarding her late hours. Ten-thirty at night, I feel, is rather late for a young woman of twenty to be coming home, when she must be at the Ferry Building the next morning before seven to catch the Oakland boat for a full day of classes at Mills College.

"He will break that promise, my dear, if you insist upon staying out at night until ten-thirty."

"My husband, unlike my father, will not be a tyrant."

"I apologize. Henceforth, I shall express fatherly anxiety only if you should not return home at all in the evening— before the wedding, that is."

Marina colored slightly, but she also showed by a droll smile that she appreciated my remark. When she was growing up, Marina and I rarely discussed the birds and the bees. My intuition, however, tells me that her appetites and expectations in this very vital department of human experience are proceeding on course.

"If God made us, then God must be both a man and a woman," Marina once announced to me when she was about six years old. "It takes a man and a woman to make a baby. You and mother made me, then mother died."

Marina was obviously working out a number of things in her mind: the nature of God and human procreation, and the cause of her own partial orphanhood. Agnes Tobin, the woman Marina was most fond of as a child, has had enormous influence on Marina's character. Take Marina's bookishness, for instance, and her spirited personal style: both these traits existed in Agnes Tobin with communicative intensity. I refer, of course, to the Agnes Tobin of yore; for ever since Agnes broke off her friendship with Alice Meynell, around ten years ago, she has grown distracted and reclusive. Today, she virtually leads the cloistered life of a Carmelite nun. After nearly a year living in San Francisco at the Tobin townhouse, Alice Meynell abruptly packed her bags and returned to her husband in London. Distraught at the loss of her friend, Agnes went into decline, like a spurned lover, and has not been the same ever since. Whatever it is (and no one knows for certain), Agnes's Secret has wasted her resilience, her capacity for living, as consumption once wasted Sybil.

Marina and John look forward to a long and happy life

792

together, which I do truly hope they have. "Like Nana and Grampa" is Marina's way of summing up her hopes. She remembers my parents rather well, being all of ten and eleven when they died, a year apart. Mayor Schmitz arranged for a most impressive civic funeral for Father. Attired in his full-dress uniform, Father's body lay in state in the rotunda of City Hall before being taken to St. Mary's Cathedral on Van Ness Avenue, where Archbishop Riordan himself celebrated the funeral mass. After the ceremony, I escorted Mother down the aisle behind the casket. She held on to my arm for support. A wide-eyed Marina held her Nana's other hand.

"I'll not be lasting much longer myself, Sebastian," Mother remarked as we rode in a closed horse-drawn carriage towards the train station where we would meet Father's body, being transported there atop one of the department's largest equipment wagons, pulled by a half-dozen fine horses, the wagon draped in black crepe and a fire bell tolling slowly all the while. "We've been together nearly sixty years and I can't be imagining life without him."

"Nonsense, Mother," I said. "The best way to be with Pa is to stay alive and keep his memory green. And besides: Marina needs you."

I feel that Mother might very well be alive today, a spry old lady in her mid-eighties, had she not stepped accidentally into the path of a streetcar on Market Street. A spear-sharp broken rib punctured her lung; the lung filled with fluid, and then pneumonia set in, compounding the disaster. Not having had a normal family life, Marina grew up especially sensitive to the way Grandpa and Nana behaved towards each other. I flatter myself that had Virginia lived, Marina might have had equally beneficial models in her mother and father; for Virginia and I were most compatible in our brief time together.

I called upon Virginia as soon as I had escorted my trunks to my parents' house and said hello to Mother and Father after four years. One trunk, crammed full of notes, half-drafts of articles, and difficult-to-secure books, had rarely left my sight since Paris: whatever I had to show for the years 1890–1894

793

was contained therein. When I arrived home, my parents were eating lunch in the kitchen. Father wore a collarless shirt, its starched whiteness broken by a run of broad suspenders. Mother wore a light brown dress and a white apron. Neither of them had changed drastically in four years, although on second glance I could see that they were both grayer and a little more lined in the face. Father's hands, I noticed when he reached out to shake mine, were splotched with brown spots, and Mother's back showed the discernible beginnings of a hump.

"It seems that we're always either sending you off or saying hello," Father said, shaking my hand. Mother embraced me, crying a little all the while, then went to the cupboard for another plate.

"We're eating leftover stew," she said. "Join us for lunch." With my stomach so nervous over the prospect of seeing Virginia, who lived but a ten-minute walk away, I was in no mood for warmed-over lamb stew, but I sat down anyway out of filial reverence and managed a half-dozen mouthfuls.

"Did you accomplish your goals, lad?" Father asked, oblivious to the irony of calling his forty-six-year-old son "lad."

"I did, Father," I said. "I've brought home four trunkfuls of research."

"That's good, my boy. Your mother and I loved your letters. We've saved them all, with all of their beautiful stamps and postmarks. Your mother, by the way, was frightened that you'd be fixing to become a monk at Chartreuse and that she'd not be seeing you again, but I assured her that becoming a monk was not in your nature."

"Virginia Walsh was as frighted as myself," Mother said. "She'd come by here and read all your letters, especially the last ones from the Carthusians, looking for a hint of your intentions. She was most distressed by your sudden piety." Mother laughed, and Father joined in, the two of them enjoying their little joke together.

"What are you doing with us old folks?" Father finally asked. "Haven't you got calls to be making?"

794

"Change your shirt first," Mother said. "It's as yellow as parchment and your collar looks like an old playing card."

"A Jack of Hearts," Father guffawed. Like a schoolgirl, Mother joined him in the laughter.

How could two people still perform for each other after nearly fifty years?, I remember asking myself as I went upstairs. What miracle had preserved such mutual interest after the infinite repetitions of meals, talks, nights' sleep, couplings, daily routines—each repeated more than ten thousandfold across some forty-odd years? Retying my cravat over a fresh shirt and a stiff white collar, I began to understand that their feeble humor, their gentle chiding of their overaged son, constituted a species of triumph between them. From the wayside pub called the Armagh Chalice where they first met so long ago, through New York and San Francisco, something defiant of time and monotony had survived in their relationship, capable of adding an element of companionship, of shared drollery, to their midday kitchen meal of last night's lamb stew, warmed over. Grabbing Father around the neck as a barefoot girl of sixteen, Mother had promised to go to hell itself for him if necessary. All that had been required, however, had been that she keep him company in the kitchen when they had both grown old.

Heading for the Tobin mansion, I climbed the steep incline of California Street, grateful for the level block between Mason and Taylor where I could catch my breath. Looking to my left as I crossed Taylor, I saw Virginia halfway up the hill, walking in my direction, a bag of groceries in one arm. Indecisive as to whether to go down to her or wait for her to reach the top of the hill, I stood paralyzed in the middle of the block. Virginia was wearing a broad-brimmed hat with a light veil falling before her face; despite the veil, however, I knew for certain that it was she mounting the sidewalk steps of Taylor Street: deliberately, as she did everything, one step at a time, heading unawares towards me, her would-be affianced who had taken so long to recognize his feelings for her. Reaching the top of the hill, Virginia looked in my direction. She smiled in

795

recognition. I resisted a temptation to drop then and there to my knees, right in the middle of the street, and risk being hauled off for a madman, which in my own way, I was: mad with anxiety as to whether or not it was all too late, whether the past had been irretrievably discarded.

"Halfway up the hill," Virginia said with only the slightest belaborment to her breathing, "I asked myself what sort of an odd duck would be standing in the middle of the street, oblivious to the traffic."

"A dumbstruck duck," I said, taking the bag of groceries from her, "tired and bewildered from his long journey, a duck who is pleased to be home and to be able to see you again."

"Let's sit in the park for a minute," she said. Crossing California Street we found benches in the Huntington Park, facing a splashing Italian fountain donated to the city by Mrs. Arabella Huntington. A cluster of Chinese children in multicolored silken pajamas were playing a game of jump-rope that seemed to involve at least four whirring strands which they pranced in and out of with amazing alacrity.

"We said goodbye in a playground park," I said.

"And I implored you not to go."

"I had ears," I said, "but I did not hear."

"You should have listened to your heart."

"I heard my heart very clearly in the cloister silence of the Grand Chartreuse," I said, "and I listened to what my heart told me."

"So you wrote in your letter," she said, noncommittally.

"I wrote much else besides," I said, made fearful by her composure.

"Your proposal of marriage, you mean?"

She sat silently for a moment, observing the Chinese children at play from behind the semiobscurity of her veil. A fearsome hatpin held her hat affixed to her thick dark-blond hair, drawn behind her head in a bun that had loosened slightly under the disturbance of her afternoon's shopping. The velvet collar of her coat added a note of elegance to her otherwise routine *ensemble*. That collar, I thought to myself, was Virginia's sign of adopted Tobinhood, differentiating her

796

from the other women visiting the market on an ordinary weekday afternoon.

"Yes, my proposal. But before you say anything, listen, please, to what I've been thinking. First of all, I love you. I have loved you for a long time without ever recognizing it. Unless your hurt and anger is now too great, I am confident that you will admit that you once loved me—and that you might yet love me once again. Marry me, Virginia, please marry me. We'll make a new start in life—all on our own, the two of us. I have spent time in France, Italy, and Spain observing vineyards and wineries. I think I understand the details of viticulture. Join me in the Napa Valley! I have enough money for a down payment on a small ranch. We can make a new start as grape-growers and winemakers, together, the two of us!"

"I'm not the same person that you left," she said.

The thought crossed my mind that she had perhaps found another *beau*. She was, after all, a handsome woman, and a Tobin by adoption. Other—younger!—men might very well have become interested in her during my absence. "I am thirty-four years of age, for one thing, and have grown accustomed to being unmarried."

"I am forty-six," I said, "and I am sick to death of being alone."

"But you are a man," she said. "You can alter your condition at will. Women must remain passive until opportunities present themselves. But to return to my point: I could live out the rest of my life as a single person if the other choice confronting me was to marry a man I did not love or who did not love me."

"No such man sits near you now," I said.

"Were a man to ask me to marry him just because that man had grown tired of his sinful ways and had suddenly found religion," Virginia said, removing her veil from her face and lifting it up over her hat, "I frankly wouldn't be very much interested."

As if for the first time, I realized with a drying in my throat and quickening of my pulse what a handsome woman I had left behind in San Francisco to be courted by other men. What bold Irish lines was her face structured upon! Such a lifting high of cheekbone, such generosity of mouth, such a drama of Irish eyes!

"I'd as lief be a single woman as some man's joyless duty," she continued.

"A man who had you," I said, "would possess joy itself."

"A man who had me would possess an ordinary Irish woman," Virginia said. "Even so, I'm worth the having, even if some whom I know be heedless of the opportunity."

"I realize that now," I said. "I only hope that I am not too late."

"What do you think these past four years have been like for me?" she asked.

Saying nothing (what could be said?), I looked away from her, my gaze focusing first upon the stone façade of the Crocker mansion, then over to the Huntington fountain where the Chinese children were floating little paper boats.

"Some day I shall tell you about it," Virginia said, "about the last four years, I mean."

"I am so sorry," I said.

"Never mind," she said. "I must be getting home. Our new cook bears watching. What book shall we read for next Saturday?"

At this, I broke into uncontrollable sobs. Right there in the park, before the puzzled gaze of the Chinese children, I knelt in the gravel before Virginia, and, shuddering with sobs, I took her hands in mine, covering them with kisses.

"Now, now, Sebastian," Virginia said with almost maternal tenderness, "you are not being very articulate. Compose yourself. Saturday will soon be here and we both must get busy on a new book."

"Grape Culture, Wines, and Wine-Making," I managed to whisper, "by Agoston Haraszthy."

"What an outlandish name!"

"It's Hungarian," I said, rising and resuming my seat on the bench next to her. "Most Hungarian names are outlandish."

798

Regaining my composure, I fumbled in my coat pocket for my pencil and wrote down the title of Haraszthy's book on a slip of paper in my notebook, which I tore out and handed to her.

"I'll go to the Mechanics' Library tomorrow morning and check the book out," Virginia said, putting the paper into her purse.

"I'll call on you very early Saturday," I said, "around seven o'clock, if that does not prove a hardship."

"Good Lord, Sebastian, where will we be going at that ungodly hour?"

"St. Helena, in Napa County," I said, kissing her hand once more.

Saturday, Virginia and I caught the seven-thirty ferry to Benicia; and from there, the one-passenger-car train servicing Vallejo, Napa, St. Helena, and points further north. As befits a gentleman a-courting, I spruced myself up as best I could, having treated myself previously that week to a haircut and a beard trim at the barber parlor of the St. Dunstan Hotel. Surveying my wardrobe, I selected a white linen suit and straw boater for the day's excursion. Examining myself in my mirror, I decided that, all things considered, I did not look half bad for a gentleman of forty-six, about to embark upon a springtime picnic with a young lady of thirty-four. Drinking had thickened me somewhat, but not to the point of disconcerting obesity. There were more than a few streaks of gray in my beard, but I had a full head of hair and all my teeth—which I proceeded to examine in the mirror as I tied a rather jaunty bow tie. After considerable debate, I decided that spats would be in order to protect my shoes from the Napa Valley dust—so I told myself. Freshly shaved, talcumed, and pomaded, and with three cups of coffee sloshing on my empty stomach, I was about to step out to the street when Mother and Father came downstairs in their bathrobes. Mother was yet wearing her nightcap.

"Now don't you look something?" Mother said.

"You'll be out dancing this early in the morning?" Father

asked. "Or are you sneaking in from the night before?" The two of them tittered quietly. Here I was, near fifty, and an object of wry amusement to my aged parents.

"I'm off to Napa with Virginia," I said. "We're going on a picnic and we shall also be looking over some property."

"Can I give you some advice, son?" Father asked. "Take them spats off. Country people don't truck to cityfolk wearing spats in the country. Put some good boots on instead, especially if you be thinking of walking the fields, and discussing a little business." I went upstairs and removed my spats as Father suggested. I also put on a heavier pair of shoes. Virginia was already standing in front of the Tobin townhouse when I arrived, a large picnic basket at her feet.

"I didn't want the doorbell ringing and the dog barking this early on Saturday morning," she said.

We caught a cable car down to Market Street, then walked the few remaining blocks to the Ferry Building. Crossing to Benicia, we had the entire boat to ourselves aside from five or so Portuguese and Chinese truck farmers, returning with empty wagons to the East Bay after having disposed of their produce to the wholesalers at the Farmers' Market. We stood together on deck, enjoying the sea and the receding cityscape and the beginnings of the April day. As if by agreement, Virginia was wearing a straw boater similar to mine, and a well-tailored hiking suit, the skirt cut shorter than usual and with an ample kick pleat. She wore tan boots, laced high, very appropriate for the country. I found myself thinking just exactly how young forty-six really was, of how many good years might very well be remaining to us both. How fresh and healthy Virginia looked, tilting her face slightly so as to feel the morning sun on her face! And as for myself—I felt perfectly splendid! My life had miraculously edged itself into a second spring. Once again, despite the fact that I had squandered other April mornings such as this, I had come into a middle-aged rendezvous with spring. I was reborn to love, to a lyrical appreciation of the sheer miracle of my existence in this lovely world, with this beautiful good woman beside me!

On the train, we found two seats facing each other. I sat

800

before Virginia, the picnic basket at her side. Leaning over, I adjusted her boater from its straightforward position to an insouciant angle. She laughed shyly as I tilted her brim forward. The train lurched out of the little Benicia station, beginning its milk run to Vallejo and from there up through the Napa Valley.

"Now then," Virginia said, "the Haraszthy book. I have read it and I await your comments."

"Did you like it?" I asked.

"I enjoyed much of the commentary and I loved the engravings," she said, "but I became lost in the technical details relating to winemaking."

"Haraszthy was a Hungarian count, or so he claimed," I said. "The Legislature sent him to Europe in 1861 to investigate the prospects of bringing the European wine industry to California. Haraszthy sent back thousands of cuttings. In 1862 he published this book, calling for the development of vineyards and wineries in California. You might call this book the bible of California viticulture."

"Are you serious, Sebastian, about moving to the Napa Valley?"

"I am very serious, Virginia, about beginning my life over again in healthy circumstances, and this seems the best way. I want to experience life on the land as I did at *La Grande Chartreuse*. At the same time, I hope to continue my writing. Winemaking offers me both possibilities, if I, if we, can make a go of it."

Around eleven o'clock we entered the Napa Valley. Vineyards stretched away on all sides of us, reaching towards the foothills on the eastern and western edges of the valley. To our left, we could see the Inglenook Winery of Captain Gustav Niebaum, a stone fantasy resembling the castle of an Eastern European fairytale. Chateau Montelena and Chateau Beaulieu—next seen—evoked the South of France. We passed the great stone winery built by the Beringers, a Gothic-like affair, three stories tall, reminding me of the Rhineland. Greystone Cellars, done in the grand manner of Richardsonian Romanesque and set on a commanding knoll, dominates the central Napa Valley like a great cathedral devoted to the worship of the vine.

"Greystone Cellars cost some two million dollars to build," I told Virginia as our train rolled past the massive pile. "For us, I have a more modest beginning in mind."

Detraining at St. Helena, we found a hired horse and buggy waiting for us at the station as per my contract made earlier in the week by telegraph. Passing through the sleepy town, we headed west through a landscape of vineyards—the leafy vines just beginning to send forth their tender berries—towards the foothills of the Mayacamas range dividing Napa Valley from Sonoma.

"You haven't told me where we're going," Virginia said.

"To a special place," I said. "To a place I hope will be our home."

Avila Vineyards (so named after it came into our possession) is a smallish mountainside property developed by Arpad Haraszthy, the son of the Count (and a founding member of the Bohemian Club), in the mid-Seventies. Planting some hundred acres in Johannesberg Riesling, White Muscat, Flame Tokay, and Zinfandel, Arpad in turn sold the property in the mid-Eighties to its most recent owner, the recently deceased Senhor Pedro Freitas, a Portuguese. His childless widow, a leathery-faced woman in her early sixties, burnt brown by a lifetime in the sun, had no intention of managing the vineyard on her own. She preferred, rather, to sell it at a good price, then move to Livermore Valley where her widower brother had a ranch and needed someone to keep house, preferably a younger sister, devoted to his best interests.

All this Virginia and I learned in the course of our visit to Senhora Freitas, who had been recommended to me, incidentally, by the Bank of Napa, which held the mortgage on the property. I had written the president of the bank from Paris, asking him to keep me informed upon my return as to smaller properties up for sale. The bank's letter, informing me of the Senhora Freitas's desire to sell, awaited my arrival in San Francisco. Senhora Freitas dressed herself completely in black, despite the bright sunshininess of the day. She also wore a black bandanna around her head. Virginia and I followed her about the property, inspecting the fields, the winery proper—a whitewashed Mediterranean-style building, roofed in red tile—and the ranch house, a two-story cottage in the General Grant style, surrounded on three sides by a screened-in porch. Returning from a tour of the vines, we passed a live oak tree set atop a slight knoll. In an opening in the oak tree, the late Senhor Freitas had emplaced a shrine to Our Lady of Mount Carmel. Leaving the Senhora to her afternoon nap, Virginia and I returned to the oak-shaded spot for our picnic. We sat on a canvas tarpaulin lent us by the Senhora. From her also came two bottles of vineyard wine, a Riesling and a Zinfandel, which we drank out of heavy kitchen tumblers, washing down our luncheon of biscuits, honey, apples, and cheese.

"The entire property sells for fifteen thousand," I said. "I could get it for three thousand down, provided the Bank of Napa approves the loan."

"Is that Our Lady of Mount Carmel?" Virginia asked, looking up at the statue that stood in the cleft of the tree trunk, enshrined beneath a shelter of redwood shingle.

"Yes, I am almost certain," I said.

"Then the property should be given a Carmelite name," Virginia said. "Perhaps something in honor of St. Teresa of Avila."

Abandoning her decorous seating (bolt upright, her skirt-covered legs tucked to one side), she stretched herself out at full length, her head propped up on one elbow, which she rested on her rolled-up jacket. The angle of her body pushed her breasts against her blouse. Reaching over, I removed her boater hat and pulled away the pin holding her hair behind her head. It fell down to one side of her shoulders in a stream of cascading gold. She blushed like a girl.

"Forgive me," I said.

"For what, Sebastian?"

"For the waste."

"In the book you recommended, Haraszthy says that a good wine takes time to mature. Perhaps the same is true of people."

"Time can enrich a wine," I said, "if the conditions are proper. Too much time, however, can make a wine go sour."

"Then we shall have to taste the wine to find out," she said. I leaned over and for the first time in our acquaintance, our lips met. Her mouth tasted of honey and Zinfandel. I heard the buzzing of bees drowsily foraging amidst the buckthorn and the sumac as I closed my eyes upon the cool silence of her face.

We were married in June—a simple affair at Old St. Mary's. The pastor, Reverend Bernard Brady of the Paulist fathers, performed the ceremony and said the nuptial mass. R. M. Tobin gave Virginia away. Jimmy Phelan stood as my best man. Virginia wore a white dress, but not a bridal veil. She insisted that we were both a little long in the tooth for a full-dress wedding. I wore a conservative suit. Father, however, insisted upon his dress uniform; and some half-dozen senior officers from the Department, many of whom I had known for years, came along in attendance, in uniform also, adding a little *esprit* to our quiet ceremony. Following the mass, Jimmy Phelan gave us a champagne breakfast at the Bohemian Club. R. M. made a very charming speech in which he narrated how upon the death of her father Virginia came to be "absorbed" into the Tobin household without conscious plan or decision; how the entire family regarded her as a sister, whom they would now fear losing, save for the fact that she was marrying a good friend of the Tobin family. Jimmy Phelan then rose to say that he rarely abused his prerogatives as president of the Bohemian Club, but that he had hurried the membership committee along a bit so that the candidacy of one Sebastian Collins might be ready by today, which it was. Handing me my letter of acceptance, Phelan expressed his hope that my membership in the club would keep me a familiar face on the San Francisco scene, despite my rustication to St. Helena with my lovely bride. Agnes then read a poem she had composed especially for the occasion, "An Epithalamium in the California Mode," which included the lovely evocation of Virginia and myself standing side by side before our cottage, surrounded by healthy children, as the sun set over Avila Vineyard in summer splendor.

Speaking of which—Avila Vineyard—I had intended my purchase of the Freitas property to be entirely my own responsibility. Virginia, however, insisted upon using two thousand dollars of the five thousand dollar dowry settled on her by the Tobins. Part of this sum derived from the remnants of Virginia's father's estate, which the Tobins had prudently invested, increasing it to a tidy amount. Thus able to make a four-thousand-dollar down payment between us, Virginia and I secured Avila Vineyards at most reasonable terms from the Bank of Napa.

We had already sent our belongings up to St. Helena by freight express the week before our marriage, so we were able to travel lightly to the wine country on the day of our wedding, having barely caught the two o'clock train from Benicia. We arrived in St. Helena by late afternoon. It was sunset by the time we headed our horse and buggy into the foothill road leading to Avila Vineyards. Rising up out of tangled copses of blackberry and buckthorn, oak and madrone trees, their trunks peeling in red bark, stood sentry along the path. With luggage tied to the buggy jumpseat, and two passengers to pull, our mare took her time along the rutted lane: a course I approved of, wanting never to end this sunset ride up along foothill vineyards, broken by live oak and madrone. Ride on, ride on forever, I thought to myself, towards a vineyard villa bathed in the roseate lightfall setting over the Mayacamas Hills. Proceed, Sebastian Collins, with newly-taken wife towards a georgic destiny of patient Virgilian toil for good wine and even finer prose. A barn owl, bent on some twilight maraud, flew across our line of vision. To our left, up along the higher vineyards, black bats crisscrossed the vermilion dusk. Now and then, our mare neighed a gentle lullaby, as the song of crickets laid the land to rest.

805

"Oh Sebastian dearest, it is so peaceful," Virginia said, entwining her arm in mine and leaning her weight against me.

"We deserve such peace," I said.

"No, not deserve," Virginia said. "We deserve nothing. This is all a gift."

While Virginia went inside the house to prepare dinner, I bedded the mare down in the barn. I remember taking extra care in doing so, stroking and patting her like a pet as she ate her oats and hay. Standing on the front porch before going inside, I could barely make out the whitewashed walls of the winery across the property. It looked like a country house in Italy or Spain. Within were the vats, coils, and cooperage of my new calling, awaiting the late summer's harvest and the crush of fall. Inhaling deeply, I convinced myself that I could smell a suggestion of new wine already on the air.

Upon her departure, Senhora Freitas had stripped the house of all her personal effects; she did leave us, however, a number of pieces of heavy, dark furniture, some of it in the animal-footed style of thirty years past. Our dining-room table, for instance, where Virginia, using the groceries we had purchased in the village, spread a repast of cucumber salad, cold chicken, sliced tomatoes, apricots, and white wine, was bolstered up by four sturdy legs ending in bear's paws. A crawling child, I thought to myself, might love poking about such a mysterious nether region.

"We'll unpack everything tomorrow," I said, sitting down to our first meal alone together as man and wife.

"It will take at least a week to do that," Virginia said. "Your books and papers alone will take a day to arrange. We'll make a study of the downstairs bedroom."

When we finished eating, I helped Virginia with the dishes, drying them with an excess of deliberation and making something of a fuss as to exactly how they should be stacked in the china cabinet. By this time, I was in shirtsleeves. Virginia had changed from her traveling suit into a simple dress. My pocket watch (glanced at discreetly while Virginia was upstairs, making our bed) said eight-forty-five.

"We have," Virginia said, coming downstairs, "a most unusual bed."

"Comfortable, I hope."

"Yes, comfortable enough, but also unusual. You shall see what I mean." We sat opposite each other, across the glow of the coal oil lamp. "I'm a little disappointed, Sebastian dear," Virginia said after what seemed an eternity of silence, broken only by the cricket-song outside the window.

"My dear, it's barely nine o'clock—rather early for a bride to be disappointed, I'd say."

"I was expecting you to carry me across the threshold, that's all. You are such a traditionalist. Why ignore this one tradition?"

"Well," I said, standing, "let me rectify my mistake." Hand in hand we walked out to the porch, awash in moonlit darkness. Somewhere off in the mountains, a coyote howled its long, mournful song, then fell silent.

"He sounds lonely," Virginia said.

"Unlike us," I said, taking her into my arms. She shuddered slightly in my embrace.

"I am a little afraid," she said. "I've lived so long—by myself."

"So have I," I said, "but I never knew it until now."

"Will it be all right, Sebastian? Will it work?"

"I, Sebastian Collins," I whispered into her ear, "do take thee, Virginia Walsh, to my lawful wife, to have and to hold, from this day forward, for better, for worse, for richer, for poorer, in sickness and in health, until death do us part."

"Oh Sebastian," Virginia said, "And I also do the same. I take you forever, with all my heart."

Picking her up, I carried her across the threshold. She almost fled from my arms to the staircase. While Virginia was upstairs preparing for bed, I dragged two trunks of books and papers from the porch into the parlor. Then I changed into my nightshirt and bathrobe, fetching them from my suitcase which was still downstairs. I hung my clothes in the foyer closet. Turning off the last lamp, I went upstairs.

807

Virginia had not exaggerated. The bed left us by Senhora Freitas as part of the purchase price was of the darkest walnut. A triumphant griffin, skillfully carved in walnut also, bestrode the six-feet-high headboard like a gargoyle atop the balustrade of a Gothic cathedral. Blowing out the candle, I doffed my bathrobe—but not my nightshirt—and climbed into bed next to Virginia. She was better prepared for our wedding night than I, as I discovered when, with great surprise and eager joy, I took her silk-cool nakedness into my arms.

We worked side by side that year, husband and wife, sharing a dream. *Wine Prospects for California* bears the entwined signature "by Sebastian and Virginia Collins" because we wrote that little book together, just as we rose at midnight together to set out flaming oil pots against an unexpected frost, or together wrapped the base of our vines with burlap sacks to frustrate the nibbling of rabbits, raccoons, and deer. In our book—jointly researched and discussed, drafted initially by myself, then rediscussed between the two of us—Virginia and I sought to express the history and Californian ideality of our undertaking. We began our book with a study of Thomas Jefferson; for Jefferson, responsible for so many wonderful American things, must also be considered the founding father of American wine. An accomplished connoisseur, Jefferson gathered the great vintages of Germany and France into his Monticello Cellar. He planted vineyards and experimented in winemaking. Eloquently and ceaselessly, he promoted wine as an agent of health, temperance, civility, and civilization. America, Jefferson argued, would never be culturally mature until it knew and used wine. Our next chapter dealt with Padre Junipero Serra, the founding father of California, who also founded the state's wine industry, planting California's first vines at Mission San Diego sometime in 1770. Jean Louis Vignes of Bordeaux came to Los Angeles in the early 1830s and established California's first commercial vineyard. Pierre and Jean Louis Sansevain, his nephews, kept the business going after their uncle retired, producing wines of remarkable quality. We devoted an entire chapter to the Sansevain story, seeing in it the foundation epic of our industry.

Visitors to California frequently observe that the wine country of California suggests Europe—as a matter of organized landscape and as a matter of the cultures of the French, Italian, and German families living among our vineyards. The entire story of wine in California is indeed a rich pageant of continuities and associations between the Old World and the New. Virginia and I also endeavored to suggest this Euro-American ideality. Wine upgrades California, we wrote, urging it onwards to further civilization. In wine, in the wine country, the American-as-Californian becomes, not only the pioneer coaxing virgin soil to fruition, but the heir to the ages, bent upon an immemorial task of translation and care.

"Wine," we wrote, "involves a practical and deeply poetic blend of agriculture, technology, and art. The wine industry reconciles the urban with the rural, the natural with the technological. In a very real way—in its commitment, that is, to agriculture, to rural industries, to civility and science—the wine country of California is Thomas Jefferson's American dream come true: a landscape of balance, repose, and aesthetic harmony, an America released by nature, subdued by art and manufacture, mellowed by a sense of European association."

"It's all a little idealistic, isn't it, Sebastian?" Virginia asked as we reviewed the manuscript one last time before sending it off to Millicent Shinn at the *Overland Monthly* in San Francisco, who had agreed to run parts of it as articles, before issuing the entire manuscript in book form. "We haven't sufficiently emphasized the hard work involved, I fear."

We might have eliminated the realities of labor from *Wine Prospects for California*, but we did not eliminate the sweat and struggle from our daily lives. Six days a week, we rose with dawn, breakfasted by sunrise, then began a morning of chores. There always seemed a hundred things to do: equipment to service; soil to be turned with mule and plow (the most onerous, backbreaking work of all!); vines to be pruned or grafted; a harvest to be contracted for with Mexican laborers, then supervised; a crush; then the long, patient work of winemaking itself: the vatting, settling, straining, and revatting; the rolling of great oaken barrels into place on their racks in the stone-cool recess of Avila Winery, there to await the patient work of nature herself. Keeping our overhead as low as possible, we did most of the work ourselves. I had to hire on a part-time basis a young Basque cooper, however; for no one can teach himself the barrelmaker's art; and I also secured the services of a professional vintner, who consulted with me during the crucial stages of the crush; for no matter how impeccable my viticultural scholarship, I was inexperienced in the practical techniques of winemaking.

We took our main meal at noon, followed by a siesta until three. Much of our lovemaking occurred then, beneath the watchful eye of the griffin, our exerted bodies refreshed by a faint breeze blowing down from the Mayacamas, billowing out the curtains of our opened bedroom window like the flying jib of a pleasure craft. How sweet to sleep for an afternoon hour in the arms of one's beloved wife after a connection of flesh by turns tender and passionate, the body's hungers satisfied and the soul sustained in conjugal innocence. What Signora Anna Amari told me in Rome eighteen years earlier proved to be so very, very true: a happy marital union is the most gratifying mode of physical love; for such a coverture engages all levels of the self—body, mind, imagination, spirit—nourishing each with appropriate gifts. In terms of physical love, Virginia satisfied me most lavishly (and after a period of mutual tutelage and self-discovery on her part, I did the same for her); yet her body was my temple as well as my pleasure garden. How often during those happy moments (or when they were over, for in the intensity of fulfillment no thought crossed my consciousness) did I remember Ryan Patrice's words, spoken at *La Grande Chartreuse*: "A monk's cell and a marriage bed, Sebastian, are both places of ascesis. The celibate snobbery of our Church has exalted the one, but no matter: be patient. The Catholicity of the future shall rediscover the sacrament of matrimony, glorying in its sensuous, procreative intent." After such wayward pilgrimage to come into such safe harbor!

810

My every ambition towards Virginia—fulfilled tenderly or in a furious rush, or remaining a passing speculation as I watched her lift her arm towards the cupboard, walk from her bath swathed in one of my oversized robes, stand scattering grain from a pan to a flock of clucking chickens, return from one of her solitary walks, a beadline of moisture across her upper lip—my every ambition, culminated in an act of love or drained off into that constant reservoir of energy between us, replenished our relationship, which seemed beyond depletion, like the bowl blessed by the god Mercury, flowing forever with milk and honey.

She first knew great pleasure on a rainy night, the two of us beneath downy quilts as water beat against the windowpane, making all within so cozy, so safe from harm. Such pleasure came, no doubt, because we were some three months into our marriage, hence a little experienced with each other and no longer shy; hence arose my courage to take my husbandly kisses beneath her belly, bringing my mouth to her there and staying a while in fervent ministration, hearing the pat, pat, pat on the glass and her gradual welling of sighs and urgent encouragements of yes, yes, yes, until—I by then being mounted above her—she exploded beneath me like a too-long delayed storm, the wind and rain without seeming feeble in comparison to those human cries that arose in her like a joyous sob: yes, yes, yes O yes: myself now having passed beyond all delusion of male mastery, content to serve her urgencies, which drained the seed from me in archings and sighs and a rush of full-mouthed kisses.

"O dearest, dearest," she said, the breath not yet returned to her, "I was so lonely while you were gone. I hated you, hated you for leaving me, for ignoring what I was trying to place before you with all the frankness I dared display. And now this! Dearest one, husband, Sebastian, let me kiss you here, and here, and here. Let me hold you like this forever, a woman complete." We slept deeply that evening: the night of Marina's conception (so I have always believed) and hence, most cruelly, the beginning of the end.

I sit here in the late afternoon before the Palace of Fine Arts, and I remember Virginia and myself, and our last nine months together. I have an hour before Marina and John are due to rendezvous with me here. I shall watch the swans gliding back and forth across the lagoon, and I shall rest myself on this bench, a man growing old, enamored of memory and regret.

Maybeck has done well with his Palace of Fine Arts: this orchestration of dome, colonnade, lagoon—meant, so Maybeck says, "to suggest an old Roman ruin, away from civilization, which two thousand years before was the center of action and full of life, and now is overgrown with bushes and trees." The Exposition Art Committee has been truly gratified by the favorable response of the public to the fifty California painters on exhibit in the Palace's California Gallery. Twenty-five years ago Virginia suggested that I not go to Europe but stay in California to write about California art. I replied that there was no California art to write about. Now I shall be hard pressed to find space for all that I wish to say about our fifty local painters in *Art in California*, the *catalogue raisonné* I am preparing for the Art Committee at the behest of John Trask, the chairman. I have spent many pleasant hours these past three months in the California Gallery, musing before the works of Dunlap, Bremer, Mathews, McComas, Stackpole, Porter, Peters, Piazzoni, Martinez, Keith, Putnam—realizing all the while that yes at last California has the beginnings of a coherent art tradition. In my *catalogue raisonné* I shall make every effort to suggest how the European training that most of our artists on exhibit received in their youth helped them to perceive and paint the landscape of California in a most charming manner. Our nativist movement, fruitfully European in influence, encourages the perception of California, not as the landscape of an untamed frontier, but a landscape that is mellow, time-soaked, smoky with human association.

More European paintings should have been on exhibit, save for the accursed European War. The torpedoing of the *Lusitania*, I fear, cinches our involvement in the conflict. Some one hundred and twenty-eight Americans were among the thousand and more passengers sent to a watery grave off the coast of Ireland, a number of them graduate students of Royce's: a fact that has driven Josie towards the edge of hysteria. Not only has his beloved Germany enslaved itself to the Prussian Hun; it now hunts down and kills his philosophy students. We San Franciscans are doing our best to conduct a world's fair despite the fact that half the world is in flames—as we ourselves were not ten years ago. The Panama-Pacific International Exposition is our city's way of telling that portion of the civilized world not embroiled in the conflict that San Francisco has recovered itself from the ashes of April 1906.

Like most of the city, I was fast asleep at five-sixteen of the morning of Wednesday, April 18, when the forty-eight-second shock wave hit the San Francisco peninsula. Marina, then just turning ten, ran immediately into my bedroom, where I was sitting bolt upright in my bed, trying to recover myself from the feeling of confusion induced by the temblor: a feeling of paralysis akin, I recall, to my first experience of artillery fire on the battlefield. Waking to find myself surrounded by broken china (a pitcher and bowl had slid off the nightstand), the pictures on my bedroom wall all topsy-turvy, my bed itself partially collapsed, I was in a state of temporary befuddlement.

"Daddy, Daddy," Marina cried, hopping into my precariously slanting double bed, "is it the end of the world?" To tell the truth, I was not certain; but I calmed her as best I could, taking her into my arms beneath the blankets.

"It's not the end of the world," I said. "It's only an earthquake."

Indeed, it *was* only an earthquake: a number nine earthquake on the seismological scale (a strength of ten constitutes geological catastrophe), which we might have survived had it not been for the fire. Residential San Francisco is built of wood, and most of our wooden residences took the shock rather well, riding out the earthquake like storm-buffeted ships, tossed about, but remaining intact. Along the waterfront, however, a number of cheaper hotels, built on mud fill, collapsed totally, accounting for a good number of the 667 bodies eventually checked into the city's makeshift morgue. The groans of the hundreds trapped beneath the rubble of collapsed hotels and tenements was horrible to hear. Those who reached such scenes in the immediate aftermath of the quake now tell me that they sometimes still have nightmares in which they hear men, women, and children crying out in agony beneath the tons of rubble. Had the shock occurred by day, when our downtown office buildings were filled, thousands upon thousands would have met equally horrible ends; a considerable number of our flimsily constructed brick-over-wood-frame commercial buildings collapsed in cascades of brick and severed timber beams. Battered as we were, however, we should have gotten by the disaster fairly easily, were it not for the fires that broke out because of overturned stoves, collapsing chimneys, and the like. The earthquake destroyed the city's two water mains and short-circuited our newly installed electrical alarm system. (Seeing this system into operation had been among Father's last official acts.) Chief Dennis O'Sullivan, Father's *protégé* in the Department, sustained mortal injuries in the immediate aftermath of the quake itself. With no water, no system of alarms, and no chief, the Department lost precious hours in organizing itself against the blazes that were breaking out in the South of Market and downtown districts of the city, where the all-night stoves of restaurants were proving especially inflammatory.

The chimney of the kitchen stove in our Taylor Street flat was totally twisted about, so I foreswore making a hot breakfast for Marina after I had calmed her and myself down following the quake. A lady at a house at Gough and Hayes streets, however, lit her stove fire and began preparing a skillet of ham and eggs. The sparks from her broken chimney (collapsed on the roof where she could not see it) soon had the entire Hayes Valley ablaze—the so-called Ham and Eggs Fire—including St. Ignatius Church and College. I had no intention, however, of reporting to work that morning.

814

Dressing Marina in a warm coat against the morning chill, I took her to an empty butte at Taylor and Green streets that rises out over the downtown area. From there, we could see the smokestreams of some thirty fires rising up over the city, but as yet there was no general conflagration. The clock on the Ferry Building read 5:16 as it did for many days afterwards. Marina and I were joined on the butte by a number of other curious onlookers; indeed, there was almost a holiday atmosphere in the air: a sense of routine interrupted, of exciting events about to occur which, while slightly fearful, were not all that unpleasant.

"They'll have it under control by noontime," I remember one gentleman observing.

Destiny had other intentions. By noon the fires showed definite signs of being out of control. By late afternoon, certain fires had coalesced into fire storms which leapt from rooftop to rooftop like bighorn sheep. That night, the sky glowed a hellish red and you could feel the heat coming up the California Street hill from the blazing South of Market and downtown area. Then the dynamiting began as the Army and the Fire Department tried to stop the oncoming fire by depriving it of rooftops to leap across. Marina slept with me that night, huddled in my arms, as the booming continued, rendering San Francisco like a city under artillery siege. A trooper from the Presidio rang our doorbell at six o'clock the next morning, saying very politely that we had four hours to evacuate our premises.

"I'll need more time," I said. "I'll need time to pack my belongings."

"That's all the time you get," he said. "Sorry—Captain's orders. We'll be dynamiting this block by noon. You'll find food and shelter at Alamo Square or Golden Gate Park— courtesy of Uncle Sam."

Uncle Sam, however, had made no provisions to help me rescue some of my worldly goods. Marina stood wide-eyed at my side as the soldier spoke, then disappeared upstairs when he left. A little later, she came downstairs dressed in her best

815

coat and carrying one of my leather satchels stuffed with a rather random assortment of her favorite dresses. In one arm she held a gigantic rag doll.

"I'm ready, Daddy," she said.

Her matter-of-factness inspired and disconcerted me. The thought of leaving behind my library and my papers, including two partially complete manuscripts (the results of years of work) drove me to the edge of panic. At fifty-eight, one does not begin one's life work anew. Leaving Marina with the elderly Alsatian couple next door (themselves in tears as they packed their worldly goods), I bolted down Pacific Street in search of a taxi. My quest seemed hopeless. Every horse-drawn vehicle in San Francisco had already been pressed into service. Hordes of Chinese were marching out of Chinatown as I moved down Dupont Street towards Bush—a ragtag parade of all ages, each adult loaded with an astonishing amount of goods. One gentleman balanced a crate of quacking ducks on his head. A young woman, a prostitute perhaps, unable to hobble fast enough along on her deliberately misshapen feet, rode piggyback on the back of an older woman. The Chinese children, like Marina, were unpanicked. I heard no crying from them; rather, they marched along with the deliberate stoicism of their elders. Streams of refugees were pouring westward from the central city. At times, it seemed as if I were the only person moving in the direction of the holocaust. I had the idea, irrational perhaps, that the best place to secure the rental of an unused vehicle was on the fringes of the disaster itself, rather than in the rear areas where most buggies, carriages, wagons, and motor cars would have already been identified and put to use. I saw no empty wagons or taxis, however; I saw only a city, abandoned by its citizenry, being destroyed by fire and dynamite. The holiday atmosphere of Wednesday morning had vanished, and in its place crept an atmosphere of shock and grief as a great city surrendered itself to the voracious embrace of what seemed a deliberately vengeful holocaust, the wrath of angered gods being poured down from the heavens.

All things considered, I saw little panic. The presence of a soldier on every block obviously stabilized the situation. Surprisingly, no soldier or policeman halted me to ask why I was heading in the opposite direction. I must have appeared to be some sort of an official, a supposition compounded by the fact that a number of firemen recognized me as I passed and shouted hello. I also knew a number of the police, and was also perhaps recognized as a friend of Mayor Phelan's.

"Good thing the old man never lived to see this," a young fireman, Thomas Patrick Collins (no relation), told me at Bush and Montgomery streets, referring to my father, whom he once served as driver. Young Collins's face was black with soot, and his eyes peered forth from his minstrel mask, bloodshot and watery with exhaustion. "Had the old man been about," he said, "we might have stopped this awful mess in the first few hours, instead of letting it get out of hand."

During an hour's search, I found only one unoccupied taxi. The owner, however, demanded four hundred dollars, cash or equivalent in gold or jewelry, to be paid within the first hour of rental. I had no such money or property on hand, and all banks, obviously, were closed or burnt to the ground, their steel safes intact beneath the rubble, but too hot to be opened for weeks after they were dug out of the ruins. Giving up in despair, and realizing that I had to return to fetch Marina within the half hour, I trudged wearily up Geary Street on my way home. In my mind I was calculating just exactly what I could carry away from the house by hand. It seemed precious little. A taxi buggy rattled up Geary Street, a phantom vehicle in a dead city. I hailed it jubilantly.

"Oh, Dr. Collins, good day to you, sir. A terrible hour! A devilish devastation! You look exhausted, sir. Might I be of service?" It was Jim Norton, the cabbie operating from the Palace Hotel whose services I had secured on many more pleasant occasions, to include my night with the ballerinas from the Grand Opera Company. Jim was unshaven and a little drunk, but I was never so glad to see anyone in my life.

"Jim, I need help to get my belongings out of my house,

817

some of them at least. I've only two hours left before the Army plans to dynamite my flat. Can you help me?"

"Can and will, governor. I'm heading home myself, by which I mean my place in the Mission. It's been a busy time, it has. The first thing when this here devilish devastation was breaking out, I realized there was money to be made. I was dozing atop my rig when the quake struck, knowing there'd be plenty of business that morning on account of the early train for New York. This here Eyetalian opera singer staying at the Palace Hotel runs out just after things began settling down, a bellboy following him with some suitcases. The Eyetalian ain't been to bed yet; I could tell this from the fact of his still having his penguin suit on, and a top hat. 'Take-a me to the boat!' he yells, kind of real excited; so I took him to the Ferry Building, no more than six blocks away, but he puts a fifty dollar gold piece in my hand, then runs for the six-thirty departure, already filling up with refugees. Right then and there I knew there was money to be made. I dashed home for an hour to check on the family, and I've been jockeying this rig almost fifteen hours a day ever since."

"I can match Mr. Caruso's price," I said. "In fact, I'll pay seventy-five dollars."

"I've been getting two hundred."

"I haven't that sort of money on hand, Jim."

"And I'm getting tired of taking it in, anyway—at least from San Franciscans. Hop up here and give me a chance to do something for one of my own for a change." Grinning, he reached down to me. I took his hamlike fist and he hoisted me up on the seat next to him. It took us little more than an hour to pack my most important books, manuscripts, documents and, with Norton's help, load them into his rig. As I worked, I blessed my decision to leave the bulk of my memorabilia and papers up in St. Helena in the attic of my Avila Vineyards home, which I use as a weekend and summer place, renting the vineyards out, however, to a winery nearby. As craftily as Norton supervised the loading of his hansom cab, seeing to it that not an inch of space was wasted, I had room for only the

818

most crucial of my books and papers. Our entire block of Taylor Street had already been abandoned, save for the Alsatian couple who had watched over Marina and whom I invited as a form of repayment to share the taxi with us.

"Sir, you must be moving along now," a sergeant announced as we were packing the last of our luggage aboard the dangerously overladen rig. "The dynamiters are finishing with the next block." The Alsatians, Marina, Jim Norton, and I all piled atop the hansom cab, its springs crushed nearly to the ground. Norton cracked his whip over his exhausted animal.

"Goodbye, San Francisco!" he called, and away we lurched at a very slow pace. Soldiers lugging cases of dynamite were moving onto our street as we rolled away.

Proceeding up to Fillmore Street, we passed Van Ness Avenue, where the fire was destined to be contained some two days later. The flames could not leap across the 120-foot width of this boulevard. Everything east of Van Ness, however, was burned to the ground. At Fillmore and Hayes, the Alsatian couple left us for the refugee camp being established by the Army at Alamo Square. At Mr. Norton's invitation, I decided to continue with him out to the Mission District, where he assured me I could rent a room temporarily from his own landlady, who owned a row of houses on Alabama Street. We could not, however, an army sentry informed us, proceed at once as we intended down Divisadero to the Upper Market area, and thence to the Mission. No unescorted vehicles were being allowed to pass. There had been some incidents, the sentry said—robberies, the expropriation of carriages, a shooting or two. A caravan under army escort, leaving from Alamo Square, would cross to the Mission District in forty-five minutes and we were welcome to join it with the other refugees heading in that direction.

While Norton attended to his exhausted horse and while Marina slept inside the cab, wrapped in Norton's outside blanket, which he wrapped around his legs and waist as he pushed his hack through the chilly mornings and evenings of San Francisco, I crossed Fillmore Street and entered Sacred

Heart Church. Poised on the upper edge of Hayes Valley, Sacred Heart Church has a commanding east-west and north-south view of San Francisco. Its outsized yellow brick Lombard bell tower is a landmark, visible from many parts of the city. The church was packed with refugees, a number of them asleep on pews, others eating bowls of soup being served by a group of nuns near a side entry. Babies were crying, and the church echoed with the babble of a hundred excited voices.

On instinct, wishing one last look at the devastation, I wound my way up the circular steps of the Church's soaring campanile until I reached the observation platform at its summit. There I beheld the penultimate stages of San Francisco's death agony. Fires raged everywhere. A funnel of smoke (later estimated as a mile and a half in height) rose up from the city like a tornado cloud. Haze and smoke totally obscured entire portions of the South of Market area. Other districts were only partially visible; and what could be seen was not a pretty picture: the charred frames of thousands of burnt buildings; the gutted facades of those few office buildings in the downtown district that still stood; other blocks yet burning out of control. The intermittent thundering of dynamite echoed from hill to hill, an ominous *basso profundo* against the strident soprano of the clanging bells of fire wagons racing desperately towards the uneven struggle. The most poignant symbol of the disaster was the total ruin of our City Hall, which had taken San Francisco some thirty years to build. Its dome remained oddly intact atop a framework of steel girders; the walls of the building, however, shaken by the fury of the earthquake, had peeled away from the understructure and crashed to the ground in a pile of rubble. Immediately east of me, I could see that the fire was reaching out to engulf the buildings of the old St. Ignatius College at Hayes and Van Ness. Mentally, I said goodbye to the personal possessions in my office—fortunately not of great value, my little cubbyhole being of little use for aught save student conferences.

Like myself, an entire city was losing the physical substance

820

of its past. Why, I asked myself as flames engulfed the college where I had worked so happily since my return from Napa in 1896, why was this happening? Why was the flesh of San Francisco being so immolated? Why was our city being purged by fire? Was it because of our sins? Had San Francisco sunk into some monstrous iniquity that only the chastisement of heaven itself might rectify? What could these sins be? Murder? Certainly not murder, for there was killing aplenty in other cities as well. Drunkenness? Opium? Gambling? Whoredom? Although San Francisco had raised these foibles to the level of a local art form, were they not endemic to the human condition? Graft and corruption? Had we not, under Mayor Phelan, made every effort to reform ourselves? Were our civic corruptions greater, say, than Chicago, New Orleans, New York? For all our faults, had we not built a superb city on the edge of the far western wilderness: a place of churches, schools, libraries, theaters, parks: a City of Man, replete with human achievement and promise? Why, then, should the earth itself shake us so in anger? Why should fire waste the work of sixty years, obliterating all signs of our human culture, reducing to ashes those cherished, pitiably few symbols of our earthly sojourn: the faded daguerreotype of parents who came around the Horn in '49; a family Bible; an *armoire* of redwood; a carpet whose intricate patterns we mused upon in an idle hour?

Stripped naked, deprived of our material past, we San Franciscans were being born again, rebaptized in flame. This fire was no punishment for our sins. This was a burnt offering, a sacrifice. The holocaust was bringing all our past forward to one present apocalyptic moment, then consuming that amalgamated past and present in a white-hot heat that would leave only a condensed bright hardness, a jewel-like identity, behind. Surrendering our city to the devouring flames, we were in turn repossessing a flame-forged San Francisco, a spiritualized essence, a city-soul capable of transcendent survival without a body of mortar and brick. Deprived of its monuments, our past would survive in memory and myth. San Francisco was now a diamond, forged in the heat of the earth.

821

A city does not die because its walls fall and its trophies are consigned to the flames. A city only dies when its soul dies, and San Francisco's soul was by no means dead. Like the mythic phoenix, that soul would rise from its very ashes, clothed in even more splendid plumage. I would sorely miss the city of my youth and middle age; but already, standing in the bell tower of Sacred Heart Church, transfixed by the holocaust unfolding beneath me, I looked forward to building the new San Francisco. I also determined that I had done enough to save myself and my own. I now owed attendance at the stricken queen's deathbed. I should be there when the death rattle came.

Descending the tower, I rejoined Marina and Mr. Norton. Awakened from her impromptu nap, Marina was sitting next to the burly Irish cabbie on the driver's seat, her rag doll in her lap. The two of them were munching on rather haphazard sandwiches.

"I was hungry, Daddy," Marina said. "Mr. Norton got some bologna sandwiches from the sisters' picnic kitchen in the church."

"The escorted caravan leaves for the Mission in ten minutes, Dr. Collins," Mr. Norton said. "A soldier just came by telling us all to start lining up."

Reaching into my coat pocket, I extracted my wallet. I counted some fifty dollars out, all that I had on hand. "Mr. Norton," I said, "would you keep Marina with you until I can rejoin you this evening? I want to see if I can be of use downtown."

"No problem, governor," Norton said. "But keep your money. You might need it. We can square accounts later on. I'll bring this little gal home to the missus, where she can wait for you snug as you please."

"O, what a good time, Daddy!" Marina bubbled. "Can I ride up here with Mr. Norton?"

"You bet you can, little poppet," Norton volunteered.

A squad of cavalry soldiers clattered up. The soldiers proceeded to organize the caravan. There was some confusion at first, as inexperienced teamsters wrestled with their exhausted, reluctant horses; but within five minutes a long line of carriages, buggies, taxis, draywagons, a motor car or two, and an assortment of lesser carts had formed itself. The sergeant in charge blew his whistle, and the bedraggled entourage began snaking its way down Fillmore Street towards the southern portion of the city. Perched atop the hansom next to Mr. Norton, Marina turned to wave once before her vehicle dropped out of sight. Holding her doll up high, she made one of its arms move up and down in farewell.

Having secured a pass from the medical lieutenant in charge of the Alamo Square relief camp, I walked down Hayes Street towards the City Hall where, I was told, volunteers were being received and assigned. I arrived just as Mayor Schmitz and General Funston, joined by many of the leading citizens of the city, including Phelan, were concluding an open-air meeting concerning the city-wide organization of relief groups. Anxious to join his firemen on the front lines, Mayor Schmitz appointed Mayor Phelan his authorized deputy to supervise all relief work in the city, public and private. Phelan, in turn, asked me to serve as secretary to his committee. Secure concerning Marina's safety, I accepted. I was relieved to have something worthwhile to do in the crisis. One can brood only so long, after all, about a house and furniture and a few hundred books—dynamited, then consumed by flames.

I sit here in the impending dusk, watching the swans glide back and forth across the lagoon that fronts Maybeck's Piranesian dome. A half hour remains until Marina and John are due to fetch me for dinner at the Tivoli. They will not be late. Like her mother, Marina has an instinctive apprehension of time. In a world without watches or clocks, either of them could match the sun for precision of movement.

A moment ago, I was remembering the Fire. One of the few possessions I threw into my satchel as Mr. Norton's hansom cab waited outside the door was a framed photograph of Virginia I then kept on my bedstand, as I yet do today. It shows Virginia standing next to a carved wooden sign, "Avila Vineyards," affixed to a post at the entrance to the road leading to our ranch. Squinting slightly into the sunlight beneath the hand she is holding over her eyes for shade, Virginia smiles—indeed, laughs almost audibly. I snapped the photograph myself with a Kodak box camera and I cherish it because its very informality reminds me of the affectionate spontaneity of those vineyard days under the golden Napa sun.

Virginia had a way of managing everything perfectly, which was what she did for the Tobins for more than ten years: make a household run like clockwork. Even the most inconsequential meal we took together—a hasty breakfast before heading out to the fields, a cold supper just before bed after a long day's work—had a note of preparation and grace to it: the hot toast covered just so under a pile of napery to preserve its warmth, the fancifully curled radishes garnishing the late evening cold plate of sliced lamb and potato salad—a touch of art, of caring, added to a meal taken together in the happy silence following a day's harvest that had continued into the twilight. Fresh bedclothes and towels were always stacked high in our linen closet; and the latest issues of my favorite journals always stood next to my easy chair, kept up to date by our household's silent librarian.

Speaking of which—books—we contrived a snug study on the first floor of the cottage: bookcases, two writing desks (one for each of us), and two stuffed leather reading chairs. On weekdays when the work of the ranch had not overly exhausted us, or on the weekends, when we tried not to work, Virginia and I labored together on *Wine Prospects for California*. In her clear, graceful hand, Virginia made extracts from books, periodicals, or other research materials according to how I had marked the margins with a soft lead pencil. I would then do a first draft from her notes. Together, we would polish the manuscript into its final form.

Virginia and I loved to read aloud to each other in the evening. We had our own special system of doing so. Obtaining two copies of the book we happened to be reading (in our year together we finished *Les Misérables, Vanity Fair*, and three quarters of *The Red and the Black*), we would assign each other parts—male, female, narrator—which we alternated between us, Virginia taking all the female parts. We thus put on many a lively performance for each other, happy in our company and under the spell of Hugo, Thackeray, or Stendhal. As the evening drew on, I would watch Virginia shadowed in the soft light of her kerosene reading lamp, her face animated by a particularly masterful piece of dialogue. I could hardly believe my luck that we had found such safe haven together. On certain evenings, if I were struck overmuch by the way a strand of her hair fell over her forehead as she did her best to render Becky Sharp, or if I noticed a particularly sulky quality to her voice as she presented Mathilde de La Mole in a touching love scene with Julien Sorel (I playing that adventuring ecclesiastic), then we became as Francesca and Paolo in Dante's *Divine Comedy*. We read no more. Unlike Dante's lovers, however, our happiness was shadowed over by no touch of sin, no anxiety about discovery, only conjugal surrender, each act more glorious because it was open to the transmission of life, followed by deep sleep and the dawn of a new day together.

Although I did not think about it then, I can now see many similarities between Virginia and my mother. Both women possessed the same instinctive orderliness, together with the same love of reading and naive delight in new words. Virginia occupied a higher social niche than did Mother on our local social ladder, being a banker's daughter of some education and Tobin polish; nevertheless, the comparison holds. A successful marriage, I suppose, must incorporate an element of paternal and maternal nurture between the husband-father and the mother-wife. I felt, in any event, a great conviction of security and calm in our household of two, akin to what I knew as a boy, and I attribute it to Virginia. I myself have always been of an extremely nervous disposition.

Sitting here before this fantasy palace, this shrine of memory and regret, I can see Virginia in my mind's eye like a rustic Roman matron against a vine-covered landscape ablaze in autumnal color. The skimmed cream of our fields, the fruit of that one vintage year destiny would afford us, rests in oaken casks inside the stone-secured coolness of Avila Winery, awaiting the fermentation of the impending season. Standing atop the oak-crowned knoll on our property, Virginia faces into a late afternoon breeze that bears with its coming a suggestion of winter. Pushing against her hips, the autumnal vector whips Virginia's skirts out back behind her, her fine female form becoming a trim schooner running ahead of its sail. Within her lies the seed of life, received in a moment of loving surrender. Like the vine, Virginia's womb nurtures the tender berry-growth of future harvest: a ganglion of ovum and welcomed sperm clinging precariously to a welcoming wall of mother flesh; but in the fullness of time a girl child, made to the image and likeness of God, destined one day to fill the space around her with sweetness and bright talk. With the procession of the seasons—autumn to winter, winter to spring—the berry assumes a fish shape, then struggles upwards to amphibian ascendancy. Oversized eyes stare unblinkingly at a dark amniotic sea. Pollywog tendrils develop fingers, a thumb. Grasping and ungrasping begins, as if the future on the other side of the protective wall of bone and flesh were being reached out for, as if the human life to come were being celebrated in a happy hand-dance.

"Here, Sebastian," Virginia said one day as winter breathed its last, "feel her kick." (Virginia always referred to the baby as female. I accepted her prognosis.) Placing my hand on Virginia's firm life-rich belly, I felt the soft thud, thud, thud of my daughter's kicking.

When all is said and done, what do I have to show for this long life of mine? I am neither wealthy nor famous, nor highly situated. With Marina's forthcoming marriage, I face the prospect of being left alone to rattle about an overlarge flat: rattle at first, with an old man's boisterousness, but soon shuffle about in carpet slippers, seedy, neglected, the dribbled remnants of a month of morning eggs hardening on my bathrobe lapel, all alone with the few pathetic trophies that prove that I once did indeed exist, robustly, filling the world with my energetic presence, my hopes and my dreams. What a cruel joke life is! Perceived from a skeptical perspective, what is this insubstantial pageant anyway, but a brief series of disillusionments, as hope after hope fails of fulfillment and the body weakens into debilitated loathsomeness?

Such a perspective tempts faith. Growing older, I cling even more desperately to the possibility that the vast symbologies of my religion might indeed signify something that partakes of truth. After nearly seventy years on this planet, I accept the fact that I personally cannot feel the incandescent heat and light of faith save only as religion speaks to me through the senses. My imagination is incarnational—which is why I was fortunate to be born Roman and to have known Italy in my youth. My nature required the theatrical consolations of the baroque. I am a sensualist and a skeptic by nature, passionately addicted to the present, enslaved by the sensuously aesthetic, tempted to disbelief when the radiant golden monstrance is hidden in the secret recesses of the tabernacle. In this, in my enmeshment in the cultural pageantry of faith, I stand in such contrast to Ryan Patrice and Merry del Val, both of whom, at one time or another, took responsibility for the direction of my compromised soul. In their differing ways, these men, Carthusian and Cardinal, passed through the veil of sense to something more austere and transcendant.

Throughout my life, I have loved whatever feeble honors I have been offered. I have never fled from the little recognition that has come my way. Each bit of praise, each gesture of approval, re-evokes for me that sweet, sweet moment so long ago when Jessie Benton Fremont took my hand so warmly and led me across the lawn to meet the General. O exquisite acknowledgement—from such a superb lady, at such a receptive time of my youth! Perhaps it is because I am a provincial of lower-middle-class origins that I so love praise, or it might be more a matter of temperament, transcending motivations of social class or cultural geography. In all this, however, I stand in contrast to Merry del Val. Born to the nobility, he has had honors lavished upon him from birth; yet the more rapidly he gained promotion, the more he withdrew into the secret cloister of his soul. Denied his first desire—to become a parish priest in England—he stole scattered hours from his duties as secretary of state to hear confessions in San Silvestro in Capite, the English church in Rome, or to work among the orphans of Scuola Mastai, the Christian Brothers hostelry in Trastevere, the working-class district of Rome. Born at the luxuriant center of everything I have ever aspired to—indeed grubbed after so naively and with such an overreaching of my caste!—Merry del Val regarded the baroque splendor of his circumstances with a *contemptus mundi* characteristically Spanish. While I fed greedily off plates of heavy crockery, my confessor dined on bread and unsalted vegetables in his Vatican apartment, using—perforce—good china and cutlery of the finest silver. I would not be surprised but that Merry del Val wears a hair shirt beneath his scarlet robes.

"It took me years to see beyond cultural circumstances, Sebastian," Ryan Patrice confessed to me at *La Grande Chartreuse*. "Indo-China cured me of ultramontanism: of seeing the Church as the spiritually militant striking force of the Latin Christian West. I joined the Paris Foreign Mission Society because I loved its two-hundred-year-old involvement in the spread of French Catholicism to Southeast Asia, and wanted to play a part in that drama of expansion. After a half-dozen years on the scene, however, I recognized that something was very wrong: that our missionary effort succeeded only when it was protected by the force of French arms. A hundred years ago, a brilliant member of my Society, Monsignor Pierre-Joseph Pigneau de Béhaine, went so far as to engineer the establishment of the Annamite empire with the help of a French army, so as to secure a favorable environment for our missionaries. Blood, blood, blood—such was the experience of the Portuguese missionaries in the sixteenth century, the Jesuits in the seventeenth century, the Spanish Dominicans and the Paris Society these past two hundred years. Why? God's will, for one thing: Indo-China has been drenched in the blood of martyrs. But was so much slaughter necessary? Could we not have presented ourselves to these people in a manner and a mode that was separate from our civilization, that preached Jesus Christ as other than the presiding divinity of French imperialism? My own work in Hanoi, I must admit, truly thrived only after my province became a colonial protectorate of France. That happened in 1886. Before that, I stood in constant peril of my life. Four years earlier, in 1882, a punitive expedition of the French army from Saigon seized Hanoi for a few weeks before being repulsed. I was away at the time, visiting some catechetical outposts, or else I also, as my colleague Father Bechet and his catechists, would have lost my head to the Annamite swordsmen."

Patrice and I were stacking stones in a hand-pushed cart as we spoke; or rather, as he spoke and I listened with fascination to his discourse. We had spent the previous week moving the stones into intermediate piles throughout a meadow scheduled for conversion to an arable field. For a man nearing sixty, Patrice worked with admirable energy. What a contrast, I noted, was this perspiring Carthusian oblate to the suave ecclesiastic I had known at Harvard: his red beard elegantly trimmed, his Prince Albert coat perfect in tailoring.

"The mass executions in Hanoi drove me to a near insanity of confusion and grief," Patrice continued, wiping his scanty gray beard with a swooping motion of his sleeve. "I thought seriously of returning home, perhaps even of resigning from the Society and retiring to a nuns' chaplaincy in my native province."

"What dissuaded you?" I asked. Together we had just lifted one rather troublesome rock onto the cart and were resting for a moment in silence.

"Emptiness," he said at last.

"What is emptiness?" I asked.

"I shall tell you another time," he said, "when you are ready to listen to me. Suffice to say that I did not leave my Society. I began, however, to pay more attention to prayer and to practice interior recollection—and now, as you can see, I am here."

"Hauling stones with a drunkard whoremonger," I said.

"Who is trying to reform himself," Patrice said.

"Will you ever go back?" I asked.

"To Indo-China? Perhaps one day—if I have not grown too old—when I understand better."

"Understand what?"

"Belief, faith—what its essence is, Who its essence is—lest in preaching to the Annamites I myself become a castaway. For the while, however, I have the permission of my superiors to remain here, seeking to regain my faith. There is so much I want to understand! I feel that my life is only beginning. I feel like a child!"

"You could have been a bishop," I said. "You could have been superior general."

"I left ambition in Rome twenty-five years ago. I wanted only a missionary's life. And now—so late, so early—I am being led on further . . . to something else."

"Let us hope that the path you are traveling does not lead to further emptiness," I said.

"If it does," Ryan Patrice said, "I shall pray for patience. I have faced the emptiness before and I have found the Self Who is there."

When my own emptiness came, I did not pray. I raged in anger. I cursed the heavens for the cruel joke that had been played upon Virginia and myself: the bestowal of one life at the cost of another, her life, my wife's life, Virginia's life!

I must compose myself. What is done is done. Acceptance and resignation are our only course. A rupture, the escape of some contamination into her bloodstream—and then the announcement, made to me by the physician from the Stanford Hospital whom Phelan had sent up from San Francisco when I telegraphed him that all was not well and that our country

830

doctor needed consultation. "Blood poisoning" is not a pleasant word, yet not necessarily a fatal word either; so I seized upon that possibility when the announcement came, the three of us, country doctor, professor of medicine, and myself, sitting in the study where, such a short while ago, Virginia and I had sat of an evening reading *Vanity Fair* out loud.

"She'll recover?" I asked—no, not asked—I pleaded. Tell me, tell me, doctor, that death cannot come into our vineyard paradise and take off one so young, whom happiness has found at last!

"The next twenty-four hours should tell," the specialist said.

She never recovered. She sank into a coma that very evening, regaining consciousness only once, in the hour before the dawn. And in the final minutes of her awareness she looked at me with a look that I shall never forget. In the silent language of eyes, Virginia pleaded to me for the life that was not mine to give her. Delivered two weeks earlier of a perfect female child, my wife, my young mother, did not wish to die. I saw no resignation in her face. I saw struggle—and resentment. I saw an element of anger that cut into my heart and my bowels like a butcher knife. I held her hand, and she did not take it away (did she have the strength to move it?): which meant, I prayed, that she did not consider me the author of her woe. Dying at the midpoint of her life, however, she had no tolerance for balanced contemplation. She struggled with furies, and the contest showed in her eyes. She slipped into the last unconsciousness as a priest from the nearby Carmelite monastery arrived with the holy oils.

In the days before her death, as I vacillated between despair and hope, I asked myself whether I was being punished for Mentana, for the shaft of steel I had once driven into another man's gut, sending him to the untimely death that now loomed before my wife. Like Virginia, he had no wish to perish while the taste of time was yet sweet on his lips. In the early years of my bereavement, that superstitious query often tempted me: namely, that since I wedded him with my bayonet of steel, and he died in my embrace, did the bride of my flesh fall away from our coupling in a deathly swoon, killed by the plasm I had implanted within her, in some enactment of nature's forfeit? I reject that notion now. However horrible the deed at Mentana, I killed there not in anger, but in self-defense on the field of battle, taking my chances with the rest of them.

Virginia died. After twenty years I accept the fact of her death—most of the time, save when the fearsome loneliness comes, leading to resentment. Virginia died because it was God's will that she be gathered to Him. Her life had reached its natural and supernatural arc of completion.

"O Sebastian, I am so happy here with you," she had said some two weeks before her confinement. "We are so lucky. We have everything. And now—we shall have someone to share our happiness with!"

She died in the spring, in the fullness of her young life, after giving life to another. She did not die content or resigned to her death. She was too Irish for that! But she did die at the apex of her existence, generous, loving, and good. We buried her beneath the oak tree on the knoll where we had picnicked in the early April of 1894 on our first day together at the Avila Vineyard, and where I had first tasted the Zinfandel sweetness of her mouth.

See, see where my lost wife comes towards me now, reborn as Marina—and next to her John, escorting my daughter about San Francisco as I escorted her mother on those Saturdays so long ago when we rambled about the city together discussing books. Marina has Virginia's stride, her broadness of shoulders, her assertiveness of feature. Like her mother, Marina loves order. My sorted and catalogued papers attest to that! Such good women, these two, the one reborn in the other—down to a run of freckles across their noses. In those final days, just before her last strength ebbed away, Virginia would insist upon holding Marina long after the doctor wanted her to rest.

"I knew that she would be a girl, Sebastian, didn't I?"

"Yes, Virginia, you knew. You always knew."

Someday soon I shall rejoin Virginia; for a marriage such as ours—blessed by the Church, consummated in passionate surrender—outlasts physical death. Such a union bears the stamp of eternity. I consoled myself with that notion of the sacramental survivability of our relationship in the immediate aftermath of my first grief, when rage had subsided and I was trying to reintegrate what had happened into some framework of meaning. Then for certain I knew firsthand that long emptiness Ryan Patrice and I had discussed that day in an Alpine meadow as we were lugging stones.

"You wait and wait," Patrice had said, "and you come very close to despair. Nothingness is everywhere. Your hopes are mocked by the void. With one last desperate gamble, you cast yourself headlong on the abyss and you beg for an answer. His response is born miraculously from your anguished petition. For in that last act of entreaty, you reach the Self beyond the abyss. He was there all the time, Sebastian. He is everywhere—even when He seems most lost. To beseech Him when all else has failed is to discover that He has always been at your side."

Well then, let Him come to me. Let Him come to Sebastian Collins of San Francisco! Let Him approach in His human guise—as Marina and John now draw near, arm in arm, across a plaza filled with early evening visitors to our Dream City. I shall discuss my life with Him. I shall tell Him of the people I have known and the places I have seen and the men and women I have loved. I shall speak to Him of San Francisco, where I have worked to achieve a foreshadowing of the Heavenly City, the New Jerusalem, walled in righteousness, its streets paved in diamonds and pearls and gold. I shall thank Him for this long life of mine—for parents, benefactors, lovers and friends, for my wife and my daughter. I shall thank Him for this lovely city, reborn from its ashes. I shall thank Him for all the wondrous beauties of nature and of art I have enjoyed, for the taste of wine and food on my palate. I shall welcome Him as I now welcome Marina and John—with arms outstretched, and with a deep, deep love overflowing in my heart.

Come now, dear children. Walk into this old man's embrace. Feel my body that has known such delight. Embrace the human flesh through which we all struggle towards our destiny—which is the destiny of spirit. Let me embrace the two of you! Let us feel all around us that awesome, transforming energy pulsating at the core of creation itself: that Love at once flesh, fire, and heart—whose face is the radiant whiteness of the moon, whose eyes are stars, whose breath keeps the heavens in motion, and from whose mouth comes an awesome galactic song.

Chapter 19

T O THE SURPRISE of no one, Andy Soutane has won the Democratic gubernatorial nomination, and John Como has been elected the fortieth mayor of San Francisco. On election night most of the Mayor's immediate staff, including myself, sat together in a suite at the Del Webb Townehouse Hotel on Market Street and glumly watched the television reports. Soutane was leading Carpino in every county except Del Norte, Siskiyou, and Modoc, the three counties that rim the extreme northern edge of the state.

"Maybe we could get them to secede from California," Terry Shane observed, digging into a crumpled pack of Marlboros. "Then Carpino could be governor of the newly-formed state of Arctic California."

"We could have our capital at Yreka," Danny Pappas said. "I've always wanted to raze and redevelop Yreka."

The television newscaster, with gushing enthusiasm, announced that as of eight o'clock that evening, of the precincts reporting, Andy Soutane seemed to be heading for a two-to-one victory over his rival, Claudio Carpino, the mayor of San Francisco. The program then switched to the Soutane headquarters at the Beverly Plaza in Los Angeles. A United States senator, the mayor of Los Angeles, and the congressman from Riverside were all noting their satisfaction with Andy Soutane's overwhelming victory.

835

"I'm an old track man," said United States Senator Layman Pate, "and it's clear to me that Andy Soutane has left Claudio Carpino back at the starting block."

Mayor Carpino himself, meanwhile, was at his home in Sea Cliff, dining *en famille* with Esmeralda, their children, their children's spouses, and their grandchildren. If they had their television on, which I suppose they did, then they, like us, would have been treated—following the Senator Pate interview—to a rerun of Esmeralda's famous press conference the day of her return from her holiday. There she was once again, through the miracle of television, in full glorious color, rubbing her husband's denuded dome as she rehearsed the history of her disillusionment with politics.

"Adjust the color tuner will you, Norton," Barry Scorse said, "I don't think that the red of Esmeralda's hair is quite right. Match it up with Ursula here."

"I'll match it up with the red on the Mayor's face," I said.

"Listen, dearie," Ursula Iraslav said, "my hair color is real. The phantom First Lady gets hers from a bottle."

"Speaking of bottles," Jimmy Driscoll said, "let's order more booze from room service and charge it to the campaign. We might as well make a party of it."

"That's right, Jimmy," I said. "We'll treat the rest of the evening like an old-fashioned Irish wake."

It was a wake, of course: our futures on the public dole were dying along with Claudio Carpino's political career. Strangely enough, it was also fun, a party. Defeat, together with the imminent prospect of our breakup as a team, brought everyone together. I sensed a mood of regret, indeed elegiac nostalgia, the moment I walked into the Las Vegas-style suite. Throughout the evening, the barbs flying back and forth among us lacked their usual bite, as if, realizing that our days together were numbered, we were each taking a second look at the men and women with whom we had shared eight exciting years at the helm of a great American city. Audrey Yee, for instance, usually can't stand Inspector Ted Potelli, who calls her "sweetheart" and "doll" and who once, according to Audrey, unsuccessfully tried to cop a feel off her in the front seat of the mayoral limousine. Audrey, however, seemed to be chatting it up with Potelli rather amiably that evening: rather fetching (Audrey, not Potelli!) in a brightly colored Chinese jacket and one of those *cheong sam* dresses that Asian women wear on special occasions. Potelli, on his part, was doing his best not to ogle overlong Audrey's superb thighs, which extended their black-stockinged length from each side of her split skirt as she sat primly on the sofa, looking for all the world like a character out of "Terry and the Pirates." Barry Scorse was making less noise than usual: which is to say that he kept his comments down to the decibel level of a solitary jackhammer, as opposed to his usual Concorde on takeoff.

"What time the Mayor say he's getting here?" Scorse asked Ursula Iraslav.

"He didn't say exactly, dearie."

"The best time to concede is eleven o'clock eastern standard time," Nadia North said. "That way you get the late-news audience and the switch-overs from the evening movie in the East, and the just-sitting-down-to-watch-television people in California."

"Who cares?" Danny Pappas asked. "Why worry about a crowd when you've already fallen for the count?"

"Even in defeat," Nadia said, "a politician likes an audience."

"Terry," I said, "when you brief the Mayor on his remarks, have him try this one out: 'You'll no longer have Claudio Carpino to kick around!'"

"It's been used before," Shane said "by Fiorello La Guardia—or was it Richard Daley?"

"No, it was Frank Skeffington," said Nadia North, opening the suite door which had just been buzzed. A red-jacketed barman wheeled in a set-up that included a couple of bottles of good booze, glasses, mix, and a silver bucket of ice.

"Skeffington?" Jimmy Driscoll said. "Yeah, that is us, the last hurrah, the last big-city administration to be run by hulking ethnics."

"Speak for yourself," Nadia North said. "I'm a WASP, not an ethnic; and I try not to hulk."

837

"He is definitely thinking of Ted Potelli," I said. "The Inspector is ethnic and he definitely hulks. Come on, Ted. Hulk for us—just once."

"Better hulk than swish, sweetheart," Ted Potelli said.

"Quiet, you two," Ursula Iraslav hissed. "The mayoral candidates are coming on."

One by one, reporters from the Channel 5 news team came on screen from remote pickups at the various mayoral campaign headquarters, interviewing the defeated candidates. Supervisor Sandra Van Dam, her voice more whiskey-throated than usual, said that she felt that she had run a good campaign but that San Francisco just wasn't ready yet for a woman mayor. State Senator Mortimer Engels said that he didn't have any time to brood over his defeat because he was going to run for Congress in the next election. Superior Court Judge Charles Fessio said that San Francisco was a great place and that he was happy to serve the city as a judge, which seemed to be what the voters wanted him to do. Supervisor Al Tarsano, wearing his usual red bow tie, and backed by his brood of boys, all wearing red bow ties, refused to concede defeat.

"It's too early to tell," he claimed. "The votes from the outer Mission district haven't been counted yet."

"You've had it, baby," Jimmy Driscoll said to the television set, a refilled glass of Scotch in his hand.

"So have we," said Terry Shane, "but unlike Tarsano, we know it."

"Here comes the future," said Nadia North as Channel 5 switched to John Como headquarters at Ashbury Hall in the Haight-Ashbury. Beaming, as sleek as a seal, Como was acknowledging the cheers of the crowd, his eyes sparkling with pleasure behind his aviator glasses. In the movie, he'd have to be played by Warren Beatty. Mrs. Como was boosted onto the stage and the two of them kissed, bringing the crowd to even higher decibels of approbation. "Como! Como! Como!" the crowd chanted. "Como! Como!"

"I think they're trying to tell us something," Barry Scorse said.

"Your people, sir," Terry Shane said, "is a great beast."

"Don't quote Alexander Hamilton," Nadia North said. "He wasn't a Democrat."

"He was right, however," I said, "in this instance at least."

"No doubledome sour grapes, you doubledomes," Barry Scorse said. "You buy your ticket and you take your chances."

"Citizens of San Francisco," John Como hollered into the microphone over the roar of the crowd. As he began to talk the noise leveled off. "This is a real thrill for both of us." He lifted his wife's arm up as if she had just won the heavyweight championship of the world, and the crowd returned for an interval to its cry of "Como! Como! Como!"

"All right already," said Audrey Yee, pushing Potelli's heavy ethnic arm off her shoulder, where it had surreptitiously fallen from the sofa cushion.

"Audrey, dear," Ursula Iraslav said, "just let me know if Officer Potelli is up to his old tricks."

"I'm an inspector, not a patrolman," Potelli said.

"Well, inspect someone else," Audrey Yee said, remaining, however, in position.

"There's a new day ahead for San Francisco," John Como orated over the crowd. "This city once again belongs to the people, the ordinary, everyday people."

"Yeah, the fruits, the draft dodgers, and the welfare chiselers," said Inspector Ted Potelli of the SFPD.

"For too many years now," Como continued, warming to his subject, "San Francisco has belonged to Big Business and Big Labor. We're going to give San Francisco back to the ordinary citizen. We're going to bring new kinds of people on our governmental commissions—gays, lesbians, minorities, single parents."

"See, what did I tell you," Potelli said. "It's going to be even worse than I predicted. I'll bet there isn't an ordinary citizen in that crowd."

"We're going to make San Francisco an example to the rest of the nation," Como perorated, "of liberal modernity, of flexibility and accommodation."

"Of kookery and catastrophe," Terry Shane said.

"A city where everyone feels welcome," John Como said.

"Except normal people like me," said Ted Potelli.

"You're not normal," Audrey Yee said. "You're just unimaginative."

"San Francisco is once again going to be where the action is," John Como concluded. Cheers and more waving. A banjo band broke into "San Fran-cis-co, open your golden gate!" whereupon the screen switched to a studio location. *Express* columnist Harry Shaw and Assemblyman Jeremiah Jones sat talking to anchorman Dave Fowler, who introduced them, then asked: "Gentlemen, what does the victory of John Como mean for San Francisco?"

"It means that minorities will start to have a say about how this town is run," Jeremiah Jones volunteered, "and by that I mean black people especially. The precinct count will show, I'm certain, that the black people of San Francisco put John Como into office. The new mayor won't forget this."

"Or you'll have his ass," Jimmy Driscoll said admiringly to the flickering sepia image of Jeremiah Jones. "Those black cats are learning fast. It took us Irish twice as long."

"And we haven't really learned yet," I said.

"I'd say that the election of John Como signals the last hurrah of the old coalition," Harry Shaw said. "By this I mean the alliance among Big Labor, the City Hall politicians, the Irish and the Italians and Downtown that ruled this city for the last seventy years—since the Fire and Earthquake."

"And made it great," Danny Pappas said. "That's the coalition that put this town together. Except for the Greeks—he forgot to mention the Greeks."

"And the Yugoslavians," said Ursula Iraslav. "We Serbo-Americans are sick and tired of getting pushed around."

"What about the Chinese?" Audrey Yee asked. "We built the railroad. We did all the laundry."

"What about us WASPs?" Nadia North asked. "We're tired of being blamed for everything that goes wrong. After all, we started the goddammed country,"

"There's a new ethnicity around San Francisco today," Harry Shaw was saying, "and this ties in with the gay movement as well. San Francisco will be the showcase of the new politics." The suite telephone rang. Terry Shane answered it.

"If it's the Mayor," Danny Pappas said, "tell him that he lost."

"It's for you, Norton," Shane said. "It's a woman."

"Probably a fruit in drag," Inspector Ted Potelli said.

"Hi," Deborah said. "I'm downstairs. What a hotel! Shall I come up?"

"Have her come up," Inspector Potelli said behind me. "If she's not a fruit in drag, she'll probably like to meet a real man."

"No," I said. "I'll meet you in the ballroom. Follow the signs that say Claudio Carpino for Governor."

I found Deborah waiting for me at the entrance to the dispiritedly near-empty grand ballroom of the Del Webb Townehouse. An orchestra of some dozen graying middle-aged men in maroon dinner jackets with oversized shawl lapels and clip-on maroon bow ties were playing "Alexander's Ragtime Band" to a dance floor only one-third occupied. A couple of older women in floral print dresses, volunteers from the campaign, lacking partners, were dancing with each other. I spotted a half dozen third-level political freeloaders in the crowd, but no one of great importance in local politics.

"I don't sense victory in the air," Deborah said.

"Soutane has to accept the nomination within the next ten minutes," I said, "if he wants to make the late-night news in the East. Let's go find a television set."

We found a TV monitor adjacent to the no-host bar at one end of the semicavernous ballroom, which we crossed diagonally, not having to worry about getting in the way of too many dancers. Just as I suspected, Soutane was acknowledging his victory in time to make the late-night news in Washington and New York. Dressed conservatively, like a professor at the Stanford Business School, in a pinstripe suit, white shirt, and blue-and-white polka dot tie, Andy Soutane stood at a podium conspicuously dominated by the Beverly Plaza logo, waving to an unseen, but highly voluble crowd. Fashion model Tara Malone—almost certainly the future Mrs. Andy Soutane, so the *Los Angeles Times* had reported that morning—stood next to her man, looking both sexy and quasi-conjugal in a rather daring amount of cleavage. Her moist mouth, with its dramatic bee-stung lower lip, puckered and unpuckered with pollywoggish, fellatic glee. In deference to the occasion, Malone—who according to *Us* magazine usually prefers blue jeans and a plaid shirt knotted well above her waist to reveal a yummy tummy and fetching belly button—wore a silver sheath dress, with more than a hint of Warhol in its glittering spangles. Warmed by the television lights, the spangles refracted off the surface of the television screen with iridescent playfulness. Between Soutane's Brooks Brothers suit and Tara Malone's Cher Bono dress, the special dualities of California—city/country, Hollywood/Midwest, San Francisco/ Los Angeles—were evoked, acknowledged and complimented. Viewers in either Hillsborough or El Centro could identify. Behind Andy Soutane and Tara Malone crowded the array of semianonymous hangers-on who always seem able to get on platforms on election nights, together with the usual platoon of politicians showing the flag of unity in the camp of the winner: in Soutane's case, two United States senators, a congressman or two, and the mayor of Los Angeles. I expected to catch a glimpse of Cole O'Halloran—which I did, in the course of a wide-angle shot of the entire stage. Cole's high coloring, made more flushed no doubt by a liberality of election day libations, showed up well on color television, as did his powder-blue suit. The sight of Tiny Roncola, however, standing next to Cole and like him cheering and applauding lustily, came as a pleasant surprise. Come November, I might have a friend in high places.

"This is the Bicentennial Year," Andy Soutane was saying. "The first two hundred years of this nation's history were dominated by the eastern seaboard. The next hundred years is our turn. The cutting edge of the American experiment is right here in California. The sort of society we are building

842

will provide the rest of the nation with a model for its future. That's a big responsibility. That's why we need new leadership in Sacramento. California needs a prudently progressive leadership, and so does the rest of America."

"That dude ain't even elected governor yet and he's already running for president of the United States," said the black bartender enshrined behind the no-host bar of the ballroom.

"I'm glad it's all over," I said to Deborah a few days later. "It's been a busy year." We were lunching at the San Domenico on Pacific in the North Beach area, where, as I mentioned to her sentimentally over a kir, we had had our first date some thirteen months ago.

"Glad what's over?" Deborah asked, crunching into a buttered baguette topped by country paté.

"The election."

"I hadn't noticed, really. There's too much else of interest going on."

"Like what?"

"Like us, for instance."

"That's my line," I said.

"I have decided to accept your oft-repeated offer of marriage."

An involuntary jerk of my arm spilled a half-filled water glass into my lap. I stood up halfway out of my seat, my pants embarassingly drenched, dabbing at my wet fly clumsily with a napkin.

"This is where I came in," Deborah said. "You did the same thing a year ago."

"I accept your offer," I said. "Mother will be so happy that you're at last making an honest man of me."

"You'll never amount to much unless I take you in hand. Also, I'm tired of a backstairs romance. I prefer that you make an honest woman of me. It's more wholesome for both of us."

"But what about all the doubts you have?" I said, finishing off my kir in three nervous swallows.

"I don't remember any doubts."

"I mean about the future and the fact that everybody who is married seems to be getting divorced. You once said that trust and fidelity are impossible in today's ratty world. No one believes in anything anymore. You said it. I remember clearly."

"That was before I went into the hospital," she said. "When I was there, I spent some time thinking about our relationship. I analyzed your strengths and your weaknesses—and my own. I've decided that it's time for both of us to grow up and take our chances. Who cares what everyone else is doing, or the fact that modern marriage is a disaster? We can create our own center of gravity. Besides, I have a suspicion that commitment will once again be the in thing and promiscuity is very soon going to be passé. The New Chastity I call it. You know how I love to keep up with trends; so marry me and we'll both once again be chaste."

"I'm substantial enough for that—gravity, I mean; and monogamy is my second nature."

"You and I are from cultures that prize stability between men and women, or used to."

"Our life, you realize, could turn into a disaster movie."

"It might do that anyway," she said. "There are never any guarantees, are there?—especially when the male in the relationship is so inherently indecisive."

"I am not indecisive," I said. "I'm just cautious."

"Thirty-six is awfully cautious—almost weird."

Our lunch arrived—shrimp Louis, piled high over an extravagant bed of lettuce, San Francisco-style. As a mark of friendship, the owner, Dominic St. Pierre himself, came over to our table and filled our wine glasses with Christian Brothers Sauvignon Blanc. As a conservative, I have never succumbed to the heresy that popular wines can't be good wines. One judges a viticultural region by its popular wines as well as by its premium vintages.

"We've just gotten engaged," I said.

"You're the second couple to tell me that this week." Dominic said. "It must be some sort of trend."

844

I offered a toast. "To the future," I said, "to whatever measure of pleasure and pain comes our way."

"To happiness," Deborah said, "to sticking together, to trying to live with a little style—and not throwing away the ordinary chances for happiness."

"Like lunch together," I said.

"Like a nice word, a good film or a book, a walk in the park, a ride in the country—anything and everything."

"So long as it's fun," I said, "and we do it together."

"So long as we try to live, really live, instead of just talking about it."

We drank. Brother Timothy the Cellarmaster had chosen well. The Sauvignon Blanc was spicy, a little pearish, but dry, and perfectly chilled. Like the Christian Brothers, Deborah and I had set ourselves upon an heroic course. We would try to make the ordinary thing work well.

"Here's looking at you, kid," I said.

The last job I did for Mayor Claudio Carpino, the soon-to-be-former mayor of San Francisco, was to ride with him in the limo out to the Presidio where he was scheduled to address the luncheon honoring the two-hundredth anniversary of the founding of San Francisco. The last time I had seen the Mayor before that day had been on election night: standing bravely before the sparse but noisy crowd in the ballroom of the Del Webb Townehouse, waving his arm like a winner and smiling broadly as the already tired orchestra launched into the evening's tenth rendition of "Alexander's Ragtime Band." Esmeralda had a forced smile on her face, degenerating every other moment into a grimace, now and then setting itself into a pharaonic stare. Standing behind their parents, the Carpino sons, dressed in black as for a funeral, stared at the crowd impassively. Only Barbara Carpino had the political ritual of a game and plucky acceptance of defeat down pat. Holding one of her children in her arms, a boy of three dressed in a sailor suit, she smiled broadly as the little tyke waved his arm to the music of an orchestra having no trouble overcoming the hoarse

845

cheers of the inadequate crowd. That was ten days ago. The look of subdued humiliation on Claudio Carpino's face that night—as a year's work, more than a million dollars, and his political future went down the drain—had given way to a demeanor of calm resignation, broken intermittently with flashes of the old optimism.

"Now what about it, Jimmy boy, give me the scoop about the founding of San Francisco," the Mayor said as Inspector Ted Potelli steered the sleek black Cadillac out Van Ness Avenue.

"Here are your pertinent facts," I said, handing him some half dozen three-by-five cards on which I had typed the basic data relating to the Anza Expedition. "You can extemporize from these in your usual fashion." For a moment it seemed like old times: as if I were just beginning my appointment in the Carpino administration and was still feeling thrilled about riding with the mayor of San Francisco around his city in a big black limo, everyone recognizing us and waving from the sidewalk or honking their car horns in salute. We'd be off to one event or another, talking excitedly—Shane, Scorse, Driscoll, or myself—about one or another piece of impending business. We had years ahead of us, after all, time enough for a hell of a good time, and a chance to get a lot done for San Francisco.

As quickly as possible, I briefed the Mayor on the expedition of men, women, and children which started out from Tubac, State of Sonora, northern Mexico, in September of 1775, Lieutenant Colonel Juan Bautista de Anza of the Spanish frontier forces commanding officer in charge. Eight babies, I told the Mayor, were born on the nine-month trek. What few horses the Anza Expedition possessed were stolen by Apaches, so nearly everyone was forced to walk the more than a thousand miles—much of it hostile desert, burning by day, shivering cold by night—between Tubac and the peninsula of San Francisco. On 27 June 1776, two hundred years before the day and the hour Inspector Ted Potelli of the SFPD, heading for the Presidio Officers' Club, swung the limo of the mayor of

846

San Francisco, headed for one of the last ceremonial occasions of his lame-duck administration, through the Presidio gate, some two hundred Mexican colonists made camp on a site chosen earlier by Anza, who had rushed out ahead of the expedition as it rested at Monterey. A small creek, *Laguna de Nuestra Señora de los Dolores*, ran through the campsite. The area had also been selected by the padres of the expedition as the site for a new mission.

"That's good," the Mayor said, running his eye down the typed index cards as I spoke. "I like the part about the babies. You've done a good job as usual."

How sad it all seemed: a pat on the head for the no-longer young staffer of a doomed politico. Is this all that my public service career had—would—could—come to? You don't need to be a Ph.D. from Harvard to list a few rudimentary facts on slips of paper. Where were all my bright dreams of a rejuvenated city? Where was the early promise of the Claudio Carpino administration?

"I know what you're thinking," the Mayor said, as if reading my mind, "but don't worry: it hasn't been wasted. We've accomplished a lot."

Tell me what, I wanted to say. But why bother? The past is past. I've got the future to look forward to.

"We took San Francisco into its new era," the Mayor continued, as if rehearsing something in his own mind. "We made sure that San Francisco wouldn't be a Pacific Coast Williamsburg, a boutique city for limousine liberals. We've helped keep the city in the competition." He paused to wave to a Muni driver who had saluted us with three long blasts of his trolley horn. As in an exchange of salutes, Inspector Ted Potelli of the SFPD beat out a shave-and-haircut-six-bits on the limo horn in reply

"I know what you're thinking," the Mayor said returning to his discourse. "You're a librarian, a species of academic. You've written a book about San Francisco; but running a city is different from writing about it. The changes come slower, and your control over your material is a lot more difficult.

847

You'll see. In the long run, we've made a transition these past eight years that is for the best. We've kept our old businesses and we've brought in new jobs. We gave the blacks a piece of the action so some of their crazy leaders wouldn't encourage them to burn down the place. We opened a rapid transit system and built a hell of a lot of beautiful buildings. So much has happened, in fact, that people got a little scared and they pushed a panic button marked John Como. But wait and see. Six months in office and Como will have reversed his no-growth attitude. He'll be meeting with the chamber of commerce and making speeches about luring development to San Francisco. Unless he wants his entire city on welfare, a mayor has got to go out and hustle the jobs and paychecks for his people."

The limo pulled up to the Presidio Officer's Club, a wall of which dates from the Presidio's founding in 1776. "In a way," the Mayor continued, "all big cities are ungovernable. Great ones, however, have a way of running themselves. You can say this for me: I never stood in the way of San Francisco's running itself, and I spent a lot of time keeping us economically prosperous. The time will come that the citizens will remember this and be grateful. Who knows? I may run again four years from now."

"If you do—and you win," I said, surprised by my boldness, "concentrate more on being mayor than upon running for higher office. Being mayor of San Francisco is a big enough job for anyone."

"So is being a good city librarian," the Mayor said, pulling at the door handle before the limo had fully stopped. "Spend the next four years learning where the books are. When I'm back in office, I may keep you on—provided you survive John Como."

He sprang from the limo and with his old verve walked briskly into the building, eager once again to play his mayoral role with his customarily exuberant style. I suspect that his homily to me had been in part an effort to buoy himself up for his first public appearance following his defeat in the gubernatorial primary. Whatever the causes, however, he and I had just completed the first and perhaps only candid conversation of our acquaintance.

My Lord, did he play rhetorical variations on the Anza theme! "It's like the old days," Jimmy Driscoll muttered to the staff table. "He's got them eating out of his hand. That bit about the eight babies born on the trail being the first native San Franciscans was dynamite. We're too good to die. We need another four years in office."

I felt rather good about life that evening as I stood on my balcony, sipping a snifter of brandy and watching the lights on the bay. Deborah had just called from Arizona to say that her parents had relented and would not insist upon a Phoenix wedding.

"Also—I've resigned from the Library. It would be tacky of me to stay there after next month. I've gotten a job as director of recreation services for the children patients at the University of California Medical Center. I even make more money."

"That's not too hard to do," I said.

"I've been talking over your situation with Mom and Dad," Deborah said. "They both agree that you'd be crazy to give up your job to write. Mayor Como has already said in Harry Shaw's column that he intends to keep you on. Dad says this—and I quote: 'If he wants to write, let him go to bed early and get his fat ass out of bed in the morning to write before work, and let him write on weekends.' Mother is also reluctant for her daughter to attach herself to someone who is unemployed. That's a dirty word down here in Phoenix."

"I suspect that I am acquiring a strong set of in-laws," I said.

"They have our best interest at heart."

"Tell your father that I agree. Tell him I'm going to spend this weekend on the Sebastian Collins biography."

"That's a good boy," Deborah said. "Neither of us was cut out for a garret in the Haight-Ashbury. Besides, if you didn't work, you wouldn't write any more. You'd just have longer and longer lunches."

I look forward to the challenge of getting my life more together under Deborah's influence. Deborah hates sloppiness and waste! I'm having lunch next week with an editor from the University of California Press who has heard about the Sebastian Collins project. He says he's interested. If I sign a contract, there will be the pressure of a deadline; but no matter, deadlines have a way of helping work to get done. Sebastian Collins deserves a good biography.

The lights of Berkeley sparkled across the bay. A tanker stole silently towards an Oakland berth. God—but this peninsula and this bay must have seemed a beautiful place that day two hundred years ago when the Anza Expedition pitched its tents and went about the business of founding a city. It also could have seemed rather frightening—seven bare, windswept hills huddled on the edge of an unsettled half-continent and an unexplored Pacific. Things haven't changed. Like those Spanish and Mexican pioneers, we San Franciscans can still feel the beauty and the fear. With two hundred years behind us, however, we can also find much reason for hope; and hope, in and of itself, is a form of wisdom.

This place is truly Land's End, I thought to myself. You can almost feel the surging aspiration of the continent behind us. You can almost feel a nation's desperate hope breaking against us, just as the Pacific breaks off Land's End. Maybe that was the way it was even two hundred years ago when the Anza party got here—overloaded with expectation, I mean, and hence doomed to disappointment. Perhaps that's my luck—or misfortune—in being a San Franciscan. I suppose that I am guilty of pushing it all a little too insistently, of demanding that it all come true for me here and now. But when you are at the end of America, where else is there to go?

It's probably a good thing that I stay at the Library. I've chosen this profession and I have to stick with it. I want to stick with it, in fact, even if it means putting up with the likes of Mabel Storm. Sebastian Collins never threw in the towel. I've got to do justice to the story of his last romance and how he went to Rome to testify at the Vatican on behalf of the cause

850

of Ryan Patrice for canonization, and how he worked and worked as a library commissioner until he was literally too old and too weak to travel downtown. Sebastian Collins never lost hope in San Francisco, even when the Atheneum project fell through. Self-pity is the enemy—throwing up your arms in despair and saying that the San Francisco envisioned by Sebastian Collins is over and done with. Dreams never come fully true; but then again, they don't fully disappear either. Collins watched this same bay from this same hill and felt this same dream of a city at Land's End that might have something to say to the rest of America. We are not saying much now, I'll admit. We've lost our history, and a certain disorder of spirit is eating away at our collective soul. I sometimes fear that something horrible will happen in San Francisco. I don't possess an exact image for my fear, but it involves a collective act of murder and self-destruction. Best not to think of it. Best to have hope. Best to resist the temptations of antiquarianism on the one hand, and orchidaceous hedonism on the other. Like Sebastian Collins, I've got work to do. I must play my part in the buildling of a city.

Deborah Tanner and I were married on the last Saturday of July 1976 in the small community chapel of the Paulist Fathers' rectory adjacent to the venerable church of Old St. Mary's in Chinatown. The pastor, Father Thomas J. Connellan, C.S.P., performed the ceremony and said a nuptial low mass. Terry Shane and Toby Wain stood as my best men. I told Father Connellan that since I was all of thirty-six, and never married, I needed two best men to see me through the ordeal.

Deborah asked Erma, the young black woman with whom she had shared a room in the hospital, to serve as her maid of honor. Erma had gone through a period of deep depression following her surgery, Deborah told me, but of late her spirits had been on the upswing. Erma had at first been convinced that she was now out of the running as far as men were concerned. Deborah, however, fixed her up with Danny

Parker, the Library's affirmative action officer, and the two of them seemed to be hitting it off. Danny, in any event, seemed pleased with Erma and with life in general as he escorted Erma into the Paulist Fathers' rectory for the ceremony.

Mother arrived at the same time as Danny and Erma. This made me a little nervous at first because Mother sometimes uses the phrase "colored people," which she thinks is refined but which, I'm told, is at present considered insulting by black Americans. Danny Parker, however, seemed at once to intuit Mother's situation and handled her beautifully, for which I was most grateful. The Tanners arrived from the Clift Hotel in a taxicab, looking tanned and fit and well-tailored, as usual. Deborah was supposed to be arriving with them, but was nowhere in sight. For a panic-stricken moment, I thought that I might be left jilted at the altar.

"I told Deborah to stay out of sight," Mrs. Tanner said. "We let her out of the cab around the corner on Grant Avenue—at the side entrance to the church. She's in the sacristy with Father Connellan. I really don't think that it's a real wedding unless the bride makes a dramatic entrance, do you? Even if the couple has—shall we say—anticipated some of the privileges of matrimony, there should be a sense of excitement, of anticipation, in a wedding, don't you think?"

I gasped with fear and delight as Spencer Tanner brought his daughter to me at the altar. She seemed so young and tall and strong and beautiful, like the heroine of a long narrative poem by Sir Walter Scott. She wore a simple white dress. A crown of miniature white rosebuds encircled the Medusa ringlets of her copper-colored hair. Neither of us faltered when it came time to promise "until death do us part."

"Have fun, kids," Mother said after the ceremony. "Have a wonderful time. That's your mother's philosophy."

In the late afternoon, we drove up to the Napa Valley and registered in the Burgundy Inn at Yountville, a former stone winery refurbished with local antiques into an old-fashioned wine-country hostelry. The bed in our room was a most unusual affair—massive and dark, of walnut, and surmounted

852

on the height of its six-foot-high headboard with a cunningly carved griffin, its wings flaring dramatically, one paw held high as if the creature were on the march. That night under the griffin's guardianship, we made love as unfalteringly as we had pronounced our vows that morning. Whatever else had previously passed between us was in the nature of a clumsy rehearsal. Afterward, we lay side by side as moonlight flooded our room.

"I need one of those sleeveless T-shirts," I said, "and I should be smoking a Gauloise cigarette."

"You're no Jean-Paul Belmondo," Deborah said, "but you'll do—with a little more practice."

The next morning, after coffee and croissants in the inn's kitchen, we drove up to the monastery of Mount La Salle for eleven o'clock mass. Sherry-golden sunlight flooded the creamy-walled Spanish Renaissance-style church, making the delightful banners hung along the whitewashed walls even more bright. "Peace," proclaimed one of the pennants. "Love," announced another. A discalced Carmelite priest from Oakville said the mass, and a choir of black-robed Christian Brothers sang a most beautiful mixture of modern hymns and Gregorian chant. After luncheon at La Belle Hélène in St. Helena, we drove out through a landscape of georgic splendor towards the foothills, in search of Avila Vineyards. We found the old house in pretty good shape. It is occupied by the field foreman of the large winery that has long since absorbed the property. The store cellar of Avila Vineyards is now used exclusively for the aging of champagne. An ancient oak tree watches over the property from a nearby knoll. Hand in hand, Deborah and I headed toward it along a bee-buzzed footpath, edged on either side by banks of orange-gold California poppies. Across the horizon stretched row upon row of green-leafed vines, their purple grapes, sixty days from harvest, gathering a final measure of strength from the sun of summer. The druid oak tree offered us welcome shade from the considerable heat of a high afternoon in July. Before we sat down beneath its coolness, however, we stood silently before the twin stones that lie there in the ground side by side. One is grimed with age. The other yet possesses a suggestion of its once-shiny marble surface. Virginia Walsh Collins, 1860–1895, says the more mossy of the two slabs. Sebastian Collins, 1848–1940, says the other. From the knoll, incidentally, you look out across a landscape luxuriant with the golden promise of California.